JAMES HOGG

# *Altrive Tales*

*Collected among the Peasantry of Scotland and from Foreign Adventurers*

*By The Ettrick Shepherd*

*With Illustrations by George Cruikshank*

Edited by

Gillian Hughes

EDINBURGH UNIVERSITY PRESS

2005

Edinburgh University Press
22 George Square
Edinburgh
EH8 9LF

Typeset at the University of Stirling
Printed and bound in Great Britain by
The Cromwell Press, Trowbridge, Wilts

ISBN 0 7486 2087 7



A CIP record for this book is available from the British Library

The publisher acknowledges support from

towards the publication of this volume

# Hogg Rediscovered

## A New Edition of a Major Writer

This book forms part of a series of paperback reprints of selected volumes from the Stirling / South Carolina Research Edition of the Collected Works of James Hogg (S/SC Edition). Published by Edinburgh University Press, the S/SC Edition (when completed) will run to some thirty-four volumes. The existence of this large-scale international scholarly project is a confirmation of the current consensus that James Hogg (1770–1835) is one of Scotland's major writers.

The high regard in which Hogg is now held is a comparatively recent development. In his own lifetime, he was regarded as one of the leading writers of the day, but the nature of his fame was influenced by the fact that, as a young man, he had been a self-educated shepherd. The second edition (1813) of his long poem *The Queen's Wake* contains an 'Advertisement' which begins as follows.

> The Publisher having been favoured with letters from gentlemen in various parts of the United Kingdom respecting the Author of the *Queen's Wake*, and most of them expressing doubts of his being a Scotch Shepherd; he takes this opportunity of assuring the Public, that *The Queen's Wake* is really and truly the production of *James Hogg*, a common shepherd, bred among the mountains of Ettrick Forest, who went to service when only seven years of age; and since that period has never received any education whatever.

This 'Advertisement' is redolent of a class prejudice also reflected in the various early reviews of *The Private Memoirs and Confessions of a Justified Sinner*, the book by which Hogg is now best known. This novel appeared anonymously in 1824, but many of the early reviews identify Hogg as the author, and see the *Justified Sinner* as presenting 'an incongruous mixture of the strongest powers with the strongest absurdities'. The Scotch Shepherd was regarded as a man of powerful and original talent, but it was felt that his lack of education caused his work to be marred by frequent failures in discretion, in expression, and in knowledge of the world. Worst of all was Hogg's lack of what was called 'delicacy', a failing which caused him to deal in his writings with subjects (such as prostitution) that were felt to be unsuitable for mention in polite literature. Hogg was regarded by these reviewers, and by his contemporaries in general, as a man of undoubted genius, but his genius was felt to be seriously flawed.

A posthumous collected edition of Hogg was published in the late 1830s. As was perhaps natural in all the circumstances, the publishers (Blackie & Son of Glasgow) took pains to smooth away what they took to be the rough edges of Hogg's writing, and to remove his numerous 'indelicacies'. This process was taken even further in the 1860s, when the Rev. Thomas Thomson prepared a revised edition of Hogg's *Works* for publication by Blackie. These Blackie editions present a bland and lifeless version of Hogg's writings. It was in this version that Hogg was read by the Victorians, and, unsurprisingly, he came to be regarded as a minor figure, of no great importance or interest. Indeed, by the first half of the twentieth century Hogg's reputation had dwindled to such an extent that he was widely dismissed as a vain, talent-free, and oafish peasant.

Nevertheless, the latter part of the twentieth century saw a substantial revival of Hogg's reputation. This revival was sparked by the republication in 1947 of an unbowdlerised edition of the *Justified Sinner*, with an enthusiastic Introduction by André Gide. During the second half of the twentieth century Hogg's rehabilitation continued, thanks to the republication of some of his texts in new editions. This process entered a new phase when the first three volumes of the S/SC Edition appeared in 1995, and the S/SC Edition as it proceeds is revealing a hitherto unsuspected range and depth in Hogg's achievement. It is no longer possible to regard him as a one-book wonder.

Some of the books that are being published in the S/SC Edition had been out of print for more than a century and a half, while others, still less fortunate, had never been published at all in their original, unbowdlerised condition. Hogg is now being revealed as a major writer whose true stature was not recognised in his own lifetime because his social origins led to his being smothered in genteel condescension; and whose true stature has not been recognised since, because of a lack of adequate editions. The poet Douglas Dunn wrote of Hogg in the *Glasgow Herald* in September 1988: 'I can't help but think that in almost any other country of Europe a complete, modern edition of a comparable author would have been available long ago'. The Stirling / South Carolina Research Edition of James Hogg, from which the present paperback is reprinted, seeks to fill the gap identified by Douglas Dunn.

**Douglas S. Mack**

# General Editors' Acknowledgements

The work of the Stirling / South Carolina Edition of James Hogg is being greatly assisted by a major Research Grant awarded in 2002 by the United Kingdom's Arts and Humanities Research Board. This grant is of crucial importance for the Hogg Edition, and its benefits will be wide-ranging. Among other things, it has enabled Gillian Hughes to complete the present edition of *Altrive Tales* much more quickly than would otherwise have been possible. We are likewise grateful for the funding and other support made available to the Hogg Edition over the years by the University of Stirling and the University of South Carolina. Valuable grants and donations have also been received from the Association for Scottish Literary Studies, the Carnegie Trust for the Universities of Scotland, the Glenfiddich Living Scotland Awards, the James Hogg Society, and the Modern Humanities Research Association. The work of the Edition could not have been carried on without the support of these bodies.

# Volume Editor's Acknowledgements

This volume could not have been completed without the help of a large number of individuals and institutions. My first thanks must go to other scholars working on the Stirling/ South Carolina Edition and particularly to Peter Garside (General Editor for the volume) for his never-failing encouragement, detailed guidance, and timely information, and to Douglas Mack who is a constant source of help and information to myself as to all Hogg scholars. Richard Jackson provided valuable information and invaluable practical help, while Meiko O'Halloran also undertook the task of proof-reading the text. I am grateful to Suzanne Gilbert for her help, and to Janette Currie for extra information about Mrs Izett. Thanks are due for particular help to Helen Beardsley, Jacqueline Belanger, Mike Bott, Ian Duncan, Penny Fielding, Susan Harris, Janet Horncy, Mike Kelly, Donald Kerr, Tom McKean, Anthony Mandal, Jane Millgate, Jean Moffat, Virginia Murray, Murray Pittock, Sharon Ragaz, David Retter, the late Jill Rubenstein, Patrick Scott, and Gordon Willis. I particularly wish to thank Hogg's descendants Chris Gilkison, Liz Milne, and David Parr for their support.

I have been enabled to travel to examine Hogg's letters and literary manuscripts in North America and New Zealand by generous grants from the Bibliographical Society and the Carnegie Trust for the Universities of Scotland. During October 2001 I was fortunate enough to be the Frederick A. & Marion S. Pottle visiting research fellow at the Beinecke Rare Book and Manuscript Library, Yale University.

I wish to thank the following for permission to cite manuscript materials in their care: the Alexander Turnbull Library, National Library of New Zealand, Te Puna Matauranga o Aotearoa; the Beinecke Rare Book and Manuscript Library, Yale University; the Bodleian Library, University of Oxford; the British Library; the Poetry/Rare Books Collection, University Libraries, University of Buffalo, State University of New York; the Directors of Coutts & Co.; Fales Library & Special Collections, New York University; the Historical Society of Pennsylvania; the Houghton Library, Harvard University; the Huntington Library, San Marino, California; the John Murray Archive; the Department of Special Collections, Kenneth Spencer Research Library, University of Kansas; Liverpool Record Office, Liverpool Libraries and Information Services; the University of London Library; The Newberry Library, Chicago; the Society of Antiquaries of Newcastle upon Tyne and Northumberland Record Office; the Trustees of the National Library of Scotland; the Pierpont Morgan Library, New York; Princeton University Library; the Miscellaneous Collection of the Queen's University Archives, Kingston, Ontario; Reading University Library; Special Collections, University of Otago Library, Dunedin, New Zealand; Stirling University Library; the Scottish Borders Archive and Local History Centre, Scottish Borders Library Service, St Mary's Mill, Selkirk; and the Wordsworth Trust. Material in the Boston Public Library/Rare Books Department is cited by Courtesy of the Trustees, and from the Byron-Lovelace papers belonging to Lord Lytton by permission of Pollingers Limited. Every effort has been made to trace all copyright holders, but if any errors or omissions have inadvertently been made, the publisher will be pleased to amend these in a future edition.

# Contents



# Illustrations

# Introduction

## 1. Genesis and Publication History

When *Altrive Tales* first appeared in April 1832, as the first volume of a twelve-volume set, it seemed that Hogg had successfully brought to fruition a long-standing plan to preserve his prose fiction in print in the form of a collection of matching volumes.

Some of the earliest of Hogg's prose tales were published in his own essay-periodical *The Spy* of 1810–11, and Ian Duncan has traced the continuation of Hogg's writings in this form in his S/SC edition of Hogg's *Winter Evening Tales* of 1820. As Duncan remarks:

> In the decade following *The Spy* Hogg offered his stock of 'rural and traditionary tales' to several Edinburgh publishers, including Constable and Blackwood, before Oliver and Boyd brought out *Winter Evening Tales* in the spring of 1820.[1]

As Douglas Mack had previously noted, Hogg's original collection seems to have been divided and reformed into his two separate volume publications of fiction, *The Brownie of Bodsbeck; and Other Tales* (1818) and *Winter Evening Tales* (1820).[2] Duncan sees the title of the second of these as 'the generic title for a loose, capacious, fluid stock of narratives that Hogg drew upon, reworked and recombined throughout his career as opportunity arose', pointing to a subsequent attempt by Hogg in October 1822 to reunite the two collections under the title of the second and more commercially successful publication.[3] Earlier that year Hogg had achieved the professional dignity of a collected edition of his poetry with the publication by the prestigious Constable firm of a four-volume *The Poetical Works of James Hogg*. It was therefore natural that he should seek the preservation and endorsement of his work in prose in similar fashion, and there is indeed a surviving letter to him from the Constable firm of 21 October 1822 declining 'a collected edition of your Novels uniform with the Poetry'.[4] It is at first sight surprising that almost a decade should pass before the partial realisation of this ambition.

Hogg's career as a fiction writer contrasts sharply with that of his literary mentor, Sir Walter Scott, who rapidly produced novel after novel that could be bound uniformly and grouped together on the library shelf even as first editions, and which were from time to time reissued as sets under such generic titles as 'Novels and Tales' or 'Historical Romances' even before the canonical *magnum opus* edition of the Waverley Novels began to appear towards the end of his career. Scott was a master of the three-volume format that dominated the production of fiction at this time, using it to structure and develop his novels with care and skill. Hogg, on the other hand, was clearly more comfortable with the shorter form of the traditional tale and with the more adaptable length and looseness of the novella. Ian Duncan has remarked upon Hogg's preference for 'old tales', arguing that they placed a healthy emphasis on 'a vital regenerative principle which urbane cultures relegating to childhood and to a superseded cultural past, are in danger of forgetting'.[5] But this preference did not sort well with a dominant publication practice of the 1820s. Hogg's volume publications often consist of two-volume collections of tales, and when he did publish a three-volume work, he often subverted it in favour of his preferred forms. *The Three Perils of Man* (1822), for instance, includes a prize tale-telling contest after the pattern of the contention of the minstrels for Queen Mary's harp in *The Queen's Wake*. *The Three Perils of Woman* (1823) bears the subtitle of 'A Series of Domestic Scottish Tales' and divides into at least two parts, one relating to events around the Jacobite Rising of 1745 and one relating to the Scotland of the 1820s. It also seems that Hogg would have preferred to spread his materials into a fourth volume had not his London publisher Longmans disapproved, remarking in a letter to him of 5 May 1823:

> As to the number of Volumes, we consider the work equally valuable to us in three volumes as in four; and, if you extend the work to the latter number, we are sorry to say that we cannot extend the remuneration to the author. A novel in three volumes we always consider more saleable than one in four; so that what is gained in one way is lost in another.

Just as *The Three Perils of Woman* was probably truncated to fit the three-volume format demanded by its publisher, Hogg's later collection of *Tales of the Wars of Montrose* was unsuitably and grudgingly expanded to that length.[6] Perhaps Hogg's unease with the three-volume format partly explains his avoidance of the word 'novel' and preference for 'tale' and 'romance' throughout his career.

*Winter Evening Tales* of 1820 was Hogg's most successful collection of fiction, as Duncan indicates, but the appearance of a second edition in the following year was probably a mixed blessing. Unsold copies of this edition seem to have blocked Hogg's subsequent attempts to publish a collected edition of his tales in the years that followed. For instance, his letter of 18 December 1824 to G. & W. B. Whittaker, the London partners of Oliver and Boyd in the publication, shows him asking for permission to select some tales from *Winter Evening Tales* for inclusion in the projected collection:

> I made an agreement last year for an edition of all my tales in 8 vols but to my disappointment found that a part of the second edition of The Winter Evening Tales were still unsold.[7]

A subsequent letter of Hogg's to William Blackwood of 5 January 1825 (NLS MS 4012, fol. 179) indicates that both Oliver and Boyd in Edinburgh and Whittaker in London had refused to permit this. No doubt both publishers feared that the appearance of a collected tales would slow down the already sluggish sales of copies of the earlier work in their hands. Hogg's frustration is evident when he suggests to Blackwood that he might proceed even without the permission of the publishers of the second edition of *Winter Evening Tales*, by making some minor alterations to the tales selected: 'Whitaker has refused also! I would not care to select a few and alter them throughout and let him seek his amends'. His willingness to risk a dispute about publication rights was, however, most unlikely to be shared by the prudent Edinburgh publisher.

The idea of a collected edition of tales was revived by Hogg in 1826, after the failure of the publishing firm of Archibald Constable. This failure had ruined several of Hogg's literary associates, among them John Aitken and, most notably of course, Sir Walter Scott himself. Hogg's credit was also stretched beyond its limits, as he sought to find the rent for the large and inadequately-stocked farm of Mount Benger that he held from 1821 to 1830 on a lease from the Buccleuch estate. Unfortunately, 1826 saw something of a decline for Edinburgh as a centre of novel publication, following a serious financial crisis in the book-trade. Peter Garside has indicated that the optimum period for the production of novels in Scotland was between 1822 and 1825, with Blackwood, for example, producing only eight new novels between 1827 and 1829 compared with twenty-one between 1822 and 1825.[8] From William Blackwood's point of view Hogg's suggestion in his letter to him of 19 March [1826] was therefore ill-timed:

> I think it is high time you were beginning some publication of mine to liquidate all or part of my debt and I think the whole of my select Scottish tales should be published in

> Numbers one every month with the Magazine to be packed with it and a part of the first No sent gratis to some of your principal readers. (NLS MS 4017, fol. 138)

Hogg had found the benefits of this type of strategy more than fifteen years earlier in publicising the first number of his weekly essay-periodical, *The Spy* (1810–11), and his scheme to publish a longer work in magazine-type monthly instalments also anticipates the success of specialists in number publications (i. e. serialised in parts) such as Blackie and Son of Glasgow in reaching out to a lower-middle-class mass market in the early Victorian era. Blackwood, though, like other publishers in 1826, had taken the Constable failure as a warning against expansionist speculations and had drawn in his horns accordingly. Undaunted, Hogg again proposed a multi-volume collection of his prose tales six months later, on the back of the success of his series of 'The Shepherd's Calendar' within the pages of *Blackwood's Edinburgh Magazine*. This time he suggested that Blackwood might share the risk with his customary London partners Cadell and Davies, and offered the assistance of his nephew Robert Hogg to purge his work of errors of taste and delicacy. His letter of 12 September 1826 states:

> I therefore wish that at all events you and Davis would publish an edition of my Scottish tales revised in four close printed volumes and the Shepherd's Callendar in two [...] I should like above all things that my nephew Robert took the charge of the edition but there are many large curtailments that I only can manage but if you think it would answer better to have it printed in London that can easily be managed (NLS MS 4017, fols 139–40)

Hogg's manoeuvring here is particularly interesting, the suggestion that a London printer might be employed running counter to all his previous experience in publishing his fiction–even with a London publisher like Longmans he had hitherto seemed anxious to use an Edinburgh printer. This is probably to be interpreted as the first of several hints that his work could be published in London if suitable arrangements were not made in Edinburgh. If so, the reminder was partially effective, for Blackwood's reply of 23 September was conciliatory, emphasising his eagerness to oblige insofar as the stagnation of the publishing trade would allow, and holding out hopes that he would undertake a collected edition of Hogg's prose fiction at some not-too-distant future time:

> I wish much it were in my power to assist you by getting speedily forward an edition of your Tales. I still think that an edition in a cheap form revised and altered as we talked of, assisted by your Nephew would answer very well. Every thing however is so dull and I have such heavy demands upon me that I cannot well venture upon much just now, but I hope in a very short time things will get better. At present there is such a stagnation as I have never seen since I have been in business. (NLS MS 30309, pp. 385–87)

For the time being Hogg seems to have accepted this decision, pushing instead for the limited goal of a volume republication of 'The Shepherd's Calendar' series, which if successful would be the harbinger of the collected fiction. In complaining to Blackwood on 29 January 1828 about the delay in publishing *The Shepherd's Calendar* in two volumes, Hogg remarked:

> Had they been published last year my other tales in six vols might have been required this year which might have been of great advantage to me Were these properly revised there is no doubt that they have more interest and nature than tales in general (NLS MS 4021, fols 273–74)

Douglas Mack has given a full account of the delays preceding the publication by Blackwood of *The Shepherd's Calendar* in two volumes in late February or early March 1829. As he remarks, 'Naturally enough, Blackwood did not wish another publisher to bring out a book containing the contributions to *Blackwood's* of the star turn of the "Noctes Ambrosianae"', even though he was not particularly eager to publish it himself.[9] Perhaps too Blackwood sensed that an early publication of *The Shepherd's Calendar* would only lead to reiterated and more energetic demands for the speedy publication of the larger prose fiction collection. Hogg's subsequent account of this period in his 'Memoir' is one of constant postponements on Blackwood's part that never amounted to a decisive refusal. Although he dates his first mention of the project to Blackwood to 'the spring of 1829' (p. 59), it had in fact surfaced occasionally for years before that date.

A new urgency enters Hogg's correspondence on this issue with the conclusion of his tenancy of the Mount Benger farm at Whitsunday 1830. Payment was then due to Hogg's numerous creditors, including the Buccleuch estate to whom back-lying rent was owing. At this point the scale of Hogg's debts was openly revealed, both to himself and other people. On 28 April, as the end of the lease drew near, Hogg had enquired of Blackwood, 'Do you not think that in London I could be well employed in some literary capacity?' (NLS MS 4027, fols 185–86); and on 26 May he spelled out again the alternatives before him:

> You must contrive some literary plan to replenish my purse a little once more in the course of the year else I must go straight to London and become what De-quinsey [*sic*] calls *a literary hack* and this in sooth appears to me the only plan by which I can make a tolerable shift. There is another which I think might raise me a supply It is to publish all my tales in numbers like Sir W Scott's to re-write and sub divide them and they being all written off hand and published without either reading or correction I see I could improve them prodigiously. But as my good taste has been watched with a suspicious eye by the literati I would have the work published under the sanction of Lockhart [...] I think an edition of my Scottish tales by Lockhart for behoof of the author would have some effect. [...] If the tales included the lives of Col Aston Bailley Sydserf Col Cloud &c &c they would not amount to less than twelve numbers one for every month of the year of the same size as Sir Walter's. [...] But I will not write to Lockhart or any other body concerning it till I hear your opinion which I know will be a candid one. (NLS MS 4036, fols 102–03)

This letter neatly offers Blackwood the choice of publishing Hogg's collected prose fiction or losing the Shepherd of the 'Noctes Ambrosianae' to the literary marketplace of London. Significantly, a new periodical entitled *Fraser's Magazine* had been published in London that February: the new periodical sought to recapture the early wildness of *Blackwood's* and welcomed its contributors, among them the Ettrick Shepherd, with great eagerness. Hogg's letter also touches upon several other vital issues for the production of what became the 'Altrive Tales' series. Firstly, while Hogg continues to emphasise the 'Scottish tales' aspect of the collection, and therefore its continuities with both *Winter Evening Tales* and *The Shepherd's Calendar*, the tales he names for inclusion are mostly unpublished fictions of novella length. During the later 1820s these must have been much harder to place than the shorter tales, for which there was a ready market as magazine contributions. It is significant that while *Winter Evening Tales* of 1820 had been subtitled 'Collected among the Cottagers of the South of Scotland' the first volume of *Altrive Tales* was to be subtitled 'Collected among the Peasantry of Scotland, and from Foreign Adventurers'. The new phrase signalled the inclusion of longer and previously unpublished novellas outside the realm of tales of peasant life and tradition or semi-fictionalised autobiography, and it nods towards Defoe as much as Burns. In his letter to Blackwood Hogg also markedly attempts to increase his guarantee of respectability by naming as the editor of the series John Gibson Lockhart, the son-in-law of Scott and editor of the prestigious London-based *Quarterly Review*. And of course Blackwood is offered Sir Walter Scott's *magnum opus* edition of the Waverley Novels as a tantalisingly successful precedent.

By securing the copyright to all Scott's novels in 1828, Robert Cadell found himself in a position to bring out a collected edition, including fresh editorial matter by Scott himself and high-quality engravings, now known as Scott's *magnum opus* edition. The monthly volumes which had begun to appear in June 1829 were designed to appeal to a new middle-class market and sold for only five shillings each, the high costs of production being offset by huge sales in a relatively untapped market. Sales rose as high as 30,000 copies, so that, in Peter Garside's words, '1829 marks a watershed in the production of fiction in Britain, with the first clear realization of an extended middle-class market'.[10] The *magnum opus* edition of the Waverley Novels seemed likely to clear Scott's enormous debts, and Hogg must have hoped that the collected tales of the Ettrick Shepherd would clear his own more modest liabilities and enable him to make a decent financial provision for the future of his widow and four young children, soon to be increased to five with the birth of Mary Gray Hogg in August 1831.

Blackwood's reaction seems to have been cautiously favourable, at least to begin with, and he was certainly willing to go to some trouble to consult with Lockhart about the feasibility of such a series. Lockhart and his family were in Scotland in the summer of 1830, arriving in Edinburgh at the end of May and leaving within days for Chiefswood, their holiday home on Scott's Abbotsford estate.[11] Hogg was in town himself during the second week in June, but evidently missed seeing Lockhart at that time. However, it was arranged that Hogg and Blackwood should visit Chiefswood on 3 July to discuss the proposed publication with him. Writing to Blackwood on 21 June 1830 to announce his safe return to Yarrow, Hogg assured the publisher, 'I reccollect my tryste at Mr Lockhart's on the 3d of July and will probably be there a day or two sooner as I have to be at Selkirk on the 30th' (NLS MS 4027, fols 188–89).

The visit was certainly made, as Hogg was still at Chiefswood on 7 July.[12] No definite arrangements for the publication were made, and it seems likely that Lockhart was unwilling to appear as Hogg's editor, or to commit his time to such a project. This is reflected in the discussion Hogg had with Scott on the matter at their last meeting on 28 September 1830. Hogg later gave two accounts of Scott's reaction to the plan, the first of which was written only two days afterwards in his letter to Blackwood of 30 September:

> I had a long chat with Sir Walter the day before yesterday here about our proposed publication of my Scottish tales in monthly numbers. He seemed to think that a good deal of selection would be required; confessed he had forgot many of them and mentioned *The Brownie!* as having had a high character and as much too long out of the market. But he said if you entered heartily into the speculation there was no fear of it and he should answer for Lockhart's assistance only it was not possible that he could do all and that as little as possible should be left to him. (NLS MS 4027, fols 194–95)

Scott's opinion is presented more negatively in the accounts given in Hogg's subsequent 'Anecdotes of Sir W. Scott' and *Familiar Anecdotes of Sir Walter Scott*, the two versions of his recollections of their friendship written after Scott's death. These narratives give the same account essentially, and the first-written is as follows:

> Before we parted I mentioned my plan to him of trusting an edition of my tales to Lockhart. He disapproved of it altogether and said he would not for any thing that Lockhart should enter on any such responsibility for that considering my ram-stam way of writing the responsibility was a heavy and a dangerous one. I use his very words. And then turning half round leaning on his crutch and fixing his eyes on the ground after hanging down his large eye-brows for a good long space he said "you have written a great deal that might be made available Hogg with proper attention. And I am certain that day or other [*sic*] it will become available to you or your family But in my opinion this is not the proper season. I wish you could drive off the experiment until a time when the affairs of the nation are in better keeping For at present all things and in particular literature are going straight down hill to ruin."[13]

In both accounts Scott praises some part of Hogg's work, but in neither of them does he encourage the production of a collected edition in 1830, despite the success of his own *magnum opus* edition. He appears in both as dubious about the inclusion of Lockhart in the scheme. It seems likely that the second and later account is the more accurate of the two, because in writing to Blackwood Hogg would naturally wish to present Scott's opinion of his project in the most favourable light possible. Lockhart, paying a visit to Hogg a few days before leaving Scotland in October, noted his depression, subsequently describing him as 'wet, weary & melancholy'.[14] Hogg, in urgent need of money, seems to have decided to let the question of his collected prose fiction rest for a few months and in the interim to press Blackwood to publish a smaller work. On 20 October he wrote:

> I still hope that my 'Scottish Tales' published in 12 No's with a preface by Lockhart and some pains taken in the arrangement may be made available by and by but in the mean time I should have something going on to keep *the banes green.* (NLS MS 4027, fols 198–99)

Blackwood agreed to publish a selection of Hogg's best songs in a single volume designed for the gift-book market. *Songs by the Ettrick Shepherd* was published at the beginning of 1831, and soon afterwards brought a welcome payment of seventy pounds to the author and the promise of another fifty pounds when a thousand of the fifteen hundred copies printed had been sold.[15] The preparation and printing of *A Queer Book*, a selection of Hogg's ballads and other periodical poetry, then occupied Hogg's energies until the summer of 1831,[16] but when publication of this second shorter work appeared to be imminent Hogg once more reverted to pressing his scheme for a collected prose fiction on his Edinburgh publisher.

At this point a new factor evidently came into play, since Hogg mentions in his letter to Blackwood of 29 June 1831 that a London publisher had expressed an interest in his work:

> You have never told me expressly what you think of my *Scottish Tales* in twelve monthly volumes with decorations Every volume to commence with an original tale or otherwise as may be deemed most meet. Would you like to try them yourself or shall I venture to correspond with another. I had a letter from apparently a new London firm the other day requesting to publish something for me. I have not seen Lockhart yet but hope to see him soon. (NLS MS 4029, fol. 255)

The 'new London firm' may well have been that of James Cochrane, the eventual publisher of *Altrive Tales.* It is unclear how Hogg first made contact with his London publisher, and a picture can be built up only tentatively from scattered hints. According to a subsequent letter to Lockhart Hogg made the first approach to Cochrane 'on the advice of some friends', while by Cochrane's own account his name was first drawn to Hogg's attention by 'John Anderson'.[17] John Anderson, Junior was an Edinburgh bookseller with premises on the North Bridge. As a partner in the firm of Fairbairn and Anderson he had in 1819 published *Selecta Latine*, passages for the use of students as selected by Hogg's friend James Gray of the Edinburgh High School, and, two years later, an edition of the poems of Robert Fergusson with a life by Gray. Hogg's protégé Henry Scott Riddell published his 'Stanzas on the Death of Lord Byron' with Anderson in 1825, and at one time it seems that Hogg himself intended to contribute a preface to one of the volumes of Anderson's Cabinet Edition of *The Poets of Scotland.* Little is known of Cochrane's history, but according to an anonymous pamphlet written by Dr James Browne in 1832 his firm was at that time 'a junior publishing house in London, about a year old'.[18] Cochrane seems to have been anxious to become known as a publisher in Edinburgh circles at this time, as the following notice in the *Edinburgh Weekly Chronicle* of 29 October 1831 (p. 348) indicates:

> ARTISANS' READING ROOM.–We understand that Mr Cochrane, publisher, London, has presented this interesting institution with a copy of the beautiful work which he has just published, viz. Fletcher's History of Poland. This is the second donation that spirited publisher has made to the Artisans' Reading Room.

Hogg's attention might also have been drawn to Cochrane as a partner in the firm of Cochrane and Pickersgill, the publishers of *The Club-Book*, a collection of tales contributed by different well-known writers under the editorship of the Scottish writer Andrew Picken (1788–1833). Hogg's enthusiastic response to Picken's invitation to him to contribute is dated 20 November 1830, and two of his tales, 'The Laidlaws and the Scotts. A Border Tradition' and 'The Bogle o' the Brae. A Queer Courting Story' were published in *The Club-Book* in July 1831.[19] Cochrane's own periodical, *The Metropolitan,* in reviewing the work in the August issue praised Hogg's poetry above his prose, but was careful to add that although his prose tales were sometimes in questionable taste 'they generally have their root in something that is good, and many of them are quite delightful for their *naive* and abundant fancy–particularly when the poet gets to ride on the airy broomstick of Scotch superstition'.[20] It may well be that this was part of an effort by Cochrane to attract the attention of the well-known Scottish author.

Any expression of interest by a London firm in the summer of 1831 was likely to have fuelled Hogg's impatience, especially in view of Blackwood's dilatoriness in publishing *A Queer Book*. Contrary to Hogg's expectations Blackwood, having printed this poetry collection, then refused to set a date for publishing it on the grounds that the political agitation preceding the passage of the 1832 Reform Act was seriously hampering his publishing business. This was probably not untrue, since Blackwood not only said this to Hogg but wrote to the same effect on 24 October 1831 to his son William in India:

> This cursed Reform Bill has caused a dreadful stagnation in every kind of business for the whole of this year. There never has been so slack a year in our trade ever since I have been in business. Had it not been for the Magazine we should have had nothing to do.[21]

Hogg is hardly to be blamed, however, if he saw this as a pretext to avoid publishing his work. Having been told in 1826 that Constable's failure had rendered the times unpropitious for the appearance of his collected prose fiction, he was now being told that they were still unpropitious because of the Reform Bill–and this at the very time that Scott's *magnum opus* edition was breaking all records for the sale of popular fiction. And while Hogg lay under a burden of debt and the sore reflection that in the event of his death his young family were virtually unprovided for, Blackwood had recently moved his business from Princes Street into even more handsome premises in George Street, and his family residence from suburban Newington to fashionable Ainslie Place in the New Town.[22]

Hogg's letter to Lockhart of 11 August [1831], written shortly before the birth of his youngest child, shows his anxiety to make a firm arrangement to begin his series of collected prose tales, either with Blackwood or a London publisher. Blackwood would be a useful consultant as to the proposed revisal, interestingly referred to as a purgation:

> I am still depending on your writing a preface for me and taking the responsibility of my new edition of Scottish tales. My principal hope is anchored there and I intend to purge

> thoroughly and improve greatly and submit every thing to Robt Hogg Ebony and a third one; and if there ever should occur any doubt or difference of opinion to appeal to you for I could not desire you to superintend the whole press. Do you not think that a London publisher would be best? I want to publish my first No. in Janr and continue till my tales are exhausted. (NLS MS 924, No. 84)

As the autumn progressed, however, it became clear that neither Blackwood nor Lockhart was particularly enthusiastic about Hogg's collected prose fiction,[23] and that Hogg was becoming correspondingly despondent about the possibility of an Edinburgh publication and looking more and more to London. On 2 November he wrote testily to Blackwood:

> I think it ridiculous to have books so long lying out of print. I shall have my tales commenced this winter by some publisher since you are so faint hearted about publishing. I never had so much need of making something. [...] I wish you would sell off the Shepherd's Calander at some sale as I wish to select some of the best tales and mingle them with my large work. (NLS MS 4029, fols 266–67)

It may well have been at this point that he entered into serious discussions and negotiations with James Cochrane. No details of these have apparently survived, and the negotiations are merely a matter for speculation. When the inevitable breach with Blackwood came on 6 December Hogg seems to have decided almost at once that he would go to London to superintend the publication of the first volumes of the series, writing to his nephew James Gray on the following day, 'I am thinking of going to London for a few months'.[24] A week later he alerted Lockhart to his imminent arrival, and asked him for his advice regarding the proposed collected edition:

> I have taken the resolution of coming up to you forthwith and setting my tales a going at least under your auspices. I find that I cannot subsist my family any longer without doing something and the Baillie [i.e. Blackwood] will do nothing I will ask no more than you think prudent to do but if it were only the assisting me with your advice in the arrangement and selection it would be a great matter. If you were to write a preface and publish it as your edition I would be sure of success or even a preface saying that you *advised* the publication would avail. However I can effect nothing here

> and must try for once what I can do in London so that it is likely I shall be with you by the close of the year [...] Please consider in the first place whether "Winter Evening Tales *a new series* [*sic*] "The Tales of Altrive" or "The select prose works of &c &c are the best titles. They have all been proposed to me by friends with sundry others besides.

And with a final parting shot to Blackwood of 'You have starved me fairly out of my house and country'[25] Hogg departed from Edinburgh by sea to London on Friday, 23 December arriving over a week later on the last day of the year.

Hogg must have had an understanding with Cochrane previous to his arrival in London, for in noticing the event the *Morning Chronicle* of 2 January 1832 states, 'We understand that Mr. Hogg has arranged with his new publisher (Messrs. Cochrane and Co., of Waterloo-place) for the speedy appearance of a series of "Altrive Tales, by the Ettrick Shepherd," which are to be printed in London'. Hogg was also able to write reassuringly to his wife the very day after his arrival, 'I have seen Cochrane and Lockhart, and everything is likely to be amicably arranged'.[26]

The literary business engaged in by Hogg during his London visit from January to March 1832 has been less well documented than his public social triumphs, and Hogg's own letters tend to give the impression that he was far more idle in this respect than can actually have been the case. It is comparatively easy to write about parties, dinners, and other social functions, and much more difficult to describe in an interesting way those solitary hours spent scribbling at a desk. Hogg's starring role at the Burns dinner at the Freemasons' Hall on 25 January and similar events must have flattered him personally and provided good publicity for the forthcoming first volume of his *Altrive Tales*, but the literary work of preparing that volume for the press was by no means forgotten. By mid-January Hogg was living at his publisher's establishment at 11 Waterloo Place and sending for copies of his periodical articles and published works so that he could revise his work for the new publication. An exchange of notes with Lockhart provides some details of Hogg's progress with the prefatory 'Memoir of the Author's Life' and 'Reminiscences of Former Days' during February, and internal evidence indicates clearly that these were prepared for publication during Hogg's London visit.[27] The printing of *A Father's New Year's Gift*, a 'stitched sixpenny trifle' of Hogg's prayers and hymns for children, would have familiarised him with his new publisher's correctors of the press and with the printing firm of A. &. J. Valpy of Red Lion Court, Fleet

Street, also employed as the printers of *Altrive Tales*.[28]

The first volume of *Altrive Tales* was announced in *The Times* of 16 February as to be published on 1 March 1832, while notices in *The Athenaeum* and *The Metropolitan* in February gave details of the contents of the volume, specifying the frontispiece engraving of a portrait of Hogg by Fox and the inclusion of an illustration by George Cruikshank.[29] Any delays in the production of the first volume seem to have been due as much to the publisher's financial circumstances as to the author's socialising. As early as 17 January Hogg comments in a letter to his wife on Cochrane's reluctance in pushing on the printing and expresses doubts about his solvency:

> For I am afraid that this connection of mine with Mr Cochrane may turn out a hoax. Several of my literary friends have been hinting to me that he is venturing far beyond his capital and that his credit is already tottering. Lockhart on the other hand thinks quite the contrary and none of the Booksellers and I have been in company with very many have ever hinted at the thing. I rather however begin to suppose it as he is not pushing the work through the press with any degree of vigour but rather as it were waiting for something and I dare not push him till I see how his accounts for the year are settled.[30]

Hogg clearly suspected that Cochrane was so straitened financially as to be unable to cover the expenses of paper, printing, binding, illustrations, and advertising immediately. Since the cost of producing and printing illustrations from engraved steel-plates was high, and the volumes were to sell at a comparable price to Scott's *magnum opus* edition, a larger print run was probably necessary. Hogg, however, clearly found this alarming. He reported to Blackwood on 5 February, 'Cochrane is printing off 4000 of the first volume of my tales of which he intends to make two editions I thought it nonsense and proposed only 1500 but he laughed at the idea but I cannot help thinking it a great and needless risk still' (NLS MS 4033, fols 123–24). As Hogg had not quite finished his 'Reminiscences of Former Days' on 25 February it would have been difficult for Cochrane to publish on 1 March as originally advertised, but once that date had been passed no further progress seems to have been made with the production of the volume for a fortnight afterwards. As Hogg wrote to his wife on 14 March, 'My publication has not proceeded one step these two weeks. I cannot understand it'.[31] A prefatory advertising leaf in the published volume suggests that the work was then scheduled to appear on 31 March (shortly after Hogg's departure for Scotland) as the first of a projected twelve volumes, one to be published every other month at six shillings with illustrations by George Cruikshank.

Hogg departed from London for Scotland towards the end of March, shortly before the publication of the first volume of his proposed 'Altrive Tales' series. He intended that during his absence Allan Cunningham, Lockhart, and Thomas Pringle should take the charge of the press off his hands, since it would have been expensive and time-consuming to have proofs sent to Scotland (Garden, pp. 247–48). The proposed contents of the first seven volumes are set out in a list of 19 March, apparently left with Roscoe and Richie, Cochrane's correctors of the press:

The Altrive Tales

---

Vol. 1st Memoir of the Author
Adventures of Capt. Lochy
The Pongos
Marrion's Jock

---

Vol 2d Adventures of Col. Aston
The Brownie of Bodsbeck

---

Vol 3d The Seige [*sic*] of Roxburgh

---

Vol 4th An Original Tale to be sent from Scotland and the remainder selected from the Winter Evening Tales and Shepherd's Calender [*sic*]

---

Vol 5th An Original Tale to be sent from Scotland
The Wool-Gatherer and
The Hunt of Eildon
If any thing more wanted to be selected from The Winter Evening Tales and Shepherd's Calender

---

Vol. 6th
The Confessions of a Sinner
If any more wanted to be selected from The Winter Evening tales and Shepherd's Calendar

---

Vol 7th
An Original Tale to be sent

> The rest to be selected from The Winter Evening Tales and Shepherd's Calender
>
> ---
>
> The rest I will come and superintend[32]

The final words appear to indicate that Hogg intended to make another visit to London about the same time the following year, when he would plan the remainder of the series. The terms and other specific details of publication remain to some extent unclear, since there is apparently no surviving publisher's record, and scattered references to the work in letters are not always entirely consistent with one another. Hogg's letter to Blackwood of 5 February (quoted above) had suggested that Cochrane intended to print four thousand copies of the first volume, but only three thousand were apparently printed, and these seem to have been divided by Cochrane into several tranches. Hogg states in his letter to M'Donald that of the printed copies 'there is only an edition of 1000 published', although when he offered the work to Oliver and Boyd subsequently he wrote, 'There are 1500 of the 3000 printed remaining ready for a second edition'.[33] The second figure, suggesting that Cochrane intended two editions each of 1500 copies, is supported by his later assertion to Fullarton of 14 October 1832 that 'There was 1500 of the first vol. sold in 12 days'.[34] Hogg's letter to Alexander Elder of 14 January 1833 mentions that Cochrane had published the work on the understanding that Hogg's author's share was to be 'one sixth part of the retail price over the whole edition in bills at eighteen months on the publication of each number. Or one sixth part of the copies sold, in cash, at the publication of each new number, optional'. His letter to M'Donald states that if an edition consisted of more than 2000 copies then the author's share would be a fifth of the total retail price, and another letter implies that Cochrane had in fact promised him a fifth share.[35] On an edition of 1500 copies selling for five shillings each Hogg would then expect to receive £54-3-4 for each volume as a sixth part of the price or £75 as a fifth part of the price.

Hogg's standing as the literary lion of the London season that winter would appear to augur a brisk sale for the volume, and in fact he claimed subsequently that 1500 copies had been sold within twelve days of publication.[36] There are indications, however, that publication was delayed for something like a fortnight beyond the advertised date of 31 March. The first of a two-part review appeared in *The Literary Gazette* of 31 March, but this appears to have been written on the basis of a pre-publication copy. In printing the second part a week later the reviewer commented that as 'some requisite alterations have prevented the appearance of this volume at the appointed time, [...] it is still a sealed book to the generality'. *The Athenaeum* of 14 April 1832 grumbled that 'the publisher thought it proper to give the book to one of our brethren a full fortnight before he sent it to us, and the consequence was, that passage after passage came pouring from the pages of Jerdan [editor of *The Literary Gazette*], through all those inferior papers which live, like caterpillars, on the green leaves of the *Gazette* and the *Athenaeum*. With us this discourtesy is as dust in the balance, when the welfare of such a man as he of Ettrick is concerned'. The delay had been previously noted by *The Athenaeum* of 7 April:

> We hear that some inconsiderate expressions in Hogg's autobiography respecting a worthy bookseller have occasioned the unlooked-for and injurious delay in the publication of the Altrive Tales. We are sorry that a man who is not at all sensitive should say anything galling of another who shrinks at a gentle touch: but we are still more concerned to think that the correction of this error, which is reported not to have been of a very heinous nature, will tend to hurt the sale of a work which an author of no every-day qualities depends upon for bread. Blackwood is not treated with much respect, neither is the memory of Constable; nay, Lockhart himself, the steady and unflinching friend of the Shepherd, has epithets bestowed on him which it requires no little after-praise to qualify: yet we hear of no complaints from any of these quarters.[37]

Evidently then, William Blackwood was not the publisher who demanded the cancellation of statements about himself from Hogg's 'Memoir' in *Altrive Tales* (1832). From scattered hints it seems that the volume, as originally printed, had included offensive allegations about Owen Rees, partner in the Longman publishing firm. The first part of the *Literary Gazette* review had concluded, 'The only very objectionable passage we have to censure, is an allusion to Mr. Owen Rees, in which the Shepherd is terribly mistaken'. James Browne in his anonymous pamphlet, *The 'Life' of the Ettrick Shepherd Anatomized* (1832) says in discussing Hogg's relations with the Longmans firm:

> We happen to know, however, that the copies of the 'Memoir,' as originally printed, contained insinuations against one of the individual partners, of so gross a kind, that Hogg, or his

> publishers, were compelled to cancel the offensive matter; a circumstance which occassioned a fortnight's delay in the shipment of the copies for Scotland.[38]

The volume as published certainly contains a section concerning Hogg's dealings with the Longman firm (pp. 55–57 in the present edition), but Owen Rees is not mentioned by name, and it seems probable that Cochrane agreed to print a replacement for the section containing the objectionable remarks.[39]

Cochrane's own shaky financial standing was far more detrimental to Hogg's plan for a multi-volume collection of his prose fiction than a small delay caused by a bookseller aggrieved at his treatment in the 'Memoir'. It has been noted already that Hogg expressed his doubts as to the soundness of Cochrane's financial position as early as 17 January, and he continued to do so from time to time in his letters. Notifying William Blackwood on 2 March of his attempts to get a London publisher to take over the publication of his *Songs by the Ettrick Shepherd* and *A Queer Book*, Hogg wrote 'Cochrane would give £100 for them and take the other at your own price which is certainly very reasonable but I am afraid the cash would hardly be forthcoming'. It seems probable that he had also been warned by Lockhart of the danger of an imminent failure by Cochrane.[40] Another sign that Hogg was aware of Cochrane's shortage of necessary capital is provided by his attempt to find him a partner with some money to invest in the firm. From Cochrane's later account it is clear that it was Hogg himself who effected the fateful introduction of the young and ambitious John M'Crone, at that time employed by the musical publisher Samuel Chappell of New Bond Street as a shopman:

> [...] he was introduced to me by the Ettrick Shepherd, who had been accidentally acquainted with him, while Shopman in Chappell's the music shop–in Bond Street. He represented to me that he had some capital & would be glad to join me in business [...][41]

Hogg seems to have deliberately ignored his own misgivings and the warnings of others, and to have shut his eyes to the financial instability of his London publisher. As he returned home to Yarrow he no doubt hoped for the best with respect to the continuation of his 'Altrive Tales' series.

Cochrane's business collapsed about a month after Hogg's departure from London on 25 March. The bookseller Sir Richard Phillips (1767–1840) wrote to Hogg at Altrive on 27 April with the news, as follows:

> [...] my sympathy is specially aroused by what has been passing within a few days at the house of your publisher in Waterloo Place I hear of Executions, Seizures, Attachments, Arrests, &c &c [...]
>
> The day before yesterday he was not in his business the whole day, a man from the Sheriff being in possession, nothing being to be delivered on credit, & the man receiving all money. Another Execution, but a few days since nearly swept the premises [...][42]

A notice of a fiat of bankruptcy 'against James Cochrane, of No. 11, Waterloo-Place, Pall-Mall' duly appeared in the *London Gazette* of 8 May 1832, the firm's creditors being requested to attend a court of bankruptcy to give in their claims against him on 19 June. Hogg appears to have received the news as early as 2 May, and wrote to Cochrane himself on the following day asking him to secure the remaining copies of *Altrive Tales* for himself as author and to find another London firm to publish them on commission for him until Cochrane was permitted to set up his own business once more. On the same day he also consulted Lockhart, who had in many respects inherited Scott's role of literary advisor in Hogg's eyes now that his old mentor was in feeble health both bodily and mentally:

> As you dreaded Mr Cochrane is knocked up and now I know not what to do. I have been inveigled most shamefully and yet I cannot blame him for at the advice of some friends I applied to him first. [...] I hope that as Goldie's turned out so good a concern for me ultimately so may this but the present time is the worst. (NLS MS 924, No. 86)

Hogg's mind reverted to 1814, when George Goldie's bankruptcy had halted sales of the third edition of his most successful work to date, *The Queen's Wake*. At that time the bankrupt's trustees had agreed to make the copies over to the author, William Blackwood and John Murray had sold them for him, and the end result had been that Hogg received more for those copies than he would have done had Goldie continued in business.[43] Hogg's characteristic optimism was hardly justified in 1832, however, as he failed to find a publisher who was prepared to continue the publication on terms that he regarded as satisfactory.

At first sight this is extremely surprising, given high initial sales and Hogg's status as the London literary lion of the preceding winter season. Hogg's agent in London, John M'Donald, appears to have received a curt refusal from the firm of Richard Bentley and a proposal from Smith and Elder to publish them on the author's behalf only if Hogg could place securities in their hand to the amount of £200. Hogg considered this insulting to him as an established author, and declined a proposal which in any case he could hardly have accepted given his financial situation. Over the next few months he himself offered the work to two Scottish publishing firms, Archibald Fullarton and Oliver and Boyd, but without success and the momentum of the series broke down completely.[44]

The remaining copies of the first volume of *Altrive Tales* appear to have been sold at intervals over the next few years, some of them at least without Hogg's knowledge and consent. Examination of multiple copies of *Altrive Tales* indicates that two separate attempts were made to disguise for resale the fact that the volume had been originally intended as the first of a multi-volume set. In the first of these reissues there is no half-title with 'VOL. I.' and the title-page dated 1832 also omits 'VOL. I.', while the final leaf, although textually identical with the final leaf of the original publication, is a cancel and omits the phrase 'END OF VOL. I.'. In the second reissue the half-title is missing, while the title page is dated 1835 and omits 'VOL. I.', and the last leaf, though textually identical to the original publication, has 'THE END' rather than 'END OF VOL. I'. This 1835 reissue additionally omits the prefatory leaf with 'Contents of the First Volume' on the recto, and 'Illustrations to the First Volume' on the verso.[45] It seems unlikely that Hogg himself would have consented to the first of these reissues at least, which was apparently made in 1832 itself when he was still hoping to continue with the projected twelve-volume series. This would appear to be confirmed by his letter of 12 May 1833 to John M'Crone, who was about to become Cochrane's new partner, asking, 'What are become of all the vols of my tales which Cochrane and Mason contrived to preserve for me? Am I never to realize any thing from them?'[46] Mason is perhaps the F. J. Mason, who advertised the volume at a bargain price of three shillings and sixpence among a list of other works available in Edinburgh at Stillies' Library, 140 High Street in the *Edinburgh Evening Post* of 23 August 1834. A novel published by Mason in 1834 gives his address as 444, West Strand in London.[47] His advertisement for *Altrive Tales* gives no indication that the volume had been intended as the first of a multi-volume series, and the price implies that the work had been remaindered at this time, which was a significant one for James Cochrane.

After his bankruptcy in early May 1832 Cochrane clearly hoped to re-establish himself as a publisher in partnership with the young John M'Crone. M'Crone's lengthy visit to Altrive that autumn to collect materials for a book about the recently-deceased Sir Walter Scott also served to make Hogg acquainted with their plans for the projected partnership and to secure him for the firm's list of authors. In a letter handed to M'Crone for delivery to Cochrane Hogg expressed his willingness to oblige but pointed out, 'I cannot make a bargain with a company which does not yet exist'.[48] Cochrane, from his reply of 10 December, seemed eager to retain Hogg for his author's list, offering the concession of employing Andrew Shortreed, the Edinburgh printer of *A Queer Book*:

> We shall wait upon the dons of the Trade ourselves & if we cannot get Duncan & other Scotch houses to join in the work, I trust I shall be enabled to go on with it without them.–Now that we have a Volume to shew as a specimen–your friend Shortreed of Edin[r] could print the work & I should be prepared to pay in Cash one volume under another–that is to publish every two months & to pay for one vol. when another was ready.–The no might be limited to 1500.[49]

More cautious than he had been at the start of the year, Cochrane was now willing to print only half the number of copies that had been produced of the first volume, and would clearly prefer to have a Scottish partner to share in the risk involved. He subsequently wrote to Hogg on 13 January 1833 to say that the partnership with M'Crone had been effected (NLS MS 2245, fols 218–19). The new firm, however, was apparently less enthusiastic about the 'Altrive Tales' series than the old one, as the matter appeared to hang fire then for several months. Perhaps M'Crone was less interested in Hogg's tales than in his anecdotes of his friend and literary mentor, Scott. By the beginning of February 1833 Hogg was in Edinburgh, opening negotiations for another series of his collected prose fiction with Blackie and Son of Glasgow under the old title of 'Winter Evening Tales'. No agreement was reached at this point, and it seems probable that there were several negative factors here. Firstly Hogg was offered only a twelfth of the price of the edition as his author's share, about half what he hoped to receive. Secondly, the Blackie enterprise printed and distributed their own books, so that they were not particularly receptive to Hogg's requests to have the work printed in Edinburgh by Oliver and Boyd, and to give Cochrane and M'Crone's London publishing house a share of the work.[50] When he wrote to M'Crone on 12 May 1833, however, Hogg was still hoping for some sort of partnership between Glasgow and London:

> I have likewise put off the Messrs Blackie for two or three months until I see how you come on. I would like at all events if practicable that your names were in as publishers and as the Blackies are good men and sell to all the *trade* at half price you cannot be wrong in taking a few hundreds of each vol.[51]

M'Crone paid another visit to Altrive in June 1833, and returned to London with a letter from Hogg offering Cochrane and himself a new single-volume publication of 'Genuine Tales of the days of Montrose' together with Hogg's manuscript for it. Cochrane was pleased at this mark of Hogg's confidence in the new firm, but his letter of acceptance of 24 July makes it plain that he was by now reluctant to act as the chief publisher of the 'Altrive Tales' series:

> I was in hopes you would have ere this closed with the Scotch House to continue the Altrive Tales–stipulating for us to be the London Publishers–we engaging to take 500 Copies certain. I feel convinced this would be the most beneficial mode for you–You are so popular in Scotland that an active house in Glasgow would effect wonders–There would be no difficulty as to size, or type, the first volume being an excellent specimen. I shall enclose half a dozen copies for you in a parcel for Edinburgh in a few days. Times are now so altered in the Book Trade, that we can no longer venture on such a work single handed. (NLS MS 2245, fols 228–29)

Hogg's response was to suggest that perhaps the 'Montrose' work might be published with some previously-published shorter tales from *The Shepherd's Calendar*, as the second and third volumes of the 'Altrive Tales' series, and this arrangement was initially agreed to by Cochrane. Although Cochrane's letter of 9 August states that the firm might print 1500 copies of the second and third volumes it also reveals that he was depending on a Scottish firm, either Fullarton or Blackie and Son, as partners in the work. Such an arrangement, though, would be quite unacceptable to these numbers publishers, who kept a tight control over every aspect of book production and distribution. Cochrane reports, 'I have written to Blackie & Fullarton–If they could be induced to push the work in Scotland–there would be no fear of the result'.[52] Presumably an unpropitious reply to this offer of partnership effectively put a stop to plans to revive the 'Altrive

Tales' series. Hogg, however, seems to have envisaged the publication of two collected prose fiction series, with the possibility of 'Winter Evening Tales' being published by Blackie and Son in Glasgow, and 'Altrive Tales' by Cochrane and M'Crone in London. Writing to Lockhart on 17 September 1833 he states:

> I have got an offer from a Glasgow subscribing Co. for a dozen vol's of tales of which they calculate they can sell 20=000!! in numbers but their offer is so small (one twelfth of the retail price) that I have hitherto refused it. I am likewise trusting Cochrane and M,Crone with two or three vols of the Altrive Tales till I see how they come on. I like the men and would like to be of use to them if I could. I find that my tales in MS and print even with a great deal extracted as *balaam* [i.e. space-filling material] will amount to 24 vols. (NLS MS 934, fols 219–20)

Hogg had been visited by 'Blackie' (presumably Blackie senior, though the visitor may have been his son) by early November. He had then 'bargained with him for six Vols of Tales offering him *sixteen* more which he declined contrary to every rule of Grammar'. On 11 November Hogg sent the Glasgow firm a corrected copy of *The Brownie of Bodsbeck; and Other Tales* as his first instalment of copy for the projected work. This engagement would naturally put an end to Cochrane's hopes of continuing the 'Altrive Tales' series in partnership with the Glasgow firm, and Cochrane seems to have told Hogg subsequently that he was willing to consider only a limited edition of 750 copies of the forthcoming volumes. Hogg's anger is palpable in his letter to Cochrane of 1 March 1834:

> I am exceedingly averse to the stopping of the unfortunate Altrive Tales with one vol. which I meant should at least have been twelve. And moreoever there never was an edition of 750 of any work of mine published and I shall not begin now. [...] the whole business is a whim of Johnie M,Crone's but he will find that he has met with one *at least* as obstinate as himself *I will not do it*. [...] as for bereaving a dozen volumes of all the original matter for a poor shabby edition of 750!! O lord that will never go down with the old Shepherd![53]

This appears to have been the effective end of the 'Altrive Tales' series, though M'Crone's letter to Hogg of 23 June implies that the firm was still interested in publishing his work:

> We are getting on very well here–and you may chance to see one or other of us this autumn–We can then renew our old Compacts over a *cheerer*, and rivet our connection closer. (NLS MS 2245, fols 243–44)

The promised visit never took place, however, as by the time M'Crone was in the district Margaret Hogg refused to have him in the house. James Cochrane had discovered that his young partner was conducting an adulterous affair with his wife, and the business partnership was accordingly dissolved. Significantly, it appears to have been during August 1834 that some of the stock of copies of the first volume of *Altrive Tales* was remaindered by T. J. Mason. Hogg, with his wife's support, subsequently promised his 'Montrose' tales to the injured husband, and *Tales of the Wars of Montrose* was eventually published by James Cochrane early in 1835.[54] The posthumous and heavily bowdlerised six-volume *Tales and Sketches by the Ettrick Shepherd* published by Blackie and Son between December 1836 and December 1837 is a poor shadow of Hogg's original conception of a twelve-volume collected prose works in 'Altrive Tales', and the resemblance of the volume of *Tales and Sketches* edited by Thomas Thomson in 1865 is yet more tenuous. Fortunately Hogg's ambitions for a collected edition of his prose work are now being gradually fulfilled with the publication of the successive volumes of the Stirling/South Carolina Research Edition of the Collected Works of James Hogg.

## 2. Hogg as a Collected Author

During his lifetime Hogg made several attempts to achieve the established status of author of a collected edition for himself, most notably in his four-volume *Poetical Works* of 1822. John Murray had published a *Poetical Works* for Byron in 1815, and closer to home Scott had published a twelve-volume *Poetical Works* in 1820, and a ten-volume *Poetical Works* in 1821. It was natural for Hogg to wish to emulate the achievements of the leading poets of the day, preserving and dignifying his own poetry in similar fashion. The publisher Robert Cadell also thought that it would be a desirable thing for Hogg's name and other works, even though telling him that 'it will take a good deal of pushing' and that 'the advertising will be considerable in order to start you as a collected author'.[55] The appearance of *Altrive Tales* as the first of a collected prose works was an assertion by Hogg that his tales also merited inclusion among the best writing of the age. That it was published almost ten years after a collected edition of his poetry reflects, among other things, the higher status traditionally accorded to poetry and to drama and the general feeling that verse was the proper mode of expression for an original genius and peasant poet.[56]

The definition of classic status was gradually expanding and being modernised during the years preceding the publication of *Altrive Tales*. Traditionally classic status was granted primarily to the Latin and Greek writers of antiquity, such as Homer and Sophocles, Virgil and Pindar. However, Samuel Johnson's *The Lives of the Poets* (1779–1781) is an early indicator that British poets of the past were increasingly regarded in the same way, while Scott's involvement with 'Ballantyne's Novelist's Library' a generation later shows that the status of fiction was rapidly rising. The appearance of the first volume of Scott's *magnum opus* edition of the Waverley Novels in June 1829 implicitly claimed this classic status for the work of a living rather than a dead author, and was therefore, as Jane Millgate has indicated, an audacious as well as a novel development:

> [...] in collecting and annotating his writings in this way Scott was implicitly assigning to fiction a status previously reserved for poetry and drama, and to the productions of a living author a treatment normally accorded only to the achievements of the great masters of the past.[57]

Scott could have been considered unduly egotistical in editing his own work and in urging its claims to classic status, and Millgate argues that the 'engagingly modest and even self-deprecating' tone of his introduction and notes are part of a strategy to evade this charge. The expected account of the author's life and the composition of his work was also successfully diffused over a sequence of volumes that included his collected poetry as well as prose fictions, minimising the apparent egotism of autobiography.[58] Scott in his *magnum opus* edition acquiesces gracefully in the valuation previously placed on his work by the purchasing and reading public, and his strategy was eminently successful.

The success of the *magnum opus* edition set a fashion for collected editions in monthly volumes, handsomely printed and bound in a pocket-sized format and including steel-plate engravings, for the modest sum of five or six shillings per volume. The aim of their publishers was to produce volumes 'cheap enough for the deal shelves of the mechanic, and handsome enough for the boudoir of a lady',[59] and which could be reliably built into handsome sets. Regularity of publication was essential, since the purchaser would naturally be unwilling to begin to assemble a set which might never be completed, and is emphasised in advertisements for several of these series. John Murray, for example, felt that an apology and justification was due for the late appearance of even the final volume of a seventeen-volume set of Byron's works:

> The punctuality with which this popular publication has appeared on the first of every month, since its commencement in January 1832, has been accomplished by great efforts on the part of the Editor and Publisher, and they are only induced to depart from it in this instance in order that the concluding Volume [...] may be made as accurate and perfect as possible.[60]

In this context the postponement of the publication of the first volume of Hogg's *Altrive Tales* (noted above) from 1 March to 31 March, and then the withdrawal of copies from the market for a further fortnight after publication, would have seriously compromised its appeal to purchasers. Cochrane's bankruptcy halted a series whose regularity of publication must have appeared unpromising from the start.

Some of the monthly editions built up to form a collected set of the writings of one particular author, and others claimed to embody the best and most popular fiction of a particular epoch. Few of them consisted of new and hitherto unpublished work, though there were occasional exceptions such as Leitch Ritchie's 'Library of Romance'.[61] In general, though, the monthly sets claimed to recognise the classic status already granted by the reading public to individual works or celebrated authors.

One of the earliest series claiming to draw together the best fiction of the age was the 'Standard Novels' series of Henry Colburn and Richard Bentley. Early in 1831 they advertised a monthly 'National Library–Series of Standard Novels. Uniform with the Waverley Novels'. The first volume, J. F. Cooper's *The Pilot*, was to appear on 1 March, the first of a six-shilling series, 'beautifully printed and embellished, and neatly bound'. The 'Standard Novels' were to 'consist solely of those works of fiction which have been established in public estimation by the unerring voice of fame; and to the novels of each writer will be prefixed a biographical and critical Essay'. Subsequent advertisements stress regularity of appearance of the successive volumes on the first day of the month, and their bargain price. The volumes 'will range in the library with the Waverley

Series, but they will contain a much greater quantity of matter–a quantity indeed equal to two, and sometimes to three ordinary volumes'.[62] Such series were clearly designed to appeal to (and partly form the cultural aspirations of) the modestly comfortable middle-class household, invited to create its own elegant library in monthly bargain-priced instalments, in addition to subscribing to a circulating library. In February 1833 *The Literary Gazette* reflected enthusiastically upon the progress of the series in reviewing its twenty-fourth number, commenting on the authors chosen to appear under the 'Standard' label, who included Cooper, Godwin, Austen, Jane Porter, Mary Brunton, and John Galt:

> The selection before us has one great merit–it is perfectly unexceptionable; and to this negative qualification we must add much warmer praise; for the volumes well deserve the 'standard' place assigned to them in English literature.

The paper conceded that the 'plan of the circulating libraries is good, as far as it goes; we are enabled, at an astonishingly cheap rate, to keep pace with the novelties of the day' but commended the new fashion as a necessary supplement to this practice:

> We entirely approve of the system of reprints; the neat and cheap editions now appearing are the very things for the family bookcase, and for the shelves of the young people; and no pages are like those of our own library, whether numerous or scanty–a familiar face is as great a merit in a book as in a friend.[63]

Colburn and Bentley tempted the purchaser of Scott's *magnum opus* edition with a supplementary set of fictions by other popular and decorous contemporary novelists, also handsomely produced at modest cost. They also emphasised that 'authors of the volumes already published have been induced to revise their works, and to write Notes and new Introductions expressly for the series'.

Another series, beginning monthly publication on 2 May 1831, 'Roscoe's Novelist's Library', focused on the standard fiction of the previous age, and was viewed as a useful counterpart to the 'Standard Novels' series:

> WHEN the series of Standard Novels and Romances was announced by Messrs. Colburn & Bentley, we most heartily recommended it to that patronage it so well deserved, and which we have great pleasure in hearing it has so largely received. We could not, however, but express our regret

> that the plan did not include the works of Fielding and Smollett, De Foe, and others, the elder masters of fiction [...]. The hint, we are most happy to say, has been taken by Messrs. Cochrane & Pickersgill, and a series is announced, to be *confined* to these classical works. This is well, and looks like judgment in the new firm. There can be no clashing in the two series; the one was wanting to complete the other.[64]

The 'Novelist's Library', edited by Thomas Roscoe, was less revolutionary than either Scott's *magnum opus* edition or the 'Standard Novels' series, because it comprised the fiction of a previous age. However, it is of particular relevance to Hogg's own collected fiction because James Cochrane was its publisher. While the immediate inspiration for *Altrive Tales* in Hogg's mind and that of his publisher was Scott's *magnum opus* edition, Cochrane's experience in publishing 'Roscoe's Novelist's Library' clearly informed *Altrive Tales* itself. 'Roscoe's Novelist's Library' was itself described as uniform with the Waverley Novels, a classic collection planned to include works by Smollett, Fielding, Cervantes, Goldsmith, Sterne, Swift, Frances Burney, Le Sage, and Henry Mackenzie, handsomely produced but for a more popular market than previous editions. As an advertisement in the volume containing *Humphry Clinker*, published on 1 July 1831, explains:

> The best uniform Editions of these celebrated works have hitherto been published in forms and at prices which have placed them beyond the reach of any but the wealthier classes of readers. To remove this inconvenience, and supply wants which the Public have long felt, the Proprietors intend to publish the present Edition in Monthly Volumes, beautifully printed, and embellished with Plates, at the cheap price of five shillings per volume, neatly bound. Each Author can be purchased separately.
>
> [...] George Cruikshank [...] is engaged to illustrate the whole series of the Novelist's Library.[65]

The emphasis on Cruikshank's continuing involvement is significant, for the success of the series was heavily dependent upon its engravings and general appearance of elegance to distinguish it from previous editions. Two previous volumes, an edition of *Robinson Crusoe*, had received disappointing reviews focusing on unsatisfactory engravings by J. G. Strutt, and effectively the series was relaunched by Cochrane and Pickersgill on 1 July after George Cruikshank was secured to illustrate all the remaining volumes. The new first volume, comprising Smollett's *Humphry Clinker*, featured an engraved frontispiece portrait of Smollett and four other engraved illustrations, while succeeding volumes similarly included either four or five plates each. The monthly volumes were printed by the firm of A. J. Valpy in gatherings of eight leaves and bound in a yellow watered silk with gold and navy paper spine labels.[66] It is unclear how many volumes were published altogether, but the series appears to have been successful enough to survive Cochrane's bankruptcy in the spring of 1832. A review of volume XIII, the first part of *Don Quixote*, published by Effingham Wilson, Royal Exchange, London, opens by expressing pleasure that the series has been 're-suscitated', and Wilson appears to have published at least four more volumes, the rest of *Don Quixote* (XIV and XV), and a two-part edition of *Gil Blas*, all forming part of 'Roscoe's Novelist's Library' and with illustrations by Cruikshank.[67]

The first volume of *Altrive Tales* was not dissimilar to a volume of 'Roscoe's Novelist's Library', though slightly less luxurious in appearance and costing an extra shilling, these elements perhaps reflecting the necessary inclusion of the author's royalty in calculating costs. It too was printed by the Valpy firm in gatherings of eight leaves, bound in a ribbed green cloth with gold and navy paper spine labels, claiming likewise to be printed uniformly with the Waverley Novels. It provided a frontispiece engraved portrait of the author and one illustration by Cruikshank. A volume of the 'Altrive Tales' series was to appear every other month rather than monthly, but the prefatory advertisement similarly emphasises the classic status of the twelve-volume series. It declares that 'the writings, genius, and character of Mr. Hogg are now co-extensive with the national feeling', and that the author has been induced to publish the collection 'as an Inheritance to his Children and a Legacy to his Country'.

The emphasis on 'national feeling' in describing Hogg's proposed 'Altrive Tales' series is of particular interest. Several reprint editions had a national aspect, in keeping with Scott's status as premier Scottish novelist in his Waverley Novels. 'The Romance of History', for instance, costing six shillings per volume and advertised as uniform with the Waverley Novels was subdivided into four series, each of three volumes, by nation, 'England' by Henry Neele, 'France' by Leitch Ritchie , 'Italy' by Charles Macfarlane, and 'Spain' by M. Trueba. As the advertisements explained, 'These Works illustrate the Romantic Annals of every Age [...] and comprise also a short History of each Country'.[68] A similar impulse to summarise national achievement appears to inform several of the series of fictions that followed the *magnum opus* edition of Scott. Colburn and Bentley offered as a subset of their 'Standard Novels' series a 'Cheap Edition of Cooper's Novels', *The Spy, The Pilot, The Last of the Mohicans, The Pioneers,* and *The Prairie* all appearing in six-shilling volumes 'beautifully embellished' and with 'a new Introduction by the Author'.[69] The work of James Fenimore Cooper (1789–1851) was clearly being promoted as the acme of contemporary American fiction. The Irish equivalent was 'Miss Edgeworth's Tales and Novels, in Monthly Volumes, with superb Engravings', described as 'uniform in size and appearance with the Waverley Novels and Lord Byron's Life and Works', the first of eighteen monthly volumes being published on 1 May 1832.[70]

Of the single author series, the most influential after the *magnum opus* edition itself were probably the above-mentioned works of Lord Byron and those of Maria Edgeworth, both of them making an appearance slightly later than the first volumes of 'Standard Novels' and 'Roscoe's Novelist's Library'. A prospectus for the fourteen-volume 'First Complete and Uniform Edition of the Works of Lord Byron, with his Letters and Journals, and his Life by Thomas Moore' was issued by John Murray in the autumn of 1831, and the first volume published at the start of 1832. Byron's heroic death at Missolonghi in 1824 had purged his image of scandal and moral taint, and reinforced his identification with his own Romantic heroes, firing the Byronic myth for the next generation. Cheaply-produced French editions were threatening Murray's control of Byron's work, and must have provided a major impetus towards the monthly multi-volume edition, each with an engraved frontispiece and title-page and selling at a modest five shillings. This was a more traditional project in conception than Scott's *magnum opus* edition (since Byron was a dead poet and the biography written by an editor), if not in terms of marketing.[71] Murray's edition was hugely successful: an advertisement for the third volume states that owing 'to the great demand for former Volumes, the Plates have been re-engraved', and gradually the scope of the edition was widened to include 'such notes and illustrations to Lord Byron's text, as are usually appended to the pages of a deceased author of established and permanent popularity', so that the total number of volumes published was in the end seventeen, including a substantial index. The edition came to include by means of its substantial notes a brief history of the initial reception of his individual poems. A reviewer of the eleventh volume alluded to remarks by Jeffrey and Wilson, and commented:

> *Manfred* had the good fortune to be reviewed at the time by several of the ablest critics of the day in their best respective manners; and it is extremely interesting *now* to look back to and compare the several observations of such minds.

The edition became a model for future editors, the same reviewer declaring that 'whosoever may have to edit, *post mortem*, the *opera omnia* of any one of the true poets of this age, can follow no better model than what is afforded them in this edition of Byron'.[72]

The early volumes of the Byron edition were starting to appear during Hogg's London visit, and must have increased his awareness that there was an implicit immodesty in the production of a collected works within the author's lifetime. He must also have drawn comparisons between the claims to fame of the aristocratic Lord Byron and the plebeian Ettrick Shepherd. He jokes, for example, in *Altrive Tales* itself about Dr Scott the Odontist's spurious reputation as a poet and a wit, commenting, 'Had he lived till now, I am persuaded his works would have swelled out to volumes, and would have been published in his name, with his portrait at the beginning' (p. 76). The tales that follow Hogg's autobiographical reminiscences are (unlike the Odontist's poems) the genuine work of the author, but in other respects the notional publication is a comic travesty of Hogg's own enterprise, which also has the author's portrait at the beginning and is designed to swell out to volumes. Hogg is drawing attention to the formal properties of a collected works in *Altrive Tales*, with its portrait of the author, dedication, and prefatory biographical introduction.

The first of the eighteen monthly volumes of *Tales and Novels by Maria Edgeworth* was not published until 1 May 1832, after the appearance of Hogg's *Altrive Tales*, although the series was advertised before that date and Hogg must have been aware during his London visit that such a series was projected. Like the Byron edition, each volume of the Edgeworth series contained an engraved frontispiece and title-page and had a retail price of five shillings. Edgeworth's tales were asserted to have 'taken an enduring position in the literature of the country', and although 'they cannot be said, strictly, to be Historical, yet they will be found to resemble no contemporary works in the department of Romance so much as the earlier novels of the Author of Waverley'.[73]

Within this context the status of *Altrive Tales* was problematic. Hogg could hardly assert that his fiction was the best of Scottish fiction, when earlier publications such as *The Brownie of Bodsbeck* had been viewed as secondary Scottish novels, falling short of a standard set by Scott himself. Ian Duncan has argued that Hogg's *Winter Evening Tales* represents 'a vibrant demotic alternative to the culturally and commercially dominant form of the historical novel established [...] by Walter Scott'. A similar alternative view of Scottish fiction appears to underlie the title *Altrive Tales*, as 'collected among the Peasantry of Scotland, and from Foreign Adventurers'.[74] There is a certain tension, however, in offering an alternative to the dominant mode of national fiction in a form associated with and founded upon general acceptation and classic status. A brief description of the three tales in the first and only volume of *Altrive Tales* is revealing: they were a longer tale that he had not been able to publish previously at all ('The Adventures of Captain John Lochy'); a magazine contribution that might not otherwise have been permanently preserved ('The Pongos'); and a tale rescued from the previous context of a comparatively unsuccessful longer fiction ('Marion's Jock'). Hogg's claim to be a classic author was particularly bold, as the author of the anonymous pamphlet attack entitled *The 'Life' of the Ettrick Shepherd Anatomized* did not fail to remark. He commented sarcastically that the volume was 'intended, doubtless, to rival the Waverley Novels and the works of Byron, and modestly published at a price *one fifth* more than that of these standard and classical works'.[75]

Hogg's insecure claim to classic status is surely reflected in the inclusion in the volume of his reminiscences of eminent literary contemporaries. They provide evidence of association with major literary figures, but at the same time Hogg himself almost always appears as a subordinate figure, most pointedly in his reminiscences of Wordsworth who unfairly denies Hogg due recognition as a poet. Visiting Wordsworth at Rydal Mount Hogg, his host, and a number of other poets walk upon the terrace to admire an unusual arch of light in the sky. When Hogg remarks to Dorothy Wordsworth that this is a triumphal arch celebrating the meeting of the poets, Wordsworth deflates his pretensions with the comment, 'Where are they?' (see p. 68). Advertisements for *Altrive Tales* encapsulate this insecurity rather neatly, by describing the volume as 'containing the Autobiography of the Author, brought down to the present time, with Reminiscences of Sir Walter Scott, Southey, Wordsworth, Lockhart, Cunningham, Galt &c.'[76] Hogg's association with the likes of Scott, Southey and Wordsworth seems more important and prominent than the rest of his autobiography. Extracts subsequently published in newspapers also tend to focus on this part of *Altrive Tales* (see pp. liv–lv below).

Hogg had originally hoped to separate the traditional roles of author and editor, daringly united by Scott. His mention in the 'Memoir' itself of Lockhart's refusal to act as editor may therefore be a form of self-defence. 'He said that he would cheerfully assist me [...] but that it was altogether without a precedent for one author to publish an edition of the works of another while the latter was still alive, and better qualified than any other person to arrange the work' (p. 59). The illustrious example of Lockhart's father-in-law implicitly justifies Hogg's own practice in *Altrive Tales*. Scott also endorses the 'Memoir' more directly. A letter from him appears at the very start of Hogg's literary autobiography arguing that it is valuable as it shows 'the efforts of a strong mind and vigorous imagination, to develop themselves even under the most disadvantageous circumstances' and because it offers novelties such as a depiction of 'real shepherds actually contending for a poetical prize' (p. 11). This letter was originally published anonymously at the start of the 'Memoir' included in Hogg's 1807 edition of *The Mountain Bard*, and his inclusion of it here (Scott's name being given for the first time) surely argues some insecurity in Hogg's mind about the classic status he is claiming and a real defensiveness about the egotism of autobiography. Scott's influence and example is inescapable in any consideration of Hogg's methods and objectives in *Altrive Tales*.

A more interesting and ultimately more successful response to any charge of egotism was Hogg's open and cheerful plea of guilty at the very start of what he terms 'this *important* Memoir':

> I LIKE to write about myself: in fact, there are few things which I like better; it is so delightful to call up old reminiscences. Often have I been laughed at for [...] my good-natured egotism [...] and I am aware that I shall be laughed at again. (p. 11)

This is Hogg at his most playful, both mocking and utilising formal convention and reader expectations. His autobiography will be entertaining as well as egotistical, 'containing much more of a romance than mere fancy could have suggested'. In effect, it will be a true tale preceding his fictional tales and the reader's amusement is the best justification for publishing and preserving both.

## 3. Diversity of Fictions

The publication history of *Altrive Tales* as the start of a collected prose fiction series has always tended to obscure as much as illuminate the nature of the existing volume. Hogg's achievement has been necessarily viewed as incomplete, and discussion has tended to centre on the narrative of the 'Memoir of the Author's Life' while treating the three tales of the volume as almost incidental and arbitrary components of the volume. This is in keeping with the conventional view that Hogg's own collections of tales and sketches have no definite plan, a view which is now being seriously challenged by successive volumes of the Stirling/South Carolina Edition.[77] Hogg must have been aware that sales of the first volume of his projected series would crucially affect demand for the subsequent volumes, and it would therefore be surprising if he had not chosen the tales for the first volume with some care. The three component tales neatly reflect the subtitle of the collection, 'Collected among the Peasantry of Scotland, and from Foreign Adventurers': 'Marion's Jock' is a virtuoso exercise in Scots and in Hogg's ability to communicate the peasant lifestyle of his native Border district; 'The Adventures of Captain John Lochy' is an historical fiction linking Scotland to Russia, the Netherlands, and Sweden; and 'The Pongos' takes a look at Scottish involvement in the British empire in a comic parody of Enlightenment notions about the nature of man and of society. Hogg's own statement in the 'Memoir' about the tales to follow is apparently casual, but also expresses pride in the range as well as the quality of his achievement:

> In the following volumes I purpose to give the grave and gay tales, the romantic and the superstitious, alternately, as far as is consistent with the size of each volume. At all events I think I can promise my readers that I shall present them with a series of stories which they shall scarcely feel disposed to lay aside until a rainy Sunday; and with a few reminiscences relating to eminent men [...] I once more bring this Memoir, it may be hoped, to a partial conclusion. (p. 60)

While the typography of the volume apparently separates the 'Memoir of the Author's Life' from the tales that follow it, by the use of a separate pagination sequence, a rule, and a fresh heading (p. 79), there are a number of cross-references from the literary life to the literary work. In one place, for example, Hogg suggests that the reader who wishes to know more about his own youthful love experiences 'will find some of the best of them in those of "George Cochrane," in the following tales' (p. 55). It is also significant that this first-person 'Memoir' is followed in *Altrive Tales* by 'The Adventures of Captain John Lochy', another 'autobiography' written in the first person. In this tale Hogg plays with the conventions of the genre much as he had done earlier in the conclusion of Robert Wringhim's narrative in *The Private Memoirs and Confessions of a Justified Sinner.*[78]

Although the conventional and expected closure of a person's life is his death, Hogg acknowledges that this event can hardly occur within the confines of a first-person narrative account of it. In the passage from the 'Memoir' quoted above Hogg focuses on the fact that as he is alive his narrative is necessarily incomplete, but offers the reader and purchaser of the volume the option of another satisfactory closure. His narrative has recounted his peasant origins, his struggles first for literacy and then his partial successes and frequent disappointments as a professional author, culminating in his endeavours to produce the 'Altrive Tales' series. Hogg's readership must determine whether the plot is to conclude with a final crushing disappointment or a long-delayed triumph and vindication of his struggle for literary recognition.

'The Adventures of Captain John Lochy' is also incomplete, and offers a similar choice of endings to the life of an eminent man. Although the events recounted finish in 1715, Lochy clearly survived the Jacobite Rising of that year since he dates the composition of one section of the narrative itself precisely to 7 February 1731 (p. 139). In the final pages he hesitates between buying an estate in Hogg's own native district and returning to the life of a military adventurer abroad, after which his account ceases abruptly and the intervention of Hogg as author and supposed editor of Lochy's journal is required to finish it. Hogg as editor also fails to provide the expected narrative closure. He simply reiterates the two possible conclusions already posited by Lochy himself, a life rooted in a local society or one of further displacement and wandering. Hogg's indecision on this issue is all the more striking in close proximity with his successful resolution of the mystery surrounding Lochy's birth. His tongue-in-cheek concluding sentence is, 'But I only regret that our intrepid hero did not write out his autobiography to the last of his life; yet perhaps he did, as I know not what became of him' (p. 159). When 'The Adventures of Captain John Lochy' is read immediately after the 'Memoir of the Author's Life' the two texts reverberate strongly together. Their juxtaposition makes the reader aware that the 'Memoir' is a narrative construct with resemblances to Hogg's avowed fictions, and that the different parts of the work when read in succession may qualify and reinforce one another in various ways.

*Altrive Tales* opens up serious questions about the nature of man and society by means of a series of such juxtapositions, relating the personal experience of autobiography to more obviously crafted fictions. Among its major themes are the relationship between the individual and society, and what it is to be human. The volume opens in the verse Dedication with a most confident and positive celebration of an organic, ordered society in Hogg's native district centred around the local leadership of a great family, that of Hogg's patrons, the Dukes of Buccleuch. Lady Anne Scott provides material assistance to the local people in times of distress and is receptive to local legends and the power of the local landscape. Hogg's recollections of a specific evening at Bowhill contrast the threatening storm outside the mansion with the domestic and social harmony within:

> With all these scenes before his eyes,
> A family's and a nation's ties–
> Bonds which the heavens alone can rend,
> With chief, with father, and with friend. (ll. 218–21)

A similar note is apparently sounded at the beginning of 'Reminiscences of Former Days' when Hogg mentions the Duke's grant to him of the small farm of Altrive Lake in Yarrow:

> [...] never was a more welcome one conferred on an unfortunate wight, as it gave me once more a habitation among my native moors and streams, where each face was that of a friend, and each house was a home, as well as a residence for life to my aged father. (p. 53)

Between the passage from the Dedication and this similar one in 'Reminiscences of Former Days', however, the reader has learned of incidents that collectively cast doubt on its rosy picture of an organic society in the Scottish Borders. Intervening sections of the 'Memoir' have described how Hogg was turned out of his family home as a child (p. 12), and that while working for one shepherd he was 'often nearly exhausted with hunger and fatigue' (p. 14). After a period of unsuccessful farming in Dumfriesshire he found 'the countenances of all my friends altered; and even those whom I had loved, and trusted most, disowned me, and told me so to my face' (p. 23). Having read much of the preceding 'Memoir' it is not easy to accept unquestioningly that in this society 'each face was that of a friend, and each house was a home'. A retrospective shadow is cast on the idyllic portrayal of that society in the Dedication too: the 'rude boy of rustic form,/ And robe all fluttering to the storm' (ll.

17–18) seeming markedly less picturesque and more materially deprived than he at first appeared to be.

Scattered passages of the 'Memoir' depict Hogg as a dispossessed person rather than as an integrated and valued member of an organic community. In one well-known passage, for instance, Hogg describes himself as an intruder in the literary world:

> For my own part, I know that I have always been looked on by the learned part of the community as an intruder in the paths of literature, and every opprobrium has been thrown on me from that quarter. The truth is, that I am so. The walks of learning are occupied by a powerful aristocracy, who deem that province their own peculiar right; else, what would avail all their dear-bought collegiate honours and degrees? No wonder that they should view an intruder, from the humble and despised ranks of the community, with a jealous and indignant eye, and impede his progress by every means in their power. (p. 46)

Awareness of the succeeding tale of 'The Adventures of Captain John Lochy' tends to give special prominence to these passages. Several critics, notably Douglas Gifford and David Groves, have persuasively linked 'The Adventures of Captain John Lochy' with *The Private Memoirs and Confessions of a Justified Sinner* and with a projected collection of Hogg's tales of the 1820s under the title of 'Lives of Eminent Men'. Lochy's birth, like that of Robert Wringhim, is carefully positioned around 1689, a pivotal year in Scottish history, and both men exhibit symptoms of paranoia or alternatively do indeed suffer a mysterious persecution. Perceptively, Gifford goes on to relate Lochy's feeling that he has been 'a tennis-ball of fortune in a pre-eminent degree' to Hogg's powerlessness in literary Edinburgh, where he too seemed to be 'a tennis-ball between contending parties'.[79] John Lochy's feelings do indeed relate to those of James Hogg, and most clearly of all by comparison with the preceding 'Memoir' within *Altrive Tales*. Both protagonists sense that they are stumbling along in a society to which they do not fully belong, and subject to a network of relationships they do not participate in and rules they do not fully comprehend. Defensively, Hogg argues that 'I am so ignorant of the world, that it can scarcely be expected I should steer clear of all inadvertencies' (p. 50), or remarks that 'the whole of that trifling business has to this day continued a complete mystery to me' (p. 56). When he tries to arrange for the publication of his poem *The Pilgrims of the Sun* a mysterious understanding appears to exist between Constable and Miller (p. 38). Creating a suppositious literary family around Scott, Hogg envisages Lockhart as truly belonging by right of blood as 'a legitimate younger brother' and himself only by adoption as 'a step-son' (p. 75). There is a real if occasional sense in the 'Memoir' that Hogg's genius in combination with his birth has left him adrift in the world.

The career of John Lochy is also founded upon questions of legitimacy, reiterated on a political level by the many Jacobite references within the tale. Lochy is born at the time of the Revolution, is due to be hanged on Oak Apple Day, and is uncertain whether to adhere to the cause of the Stuarts or that of the Hanoverians. A foundling of aristocratic but undefined parentage, he is alternately threatened and protected by mysterious agencies whose motivation and actions he does not comprehend. A reprieve is obtained 'by whom [...] I never knew' (p. 85), a horse and a military commission arrive 'by whom [...] I was kept in profound ignorance' (p. 88), and a mysterious understanding appears to exist between his devoted servant Finlay and his unknown female protector (p. 98). Cast out of Scotland, he moves from war to war and country to country, fighting for the English at Blenheim, and passing into Russia with the army of Charles XII of Sweden. His dispossession, unlike that of his friend Prince Iset, appears to be a permanent condition, and when Iset is returned to his family and nation taking the beautiful Araby with him as a bride Lochy feels the contrast acutely:

> [...] I felt a blank in my heart, and as if I had been a creature deserted,–an isolated and lonely being, who seemed thrown upon the world to be a football in it; a creature,–the sport of every misadventure that could fall to the lot of man. (p. 139)

He returns to Scotland only when the country is in a state of civil war, and without family ties he feels he has no natural allegiance to either party in the 1715 Jacobite Rising. Lochy's ultimate adherence to the Hanoverian side is motivated largely by the general recognition of his strong physical resemblance to the Duke of Argyll, and his conclusion that there must consequently be a close bond of blood between them. He says that 'ever since I was made to believe that I was the duke's brother, I had an insatiable desire to be acquainted with him, to serve and to oblige him' (p. 145), adding subsequently 'my heart clung to him' (p. 149), an attraction which is clearly not determined by Argyll's reluctant and suspicious response to his overtures of support. While other passages of Hogg's 'Memoir' stress his happiness despite lack of worldly success, those which hint at alienation and a feeling of dispossession are accentuated by association with the succeeding narrative.

The second tale of the volume, 'The Pongos', is a brilliant example of Hogg's gift for unsettling his reader's expectations by an instability of tone–a technique that characterises many of his major fictions, *The Three Perils of Woman* being a prominent example. This tall tale of a child raised by apes is an early version of the Tarzan story as Douglas Gifford has noted.[80] In the context of *Altrive Tales* as a whole it comes in the wake of Hogg's account in the 'Memoir' of the training he received in the debating club of the Forum, which he emphasises as an important part of his education as a writer:

> [...] I never was so much advantaged by any thing as by that society; for it let me feel, as it were, the pulse of the public, and precisely what they would swallow, and what they would not. [...] Of this I am certain, that I was greatly the better for it, and I may safely say I never was in a school before. I might and would have written the 'Queen's Wake' had the Forum never existed, but without the weekly lessons that I got there I could not have succeeded as I did. (pp. 27–28)

The verb 'swallow' suggests feeding, in this case 'cramming' or deceiving with lies, a process Hogg describes elsewhere in the 'Memoir' as characteristic of Edinburgh literary society. Lockhart, for instance, is reported by Hogg as one who 'never tauld me the truth a' his days but aince, an' that was merely by chance, an' without the least intention on his part' (p. 74). A narrative is both a lie and a story, and Hogg's passage from primitive bard to professional literary man involves careful training in performance art, unsympathetically described as public deception. Hogg's emphasis on feeding his audience should alert the reader to the artfulness of the 'Memoir' itself, highlighted by the wider context of *Altrive Tales*.

'The Pongos', a supposedly genuine letter from a Scottish colonist in South Africa, signals its fictitious nature in the opening paragraph: it is 'one of those stories which, were it to occur in a romance, would be reckoned quite out of nature, and beyond all bounds of probability' (p. 160). Hogg's status as a sort of missing link, a living connection between primitive orality and Edinburgh literary society, is both asserted and interrogated in several new passages in the 1832 'Memoir'. One of the more interesting of these is his account of how he first heard of Burns and resolved to succeed him as a Scottish poet. Hogg slyly writes this account of literary innocence and awakening in a consciously knowing and conventional fashion. His first readers would have been well accustomed to spiritual autobiographies, with their emphasis on spiritual awakening, and Hogg's first encounter with Burns's poetry is a secular version of this, 'a new epoch' in his life as he discovers his true vocation as an author:

> I wept, and always thought with myself–what is to hinder me from succeeding Burns? I too was born on the 25th of January, and I have much more time to read and compose than any ploughman could have, and can sing more old songs than ever ploughman could in the world. But then I wept again because I could not write. However, I resolved to be a poet, and to follow in the steps of Burns. (p. 18)

Beneath the apparently naive and innocent narrative of 'The Pongos' lies another informed literary reference, this time to the eighteenth-century fascination with the orang-outang.[81] Despite the creature's apparent likeness to a human being the French naturalist Buffon concluded that it should be classified among the brute creation, whereas the Scots Lord Monboddo decided that it represented man at the most primitive stage of social and intellectual development. Hogg's tale frequently alludes to individual points of evidence cited in this dispute, such as the ability to speak, to make fire, and to live in houses, but mocks his sources by demonstrating that a pongo is a good deal more civilised than a colonist. Although the narrator terms the pongo 'horrible monster' (p. 162) and 'hideous brute' (p. 164) it is the colonists who are aggressive and deceitful, and they who display symptoms of wishing to enslave both the pongos and the native African population (one tribe of which is interestingly called 'the Lockos', echoing the 'John Lochy' of the preceding tale). It is the pongos rather than the colonists that live together harmoniously, and display a generous concern for the well-being of those with whom they associate. At times a pongo can be exaggeratedly civilised in Hogg's tale. For instance, not only does a pongo understand the European code of duelling, but he adheres to it when his European opponent breaches it. The naivete of 'The Pongos', like that of the 'Memoir', is more apparent than real.

The final story in *Altrive Tales*, 'Marion's Jock', has obvious thematic links with the one that precedes it. The harsh life of the subsistence farmer in Hogg's native Borders contrasts unfavourably with the idyllic existence of the Pongos in this story of a half-starved and greedy servant lad who kills a pet lamb belonging to his master so that he may feast on it. When the narrator of 'The Pongos' arrives with a party of colonists to rescue his son William and daughter Beatrice from the nurturing creatures, 'the children fled from us, crying for their mother, and took shelter with their friends the pongos' (p. 168). The excessive greed and emotional deadness of Jock, on the other hand, is shown to result from life-long deprivation: he is referred to, often in his presence, as 'the creature' (p. 175), a 'savage' (p. 176), 'the dirty blackguard callant' (p. 179), and 'the menseless tike!' (p. 175). If Jock's behaviour is brutal, his carnivorousness leading to the slaughter of an innocent lamb, Hogg provides plenty of indications that he has been brutalised. Like the preceding tale, 'Marion's Jock' asks what brute nature is, and who may truly be described as savage and as civilised. As in 'The Pongos', the distinction between human and brute is uncomfortably blurred in several passages of this tale–the pet lamb takes on some of the meaning of the Christian sacrificial Lamb, whereas Jock and his master's battle for life is like that 'between an inveterate terrier and a bull-dog' (p. 185). Furthermore, Jock is threatened not just with death but butchery when his master enquires '[...] whether would you choose to have your throat cut, or to have your feet tied and be skinned alive?' (p. 184). If the pet lamb is a person murdered, Jock becomes potential butcher's meat. The final paragraph of the narrative emphasises Jock's separation from all human society, as he flies 'from all the world' while 'still flying into the world'. Specifically, he has 'no home, no kindred' and 'no hold of any thing in nature' (p. 186). These expressions link Jock, as an outsider, to John Lochy in the first tale of the volume, who similarly describes himself as feeling 'bereaved of every bond of affection', and of 'every thing that could tend to link me to my country or my race' (p. 156). It is a long way from the Borders community so confidently asserted in the Dedication to *Altrive Tales*.

By highlighting Hogg's occasional hints of the harsh treatment he received as a child, 'Marion's Jock' also qualifies Hogg's Romantic view of a Borders childhood in the 'Memoir'. The *Altrive Tales* version of the 'Memoir' includes several new passages which deliberately cater to the sentimental views of Hogg's proto-Victorian readership concerning childhood, particularly the childhood of a bard. In these additional sections, Hogg's childhood is implicitly modelled on that of James Beattie's Edwin in *The Minstrel* (1771–1774), a narrative poem tracing the development of a poet in a primitive age and a clear ancestor of Wordsworth's *Prelude*. It accords with Hogg's work for the Annuals of the 1820s and in particular with the account of his childhood given in 'The Minstrel Boy', contributed to

*Friendship's Offering* for 1829. In this poem Hogg's childhood is essentially a solitary communing with nature. Addressing the boy of the accompanying engraving, Hogg recollects a time

> When I, like thee, on a summer day
> Would fling my bonnet and plaid away,
> And toil at the leap, the race, or the stone,
> With none to beat but myself alone.
> And then would I raise my tiny lay
> And lilt the songs of a former day:
> Till I believed that over the fell
> The fairies peeped from the heather bell;[82]

The recollections of Hogg's brother William about their childhood emphasise Hogg's childish competitiveness, describing his challenging other boys to athletic contests, and his persistence despite frequent defeats.[83] By contrast a new insertion in the 'Memoir' for *Altrive Tales* follows 'The Minstrel Boy' in depicting Hogg's youthful exercises as solitary and imaginative:

> Even at that early age my fancy seems to have been a hard neighbour for both judgment and memory. I was wont to strip off my clothes, and run races against time, or rather against myself; and, in the course of these exploits, which I accomplished much to my own admiration, I first lost my plaid, then my bonnet, then my coat, and, finally, my hosen; for, as for shoes, I had none. In that naked state did I herd for several days, till a shepherd and maid-servant were sent to the hills to look for them, and found them all. (p. 13)

Similarly, Hogg's infant love for the farm-servant Betty is apparently naive but is described in firmly literary and knowing terms, recalling among other things Byron's infant passion for his nurse, May Gray, and for his cousin Mary Duff, and supporting Hogg's characterisation in *Blackwood's Edinburgh Magazine* and elsewhere as a poet with an exaggerated fondness for women. The tendency of such passages in the revised 'Memoir' to render it more sentimental than before is, however, necessarily qualified for the alert reader by the inclusion in the same volume of the harsh childhood depicted in 'Marion's Jock'.

The existing volume of *Altrive Tales* is far from being a random assemblage of items, but was clearly structured so that the three tales have thematic links with one another and with the 'Memoir' that precedes them. Each component part of the volume modifies the reader's experience of the other, while the physical and thematic proximity of the three tales to the 'Memoir' should alert the reader to the consciously literary and conventional nature of the 'Memoir' itself.

## 4. Reception

Even at the time of its publication in the spring of 1832 *Altrive Tales* received very little attention as a collection. Awareness that it was published as the first instalment of a multi-volume series of Hogg's collected prose works, and the attractions of the 'Memoir of the Author's Life', obscured the relationship between its component parts from the beginning.

Contemporary reviews naturally focused on the 'Memoir of the Author's Life', assuming that there would be ample opportunity for comment on Hogg's tales when the subsequent volumes of the series were published. As a result several reviewers fail to make any mention of the tales themselves, while others simply list them by title. The critic of *Fraser's Magazine*, after stating openly that there would be many future opportunities to discuss Hogg's tales, is flippant as well as brief about the tales of the initial volume: '[...] the story of Captain Lochy [...] is one of Hogg's best, being, indeed, a very happy imitation of De Foe' and 'the Pongos is, we believe, pleasant–but as we have not read it, we are not quite sure'.[84] A similar, though less openly avowed, lack of attention to Hogg's fiction characterises the *Mirror*, which misunderstands the nature of the series as a result. The reviewer describes it as a collection of 'the best of the grave and gay tales with which he has aided the Magazines and Annuals during the last few years',[85] a summary which ignores the important function of the series as a vehicle for the publication of the longer fiction that Hogg had found almost impossible to place within the pages of contemporary periodicals. Comment on the tales themselves tends towards puzzlement, recognising Hogg's power as a story-teller but admitting its effect is not always experienced as a pleasurable one. The *Monthly Review* characterises the tales as 'all distinguished by a wildness of imagination, which bounds from incident to incident with an enviable facility'. 'The Adventures of Captain John Lochy' displays Hogg's 'teeming fancy', but is somewhat incoherent:

> His adventures on the continent follow each other with so much rapidity, that it is difficult to remember them. We must

> say that they are too often not worth remembering, and yet the tale is upon the whole calculated to interest the reader from the very number, if not from the attractiveness of its incidents. The two other stories are short, and, though of a different character, are calculated to afford a favourable specimen of the compositions by which they are to be followed.[86]

*The Scotsman* of 2 June 1832, in a largely favourable review of the volume, nevertheless objects to the tales themselves. 'The Adventures of Captain John Lochy' is described as 'a strange, rambling, incoherent production', the matter of which is 'too indigested to leave an agreeable impression'. 'Marion's Jock' is dismissed as 'coarsely handled'.

The poetical dedication to the series, however, is termed 'elegant' (by *The Literary Rambler*), 'an exquisite performance' (by the *Mirror*), and 'of great feeling and delicacy' (by *The Athenaeum*). The reviewer of *The Literary Gazette* writes that it is 'honourable to the heart of the writer, and contains several passages of fine natural thought and poetical beauty'. The physical attractions of the volume and its engravings also receive passing comment.[87]

Almost all the passages extracted in reviews, however, and almost all the remarks made upon the volume, are concerned with the prefatory 'Memoir' and in addition several newspapers published extracts from it within their columns. The final section of 'Reminiscences of Former Days', giving Hogg's recollections of other literary men, was particularly attractive for this purpose and already divided into convenient and self-contained sections. *The Day*, for instance, gives an account of Hogg's early life from the 'Memoir' and then summarises the later portions as follows:

> In the concluding portion of this piece of autobiography, he draws the characters of the celebrated publishers, Longman & Co. Constable, Miller, and Blackwood. He sketches those of Britain's leading Literateurs, Scott, Wilson, Lockhart, Woodsworth [*sic*], Galt, and Allan Cunningham. The whole is done, if not with a powerful, at least with an original pencil, and will fully reward the reader. The fact is, the preliminary memoir is worth the price of the whole volume.[88]

Subsequent issues of this paper for 28 April and 5 May 1832 contain extracts entitled 'Hogg, Southey and Wordsworth', and 'Hogg's First Interview with Galt'. Other newspapers also filled their columns with extracts from Hogg's 'Memoir', the *Morning Advertiser*, for example, featuring 'Wonderful Memory of Sir Walter Scott' in the issue for 20 April and 'Southey' in that of 23 April 1832. Attention was given almost equally by reviewers to Hogg's early pursuit of literature under difficulties, and to the literary gossip he purveyed: reviewers not only praised the volume but were 'profuse in their extracts', as the *Ladies Museum* expresses it.[89] The critic of *The Athenaeum* feels that Hogg's 'unostentatious egotism gives to the Memoir what fragrance gives to the rose, an increase of sweetness', even while warning Hogg against expecting his work to be valued more highly on account of the difficulties under which it had been produced on the grounds that it 'matters not to the world how and in what way a work of genius is produced'.[90] Even the review in the *Mirror*, which describes the 'Memoir' as 'a most objectionable preface', consists largely of Hogg's reminiscences of his contemporaries.[91]

This concentration on the 'Memoir' was also fuelled by Hogg's frankness in discussing his contemporaries. In noting the anger shown by Hogg against William Blackwood the *Kelso Chronicle* remarks neutrally, 'We are hurt to think that two persons so long intimate as Mr. Hogg and Mr. Blackwood should part on such terms; but on reading the fact, we cannot help feeling that there must be faults on both sides'. For *Fraser's Magazine*, however, Hogg's anger against William Blackwood provides another opportunity for an attack upon its Edinburgh rival and its publisher. Hogg's account of Blackwood's financial dealings with him are reprinted and interspersed with comments such as 'Mr. Blackwood never gave him any thing for it! Of course'. The *Fraser's* reviewer declares that 'no scruple was felt in accepting his literary labours without remuneration; and Hogg did wisely in shaking off his Edinburgh trammels', subsequently terming Blackwood one of the 'paltry pilferers of the profits of genius'. As a result of such public imputations on his honesty, Blackwood later refused to make up his quarrel with Hogg without a signed statement from him acknowledging his financial probity in their past transactions, a stand which effectively barred Hogg's subsequent work from the pages of *Blackwood's Edinburgh Magazine*.[92] Hogg's comments about William Blackwood were not the only controversial parts of his 'Memoir', however. It has already been indicated that one publisher, almost certainly Owen Rees of the Longmans firm, may have caused the publication to be delayed while offensive remarks about him were cancelled (see pp. xxvi–xxviii above). George Goldie, the publisher of the early editions of *The Queen's Wake* and of Hogg's drama *The Hunting of Badlewe*, was clearly angered that allegations against his financial probity made in the 1821 version of the 'Memoir' had been published unaltered in 1832. After the publication of *Altrive Tales* he reprinted his earlier pamphlet attack on Hogg, *A Letter to a Friend* of 1821, with a new preface in which he threatens more extensive retaliation later:

> I have not done with this mean-spirited individual–for I am in possession of facts and anecdotes respecting his career, which shall one day come forth in the shape of a detailed Memoir of his Life and Character; in which I propose to shew such a picture as has seldom met the public eye.
>
> I shall feel obliged by authentic communications being sent to me relative to this man, in order that they may be incorporated in the body of my proposed book.

Under the pseudonym of 'An Old Dissector' Dr James Browne of Edinburgh also produced a stinging attack, *The 'Life' of the Ettrick Shepherd Anatomized.* The publication of this pamphlet confirms the statement it contains that the 'Memoir' had 'acquired a present and factitious notoriety', a notoriety which inevitably obscured the prose fictions in *Altrive Tales.*[93]

In view of its initial reception it is hardly surprising that *Altrive Tales* failed to survive as a collection in the nineteenth century. *Tales and Sketches by the Ettrick Shepherd*, published by the Glasgow firm of Blackie and Son between December 1836 and December 1837, formed the basis of most editions of Hogg's prose fiction for more than a hundred years subsequently, and that edition excluded all three of the stories in *Altrive Tales.* Hogg's 'Memoir' was reprinted, oddly enough, not in this prose collection but in the companion set of *Poetical Works of the Ettrick Shepherd.* This seems to have been the result of a quirk of fate, a last-minute replacement being required to make up the final volume of the five-volume set after John Wilson's biographical sketch of Hogg failed to materialise. It is referred to on the title-page as 'An Autobiography' and in view of its new context the Glasgow firm cut the paragraphs that referred directly to its old context of *Altrive Tales* thus effecting the severance between 'Memoir' and tales initiated by the collection's contemporary reception.[94] Other volumes of the Stirling/South Carolina Edition have described how the Hogg canon created by these two editions (and reinforced by others based upon them) was one which ignored and indeed virtually obliterated the collections created by Hogg himself. As a result critics such as Louis Simpson could confidently assert that 'Hogg's collections of tales and sketches were put together on no definite plan'.[95] These factors meant that the story of the reception of Hogg's *Altrive Tales* after 1832 is primarily the reception of its component parts seen in isolation from one another and not the story of the reception of the collection as such.

Until the publication of Douglas Mack's ground-breaking edition of 1972 Hogg's 'Memoir' was largely seen as a quarry from which raw material could be extracted and processed by critics and biographers. Mack recognises that the 'Memoir' and Hogg's anecdotes of Scott are 'well known as sources for the study of Scott and his period' but 'seldom read in their entirety'. By showing the development of the text through its earlier versions of 1807 and 1821 and indicating Hogg's additions, deletions, and revisions, he treats it as a work of art on a par with the prose tales. The way was then open for the reconnection of the 'Memoir' with Hogg's prose fiction, and important work by Silvia Mergenthal and Nelson C. Smith has continued Mack's examination of it as a literary construct.[96]

The modern focus on the psychological aspects of *The Private Memoirs and Confessions of a Justified Sinner* has also linked the 'Memoir' with Hogg's fiction, Barbara Bloedé, for instance, seeing in Hogg's account of his own childhood experience the seeds of his later fictional treatment of the double. Douglas Gifford's similar identification of a group of fictions written shortly after *Confessions* in which the hero suffers mysterious persecution from an arch-enemy, serves among other things to connect 'The Adventures of Captain John Lochy' with the 'Memoir' once again. David Groves also, by comparing the same story to *Confessions of a Justified Sinner*, demonstrates its renewed importance in a fresh context.[97]

Criticism of a work regarded as falling outside the established canon will always tend to be sparse. 'Marion's Jock' as it appears in the context of *Altrive Tales* has not received much attention. However, after long neglect the previous version of the tale, under the title of 'The Laird of Peatstacknowe's Tale', is now rightly regarded as a miniature masterpiece largely because of the revival of interest in *The Three Perils of Man* (1822) in which it originally appeared. Hogg's Border Romance, after disappearing from view in the bowdlerised and truncated 'The Siege of Roxburgh' of *Tales and Sketches by the Ettrick Shepherd*, was made visible again (together with this inset tale) in Douglas Gifford's edition of *The Three Perils of Man* of 1972. 'The Laird of Peatstacknowe's Tale' is now at the centre of stimulating criticism of the larger fiction by W. G. Shepherd, Ian Duncan, and others.[98] The alternative version, 'Marion's Jock' in the 1832 *Altrive Tales*, however, has largely been unjustifiably ignored or dismissed as a by-product of the author's self-censorship, an early example of the bowdlerising process.

'The Pongos' enjoyed the most interesting contemporary reception of the three tales included in the *Altrive Tales* collection, although often dismissed subsequently as a tall tale. After its first publication as 'A Letter from Southern Africa' in *Blackwood's Edinburgh Magazine* the tale achieved a certain celebrity that must have amused Hogg greatly. Hogg's daughter later recalled this, presumably from her mother's recollections:

> A story this too strange for human credulity to believe, one would think! Neverthless, the author received not one but several letters, asking if the events related had really occurred. Mrs. Hogg naturally asked him what answer he would return, and his reply was, 'None at all–if there are people so silly as to believe it, let them do so.'

When the story was republished as 'The Pongos' in *Altrive Tales* Hogg's contemporaries seem to have been again fascinated by it as a tale occupying an indeterminate position between fact and fantasy. The reviewer for the *Sunday Times* prefaced two extracts from the tale with the following puzzled summary:

> 'The Pongos,' which we suppose to be no invention of his, appears as a letter from a person of the name of Mitchell. The writer solemnly declares that what he says is true, but sensibly adds that he does not expect to be believed. His tale is one of the most extraordinary ever committed to paper.[99]

'The Pongos' was also reprinted from *Altrive Tales* in an Edinburgh literary paper, *The Schoolmaster*, for 16 February 1833 (pp. 106–09). Douglas Gifford, in recognising the tale as an early version of the Tarzan story, is one of the few modern critics to have acknowledged its powerfully mythic force.[100]

The present volume attempts, as far as possible, to reinstate the original context of *Altrive Tales* of 1832 for Hogg's verse Dedication, 'Memoir' and three tales, enabling them to be interpreted in conjunction with one another. This cannot, of course, be done entirely successfully, the modern reader being well aware that Cochrane's bankruptcy ended the series with this first volume and that the other eleven volumes of the 'Altrive Tales' series cannot succeed it. However, as Hogg's ambitions for a collected edition of his prose work are now being gradually fulfilled with the publication of the successive volumes of the Stirling/South Carolina Research Edition of the

Collected Works of James Hogg, the new context for *Altrive Tales* does provide a fortunate resemblance to the old.

## Notes

1. See the Introduction to James Hogg, *Winter Evening Tales*, ed. by Ian Duncan (S/SC, 2002), p. xi.
2. See the Introduction to James Hogg, *The Brownie of Bodsbeck*, ed. by Douglas S. Mack (Edinburgh and London: Scottish Academic Press, 1976), pp. xv–xvii.
3. James Hogg, *Winter Evening Tales*, ed. by Ian Duncan (S/SC, 2002), p. xxii.
4. Constable & Co. to Hogg, 21 October 1822, in National Library of Scotland (hereafter NLS) MS 791, p. 644. I am grateful to the Trustees of the National Library of Scotland for permission to cite manuscript and other material in their care in the present volume.
5. See the Introduction to James Hogg, *Winter Evening Tales*, ed. by Ian Duncan (S/SC, 2002), p. xxvii.
6. Longmans letter to Hogg of 5 May 1823 is in the Longman Archives in the University of Reading Library, part 1, Item 101 (Letter-Book 1820–25), fol. 357. For the publication history of the later work see *Tales of the Wars of Montrose*, ed. by Gillian Hughes (S/SC, 1996), pp. xii–xvii.
7. For Ian Duncan's account of the reception of *Winter Evening Tales* see pp. xxxii–xxxvi of his S/SC edition. Hogg's letter to Whittakers of 18 December 1824 is in the Manuscripts Division of the Department of Rare Books and Special Collections, Princeton University Library: RTCO1, Box 9. (Published with permission of the Princeton University Library.)
8. See Peter Garside, 'The English Novel in the Romantic Era: Consolidation and Dispersal', in *The English Novel 1770–1829: A Bibliographical Survey of Prose Fiction Published in the British Isles: Volume II: 1800–1829*, ed. by Peter Garside and Rainer Schöwerling (Oxford: OUP, 2000), pp. 15–103 (pp. 89–90).
9. James Hogg, *The Shepherd's Calendar*, ed. by Douglas S. Mack (S/SC, 1995), pp. xiv–xvi, the quotation being from p. xv.
10. See Garside, 'The English Novel in the Romantic Era: Consolidation and Dispersal', p. 102.
11. Edgar Johnson, *Sir Walter Scott: The Great Unknown*, 2 vols (London: Hamish Hamilton, 1970), II, 1132. Blackwood's letter to his son William of 13 June 1830 mentions seeing Lockhart on Princes Street in Edinburgh shortly after 28 May, adding that he was then at Chiefswood with his family–see Mrs Oliphant, *Annals of a Publishing House: William Blackwood and his Sons their Magazine and Friends*, 2 vols (Edinburgh, 1897), II, 98.
12. Hogg's letter to Robert Purdie of 9 June 1830 (NLS Acc. 3196) was written from Altrive, but a letter to Blackwood from Altrive dated 21 June (NLS MS 4027, fols 188–89) announces his safe arrival home again. A note to J. M. Williams of 7 July (in a copy of Hogg's *Lay Sermons* at the Huntington Library, San Marino, California: Rare Book 183591) is dated from Chiefswood. I thank the Huntington Library, San Marino, California for permission to cite this letter here.
13. James Hogg, *Anecdotes of Scott*, ed. by Jill Rubenstein (S/SC, 1999), p. 18. The text quoted is based on Hogg's manuscript.
14. In his letter to Blackwood of 26 July 1831 Lockhart recalled the powerful

impression made upon him by Hogg 'as I saw him a few days before I left Scotland in October at Altrive–wet, weary & melancholy' (NLS MS 4030, fols 76–77).

15. *Songs by the Ettrick Shepherd* was advertised as to be published 'in a few days' in the *Edinburgh Weekly Chronicle* of 5 January 1831, and reviewed in the paper for 12 January (p. 14). Blackwood's letters to Hogg of 12 and 17 March 1831 contain his terms of payment to the author–see NLS MS 30312, pp. 160–61 and 163–64.
16. For an account of the production process of *A Queer Book* see Peter Garside's edition of that work (S/SC, 1995), pp. xii–xvi, xxi–xxii. Garside's account of the delays between the completion of printing *A Queer Book* in the summer of 1831 and publication of the work in early May 1832 is on pp. xxiv–xxvi.
17. Hogg to Lockhart, 3 May 1832, in NLS MS 924, No. 86, and Cochrane to Hogg, 18 June 1835, in NLS MS 2245, fols 262–63.
18. I thank Richard Jackson for this information, given in his unpublished paper 'Two John Andersons, Edinburgh Publishers and Booksellers'. There is a book of title-pages from works published by the firm of Fairbairn and Anderson in the NLS, Shelfmark ABS.1.78.23. Browne's reference to Cochrane as a publisher is in his anonymous pamphlet, *The 'Life' of the Ettrick Shepherd Anatomized; in a Series of Strictures on the Autobiography of James Hogg, prefixed to the first volume of the 'Altrive Tales'. By An Old Dissector* (Edinburgh, 1832), p. 5.
19. Hogg's letter to Picken of 20 November 1830 is in the Beinecke Rare Book and Manuscript Library, Yale University, Osborne MSS, Folder 7421. For Hogg's tales see *The Club Book, Being Original Tales by Various Authors*, ed. by Andrew Picken, 3 vols (London, 1831), II, 143–64 and 231–64 respectively. It was listed under 'New Books' in *The Literary Gazette*, 30 July 1831, p. 492.
20. See *The Metropolitan*, 1 (August 1831), 146–48 (p. 148).
21. Cited from Mrs Oliphant, *Annals of a Publishing House*, II, 104.
22. For details of these changes arising from the flourishing Blackwood publishing business see Oliphant, II, 96–101. At the same time Blackwood set up his carriage, a real benchmark of professional success.
23. Lockhart wrote to Blackwood from Chiefswood, for instance, on 22 September 1831, declining any editorial role, 'Don't let Hogg dream I wd have anything to do w his Edition of Novels. Even if there were nothing else, I have not time for such a thing. It is quite impossible.–"None but himself can be his Editor"'–see NLS MS 4030, fols 79–80.
24. Hogg to James Gray, 7 December 1831, at the Historical Society of Pennsylvania (HSP): Dreer Collection, English Poets. I thank the Historical Society of Pennsylvania for permission to cite this letter here.
25. Hogg's letter to Lockhart of 14 December 1831 is in NLS MS 924, No. 79. His comment to Blackwood was made in a note of [19–21 December 1831] in NLS MS 4719, fol. 184.
26. See Hogg's letter to Blackwood of 6 December 1831 (NLS MS 4029, fols 268–69). The report of Hogg's departure from Edinburgh 'this day (Friday)' was made in the *Edinburgh Observer* of 23 December 1831, and cited by *The Atlas* of 1 January 1832. A letter from Hogg to his wife of 1 January 1832 from London reports that he 'landed yesterday, after a most pleasant, but tedious passage'–see Mrs Garden, *Memorials of James Hogg, the Ettrick Shepherd* (Paisley, undated), pp. 242–43 (hereafter referred to as Garden).
27. See Note on the Text, pp. 198–99, 201–03.
28. A review of *A Father's New Year's Gift* in *The Athenaeum*, 4 February 1832, p. 78,

gives some idea of the date of publication and also the price. A facsimile of this rare publication, with a brief introduction, was published in *Studies in Hogg and his World*, 8 (1997), 77–96.

29. See *The Athenaeum*, 11 and 18 February 1832, pp. 97 and 114, and also *The Metropolitan*, 3 (February 1832), 51.
30. Hogg to Margaret Hogg, 17 January 1832, in Stirling University Library, MS 25B (8). I am grateful to the Arts Librarian, Mr Gordon Willis, for permission to cite manuscript material in the University of Stirling Library in the present volume.
31. For evidence that Hogg was still writing his 'Reminiscences of Former Days' on 25 February see the Note on the Text, p. 203. An extract from his letter to his wife is given in Garden, p. 262.
32. The recipient's name is not given on Hogg's letter of 19 March 1832 in the Beinecke Rare Book and Manuscript Library, Yale University, GEN MSS 61, Box 1, Folder 17. However, a subsequent letter to John M'Donald of around 18 May 1832 regarding *Altrive Tales* (NLS MS 2245, fols 168–69) says 'I left the charge with Roscoe and Richie who were Cochrane's correctors of the press'.
33. Hogg to John M'Donald, 3 May 1832, in Garden, pp. 268–71, and Hogg to Oliver and Boyd, 7 July 1832, in NLS Acc. 5000/188.
34. Hogg to Fullarton, 14 October 1832, in the Beinecke Rare Book and Manuscript Library, Yale University, GEN MSS 61, Box 1, Folder 36.
35. Hogg to Alexander Elder, 14 January 1833, in the Beinecke Rare Book and Manuscript Library, Yale University, GEN MSS 61, Box 1, Folder 8, and Hogg to John M'Donald, [18 May 1832], in NLS MS 2245, fols 168–69. While Hogg's letter to Elder mentions a sixth of the retail price, Hogg's letter to Cochrane of 3 May 1832 refers to 'my share of one fifth of it' (Beinecke Rare Book and Manuscript Library, Yale University, GEN MSS 61, Box 1, Folder 6).
36. Hogg to Fullarton, 14 October 1832, in Beinecke Rare Book and Manuscript Library, Yale University, GEN MSS 61, Box 1, Folder 36.
37. *Altrive Tales* was reviewed in *The Literary Gazette*, 31 March and 7 April 1832, pp. 199–201 and 214–16 (p. 214). See also *The Athenaeum*, 14 April 1832, pp. 235–37 (p. 235). The delay in publication was noted in the issue for 7 April 1832, p. 227.
38. See *The Literary Gazette*, 31 March 1832, pp. 199–201 (p. 201), and [James Browne], *The 'Life' of the Ettrick Shepherd Anatomized* (Edinburgh, 1832), p. 35. Hogg left London on 25 March, and although in his letter of 1 April notifying Cochrane of his safe arrival at Altrive (NLS MS 2956, fols 159–60) he mentions receiving a letter from Cochrane in Edinburgh, there is no indication of anything amiss with publication plans for *Altrive Tales*. It seems probable that Cochrane himself was responsible for altering the sheet containing offensive remarks about Owen Rees.
39. A copy of the first edition in the Alexander Turnbull Library, Wellington (at 821.7 G) contains only stubs for the relevant two leaves (pp. xcix/c and ci/cii), and it is possible that in this copy the pages containing Hogg's remarks have been removed by the printer without the replacements having been substituted, or, alternatively, taken out by someone aware that they included inflammatory material. But none of the other copies of the first edition examined show signs of cancellation here, apart from the NLS copy at Hall. 149. a. (I am grateful to the Alexander Turnbull Library, National Library of New Zealand, Te Puna Matauranga o Aotearoa, for permission to refer to the copy in the library's collections.)

40. See Hogg to Blackwood, 2 March 1832 in NLS MS 4033, fols 125–26. His letter to Lockhart of 3 May 1832 (NLS MS 924, No. 86) in saying 'As you dreaded Mr Cochrane is knocked up', implies a previous warning by Lockhart.
41. James Cochrane to Sir Egerton Bridges, 13 October 1834, in Beinecke Rare Book and Manuscript Library, Yale University, MSS Osborn Files, Folder 3446.
42. A photocopy of Sir Richard Phillips's letter to Hogg, postmarked 27 April 1832, is owned by Mr David Parr of Nelson, New Zealand, one of Hogg's descendants. I am grateful to him for permission to quote it here. The letter is cited in part in Garden, pp. 207–08.
43. Hogg to Cochrane, 3 May 1832, in Beinecke Rare Book and Manuscript Library, Yale University, GEN MSS 61, Box 1, Folder 6. Goldie in *Letter to a Friend* (p. 15) stated that as a result of Blackwood's intervention on Hogg's behalf after his bankruptcy in 1814 Hogg received for *The Queen's Wake* 'something more than £70 over and above what he would have received'. Hogg terms it 'more than double' in his 'Memoir' (p. 32).
44. John M'Donald's letter to Hogg of 2 July 1832 with a copy of Bentley's refusal of *Altrive Tales* is in NLS MS 2245, fols 210–11. Hogg's letter to Lockhart of 4 October 1832 (NLS MS 924, No. 83) recounts, 'I authorised Mr John M,Donald in whose hands the M.S.S. are to try to conclude a bargain for me and he tried both Mr Elder and Mr Bentley but he had been too sharp with them and is ignorant of that sort of business so I debarred him from mentioning the Altrive Tales farther at present'. Hogg's letter to Oliver & Boyd of 7 July 1832, offering them the work, is in NLS Acc. 5000/188. On 14 September 1832 (NLS MS 3813, fols 66–67) he asked Fullarton, 'By the by will you take my Altrive Tales?', calling him 'a d– fool not to proceed with the Altrive Tales' in a subsequent letter of 14 October 1832 (Beinecke Rare Book and Manuscript Library, Yale University, GEN MSS 61, Box 1, Folder 36).
45. For examples of the 1832 and 1835 reissues in the National Library of Scotland see the copies at Hall.149.a and Hall.197.i respectively. Douglas Mack has written about the second of these in his 'James Hogg's Altrive Tales: an 1835 reissue', *The Bibliotheck*, 5 No. 6 (1969), 210–11.
46. Hogg to John M'Crone, 12 May 1833, in Bodleian Library, University of Oxford, Ms Autogr. d. 11, fols 321–22.
47. William T. Hayley's *Douglas D'Arcy: Some Passages in the Life of an Adventurer* was published anonymously in London in 1834 under the imprint of 'F. J. Mason, 444, West Strand'–see 'The English Novel, 1830–1836: A Bibliographical Survey of Prose Fiction Published in the British Isles', compiled by Peter Garside and Anthony Mandal (CEIR, Cardiff) and Verena Ebbes, Angela Koch, and Rainer Schöwerling (Projekt Corvey, Paderborn University), in *Cardiff Corvey*, Issue 10 (June 2003). This may be accessed electronically at http:/www.cf.ac.uk/encap/corvey/1830s.
48. Hogg to James Cochrane, 4 November 1832, in Beinecke Rare Book and Manuscript Library, Yale University, GEN MSS 61, Box 1, Folder 6. The letter has a postscript written by Hogg ten days subsequently.
49. Cochrane to Hogg, 10 December 1832, in NLS MS 2245, fols 216–17. Cochrane also urged Hogg to return to London, promising, 'You shall have no puffing this time–to serve the views of literary spend-thrifts'.
50. A full account of Hogg's relations with the Glasgow firm of Blackie and Son, and of the production of the six-volume *Tales and Sketches by the Ettrick Shepherd* between December 1836 and December 1837 has been prepared by

Peter Garside and Gillian Hughes.

51. Hogg to M'Crone, 12 May 1833, in Bodleian Library, University of Oxford, MS Autogr. d.11, fols 321–22.
52. Hogg's proposal is contained in his letter to John M'Crone of 3 August 1833, owned by the Society of Antiquaries of Newcastle upon Tyne: Brooks Collection, Volume VI, fol. 83A. (I thank the Society of Antiquaries of Newcastle upon Tyne and the Northumberland Record Office for permission to cite it here.) Cochrane's reply of 9 August is in NLS MS 2245, fols 230–31.
53. Hogg's letter to Janet Laidlaw of 4 November 1833 (Miscellaneous Collection, Queen's University Archives, Kingston, Ontario) records a recent Blackie visit to Altrive to bargain for the 'Winter Evening Tales' collection, and his letter to Blackies of 11 November (NLS MS 807, fol. 20) was accompanied by the marked-up copy of *The Brownie of Bodsbeck*. Hogg's indignant letter to Cochrane of 1 March 1834 is at the Houghton Library, Harvard University: Autograph File *44M-161. Publication is by permission of the Houghton Library, Harvard University.
54. The breakdown of the Cochrane marriage and subsequently of the business partnership between Cochrane and M'Crone is difficult to date precisely. Cochrane clearly wrote to inform Hogg of the break up of his business partnership with M'Crone in a letter dated 3 November 1834. This has not survived but is alluded to in Hogg's reply of 8 November (Beinecke Rare Book and Manuscript Library, Yale University, GEN MSS 61, Box 1, Folder 6) as 'so heart-breaking that the circumstances shall never more be alluded to by me'. Hogg wrote to Cunningham on the same day asking for more details of the adultery, but Cunningham's reply of 15 November (NLS MS 2245, fols 249–50) suggests that the events referred to had happened some weeks previously. Cunningham mentions that the partnership had been dissolved by this date, that M'Crone was about to be married to the daughter of a Professor Bordwine, that he had refused to receive M'Crone at his house despite the urging of friends, and that he had 'adhered in Book matters to Cochrane'. Hogg himself had perhaps heard of the adultery by 13 October 1834 when he wrote that 'M'Crone was not here poor fellow and I was sorry for it for I think he esteemed me; but Margt caused me forbid him the house' (NLS MS 10998, fol. 178). It seems unlikely that Margaret Hogg would otherwise have behaved with such uncharacteristic inhospitality, especially when M'Crone had paid lengthy visits to Altrive during the two previous autumns. The publication history of *Tales of the Wars of Montrose* is given by Gillian Hughes in the relevant S/SC volume (S/SC, 1996), pp. xii–xvii.
55. Cadell to Hogg, 2 February 1822, in NLS MS 2245, fols 74–75. Cadell was then a partner in the firm of Archibald Constable & Co., on whose behalf he was responding.
56. Hogg's status as self-educated peasant was thought to limit his range even in verse. With reference to the epic *Queen Hynde* Douglas Mack states that as the epic was the highest and noblest of all the various poetic genres 'who could regard a self-educated farm-worker as a person to be taken seriously as a rival to Homer and Virgil?'–see *Queen Hynde*, ed. by Suzanne Gilbert and Douglas S. Mack (S/SC, 1998), p. xi.
57. Jane Millgate, *Scott's Last Edition: A Study in Publishing History* (Edinburgh: Edinburgh UP, 1987), p. vii.
58. Millgate, pp. vii, 111.
59. See the review of the first volume of Edgeworth's *Tales and Novels* in *The Athenaeum*, 28 April 1832, p. 273.

60. Murray's announcement of the delayed publication of volume XVII of his edition of Byron is in *The Literary Gazette*, 20 April 1833, p. 256.
61. *The Ghost-Hunter and his Family. By the O'Hara Family* was published at six shillings, cloth-bound, by Smith, Elder, and Co. of London at the start of 1833, as the first volume of 'The Library of Romance, Edited by Leitch Ritchie'. According to the Preface (pp. [iii]–xii) the series was to include original novels by well-known and unknown authors, as well as translations and adaptations of novels in foreign languages and reprints and adaptations of American novels. I am grateful to Peter Garside for this information about 'The Library of Romance' series.
62. The advertisement for the forthcoming series of 'Standard Novels' is in *The Literary Gazette*, 19 February 1831, p. 128. Further details are taken from a subsequent notice in the same paper for 12 March 1831, p. 176.
63. See *The Literary Gazette*, 16 February 1833, pp. 102–03 (p. 102). The reviewer declares, 'Here are twenty-four volumes, neatly bound, prettily embellished, and all by writers of established popularity, for what at original prices would have cost thirty or five-and-thirty pounds'. The purchaser of the 'Standard Novels' to date would in fact have paid six pounds four shillings.
64. See *The Athenaeum*, 2 April 1831, pp. 216–17.
65. The date of publication of *Humphry Clinker* is given in the prefatory leaf of the second of volumes 1–4 of 'Roscoe's Novelist's Library', in their original binding in the Hugh Sharpe collection of the National Library of Scotland, shelfmark H. S. 877–880. Details of the physical appearance of the volumes are taken from this set.
66. An advertisement for the original first volume of 'Roscoe's Novelist's Library', the first part of *Robinson Crusoe* illustrated by Strutt, appears in *The Literary Gazette* of 9 April 1831, p. 240. The same paper reviewing it on 7 May 1831 commented that the illustrations were 'slight' and 'might be better', and rejoiced in the news that Cruikshank had been engaged to illustrate the remainder of the series (p. 296).
67. *The Literary Gazette* of 2 February 1833 (p. 72) declares, 'We are glad to see this "Library" resuscitated, and with a production so everlastingly popular in every shape and form as that of the inimitable Cervantes'. An advertisement for the volume giving the publisher as Effingham Wilson had appeared in the paper for 26 January 1833 (p. 61).
68. See the advertisement in *The Literary Gazette*, 4 February 1832, p. 78. It was advertised as having been published on 1 February in the issue for 10 March 1832, p. 160.
69. Cooper's works were advertised in the *Edinburgh Evening Courant* of 14 July 1832.
70. 'Miss Edgeworth's Tales and Novels' were advertised in *The Literary Gazette*, 14 April 1832, p. 240.
71. *The Literary Gazette* of 5 November 1831 (p. 720) informs readers that a prospectus for the series and specimens of the letter-press and engravings may be had from John Murray, and advertises the first five-shilling volume for 1 January 1832. *The Athenaeum* of 31 December 1831, reviewing this, remarks, 'we have heard, that to a wish to drive the smuggling French out of the market, we owe this elegant reprint' (p. 841).
72. See *The Literary Gazette* of 3 March 1832 (p. 144) for the advertisement of the third volume. Murray's extension of his original plan to include substantial notes is explained in the prefatory 'Advertisement' to the thirteenth volume of the series, and is end-dated 'London, December 12. 1832'–see *The Works of Lord Byron, with his Letters and Journals, and his Life by Thomas*

*Moore, Esq.*, 17 vols (London, 1832–33), XIII, v–vi. The review of the eleventh volume is in *The Literary Gazette*, 27 October 1832, pp. 678–80 (p. 679).

73. The description of and justification for the series is taken from the publisher's advertisement prefacing the first volume, end-dated 'April 30, 1832'–see *Tales and Novels by Maria Edgeworth*, 18 vols (London, 1832–33), I, v–viii (pp. viii, vi). There was an advertisement for the first volume of 'Miss Edgeworth's Tales and Novels' in *The Literary Gazette* of 14 April 1832 (p. 240), and Hogg mixing in London with many publishers and literary men might be supposed to have heard of the series beforehand.
74. See, for instance, 'Scotch Novels of the Second Class. No. II. Hogg's Brownie of Bodsbeck–Winter Tales–Three Perils of Man–Three Perils of Woman', *Edinburgh Magazine*, 13 (October 1823), 485–[91]. For Ian Duncan's comment, see the Introduction to *Winter Evening Tales*, ed. by Ian Duncan (S/SC, 2002), p. xi.
75. [James Browne], *The 'Life' of the Ettrick Shepherd Anatomized* (Edinburgh, 1832), p. 5.
76. See, for instance, the advertisement in the *Edinburgh Evening Courant* of 21 April 1832.
77. For specific examples, see the Introduction to *Tales of the Wars of Montrose*, ed. by Gillian Hughes (S/SC, 1996), pp. xiv–xv, and Douglas Mack's account of the way in which Hogg's 'Shepherd's Calendar' stories 'combine, like the stories of Joyce's *Dubliners*, into a resonant and convincing portrait of the life and spirit of a particular society'–see *The Shepherd's Calendar*, ed. by Douglas S. Mack (S/SC, 1995), p. xix.
78. There was surely an oddity, for example, in Robert's persistent scribbling in his journal at the very moment at which his diabolical nemesis approaches in the person of Gil-Martin: 'But, ah! who is yon that I see approaching furiously–his stern face blackened with horrid despair. My hour is at hand. [...] I will now seal up my little book, and conceal it [...]'–see James Hogg, *The Private Memoirs and Confessions of a Justified Sinner*, ed. by P. D. Garside (S/SC, 2001), p. 165.
79. See Douglas Gifford, *James Hogg* (Edinburgh: The Ramsay Head Press, 1976), pp. 195–96. Gifford's argument is developed further in 'The Basil Lee Figure in James Hogg's Fiction', *Newsletter of the James Hogg Society*, 4 (1985), pp. 16–27. See also David Groves, 'The *Confessions* and *The Adventures of Captain John Lochy*', *Newsletter of the James Hogg Society*, 6 (1987), 11–13.
80. See Douglas Gifford, *James Hogg* (Edinburgh: The Ramsay Head Press, 1976), p. 201.
81. Specific references in Hogg's tale to the eighteenth-century dispute about the nature of the great apes are indicated in the explanatory Notes to the present edition. For a discussion of Scott's allusions to it in *Count Robert of Paris*, see Clare Simmons, 'A Man of Few Words: The Romantic Orang-Outang and Scott's *Count Robert of Paris*', *Scottish Literary Journal*, 17 No. 1 (May 1990), 21–34. Ian Duncan discusses the Enlightenment background to the debate with particular reference to *Rob Roy* in 'Primitive Inventions: *Rob Roy*, Nation, and World System', *Eighteenth-Century Fiction*, 15 No. 1 (October 2002), 81–102.
82. See James Hogg, 'The Minstrel Boy', in *Friendship's Offering* (London, 1829), pp. 209–13 (p. 211).
83. William Hogg's letter to James Gray of 20 November 1814 recalling his brother's childhood states 'among his fellows he was always forward at every diversion that required agility and vigour, but did not much mind

whether he was victor or not', and illustrates this statement by a specific incident where a shepherd observed the local boys playing together and encouraged them to run a series of races against one another (Beinecke Rare Book and Manuscript Library, Yale University, GEN MSS 61, Box 1, Folder 19).

84. *Fraser's Magazine*, 5 (May 1832), 482–89 (p. 482).
85. *The Mirror of Literature, Amusement and Instruction*, 21 April 1832, pp. 254–56 (p. 254).
86. *Monthly Review*, new series, 2 (May 1832), 82–100 (pp. 82–83).
87. See *Literary Rambler*, 11 May 1832, p. 6; *The Mirror of Literature, Amusement and Instruction*, 21 April 1832, pp. 254–56 (p. 254); *The Athenaeum*, 14 April 1832, pp. 235–37 (p. 235); and *The Literary Gazette*, 31 March and 7 April 1832, pp. 199–201, 214–16 (p. 199).
88. See *The Day*, for 23 April 1832, p. 386, for 28 April 1832, pp. 410–11, and for 5 May 1832, p. 7.
89. *Morning Advertiser* for 20 and 23 April 1832, and *Ladies Museum*, new series, 3 (May 1832), 226.
90. *The Athenaeum*, 14 April 1832, pp. 235–37 (p. 235).
91. See *The Mirror of Literature, Amusement and Instruction*, 21 April 1832, pp. 254–56 (p. 254).
92. See *Kelso Chronicle*, 27 April 1832, p. 27, and *Fraser's Magazine*, 5 (May 1832), 482–89 (p. 487). In his letter to John Grieve of 13 February 1833 (NLS MS 30313, pp. 80–83) Blackwood stated, 'Unfortunately however he in an evil hour printed in his Memoirs some statements not only unfriendly to me but most unjust to my character as a man of business, and as these have gone forth to the world it is impossible that I can resume my connection with M[r] Hogg, unless he writes me a letter expressive of the strong sense he has of the honourable nature of the whole of my transactions with him'.
93. See the prefatory leaf in George Goldie, *A Letter to a Friend*, second edition (Edinburgh, 1832), and [James Browne], *The 'Life' of the Ettrick Shepherd Anatomized* (Edinburgh, 1832), p. 8.
94. The fifth volume of some early sets of *Poetical Works of the Ettrick Shepherd*, 5 vols (Glasgow: Blackie and Son, 1838–40) have a separate notice to subscribers dated May 1840 pasted to the front end-papers to explain the substitution of Hogg's own memoir of his life for the promised memoir by Wilson, with a facsimile of Wilson's autograph promise that 'a Memoir of Mr Hogg, on a more extensive scale than was at first contemplated, is now in preparation by Professor Wilson, and will be published [...] within a few Months, in the same style & form as these volumes'. The work, however, never appeared. Hogg's 'Autobiography' finishes at the writing of *The Royal Jubilee* with the words 'and I have preserved it as a relic' (p. xci–p. 59 in the present edition). Details of Hogg's endeavours to publish *Altrive Tales* and a reference to 'the following volumes' of tales (pp. 59–60) were presumably omitted as inappropriate to the new context of a posthumous edition of Hogg's poetry, and are replaced by a brief summary of the failure of the 'Altrive Tales' series, the final years of his life, his death, and a character assessment. The Editor explains, 'As Mr Hogg's autobiography breaks off several years before his literary labours terminated, it will be proper to continue the narrative very shortly down to the time of his death' (p. xcii) but does not indicate that 'END OF THE AUTOBIOGRAPHY' on p. xci was not the end of the 1832 'Memoir' from *Altrive Tales*.
95. See, for example, the 'Note on the Text' to *Tales of the Wars of Montrose*, ed. by Gillian Hughes (S/SC, 1996), pp. 236–39, and also Louis Simpson, *James*

*Hogg: A Critical Study* (Edinburgh and London: Oliver & Boyd, 1962), p. 112.

96. See the Preface to James Hogg, *Memoir of the Author's Life* and *Familiar Anecdotes of Sir Walter Scott*, ed. by Douglas S. Mack (Edinburgh and London: Scottish Academic Press, 1972), and also Silvia Mergenthal, *James Hogg: Selbstbild und Bild: Zur Rezeption des 'Ettrick Shepherd'* (Frankfurt am Main: Peter Lang, 1990) and Nelson C. Smith, *James Hogg*, Twayne's English Authors Series 311 (Boston: Twayne Publishers, 1980), pp. 32–38.
97. Barbara Bloedé, 'James Hogg's *Private Memoirs and Confessions of a Justified Sinner*: The Genesis of the Double', *Etudes Anglaises*, 26 (1973), 174–86; Douglas Gifford, 'The Basil Lee Figure in Hogg's Fiction', *Newsletter of the James Hogg Society*, 4 (1985), pp. 16–27; David Groves, 'The *Confessions* and *The Adventures of Captain John Lochy*', *Newsletter of the James Hogg Society*, 6 (1987), pp. 11–13.
98. See James Hogg, *The Three Perils of Man: War, Women and Witchcraft*, ed. by Douglas Gifford (Edinburgh and London: Scottish Academic Press, 1972); W. G. Shepherd, 'Fat Flesh: The Poetic Theme of *The Three Perils of Man*', *Studies in Hogg and his World*, 3 (1992), 1–9; and Ian Duncan, 'Scott, Hogg, Orality and the Limits of Culture', *Studies in Hogg and his World*, 8 (1997), 56–74.
99. See Garden, p. 157, and also the *Sunday Times* for 29 April 1832.
100. Douglas Gifford, *James Hogg* (Edinburgh: The Ramsay Head Press, 1976), p. 201.

# Select Bibliography

### Editions of *Altrive Tales*

The present edition is a paperback reprint of the hardback Stirling / South Carolina edition of *Altrive Tales* (2003), the only alternative to the first edition published by James Cochrane of London in 1832. Hogg's *Memoir of the Author's Life* was edited (with *Familiar Anecdotes of Sir Walter Scott*) by Douglas S. Mack, and published by Scottish Academic Press in Edinburgh in 1972.

### Collected Editions

The Stirling / South Carolina Research Edition of the Collected Works of James Hogg (Edinburgh: Edinburgh University Press, 1995–), now underway but not yet complete, is a modern scholarly edition. Previous editions which are useful but bowdlerised are *Tales and Sketches by the Ettrick Shepherd*, 6 vols (Glasgow: Blackie and Son, 1836–37), *The Poetical Works of the Ettrick Shepherd*, 5 vols (Glasgow: Blackie and Son, 1838–40), and *The Works of the Ettrick Shepherd*, ed. by Thomas Thomson, 2 vols (Glasgow: Blackie and Son, 1865).

### Bibliography

Edith C. Batho's Bibliography in *The Ettrick Shepherd* (Cambridge: Cambridge University Press, 1927), is still useful, together with her supplementary 'Notes on the Bibliography of James Hogg, the Ettrick Shepherd', in *The Library*, 16 (1935–36), 309–26. Two more modern and reader-friendly bibliographies are Douglas S. Mack, *Hogg's Prose: An Annotated Listing* (Stirling: The James Hogg Society, 1985), and Gillian Hughes, *Hogg's Verse and Drama: A Chronological Listing* (Stirling: The James Hogg Society, 1990). Subsequent information about recently-discovered Hogg items may be gleaned from various articles in *The Bibliotheck* and *Studies in Hogg and his World*.

### Biography

Karl Miller's perceptive and illuminating *Electric Shepherd: A Likeness of James Hogg* (London: Faber, 2003) contains much biographical information. Gillian Hughes is currently writing a detailed biography: her forthcoming *James Hogg: A Life* (Edinburgh University Press) will draw on her three-volume edition of Hogg's *Collected Letters*, the first volume of which was published by Edinburgh University Press in 2004. Hogg's life up to 1825 is covered by Alan Lang Strout's

*The Life and Letters of James Hogg, The Ettrick Shepherd Volume 1 (1770–1825)*, Texas Technological College Research Publications, 15 (Lubbock, Texas: Texas Technological College, 1946). Much valuable information may be obtained from Mrs M. G. Garden's memoir of her father, *Memorials of James Hogg, the Ettrick Shepherd* (London: Alexander Gardner, 1885), and from Mrs Norah Parr's account of Hogg's domestic life in *James Hogg at Home* (Dollar: Douglas S. Mack, 1980). Also useful are Sir George Douglas, *James Hogg*, Famous Scots Series (Edinburgh: Oliphant Anderson & Ferrier, 1899), and Henry Thew Stephenson's *The Ettrick Shepherd: A Biography*, Indiana University Studies, 54 (Bloomington, Indiana: Indiana University, 1922).

## General Criticism

Edith C. Batho, *The Ettrick Shepherd* (Cambridge: Cambridge University Press, 1927)

Louis Simpson, *James Hogg: A Critical Study* (Edinburgh and London: Oliver & Boyd, 1962)

Douglas Gifford, *James Hogg* (Edinburgh: The Ramsay Head Press, 1976)

Nelson C. Smith, *James Hogg*, Twayne's English Authors Series (Boston: Twayne Publishers, 1980)

Thomas Crawford, 'James Hogg: The Play of Region and Nation', in *The History of Scottish Literature: Volume 3 Nineteenth Century*, ed. by Douglas Gifford (Aberdeen: Aberdeen University Press, 1988), pp. 89–105

David Groves, *James Hogg: The Growth of a Writer* (Edinburgh: Scottish Academic Press, 1988)

Silvia Mergenthal, *James Hogg: Selbstbild und Bild*, Publications of the Scottish Studies Centre of the Johannes Gutenberg Universität Mainz in Germersheim, 9 (Frankfurt-am-Main: Peter Lang, 1990)

Penny Fielding, *Writing and Orality: Nationality, Culture, and Nineteenth-Century Scottish Fiction* (Oxford: Clarendon Press, 1996)

Karl Miller, *Electric Shepherd: A Likeness of James Hogg* (London: Faber, 2003)

## Criticism on *Altrive Tales*

Little attention has been paid to *Altrive Tales* to date, and most relevant criticism relates to individual components of it seen in other contexts. Of this the following articles are particularly helpful:

Douglas S. Mack, 'James Hogg's Altrive Tales: an 1835 reissue',

*The Bibliotheck*, 5 no. 6 (1969), 210–11

Barbara Bloedé, 'James Hogg's *Private Memoirs and Confessions of a Justified Sinner:* the Genesis of the Double', *Etudes Anglaises*, 26 no. 2 (1973), 174–86

Douglas Gifford, 'The Basil Lee Figure in Hogg's Fiction', *Newsletter of the James Hogg Society*, 4 (1985), 16–27

David Groves, '*The Confessions* and *The Adventures of Captain John Lochy*', *Newsletter of the James Hogg Society*, 6 (1987), 11–13

Silvia Mergenthal, '*Naturae Donum:* Comments on Hogg's Self-Image and Image', *Studies in Hogg and his World*, 1 (1990), 71–79

W. G. Shepherd, 'Fat Flesh: The Poetic Theme of *The Three Perils of Man*', *Studies in Hogg and his World*, 3 (1992), 1–9

Ian Duncan, 'Scott, Hogg, Orality and the Limits of Culture', *Studies in Hogg and his World*, 8 (1997), 56–74

Robin MacLachlan, 'Hogg and the Art of Brand Management', *Studies in Hogg and his World*, 14 (2003), 5–15

Meiko O'Halloran, 'Hogg's Kaleidoscopic Art: Identity, Tradition, and Legitimacy in the Work of James Hogg' (unpublished D. Phil. thesis, University of Oxford, 2004)

# Chronology of James Hogg

**1770** On 9 December James Hogg is baptised in Ettrick Church, Selkirkshire, the date of his birth going unrecorded. His father, Robert Hogg (*c.*1729–1820), a former shepherd, was then tenant of Ettrickhall, a modest farm almost within sight of the church. His mother, Margaret Laidlaw (1730–1813), belonged to a local family noted for their athleticism and also for their stock of ballads and other traditional lore. Hogg's parents married in Ettrick on 27 May 1765, and had four sons, William (b.1767), James (b.1770), David (b.1773), and Robert (b.1776).

**1775–76** Hogg attends the parish school kept by John Beattie for a few months before his formal education is abruptly terminated by his father's bankruptcy as a stock-farmer and sheep-dealer and the family's consequent destitution. Their possessions are sold by auction, but a compassionate neighbour, Walter Bryden of Crosslee, takes a lease of the farm of Ettrickhouse and places Robert Hogg there as his shepherd.

**1776–85** Due to his family's poverty Hogg is employed as a farm servant throughout his childhood, beginning with the job of herding a few cows in the summer and progressing as his strength increases to general farmwork and acting as a shepherd's assistant. He learns the Metrical Psalms and other parts of the Bible, listens eagerly to the legends of his mother and her brother William (*c.*1735–1829), of itinerants who visit the parish, and of the old men he is engaged with on the lightest and least demanding farm-work.

**1778** Death on 17 September of Hogg's maternal grandfather, William Laidlaw, 'the far-famed Will o' Phaup', a noted athlete and reputedly the last man in the district to have spoken with the fairies.

***c.* 1784** Having saved five shillings from his wages, at the age of fourteen Hogg purchases an old fiddle and teaches himself to play it at the end of his day's work.

**1785** Hogg serves a year from Martinmas (11 November) with Mr Scott, the tenant-farmer of Singlee, at 'working with horses, threshing, &c.'

**1786** Hogg serves eighteen months from Martinmas with Mr Laidlaw at Elibank, 'the most quiet and sequestered place in Scotland'.

**1788** The father of Mr Laidlaw of Elibank, who farms at Willenslee, gives Hogg his first engagement as a shepherd from Whitsunday (15 May); here he stays for two years and begins to read while tending the ewes. His master's wife lends him newspapers and theological works, and he also reads Allan Ramsay's *The Gentle Shepherd* and William Hamilton of Gilbertfield's paraphrase of Blind Harry's *The Life and Adventures of William Wallace*.

**1790** Hogg begins a ten-years' service from Whitsunday as shepherd to James Laidlaw of Blackhouse farm, whose kindness he later described as 'much more like that of a father than a master'. Hogg reads his master's books, as well as those of Mr Elder's Peebles circulating library, and begins to compose songs for the local lasses to sing. He makes a congenial and life-long friend in his master's eldest son, William Laidlaw (1779–1845), and with his elder brother William and a number of cousins forms a literary society of shepherds. Alexander Laidlaw, shepherd at Bowerhope in Yarrow, is also an intimate friend who shares Hogg's efforts at self-improvement. 'The Mistakes of a Night', a Scots poem, is published in the *Scots Magazine* for October 1794, and in 1797 Hogg first hears of Robert Burns (1759–96) when a half-daft man named Jock Scott recites 'Tam o' Shanter' to him on the hillside. Towards the end of this period Hogg composes plays and pastorals as well as songs. His journeying as a drover of sheep stimulates an interest in the Highlands of Scotland, and initiates a series of exploratory tours taken in the summer over a succession of years.

**1800** At Whitsunday Hogg leaves Blackhouse to look after his ageing parents at Ettrickhouse. Going into Edinburgh in the autumn to sell sheep he decides to print his poems: his *Scottish Pastorals* is published early in the following year and receives favourable attention in the *Scots Magazine* for 1801. More popular still is his patriotic song of 'Donald Macdonald' also composed at about this time, in fear of a French invasion.

**1802** Hogg is recruited by William Laidlaw in the spring as a ballad-collector for Scott's *Minstrelsy of the Scottish Border*, and meets Walter Scott himself (1771–1832) later in the year. He begins to contribute to the *Edinburgh Magazine*, and keeps a journal of his Highland Tour in July and August that is eventually published in the *Scots Magazine*.

**1803** The lease of Ettrickhouse expires at Whitsunday and Hogg uses his savings to lease a Highland sheep farm, signing a five-year lease for Shelibost in Harris on 13 July, to begin from Whitsunday 1804. On his journey home he stops at Greenock where he meets the future novelist John Galt (1779–1839) and his friend James Park. He is now a regular contributor to the *Scots Magazine*, and also earns prizes from the Highland Society of Scotland for his essays on sheep.

**1804** Hogg loses his money and fails to gain possession of Shelibost through a legal complication, retiring into England for the summer. On his return home he fails to find employment, but occupies himself in writing ballad-imitations for the collection published in 1807 as *The Mountain Bard*.

**1805–1806** Hogg is engaged from Whitsunday 1805 as a shepherd at Mitchelslacks farm in Closeburn parish, Dumfriesshire: his master Mr Harkness belongs to a local family famous for their support of the Covenanters. He is visited on the hillside by the young Allan Cunningham (1784–1842), and becomes friendly with the whole talented Cunningham family. Around Halloween 1806 (31 October) he becomes the lover of Catherine Henderson. Towards the end of the year Hogg signs leases on two farms in Dumfriesshire, Corfardin and Locherben, to begin from Whitsunday 1807.

**1807** *The Mountain Bard* is published by Archibald Constable (1774–1827) in Edinburgh in February. At Whitsunday Hogg moves to Corfardin farm in Tynron parish. *The Shepherd's Guide*, a sheep-farming and veterinary manual, is published in June. Hogg acknowledges paternity of Catherine Henderson's baby, born towards the end of the summer and baptised Catherine Hogg on 13 December.

**1808–09** As a result of trips to Edinburgh Hogg becomes acquainted with James Gray (1770–1830), classics master of the Edinburgh High School and his future brother-in-law. He also meets a number of literary women, including Mary Peacock, Jessie Stuart, Mary Brunton, and Eliza Izett. After the death of his sheep in a storm Hogg moves to Locherben farm and tries to earn a living by grazing sheep for other farmers. His debts escalate, he becomes increasingly reckless, and around Whitsunday 1809 becomes the lover of Margaret Beattie. In the autumn Hogg absconds from Locherben and his creditors, returning to Ettrick where he is considered to be disgraced and unemployable.

**1810** In February Hogg moves to Edinburgh in an attempt to pursue a career as a professional literary man. In Dumfriesshire Margaret Beattie's daughter is born on 13 March, and her birth is recorded retrospectively as Elizabeth Hogg in June, Hogg presumably having acknowledged paternity. Later that year Hogg meets his future wife, Margaret Phillips (1789–1870), while she is paying a visit to her brother-in-law James Gray in Edinburgh. He explores the cultural life of Edinburgh, and is supported by the generosity of an Ettrick friend, John Grieve (1781–1836), now a prosperous Edinburgh hatter. A song-collection entitled *The Forest Minstrel* is published in August. On 1 September the first number of Hogg's own weekly periodical *The Spy* appears, which in spite of its perceived improprieties, continues for a whole year.

**1811–12** During the winter of 1810–11 Hogg becomes an active member of the Forum, a public debating society, eventually being appointed Secretary. This brings him into contact with John M'Diarmid (1792–1852), later to become a noted Scottish journalist, and the reforming mental health specialist Dr Andrew Duncan (1744–1828). With Grieve's encouragement Hogg takes rural lodgings at Deanhaugh on the outskirts of Edinburgh and plans a long narrative poem centred on a poetical contest at the court of Mary, Queen of Scots.

**1813** Hogg becomes a literary celebrity in Edinburgh when *The Queen's Wake* is published at the end of January, and makes new friends in R. P. Gillies (1788–1858) and John Wilson (1785–1854), his correspondence widening to include Lord Byron (1788–1824) early the following year. Hogg's mother dies in the course of the summer. Hogg tries to interest Constable in a series of Scottish Rural Tales, and also takes advice from various literary friends on the suitability of his play, *The Hunting of Badlewe*, for the stage. In the autumn during his customary Highland Tour he is detained at Kinnaird House near Dunkeld by a cold and begins a poem in the Spenserian stanza, eventually to become *Mador of the Moor*.

**1814** Hogg intervenes successfully to secure publication of the work of other writers such as R. P. Gillies, James Gray, and William Nicholson (1782–1849). George Goldie publishes *The Hunting of Badlewe* in April, as the Allies enter Paris and the end of the long war with France seems imminent. During the summer Hogg meets William Wordsworth (1770–1850) in Edinburgh, and visits him and other poets in an excursion to the Lake District. He proposes a poetical repository, and obtains several promises of contributions from important contemporary poets, though the project leads to a serious quarrel with Scott in the autumn. The bankruptcy of George Goldie halts sales of *The Queen's Wake*, but introduces Hogg to the publisher William Blackwood (1776–1834). Having offered Constable *Mador of the Moor* in February, Hogg is persuaded by James Park to publish *The Pilgrims of the Sun* first: the poem is brought out by John Murray (1778–1843) and William Blackwood in Edinburgh in December. Towards the end of the year Hogg and his young Edinburgh friends form the Right and Wrong Club which meets nightly and where heavy drinking takes place.

**1815** Hogg begins the year with a serious illness, but at the end of January is better and learns that the Duke of Buccleuch has granted him the small farm of Eltrive Moss effectively rent-free for his lifetime. He takes possession at Whitsunday, but as the house there is barely habitable continues to spend much of his time in Edinburgh. He writes songs for the Scottish collector George Thomson (1757–1851). Scott's publication of a poem celebrating the ending of the Napoleonic Wars with the battle of Waterloo on 18 June prompts Hogg to write 'The Field of Waterloo'. Hogg also writes 'To the Ancient Banner of Buccleuch' for the local contest at football at Carterhaugh on 4 December.

**1816** Hogg contributes songs to John Clarke-Whitfeld's *Twelve Vocal Melodies*, and plans a collected edition of his own poetry. *Mador of the Moor* is published in April. Despairing of the success of his poetical repository Hogg turns it into a collection of his own parodies, published in October as *The Poetic Mirror*. The volume is unusually successful, a second edition being published in December. The Edinburgh musician Alexander Campbell visits Hogg in Yarrow, enlisting his help with the song-collection *Albyn's Anthology* (1816–18). William Blackwood moves into Princes Street, signalling his intention to become one of Edinburgh's foremost publishers.

**1817** Blackwood begins an *Edinburgh Monthly Magazine* in April, with Hogg's support, but with Thomas Pringle and James Cleghorn as editors it is a lacklustre publication and a breach between publisher and editors ensues. Hogg, holding by Blackwood, sends him a draft of the notorious 'Chaldee Manuscript', the scandal surrounding which ensures the success of the relaunched *Blackwood's Edinburgh Magazine*. Hogg's two-volume

*Dramatic Tales* are published in May. Hogg spends much of the summer at his farm of Altrive, writing songs for *Hebrew Melodies*, a Byron-inspired collection proposed by the composer W. E. Heather. In October George Thomson receives a proposal from the Highland Society of London for a collection of Jacobite Songs, a commission which he passes on to Hogg.

**1818** *The Brownie of Bodsbeck; and Other Tales* is published by Blackwood in March, by which time Hogg is busily working on *Jacobite Relics*, his major preoccupation this year. A modern stone-built cottage is built at Altrive, the cost of which Hogg hopes to defray in part by a new one guinea subscription edition of *The Queen's Wake*, which is at press in October though publication did not occur until early the following year.

**1819** On a visit to Edinburgh towards the end of February Hogg meets again with Margaret Phillips; his courtship of her becomes more intense, and he proposes marriage. Hogg's song-collection *A Border Garland* is published in May, and in August Hogg signs a contract with Oliver and Boyd for the publication of *Winter Evening Tales*, also working on a long Border Romance. The first volume of *Jacobite Relics* is published in December.

**1820** During the spring Hogg is working on the second volume of his *Jacobite Relics* and also on a revised edition of *The Mountain Bard*, as well as planning his marriage to Margaret Phillips, which takes place on 28 April. His second work of fiction, *Winter Evening Tales,* is published at the end of April. Very little literary work is accomplished during the autumn: the Hoggs make their wedding visits in Dumfriesshire during September, and then on 24 October Hogg's old father dies at Altrive.

**1821** The second volume of *Jacobite Relics* is published in February and a third (enlarged) edition of *The Mountain Bard* in March. The inclusion in the latter of an updated 'Memoir of the Author's Life' raises an immediate outcry. Hogg's son, James Robert Hogg, is born in Edinburgh on 18 March and baptised on the couple's first wedding anniversary. Serious long-term financial troubles begin for Hogg with the signing of a nine-year lease from Whitsunday of the large farm of Mount Benger in Yarrow, part of the estates of the Duke of Buccleuch–Hogg having insufficient capital for such an ambitious venture. In June Oliver and Boyd's refusal to publish Hogg's

Border Romance, *The Three Perils of Man*, leads to a breach with the firm. Hogg also breaks temporarily with Blackwood in August when a savage review of his 'Memoir of the Author's Life' appears in *Blackwood's Edinburgh Magazine*, and begins again to write for Constable's less lively *Edinburgh Magazine*. In September there is a measles epidemic in Yarrow, and Hogg becomes extremely ill with the disease. By the end of the year Hogg is negotiating with the Constable firm for an edition of his collected poems in four volumes.

**1822** The first of the 'Noctes Ambrosianae' appears in the March issue of *Blackwood's Edinburgh Magazine*: Hogg is portrayed in this long-running series as the Shepherd, a 'boozing buffoon'. June sees the publication of Hogg's four-volume *Poetical Works* by Constable, and Longmans publish his novel *The Three Perils of Man*. There is great excitement in Edinburgh surrounding the visit of George IV to the city in August, and Hogg marks the occasion with the publication of his Scottish masque, *The Royal Jubilee*. A neighbouring landowner in Ettrick Forest, Captain Napier of Thirlestane, publishes *A Treatise on Practical Store-Farming* in October, with help from Hogg and his friend Alexander Laidlaw of Bowerhope. James Gray leaves Edinburgh to become Rector of Belfast Academy.

**1823** In debt to William Blackwood Hogg sets about retrieving his finances with a series of tales for *Blackwood's Edinburgh Magazine* under the title of 'The Shepherd's Calendar'. His daughter Janet Phillips Hogg ('Jessie') is born on 23 April. That summer a suicide is exhumed in Yarrow, and Hogg writes an account for *Blackwood's*. *The Three Perils of Woman*, another novel, is published in August, and Hogg subsequently plans to publish an eight-volume collection of his Scottish tales.

**1824** Hogg is working on his epic poem *Queen Hynde* during the spring when his attention is distracted by family troubles. His once prosperous father-in-law is in need of a home, so Hogg moves his own family to the old thatched farmhouse of Mount Benger leaving his new cottage at Altrive for the old couple. *The Private Memoirs and Confessions of a Justified Sinner*, written at Altrive during the preceding months, is published in June. Hogg contributes to the *Literary Souvenir* for 1825, this signalling the opening of a new and lucrative market for his work in Literary Annuals. In November a major conflagration destroys part of Edinburgh's Old Town. *Queen Hynde* is published early in December.

**1825** Another daughter is born to the Hoggs on 18 January and named Margaret Laidlaw Hogg ('Maggie'). Hogg turns his attention to a new work of prose fiction, 'Lives of Eminent Men', the precursor of his *Tales of the Wars of Montrose.* In December John Gibson Lockhart (1794–1854), Scott's son-in-law and a leading light of *Blackwood's*, moves to London to take up the post of editor of the *Quarterly Review*, accompanied by Hogg's nephew and literary assistant Robert Hogg.

**1826** Hogg is in arrears with his rent for Mount Benger at a time which sees the failure of the Constable publishing firm, involving Sir Walter Scott and also Hogg's friend John Aitken. By July Hogg himself is threatened with arrestment for debt, while the Edinburgh book trade is in a state of near-stagnation. James Gray is also in debt and leaves Belfast for India, leaving his two daughters, Janet and Mary, in the care of Hogg and his wife.

**1827** Hogg's financial affairs are in crisis at the beginning of the year when the Buccleuch estate managers order him to pay his arrears of rent at Whitsunday or relinquish the Mount Benger farm. However, 'The Shepherd's Calendar' stories are appearing regularly in *Blackwood's Edinburgh Magazine* and Hogg is confident of earning a decent income by his pen as applications for contributions to Annuals and other periodicals increase. The death of his father-in-law Peter Phillips in May relieves him from the expense of supporting two households. Hogg founds the St Ronan's Border Club, the first sporting meeting of which takes place at Innerleithen in September. The year ends quietly for the Hoggs, who are both convalescent–Margaret from the birth of the couple's third daughter, Harriet Sidney Hogg, on 18 December, and Hogg from the lameness resulting from having been struck by a horse.

**1828** Although a more productive year for Hogg than the last, with the publication of his *Select and Rare Scotish Melodies* in London in the autumn and the signing of a contract with Robert Purdie for a new edition of his *Border Garland*, the book-trade is still at a comparative standstill. Hogg's daughter Harriet is discovered to have a deformed foot that may render her lame. A new weekly periodical entitled the *Edinburgh Literary Journal* is started in Edinburgh by Hogg's young friend, Henry Glassford Bell (1803–74).

**1829** Hogg continues to write songs and to make contributions to Annuals and other periodicals, while the spring sees the publication of *The Shepherd's Calendar* in book form. Hogg continues to relish shooting during the autumn months and the country sports of the St Ronan's Border Club.

**1830** Hogg's lease of the Mount Benger farm is not renewed, and the family return to Altrive at Whitsunday. Inspired by the success of Scott's *magnum opus* edition of the Waverley Novels, Hogg pushes for the publication of his own tales in monthly numbers. Blackwood agrees to publish a small volume of Hogg's best songs, and Hogg finds a new outlet for his work with the foundation in February of *Fraser's Magazine*. Towards the end of September Hogg meets with Scott for the last time.

**1831** *Songs by the Ettrick Shepherd* is published at the start of the year, and a companion volume of ballads, *A Queer Book*, is printed, though publication is held up by Blackwood, who argues that the political agitation surrounding the Reform Bill is hurtful to his trade. He is also increasingly reluctant to print Hogg's work in his magazine. Hogg's youngest child, Mary Gray Hogg, is born on 21 August. Early in December Hogg quarrels openly with Blackwood and resolves to start the publication of his collected prose tales in London. After a short stay in Edinburgh he departs by sea and arrives in London on the last day of the year.

**1832** From January to March Hogg enjoys being a literary lion in London while he forwards the publication of his collected prose tales. Within a few weeks of his arrival he publishes a devotional manual for children entitled *A Father's New Year's Gift*, and also works on the first volume of his *Altrive Tales*, published in April after his return to Altrive. Blackwood, no doubt aware of Hogg's metropolitan celebrity, finally publishes *A Queer Book* in April too. The Glasgow publisher Archibald Fullarton offers Hogg a substantial fee for producing a new edition of the works of Robert Burns with a memoir of the poet. The financial failure of Hogg's London publisher, James Cochrane, stops the sale and production of *Altrive Tales* soon after the publication of the first (and only) volume. Sir Walter Scott dies on 21 September, and Hogg reflects on the subject of a Scott biography. In October Hogg is invited to contribute to a new cheap paper, *Chambers's Edinburgh Journal*.

**1833** During a January visit to Edinburgh Hogg falls through the ice while out curling and a serious illness results. In February he tries to interest the numbers publisher Blackie and Son of Glasgow in a continuation of his collected prose tales. He tries to mend the breach with Blackwood, who for his part is seriously offended by Hogg's allusions to their financial dealings in the 'Memoir' prefacing *Altrive Tales.* Hogg sends a collection of anecdotes about Scott for publication in London but withdraws them in deference to Lockhart as Scott's son-in-law, forwarding a rewritten version to America in June for publication there. He offers Cochrane, now back in business as a publisher, some tales about the wars of Montrose, and by November has reached an agreement with Blackie and Son. The young Duke of Buccleuch grants Hogg a 99-year lease for the house at Altrive and a fragment of the land, a measure designed to secure a vote for him in elections but which also ensures a small financial provision for Hogg's young family after his death.

**1834** Hogg's nephew and literary assistant Robert Hogg dies of consumption on 9 January, aged thirty-one. Hogg revises his work on the edition of Burns, now with William Motherwell as a co-editor. His *Lay Sermons* is published in April, and the same month sees the publication of his *Familiar Anecdotes of Sir Walter Scott* in America. When a pirated version comes out in Glasgow in June Lockhart breaks off all friendly relations with Hogg. The breach with William Blackwood is mended in May, but Blackwood's death on 16 November loosens Hogg's connection both with the publishing firm and *Blackwood's Edinburgh Magazine.*

**1835** *Tales of the Wars of Montrose* is published in March. Hogg seems healthy enough in June, when his wife and daughter, Harriet, leave him at Altrive while paying a visit to Edinburgh. Even in August he is well enough to go out shooting on the moors as usual and to take what proves to be a last look at Blackhouse and other scenes of his youth. Soon afterwards, however, his normally excellent constitution begins to fail and by October he is confined first to the house and then to his bed. He dies on 21 November, and is buried among his relations in Ettrick kirkyard a short distance from the place of his birth.

# *Altrive Tales*

THE ETTRICK SHEPHERD.

(AGED 60)

London Published by James Cochrane & Co 1832

# ALTRIVE TALES:

COLLECTED

AMONG THE PEASANTRY OF SCOTLAND,

AND

FROM FOREIGN ADVENTURERS.

BY

THE ETTRICK SHEPHERD.

WITH ILLUSTRATIONS BY GEORGE CRUIKSHANK.

LONDON:

JAMES COCHRANE AND CO.,

11, WATERLOO PLACE, PALL MALL.

1832.

# DEDICATION

TO

THE RIGHT HONOURABLE

## LADY ANNE SCOTT, OF BUCCLEUGH

To her, whose bounty oft hath shed
Joy round the peasant's lowly bed,
When trouble press'd and friends were few,
And God and angels only knew:
To her, who loves the board to cheer,
And hearth of simple cottager;
Who loves the tale of rural hind,
And wayward visions of his mind,—
I dedicate, with high delight,
The themes of many a winter night.

What other name on Yarrow vale
Can Shepherd choose to grace his tale?
There other living name is none
Heard with one feeling–one alone.
Some heavenly charm must name endear
That all men love, and all revere!
Even the rude boy of rustic form,
And robe all fluttering to the storm,
Whose roguish lip and graceless eye
Incline to mock the passer by,
Walks by the maid with softer tread,
And lowly bends his burly head,
Following with eye of milder ray
The gentle form that glides away.
The little school-nymph, drawing near,
Says, with a sly and courteous leer,
As plain as eye and manner can,
"Thou lov'st me–bless thee, Lady Anne!"
Even babes will catch the 'loved theme,
And learn to lisp their Lady's name.

The orphan's blessing rests on thee;
Happy thou art, and long shalt be!
'Tis not in sorrow, nor distress,
Nor fortune's power to make thee less.
The heart, unalter'd in its mood,
That joys alone in doing good,
And follows in the heavenly road,
And steps where once an angel trod;–
The joys within such heart that burn,
No loss can quench, nor time o'erturn!
The stars may from their orbits bend,
The mountains rock, the heavens rend,
The sun's last ember cool and quiver,
But these shall glow, and glow for ever!

Then thou, who lov'st the Shepherd's home,
And cherishest his lowly dome,
O list the mystic lore sublime
Of fairy tales of ancient time.
I learn'd them in the lonely glen,
The last abodes of living men;
Where never stranger came our way
By summer night, or winter day;
Where neighbouring hind or cot was none,
Our converse was with heaven alone,
With voices through the cloud that sung,
And brooding storms that round us hung.

O Lady, judge, if judge you may,
How stern and ample was the sway
Of themes like these, when darkness fell,
And gray-hair'd sires the tales would tell!
When doors were barr'd, and eldron dame
Plied at her task beside the flame,
That through the smoke and gloom alone
On dim and umber'd faces shone;
The bleat of mountain goat on high,
That from the cliff came quavering by;
The echoing rock, the rushing flood,
The cataract's swell, the moaning wood;
That undefined and mingled hum–
Voice of the desart, never dumb;

All these have left within this heart
A feeling tongue can ne'er impart;
A wilder'd and unearthly flame,
A something that's without a name.

And, lady, thou wilt never deem
Religious tale offensive theme;
Our creeds may differ in degree,
But small that difference sure can be.
As flowers which vary in their dyes,
We all shall bloom in Paradise.
As sire, who loves his children well,
The loveliest face he cannot tell,–
So 'tis with us; we are the same,
One faith, one Father, and one aim.

And hadst thou lived where I was bred,
Amid the scenes where martyrs bled,
Their sufferings all to thee endear'd,
By those most honour'd and revered;
And where the wild dark streamlet raves,
Hadst wept above their lonely graves,
Thou wouldst have felt, I know it true,
As I have done, and aye must do:
And for the same exalted cause,
For mankind's right, and nature's laws,
The cause of liberty divine,
Thy fathers bled as well as mine.

Then be it thine, O noble maid,
On some still eve these tales to read;
And thou wilt read, I know full well,
For still thou lov'st the haunted dell;
To linger by the sainted spring,
And trace the ancient fairy ring,
Where moonlight revels long were held
In many a lone sequester'd field,
By Yarrow dens and Ettrick shaw,
And the green mounds of Carterhaugh.
O! for one kindred heart, that thought
As minstrel must and lady ought;
That loves, like thee, the whispering wood,

And range of mountain solitude!
Think how more wild the mountain scene,
If times were still as they have been;
If fairies, at the fall of even,
Down from the eyebrow of the heaven,
Or some aërial land afar,
Came on the beam of rising star;
Their lightsome gambols to renew,
From the green leaf to quaff the dew,
Or dance with such a graceful tread,
As scarce to bend the gowan's head.

Think if thou wert, some evening still,
Within thy wood of green Bowhill–
Thy native wood!–the forest's pride!
Lover or sister by thy side;
In converse sweet the hour t' improve,
Of things below and things above;
Of an existence scarce begun;
And note the stars rise one by one.
Just then, the moon and day-light blending,
To see the fairy bands descending,
Wheeling and shivering as they came,
Like glimmering shreds of human frame;
Or sailing, mid the golden air,
In skiffs of yielding gossamer.
O! I would wander forth alone,
Where human eye hath never shone,
Away, o'er continents and isles,
A thousand and a thousand miles,
For one such eve to sit with thee,
Their strains to hear and forms to see!
Absent the while all fears of harm,
Secure in Heaven's protecting arm;
To list the songs such beings sung,
And hear them speak in human tongue;
To see in beauty, perfect, pure,
Of human face the miniature,
And smile of beings free from sin,
That had not death impress'd within.
Ah! can it ever be forgot,
What Scotland had, and now has not!

Such scenes, dear lady, now no more
Are given, or fitted, as before,
To eye or ear of guilty dust;
But when it comes, as come it must,
The time when I, from earth set free,
Shall turn the sprite I fain would be;
If there's a land, as grandsires tell,
Where brownies, elves, and fairies dwell,
There my first visit shall be sped.–
Journeyer of earth, go hide thy head!
Of all thy travelling splendour shorn,
Though in thy golden chariot borne!
Yon little cloud of many a hue
That wanders o'er the solar blue,
That curls, and rolls, and fleets away
Beyond the very springs of day,
That do I challenge and engage
To be my travelling equipage;
Then onward, onward, far to steer,
The breeze of heaven my charioteer;
By azure blue and orient sheen,
By star that glimmers red and green,
And hangs like emerald polish'd bright
Upon the left cheek of the night,
The soul's own energy my guide,
Eternal hope my all beside.
At such a shrine who would not bow?
Traveller of earth, where art thou now?

Then let me for these legends claim
My young, my honour'd Lady's name;
That honour is reward complete,
Yet I must crave, if not unmeet,
One little boon–delightful task
For maid to grant, or minstrel ask!

One day, thou may'st remember well,
For short the time since it befel,
When o'er thy forest bowers of oak
The eddying storm in darkness broke;
Loud sung the blast a-down the dell,
And Yarrow lent her treble swell;

The mountain's form grew more sublime,
Wrapt in its wreaths of rolling rime;
And Newark cairn, in hoary shroud,
Appear'd like giant o'er the cloud;
The eve fell dark, and grimly scowl'd,
Loud and more loud the tempest howl'd;
Without was turmoil, waste, and din,
The kelpie's cry was in the linn!
But all was love and peace within.
And aye between, the melting strain
Pour'd from thy woodland harp amain,
Which, mixing with the storm around,
Gave a wild cadence to the sound.

That mingled scene, in every part,
Hath so impress'd thy Shepherd's heart
With glowing feelings, kindling, bright,
Some filial visions of delight,
That almost border upon pain,
And he would hear those strains again.
They brought delusions not to last,
Blending the future with the past;
Dreams of fair stems, in foliage new,
Of flowers that spring where others grew,
Of beauty ne'er to be outdone,
And stars that rise when sets the sun;
The patriarchal days of yore,
The mountain music heard no more,
With all these scenes before his eyes,
A family's and a nation's ties–
Bonds which the heavens alone can rend,
With chief, with father, and with friend.
No wonder that such scene refined
Should dwell on rude enthusiast's mind;
Strange his reverse!–he little wist–
Poor inmate of the cloud and mist!
That ever he, as friend, should claim
The proudest Caledonian name.

# MEMOIR
## OF
## THE AUTHOR'S LIFE

I LIKE to write about myself: in fact, there are few things which I like better; it is so delightful to call up old reminiscences. Often have I been laughed at for what an Edinburgh editor styles my good-natured egotism, which is sometimes any thing but that; and I am aware that I shall be laughed at again. But I care not: for this *important* Memoir, now to be brought forward for the fourth time, at different periods of my life, I shall narrate with the same frankness as formerly; and in all, relating either to others or myself, speak fearlessly and unreservedly out. Many of those formerly mentioned are no more; others have been unfortunate; but of all I shall tell the plain truth, and nothing but the truth. So, without premising further, I shall proceed with an autobiography, containing much more of a romance than mere fancy could have suggested; and shall bring it forward to the very hour at which I am writing. The following note was prefixed by SIR WALTER SCOTT to the first edition of the Memoir in 1806.

"THE friend to whom Mr. Hogg made the following communication had some hesitation in committing it to the public. On the one hand, he was sensible, not only that the incidents are often trivial, but that they are narrated in a style more suitable to their importance to the Author himself, than to their own nature and consequences. But the efforts of a strong mind and vigorous imagination, to develop themselves even under the most disadvantageous circumstances, may be always considered with pleasure, and often with profit; and if, upon a retrospect, the possessor be disposed to view with self-complacency his victory under difficulties, of which he only can judge the extent, it will be readily pardoned by those who consider the Author's scanty opportunities of knowledge,– and remember, that it is only on attaining the last and most recondite recess of human science, that we discover how little we really know. To those who are unacquainted with the pastoral scenes in which our Author was educated, it may afford some amusement to find real shepherds actually contending for a poetical prize, and to remark some other peculiarities in their habits and manners. Above all, these Memoirs ascertain the authenticity of the publication, and are therefore entitled to be prefixed to it."

My dear Sir,

Mitchell-Slack, Nov. 1806.

According to your request, which I never disregard, I am now going to give you some account of my manner of life and *extensive* education. I must again apprize you, that, whenever I have occasion to speak of myself and my performances, I find it impossible to divest myself of an inherent vanity: but, making allowances for that, I will lay before you the outlines of my life,–with the circumstances that gave rise to my juvenile pieces, and my own opinion of them, as faithfully

As if you were the minister of heaven
Sent down to search the secret sins of men.

I am the second of four sons by the same father and mother; namely, Robert Hogg and Margaret Laidlaw, and was born on the 25th of January, 1772. My progenitors were all shepherds of this country. My father, like myself, was bred to the occupation of a shepherd, and served in that capacity until his marriage with my mother; about which time, having saved a considerable sum of money, for those days, he took a lease of the farms of Ettrick House and Ettrick Hall. He then commenced dealing in sheep–bought up great numbers, and drove them both to the English and Scottish markets; but, at length, owing to a great fall in the price of sheep, and the absconding of his principal debtor, he was ruined, became bankrupt, every thing was sold by auction, and my parents were turned out of doors without a farthing in the world. I was then in the sixth year of my age, and remember well the distressed and destitute condition that we were in. At length the late worthy Mr. Brydon, of Crosslee, took compassion upon us; and, taking a short lease of the farm of Ettrick House, placed my father there as his shepherd, and thus afforded him the means of supporting us for a time. This gentleman continued to interest himself in our welfare until the day of his untimely death, when we lost the best friend that we had in the world.

At such an age, it cannot be expected that I should have made great progress in learning. The school-house, however, being almost at our door, I had attended it for a short time, and had the honour of standing at the head of a juvenile class, who read the Shorter Catechism and the Proverbs of Solomon. At the next Whitsunday after our expulsion from the farm I was obliged to go to service; and, being only seven years of age, was hired by a farmer in the neighbourhood to herd a few cows; my wages for the half year being a ewe lamb and a pair of new shoes. Even at that early age my fancy seems to have been a hard neighbour for both judgment and memory. I was wont to strip off my clothes, and run races against time, or rather against myself; and, in the course of these exploits, which I accomplished much to my own admiration, I first lost my plaid, then my bonnet, then my coat, and, finally, my hosen; for, as for shoes, I had none. In that naked state did I herd for several days, till a shepherd and maid-servant were sent to the hills to look for them, and found them all. Next year my parents took me home during the winter quarter, and put me to school with a lad named Ker, who was teaching the children of a neighbouring farmer. Here I advanced so far as to get into the class who read in the Bible. I had likewise, for some time before my quarter was out, tried writing; and had horribly defiled several sheets of paper with copy-lines, every letter of which was nearly an inch in length.

Thus terminated my education. After this I was never another day at any school whatever. In all I had spent about half a year at it. It is true, my former master denied this; and when I was only twenty years of age, said, if he was called on to make oath, he would swear I never was at his school. However, I know I was at it for two or three months; and I do not choose to be deprived of the honour of having attended the school of my native parish; nor yet that old John Beattie should lose the honour of such a scholar. I was again, that very spring, sent away to my old occupation of herding cows. This employment, the worst and lowest known in our country, I was engaged in for several years under sundry masters, till at length I got into the more honourable one of keeping sheep.

It will scarcely be believed that at so early an age I should have been an admirer of the other sex. It is nevertheless strictly true. Indeed I have liked the women a great deal better than the men ever since I remember. But that summer, when only eight years of age, I was sent out to a height called Broad-heads with a rosy-cheeked maiden to herd a flock of new-weaned lambs, and I had my mischievous cows to herd besides. But, as she had no dog and I had an excellent one, I was ordered to keep close by her. Never was a master's order better obeyed. Day after day I herded the cows and the lambs both, and Betty had nothing to do but to sit and sew. Then we dined together every day at a well near to the Shiel-sike head, and after dinner I laid my head down on her lap, covered her bare feet with my plaid, and pretended to fall sound asleep. One day I heard her say to herself, "Poor little laddie! he's joost tired to death," and then I wept till I was afraid she would feel the warm tears trickling on her knee. I wished my master, who was a handsome young man, would fall in love with her and marry her, wondering how he could be so blind and stupid as not to do it. But I thought if I were he, I would know well what to do.

There is one circumstance which has led some to imagine that my abilities as a servant had not been exquisite; namely, that when I was fifteen years of age I had served a dozen masters; which circumstance I myself am rather willing to attribute to my having gone to service so young, that I was yearly growing stronger, and consequently adequate to a harder task and an increase of wages: for I do not remember of ever having served a master who refused giving me a verbal recommendation to the next, especially for my inoffensive behaviour. This character, which I, some way or other, got at my very first outset, has, in some degree, attended me ever since, and has certainly been of utility to me; yet, though Solomon avers that "a good name is rather to be chosen than great riches," I declare that I have never been so much benefited by mine, but that I would have chosen the latter by many degrees. From some of my masters I received very hard usage; in particular, while with one shepherd, I was often nearly exhausted with hunger and fatigue. All this while I neither read nor wrote; nor had I access to any book save the Bible. I was greatly taken with our version of the Psalms of David, learned the most of them by heart, and have a great partiality for them unto this day. Every little pittance of wages that I earned was carried directly to my parents, who supplied me with what clothes I had. These were often scarcely worthy of the appellation. In particular, I remember being exceedingly bare of shirts: time after time I had but two, which often grew so bad that I was obliged to leave wearing them altogether. At these times I certainly made a very grotesque figure; for, on quitting the shirt, I could never induce my trews, or lower vestments, to keep up to their proper sphere, there being no braces in those days. When fourteen years of age I saved five shillings of my wages, with which I bought an old violin. This occupied all my leisure hours, and has been my favourite amusement ever since. I had commonly no spare time from labour during the day; but when I was not over-fatigued, I generally spent an hour or two every night in sawing over my favourite old Scottish tunes; and my bed being always in stables and cow-houses, I disturbed nobody but myself and my associate quadrupeds, whom I believed to be greatly delighted with my strains. At all events they never complained, which the biped part of my neighbours did frequently, to my pity and utter indignation. This brings to my remembrance an anecdote, the consequence of one of these nocturnal endeavours at improvement.

When serving with Mr. Scott of Singlee, there happened to be a dance one evening, at which a number of the friends and neighbours of the family were present. I, being admitted into the room as a spectator, was all attention to the music; and, on the company breaking up, I retired to my stable-loft, and fell to essaying some of the tunes to which I had been listening. The musician going out to a short distance from the house, and not being aware that another of the same craft was so near him, was not a little surprised when the tones of my old violin assailed his ears. At first he took it for the late warbles of his own ringing through his head; but, on a little attention, he, to his horror and astonishment, perceived that the sounds were real,–and that the tunes, which he had lately been playing with so much skill, were now murdered by some invisible being hard by him. Such a circumstance at that dead hour of the night, and when he was unable to discern from what quarter the sounds proceeded, convinced him all at once that it was a delusion of the devil; and, suspecting his intentions from so much familiarity, he fled precipitately into the hall, speechless with affright, and in the utmost perturbation, to the no small mirth of Mr. Scott, who declared that he had lately been considerably annoyed himself by the same discordant sounds.

From Singlee I went to Elibank upon Tweed, where, with Mr. Laidlaw, I found my situation more easy and agreeable than it had ever yet been. I staid there three half-years–a term longer than usual; and from thence went to Willenslee, to Mr. Laidlaw's father, with whom I served as a shepherd two years,–having been for some seasons preceding employed in working with horses, threshing, &c.

It was while serving here, in the eighteenth year of my age, that I first got a perusal of "The Life and Adventures of Sir William Wallace," and "The Gentle Shepherd;" and though immoderately fond of them, yet (what you will think remarkable in one who hath since dabbled so much in verse) I could not help regretting deeply that they were not in prose, that every body might have understood them; or, I thought if they had been in the same kind of metre with the Psalms, I could have borne with them. The truth is, I made exceedingly slow progress in reading them. The little reading that I had learned I had nearly lost, and the Scottish dialect quite confounded me; so that, before I got to the end of a line, I had commonly lost the rhyme of the preceding one; and if I came to a triplet, a thing of which I had no conception, I commonly read to the foot of the page without perceiving that I had lost the rhyme altogether. I thought the author had been straitened for rhymes, and had just made a part of it do as well as he could without them. Thus, after I got through both works, I found myself much in the same predicament with the man of Eskdalemuir, who had borrowed Bailey's Dictionary from his neighbour. On returning it, the lender asked him what he thought of it. "I dinna ken, man," replied he; "I have read it all through, but canna say that I understand it; it is the most confused book that ever I saw in my life!" The late Mrs. Laidlaw of Willenslee took some notice of me, and frequently gave me books to read while tending the ewes; these were chiefly theological. The only one, that I remember any thing of, is "Bishop Burnet's Theory of the Conflagration of the Earth." Happy it was for me that I did not understand it! for the little of it that I did understand had nearly overturned my brain altogether. All the day I was pondering on the grand millennium, and the reign of the saints; and all the night dreaming of new heavens and a new earth–the stars in horror, and the world in flames! Mrs. Laidlaw also gave me sometimes the newspapers, which I pored on with great earnestness–beginning at the date, and reading straight on, through advertisements of houses and lands, balm of Gilead, and every thing; and, after all, was often no wiser than when I began. To give you some farther idea of the progress I had made in literature–I was about this time obliged to write a letter to my elder brother, and, having never drawn a pen for such a number of years, I had actually forgotten how to make sundry letters of the alphabet; these I had either to print, or to patch up the words in the best way I could without them.

At Whitsunday 1790, being still only in the eighteenth year of my age, I left Willenslee, and hired myself to Mr. Laidlaw of Black House, with whom I served as a shepherd ten years. The kindness of this gentleman to me it would be the utmost ingratitude in me ever to forget; for, indeed, it was much more like that of a father than a master,–and it is not improbable that I should have been there still, had it not been for the following circumstance.

My brother William had, for some time before, occupied the farm of Ettrick House, where he resided with our parents; but, having taken a wife, and the place not suiting two families, he took another residence, and gave up the farm to me. The lease expiring at Whitsunday 1803, our possession was taken by a wealthier neighbour.

The first time that I attempted to write verses was in the spring of the year 1796. Mr. Laidlaw having a number of valuable books, which were all open to my perusal, I about this time began to read with considerable attention;–and no sooner did I begin to read so as to understand, than, rather prematurely, I began to write. For several years my compositions consisted wholly of songs and ballads made up for the lasses to sing in chorus; and a proud man I was when I first heard the rosy nymphs chaunting my uncouth strains, and jeering me by the still dear appellation of "Jamie the poeter."

I had no more difficulty in composing songs then than I have at present; and I was equally well pleased with them. But, then, the writing of them!–that was a job! I had no method of learning to write, save by following the Italian alphabet; and though I always stripped myself of coat and vest when I began to pen a song, yet my wrist took a cramp, so that I could rarely make above four or six lines at a sitting. Whether my manner of writing it out was new, I know not, but it was not without singularity. Having very little spare time from my flock, which was unruly enough, I folded and stitched a few sheets of paper, which I carried in my pocket. I had no inkhorn; but, in place of it, I borrowed a small vial, which I fixed in a hole in the breast of my waistcoat; and having a cork fastened by a piece of twine, it answered the purpose fully as well. Thus equipped, whenever a leisure minute or two offered, and I had nothing else to do, I sat down and wrote out my thoughts as I found them. This is still my invariable practice in writing prose. I cannot make out one sentence by study, without the pen in my hand to catch the ideas as they arise, and I never write two copies of the same thing.

My manner of composing poetry is very different, and, I believe, much more singular. Let the piece be of what length it will, I compose and correct it wholly in my mind, or on a slate, ere ever I put pen to paper; and then I write it down as fast as the A, B, C. When once it is written, it remains in that state; it being, as you very well know, with the utmost difficulty that I can be brought to alter one syllable, which I think is partly owing to the above practice.

It is a fact, that, by a long acquaintance with any poetical piece, we become perfectly reconciled to its faults. The numbers, by being frequently repeated, wear smoother to our minds; and the ideas having been expanded, by our reflection on each particular scene or incident therein described, the mind cannot, without reluctance, consent to the alteration of any part of it.

The first time I ever heard of Burns was in 1797, the year after he died. One day during that summer a half daft man, named John Scott, came to me on the hill, and to amuse me repeated Tam o'

Shanter. I was delighted! I was far more than delighted–I was ravished! I cannot describe my feelings; but, in short, before Jock Scott left me, I could recite the poem from beginning to end, and it has been my favourite poem ever since. He told me it was made by one Robert Burns, the sweetest poet that ever was born; but that he was now dead, and his place would never be supplied. He told me all about him, how he was born on the 25th of January, bred a ploughman, how many beautiful songs and poems he had composed, and that he had died last harvest, on the 21st of August.

This formed a new epoch of my life. Every day I pondered on the genius and fate of Burns. I wept, and always thought with myself–what is to hinder me from succeeding Burns? I too was born on the 25th of January, and I have much more time to read and compose than any ploughman could have, and can sing more old songs than ever ploughman could in the world. But then I wept again because I could not write. However, I resolved to be a poet, and to follow in the steps of Burns.

I remember in the year 1812, the year before the publication of the "Queen's Wake," that I told my friend, the Rev. James Nicol, that I had an inward consciousness that I should yet live to be compared with Burns; and though I might never equal him in some things, I thought I might excel him in others. He reprobated the idea, and thought the assumption so audacious, that he told it as a bitter jest against me in a party that same evening. But the rest seeing me mortified, there was not one joined in the laugh against me, and Mr. John Grieve replied in these words, which I will never forget, "After what he has done, there is no man can say *what* he may do."

My friend, Mr. William Laidlaw, hath often remonstrated with me, in vain, on the necessity of a revisal of my pieces; but, in spite of him, I held fast my integrity: I said I would try to write the next better, but that should remain as it was. He was the only person who, for many years, ever pretended to discover the least merit in my essays, either in verse or prose; and, as he never failed to have plenty of them about him, he took the opportunity of showing them to every person, whose capacity he supposed adequate to judge of their merits: but it was all to no purpose; he could make no proselytes to his opinion of any note, save one, who, in a little time, apostatized, and left us as we were. He even went so far as to break with some of his correspondents altogether, who persisted in their obstinacy. All this had not the least effect upon me; as long as I had his approbation and my own, which last never failed me, I continued to persevere. At length he had the good fortune to appeal to you, who were pleased to back him; and he came off triumphant, declaring, that the world should henceforth judge for themselves for him.

I have often opposed his proposals with such obstinacy, that I was afraid of losing his countenance altogether; but none of these things had the least effect upon him; his friendship continued unimpaired, attended with the most tender assiduities for my welfare; and I am now convinced that he is better acquainted with my nature and propensities than I am myself.

I have wandered insensibly from my subject: but to return.–In the spring of the year 1798, as Alexander Laidlaw, a neighbouring shepherd, my brother William, and myself, were resting on the side of a hill above Ettrick church, I happened, in the course of our conversation, to drop some hints of my superior talents in poetry. William said, that, as to putting words into rhyme, it was a thing which he never could do to any sense; but that, if I liked to enter the lists with him in blank verse, he would take me up for any bet that I pleased. Laidlaw declared that he would venture likewise. This being settled, and the judges named, I accepted the challenge; but a dispute arising respecting the subject, we were obliged to resort to the following mode of decision: Ten subjects having been named, the lots were cast, and, amongst them all, that which fell to be elucidated by our matchless pens, was, *the stars!*–things which we knew little more about, than merely that they were burning and twinkling over us, and to be seen every night when the clouds were away. I began with high hopes and great warmth, and in a week declared my theme ready for the comparison; Laidlaw announced his next week; but my brother made us wait a full half year; and then, on being urged, presented his unfinished. The arbiters were then dispersed, and the cause was never properly judged; but those to whom they were shown rather gave the preference to my brother's.–This is certain, that it was far superior to either of the other two in the sublimity of the ideas; but, besides being in bad measure, it was often bombastical. The title of it was "Urania's Tour;" that of Laidlaw's, "Astronomical Thoughts;" and that of mine, "Reflections on a view of the Nocturnal Heavens."

Alexander Laidlaw and I tried, after the same manner, a paraphrase of the 117th Psalm, in English verse. I continued annually to add numbers of smaller pieces of poetry and songs to my collection, mostly on subjects purely ideal, or else legendary. I had, from my childhood, been affected by the frequent return of a violent inward complaint; and it attacked me once in a friend's house, at a distance from home, and, increasing to an inflammation, all hopes were given up of my recovery. While I was lying in the greatest agony, about the dead of the night, I had the mortification of seeing the old woman, who watched over me, fall into a swoon, from a supposition that she saw my *wraith*:–a spirit which, the vulgar suppose, haunts the abodes of such as are instantly to die, in order to carry off the soul as soon as it is disengaged from the body: and, next morning, I overheard a consultation about borrowing sheets to lay me in at my decease; but Almighty God, in his providence, deceived both them and the officious spirit; for, by the help of an able physician, I recovered, and have never since been troubled with the distemper.

My first published song was "Donald M'Donald," which I composed this year, 1800, on the threatened invasion by Buonaparte. The first time I sung it was to a party of social friends at the Crown Tavern, Edinburgh. They commended it, on which I proffered it to one of them for his magazine. He said it was much too good for that, and advised me to give it to Mr. John Hamilton, who would set it to music and get it engraved. I did so, and went away again to the mountains, where I heard from day to day that the popularity of my song was unbounded, and yet no one ever knew or inquired who was the author.

There chanced to be about that time a great masonic meeting in Edinburgh, the Earl of Moira in the chair; on which occasion, Mr. Oliver, of the house of Oliver and Boyd, then one of the best singers in Scotland, sung "Donald M'Donald." It was loudly applauded, and three times encored; and so well pleased was Lord Moira with the song, that he rose, and in a long speech descanted on the utility of such songs at that period–thanked Mr. Oliver, and proffered him his whole interest in Scotland. This to the singer; yet, strange to say, he never inquired who was the author of the song!

There was at that period, and a number of years afterwards, a General M'Donald, who commanded the northern division of the British army. The song was sung at his mess every week-day, and sometimes twice and thrice. The old man was proud of, and delighted in it, and was wont to snap his thumbs and join in the chorus. He believed, to his dying day, that it was made upon himself; yet neither he nor one of his officers ever knew or inquired who was the author–so thankless is the poet's trade! It was, perhaps, the most popular song that ever was written. For many other comical anecdotes relating to it, see a collection of my songs published by Mr. Blackwood last year.

In 1801, believing that I was then become a grand poet, I most sapiently determined on publishing a pamphlet, and appealing to the world at once. This noble resolution was no sooner taken than executed; a proceeding much of a piece with many of my subsequent transactions. Having attended the Edinburgh market one Monday, with a number of sheep for sale, and being unable to dispose of them all, I put the remainder into a park until the market on Wednesday. Not knowing how to pass the interim, it came into my head that I would write a poem or two from my memory, and get them printed. The thought had no sooner struck me than it was put in practice; and I was obliged to select, not the best poems, but those that I remembered best. I wrote several of these during my short stay, and gave them all to a person to print at my expense, and, having sold off my sheep on Wednesday morning, I returned to the Forest. I saw no more of my poems until I received word that there were one thousand copies of them thrown off. I knew no more about publishing than the man of the moon; and the only motive that influenced me was, the gratification of my vanity by seeing my works in print. But, no sooner did the first copy come to hand, than my eyes were open to the folly of my conduct; for, on comparing it with the MS. which I had at home, I found many of the stanzas omitted, others misplaced, and typographical errors abounding in every page.

Thus were my first productions pushed headlong into the world, without either patron or preface, or even apprising the public that such a thing was coming, and "unhousell'd, unanointed, unaneled, with all their imperfections on their heads." "Will an' Keatie," however, had the honour of being copied into some periodical publications of the time, as a favourable specimen of the work. Indeed, all of them were sad stuff, although I judged them to be exceedingly good.

The truth was, that, notwithstanding my pride of authorship, in a few days I had discernment enough left to wish my publication heartily at the devil, and I had hopes that long ago it had been consigned to eternal oblivion; when, behold! a London critic had in malice of heart preserved a copy, and quoted liberally out of it last year, to my intense chagrin and mortification.

On the appearance of "The Minstrelsy of the Scottish Border," I was much dissatisfied with the imitations of the ancient ballads contained in it, and immediately set about imitating the ancient ballads myself–selected a number of traditionary stories, and put them in metre by chanting them to certain old tunes. In these I was more successful than in any thing I had hitherto tried, although they were still but rude pieces of composition.

---

THE above is the substance of three letters, written in the same year, and alluding mostly to Poetical Trifles. Since that time I have experienced a very unexpected reverse of fortune. After my return from the Highlands in June last, I put every thing in readiness for my departure to settle in Harris; and I wrote and published my "Farewell to Ettrick," wherein the real sentiments of my heart at that time are simply related, which constitute its only claim to merit. It would be tedious and trifling, were I to relate all the disagreeable circumstances which ensued; suffice it to say, that my scheme was absolutely frustrated.

Miserably disappointed, and vexed at having been thus baffled in an undertaking about which I had talked so much, to avoid a great many disagreeable questions and explanations, I went to England during the remainder of the summer. On my return to Scotland, having lost all the money that I had made by a regular and industrious life, and in one week too, I again cheerfully hired myself as a shepherd, with Mr. Harkness of Mitchell-Slack, in Nithsdale. It was while here that I published "The Mountain Bard," consisting of the above-mentioned ballads. Sir Walter, then Mr. Scott, had encouraged the publication of the work in some letters that he sent me; consequently I went to Edinburgh to see about it. He went with me to Mr. Constable, who received me very kindly, but told me frankly that my poetry would not sell. I said I thought it was as good as any body's I had seen. He said that might be, but that nobody's poetry would sell; it was the worst stuff that came to market, and that he found; but, as I appeared to be a gay queer chiel, if I would procure him two hundred subscribers he would publish my work for me, and give me as much for it as he could. I did not like the subscribers much; but, having no alternative, I accepted the conditions. Before the work was ready for publication I had got above five hundred subscribers; and Mr. Constable, who, by that time, had conceived a better opinion of the work, gave me half-guinea copies for all my subscribers, and a letter for a small sum over and above. I have forgot how much; but, upon the whole, he acted with great liberality. He gave me, likewise, that same year, eighty-six pounds for that celebrated work, "Hogg on Sheep;" and I was now richer than I had ever been before.

I had no regular plan of delivering those copies that were subscribed for, but sent them simply to the people, intending to take their money in return; but though some paid me double, triple, and even ten times the price, about one-third of my subscribers thought proper to take the copies for nothing, never paying for them to this day.

Being now master of nearly three hundred pounds, I went perfectly mad. I first took one pasture farm, at exactly one half more than it was worth, having been cheated into it by a great rascal, who meant to rob me of all I had, and which, in the course of one year, he effected by dint of law. But, in the mean time, having taken another extensive farm, I found myself fairly involved in business far above my capital. It would have required at least one thousand pounds for every one hundred pounds that I possessed, to have managed all I had taken in hand; so I got every day out of one strait and confusion into a worse. I blundered and struggled on for three years between these two places, giving up all thoughts of poetry or literature of any kind. I have detailed these circumstances in a larger MS. work; but, though they are most laughable, they must be omitted here, as it is only a short sketch of my *literary life* that I can include in this introduction.

Finding myself, at length, fairly run aground, I gave my creditors all that I had, or rather suffered them to take it, and came off and left them. I never asked any settlement, which would not have been refused me; and severely have I smarted for that neglect since. None of these matters had the least effect in depressing my spirits–I was generally rather most cheerful when most unfortunate. On returning again to Ettrick Forest, I found the countenances of all my friends altered; and even those whom I had loved, and trusted most, disowned me, and told me so to my face; but I laughed at and despised these persons, resolving to show them, by and by, that they were in the wrong. Having appeared as a poet, and a speculative farmer besides, no one would now employ me as a shepherd. I even applied to some of my old masters, but they refused me, and for a whole winter I found myself without employment, and without money, in my native country; therefore, in February 1810, in utter desperation, I took my plaid about my shoulders, and marched away to Edinburgh, determined, since no better could be, to push my fortune as a literary man. It is true, I had estimated my poetical talent high enough, but I had resolved to use it only as a staff, never as a crutch; and would have kept that resolve, had I not been driven to the reverse. On going to Edinburgh, I found that my poetical talents were rated nearly as low there as my shepherd qualities were in Ettrick. It was in vain that I applied to newsmongers, booksellers, editors of magazines, &c. for employment. Any of these were willing enough to accept of my lucubrations, and give them publicity, but then there was no money going–not a farthing; and this suited me very ill.

I again applied to Mr. Constable, to publish a volume of songs for me; for I had nothing else by me but the songs of my youth, having given up all these exercises so long. He was rather averse to the expedient; but he had a sort of kindness for me, and did not like to refuse; so, after waiting on him three or four times, he agreed to print an edition, and give me half the profits. He published one thousand copies, at five shillings each; but he never gave me any thing; and as I feared the concern might not have proved a good one, I never asked any remuneration.

The name of this work was "The Forest Minstrel;" of which about two-thirds of the songs were my own, the rest furnished by correspondents–a number of them by the ingenious Mr. T. M. Cunningham. In general they are not good, but the worst of them are all mine, for I inserted every ranting rhyme that I had made in my youth, to please the circles about the firesides in the country; and all this time I had never been once in any polished society–had read next to nothing–was now in the 38th year of my age–and knew no more of human life or manners than a child. I was a sort of natural songster, without another advantage on earth. Fain would I have done something; but, on finding myself shunned by every one, I determined to push my own fortune independent of booksellers, whom I now began to view as enemies to all genius. My plan was, to begin a literary weekly paper, a work for which I certainly was rarely qualified, when the above facts are considered. I tried Walker and Greig, and several printers, offering them security to print it for me.–No; not one of them would print it without a bookseller's name to it as publisher. "D–n them," said I to myself, as I was running from one to another, "the folks here are all combined in a body." Mr. Constable laughed at me exceedingly, and finally told me he wished me too well to encourage such a thing. Mr. Ballantyne was rather more civil, and got off by subscribing for so many copies, and giving me credit for ten pounds worth of paper. David Brown would have nothing to do with it, unless some gentleman, whom he named, should contribute. At length, I found an honest man, James Robertson, a bookseller in Nicolson Street, whom I had never before seen or heard of, who undertook it at once on my own terms;

and on the 1st of September, 1810, my first number made its appearance on a quarto demy sheet, price fourpence.

A great number were sold, and many hundreds delivered gratis; but one of Robertson's boys, a great rascal, had demanded the price in full for all that he was to have delivered gratis. They showed him the imprint, that they were to be delivered gratis: "So they are," said he; "I take nothing for the delivery; but I must have the price of the paper, if you please."

This money that the boy brought me, consisting of a few shillings and an immense number of halfpence, was the first and only money I had pocketed of my own making since my arrival in Edinburgh in February. On the publication of the first two numbers, I deemed I had as many subscribers as, at all events, would secure the work from being dropped; but, on the publication of my third or fourth number, I have forgot which, it was so indecorous, that no fewer than seventy-three subscribers gave up. This was a sad blow for me; but, as usual, I despised the fastidiousness and affectation of the people, and continued my work. It proved a fatal oversight for the paper, for all those who had given in set themselves against it with the utmost inveteracy. The literary ladies, in particular, agreed, in full divan, that I would never write a sentence which deserved to be read. A reverend friend of mine has often repeated my remark on being told of this–"Gaping deevils! wha cares what they say? If I leeve ony time, I'll let them see the contrair o' that."

My publisher, James Robertson, was a kind-hearted, confused body, who loved a joke and a dram. He sent for me every day about one o'clock, to consult about the publication; and then we uniformly went down to a dark house in the Cowgate, where we drank whisky and ate rolls with a number of printers, the dirtiest and leanest-looking men I had ever seen. My youthful habits having been so regular, I could not stand this; and though I took care, as I thought, to drink very little, yet, when I went out, I was at times so dizzy, I could scarcely walk; and the worst thing of all was, I felt that I was beginning to relish it.

Whenever a man thinks seriously of a thing, he generally thinks aright. I thought frequently of these habits and connexions, and found that they never would do; and that, instead of pushing myself forward, as I wished, I was going straight to the devil. I said nothing about this to my respectable acquaintances, nor do I know if they ever knew or suspected what was going on; but, on some pretence or other, I resolved to cut all connexion with Robertson; and, sorely against his will, gave the printing to the Messrs. Aikman, then proprietors of the Star newspaper, showing them the list of subscribers, of which they took their chance, and promised me half profits. At the conclusion of the year, instead of granting me any profits, they complained of being minus, and charged me with the half of the loss. This I refused to pay, unless they could give me an account of all the numbers published, on the sale of which there should have been a good profit. This they could not do; so I paid nothing, and received as little. I had, however, a good deal to pay to Robertson, who likewise asked more; so that, after a year's literary drudgery, I found myself a loser rather than a gainer.

The name of this periodical work was "The Spy." I continued it for a year, and to this day I cannot help regarding it as a literary curiosity. It has, doubtless, but little merit; but yet I think that, all circumstances considered, it is rather wonderful. In my farewell paper I see the following sentence occurs, when speaking of the few who stood friends to the work:–

"They have, at all events, the honour of patronising an undertaking quite new in the records of literature; for, that a common shepherd, who never was at school; who went to service at seven years of age, and could neither read nor write with any degree of accuracy when thirty; yet who, smitten with an unconquerable thirst after knowledge, should leave his native mountains, and his flocks to wander where they chose, come to the metropolis with his plaid wrapped about his shoulders, and all at once set up for a connoisseur in manners, taste, and genius–has much more the appearance of a romance than a matter of fact; yet a matter of fact it certainly is;– and such a person is the editor of 'The Spy.'"

I begun it without asking, or knowing of any assistance; but when Mr. and Mrs. Gray saw it was on foot, they interested themselves in it with all their power, and wrote a number of essays for it. Several other gentlemen likewise contributed a paper quietly now and then, and among others Robert Sym, Esq., which I never discovered till after the work was discontinued. Professor T. Gillespie, the Rev. Wm. Gillespie, J. Black of the Morning Chronicle, and sundry others, lent me an occasional lift. The greater part, however, is my own writing, and consists of four hundred and fifteen quarto pages, double columned,–no easy task for one person to accomplish in a year. I speak of this work as of one that *existed*, for it flew abroad, like the sibyl's papers, every week, and I believe there are not above five complete copies existing, if indeed there is one; and, as it never will be reprinted, if the scarcity of a work makes it valuable, no one can be more so, to exist at all.

All this while there was no man who entered into my views, and supported them, save Mr. John Grieve, a friend, whose affection neither misfortune nor imprudence could once shake. Evil speakers had no effect on him. We had been acquainted from our youth; and he had formed his judgment of me as a man and a poet; and from that nothing could ever make him abate one item. Mr. Grieve's opinion of me was by far too partial, for it amounted to this, that he never conceived any effort in poetry above my reach, if I would set my mind to it; but my carelessness and indifference he constantly regretted and deprecated. During the first six months that I resided in Edinburgh I lived with him, and his partner, Mr. Scott, who, on a longer acquaintance, became as firmly attached to me as Mr. Grieve; and, I believe, as much so as to any other man alive. We three have had many very happy evenings together; we indeed were seldom separate when it was possible to meet. They suffered me to want for nothing, either in money or clothes; and I did not even need to ask these. Mr. Grieve was always the first to notice my wants, and prevent them. In short, they would not suffer me to be obliged to any one but themselves for the value of a farthing; and without this sure support I could never have fought my way in Edinburgh. I was fairly starved into it, and if it had not been for Messrs. Grieve and Scott, would, in a very short time, have been starved out of it again.

The next thing in which I became deeply interested, in a literary way, was the FORUM, a debating society, established by a few young men, of whom I, though far from being a young man, was one of the first. We opened our house to the public, making each individual pay a sixpence, and the crowds that attended, for three years running, were beyond all bounds. I was appointed secretary, with a salary of twenty pounds a year, which never was paid, though I gave away hundreds in charity. We were exceedingly improvident; but I never was so much advantaged by any thing as by that society; for it let me feel, as it were, the pulse of the public, and precisely what they would swallow, and what they would not. All my friends were averse to my coming forward in the Forum as a public speaker, and tried to reason me out of it, by representing my incapacity to harangue a thousand people in a speech of half an hour. I had, however, given my word to my associates, and my confidence in myself being unbounded, I began, and came off with flying colours. We met once a week. I spoke every night, and sometimes twice the same night; and, though I sometimes incurred pointed disapprobation, was in general a prodigious favourite. The characters of all my brother members are given in the larger work, but here they import not. I have scarcely known any society of young men who have all got so well on. Their progress has been singular; and, I am certain, people may say what they will, that they were greatly improved by their weekly appearances in the Forum. Private societies signify nothing; but a discerning public is a severe test, especially in a multitude, where the smallest departure from good taste, or from the question, was sure to draw down disapproval, and where no good saying ever missed observation and applause. If this do not assist in improving the taste, I know not what will. Of this I am certain, that I was greatly the better for it, and I may safely say I never was in a school before. I might and would have written the "Queen's Wake" had the Forum never existed, but without the weekly lessons that I got there I could not have succeeded as I did. Still our meetings were somewhat ludicrous, especially the formality of some of the presidents. To me they were so irresistible, that I wrote a musical farce, in three acts, called "The Forum, a Tragedy for Cold Weather," wherein all the members are broadly taken off, myself not excepted, and some of our evening scenes depicted. I believe it is a good thing of the kind, at least I remember thinking so at the time; but it was so severe on some of my friends, who had a few peculiarities about them, that I never showed it to any one. I have it by me; but I believe never man saw it save myself. About the same time I wrote another musical drama of three acts, and showed it to Mr. Siddons. He approved of it very highly, with the exception of some trivial scene, which I promised to alter, and he undertook to have it acted on the return of the season; but I never saw him again. He was always kind and friendly to me, and made me free to the theatre from year to year.

During the time that the Forum was going on the poetry of Mr. Walter Scott and Lord Byron was exciting general attention. I had published some pieces in "The Spy" that Grieve thought exceedingly good; and nothing would serve him but that I should take the field once more as a poet, and try my fate with others. I promised; and having some ballads or metrical tales by me, which I did not like to lose, I planned the "Queen's Wake," in order that I might take these all in, and had it ready in a few months after it was first proposed. I was very anxious to read it to some person of taste; but no one would either read it, or listen to my reading it, save Grieve, who assured me it would do. As I lived at Deanhaugh then, I invited Mr. and Mrs. Gray to drink tea, and to read a part of it with me before offering it for publication. Unluckily, however, before I had read half a page, Mrs. Gray objected to a word, which Grieve approved of and defended, and some high disputes arose; other authors were appealed to, and notwithstanding my giving several very broad hints, I could not procure a hearing for another line of my new poem. Indeed, I was sorely disappointed, and told my friends so on going away; on which another day was appointed, and I took my manuscript to Buccleugh Place. Mr. Gray had not got through the third page when he was told that an itinerant bard had entered the lobby, and was repeating his poetry to the boarders. Mr. Gray went out and joined them, leaving me alone with a young lady, to read, or not, as we liked. In about half an hour he sent a request for me likewise to come: on which I went, and heard a poor crazy beggar repeating such miserable stuff as I had never heard before. I was terribly affronted; and putting my manuscript in my pocket, I jogged my way home in very bad humour. Gray has sometimes tried to deny the truth of this anecdote, and to face me out of it, but it would not do. I never estimated him the less as a friend; but I did not forget it, in one point of view; for I never read any more new poems to him.

I next went to my friend Mr. Constable, and told him my plan of publication; but he received me coldly, and told me to call again. I did so–when he said he would do nothing until he had seen the MS. I refused to give it, saying, "What skill have you about the merits of a book?"–"It may be so, Hogg," said he; "but I know as well how to sell a book as any man, which should be some concern of yours; and I know how to buy one, too, by G—!"

Finally, he told me, that if I would procure him two hundred subscribers, to insure him from loss, he would give me £100 for liberty to print one thousand copies; and more than that he would not give. I felt I should be obliged to comply; and, with great reluctance, got a few subscription-papers thrown off privately, and gave them to friends, who soon procured me the requisite number. But, before this time, one George Goldie, a young bookseller in Princes Street, a lad of some taste, had become acquainted with me at the Forum, and earnestly requested to see my MS. I gave it to him with reluctance, being predetermined to have nothing to do with him. He had not, however, well looked into the work till he thought he perceived something above common-place; and, when I next saw him, he was intent on being the publisher of the work, offering me as much as Mr. Constable, and all the subscribers to myself over and above. I was very loath to part with Mr. Constable; but the terms were so different, that I was obliged to think of it. I tried him again; but he had differed with Mr. Scott, and I found him in such bad humour, that he would do nothing farther than curse all the poets, and declare that he had met with more ingratitude from literary men than all the rest of the human race. Of course Goldie got the work, and it made its appearance in the spring of 1813.

As I said, nobody had seen the work; and, on the day after it was published, I went up to Edinburgh as anxious as a man could be. I walked sometimes about the streets, and read the title of my book on the booksellers' windows, yet I durst not go into any of the shops. I was like a man between death and life, waiting for the sentence of the jury. The first encouragement that I got was from my countryman, Mr. William Dunlop, wine and spirit merchant, who, on observing me going sauntering up the plainstones of the High Street, came over from the Cross, arm-in-arm with another gentleman, a stranger to me. I remember his salutation, word for word; and, singular as it was, it made a strong impression; for I knew that Mr. Dunlop had a great deal of rough common sense.

"Ye useless poetical deevil that ye're!" said he, "what hae ye been doing a' this time?"–"What doing, Willie! what do you mean?"–"D–n your stupid head, ye hae been pestering us wi' fourpenny papers an' daft shilly-shally sangs, an' bletherin' an' speakin' i' the Forum, an' yet had stuff in ye to produce a thing like this!"–"Ay, Willie," said I; "have you seen my new beuk?"–"Ay, faith, that I have, man; and it has lickit me out o' a night's sleep. Ye hae hit the right nail on the head now. Yon's the very thing, sir."–"I'm very glad to hear you say sae, Willie; but what do ye ken about poems?"–"Never ye mind how I ken; I gi'e you my word for it, yon's the thing that will do. If ye hadna made a fool o' yoursel' afore, man, yon wad hae sold better than ever a book sold. Od, wha wad hae thought there was as muckle in that sheep's-head o' yours?–d–d stupid poetical deevil that ye're!" And with that he went away, laughing and miscalling me over his shoulder.

This address gave me a little confidence, and I faced my acquaintances one by one; and every thing that I heard was laudatory. The first report of any work that goes abroad, be it good or bad, spreads like fire set to a hill of heather in a warm spring day, and no one knows where it will stop. From that day forward every one has spoken well of the work; and every review praised its general features, save the Eclectic, which, in the year 1813, tried to hold it up to ridicule and contempt. Mr. Jeffery ventured not a word about it, either good or bad, himself, until the year after, when it had fairly got into a second and third edition. He then gave a very judicious and sensible review of it; but he committed a most horrible blunder, in classing Mr. Tenant, the author of "Anster Fair," and me together, as two self-taught geniuses; whereas there was not one point of resemblance. Tenant being a better educated man than the reviewer himself, was not a little affronted at being classed with me. From that day to this Mr. Jeffery has taken no notice of any thing that I have published, which I think can hardly be expected to do him any honour at the long run. I should like the worst poem that I have since published to stand a fair comparison with some that he has strained himself to bring forward. It is a pity that any literary connexion, which with the one party might be unavoidable, should ever prejudice one valued friend and acquaintance against another. In the heart-burnings of party spirit, the failings of great minds are more exposed than in all other things in the world put together.

Mr. Goldie had little capital, and less interest among the trade; nevertheless, he did all for my work that lay in his power, and sold two editions of it in a short time. About that period a general failure took place among the secondary class of booksellers, and it was reported that Goldie was so much involved with some of the houses, that it was impossible he could escape destruction. A third edition of my poem was wanted, and, without more ado, I went and offered it to Mr. Constable. We closed a bargain at once, and the book was sent to Mr. Ballantyne to print. But after a part was thrown off, Goldie got notice of the transaction, and was neither to hold nor bind, pretending that he had been exceedingly ill used. He waited on Mr. Constable one hour, and corresponded with him the next, till he induced him to give up the bargain. It was in vain that I remonstrated, affirming that the work was my own, and I would give it to whom I pleased. I had no one to take my part, and I was browbeat out of it–Goldie alleging that I had no reason to complain, as he now entered precisely into Constable's terms, and had run all the risk of the former editions. I durst not say that he was going to break, and never pay me; so I was obliged to suffer the edition to be printed off in Goldie's name. This was exceeding ill done of him–nothing could be more cruel–and I was grieved that he did so, for I had a good opinion of him. The edition had not been lodged in his premises a week before he stopped payment, and yet, in that time, he had contrived to sell, or give away, more than one half of the copies; and thus all the little money that I had gained, which I was so proud of, and on which I depended for my subsistence, and the settling of some old farming debts that were pressing hard upon me, vanished from my grasp at once.

It was on the occasion of Mr. Blackwood being appointed one of the trustees upon the bankrupt estate that I was first introduced to him. I found him and the two Messrs. Bridges deeply interested in my case. I shall never forget their kindness and attention to my interests at that unfortunate period. I applied to Mr. Samuel Aitken, who was the head trustee, with fear and trembling, for I judged of him as a severe and strict man, who I knew would do justice to me, but I expected nothing farther. When I waited on him he looked at me with his grey stiff eye. "It is all over with me here," thought I. I never was more mistaken in my life; for no sooner had I stated my case than Samuel entered into my interests with his whole heart, and said, that provided he could save the creditors from losing any thing, which he was bound to do, he saw no right they had to make any thing by my edition. He then and there consigned over to me the whole of the remaining copies, 490 in number, charging me only with the expenses of printing, &c. These, to my agreeable astonishment, amounted only to two shillings and tenpence halfpenny per volume. The work sold at twelve shillings, so that a good reversion appeared to be mine. Mr. Blackwood sold the copies for me on commission, and ultimately paid me more than double of what I was to have received from Goldie. For this I was indebted to the consideration and kindness of the trustees.

I had likewise, before this time, been introduced to most of the great literary characters in the metropolis, and lived with them on terms of intimacy, finding myself more and more a welcome guest at all their houses. However, I was careful not to abuse their indulgence; for, with the exception of a few intimate friends, I made myself exceedingly scarce. I was indebted for these introductions, in a great degree, to the Reverend Dr. Morehead, one of the most amiable men I have ever known, and to two worthy ladies of the name of Lowes. I have written out, at great length, my opinion of all the characters of these literary gentlemen, with traits of their behaviour towards each other, principally from reports on which I could depend, and what I myself knew of their plans and parties; but this would fill a volume as large as the present work.

On the appearance of Mr. Wilson's "Isle of Palms," I was so greatly taken with many of his fanciful and visionary scenes, descriptive of bliss and woe, that it had a tendency to divest me occasionally of all worldly feelings. I reviewed this poem, as well as many others, in a Scottish Review then going on in Edinburgh, and was exceedingly anxious to meet with the author; but this I tried in vain, for the space of six months. All I could learn of him was, that he was a man from the mountains in Wales, or the west of England, with hair like eagles' feathers, and nails like birds' claws; a red beard, and an uncommon degree of wildness in his looks. Wilson was then utterly unknown in Edinburgh, except slightly to Mr. Walter Scott, who never introduces any one person to another, nor judges it of any avail. However, having no other shift left, I sat down and wrote him a note, telling him that I wished much to see him, and if he wanted to see me, he might come and dine with me at my lodgings in the Road of Gabriel, at four. He accepted the invitation, and dined with Grieve and me; and I found him so much a man according to my own heart, that for many years we were seldom twenty-four hours asunder, when in town. I afterwards went and visited him, staying with him a month at his seat in Westmoreland, where we had some curious doings among the gentlemen and poets of the lakes. It is a pity I have not room here to give a description of all these scenes, being obliged, according to my plan, to return to a subject far less interesting, namely, my own literary progress.

The "Queen's Wake" being now consigned to Messrs. Murray and Blackwood, I fairly left it to its fate; and they published a fourth edition, which was in fact not a new edition, but only the remainder of Goldie's third; so that I gained an edition in the eyes of the world, although not in the weight of my purse, to which this edition in reality made no *addition*. It has, however, been a good work to me, and has certainly been read and admired much above what its merits warrant. My own opinion of it is, that it is a very imperfect and unequal production; and if it were not for three of the ballads, which are rather of a redeeming quality, some of the rest are little better than trash. But, somehow or other, the plan proved extremely happy; and though it was contrived solely for the purpose of stringing my miscellaneous ballads into a regular poem, happened to have a good effect, from keeping always up a double interest, both in the incidents of each tale, and in the success of the singer in the contest for the prize harp. The intermediate poetry between the ballads is all likewise middling good.

The same year in which I wrote the two musical dramas, I also wrote a tragedy, which was called "The Hunting of Badlewe;" but of this Goldie only printed a few copies, to see how the public relished it. It was not favourably received;–but more of this hereafter.

Although it should rather have been mentioned at a period subsequent to this, I may take notice here, that the *fifth edition* of the "Queen's Wake," in royal octavo, with plates, was a plan concocted by Mr. Blackwood to bring me in a little money. He was assisted in this undertaking by Charles Sharpe, Esq., Mr. Walter Scott, and several other friends; but most of all by the indefatigable Mr. David Bridges, junior, a man that often effects more in one day than many others can do in six, and who is, in fact, a greater prodigy than any self-taught painter or poet in the kingdom.

The only other anecdote which I have recorded in my Diary relating to this poem is one about the dedication. As it related to the amusements of a young queen, I thought I could dedicate it to no one so appropriately as to her royal and beautiful descendant, the Princess Charlotte; which I did. By the advice of some friends, I got a large paper copy bound up in an elegant antique style, which cost three guineas, and sent it as a present to her Royal Highness, directing it to the care of Dr. Fisher, bishop of Salisbury, and requesting him to present it to his royal pupil. His lordship was neither at the pains to acknowledge the receipt of the work or of my letter, nor, I dare say, to deliver it as directed. The dedication I have never had the heart to cancel, even now when she is no more, and I have let the original date remain.

During all this time I generally went on a tour into the Highlands every summer, and always made a point of tarrying some time at Kinnaird House in Athol, the seat of Chalmers Izett, Esq., whose lady had taken an early interest in my fortunes, which no circumstance has ever abated. I depended much on her advice and good taste; and had I attended more to her friendly remonstrances, it would have been much better for me. In the summer of 1814, having been seized with a severe cold while there, it was arranged that I should reside at Kinnaird House two or three weeks; and as Mrs. Izett insisted that I should not remain idle, she conducted me up stairs one morning, and introduced me into a little study, furnished with books and writing materials. "Now," said she, "I do not wish you to curtail your fishing hours, since you seem to delight so much in it, but whenever you have a spare hour, either evening or morning, you can retire to this place, either to read or write, as the humour suits you."—"Since you will set me down to write," said I, "you must choose a subject for me, for I have nothing in hand, and have thought of nothing."—"How can you be at a loss for a subject," returned she, "and that majestic river rolling beneath your eyes?"—"Well," said I, "though I consider myself exquisite at descriptions of nature, and mountain-scenery in particular, yet I am afraid that a poem wholly descriptive will prove dull and heavy."—"You may make it the shorter," said she; "only write something to prevent your mind from rusting."

Upon this I determined immediately to write a poem descriptive of the river Tay, and after spending about two hours considering in what verse I should write it, I fixed on the stanza of Spenser. "That is the finest verse in the world," said I to myself; "it rolls off with such majesty and grandeur. What an effect it will have in the description of mountains, cataracts, and storms!"

I had also another motive for adopting it. I was fond of the Spenserian measure; but there was something in the best models that always offended my ear. It was owing to this. I thought it so formed, that every verse ought to be a structure of itself, resembling an arch, of which the two meeting rhymes in the middle should represent the key-stone, and on these all the strength and flow of the verse should rest. On beginning this poem, therefore, I had the vanity to believe that I was going to give the world a new specimen of this stanza in its proper harmony. It was under these feelings that my poem of "Mador of the Moor" was begun, and in a very short time completed: but I left out to the extent of one whole book of the descriptive part. There is no doubt whatever that my highest and most fortunate efforts in rhyme are contained in some of the descriptions of nature in that poem, and in the "Ode to Superstition" in the same measure.

In the same year, and immediately on finishing the above poem, I conceived a plan for writing a volume of romantic poems, to be entitled "Midsummer Night Dreams," and am sorry to this day that a friendly advice prevented me from accomplishing my design, for of all other subjects, there were none that suited the turn of my thoughts so well.

The first of these dreams that I wrote was "Connel of Dee," now published in the "Winter Evening Tales," and the second was "The Pilgrims of the Sun." It happened that a gentleman, Mr. James Park of Greenock, on whose literary taste I had great reliance, came to Edinburgh for a few weeks about this time; and, as we had been intimate acquaintances and correspondents for a number of years, I gave him a perusal of all my recent pieces in manuscript. His approbation of the "Pilgrims of the Sun" was so decided, and so unqualified, that he prevailed upon me to give up my design of the Midsummer Night Dreams, and also that of publishing Mador, and to publish the former poem as an entire work by itself. This advice of my inestimable and regretted friend, though given in sincerity of heart, I am convinced was wrong; but I had faith in every one that commended any of my works, and laughed at those who did otherwise, thinking, and asserting, that they had not sufficient discernment. Among other wild and visionary subjects, the "Pilgrims of the

Sun" would have done very well, and might at least have been judged one of the best; but, as an entire poem by itself, it bears an impress of extravagance, and affords no relief from the story of a visionary existence. After my literary blunders and miscarriages are a few months old, I can view them with as much indifference, and laugh at them as heartily, as any of my neighbours. I have often felt, that Mary Lee reminded me of a beautiful country girl turned into an assembly in dishabille, "half-naked, for a warld's wonder," whose beauties might be gazed at, but were sure to be derided.

There were some circumstances attending the publication of this poem which show the doings and the honour of the bookselling profession in a peculiar light. I called on my old friend, Mr. Constable, from whom I was very loath to part, and told him my design and views in publishing the poem. He received me with his usual kindness, and seemed to encourage the plan: but, in the mean time, said he was busy, and that if I would call again on Saturday, he would have time to think of it, and give me an answer. With the solicitude of a poor author, I was punctual to my hour on Saturday, and found Mr. Constable sitting at his confined desk up stairs, and alone, which was a rare incident. He saluted me, held out his hand without lifting his eyes from the paper, and then, resuming his pen, continued writing. I read the backs of some of the books on his shelves, and then spoke of my new poem; but he would not deign to lift his eyes, or regard me. I tried to bring on a conversation by talking of the Edinburgh Review; but all to no purpose. "Now, the devil confound the fellow," thought I to myself, "he will sit there scribbling till we are interrupted by some one coming to talk to him of business, and then I shall lose my opportunity–perhaps it is what he wants! Hang him, if I thought he were not wanting my book, I should be as saucy as he is!" At length he turned his back to the window, with his face to me, and addressed me in a long set speech, a thing I never heard him do before. It had a great deal of speciousness in it; but with regard to its purport, I leave the world to judge. I pledge myself, that in this short Sketch of my Literary Life, as well as in the extended memoir, should that ever appear, to relate nothing but the downright truth. If any should feel that they have done or said wrong, I cannot help it.

"By G–, Hogg, you are a very extraordinary fellow!" said he– "you are a man of very great genius, sir! I don't know if ever there was such another man born!" I looked down, and brushed my hat with my elbow; for what could any man answer to such an address? "Nay, it is all true, sir; I do not jest a word–I never knew such a genius in my life. I am told that, since the publication of the "Queen's Wake" last year, you have three new poems, all as long, and greatly superior to that, ready for publication. By G–, sir, you will write Scott, and Byron, and every one of them, off the field."

"Let us alane o' your gibes, Maister Constable," said I, "and tell me at ance what ye're gaun to say about yon."

"I have been thinking seriously about your proposal, Hogg," said he; "and though you are the very sort of man whom I wish to encourage, yet I do not think the work would be best in my hands. I am so deeply engaged, my dear sir, in large and ponderous works, that a small light work has no good chance in my hands at all. For the sake of the authors, I have often taken such works in hand–among others, your friend Mr. Paterson's–and have been grieved that I had it not in my power to pay that minute attention to them, individually, that I wished to have done. The thing is impossible! And then the authors come fretting to me; nor will they believe that another bookseller can do much more for such works than I can. There is my friend, Mr. Miller, for instance–he has sold three times as many of *Discipline* as perhaps I could have done."–"No, no," said I, "I'll deal none with Mr. Miller: if you are not for the work yourself, I will find out one who will take it."–"I made the proposal in friendship," said he: "if you give the work to Miller I shall do all for it the same as if it were my own. I will publish it in all my catalogues, and in all my reviews and magazines, and I will send it abroad with all these to my agents in the country. I will be security for the price of it, should you and he deal; so that, in transferring it to Miller in place of me, you only secure for it two interests in place of one."

This was all so unobjectionable, that I could say nothing in opposition to it; so we agreed on the price at one word, which was, I think, to be eighty-six pounds for liberty to print one thousand copies. Mr. Miller was sent for, who complied with every thing as implicitly as if he had been Mr. Constable's clerk, and without making a single observation. The bargain was fairly made out and concluded; the manuscript was put into Mr. Miller's hands, and I left Edinburgh, leaving him a written direction how to forward the proofs. Week passed after week, and no proofs arrived. I grew impatient, it having been stipulated that the work was to be published in two months, and wrote to Mr. Miller; but I received no answer. I then wrote to a friend to inquire the reason. He waited on Mr. Miller, he said, but received no satisfactory answer: "the truth of the matter," added he, "is this: Mr. Miller, I am privately informed, sent out your MS. among his blue-stockings for their verdict. They have condemned the poem as extravagant nonsense. Mr. Miller has rued his bargain, and will never publish the poem, unless he is sued at law." How far this information was correct I had no means of discovering; but it vexed me exceedingly, as I had mentioned the transaction to all my friends, and how much I was pleased at the connexion. However, I waited patiently for two months, the time when it ought to have been published, and then I wrote Mr. Miller a note, desiring him to put my work forthwith to the press, the time being now elapsed; or, otherwise, to return me the manuscript. Mr. Miller returned me the poem with a polite note, as if no bargain had existed, and I thought it beneath me ever to mention the circumstance again, either to him or Mr. Constable. As I never understood the real secret of this transaction, neither do I know whom to blame. Mr. Miller seemed all along to be acting on the ground of some secret arrangement with his neighbour, and it was perhaps by an arrangement of the same kind that the poem was given up. But I only relate what I know.

Some time after this Mr. Blackwood introduced me to Mr. John Murray, the London bookseller, with whom I was quite delighted; and one night, after supping with him in Albany Street, I mentioned the transaction with Mr. Miller. He said Mr. Constable was to blame; for, as matters stood, he ought to have seen the bargain implemented; but, at all events, it should be no loss to me, for he was willing to take the poem according to Mr. Miller's bargain. There was nothing more said; we at once agreed, and exchanged letters on it; the work was put to press, and soon finished. But, alas for my unfortunate Pilgrims! The running copy was sent up to Mr. Murray in London; and that gentleman, finding his critical friends of the same opinion with Mr. Miller's blue-stockings, would not allow his name to go to the work. It was in vain that Mr. Blackwood urged that it was a work of genius, however faulty, and that it would be an honour for any bookseller to have his name to it. Mr. Murray had been informed, by those on whose judgment he could rely, that it was the most wretched poem that ever was written.

Mr. Blackwood felt a delicacy in telling me this, and got a few friends to inform me of it in as delicate a way as possible. I could not, however, conceal my feelings, and maintained that the poem was a good one. Mr. Grieve checked me, by saying it was impossible that I could be a better judge than both the literary people of Scotland and England–that they could have no interest in condemning the poem; and after what had happened, it was vain to augur any good of it. I said it would be long ere any of those persons who had condemned it could write one like it; and I was obliged to please myself with this fancy, and put up with the affront.

The poem came out, and was rather well received. I never met with any person, who really had read it, that did not like the piece; the reviewers praised it; and the Eclectic, in particular, gave it the highest commendation I ever saw bestowed on a work of genius. It was reprinted in two different towns in America, and ten thousand copies of it sold in that country. Mr. Murray very honourably paid me the price agreed on three months before it was due; but the work sold heavily here, and neither my booksellers nor I have proposed a second edition. The trade were all, except Mr. Blackwood, set against it, in defence of their own good taste. It is indeed a faulty poem, but I think no shame of it; neither, I trust, will any of my friends when I am no more.

My next literary adventure was the most extravagant of any. I took it into my head that I would collect a poem from every living author in Britain, and publish them in a neat and elegant volume, by which I calculated I might make my fortune. I either applied personally, or by letter, to Southey, Wilson, Wordsworth, Lloyd, Morehead, Pringle, Paterson, and several others; all of whom sent me very ingenious and beautiful poems. Wordsworth afterwards reclaimed his; and although Lord Byron and Rogers both promised, neither of them ever performed. I believe they intended it, but some other concerns of deeper moment interfered. In one of Lord Byron's letters he told me he was busy inditing a poem for me, and assured me that "he would appear in my work in his best breeks." That poem was "Lara," and who it was that influenced him to detain it from me, I do not know. I have heard a report of one; but the deed was so ungenerous, I cannot believe it.

I may here mention, by way of advertising, that I have lost all Lord Byron's letters to me, on which I put a very high value; and which I know to have been stolen from me by some one or other of my tourist visitors, for I was so proud of these letters, that I would always be showing them to every body. It was exceedingly unkind, particularly as they never can be of use to any other person, for they have been so often and so eagerly read by many of my friends, that any single sentence out of any one of them could easily be detected. I had five letters of his of two sheets each, and one of three. They were indeed queer *harumscarum letters*, about women, and poetry, mountains, and authors, and blue-stockings; and what he sat down to write about was generally put in the postscript. They were all, however, extremely kind, save one, which was rather a satirical, bitter letter. I had been quizzing him about his approaching marriage, and assuring him that he was going to get himself into a confounded scrape. I wished she might prove both a good *mill* and a *bank* to him; but I much doubted they would not be such as he was calculating on. I think he felt that I was using too much freedom with him.

The last letter that I received from him was shortly after the birth of his daughter Ada. In it he breathed the most tender affection both for the mother and child. Good Heaven! how I was astounded by the news that soon followed that!–Peace be to his manes! He was a great man; and I do not think that one on earth appreciated his gigantic genius so highly as I did. He sent me previous to that period all his poems as they were printed.

But to return to my publication: Mr. Walter Scott absolutely refused to furnish me with even one verse, which I took exceedingly ill, as it frustrated my whole plan. What occasioned it I do not know, as I accounted myself certain of his support from the beginning, and had never asked any thing of him in all my life that he refused. It was in vain that I represented that I had done as much for him, and would do ten times more if he required it. He remained firm in his denial, which I thought very hard; so I left him in high dudgeon, sent him a very abusive letter, and would not speak to him again for many a day. I could not even endure to see him at a distance, I felt so degraded by the refusal; and I was, at that time, more disgusted with all mankind than I had ever been before, or have ever been since.

I began, with a heavy heart, to look over the pieces I had received, and lost all hope of the success of my project. They were, indeed, all very well; but I did not see that they possessed such merit as could give celebrity to any work; and after considering them well, I fancied that I could write a better poem than any that had been sent or would be sent to me, and this so completely in the style of each poet, that it should not be known but for his own production. It was this conceit that suggested to me the idea of "The Poetic Mirror, or Living Bards of Britain." I set to work with great glee, as the fancy had struck me, and in a few days I finished my imitations of Wordsworth and Lord Byron. Like a fool, I admired the latter poem most, and contrived to get a large literary party together, on pretence, as I said, of giving them a literary treat. I had got the poem transcribed, and gave it to Mr. Ballantyne to read, who did it ample justice. Indeed, he read it with extraordinary effect; so much so, that I was astonished at the poem myself, and before it was half done all pronounced it Byron's. Every one was deceived, except Mr. Ballantyne, who was not to be imposed on in that way; but he kept the secret until we got to the Bridge, and then he told me his mind.

The "Poetic Mirror" was completely an off-hand production. I wrote it all in three weeks, except a very small proportion; and in less than three months it was submitted to the public. The second poem in the volume, namely, the Epistle to R— S—, the most beautiful and ingenious piece in the work, is not mine. It was written by Mr. Thomas Pringle, and was not meant as an imitation of Mr. Scott's manner at all. There is likewise another small secret connected with that work, which I am not yet at liberty to unfold, but which the ingenious may perhaps discover. The first edition was sold in six weeks, and another of seven hundred and fifty copies has since been sold. I do not set any particular value on any poem in the work by myself, except "The Gude Greye Katte," which was written as a caricature of "The Pilgrims of the Sun," the "Witch of Fife," and some others of my fairy ballads. It is greatly superior to any of them. I have also been told, that in England, one of the imitations of Wordsworth's Excursion has been deemed excellent.

The year following I published two volumes of Tragedies: to these I affixed the title of "Dramatic Tales, by the Author of the Poetic Mirror." I forgot, however, to mention, that the Poetic Mirror was published anonymously, and I was led to think that, had the imitations of Wordsworth been less a caricature, the work might have passed, for a season at least, as the genuine productions of the authors themselves, whose names were prefixed to the several poems. I was strongly urged by some friends, previous to the publication of these plays, to try "Sir Anthony Moore" on the stage; and once, at the suggestion of Sir Walter Scott, I consented to submit it to the players, through Mr. Ballantyne. But, by a trivial accident, the matter was delayed till I got time to consider of it; and then I shrunk from the idea of intrusting my character as a poet in the hands of every bungling and absurd actor, who, if dissatisfied with his part, had the power of raising as much disapprobation as might damn the whole piece. Consequently, my first attempts in the drama have never been offered for representation. "Sir Anthony Moore" is the least original, and the least poetical piece of the whole, and I trust it will never be acted while I live; but, if at any period it should be brought forward, and one able performer appear in the character of Old Cecil, and another in that of Caroline, I may venture my credit and judgment, as an author, that it will prove successful. The pastoral drama of "All-Hallow Eve" was written at the suggestion of the

Reverend Robert Morehead. "The Profligate Princes" is a modification of my first play, "The Hunting of Badlewe," printed by Goldie; and the fragment of "The Haunted Glen" was written off-hand, to make the second volume of an equal extent with the first.

The small degree of interest that these dramas excited in the world finished my dramatic and poetical career. I had adopted a resolution of writing a drama every year as long as I lived, hoping to make myself perfect by degrees, as a man does in his calling, by serving an apprenticeship; but the failure of those to excite notice fully convinced me, that either this was not the age to appreciate the qualities of dramatic composition, or that I was not possessed of the talents fitting me for such an undertaking: and so I gave up the ambitious design.

Before this period, all the poems that I had published had been begun and written by chance and at random, without any previous design. I had at that time commenced an epic poem on a regular plan, and I finished two books of it, pluming myself that it was to prove my greatest work. But, seeing that the poetical part of these dramas excited no interest in the public, I felt conscious that no poetry I should ever be able to write would do so; or, if it did, the success would hinge upon some casualty, on which it did not behove me to rely. So, from that day to this, save now and then an idle song to beguile a leisure hour, I determined to write no more poetry.

Several years subsequent to this, at the earnest intreaties of some literary friends, I once more set to work and finished this poem, which I entitled "Queen Hynde," in a time shorter than any person would believe. I submitted it first to Sir Walter Scott, who gave it his approbation in the most unqualified terms; so the work was put to press with every prospect of high success. I sold an edition of one thousand copies to Longman and Co.; but Mr. Blackwood, who had been chiefly instrumental in urging me to finish the poem, claimed the half of the edition, and got it. But it proved to him like the Highlandman's character–"he would have peen as petter without it." That malicious *deevil*, Jerdan, first took it up and damned it with faint praise. The rest of the reviewers followed in his wake, so that, in short, the work sold heavily and proved rather a failure.

It is said the multitude never are wrong, but, in this instance, I must take Mr. Wordsworth's plan, and maintain that they *were* wrong. I need not say how grievously I was disappointed, as what unsuccessful candidate for immortal fame is not? But it would have been well could I have refrained from exposing myself. I was invited to a public dinner given by a great number of young friends, a sort of worshippers of mine (for I have a number of those in Scotland). It was to congratulate me on my new work, and drink success to it. The president made a speech, in which, after some laudatory remarks on the new poem, he boldly and broadly asserted that it was much inferior to their beloved "Queen's Wake." I was indignantly wroth, denying his assertion both in principle and position, and maintained not only that it was infinitely superior to the "Queen's Wake," but I offered to bet the price of the edition with any or all of them that it was the best epic poem that ever had been produced in Scotland. None of them would take the bet, but as few backed me. I will however stake my credit on "Queen Hynde." It was unfortunate that the plot should have been laid in an age so early that we have no interest in it.

From the time I gave up "The Spy" I had been planning with my friends to commence the publication of a Magazine on a new plan; but, for several years, we only conversed about the utility of such a work, without doing any thing farther. At length, among others, I chanced to mention it to Mr. Thomas Pringle; when I found that he and his friends had a plan in contemplation of the same kind. We agreed to join our efforts, and try to set it a-going; but, as I declined the editorship on account of residing mostly on my farm at a distance from town, it became a puzzling question who was the best qualified among our friends for that undertaking. We at length fixed on Mr. Gray as the fittest person for a principal department, and I went and mentioned the plan to Mr. Blackwood, who, to my astonishment, I found had likewise long been cherishing a plan of the same kind. He said he knew nothing about Pringle, and always had his eye on me as a principal assistant; but he would not begin the undertaking until he saw he could do it with effect. Finding him, however, disposed to encourage such a work, Pringle, at my suggestion, made out a plan in writing, with a list of his supporters, and sent it in a letter to me. I inclosed it in another, and sent it to Mr. Blackwood; and not long after that period Pringle and he came to an arrangement about commencing the work, while I was in the country. Thus I had the honour of being the beginner, and almost sole instigator of that celebrated work, "Blackwood's Magazine;" but from the time I heard that Pringle had taken in Cleghorn as a partner I declined all connexion with it, farther than as an occasional contributor. I told him the connexion would not likely last for a year, and insisted that he should break it at once; but to this proposal he would in nowise listen. As I had predicted, so it fell out, and much sooner than might have been expected. In the fourth month after the commencement of that work, I received a letter from Mr. Blackwood, soliciting my return to Edinburgh; and when I arrived there, I found that he and his two redoubted editors had gone to loggerheads, and instead of arguing the matter face to face, they were corresponding together at the rate of about a sheet an hour. Viewing this as a ridiculous mode of proceeding, I brought about two meetings between Mr. Blackwood and Mr. Pringle, and endeavoured all that I could to bring them to a right understanding about the matter. A reconciliation was effected at that time, and I returned again into the country. Soon, however, I heard that the flames of controversy, and proud opposition, had broken out between the parties with greater fury than ever; and, shortly after, that they had finally separated, and the two champions gone over and enlisted under the banners of Mr. Constable, having left Mr. Blackwood to shift for himself, and carried over, as they pretended, their right to the Magazine, with all their subscribers and contributors, to the other side.

I received letters from both parties. I loved Pringle, and would gladly have assisted him had it been in my power; but, after balancing fairly the two sides, I thought Mr. Blackwood more sinned against than sinning, and that the two editors had been endeavouring to bind him to a plan which could not possibly succeed; so, on considering his disinterested friendship for me, manifested in several strong instances, I stuck to him, expecting excellent sport in the various exertions and manœuvres of the two parties for the superiority.

I know not what wicked genius put it into my head, but it was then, in an evil hour, when I had determined on the side I was to espouse, that I wrote the "Chaldee Manuscript," and transmitted it to Mr. Blackwood from Yarrow. On first reading it, he never thought of publishing it; but some of the rascals to whom he showed it, after laughing at it, by their own accounts till they were sick, persuaded him, nay almost forced him, to insert it; for some of them went so far as to tell him, that if he did not admit that inimitable article, they would never speak to him again so long as they lived. Needless however it is now to deny, that they interlarded it with a good deal of deevilry of their own, which I had never thought of; and one who had a principal hand in these alterations has never yet been named as an aggressor.

Certain of my literary associates call me *The Chaldee Shepherd*, and pretend to sneer at my assumption of being the author of that celebrated article. Certes they have long ago persuaded the country that I was not. Luckily, however, I have preserved the original proof slips and three of Mr. Blackwood's letters relating to the article. These proofs show exactly what part was mine, which, if I remember aright (for I write this in London), consists of the first two chapters, part of the third, and part of the last. The rest was said to have been made up conjointly in full divan. I do not know, but I always suspected Lockhart of a heavy responsibility there.

I declare I never once dreamed of giving anybody offence by that droll article, nor did I ever think of keeping it a secret either from Mr. Constable or Mr. Pringle: so far from that, I am sure, had I been in town, I would have shown the manuscript to the latter before publication. I meant it as a sly history of the transaction, and the great literary battle that was to be fought. All that I expected was a little retaliation of the same kind in the opposing magazine; and when I received letter after letter, informing me what a dreadful flame it had raised in Edinburgh, I could not be brought to believe that it was not a joke. I am not certain but that I confessed the matter to Mr. George Thomson, in the course of our correspondence, before I was aware of its importance. No one ever suspected me as the author. When I came to town, every one made his remarks, and pronounced his anathemas upon it, without any reserve, in my hearing, which afforded me much amusement. Still I could not help viewing the whole as a farce, or something unreal and deceptive; and I am sure I never laughed so much in my life as at the rage in which I found so many people.

So little had I intended giving offence by what appeared in the Magazine, that I had written out a long continuation of the manuscript, which I have by me to this day, in which I go over the painters, poets, lawyers, booksellers, magistrates, and ministers of Edinburgh, all in the same style; and with reference to the first part that was published, I might say of the latter as king Rehoboam said to the elders of Israel, "My little finger was thicker than my father's loins." It took all the energy of Mr. Wilson and his friends, and some sharp remonstrances from Sir Walter Scott, as well as a great deal of controversy and battling with Mr. Grieve, to prevent me from publishing the whole work as a large pamphlet, and putting my name to it.

That same year I published "The Brownie of Bodsbeck, and other Tales," in two volumes. I suffered unjustly in the eyes of the world with regard to that tale, which was looked on as an imitation of the tale of "Old Mortality," and a counterpart to that; whereas it was written long ere the tale of "Old Mortality" was heard of, and I well remember my chagrin on finding the ground, which I thought clear, pre-occupied before I could appear publicly on it, and that by such a redoubted champion. It was wholly owing to Mr. Blackwood that this tale was not published a year sooner, which would effectually have freed me from the stigma of being an imitator, and brought in the author of the "Tales of My Landlord" as an imitator of me. That was the only ill turn that ever Mr. Blackwood did me; and it ought to be a warning to authors never to intrust booksellers with their manuscripts.

I mentioned to Mr. Blackwood that I had two tales I wished to publish, and at his request I gave him a reading of the manuscript. One of them was "The Brownie," which, I believe, was not quite finished. He approved of it, but with "The Bridal of Polmood" he would have nothing to do. Of course, my manuscripts were returned, and I had nothing else for it but to retire to the country, and there begin and write two other tales in place of the one rejected. "The Bridal of Polmood," however, was published from the same copy, and without the alteration of a word, and has been acknowledged by all who have read it as the most finished and best written tale that I ever produced. Mr. Blackwood himself must be sensible of this fact, and also, that in preventing its being published along with "The Brownie of Bodsbeck," he did an injury both to himself and me. As a farther proof how little booksellers are to be trusted, he likewise wished to prevent the insertion of "The Wool-Gatherer," which has been a universal favourite; but I know the source from whence it proceeded. I would never object trusting a bookseller, were he a man of any taste; for, unless he wishes to reject an author altogether, he can have no interest in asserting what he does not think. But the plague is, they *never read works themselves*, but give them to their minions, with whom there never fails to lurk a literary jealousy; and whose suggestions may uniformly be regarded as any thing but the truth. For my own part, I know that I have always been looked on by the learned part of the community as an intruder in the paths of literature, and every opprobrium has been thrown on me from that quarter. The truth is, that I am so. The walks of learning are occupied by a powerful aristocracy, who deem that province their own peculiar right; else, what would avail all their dear-bought collegiate honours and degrees? No wonder that they should view an intruder, from the humble and despised ranks of the community, with a jealous and indignant eye, and impede his progress by every means in their power.

I was unlucky therefore in the publication of my first novel, and what impeded me still farther, was the publication of "Old

Mortality;" for, having made the redoubted Burley the hero of my tale, I was obliged to go over it again, and alter all the traits in the character of the principal personage, substituting John Brown of Caldwell for John Balfour of Burley, greatly to the detriment of my story. I tried also to take out Clavers, but I found this impossible. A better instance could not be given of the good luck attached to one person, and the bad luck which attended the efforts of another.

I observe that in the extended MS. I had detailed all the proceedings of a club, the most ridiculous perhaps that ever was established in any city, and, owing to some particular circumstances, I cannot refrain from mentioning them here. This club was established one night, in a frolic, at a jovial dinner party, in the house of a young lawyer, now of some celebrity at the bar, and was christened *The Right and Wrong Club.* The chief principle of the club was, that whatever any of its members should assert, the whole were bound to support the same, whether *right or wrong*. We were so delighted with the novelty of the idea, that we agreed to meet the next day at Oman's Hotel, and celebrate its anniversary. We were dull and heavy when we met, but did not part so. We dined at five, and separated at two in the morning, before which time the club had risen greatly in our estimation; so we agreed to meet next day, and every successive day for five or six weeks, and during all that time our hours of sitting continued the same. No constitutions on earth could stand this. Had our meetings been restricted to once a month, or even once a week, the club might have continued to this day, and would have been a source of much pleasure and entertainment to the members; but to meet daily was out of the question. The result was, that several of the members got quite deranged, and I drank myself into an inflammatory fever. The madness of the members proved no bar to the hilarity of the society; on the contrary, it seemed to add a great deal of zest to it, as a thing quite in character. An inflammatory fever, however, sounded rather strange in the ears of the joyous group, and threw a damp on their spirits. They continued their meetings for some days longer, and regularly sent a deputation at five o'clock to inquire after my health, and I was sometimes favoured with a call from one or more of the members, between two and three in the morning, when they separated. The mornings after such visits I was almost sure to have to provide new knockers and bell-handles for all the people on the stair. Finding, however, that I still grew worse, they had the generosity to discontinue their sittings, and to declare that they would not meet again until their poet was able to join them; and if that should never happen, they would never meet again. This motion (which was made by a newly-initiated member, Mr. John Ballantyne,) was hailed with shouts of approbation, and from that hour to this *The Right and Wrong Club* never more met. It was high time that it should have been given up, for one term at least. It proved a dear club to me. I was three weeks confined to my bed, and if it had not been for Dr. Saunders, I believe I should have died. Its effect turned out better with regard to several of the other members, as it produced a number of happy marriages. During the period of high-excitation, the lads wrote flaming love-letters to young ladies of their acquaintance, containing certain proffers, which, with returning reflection, they found they could not with propriety retract. It made some of them do the wisest acts that ever they did in their lives.

This brings me to an anecdote which I must relate, though with little credit to myself; one that I never call to mind without its exciting feelings of respect, admiration, and gratitude. I formerly mentioned that I had quarrelled with Sir Walter Scott. It is true, I had all the quarrel on my own side: no matter for that; I was highly offended, exceedingly angry, and shunned all communication with him for a twelvemonth. He heard that I was ill, and that my trouble had assumed a dangerous aspect. Every day, on his return from the Parliament-House, he called at Messrs. Grieve and Scott's to inquire after my health, with much friendly solicitude; and this, too, after I had renounced his friendship, and told him that I held both it and his literary talents in contempt! One day in particular, he took Mr. Grieve aside, and asked him if I had proper attendants and an able physician. Mr. Grieve assured him that I was carefully attended, and had the skill of a professional gentleman, in whom I had the most implicit confidence. "I would fain have called," said he, "but I knew not how I would be received. I request, however, that he may have every proper attendance, and want for nothing that can contribute to the restoration of his health. And in particular, I have to request that you will let no pecuniary consideration whatever prevent his having the best medical advice in Edinburgh, for I shall see it paid. Poor Hogg! I would not for all that I am worth in the world that any thing serious should befall him."

As Mr. Grieve had been enjoined, he never mentioned this circumstance to me. I accidentally, however, came to the knowledge of it some months afterwards. I then questioned him as to the truth of it, when he told me it all, very much affected. I went straight home, and wrote an apology to Sir Walter, which was heartily received, and he invited me to breakfast next morning, adding, that he was longing much to see me. The same day, as we were walking round St. Andrew's Square, I endeavoured to make the cause of our difference the subject of conversation, but he eluded it. I tried it again some days afterwards, sitting in his study, but he again parried it with equal dexterity; so that I have been left to conjecture what could be his motive in refusing so peremptorily the trifle that I had asked of him. I know him too well to have the least suspicion that there could be any selfish or unfriendly feeling in the determination that he adopted, and I can account for it in no other way, than by supposing that he thought it mean in me to attempt either to acquire gain, or a name, by the efforts of other men; and that it was much more honourable, to use a proverb of his own, "that every herring should hang by its own head."

Mr. Wilson once drove me also into an ungovernable rage, by turning a long and elaborate poem of mine, on "The Field of Waterloo," into ridicule, on learning which I sent him a letter, which I thought was a tickler. There was scarcely an abusive epithet in our language that I did not call him by. My letter, however, had not the designed effect: the opprobrious names proved only a source of amusement to Wilson, and he sent me a letter of explanation and apology, which knit my heart closer to him than ever. My friends in general have been of opinion that he has amused himself and the public too often at my expense; but, except in one instance, which terminated very ill for me, and in which I had no more concern than the man in the moon, I never discerned any evil design on his part, and thought it all excellent sport. At the same time, I must acknowledge, that it was using too much freedom with any author, to print his name in full, to poems, letters, and essays, which he himself never saw. I do not say that he has done this; but either he or some one else has done it many a time.

My next literary undertaking was the "Jacobite Relics of Scotland." Of this work it is proper to mention, that it was first proposed in the Highland Society of London, His Royal Highness the Duke of Sussex being in the chair; yet, for all that, the native Highlanders were so jealous of a Sassenach coming plodding among them, gathering up their rebellious scraps, that, had it not been for the influence of the ladies over the peasantry of their respective districts, I could never have succeeded. But, in the end, I am sure I produced two volumes of Jacobite Relics, such as no man in Scotland or England could have produced but myself. I assert it, and can prove it; for besides the songs and histories of events and persons, I collected all the original airs over a whole kingdom, many of them among a people whose language I did not understand; and that work I dedicated to the Highland Society of London in a poetical epistle.

I published the first volume in 1819, reserving the second volume until the following year, in the hope of collecting every remnant that was worthy of preservation. The task was exceedingly troublesome, but far from being unmixed with pleasure. The jealousy of the Highlanders was amusing beyond conception. I shall never forget with what sly and disdainful looks Donald would eye me, when I told him I was gathering up old songs. And then he would say, "Ohon, man, you surely haif had very less to do at home; and so you want to get some of the songs of the poor repellioners from me; and then you will give me up to King Shorge to be hanged? Hoo, no!–Cot tamn!–that will never do."

In the interim between the publication of the first and second volumes I collected and arranged for publication "The Winter Evening Tales," which were published by Oliver and Boyd in 1820, in two volumes, closely printed. The greater part of these Tales was written in early life, when I was serving as a shepherd lad among the mountains, and on looking them over, I saw well enough that there was a blunt rusticity about them; but I liked them the better for it, and altered nothing. To me they appeared not only more characteristic of the life that I then led, but also of the manners that I was describing. As to the indelicacies hinted at by some reviewers, I do declare that such a thought never entered into my mind, so that the public are indebted for these indelicacies to the acuteness of the discoverers. Wo be to that reader who goes over a simple and interesting tale fishing for indelicacies, without calculating on what is natural for the characters with whom he is conversing; a practice, however, too common among people of the present age, especially if the author be not a blue-stocking. All that I can say for myself in general is, that I am certain I never intentionally meant ill, and that I hope to be forgiven, both by God and man, for every line that I have written injurious to the cause of religion, of virtue, or of good manners. On the other hand, I am so ignorant of the world, that it can scarcely be expected I should steer clear of all inadvertencies.

The following list of works may appear trifling in the eyes of some, but when it is considered that they have been produced by a man almost devoid of education, and principally, in his early days, debarred from every advantage in life, and possessed only of a quick eye in observing the operations of nature, it is certainly a sufficient excuse for inserting them here, more especially as some of them run a great risk of being lost. I am proud of it myself, and I do not deny it; nor is there one in the list, for the contents of which I have any reason to blush, when all things are taken into account. I was forty years of age before I wrote the "Queen's Wake." That poem was published in 1813; so that in that and the next six years I wrote and published

| | Vols. |
|---|---|
| The Queen's Wake | 1 |
| Pilgrims of the Sun | 1 |
| The Hunting of Badlewe | 1 |
| Mador of the Moor | 1 |
| Poetic Mirror | 1 |
| Dramatic Tales | 2 |
| Brownie of Bodsbeck | 2 |
| Winter Evening Tales | 2 |
| Sacred Melodies | 1 |
| Border Garland, No. I | 1 |
| Jacobite Relics of Scotland | 2 |

Making fifteen volumes in seven years, besides many articles in periodical works. To these may now be added

| | Vols. |
|---|---|
| The Spy | 1 |
| Queen Hynde | 1 |
| The Three Perils of Man | 3 |
| The Three Perils of Women | 3 |
| Confessions of a Sinner | 1 |
| The Shepherd's Calendar | 2 |
| A Selection of Songs | 1 |
| The Queer Book | 1 |
| The Royal Jubilee | 1 |
| The Mountain Bard | 1 |
| The Forest Minstrel | 1 |

Making in all about thirty volumes, which, if the quality were at all proportioned to the quantity, are enough for any man's life.

I omitted to mention formerly, that in 1815, I was applied to by a celebrated composer of music, in the name of a certain company in London, to supply verses, suiting some ancient Hebrew Melodies, selected in the synagogues of Germany. I proffered to furnish them at a guinea a stanza, which was agreed to at once, and I furnished verses to them all. The work was published in a splendid style, price one guinea; but it was a hoax upon me, for I was never paid a farthing.

In this short Memoir, which is composed of extracts from a larger detail, I have confined myself to such anecdotes only as relate to my progress as a writer, and these I intend to continue from year to year as long as I live. There is much that I have written which cannot as yet appear; for the literary men of Scotland, my contemporaries, may change their characters, so as to forfeit the estimate at which I have set them, and my social companions may alter their habits. Of my own productions, I have endeavoured to give an opinion, with perfect candour; and, although the partiality of an author may be too apparent in the preceding pages, yet I trust every generous heart will excuse, and make due allowance for the failing.

# REMINISCENCES
## OF FORMER DAYS

I MUST now proceed with my reminiscences at random, as from the time the last journal was finished and published I ceased keeping any notes. From 1809 until 1814 I resided in Edinburgh, having no home or place of retirement in my native district of Ettrick Forest, a want which I felt grievously in summer. But in the course of the last-mentioned year I received a letter from the late Duke Charles of Buccleugh, by the hands of his chamberlain, presenting me with the small farm of Altrive Lake, in the wilds of Yarrow. The boon was quite unsolicited and unexpected, and never was a more welcome one conferred on an unfortunate wight, as it gave me once more a habitation among my native moors and streams, where each face was that of a friend, and each house was a home, as well as a residence for life to my aged father.

The letter was couched in the kindest terms, and informed me that I had long had a secret and sincere friend whom I knew not of, in his late Duchess, who had in her lifetime solicited such a residence for me. In the letter he said, "The rent shall be nominal;" but it has not even been nominal, for such a thing as rent has never once been mentioned. Subsequently to that period I was a frequent guest at his Grace's table; and, as he placed me always next him, on his right hand, I enjoyed a good share of his conversation, and I must say of my benefactor, that I have never met with any man whom I deemed his equal. There is no doubt that he was beloved and esteemed, not only by his family and friends, but by all who could appreciate merit; yet, strange to say, Duke Charles was not popular among his tenantry. This was solely owing to the change of times, over which no nobleman can have any controul, and which it is equally impossible for him to redress; for a more considerate, benevolent, and judicious gentleman I never saw. It is natural to suppose that I loved him, and felt grateful towards him; but exclusive of all feelings of *that* nature, if I am any judge of mankind, Duke Charles had every qualification both of heart and mind, which ought to endear a nobleman to high and low, rich and poor. From the time of his beloved partner's death his spirits began to droop; and, though for the sake of his family he made many efforts to keep them up, the energy that formerly had supported them was broken, and the gnawings of a disconsolate heart brought him to an untimely grave. Blessed be the memory of my two noble and only benefactors! they were lovely in their lives, and in their deaths they were but shortly divided.

I then began and built a handsome cottage on my new farm, and forthwith made it my head-quarters. But not content with this, having married in 1820 Miss Margaret Phillips, youngest daughter of Mr. Phillips, late of Longbridge-moor, in Annandale, and finding that I had then in the hands of Mr. Murray, Mr. Blackwood, Messrs. Oliver and Boyd, and Messrs. Longman and Co., debts due, or that would soon be due, to the amount of a thousand pounds, I determined once more to farm on a larger scale, and expressed my wish to the Right Honourable Lord Montague, head trustee on his nephew's domains. His lordship readily offered me the farm of Mount-Benger, which adjoined my own. At first I determined not to accept of it, as it had ruined two well qualified farmers in the preceding six years; but was persuaded at last by some neighbours, in opposition to my own judgment, to accept of it, on the plea that the farmers on the Buccleugh estate were never suffered to be great losers, and that at all events, if I could not *make* the rent, I could write for it. So accordingly I took a lease of the farm for nine years.

I called in my debts, which were all readily paid, and amounted to within a few pounds of one thousand; but at that period the sum was quite inadequate, the prices of ewes bordering on thirty shillings per head. The farm required stocking to the amount of one thousand sheep, twenty cows, five horses, farming utensils of all sorts, crop, manure, and, moreover, draining, fencing, and building, so that I soon found I had not half enough of money; and though I realized by writing, in the course of the next two years, seven hundred and fifty pounds, beside smaller sums paid in cash, yet I got into difficulties at the very first, out of which I could never redeem myself till the end of the lease, at which time live stock of all kinds having declined one half in value, the speculation left me once more without a sixpence in the world–and at the age of sixty it is fully late enough to begin it anew.

It will be consolatory however to my friends to be assured that none of these reverses ever preyed in the smallest degree on my spirits. As long as I did all for the best, and was conscious that no man could ever accuse me of dishonesty, I laughed at the futility of my own calculations, and let my earnings go as they came, amid contentment and happiness, determined to make more money as soon as possible, although it should go the same way.

One may think, on reading over this Memoir, that I must have worn out a life of misery and wretchedness; but the case has been quite the reverse. I never knew either man or woman who has been so uniformly happy as I have been; which has been partly owing to a good constitution, and partly from the conviction that a heavenly gift, conferring the powers of immortal song, was inherent in my soul. Indeed so uniformly smooth and happy has my married life been, that on a retrospect I cannot distinguish one part from another, save by some remarkably good days of fishing, shooting, and curling on the ice. Those who desire to peruse my youthful love adventures will find some of the best of them in those of "George Cochrane," in the following tales.

Now, as I think the best way of writing these by-gone reminiscences is to finish the subject one is on, before beginning another, I must revert to several circumstances of importance to no body but myself. In 1822, perceiving that I was likely to run short of money, I began and finished in the course of a few months, "The Three Perils of Man, viz. War, Women, and Witchcraft!" Lord preserve us! what a medley I made of it! for I never in my life re-wrote a page of prose; and being impatient to get hold of some of Messrs. Longman and Co.'s money or their bills, which were the same, I dashed on, and mixed up with what might have been made one of the best historical tales our country ever produced, such a mass of diablerie as retarded the main story, and rendered the whole perfectly ludicrous. But the worst thing of all effected by this novel, or at least by the novel part of an authentic tale, was its influencing the ingenious Allan Cunningham to follow up the idea, and improve the subject; whereas, he made matters rather worse. I received one hundred and fifty pounds for the edition of one thousand copies as soon as it was put to press. The house never manifested the least suspicion of me, more than if I had been one of their own firm.

The next year I produced "The Three Perils of Women," also in three volumes, and received the same price likewise, in bills, as soon as it was put to press. There is a good deal of pathos and absurdity in both the tales of this latter work; but I was all this while writing as if in desperation, and see matters now in a different light.

The next year, 1824, I published "The Confessions of a Sinner;" but it being a story replete with horrors, after I had written it I durst not venture to put my name to it: so it was published anonymously, and of course did not sell very well–so at least I believe, for I do not remember ever receiving any thing for it, and I am sure if there had been a reversion I should have had a moiety. However, I never asked any thing; so on that point there was no misunderstanding. Perhaps I may bring the parties to account for it still, which they will like very ill.

But the same year I offered them two volumes 12mo of "The Lives of Eminent Men;" to which they answered, "that my last publication had been found fault with in some very material points, and they begged leave to decline publishing the present one until they consulted some other persons with regard to its merits." Oho! thinks I, since my favourite publishers thus think proper to take two thousand volumes for nothing, ("Queen Hynde" and the "Confessions of a Sinner,") and then refuse the third, it is time to give them up; so I never wrote another letter to that house.

I confess that there was a good deal of wrangling between Mr. Blackwood and me with regard to a hundred pound bill of Messrs. Longman and Co.'s, advanced on the credit of these works. When Mr. Blackwood came to be a sharer in them, and to find that he was likely to be a loser of that sum, or a great part of it, he caused me to make over a bill to him of the same amount, which he afterwards charged me with, and deducted from our subsequent transactions:– so that, as far as ever I could be made to understand the matter, after many letters and arguments, I never received into my own hand one penny for these two works. I do not accuse Mr. Blackwood of dishonesty; on the contrary, with all his faults, I never saw any thing but honour and integrity about him. But this was the fact. Messrs. Longman and Co. advanced me one hundred pounds on the credit of one or both of the works: I drew the money for the note, or rather I believe Mr. Blackwood drew it out of the bank for me. But he compelled me, whether I would or not, to grant him my promissory note for the same sum, and I was to have a moiety of the proceeds from both houses. The account was carried on against me till finally obliterated; but the proceeds I never heard of; and yet, on coming to London, I find that Messrs. Longman and Co. have not a copy of either of the works, nor have had any for a number of years. It is probable that they may have sold them off at a trade sale, and at a very cheap rate too; but half of the edition was mine, and they ought to have consulted me, or, at least, informed me of the transaction. It was because I had an implicit confidence in Blackwood's honour that I signed the bill, though I told him I could not comprehend it. The whole of that trifling business has to this day continued a complete mystery to me. I have told the plain truth, and if any of the parties can explain it away I shall be obliged to them. If the money should ever by any chance drop in, "better late than never" will be my salutation.

In 1822 I bargained with Constable and Co. for an edition of my best poems in four volumes, for which they were to pay me two hundred pounds. It was with Mr. Robert Cadell that I made the bargain. He was always a near and intimate friend of mine, but one whom at our club we reckoned a perfect Nabal; and in all our social parties we were wont to gibe him about his niggardly hardness, which he never took the least amiss. He offered not the smallest objection to the conditions; but he made a reserve (as I needed a bill at a short date) that if there were not above five hundred copies of the work sold when the bill became due, he was entitled to a renewal of the bill for six months. Accordingly, I attended the day before the bill became due and offered to accept of the renewal. Cadell took up the missive, read it over, and standing upright, he lifted his large eyes toward the cornice, his pale face looking more cadaverous than usual. He then conversed shortly with Mr. Fyffe, his cashier, studied the letter again for a good while, and then said, "And what are you going to do with the money, Hogg, that you draw out of the bank to-day on our bill?"

"I am gaun to bring it to you ye see," says I, "to lift the other bill wi'. An' I'll pay the four per centage out o' my ain pouch wi' great cheerfulness, for the good I hae gotten o' the siller."

"You have got full payment for the edition, have you?"

"Yes, I hae. Think ye I'm gaun to deny that?"

"And what did you do with it?"

"Od man, ye're no blate to speer. But the truth is that I gae it away in rent."

"Then you have no chance ever to get it again?"

"Deil a grain."

"And do you consider that by this transaction you will change the sterling value that is already in your hand for our paper?"

"Ay, an' excepting the bit interest they are the very same to me."

"But, Hoggy, my man, I won't trust you to make the experiment. There's your missive. Keep hold of what you have, and I'll pay the bill when it is presented."

"There are some waur chaps than Bob Cadell, for as sairly as I hae misca'd him whiles," thought I, as I went down stairs.

I have recorded every word that passed here, for I thought very highly of his conduct at the time; and when I saw what soon after followed, I thought ten times more of it, and never reported Cadell as a scrub again. Sir Walter Scott at the same time sent me a credit order on his banker for a hundred pounds for fear of any embarrassment; so that altogether I find I lost upwards of two thousand pounds on Mount-Benger lease,–a respectable sum for an old shepherd to throw away.

Having been so much discouraged by the failure of "Queen Hynde," I gave up all thoughts of ever writing another long poem, but continued for six years to write fairy tales, ghost stories, songs, and poems for periodicals of every description, sometimes receiving liberal payment, and sometimes none, just as the editor or proprietor felt disposed. It will be but justice to give a list of such as pay and such as do not, and their several grades, which I may add to this by and by.

In 1829 Baillie Blackwood published a selection of my best songs that could be recovered, with notes, consisting of about one hundred and forty. The work was exceedingly well received, and has paid me a good sum already. In the following year, that is, the year before last, the baillie also ventured to *print* one thousand copies of a miscellaneous work of mine, which, for fear of that great bugbear, REFORM, he has never dared to publish, and I am convinced never will.

I have had many dealings with that gentleman, and have been often obliged to him, and yet I think he has been as much obliged to me, perhaps a good deal more, and I really believe in my heart that he is as much disposed to be friendly to me as to any man; but there is another principle that circumscribes that feeling in all men, and into very narrow limits in some. It is always painful to part with one who has been a benefactor even on a small scale, but there are some things that no independent heart can bear. The great fault of Blackwood is, that he regards no man's temper or disposition; but the more he can provoke an author by insolence and contempt, he likes the better. Besides, he will never once confess that he is in the wrong, else any thing might be forgiven; no, no, the thing is impossible that he can ever be wrong! The poor author is not only always in the wrong, but, "Oh, he is the most insufferable beast!"

What has been the consequence? He has driven all his original correspondents from him that first gave Maga her zest, save one, who, though still his friend, can but seldom write for him, being now otherwise occupied, and another, who is indeed worth his weight in gold to him; but who, though invaluable, and I am sure much attached, yet has been a thousand times at the point of bolting off like a flash of lightning. I know it well, and Ebony, for his own sake, had better take care of this last remaining stem of a goodly bush, for he may depend on it that he has only an eel by the tail.

For my part, after twenty years of feelings hardly suppressed, he has driven me beyond the bounds of human patience. That Magazine of his, which owes its rise principally to myself, has often put words and sentiments into my mouth of which I have been greatly ashamed, and which have given much pain to my family and relations, and many of those after a solemn written promise that such freedoms should never be repeated. I have been often urged to restrain and humble him by legal measures as an incorrigible offender deserves. I know I have it in my power, and if he dares me to the task, I want but a hair to make a tether of.

I omitted to mention that I wrote and published a Masque or Drama, comprehending many songs, that summer the king was in Scotland. It was a theme that suited me to a tittle, as I there suffered fancy to revel free. Mr. Blackwood never gave me any thing for it; but I got what I held in higher estimation, his Majesty's thanks, for that and my other loyal and national songs. The note is written by Sir Robert Peel, in his Majesty's name, and I have preserved it as a relic.

In the spring of 1829 I first mentioned the plan of the "Altrive Tales" to Mr. Blackwood in a letter. He said, in answer, that the publication of them would be playing a sure card, if Mr. Lockhart would edit them. He and I waited on Mr. Lockhart subsequently, at Chiefswood, and proposed the plan to him. He said that he would cheerfully assist me both in the selection and correction, but that it was altogether without a precedent for one author to publish an edition of the works of another while the latter was still alive, and better qualified than any other person to arrange the work. Blackwood then requested me to begin writing and arranging forthwith, that we might begin publishing about the end of the year. But when the end of the year came, he put off and put off until the next spring, and then desired me to continue my labours till November next, as I should still be making the work the better, and would ultimately profit by so doing. Then when last November came, he answered a letter of mine in very bad humour, stating that he would neither advance me money on the work that had lain a year unpublished, nor commence a new work in a time of such agitation–and that I *must not* think of it for another year at least.

I then began to suspect that the whole pretence had all along been only a blind to keep me from London, whither I had proposed going, and keep me entirely in his own power. So, rather than offer the series to any other Scottish bookseller, I carried it at once to

London, where it was cordially accepted on my own terms, without the intervention or assistance of any body. It was not without the greatest reluctance that I left my family in the wilderness; but I had no alternative. It behoved me either to remain there and starve, or try my success in the metropolis of the empire, where I could have the assistance of more than one friend on whose good taste and critical discernment I could implicitly rely.

In the following volumes I purpose to give the grave and gay tales, the romantic and the superstitious, alternately, as far as is consistent with the size of each volume. At all events I think I can promise my readers that I shall present them with a series of stories which they shall scarcely feel disposed to lay aside until a rainy Sunday; and with a few reminiscences relating to eminent men, which I deem may be interesting to many, I once more bring this Memoir, it may be hoped, to a partial conclusion.

## SIR WALTER SCOTT

One fine day in the summer of 1801, as I was busily engaged working in the field at Ettrick House, Wat Shiel came over to me and said, that "I boud gang away down to the Ramseycleuch as fast as my feet could carry me, for there war some gentlemen there wha wantit to speak to me."

"Wha can be at the Ramseycleuch that want me, Wat?"

"I couldna say, for it wasna me that they spak to i' the byganging. But I'm thinking it's the Shirra an' some o' his gang."

I was rejoiced to hear this, for I had seen the first volumes of the "Minstrelsy of the Border," and had copied a number of old ballads from my mother's recital, and sent them to the editor preparatory for a third volume. I accordingly went towards home to put on my Sunday clothes, but before reaching it I met with THE SHIRRA and Mr. William Laidlaw coming to visit me. They alighted and remained in our cottage for a space better than an hour, and my mother chanted the ballad of Old Maitlan' to them, with which Mr. Scott was highly delighted. I had sent him a copy, (not a very perfect one, as I found afterwards, from the singing of another Laidlaw,) but I thought Mr. Scott had some dread of a part being forged, that had been the cause of his journey into the wilds of Ettrick. When he heard my mother sing it he was quite satisfied, and I remember he asked her if she thought it had ever been printed; and her answer was, "Oo, na, na, sir, it was never printed i' the world, for my brothers an' me learned it frae auld Andrew Moor, an' he learned it, an' mony mae, frae auld Baby Mettlin, that was housekeeper to the first laird o' Tushilaw."

"Then that must be a very auld story, indeed, Margaret," said he.

"Ay, it is that! It is an auld story! But mair nor that, except George Warton and James Steward, there was never ane o' my sangs prentit till ye prentit them yoursell, an' ye hae spoilt them a'thegither. They war made for singing, an' no for reading; and they're nouther right spelled nor right setten down."

"Heh–heh–heh! Take ye that, Mr. Scott," said Laidlaw.

Mr. Scott answered by a hearty laugh, and the recital of a verse, but I have forgot what it was, and my mother gave him a rap on the knee with her open hand, and said "It is true enough, for a' that."

We were all to dine at Ramseycleuch with the Messrs. Brydon; but Mr. Scott and Mr. Laidlaw went away to look at something before dinner, and I was to follow. On going into the stable-yard at Ramseycleuch, I met with Mr. Scott's liveryman, a far greater original than his master, at whom I asked if the Shirra was come?

"O, ay, lad, the Shirra's come," said he. "Are ye the chiel that maks the auld ballads and sings them?"

I said I fancied I was he that he meant, though I had never made ony very *auld* ballads.

"Ay, then, lad, gae your ways in an' speir for the Shirra. They'll let ye see where he is. He'll be very glad to see you."

During the sociality of the evening, the discourse ran very much on the different breeds of sheep, that curse of the community of Ettrick Forest. The original black-faced forest breed being always called *the short sheep*, and the Cheviot breed *the long sheep*, the disputes at that period ran very high about the practicable profits of each. Mr. Scott, who had come into that remote district to preserve what fragments remained of its legendary lore, was rather bored with the everlasting question of the long and the short sheep. So at length, putting on his most serious calculating face, he turned to Mr. Walter Brydon and said, "I am rather at a loss regarding the merits of this *very* important question. How long must a sheep actually measure to come under the denomination of *a long sheep?*"

Mr. Brydon, who, in the simplicity of his heart, neither perceived the quiz nor the reproof, fell to answer with great sincerity,–"It's the woo, sir–it's the woo that makes the difference. The lang sheep hae the short woo, and the short sheep hae the lang thing; and these are just kind o' names we gie them like." Mr. Scott could not preserve his grave face of strict calculation; it went gradually awry, and a hearty guffaw followed. When I saw the very same words repeated near the beginning of the Black Dwarf, how could I be mistaken of the author? It is true, Johnnie Ballantyne persuaded me into a nominal belief of the contrary, for several years following, but I could never get the better of that and several similar coincidences.

The next day we went off, five in number, to visit the wilds of Rankleburn, to see if on the farms of Buccleuch there were any relics of the Castles of Buccleuch or Mount-Comyn, the ancient and original possession of the Scotts. We found no remains of either tower or fortalice, save an old chapel and church-yard, and a mill and mill-dam, where corn never grew, but where, as old Satchells very appropriately says,

> Had heather-bells been corn of the best,
> The Buccleuch mill would have had a noble grist.

It must have been used for grinding the chief's black mails, which, it is known, were all paid to him in kind. Many of these still continue to be paid in the same way; and if report say true, he would be the better of a mill and kiln on some part of his land at this day, as well as a sterling conscientious miller to receive and render.

Besides having been mentioned by Satchells, there was a remaining tradition in the country that there was a font stone of blue marble, out of which the ancient heirs of Buccleuch were baptized, covered up among the ruins of the old church. Mr. Scott was curious to see if we could discover it; but on going among the ruins we found the rubbish at the spot, where the altar was known to have been, dug out to the foundation,–we knew not by whom, but no font had been found. As there appeared to have been a kind of recess in the eastern gable, we fell a turning over some loose stones, to see if the font was not concealed there, when we came to one half of a small pot, encrusted thick with rust. Mr. Scott's eyes brightened, and he swore it was an ancient consecrated helmet. Laidlaw, however, scratching it minutely out, found it covered with a layer of pitch inside, and then said, "Ay, the truth is, sir, it is neither mair nor less than a piece of a tar pat that some o' the farmers hae been buisting their sheep out o', i' the auld kirk langsyne." Sir Walter's shaggy eyebrows dipped deep over his eyes, and suppressing a smile, he turned and strode away as fast as he could, saying, that "we had just rode all the way to see that there was nothing to *be* seen."

I remember his riding upon a terribly high-spirited horse, which had the perilous fancy of leaping every drain, rivulet, and ditch that came in our way; the consequence was, that he was everlastingly bogging himself, while sometimes the rider kept his seat despite of the animal's plunging, and at other times he was obliged to extricate himself the best way he could. In coming through a place called the Milsey Bog, I said to him, "Mr. Scott, that's the maddest deil of a beast I ever saw. Can ye no gar him tak a wee mair time? He's just out o' ae lair intil another wi' ye."

"Ay," said he, "he and I have been very often, these two days past, like the Pechs; we could stand straight up and tie our shoe-lachets." I did not understand the joke, nor do I yet, but I think these were his words.

We visited the old castles of Thirlestane and Tushilaw, and dined and spent the afternoon, and the night, with Mr. Brydon of Crosslee. Sir Walter was all the while in the highest good-humour, and seemed to enjoy the range of mountain solitude, which we traversed, exceedingly. Indeed, I never saw him otherwise, in the fields. On the rugged mountains–or even toiling in Tweed to the waist, I have seen his glee not only surpass his own, but that of all other men. His memory, or, perhaps, I should say, his recollection, surpasses that of all men whom I ever knew. I saw a pleasant instance of it recorded lately, regarding Campbell's "Pleasures of Hope;" but I think I can relate a more extraordinary one.

He and Skene of Rubislaw and I were out one night, about midnight, leistering kippers in Tweed, and, on going to kindle a light at the Elibank March, we found, to our inexpressible grief, that our coal had gone out. To think of giving up our sport was out of the question; so we had no other shift, save to send Rob Fletcher home, all the way through the darkness, the distance of two miles, for another fiery peat.

While Fletcher was absent, we three sat down on a piece of beautiful greensward, on the brink of the river, and Scott desired me to sing him my ballad of "Gilmanscleuch." Now, be it remembered, that this ballad had never been either printed or penned. I had merely composed it by rote, and, on finishing it, three years before, I had sung it once over to Sir Walter. I began it at his request; but, at the eighth or ninth verse, I stuck in it, and could not get on with another line; on which he began it a second time, and recited it every word from beginning to end. It being a very long ballad, consisting of eighty-eight stanzas, I testified my astonishment. He said that he had lately been out on a pleasure party on the Forth, and that, to amuse the company, he had recited both that ballad and one of Southey's, ("The Abbot of Aberbrothock,") both of which ballads he had only heard once from their respective authors, and he believed he had recited them both without misplacing a word.

Rob Fletcher came at last, and old Laidlaw of the Peel with him, and into the foaming river we plunged, in our frail bark, with a fine blazing light. In a few minutes we came into Gliddy's Weal, the deepest pool in Tweed, when we perceived that our boat gave evident symptoms of sinking. When Scott saw the terror that Peel was in, he laughed till the tears blinded his eyes. Always, the more mischief, the better sport for him! "For God's sake, push her to the side!" roared Peel. "Oh, she goes fine!" said Scott; "An' gin the boat were bottomless, an' seven miles to row;" and, by the time he had well got out the words, down she went to the bottom, plunging us all into Tweed over head and ears. It was no sport to me at all; but that was a glorious night for Sir Walter, and the next day was no worse.

I remember leaving Altrive Lake once with him, accompanied by my dear friend William Laidlaw, and Sir Adam Fergusson, to visit the tremendous solitudes of The Grey Mare's Tail, and Loch Skene. I conducted them through that wild region by a path, which, if not rode by Clavers, was, I dare say, never rode by another gentleman. Sir Adam rode inadvertently into a gulf, and got a sad fright, but Sir Walter, in the very worst paths, never dismounted, save at Loch Skene, to take some dinner. We went to Moffat that night, where we met with some of his family, and such a day and night of glee I never witnessed. Our very perils were matter to him of infinite merriment; and then there was a short-tempered boot-boy at the inn, who wanted to pick a quarrel with him, at which he laughed till the water ran over his cheeks.

I was disappointed in never seeing some incident in his subsequent works laid in a scene resembling the rugged solitude around Loch Skene, for I never saw him survey any with so much attention. A single serious look at a scene generally filled his mind with it, and he seldom took another; but here he took the names of all the hills, their altitudes, and relative situations with regard to one another, and made me repeat them several times. It may occur in some of his works which I have not seen, and I think it will, for he has rarely ever been known to interest himself, either in a scene or a character, which did not appear afterwards in all its most striking peculiarities.

There are not above five people in the world who, I think, know Sir Walter better, or understand his character better than I do; and if I outlive him, which is likely, as I am five months and ten days younger, I shall draw a mental portrait of him, the likeness of which to the original shall not be disputed. In the mean time, this is only a reminiscence, in my own line, of an illustrious friend among the mountains.

The enthusiasm with which he recited, and spoke of our ancient ballads, during that first tour of his through the Forest, inspired me with a determination immediately to begin and imitate them, which I did, and soon grew tolerably good at it. I dedicated "The Mountain Bard" to him:–

> Bless'd be his generous heart for aye;
> He told me where the relic lay,
> Pointed my way with ready will,
> Afar on Ettrick's wildest hill;
> Watch'd my first notes with curious eye,
> And wonder'd at my minstrelsy:
> He little ween'd a parent's tongue
> Such strains had o'er my cradle sung.

## SOUTHEY

My first interview with Mr. Southey was at the Queen's Head inn, in Keswick, where I had arrived, wearied, one evening, on my way to Westmoreland; and not liking to intrude on his family circle that evening, I sent a note up to Greta Hall, requesting him to come down and see me, and drink one half mutchkin along with me. He came on the instant, and stayed with me about an hour and a half. But I was a grieved as well as an astonished man, when I found that he refused all participation in my beverage of rum punch. For a poet to refuse his glass was to me a phenomenon; and I confess I doubted in my own mind, and doubt to this day, if perfect sobriety and transcendent poetical genius can exist together. In Scotland I am sure they cannot. With regard to the English, I shall leave them to settle that among themselves, as they have little that is worth drinking.

Before we had been ten minutes together my heart was knit to Southey, and every hour thereafter my esteem for him increased. I breakfasted with him next morning, and remained with him all that day and the next; and the weather being fine, we spent the time in rambling on the hills and sailing on the lake; and all the time he manifested a delightful flow of spirits, as well as a kind sincerity of manner, repeating convivial poems and ballads, and always between hands breaking jokes on his nephew, young Coleridge, in whom he seemed to take great delight. He gave me, with the utmost readiness, a poem and ballad of his own, for a work which I then projected. I objected to his going with Coleridge and me, for fear of encroaching on his literary labours; and, as I had previously resided a month at Keswick, I knew every scene almost in Cumberland; but he said he was an early riser, and never suffered any task to interfere with his social enjoyments and recreations; and along with us he went both days.

Southey certainly is as elegant a writer as any in the kingdom. But those who would love Southey as well as admire him, must see him, as I did, in the bosom, not only of one lovely family, but of three, all attached to him as a father, and all elegantly maintained and educated, it is generally said, by his indefatigable pen. The whole of Southey's conversation and economy, both at home and afield, left an impression of veneration on my mind, which no future contingency shall ever either extinguish or injure. Both his figure and countenance are imposing, and deep thought is strongly marked in his dark eye; but there is a defect in his eye-lids, for these he has no power of raising; so that, when he looks up, he turns up his face, being unable to raise his eyes; and when he looks towards the top of one of his romantic mountains, one would think he was looking at the zenith. This peculiarity is what will most strike every stranger in the appearance of the accomplished laureate. He does not at all see well at a distance, which made me several times disposed to get into a passion with him, because he did not admire the scenes which I was pointing out. We have only exchanged a few casual letters since that period, and I have never seen this great and good man again.

## WORDSWORTH

I have forgotten what year it was, but it was in the summer that the "Excursion" was first published, when Mr. James Wilson came to me, one day, in Edinburgh, and asked me to come to his mother's house in Queen Street to dinner, and meet Mr. Wordsworth and his lady. I said I should be glad to meet any friend of his kind and venerated mother's at any time, and should certainly come. But not having the least conception that the great poet of the Lakes was in Edinburgh, and James having called him *Mr.* Wordsworth, I took it for the celebrated horse-dealer of the same name, and entertained some shrewd misgivings, how he should chance to be a guest in a house where only the first people in Edinburgh were wont to be invited.

"You will like him very much," said James; "for although he proses a little, he is exceedingly intelligent."

"I dare say he is," returned I; "at all events, he is allowed to be a good judge of horse-flesh!" The Entomologist liked the joke well, and carried it on for some time; and I found, in my tour southward with the celebrated poet, that several gentlemen fell into the same error, expressing themselves as at a loss why I should be travelling the country with a *horse-couper*. He was clothed in a grey russet jacket and pantaloons, be it remembered, and wore a broad-brimmed beaver hat; so that to strangers he doubtless had a very original appearance.

When I finally learned from James that it was the poet of the Lakes whom I was to meet, I was overjoyed, for I admired many of his pieces exceedingly, though I had not then seen his ponderous "Excursion." I listened to him that night as to a superior being, far exalted above the common walks of life. His sentiments seemed just, and his language, though perhaps a little pompous, was pure, sentient, and expressive. We called on several noblemen and gentlemen in company; and all the while he was in Scotland I loved him better and better. Old Dr. Robert Anderson travelled along with us as far as the sources of the Yarrow, and it was delightful to see the deference which Wordsworth paid to that venerable man. We went into my father's cot, and partook of some homely refreshment, visited St. Mary's Lake, which that day was calm, and pure as any mirror; and Mrs. Wordsworth in particular testified great delight with the whole scene. In tracing the windings of the pastoral Yarrow, from its source to its confluence with the sister stream, the poet was in great good-humour, delightful, and most eloquent. Indeed it was impossible to see Yarrow to greater advantage; and yet it failed of the anticipated inspiration; for "Yarrow Visited" is not so sweet or ingenious a poem as "Yarrow Unvisited;" so much is hope superior to enjoyment.

From Selkirk we were obliged to take different routes, as Wordsworth had business in Teviotdale, and I in Eskdale; and, at last, I landed at Ryedale Mount, his delightful dwelling, a day and a night before him and his lady. I found his sister there, however, a pure, ingenuous child of nature; kind, benevolent, and greatly attached to her brother. Her conversation was a true mental treat; and we spent the time with the children delightfully till the poet's arrival.

I dined with him, and called on him several times afterwards, and certainly never met with any thing but the most genuine kindness; therefore people have wondered why I should have indulged in caricaturing his style in the "Poetic Mirror." I have often regretted that myself; but it was merely a piece of ill-nature at an affront which I conceived had been put on me. It was the triumphal arch scene. This anecdote has been told and told again, but never truly; and was likewise brought forward in the "Noctes Ambrosianæ," as a joke; but it was no joke; and the plain, simple truth of the matter was thus:–

It chanced one night, when I was there, that there was a resplendent arch across the zenith, from the one horizon to the other, of something like the aurora borealis, but much brighter. It was a scene that is well remembered, for it struck the country with admiration, as such a phenomenon had never before been witnessed in such perfection; and, as far as I could learn, it had been more brilliant over the mountains and pure waters of Westmoreland than any where else. Well, when word came into the room of the splendid meteor, we all went out to view it; and, on the beautiful platform at Mount Ryedale we were all walking, in twos and threes, arm-in-arm, talking of the phenomenon, and admiring it. Now, be it remembered, that Wordsworth, Professor Wilson, Lloyd, De Quincey, and myself, were present, besides several other literary gentlemen, whose names I am not certain that I remember aright. Miss Wordsworth's arm was in mine, and she was expressing some fears that the splendid stranger might prove ominous, when I, by ill luck, blundered out the following remark, thinking that I was saying a good thing:–"Hout, me'm! it is neither mair nor less than joost a treeumphal airch, raised in honour of the meeting of the poets."

"That's not amiss.–Eh? Eh?–that's very good," said the Professor, laughing. But Wordsworth, who had De Quincey's arm, gave a grunt, and turned on his heel, and leading the little opium-chewer aside, he addressed him in these disdainful and venomous words:– "Poets? Poets?–What does the fellow mean?–Where are they?"

Who could forgive this? For my part, I never can, and never will! I admire Wordsworth; as who does not, whatever they may pretend? but for that short sentence I have a lingering ill-will at him which I cannot get rid of. It is surely presumption in any man to circumscribe all human excellence within the narrow sphere of his own capacity. The "*Where are they?*" was too bad! I have always some hopes that De Quincey was *leeing*, for I did not myself hear Wordsworth utter the words.

I have only a single remark to make on the poetry of Wordsworth, and I do it because I never saw the remark made before. It relates to the richness of his works for quotations. For these they are a mine that is altogether inexhaustible. There is nothing in nature that you may not get a quotation out of Wordsworth to suit, and a quotation too that breathes the very soul of poetry. There are only three books in the world that are worth the opening in search of mottos and quotations, and all of them are alike rich. These are, the Old Testament, Shakspeare, and the poetical works of Wordsworth, and, strange to say, the "Excursion" abounds most in them.

## ALLAN CUNNINGHAM

One day, about the beginning of autumn, some three-and-twenty years ago, as I was herding my master's ewes on the great hill of Queensberry, in Nithsdale, I perceived two men coming towards me, who appeared to be strangers. I saw, by their way of walking, they were not shepherds, and could not conceive what the men were seeking there, where there was neither path nor aim towards any human habitation. However, I stood staring about me, till they came up, always ordering my old dog Hector to silence in an authoritative style, he being the only servant I had to attend to my orders. The men approached me rather in a breathless state, from climbing the hill. The one was a tall thin man, of a fairish complexion, and pleasant intelligent features, seemingly approaching to forty, and the other a dark ungainly youth of about eighteen, with a boardly frame for his age, and strongly marked manly features–the very model of Burns, and exactly such a man. Had they been of the same age, it would not have been easy to distinguish the one from the other.

The eldest came up and addressed me frankly, asking me if I was Mr. Harkness's shepherd, and if my name was James Hogg? to both of which queries I answered cautiously in the affirmative, for I was afraid they were come to look after me with an accusation regarding some of the lasses. The younger stood at a respectful distance, as if I had been the Duke of Queensberry, instead of a ragged servant lad herding sheep. The other seized my hand, and said, "Well, then, sir, I am glad to see you. There is not a man in Scotland whose hand I am prouder to hold."

I could not say a single word in answer to this address; but when he called me SIR, I looked down at my bare feet and ragged coat, to remind the man whom he was addressing. But he continued: "My name is James Cunningham, a name unknown to you, though yours is not entirely so to me; and this is my younger brother Allan, the greatest admirer that you have on earth, and himself a young aspiring poet of some promise. You will be so kind as excuse this intrusion of ours on your solitude, for, in truth, I could get no peace either night or day with Allan, till I consented to come and see you."

I then stepped down the hill to where Allan Cunningham still stood, with his weather-beaten cheek toward me, and, seizing his hard brawny hand, I gave it a hearty shake, saying something as kind as I was able, and, at the same time, I am sure as stupid as it possibly could be. From that moment we were friends; for Allan has none of the proverbial Scottish caution about him; he is all heart together, without reserve either of expression or manner: you at once see the unaffected benevolence, warmth of feeling, and firm independence, of a man conscious of his own rectitude and mental energies. Young as he was, I had heard of his name, although slightly, and, I think, seen one or two of his juvenile pieces. Of an elder brother of his, Thomas Mouncey, I had, previous to that, conceived a very high idea, and I always marvel how he could possibly put his poetical vein under lock and key, as he did all at once; for he certainly then bade fair to be the first of Scottish bards.

I had a small bothy upon the hill, in which I took my breakfast and dinner on wet days, and rested myself. It was so small, that we had to walk in on all-fours; and when we were in, we could not get up our heads any way, but in a sitting posture. It was exactly my own length, and, on the one side, I had a bed of rushes, which served likewise as a seat; on this we all three sat down, and there we spent the whole afternoon,–and, I am sure, a happier group of three never met on the hill of Queensberry. Allan brightened up prodigiously after he got into the dark bothy, repeating all his early pieces of poetry, and part of his brother's, to me. The two brothers partook heartily, and without reserve, of my scrip and bottle of sweet milk, and the elder Mr. Cunningham had a strong bottle with him–I have forgot whether it was brandy or rum, but I remember it was excessively good, and helped to keep up our spirits to a late hour. Thus began at that bothy in the wilderness a friendship, and a mutual attachment between two aspiring Scottish peasants, over which the shadow of a cloud has never yet passed.

From that day forward I failed not to improve my acquaintance with the Cunninghams. I visited them several times at Dalswinton, and never missed an opportunity of meeting with Allan when it was in my power to do so. I was astonished at the luxuriousness of his fancy. It was boundless; but it was the luxury of a rich garden overrun with rampant weeds. He was likewise then a great mannerist in expression, and no man could mistake his verses for those of any other man. I remember seeing some imitations of Ossian by him, which I thought exceedingly good; and it struck me that that style of composition was peculiarly fitted for his vast and fervent imagination.

When Cromek's "Nithsdale and Galloway Relics" came to my hand, I at once discerned the strains of my friend, and I cannot describe with what sensations of delight I first heard Mr. Morrison read the "Mermaid of Galloway," while at every verse I kept naming the author. It had long been my fixed opinion, that if a person could once succeed in the genuine ballad style, his muse was adequate for any other; and after seeing Allan's strains in that work, I concluded that no man could calculate what he was capable of.

I continued my asseverations to all my intimate friends, *that Allan Cunningham was the author of all that was beautiful in the work*. Gray, who had an attachment to Cromek, denied it positively on his friend's authority. Grieve joined him. Morrison, I saw, had strong lurking suspicions; but then he stickled for the ancient genius of Galloway. When I went to Sir Walter Scott, (then Mr. Scott,) I found him decidedly of the same opinion as myself; and he said he wished to God we had that valuable and original young man fairly out of Cromek's hands again.

I next wrote a review of the work, in which I laid the saddle on the right horse, and sent it to Mr. Jeffrey; but, after retaining it for some time, he returned it with a note, saying, that he had read over the article, and was convinced of the fraud which had been attempted to be played off on the public, but he did not think it worthy of exposure. I have the article, and card, by me to this day.

Mr. Cunningham's style of poetry is greatly changed of late for the better. I have never seen any style improved so much. It is free of all that crudeness and mannerism that once marked it so decidedly. He is now uniformly lively, serious, descriptive, or pathetic, as he changes his subject; but formerly he jumbled all these together, as in a boiling caldron, and when once he began, it was impossible to calculate where or when he was going to end. If these reminiscences should meet his friendly eye, he will pardon them, on the score that they are the effusions of a heart that loves to dwell on some scenes of former days.

## GALT

I first met with this most original and most careless writer at Greenock, in the summer of 1804, as I and two friends were setting out on a tour through the Hebrides; so that Galt and I have been acquainted these twenty-eight years.

That was a memorable evening for me, for it was the first time I ever knew that my name had been known beyond the precincts of my native wilds, and was not a little surprised at finding it so well known in a place called Greenock, at the distance of one hundred miles. I had by some chance heard the name of the town, and had formed an idea of its being a mouldy-looking village, on an ugly coast. How agreeably was I deceived, not only in the appearance of the town, but the metal which it contained!

My two friends and I, purposing to remain there only a night, had no sooner arrived, than word had flown it seems through the town that a strange poetical chap had arrived there, and a deputation was sent to us, inviting us to a supper at the Tontine Hotel. Of course we accepted; and, on going there, found no fewer than thirty gentlemen assembled to welcome us, and among the rest was Mr. Galt, then a tall thin young man, with something a little dandyish in his appearance. He was dressed in a frock-coat and new top-boots; and it being then the fashion to wear the shirt collars as high as the eyes, Galt wore his the whole of that night with the one side considerably above his ear, and the other flapped over the collar of his frock-coat down to his shoulder. He had another peculiarity, which appeared to me a singular instance of perversity. He walked with his spectacles on, and conversed with them on; but when he read he took them off. In short, from his first appearance, one would scarcely have guessed him to be a man of genius.

The first thing that drew my attention to him was an argument about the moral tendency of some of Shakspeare's plays, in which, though he had two opponents, and one of them both obstinate and loquacious, he managed his part with such good-nature and such strong emphatic reasoning, that my heart whispered me again and again, "This is no common youth." Then his stories of old-fashioned and odd people were so infinitely amusing, that his conversation proved one of the principal charms of that enchanting night. The conversation of that literary community of friends at Greenock, as well as their songs and stories, was much above what I had ever been accustomed to hear. I formed one other intimate and highly valued acquaintance that night, which continued with increasing affection till his lamented death: I allude to James Park, Esq., junior, of that place, Mr. Galt's firm and undeviating friend. I like Galt's writings exceedingly, and have always regretted that he has depicted so much that is selfish and cunning in the Scottish character, and so little that is truly amiable, when he could have done it so well. Of my literary acquaintances in London I dare not say a word until I get back to my native mountains again, when I expect that my reminiscences of them will form a theme of great delight.

## LOCKHART

When it is considered what literary celebrity Lockhart has gained so early in life, and how warm and disinterested a friend he has been to me, it argues but little for my sagacity that I scarcely recollect any thing of our first encounters. He was a mischievous Oxford puppy, for whom I was terrified, dancing after the young ladies, and drawing caricatures of every one who came in contact with him. But then I found him constantly in company with all the better rank of people with whom I associated, and consequently it was impossible for me not to meet with him. I dreaded his eye terribly; and it was not without reason, for he was very fond of playing tricks on me, but always in such a way, that it was impossible to lose temper with him. I never parted company with him that my judgment was not entirely jumbled with regard to characters, books, and literary articles of every description. Even his household economy seemed clouded in mystery; and if I got any explanation, it was sure not to be the right thing. It may be guessed how astonished I was one day, on perceiving six black servants waiting at his table upon six white gentlemen! Such a train of Blackamoors being beyond my comprehension, I asked for an explanation; but got none, save that he found them very useful and obliging poor fellows, and that they did not look for much wages, beyond a mouthful of meat.

A young lady hearing me afterwards making a fuss about such a phenomenon, and swearing that the Blackamoors would break my young friend, she assured me that Mr. Lockhart had only *one* black servant, but that when the master gave a dinner to his friends, the servant, knowing there would be enough, and to spare, for all, invited his friends also. Lockhart always kept a good table, and a capital stock of liquor, especially Jamaica rum, and by degrees I grew not so frightened to visit him.

After Wilson and he, and Sym and I had resolved on supporting

Blackwood, it occasioned us to be oftener together; but Lockhart contrived to keep my mind in the utmost perplexity for years, on all things that related to that Magazine. Being often curious to know when the tremendous articles appeared who were the authors, and being sure I could draw nothing out of either Wilson, or Sym, I always repaired to Lockhart to ask him, awaiting his reply with fixed eyes and a beating heart. Then, with his cigar in his mouth, his one leg flung carelessly over the other, and without the symptom of a smile on his face, or one twinkle of mischief in his dark grey eye, he would father the articles on his brother, Captain Lockhart, or Peter Robertson, or Sheriff Cay, or James Wilson, or that queer fat body, Dr. Scott; and sometimes on James and John Ballantyne, and Sam Anderson, and poor Baxter. Then away I flew with the wonderful news to my other associates; and if any remained incredulous, I swore the facts down through them; so that before I left Edinburgh I was accounted the greatest liar that was in it, except one. I remember once, at a festival of the Dilletanti Society, that Lockhart was sitting next me, and charming my ear with some story of authorship. I have forgot what it was; but think it was about somebody reviewing his own book. On which I said the incident was such a capital one, that I would give a crown bowl of punch to ascertain if it were true.

"What?" said Bridges; "did any body ever hear the like of that? I hope you are not suspecting your young friend of telling you a falsehood?"

"Haud your tongue Davie, for ye ken naething about it," said I. "Could ye believe it, man, that that callant never tauld me the truth a' his days but aince, an' that was merely by chance, an' without the least intention on his part?" These blunt accusations diverted Lockhart greatly, and only encouraged him to farther tricks.

I soon found out that the coterie of my literary associates had made it up to act on O'Dogherty's principle, never to deny a thing that they had *not* written, and never to acknowledge one that they *had*. On which I determined that, in future, I would sign my name or designation to every thing I published, that I might be answerable to the world only for my own offences. But as soon as the rascals perceived this, they signed my name as fast as I did. They then contrived the incomparable "Noctes Ambrosianæ," for the sole purpose of putting all the sentiments into the Shepherd's mouth, which they durst not avowedly say themselves, and those too often applying to my best friends. The generality of mankind have always used me ill till I came to London.

The thing that most endeared Lockhart to me at that early period was some humorous poetry which he published anonymously in Blackwood's Magazine, and which I still regard as the best of the same description in the kingdom. He at length married on the same day with myself, into the house of my great friend and patron, and thenceforward I regarded him as belonging to the same family with me, I a step-son, and he a legitimate younger brother.

Of all the practical jokes that ever Lockhart played off on the public in his thoughtless days, the most successful and ludicrous was that about Dr. Scott. He was a strange-looking, bald-headed, bluff little man, that practised as a dentist, both in Glasgow and Edinburgh, keeping a good house and hospitable table in both, and considered skilful; but for utter ignorance of every thing literary, he was not to be matched among a dozen street porters with ropes round their necks. This droll old tippling sinner was a joker in his way, and to Lockhart and his friends a subject of constant mystifications and quizzes, which he partly saw through; but his uncommon vanity made him like the notice, and when at last the wags began to publish songs and ballads in his name, O then he could not resist going into the delusion! and though he had a horrid bad voice, and hardly any ear, he would roar and sing the songs in every company as his own.

Ignorant and uneducated as he was, Lockhart sucked his brains so cleverly, and crammed "The Odontist's" songs with so many of the creature's own peculiar phrases, and the names and histories of his obscure associates, that, though I believe the man could scarce spell a note of three lines, even his intimate acquaintances were obliged to swallow the hoax, and by degrees "The Odontist" passed for a first-rate convivial bard, that had continued to eat and drink and draw teeth for fifty years, and more, without ever letting the smallest corner of the napkin appear to be lifted, under which his wonderful talents had lain concealed. I suspect Captain Tom Hamilton, the original O'Dogherty, had also some hand in that ploy; at least he seemed to enjoy it as if he had, for though he pretended to be a high and starched Whig, he was always engaged with these madcap Tories, and the foremost in many of their wicked contrivances.

Well, at last this joke took so well, and went so far, that shortly after the appearance of "The Lament for Captain Patton," one of John Lockhart's best things, by-the-bye, but which was published in the doctor's name, he happened to take a trip to Liverpool in a steam-boat, and had no sooner arrived there than he was recognised and hailed as Ebony's glorious Odontist! The literary gentry got up a public dinner for him in honour of his great and versatile genius, and the body very coolly accepted the compliment, replying to the toasts and speeches, and all the rest of it. And what is more, none of them ever found him out; which to me, who knew him so well, was quite wonderful. What would I have given to have been at that meeting! I am sure Dean Swift himself never played off a more successful hit than this of "The Odontist."

He is long since dead; but he left a name behind him which has continued to this day, when I have let the secret out. Had he lived till now, I am persuaded his works would have swelled out to volumes, and would have been published in his name, with his portrait at the beginning. I never heard whether he left Lockhart any legacy or not; but he certainly ought to have done so, and both to him and Captain Hamilton. Even the acute Johnie Ballantyne was entrapped, and requested me several times to bring him acquainted with that Dr. Scott, who was one of the most original and extraordinary fellows he had ever met with in print, and he wished much to have the honour of being his publisher. In answer to this request I could only laugh in the bibliopole's face, having been for that once in the true secret. I could tell several stories fully as good as this; but as John is now a reformed character, to all appearance, I shall spare him for the present. Wilson's and his merry doings of those days would make a singular book, and perhaps I may attempt to detail them before I die.

## SYM

I first met with that noble and genuine old Tory, the renowned Timothy Tickler, in his own hospitable mansion of South Side, *alias* George's Square, in the south corner of Edinburgh, and to which I was introduced by one of his sister's sons, I think Mr. Robert Wilson, the professor's second brother.

At the very first appearance of my weekly paper "The Spy," Mr. Sym interested himself for it. Not only did his name appear first on the list of subscribers, but he recommended it strongly to all his friends and acquaintances, as a paper worthy of being patronised. Some of the fine madams pointed out to him a few inadvertences, or more properly, absurdities, which had occurred in the papers; but he replied, "O, I don't deny that; but I like them the better for these, as they show me at once the character of the writer. I believe him to be a very great blockhead; still I maintain, that there is some smeddum in him."

As the paper went on, he sent me some written advices anonymously, which were excellent, and which I tried to conform to as much as I could. He also sent me some very clever papers for the work, which appeared in it, but all the while kept himself closely concealed from me. It is natural to suppose that I had the most kindly feeling towards this friendly stranger; but it was not till I became acquainted with the Wilsons long afterwards that I knew who he was. When Mr. Robert informed me that he was his uncle, I was all impatience to see him.

A little while before the conclusion of "The Spy," Mr. Aikman, the publisher, told me one day that he suspected the friend who had interested himself so much in my success was a Mr. Sym; but I had never heard more than merely his name, and imagined him to be some very little man about Leith. Judge of my astonishment, when I was admitted by a triple-bolted door into a grand house in George's Square, and introduced to its lord, an uncommonly fine-looking elderly gentleman, about seven feet high, and as straight as an arrow! His hair was whitish, his complexion had the freshness and ruddiness of youth, his looks and address full of kindness and benevolence; but whenever he stood straight up, (for he had always to stoop about half way when speaking to a common-sized man like me,) then you could not help perceiving a little of the haughty air of the determined and independent old aristocrat.

From that time forward, during my stay in Edinburgh, Mr. Sym's hospitable mansion was the great evening resort of his three nephews and me; sometimes there were a few friends beside, of whom Lockhart and Samuel Anderson were mostly two; but we four for certain; and there are no jovial evenings of my by-past life which I reflect on with greater delight than those. Tickler is completely an original, as any man may see who has attended to his remarks; for there is no sophistry there, they are every one his own. Nay, I don't believe that North has, would, or durst put a single sentence into his mouth that had not proceeded out of it. No, no; although I was made a scape-goat, no one, and far less a nephew, might do so with Timothy Tickler. His reading, both ancient and modern, is boundless, his taste and perception acute beyond those of other men; his satire keen and biting; but at the same time his good-humour is altogether inexhaustible, save when ignited by coming in collision with Whig or Radical principles. Still, there being no danger of that with me, he and I never differed in one single sentiment in our lives, excepting on the comparative merits of some Strathspey reels.

But the pleasantest part of our fellowship is yet to describe. At a certain period of the night our entertainer knew by the longing looks which I cast to a beloved corner of the dining-room what was wanting. Then, with "O, I beg your pardon, Hogg, I was forgetting," he would take out a small gold key that hung by a chain of the same precious metal to a particular button-hole, and stalk away as tall as the life, open two splendid fiddle cases, and produce their contents, first the one, and then the other; but always keeping the best to himself. I'll never forget with what elated dignity he stood straight up in the middle of that floor and rosined his bow: there was a twist of the lip, and an upward beam of the eye, that were truly sublime. Then down we sat side by side, and began–at first gently, and with easy motion, like skilful grooms, keeping ourselves up for the final heat, which was slowly but surely approaching. At the end of every tune we took a glass, and still our enthusiastic admiration of the Scottish tunes increased–our energies of execution redoubled, till, ultimately, it became not only a complete and well-contested race, but a trial of strength to determine which should drown the other. The only feelings short of ecstasy, that came across us in these enraptured moments, were caused by hearing the laugh and joke going on with our friends, as if no such thrilling strains had been flowing. But if Sym's eye chanced at all to fall on them, it instantly retreated upwards again in mild indignation. To his honour be it mentioned, he has left me a legacy of that inestimable violin, provided that I outlive him. But not for a thousand such would I part with my old friend.

# ALTRIVE TALES

## THE ADVENTURES OF CAPTAIN JOHN LOCHY,

### WRITTEN BY HIMSELF.

I, JOHN LOCHY, was born I know not where, and I was the son of I know not whom; but my birth happened in that year in which the third William came to the throne; and that I was born of illustrious parents there can be no doubt, as the following circumstance completely and satisfactorily proves.

It happened on this wise:–As three great chiefs, with their followers, were going out on the 17th of August to hunt the deer in the forest of Glen-Lochy, in Breadalbane, at a certain pass they heard the cries of an infant, at which they were greatly amazed. They all stood still and listened, but could see nothing, for it was hardly yet day; but they heard the cries, and, following them, came to a little chest placed on the verge of the river, and there was I, lying nestled among flannels, with plenty of fine baby-clothes, and by me a small box of jewels, and this ticket on my breast:

"This boy is nobly born. His name is John. To preserve his life from his blood-thirsty relations, his mother has been compelled to leave him in the path of the gallant chief whose heart she can trust. God bless and protect my son!"

"There will be watchers near," said the chief of M'Nab; "let us spread ourselves all about and watch till sun-rise, and we shall be sure to catch them. If any perceive fliers, let them pursue and seize them, nor give up the pursuit till they are taken, though it last for a thousand miles."

They did so, and a little after daylight they perceived two riders flying westward along a height called Bovain. Several horsemen gave chase, but took a wrong direction, and lost them; but they afterwards discovered by the tracks of their horses that they had doubled back and gone down Loch-Tay, where they lost all traces of them. They took one man prisoner on the other side of the glen, apparently a peasant; but of him they could make nothing. He spoke a little of the Low Country tongue, and denied all knowledge of, or connexion with the babe. But he could give no account of what he was seeking in that country, farther than that he wanted to see a hunt.

There being three great chiefs present, it was resolved that they should cast lots for the honour of bringing up the noble boy; and the lot fell on the Earl of Breadalbane; so I was put to nurse with a poor young widow, and called John Lochy, after the river on the banks of which I was found.

This circumstance, it was said at the time, raised a great deal of curiosity, not only among the country people, but the principal gentry of the kingdom, and one or two very plausible conjectures were started, and some pains taken to trace them. But all inquiry was hushed after the earl received an anonymous letter which was put into his hand at Perth, in the midst of a great convocation of gentlemen. What that letter contained no man knows; but I was immediately removed into a place in the wilds of Glenorchy, and kept there in a farm-house in the strictest concealment for a number of years. In all that time I remember of little else save a fat old black dog, to which I was greatly attached, and a poor woman who visited the house very often, bringing the farmer's wife many presents; of small value certainly, but they had the effect of making her a welcome guest there. To me she was particularly so, for many little nic-nacs she bestowed on me, with sweetmeats, when none saw and kindly words. Her name was Mora.

There was one time in particular, that she hovered about the house like a spirit, and was seen early and late in the environs. At length she came in to the farmer and his wife with many tears, and told them that some evil awaited me, and that if I was their own son they had better look to it. If I was not their own son, she perceived from the second-sight that my danger was still the greater; and she charged them, as they valued the boy's protector, to remove me secretly to him, or send me to some other concealment for a time.

The farmer laughed at Mora's predictions, but the wife seemed much concerned. No steps being taken for my safety, I was that night taken away. The farm having been formerly possessed by two tenants, the dwelling consisted of two houses distinct from one another. In the one the farmer and his wife slept in one apartment, and a maid-servant and myself in the other; and the farmer's son and the other servants in the house opposite. At midnight a fellow stole into the house and took me, sound asleep, from the maid's bosom, without ever awakening her; and there being two other men at the door, they all three mounted on ponies and fled, taking me along with them: my favourite fat dog Cowlan, who never parted with me, also went with us.

No sooner was I taken out at the door and mounted on the little nag before the ruffian Highlander, than poor Mora awakened the farmer, for it seems she had been watching outside the house that night. He was crabbed, and bid her go about her business, for she was raving; but she persisted in assuring the pair that I was carried off to be murdered, and that if I was not rescued, every person about the house would be hanged. This being rather a serious consideration for old Donald, he ran into the other apartment and awakened the sleepy maiden, when he found poor Mora's intelligence confirmed. She had by this time roused the inmates of the other house, and all were ready for the pursuit in a few minutes. Mora perceived the route the ruffians had taken, a track not leading towards any habitation; but by a singular providence Cowlan kept barking now and then all the way behind us, and sometimes howling, which kept the pursuers close on our track. Mora pursued with the rest; and the waste being so full of pools, sharp rocks, and other impediments, the pursuers gained rapidly on the riders. The latter at length paused, and high words arose among them, when, by the cover of a deep ravine, the pursuers, consisting of the farmer, his son, a lad of eighteen, two shepherds, and poor Mora, got close to the three ruffians; so close, that they heard every word they said. Two of the men were for saving my life, sending me privately abroad, and earning the high reward. The other, the huge fellow who had held me all the way before him with very little regard for my comfort, seemed to acquiesce in the proposal, but alighted first from his pony, taking me off with him. I was wrapped in a blanket, and had a linen night-gown on; and I well remember that when the fellow alighted he fell a groping for my bare feet, and seizing one of them close by the ancle, in one moment the blanket dropped from about me, and with a tremendous swing he flung me from the precipice into the loch.

I uttered a loud shriek while flying through the air, which was responded to by one ten times louder from poor Mora, who in one moment sprung from her concealment, and, rushing forward, tumbled the gigantic ruffian over the cliff into the loch, from which he never more arose, having been brained in his fall. One of the shepherds inadvertently seized one of the other ruffians, but the two, between them, knocked the shepherd down and escaped, the attention of the party being taken up with something else.

The moment that my fall made the plash in the loch old fat Cowlan was barking and swimming. The place where the ruffian made the plunge he never regarded, but swam towards me, baying with all his energy. He was one of those loquacious animals that never could do any thing either good or bad in silence; every effort was accompanied by loud and incessant barking, and, in a time, as was said, inconceivably short, he had me at the side, trailing by the night-gown; and though he could not then bark aloud, he was still making a constant attempt at it with his mouth shut.

I lay a good while in Mora's bosom before coming to myself, and was then taken home on the pony which had belonged to the dead ruffian; so narrowly did I escape drowning in this savage place by night, owing to the sagacity of honest Cowlan.

This mountain lake into which I was cast is called Loch Dochart. It is not the Loch Dochart at the head of Breadalbane, lying at the foot of Ben More, but one situated in the rudest and wildest place of the Braes of Glenorchy, two or three miles to the westward of Inverouran. Often have I visited the scene, and stood on the top of the cliff from which I was cast. The body of the ruffian was identified as that of Alaster Campbell of Screegan in Upper Lorn, a notorious blackguard and smuggler; and the investigation of the case caused great and general astonishment.

I was shortly after removed to Inverness, and my name changed for a season. But there was a dark and mysterious plot against my existence, which it required the utmost vigilance to avert. My poor guardian angel, Mora, found me out once more, pressed me to her bosom, and wept over me, telling me that my father's, as well as my mother's kinsmen, sought my life, and had emissaries watching me for a convenient opportunity of putting their design in execution; and she assured me that unless I followed her directions I should never see the end of the week.

The next day, when I should have gone to school, I eloped with her, and for three years lived under her kind protection, wandering from one place to another, she being in constant terror for my life. I had no such terror; but being a stout boy, and fond of horses, I hired with Sir James Innes as a groom. There I remained till I was seventeen, and, as far as I remember, was regarded as a headstrong, quarrelsome, and precipitate young man. But here it seemed that I had been again discovered, and a train laid for my life.

Sir James being at that time engaged in building, a number of workmen were still coming and going about the premises, and, among the rest, a sort of genteel vagrant lingered about the house for some time as a glazier. This fellow being forward and spruce, often succeeded in engaging Sir James in conversation; and one day he says to him, "What sort of a blade is he, this dashing groom of yours?"

"I know nothing about him," said Sir James, "save that he is an active stout young fellow, who manages his horses well, and keeps his own ground with his associates."

"What is his name, if you please, Sir James?"

"They call him John, but what more I never inquired, although he has been here for several years."

"I should like well to know his name, and where he comes from; for, to tell the truth, I have some suspicions of the fellow. Does your honour think he is honest enough?"

"*Honest enough* is rather a trying term, Mr. Glazier, and applicable to few. I doubt if either you or I could be tried by that standard: for my part, I never heard aught against the young fellow's honesty."

"O! it is merely vague suspicion in me, Sir James, and I mentioned it to put so honest and confiding a gentleman on his guard. I thought I perceived a watch one day in the young rogue's possession quite unsuitable in value to his rank. I looked far wrong if it was not a gold one, and a very costly one too."

"That is quite impossible; the fellow is as poor as a buck in April," said Sir James, turning from the insidious glazier with a laugh.

"O! it is quite probable I may have been mistaken, Sir James," said the glazier, following after him, and speaking in a restrained voice. "Pray don't mention it to any body, for I wish not to do evil to any man. No, no, Sir James, far be it from me to injure any man who has his bread to win, like myself, with the sweat of his brow. I *must* have been mistaken; some gilt thing perhaps with sham jewels. Pray think no more of it."

Sir James went home, and told his lady what the glazier had insinuated against poor John. She looked a little alarmed, but said not a word, till, going to her bureau, she found her own gold watch, necklace, and jewels missing. There was no time to be lost. Sir James rode straight to Inverness, procured a warrant, and I was that same evening taken prisoner while playing at coits with the workmen. I was so perfectly unconscious of any crime, that I could not believe that it was not a trick they were playing off on me, and unluckily I stood on the defensive, and mauled the constables to some purpose. Being at last overpowered and mastered, my person was searched, and nothing of a suspicious nature being found, they demanded the key of my trunk. Without hesitation, I told them that it was sewed to the inside of my breeches pocket, for fear of losing it, and that these were lying on the lid of my trunk. They found it accordingly, searched, and, at the very first, lying openly in the shottle of my trunk they found the whole of the stolen property, with the exception of some gold pieces. I swore that the officers had brought it with them, for that it was never put there by me; but they laughed at my asseverations, led me to Inverness, and threw me into prison. But lo and behold! ere ever the investigation by the sheriff took place the glazier had vanished, and could not be produced as a witness. He was seen going up Strath-Nairn with his budget on his back; but could not be traced farther. But the evidence against me being irrefragable, I was returned to prison to stand trial at the next assizes.

This was a very melancholy time for me; but I never despaired; for though I knew very little about religion and a divine Providence, and cared less, I had some idea of a principle of justice governing the world, and conceived that I could not possibly be hanged for a crime that I had never thought of, far less committed; else it was the most enormous thing that ever was done, and sufficient to sink a whole nation.

When the day of trial arrived my advocate urged me strongly to plead guilty to the charge; which I refused with disdain, and told him that if my hands were free I would knock him down for such heinous advice. He told me if I confessed he would procure me the modified sentence of banishment for life; but if I refused I was a gone man. He knew nothing of my spirit. I would have been cut to inches before I would have confessed; so I boldly pleaded *Not Guilty*. My counsel was useless. He had no hope, and therefore made no exertion. The counsel for the Crown made a bitter speech against me, and demanded a verdict of guilty. But the judge, Lord Erskine, the only sensible man among them, in summing up the evidence took a different view of the matter, and plainly insinuated that he suspected the glazier. "Here is a fellow," said his lordship, "of whom nobody knows any thing, and who, in virtue of his profession, has access to every room in the house; and here is a simple fellow again, who has his key lying openly on the head of his trunk. It really appears to me, gentlemen, that if this young fellow had stolen the property he would have laid it more carefully by, or, at least, have secured the key better; and I am the more confirmed in this opinion from a private assurance that from some great political or selfish motive an attempt was formerly made to take away his life, and I suspect this to be another clandestine effort, proceeding from the same source. I therefore charge you to give the prisoner the advantage of these suspicious circumstances in the chain of evidence."

Quite secure now in being dealt with according to justice, I wondered what the fellows could mean in remaining so long inclosed, and keeping people's hearts and feelings on the rack, bawling and reasoning about a thing which could not admit of any doubt. At length they returned, and, to show how little a jury is to be depended upon, brought in a verdict by a majority of one voice, finding me guilty. The scoundrels! How my heart burned with indignation at their stupidity! The worthy judge, one of the Marr family, was astounded, and asked if that was really their verdict, when, being answered fiercely in the affirmative, he said that nothing then remained for him but to pronounce sentence accordingly; and there was I, as innocent of the crime as the child unborn, sentenced to be hanged by the neck on the 29th of May.

I was highly indignant at being used in this manner, and never would listen to any of their admonitions about repentance and confession; and when they asked whether I would have a Protestant or Catholic clergyman to attend me, I answered that I would neither have the one nor the other; and when any of the rascals came to pray with me I thanked them for their kindness, but begged to dispense with their services. One Parson M'Coll presuming to fall a-puling, contrary to my injunctions, I cursed him, and then sung him a Gaelic song, which soon put an end to his absurd devotions. However, after suffering all the agonies of an anticipated shameful death, at the very last a reprieve arrived from the queen for John Campbell, *alias* Lochy, by whom obtained I never knew, though most likely by Lord Erskine, my enlightened judge: a pardon soon followed.

The terms of the reprieve for John Campbell, &c. excited my curiosity exceedingly, and I judged that I could be no less than of the family either of Argyle or Breadalbane; and while indulging in these grand ideas I was visited by poor Mora, who charged me never to make any attempts at a research of that nature; but if I at all valued my life, to haste from this country as soon as liberated, for there was a power combined against my life which I could not elude, and of which I had now had dreadful evidence. As I could not but love and respect this poor woman, I resolved to follow her advice, and made a solemn promise to her that day to be guided by her direction.

The very day on which the order arrived for my liberation a carriage with the M'Kenzie's arms waited for me, and a livery servant whispered in my ear that he was sent by Mora to conduct me from my enemies in safety. The hint was sufficient. I stepped into the coach, in which was seated a lovely and splendidly dressed female, apparently below thirty years of age. She received me in silence, but regarded me with great interest. She wore a snowy veil which reached to her knee, and through that she appeared lovely beyond conception; but she took care never once to put it aside. When she spoke, her voice thrilled to my inmost soul, for it struck me that the voice was familiar to my ear. Can this be Mora? thought I to myself. Can this angelic creature be my mother, that she takes such an interest in me? The fond supposition for several minutes thrilled my soul; but the delight was almost transitory, and my heart told me that it could not be poor Mora nor my mother whom I saw there blooming in youth and beauty.

We went on board a vessel that waited for us at a bay down the firth, and the carriage returned. When we entered the cabin there was an officer's uniform lying, in which the divine creature desired me to array myself, retiring till I did so. Every thing was complete, and the sword had a basket of silver, and there was a J. and an L. engraved on it; but no appearance of a C.; and from that moment John Lochy became my confirmed name.

When the lady re-entered I took off my plumed helmet and made her a graceful bow, for I had learned good manners under Sir James, although only a groom, having a natural turn for gentility, which I suppose I had a good right to have, as you shall hear. Well, I said I made a graceful bow to the lady; so I did; but it was a humoursome one, a thing done in jest; as if I had said, "Here I am, madam, what think you of your servant now?" Instead of making me any reply, the tears burst into her eyes, and she threw her arms around my neck and kissed me. Yes, that lovely, that divine creature embraced and kissed me; and though it was through a veil of cambric lace, I never got a kiss so sweet. I would fain have returned the salutation; but she repulsed me gently, seeming to repent of what she had done. I think she must have been my mother after all.

We sailed the whole night, and yet the conversation never flagged. I implored her to tell me of my parents; and after long entreaty she told me a part, and that small part was all that ever I knew of them. I remember yet every word she said.

"Your parentage you never must know, for with that knowledge all your prospects and happiness in this world would become extinct, and most probably the day that you came to the knowledge of it would prove your last, and the last of others. One gallant knight has suffered death on your account already; and were the secret of your birth divulged, Heaven knows what would be the consequence. Enquire no more concerning it; but be assured of this, that the best blood of the kingdom flows in your veins."

"This is strange, and most oppressive!" said I. "It is not to be borne.–Of course then I am an illegitimate child?"

"No," replied she, "your father and mother were married, solemnly married; but the houses of both your parents have inadvertently, and without intending it, rendered you illegitimate, and, by an act of parliament, obtained by power in an unhallowed rage, ere ever you saw the light, made you an outcast and a vagabond on the earth; and though only one individual out of the two families knows of your existence, you see how you have been persecuted, and will be to the death. Therefore, for the sake of all that is dear to you and to me, never enquire more about your parents: in three days I will present you with a cornet's commission in Wharton's dragoons. Lord Wharton himself, the colonel's father, has procured it for you: look to him as your patron, and win your way to rank and honour in the service of your country."

Obedience and respect being my bounden duty, to such a sweet and benevolent being as this, I promised that I never would disgrace the good sword which her kindness had put in my hand, and that I would never enquire farther about my parents. I only begged to have her own address, and she should be to me father and mother, sister and brother, as well as the earthly object of my idolatry. She declined giving me it, saying it could be of no avail to me, as she was only commissioned to put me in a fair way to honour and fame, and might never have it in her power to assist me farther, or haply to see me again. With this answer I was obliged to be content, though my heart yearned for more of her dear society.

The day following the hostel boy said to me, "Captain, your horse is come;" on which I went to the stable, and found a jet-black steed of great beauty, and fully caparisoned. Of all the gifts I ever received, I valued this the most. I had a passion for beautiful horses, and cannot tell how delighted I was when I mounted that fine animal, who caprioled and cantered away so beautifully. I felt as light as the wind, and perfectly dizzy with rapture. I shall be excused for this when it is considered that I was but the other day lying chained in a dungeon, ready to be hanged, with only one dark step before me into eternity; and now, here was I bounding away upon a gallant steed, and men taking off their hats to me and calling me captain!

My commission soon arrived, signed and sealed, with a letter of instructions; but by whom either these or the horse was brought, I was kept in profound ignorance; and not having any money by me to bear my expenses on the road, I knew not what to do or where to apply. My time was limited, and I began to dread that all would go wrong together, when, on the morning of the very last day I had to remain, I heard a sweet and beloved voice below, inquiring for the young captain. I knew it to be the voice of my lovely protecting angel, and hoped that all would yet go well. Heavens! how was I astounded, when, on running to the head of the stair to welcome her, I perceived only poor old Mora in the entrance! I received such a shock of disappointment, that for a while I could not speak; which was very bad of me, for there was no one living to whom I was more indebted than to poor Mora. I at length half articulated, "Oh, poor dear Mora, is it you?"

"Yes, it is I, captain, just come to see you, and bid you farewell," said she, with a fawning accent, for the people of the house heard us: "you must give me something for a remembrance before you go away."

"Yes, Mora, I must give you something before I go away," said I, and took her into my apartment, for her accents had thrown me into a quandary. I led her to a window. I looked into her features, and studied them as if I had been going to read her fortune. They bore not the marks of age when narrowly looked into. Her eyes had the beam of youth, and her teeth were beautiful; but the features were not the features of the lovely stranger who had raised me from the depths of misery into life, light, and joy. Still every tone of that voice went to my heart, and I knew not what I was doing. She smiled at my perplexity, and said, "I must not stay with a dashing young officer, you know, as it may hurt my character, and degrade you. Here is my errand, and may the blessing of God accompany it, as shall her's, who will never forget nor forsake you!" With that she squeezed my hand, wiped her eyes, and hastened away.

I hastened to examine the contents of the parcel, and found in it a small purse well filled with gold pieces, some of them British, and some foreign coin. The next morning I began my journey, and went by Perth and Stirling to Glasgow, as directed. There I joined Lieutenant Drummond with thirty-six raw recruits, stout young fellows, but great country boobies, and bad horsemen. With these we marched southward, always gaining strength as we proceeded, till we came to Blackheath, where a great camp was formed, preparative to the sailing of an armament for Flanders to join Marlborough. This I thought a grand sight, but it was a mere drop in the bucket to what I afterwards beheld.

Drummond and I being of an age, soon found ourselves great friends; but he was a great party man, and an adherent of the banished Stuarts. I knew little about these matters, but was rather inclined to take the other side, owing to the sentiments I had imbibed with the Innes's; but there was so much enthusiasm and chivalry about this young officer in the cause of wronged royalty, and the lineal descendant of our ancient kings, that my heart joined with him, though my tongue said no.

I now entered on a new scene of existence. It was one of toil and slavery, and required a subordination, to which I found my proud spirit scarcely could submit. The passage over was one of utter confusion, noise, and outrage, and several men as well as horses were lost in landing. The Duke of Marlborough and his staff were a day behind us in landing, and the first time I saw him was at Maestricht in the Netherlands, in company with his brother and the earl of Orkney. I was greatly struck with his appearance, which manifested calmness and benignity; but his brother, the general, I thought a better looking man than he.

We lay here about a month, while every day there were fresh arrivals of troops from the various provinces and principalities, all in good order; all hearty, and careless of any thing but matters of the passing hour; in these they took a deep concern, and would have quarrelled on mere trifles. The great rage of the officers was excellence in the sword-exercise, and I could not have believed that so much science and expertness could have been attained by men. Many of them held, that to wound them was impossible; and the officers of different countries were playing with sharp swords every day. Every regiment had its fencing-masters; and these fellows fought for the pre-eminence, and slew each other without remorse in the most dashing style imaginable, without any delinquency being attached to the deed. I practised early and late to attain proficiency, and at length challenged my then master, a countryman of my own, one Corporal Renwick, whose prowess I pretended to hold cheap; but he disarmed and wounded me, making at the same time a remark which cut me to the heart. From that time forward I studied the science harder than ever, one while under the celebrated Donald Bawn, and another under Von Malloch, a Saxon; until, quite conscious of superiority, I watched a fit opportunity, when, one evening I found Renwick somewhat inebriated, and making terrible vapouring among his pupils, on which I challenged him again, and after a very few passes, slew him on the spot.

Grievously did I repent of this. A fencing-master's life was not accounted much of; but yet my brother-officers accounted this unfair, and cried shame! shame! I had not a word to say, for my heart told me it was a murder. It was malice prepense. I had prepared myself for it, and taken him at a disadvantage, when too elevated by drinking; and I found that I had done a deed which would hang like a millstone about my neck as long as I lived.

This happened after we had left the Netherlands, and were on our march to the Upper Rhine. I had been introduced to Prince Eugene, and had seen the prince of Baden, both great heroes; but the latter I never liked, nor could any of the English officers bear him; but Eugene was the darling of all ranks. The first time I saw the French, face to face, was at a strong military station in Bavaria, on the second day of June. I had a curious disagreeable sensation that day. The French nation had always been liked in Scotland, as its ancient friends, and the English hated; and here was I joined with our inveterate enemies against our old friends. Nevertheless, I was eager for the fight, and resolved to distinguish myself at all hazards. We attacked the enemy at a dreadful disadvantage, for the hill was strongly fortified, and their lines of circumvallation appeared to me almost interminable. The Dutch infantry commenced the attack on the left, and the English shortly after; but they were so hotly handled, that in fifteen minutes the Dutch lines were first staid, then driven into confusion, and beat back. Our regiment was ordered to their support, and went up the slope at a canter, cheering on the Dutch, who looked rather gruff and dispirited: but the Bavarian infantry that were opposed to us we rode over like a field of thistles, and restored that part of the field for the present. We came next upon the lines at a half-angle, which confounded us, exposing us to the fire of the lines behind. A great number fell. I saw them dropping in whole files, and among the rest, our brave young colonel fell under his horse. I was at his side in a minute, and extricated him, mounted him on my own horse, and that moment sprang on behind him, for I had no idea of being left in that confusion without a horse, and mine was the best on the field. "Lochy, I am crushed a little," said he; "take you the rein, and let us lead on. We must break the second line." Our left flank company by this time were scrambling and plunging in the second line. Ours never got the length, for we were almost a wreck. "Colonel, what shall we do?" said I. "Hem! hem!" said he. So we turned and retreated with the rest. The English had likewise given way on all points, save twelve squadrons of horse, which the Duke of Marlborough encouraged to advance, and that movement prevented a total rout. Such a confusion I had never conceived, far less seen. The shouting of orders often contrary–the thunder of the artillery–the cloud of smoke that involved us in total darkness–the curses and roars of the wounded, whom we were trampling under our feet like so much carrion, altogether presented a hideous view of the pomp and circumstance of war.

A number of horses, whose riders had fallen, were at this time hurrying by, and some foot-soldiers laying hold of them: I called out, "A horse here for the colonel. Bring that bay here, you dog!" The man obeyed, and I wondered at his fearful looks as he approached, looking up at the colonel's face. "I thinks our cornal's reather lwoking gash on't sur," said he.

"What do you mean, fellow?" said I.

"What dwos I mean? Whoy, Gwod bless the heart of thee, the man's dead. He'll never need a horse more, I assure thee, and if he tould thee he was living it was a dom'd mistake!" said the blunt Englishman, with perfect sincerity of countenance. A number of officers gathered around, and General Gower being brought forward, mortally wounded, at the same time, brought others to our side, and they all saw the dead colonel taken from my horse, out of my arms, which caused some sensation. We laid him down on the bloody field, and left him there.

The gallant Prince Eugene had by this time turned the fortune of the day, by attacking with his imperialists the enemy in flank, in such a way, that their trenches did them more evil than good. The whole British and Flemish force was then led on a second time to the attack, and a complete, but dear-bought victory was gained. A rich field of spoil fell to our share; and the next day we took the town of Donawert, and pillaged it; and at the gate of that city I was made a lieutenant. We pursued the enemy across the Danube, taking every place that came in our way.

A terrible business ensued after this, which I shall never forget while I live. The duke, from some offence taken at the Elector, ordered us out to plunder his whole country, which order was obeyed to a tittle. The whole of that fertile country was overrun and plundered, burnt, and destroyed; while the most abominable cruelty and licentiousness prevailed. We often plundered and burnt from twenty to thirty rich towns in a day; and it was said that upwards of three hundred such were utterly consumed. The riches that some men got were immense; but they were mostly in goods of high value, and a good part was again lost before they could be turned into money. For my part, I should have got very little, save in horses, for which I was always on the look out. But there was a little fellow, Finlayson, a Highland soldier's orphan boy, who had attached himself to me at Brussels, and had kept close by me as a servant ever since. That little fellow beat all beings I ever saw, for gathering up plunder. He was like a needle, and sure to be in every rich house and shop first; and having no other way of saving his plunder from stronger hands, he brought it all to my tent, and gave it me, as the only means of securing any part of it. I had by these means more riches than I knew what to do with.

But I was now guilty of a sad mistake. About the beginning of August I was one day disposing of a part of my stolen Bavarian horses, for which there was great demand, when, unfortunately, General Churchill took a fancy for my own black horse, and offered to buy him. I refused to sell him at any money. But he let me understand that he *wanted* the horse, and that I had nothing to do but to set a reasonably small price on him, for in that way the transaction was to be settled. I despised this, and told him plainly the horse was mine, and should be mine as long as he could bear me so well in my country's service! "Ay, ay! say you so?" said the general, with a sneer, and turned away.

The very next day the great duke himself called me to him, and asked me as a favour to let him have my horse, though at double value. I told him candidly that for particular reasons I could not part with my horse, and that rather than do so I would yield up my commission. "Oh, very well, 'tis all right," said he.

My friend Drummond witnessed this, and heard all that passed. As soon as the duke turned away, he said, "Good Lord! Lochy, are you mad? You have ruined yourself. That horse was worth a regiment to you; but now your doom is sealed. If you had had common sense, or the least grain of it, you would have said, 'My lord duke, though I value my horse, as a token of friendship, he is most heartily at your service without money or price; for in your hands alone can he be of the highest value to our country and to the liberties of Europe.' What a dolt you were! I wish I had had ten horses as good asked for in such a manner." The next morning at our sword-exercise I was challenged by a Colonel Scrivener, in a very saucy manner, for some pretended breach of order in our play. I offered to fight him with cut-and-thrust weapons. He said he would make one of his drummers chastise me. "Very well, colonel," said I, "I'll fight your substitute, as your substitute, whoever he is, and hope that you will at least choose a better than yourself."

We were to meet by ourselves ten minutes after sunset, for there were no seconds in repute there. I attended at the appointed time and place, where I found a figure walking to and fro wrapped in his camp-cloak. It was taller than the colonel, but seemed not to regard my approach. I unsheathed my sword. "Friend, if you are come here to meet me as Colonel Scrivener's substitute and bully," said I, "be pleased to throw off that superb cloak of thine, and betake thee to thy defences." He nodded assent–turned his back to me–loosed his cloak–stripped off his buff jerkin–drew out his sword, and felt its edge with the greatest deliberation, and then brandishing it scientifically, he turned round and faced me.

The very first look from him froze my blood;–it was Renwick, the fencing-master, whom I had so foully slain in a duel at Elchingen! He grinned ghastly at me, pointing to the wound in his breast, at the same time lifting his weapon as if to cleave me. Being quite deprived of the reasoning faculty, I ran for it with all my might; the phantom pursuing me with giant strides, close at my back, until, quite desperate, I plunged into the water at Frechingen, and swam across, and the phantom did not think proper to follow, or if it did, it sank in the brook, for I saw no more of it. My mental faculties were in a state of total derangement all that night; and the next day preparations were begun for the great battle of Blenheim, in which I acted merely as an automaton; for the only thing I remembered when that dreadful battle was over, was seeing the French cavalry drowned in the Danube. In their retreat they were hurrying over the river on two broad pontoons, guarded by a redoubt. General Wilkes called out, "A thousand crowns to the gunner who will snap the chain;" on which several tried it without effect; among the rest, an old Hessian, who missing it the first and second time, cursed and swore terribly, but loaded and pointed again with great expedition. His grey hair was streaming in the wind, and at every slight alteration that he made he grinned and swore; but getting her at last to the very point he wanted, he called to the matchman, "D–n and h–l! touch her off now!" Off went the cannon with a roar like the bursting of a mine, and threw the too eager cannoneer with a thump on the sward. Mercy, how he swore! But that moment a yell of horror arose from the Danube, for the old savage had snapped the chain neatly at one end. The pontoon turned over with the current, and throwing its whole complement of men and horses on the other one, both went down, and the whole corps perished. Thirty squadrons of men and horses were thus plunged in the river, and scarcely threescore of them made the dry land. The loss of cavalry to the enemy was greater than in the field. The old gunner swore in grand style, and clasping the huge cannon to his bosom, he kissed and blessed her one while, and cursed her another. "Ah, Saint Christopher bless thee for a noble lady!" said he, "I have manned thee these twenty years; but for all thy blustering and din, d–n thee, if ever thou gavest me a complete amends of these scoundrels till now!"

I remember also something of the great riches of the field: they were immense. Six horses could not have drawn the coined silver and gold found among the military stores alone. The other stores were incalculable. Thirty thousand French and Bavarians were killed, drowned, or taken. So that a more complete victory never was won. Little Finlayson came to my tent at night, laden with gold watches, money and trinkets; and, among other valuable things, a sword with a gold handle, which had belonged to one of the imperial generals: for Finlayson plundered all the time during these battles; friends and foes were alike to him, nor did he care a pin who gained or lost.

I believe I behaved as well as my neighbours during the engagement; that is, I acted like a machine, and obeyed such orders as reached me, never turning my back, which many a one did. Nevertheless, two days after the battle I was broken for cowardice, and turned into the ranks. It was a mere pretence, a sham trial made by the commander to be revenged on me. Colonel Scrivener, indeed, stated that I had challenged him to single combat, and durst not wait his arrival, for on reaching the appointed spot he saw me running from the field as if the devil had been at my heels. I had not one word to say for myself then. The Austrian general's sword being found in my possession, was likewise greatly against me. In short, I was pronounced an egregious coward, and the majority were for my being blown from the mouth of a cannon; but there the duke interposed, and said the more proper punishment for a proud spirit like mine was degradation; so I was condemned to serve in the ranks, my grand accoutrements and riches being all taken from me, and among other things, my noble black horse, on which I had the mortification to see General Churchill mounted the next day. Fain would I have passed a bullet through him, for as for death at that time I valued it at nothing; it would have been welcome in any shape, for in that degraded state I determined not to live.

No man condoled with me but poor Finlayson, who did not forsake me even in this low state, but bade me be of good heart, for as long as he lived I should never go the worse to my dinner for all that had befallen. I then told the little fellow in confidence that I intended deserting to the French, in order at some time to be avenged on the Duke of Marlborough. What was my astonishment when the boy told me that he understood the duke was not to blame, for that the persecution raised against me proceeded from another source altogether. "Did you ever know," said he, "that your life was eagerly sought at home?" I answered that I did. He assured me that this proceeded from the same source, though he knew not what that was; but I never should eschew it till it brought me to my end; and this he said he learned from old Andrew M'Vity, the huckster, who was telling it to another man, and who had said farther, that there were spies watching me, who would soon now bring me to a legal death, and that if I attempted deserting to the French I was gone. "Why not desert to the king of Sweden?" said the boy. "Perhaps the duke would give you leave to desert to him, for here you can never succeed."

I pondered on this intelligence all night, exceedingly irritated and unhappy, and the next day I presented a memorial to the Duke of Marlborough, stating that I hoped he was sensible that I was punished without deserving it, and that I had done my duty to my country and commander as far as lay in my power; and that, as my first commission was purchased, he would allow me to push my fortune elsewhere, for that he could hardly expect that a Scottish gentleman could serve in his ranks.

The only answer I received to this was from a corporal's guard, who came with an order to take Private John Lochy to prison, there to be confined till further orders. Accordingly I was put into a vile unhealthy prison at Philipsburg, in which there were Frenchmen, deserters, and malefactors of all sorts. There was no more attention paid to us than if we were dogs; for, in the hurry and confusion of the war, we seemed to have been totally forgotten. There was nothing but starvation, cursing, blaspheming, suffering, and death. The prisoners almost all died, for the place is surrounded by a marsh, and unhealthy in the extreme; and with that, and hunger and filth conjoined, they went fast to their long homes, unmissed and unregretted, for in war human life is no more regarded than the crops that grow in the field, hardly so much. I could not have lived in that prison a week, had it not been for poor Finlayson; but he failed me never; he never came empty handed, for he could work his way every where. The wealth of France and Germany seemed at this important period to be at his disposal. I believe little Finlayson at some times could have raised a company of men; but possession was so uncertain thus obtained, that he lost his wealth as fast as he gained it.

I lost all account of the time I was in this accursed place; but, to my great astonishment, I lost sight also of little Finlayson at one time, and gave myself quite up for lost, till one day I heard my name called from without, in broken English, and on pushing my nose through the bars, I was accosted by a very pretty maiden, who informed me, as well as she could, that my boy had sent her with money to buy me out of the prison; but that she knew not how to accomplish it, and would hand me up the purse, that I might manage it myself.

I intreated her not to do that, as I should be robbed of it instantly, for every thing that came into that place of misery was seized on as common property. But I mentioned a scheme to her that shall be nameless, on which she stood for a long time silent, as if confounded at the atrocity of the proposal. At length her eyes began to open on the probable consequences, and she gave me a nod of approbation, smiled, and vanished. The next night but two after that I was set at liberty at the dead hour of the night, charged to return at a certain hour, and committed to a guide who was to direct me how to proceed.

My guide from the prison proved to be a little old capuchin monk of slender and delicate proportions, and having a voice dwindled to treble pipes; but being covered with a gown and hood, I could not discover his lineaments. I followed close behind him along the main street, but soon found that I could not walk, there was such a feebleness about all my joints. He led me into a sort of dormitory belonging to the little monastery, where an old woman gave me some bread and wine without opening her lips. My guide then brought me armour and a sword, at the sight of which I trembled and wept for joy; but on putting it on, I could not walk one step, but fell down in a faint. The little kind-hearted capuchin disincumbered me of my armour, remarking that I stood more in need of some nourishment than these trappings of chivalry, which I could not use, but that nevertheless there was an absolute necessity for an instant escape. I was perfectly subservient, being so overcome with gratitude for my delivery from a place where I seemed to have been utterly forgotten, and left to perish by the most miserable of all deaths, that I did as I was bidden, precisely as a child does. On returning to the porch, we found two gallant steeds awaiting us, which we mounted; I with unspeakable joy, for horsemanship had always been my delight. The little monk, as I followed him, was constantly beckoning me to silence and humility of deportment. We had three gates to pass, all bolted and double guarded; but a pass-word whispered by this mysterious little fellow opened every one of them as with magic, and each of the porters bade us God speed.

"We are safe now, captain," said my guide, in good plain English: "where is it your wish to go?"

I was so petrified by the tones of the creature's voice, and the idea that I was liberated and safe, that I could make no answer; but there I sat on my horse, making faces of the most idiotical cast, which it was a mercy could not be seen for the darkness; and on the monk reiterating the question, I answered, "Any where you like, save to the allied army."

"The great duke is in England just now," said he, "and in a fine puzzle; so also is his brother; so that you are safe from their persecution. I wish I could say you were so from every other. But I think we must make our way for Darmstadt, this district being so much indented between hostile countries; and could we reach that place in safety, I expect there to meet with a gentleman who will secure our escape."

I acquiesced without remonstrance, and, feeble as I was, I never enjoyed a ride so much as this. All nature looked as if new to me, or rather like a beloved old friend with a fairer face. I did not believe that the world had contained aught so beautiful as the glorious windings of the majestic Rhine, which were constantly opening and shutting on our view as we descended. We journeyed slowly, lived well, and passed without any trouble, till we came to Darmstadt, where we were taken up and cast into prison, till we could give a more satisfactory account of ourselves. We were here hardly set, for the monk spoke bad French and no German, and I not knowing what to say, could not speak at all. We did not even know on which side the grand-duke was at that time, matters being in such confusion all along the banks of the Rhine. However, the little monk had some art with him, to me unknown, for with all his broken language and poor treble voice, he constantly gained his purpose, and was instantly liberated; but I was detained.

The next day the constable came in, chapeau in hand, and introduced Baron von Kui and Mademoiselle de Whartoong. The grand titles of my visitors confounded me, but their entrance redoubled my consternation. The baron seemed an active little fellow, covered with gold lace; but he only bowed, stood aside, and let his partner advance. It was my own guardian angel,–the adorable creature who had formerly saved my life, given me my commission, and fitted me out in Scotland! Yes, it was herself, splendidly dressed, and smiling in mature beauty. I wept like a child, pressed her to my bosom, and, without knowing what I was saying, in my delirium of joy I prayed her to tell me whether I should address her as my sister, my mother, or my wife.

"O your mother, to be sure," cried the baron, bursting into a laugh; "does it not strike your honour that she may more likely prove your daughter?" That instant the man of gold was at my knees embracing them, and I perceived then that it was my faithful Finlayson! A scene of joy and happiness ensued that cannot be described. We quite forgot that we were in a prison, but there we sat recounting our adventures. My beloved was herself the capuchin who had rescued me from thraldom, and conducted me from Philipsburg. The plan of escape had been pointed out to me by Finlayson long before, as easily to be effected, provided the Duke of Marlborough and General Churchill were at a due distance. It was at last done by and through the interest of the lovely, but most mercenary Madam Vilshoven, who could readily procure Prince Eugene's assent to any thing.

The indefatigable Finlayson had been obliged to abandon the vicinity of Philipsburg, owing to his unlicensed depredations on friends and foes; but he contrived to get word to Britain of my miserable state, and that to the only source from whence relief could have emanated. I perceived from this that there was a mysterious understanding between him and my beloved, into which I durst not inquire, since it was her will to keep it secret from me. Finlayson conducted us to his hotel, where we were introduced to his lady, the Baroness Kui, a young Bohemian of great beauty and simplicity, dressed in a style so magnificent, that to me, who knew the little fellow's origin, this whole business of titles and grandeur appeared quite ludicrous. He seemed sensible of this, and instead of putting on any airs to me, he constantly demeaned himself as my inferior; and when lording it over others, at which he was not slack, he would cast a sly look and a wink to me, to note how well he acted the great man. He was a strange character, and such a one as the Highlands of Scotland only can produce,–a being void of any moral principle, save inviolable faith and attachment to a superior.

At Darmstadt my beloved guardian took leave of me, recommending me to keep far from Britain, and not to part company with Finlayson, on whom I might depend to the last. I was again fitted out as a British captain, and, to shorten unavailing description, we took our way for Saxony, resolved to join the army of the king of Sweden. Finlayson had become too notorious on the Rhine, and was glad to get away to a distance from it; and having little to detain me there, I consented with some reluctance to accompany him. He had a carriage and horses of his own, in which we travelled; and as soon as we left the hotel he dropped his travelling foreign title, and adopted a Scottish one, for fear that in the Swedish camp I should forget, and call him by his old name; and moreover, we were both desirous to appear there as Scottish officers of rank; for ever since the days of Gustavus the Scots had been greatly caressed in Sweden.

The title which he now adopted was Sir Ranald Finlayson, with which his fair Bohemian was particularly delighted; Lady Finlayson sounded so grandly in her ears. On our way, I could not help remarking that Finlayson seemed to regard his lady with a great deal of indifference, which caused me, out of sheer civility to a very lovely woman and a foreigner, constantly to pay as much attention to her as I could. He spared no expenses on her, for she was dressed like an empress, but otherwise had very little attention paid to her, save what I did myself: the consequence of this was, that the poor girl clung to me as to a lover, and on coming to a place called Altenburg, we chanced to be alone together; and while I was merely saying some civil thing to her, without taking any thought, she came and sat down on my knee, clasped her arms about my neck, and kissed me. I was never so confounded in my life, and knew neither how to act, look, nor what to say. I pushed her gently away, and said, "My dear Lady Finlayson!" but she would not quit her hold, but held me in her embrace, and wept on my neck; and while we were in this beautiful and promising attitude, in walks the redoubted Sir Ranald Finlayson, with a swagger and a look quite indescribable. I really felt greatly abashed and out of countenance; for though I despised Finlayson in the main, and knew his tricks, yet had I been deeply obligated to him, and to appear as if endeavouring to seduce the affections of his young and simple wife was quite intolerable.

"Really, sir," said I, rising, and looking very like a fool, "really this is excessively awkward; but on my life–"

"No, no! not the least awkward," said Finlayson; "I am very happy to see you two such good friends, as it will take a great deal of the charge and trouble off my hands."

I was worse now than ever; for the lady, whose hand still held mine, squeezed it, as if delighted with the liberty granted us. What does the little precious villain mean? thought I; for I was so dumbfoundered I could not speak a word. Does he mean that I shall participate with him in the favours of his wife?

"I thank you, Sir Ranald, for your courtesy and confidence," said I, "neither of which shall ever be misused by me; and this very day I will give you a proof of my resolution." So saying, I left the room, went out and purchased a horse, and set out for Leipsic by myself, leaving them to come in their carriage by themselves, resolved to shun their company in future; for this freedom of behaviour I could not comprehend.

On reaching Leipsic, who should I meet but my countryman, Captain Drummond, formerly mentioned, who rejoiced to see me! He had come in a diplomatic capacity on behalf of the exiled Stuarts; had found a gracious reception; but despairing of the assistance of the king of Sweden, until the Czar Peter was farther humbled, he had resolved to remain with Charles, to keep him in remembrance of his promise. He introduced me to Marshall Rennyson, the greatest general of the age,* who received me with great kindness, telling me that his father was a Scotchman, and promised to introduce me to the king in a few days. In the mean time Finlayson found us, and again attached himself to me. I called him Sir Ranald, on which Drummond took a searching look of him, and said he did not know there had been a Sir Ranald Finlayson in Scotland.

"It is only a German title, sir," said Finlayson, with perfect nonchalance; "one conferred on the field of battle by Prince Eugene." I durst not ask for his lady; and, strange to say, I never saw more of her. Many a time I have wondered what the creature made of her, for I sometimes thought, if he had not killed her, she would have found us out, as we remained at Leipsic five weeks. I am almost certain she would have found means of speaking to me, and explaining some things. But nobody can comprehend what that being was capable of; he had not one virtue but an inviolable attachment to me.

On the 16th of April we were both presented to the king, as two Scottish officers who had served under the Duke of Marlborough and Prince Eugene. Charles received us, I believe, as graciously as he could; but a more disagreeable wretch I never saw. At the first look I really took him for an idiot; his head was of such a strange shape; it was by far too wide above; and his thin sandy hair stood all out in bristles; and that the man was a sort of half idiot I had no doubt then, nor have I any to this day. He had two buck teeth; that is, the two next to the foremost two protruded greatly from the semicircle; and of this peculiarity he either was ashamed, or had been so at some previous period, for he always covered them with his upper lip, so that when he laughed he was like one crying; and besides, it gave his mouth a twist, which was any thing but seemly. His eyes

* Can this be the celebrated Marshall General Renschild, whom the captain means?

were hazel, with a shade of blue, and had considerable brilliance; but then the beams seemed to be thrown inward; there was no ray of general benevolence coruscant from them; they were the windows of a dark, indignant soul, through which one saw nothing but obstinacy, pride, and revenge. His form would have been good, had he dressed like any other gentleman, but he was a boor and a sloven; and I have even seen with my own eyes the vermin creeping on his blue surtout, which had always the appearance of a second-hand one, worn by an English horse-dealer. Such was the man who was at once the admiration and terror of Europe!

But such troops I never beheld, for their evolutions were all like the work of enchantment. I question if the equal of that army ever existed, and to think that they were commanded by a headlong fool was very extraordinary. We entered his army as supernumeraries or expectants, and each of us got five hundred crowns as pocket-money. As for Finlayson, he was a mine of wealth; I believe he had more riches at this time than was contained in the treasures of some of the German princes. He offered to raise a company, and fit them out at his own expense; but the king declined admitting the Saxons into his army; so after five weeks of feasting and drilling, we set out on our route towards Lithuania, to fight Peter the Great, who had overrun that province, and all the north-east of Poland. The whole of this rapid conquest, as it will likely be particularly described by future historians, I shall take no notice of, farther than that we had in reality no fighting; for, wherever we turned our faces, the Russians fled before us like fire from flint, abandoning every thing to us; and such as chose to plunder might do so with impunity. There was a standing order against it, but subject to so many modifications, that it was seldom put in force. Finlayson pursued his old mode with such fidelity, that about the beginning of August he was fairly caught in the snare, having collected the whole treasure of Kossa, on pretence of the king's order, which he had done in more instances, and to a far greater amount; but the rapidity of our movements prevented these things coming to light, for Finlay kept always in the rear. He was tried, found guilty, and condemned to lose his head. He was not, however, in the least dispirited; and how he got the sentence altered I know not, but it was through General Rennyson; for the king never knew but that he was beheaded. He was whipped and drummed out of the army, and I did not expect ever to see him again.

Every day I was the more and more convinced of the total derangement of the king. His eagerness to humble the czar had increased to a frenzy; and when any of the officers of his guard mentioned his puissant enemy, and the confusion into which the king's movements had thrown him, then the king always uttered a demoniac laugh. Any man could have known by his countenance when he was thinking of the czar; then the right eye closed, the upper lip protruded half an inch over the under one, and his whole features were squeezed as in a vice. He had not patience to wait for his army, but, drunken with rage, he pushed on at a canter, so that only a few of his best-mounted soldiers could keep up with him. I always did for one; but I saw plainly that if it had not been for the anxiety of the guards to shield him from danger, he would have ridden straight on, and faced the czar and his army by himself.

I was present at a gallant action by night in the town of Grodno, and was one of thirty who opposed two thousand Russian cavalry, and kept them at bay for the space of ten or eleven minutes, till the king was apprised of his danger, and marshalled the army, such as it was, a mere handful; but we broke the Russians at the first onset, and killed the greater part of those who had entered the gate.

On alighting from my horse, a little before day, I fell down among the snow, and could not get up again; but there I lay lolling on the street. A guardsman lifted me; but we could not understand each other. He laughed at me, thinking I was benumbed by the frost; but, on supporting me into the house, it was found that I was wounded in the thigh, a bullet having entered near my knee on the outside, and penetrated upwards into the thickest part, where it remained close by the bone. It was immediately extracted by a Dr. Rymmer, after a cruel operation. I was not in the least aware when I received it.

The next evening, as Rymmer was dressing the wound anew, a peasant boy in the Polish dress assisted him; and was so handy, that the doctor applauded him, recommending me to retain him in my service till my wound recovered. When the surgeon retired, to my astonishment, the vulgar-looking Polish boy came up to my couch, seized my hand, let the tears fall on it, and asked me how I did. It was Finlayson, the indefatigable, kind-hearted Finlayson! He had laid aside all his riches and honours to follow me in disguise, and minister to me. I never felt more happy at any recognition, for I found that I stood greatly in need of his help, and, wicked and unprincipled as I knew him to be, when I thought of my guardian angel's charge, and of his unaltering attachment to me, what could I do but embrace him, and welcome him back? As soon as we began to converse together, he advised me to leave the service of that madman, which I refused, and reminded him of my lovely protector's charge to keep far from Britain. I said, moreover, that there was something romantic in following this meteor king, which I intended to persevere in, and, I hoped, to honour and preferment.

"Ay, the preferment of being buried in a snow wreath," said Finlayson. "What does a man seek honours and preferment for, but to spend the latter part of his life in ease and comfort? I have secured already as much treasure as will buy all the land in Scotland—I mean all that is to sell; and, if I can lay my hands on it all again, which, without your assistance, is out of my power, the whole shall be at your disposal."

I testified my astonishment, yet continued firm in my purpose to make that campaign with Charles. But nothing could retard the restless impatience of that monarch. Though in the depth of winter, and in the middle of a great snow-storm, he was off after his adversary the very next day; and there was I, left in an enemy's country, and among strangers, unable to move from my couch: but people stood in dreadful awe of Charles, and no one offered me any insult, or any thing save acts of kindness; but my poor Polish peasant boy, whom nobody regarded, was constantly paying well for every favour in his master's name.

What a strange being he was! He had brought a splendid grandee's over-dress with him, and chaperon with plumes, which I knew nothing of; and, dressed out in that style, he was every day and every night playing pranks in the town, among the Jews in particular, a great number of whom inhabit it, and many of whom he had taken in to a great amount. Both his peasant and grandee dresses were made so that he could change them in half a minute. There was at that time a Baron Steinburg in Grodno, of whom I every day heard some accounts; of his munificence, bets, and amours with certain ladies of high rank. He had, moreover, ruined certain monied men, by a species of gambling which I did not understand; but was at last caught in a married lady's bedchamber, one of great beauty and rare accomplishments, and of the very highest rank in Poland. He escaped by the window, but was hotly pursued, and was seen to take refuge in our hotel, as some alleged. The count's servants and an officer instantly besieged the door, and a strict search commenced; and there being no stranger found in the house but myself and servant boy, I was suspected, and taken prisoner; but the state of my wound, and the oaths of the good people of the house, freed me. Baron Steinburg could not be found; nor was he any more seen or heard of in Grodno, to the great disappointment of the Jews and the Count ——, the lady's husband.

He was now believed to have been the devil, as he had often been seen and disappeared in the same way. This belief saved the lady, who declared that he came into her room she knew not how, and vanished again in the same manner. But how was I astonished, long afterwards, when Finlayson told me the Baron Steinburg was himself! and when I professed myself shocked at the enormity of the crime, he laughed, and said it was only a piece of common gallantry, and that if I had seen the beauty of the dame, I would have done as he did.

"But how had you the confidence?" said I; "how durst you, for your soul, make your proposals to a lady of such beauty and rank?"

"Nothing more easy or natural," said he; "it is only the ladies of rank to whom I ever make such proposals, for they are always the most mercenary. Perhaps you will not believe me, but I have never yet met with a lady, either in Germany or Poland, whom I could not bring to my own terms at the first interview; and my infallible charm is jewellery. Money, plenty of money, will do it, but jewels are irresistible. Why, this same countess, who is really a fine woman, only had a pair of ruby ear-rings from me, in a Jew's shop one day; but then I promised her a gold chain, and the matter was settled."

I was terribly nettled at hearing the little insignificant wretch express himself in this wise; for, though I had had very little communication with ladies of the higher ranks of life, I entertained the most elevated respect for them; and this asseveration, partly authenticated by a recent fact, deranged all my sublime sentiments regarding female excellence and purity. I wished I had never heard the allegation; but comforted myself that the accused were not Scottish women.

On the 27th the Prince of Wirtemburg came upon the king's track, with three thousand men; on which, though very unfit for a campaign in such weather, I had my thigh bandaged, and Finlayson, whose name now was shortened into Fin, and I, being both well mounted, we joined the cavalcade. We found no difficulty in travelling, for the two armies had cleared the road, and the frost had made the trampled snow like a pavement. Wherever the snow had formerly been deep, we came up to great numbers of slaughtered Muscovites; for it was terribly against the czar that he had the roads to clear, not only for himself, but for his pursuers. Still, as we advanced eastward, the number of corpses increased, and Swedes were mixed with them. The Swedish army was so full of every thing, that they never stopped to rifle the slain; but Fin always tarried behind, and picked up things. His portmanteau was still on the increase wherever situated; and, among other things, he brought me a parchment one day, with the great seal of Russia on it; but I could not read the document, and paid no attention to it. In a morass, about two days' journey west of Minsk, we came to thirty Swedish waggons, which had sunk, and been abandoned by the army, in their haste to keep up with their madcap king, who issued orders every day to the rear to quicken their march. He was only intent on wreaking vengeance upon Peter, and neither seemed to know nor care what was going on behind. He was generally from fifteen to twenty miles in advance of the bulk of his army; and as his military chests, at this period, contained upwards of ten millions of specie, he was quite reckless with regard to casual losses. As a striking instance of this, Fin could not leave these thirty waggons without an interesting scrutiny of their contents: and in one baggage-waggon, which had belonged to General Levenhaupt, who was now sent on a different route, the little fellow discovered four sealed coffers of specie. One of these, filled with pieces of pure gold, Fin, after stuffing his pockets, selected for himself, and hid it; the other three he brought carefully, and delivered to the prince, who commended him greatly, and offered him a high reward, which he refused; and with a simple stupid face, said that his master had forbidden him taking any gratuities from gentlemen. The prince observed, that in no young man had he ever seen so much honesty and simplicity. Fin put his finger in his mouth, and looked so sheepish, that I was like to die with laughing.

At Minsk we joined General Horn's division of the army, who had gathered the pursuers of the right wing together, and waited the king's orders to advance, as a great battle was expected at the crossing of the river Berezine. I was exceedingly anxious to share in this battle, and observe the military tactics of this conqueror, of whom I had formed so poor an opinion. It was now the middle of summer, at least in England; but owing to the melting of the snows in the forests of White Russia, the river was flooded to a mighty torrent, and the Czar had intrenched himself in a strong position behind the river, his main body being in the town of Borissow, and a strong encampment on each flank. The only possible place of passage at any season by fording was right opposite the town, over against which there was an embankment, all bristled with cannon. Early in the morning General Horn and General Ross commenced operations at this ford, by a heavy cannonade from behind a temporary cover, attempting twice to cross the river in great force, which drew the whole puissance of the Czar's army to that spot; as on the defence of that ford all depended. The prince of Wirtemburg and I joined the king's division before day. He did not know me. When introduced by the prince, he held out his left hand, and said in Swedish, "Ha, Lochy, glad to see you again. Thought you had deserted me. True Scots gentleman. Thought of making you governor of Smolensk. Was sorry for the fate of your companion. Must have been a finished rascal though!"

From this I knew that he was not aware of the escape of Finlay. He was in high spirits on being so near his hated rival, and burning with eagerness to be at him. He led ten thousand well-mounted troops round a wood, quite out of sight of Borissow; and at sun-rise we came to a temporary pontoon, on which we crossed slowly, but in perfect safety over the roaring flood. This was ten miles above the town, and there was a strong intrenched camp before us, three miles from the town. But as soon as the king saw himself at the head of one thousand men, off he rode full drive, straight on the camp of the enemy. I never saw a more mad or precipitate action, to run headlong upon an intrenched army of thirty thousand with one thousand men! The Muscovites opened on us a heavy fire of musketry from their counterscarp, and brought down many good gentlemen around the king; on which he was obliged to wheel to the left, and attack three thousand men who guarded that position. He led his small column into the middle of them, at full gallop, and rode right through them; on which those on our left fled into a wood, and the rest into the camp; and as we were now in a line with the trenches, and some thousands more of our troops coming right in front, the Russians took fright, and fled into the town, carrying dismay and astonishment with them.

In the different lines that were here broken there might be about twelve thousand men; but their artillery had been drawn off to the defence of the ford, which was all what the French call a *ruse de guerre*, though it succeeded to the utmost. This was the first battle I had fought along with Charles by day, and it was lauded by his officers as a masterpiece; whereas I still say it was the rash and precipitate act of a madman. If he had made such an attack on any of the armies on the Rhine, he would, at the very first, have been surrounded and cut in pieces. He was a general who despised all advice and consideration, which at once showed him to be a fool: he had no quality but headlong and precipitate valour. Marlborough, scoundrel as he was, and who had proved himself so to me, was ten thousand degrees beyond Charles as a general; so was Prince Eugene.

But they had to do with their equals; the other had not.

The moment that the right wing of the Czar's army was broken by the king in person, the Muscovite troops began their flight eastward; but, in spite of all that Charles could do, Prince Gallitzin held him in check at Borissow, till Peter, by forced marches, got thirty leagues in advance. This was owing to the Swedish army having been divided by the Berezine, and the difficulty in getting over the baggage. I never saw a more furious and unreasonable being than Charles was at this delay.

For six weeks we pursued the Russians through a most abominable country, without either hill or dale, but covered with interminable woods and morasses. Charles could not now get away before his army, for all the roads and bridges were broken up by the retreating armies, and every furlong was to clear; yet, spite of all the Czar's precautions, we harassed his rear, and had fighting, less or more, every day, killing great numbers of his savage boors, whose lives were of no value; and, at the same time, losing many gallant Swedes, whose lives, in times of peril, were invaluable.

On the 7th of August we came to a river called Dobrinsk, a branch of the great river Boristhene, called by the natives Dnieper, and here we found twenty-four thousand Muscovites encamped in a spot which they deemed impregnable, but Peter was not with them. I think he was horribly afraid for himself at this time, and that this great army was left merely as a sacrifice, to gain time for himself to escape; for he could scarcely imagine that it was to turn Charles, or keep such a potent army as his long in check. The cavalry stemmed the river, to the saddle-laps, and the foot waded below them, in long lines, holding by each other; those on the lower part of the lines were drowned, the water getting above their depth; but I saw nothing of this. They were never regarded.

After the greater part of the army had got over we found that there was still an impassable morass between us and the enemy, a mile and a half over. It was a complete quagmire, a shaking fen, which no man in his right senses would have attempted to cross on horseback: but the king, as usual, despising all remonstrance, dashed into the bog, and ordered both horse and foot to follow him. Ere he had proceeded thirty yards down went his horse, head foremost. The king was thrown forward, and sunk in the mire, and the beast made such a terrible splutter and splashing, that his majesty was in great danger. I saw some officers, and his nephew the prince, in particular, laughing till they were like to fall from their horses, at seeing the greatest conqueror in the world plunging to the ears in the mire, and sweltering for life. He was terribly affronted; and when he got to his feet, without ever giving his clothes a shake, he ordered his foot to follow him, and his cavalry to keep by the water's edge, and ride round the morass. We obeyed: but he had ordered his infantry to do that which was impossible; for, in an instant, several hundreds of them were over the head in the slough. I never saw any thing in an army so ludicrous. The case was thus: the whole of the slough was partially covered with water, or rather mire; but it was all cut full of deep trenches, and these being also full of mire, they could not be discerned, till down went the king and his brave followers headlong into each, one after another. Still there was no alternative, but on they must go. When they got about half way over the Muscovites opened a heavy fire on them; but not one Swedish carbine would go off, having been all, as well as the cartridges, so well steeped in the morass; and there were they advancing in the face of an intrenched enemy, as helpless as a drove of bullocks going to the slaughter.

We had three leagues to ride round, by a horrible bad path; and before we could meet the king we had to cut our way through the right wing of the enemy. His majesty was draggled from head to foot, and as I had the good fortune to reach him first, I gave him my horse. "Thank you, thank you, Scots gentleman," said he, mounting and flying to the attack. A quarter of an hour after I saw him again, charging on foot; but by that time Fin came up with the king's own horse, which he had left in the slough. That indefatigable being, who seemed incapable of leaving any thing of value behind him, perceiving the king's grand coal-black charger wallowing in the mire, swam him out at the end of the trench, and thus extricated him with the greatest ease. When the king had his horse thus presented to him by a sheepish-looking boy, in the midst of the battle, he gave his mouth a twist, and cast on Fin a look, one would have thought, of high displeasure. "How's this? how's this? This is queer!" said he, rapidly, in Swedish, as he mounted; and that was all the thanks poor Fin got. But the Prince of Wirtemburg being present, knew Fin, and said, "That young lout is worth his weight in gold," and flung him a handful of pieces, which he gathered as greedily and as eagerly as if he had not been worth a farthing: whereas Fin had a baggage-waggon of his own coming up behind in my name, than which there was not a better stored one, nor one drawn by better horses, in the Swedish army.

The battle was now of short duration; the Muscovite lines were broken through, and a great slaughter ensued for the space of half an hour, by which time the army had vanished into the woods, and pursuit was impossible. A more gallant action than this never was fought; still it was quite manifest that the whole proceedings were those of a madman.

The beaten army retreated on the great river Boristhene, and still we pursued. The Czar also broke up his camp beyond the river, and fled towards Moscow. It was here said that he begged of Charles to enter into terms of a most advantageous peace, which the other refused, till such time as they two should meet in Moscow. For my part, I do not believe this: I heard nothing of it at the time, nor did I hear it mentioned till within these few years by Lord Keith.

It was four days before we effected our passage over the great river Boristhene, or Dnieper, and at a Muscovite town called Mohillovey the horse tarried for that space; but if the king had not been seriously indisposed from his ducking, first in the morass, and then in the river, we would not have been allowed that breathing time. He had no review there; but a complete system of plunder went on.

About the middle of September we again set out in full pursuit, all in high spirits, and bent for Moscow, a place greatly admired by Fin, because it was said the houses and churches were roofed with gold. The greater part of our road lay through forests. We had a fine broad road, with forests of wood on each hand, and here we had battles every day; for the Tartars lurked in the woods, and kept up an incessant fire from behind the trees; and, as our cavalry went foremost, great numbers fell, without being able to make any resistance. I heard, by chance one day, that this country was called Smolensko, and I then remembered that it was the place of which I was to be made governor; but I felt no interest in it.

The very next day after this intelligence, which must have been about the last week of September, for I remember thinking we had now pursued a retreating foe for exactly a twelvemonth, it was said in our army that we were not more than one hundred and sixty miles from Moscow. It was on a Sunday morning that we were called up to fight the whole Muscovite army. This was joyful tidings, for there was nothing our army longed for so much as a fair engagement with the Czar. But, as usual, the king's impatience had nearly proved the ruin of his whole army; for though quite aware that the woods were lined with an ambuscade, he dashed on the front of the enemy, with only about four thousand of his best dragoons, broke them, and kept cutting down all before him, till we were alarmed by shouts from behind. The Tartars that lined the woods had closed behind us, and cut our party off from the main army, as the Czar had cunningly devised, knowing the rashness and mad violence of his rival. We had nothing for it now but to face both ways, and fight back to back; but our force was nothing but a handful. The Tartars closed on us with an appalling shout, announcing their certainty of their prey, and rushed on like as many wild bears. They could not have mastered us, had it not been for the fire from the woods on each side, which brought down the Swedish troopers in whole files. My horse was shot through the heart, and, in plunging, threw me and himself into the ditch at one side of the road. My thigh-bone was broken; and, as I was crawling out on the other side, a Tartar struck me with a lance, and wounded me in the neck. I lay still, quite conscious that I was dying; and, though I believe but half sensible, I had an impression that I saw the Swedish van-guard cut off to a man. How the king alone escaped, is more than I can tell; but it seems that he did escape; which, when I heard of afterwards, I believed him shot-proof, like some old heroes whom I had heard of in Scotland.

I regarded the scene very little, as I thought, what had a dying man to do with these things? The road between the woods was choke-full of dead and dying, whom no man regarded, and, of course, no one regarded me; but about the fall of evening I was addressed by a Russian officer, who put up his head from the crush of carnage, and hailed me in some barbarous language, which I could not understand. I saw by his noble mien that he was of high rank. His signs indicated that he was dying of thirst; but I was obliged to make signs that I was not able to assist him, for I wondered at myself being so tenacious of life, having expected every hour to be my last since I fell. The poor fellow began to crawl towards me, but slower than a snail, for he was obliged to trail himself along the ground with his face upward; when he turned it down his head fell forward to one side. I never saw such fearful and pitiful looks, and I began to feel an inclination to live for his assistance. I could not help reflecting on the horrible system of warfare in which I was engaged, which allowed no time either for looking after the wounded or the dead, but still hurrying, hurrying on in the work of farther destruction. The poor fellow made to the side of the ditch, which, being dammed by the carcass of my horse, stood half filled up with bloody water, to which he pointed with his pallid hand, groaned, and jabbered. I could not resist the inclination to assist him, wretched and hopeless as I was; so I crawled over the dead horse, and held my canteen to his lips, which contained a portion of wine. He drank it with quaking eagerness; and when our two bloody hands met, he squeezed mine kindly and thankfully. What a vain fuming creature is man! A few hours before this we two meeting would have cut each other's throats, and exulted in the deed; now equal misfortunes joined us in mutual sympathy. He refused to drink more, but motioned to me to take it; which I did, and felt greatly refreshed, for in my agony I had forgot that I was thirsty. He had a limb shattered by a cannon-ball, and a sabre cut in his neck, which had severed one of the tendons, and made his head hang down. I tied up his head with a sword-belt, and stuffed the wound, and there did we lie groaning and drinking blood and water mixed for the whole night.

Next morning we were found by Fin, who had missed me, and suspecting the worst, came bringing his own baggage-waggon along with him, and plenty of wine, cordials, and dressings. With my own help, he set my broken thigh, and bandaged it, and washed and dressed the wound in my neck, which looked black, and very bad; and then, at my request, he reluctantly took the Russian officer with us, carrying us both to Smolensko. He turned out to be an Asiatic prince of a great people in the interior, called Baschkeirs, and his name was Iset. He had tried to seize Charles alive, but received the sabre cut which brought him down from the king's own hand. Fin carried us to the house of a Jew, named Zebulon, in which he had found a footing, as the servant of a great general of Britain, as rich as Crœsus. Zebulon was delighted to have us. When he found that he had an Asiatic prince and a British officer under his roof, he chuckled exceedingly, viewing his fortune as made.

We got such surgeons as the place afforded, and they amputated Prince Iset's limb, and bandaged his neck; and I never saw a more heroic fellow, though in the most miserable circumstances. I had no hope of his recovery. The surgeons made rather light of my wounds, telling me that I should be ready to take the field again in a few weeks: and there Iset and I lay both in the same apartment. We saw no more of our surgeons for many days, for the good people of the town and country around had now brought in great numbers of wounded soldiers; and the Protestant cathedral was given up to them as an hospital, where they lay, Russians and Swedes promiscuously, entirely at the mercy of the poor inhabitants. The week following an agent arrived from Charles with supplies, who called on me, and told me all the news, proffering every sort of assistance that I required. I had got a late supply of money, and declined any more; but Fin, by a made-up story, contrived to procure a round sum from this agent.

My broken limb gave me little trouble, save confining me in

one position; but the wound in my neck tormented me greatly. Iset fevered, and all hopes of his life were given up. He owed his preservation to the unwearied attentions of a beautiful Jewess, named Araby, the niece of old Zebulon. The latter was a complete Nabal; and coming to the knowledge that Prince Iset had no resources in monish, he grew careless of him, and harsh, letting him know that his absence would be quite agreeable. Alas! he could not be removed; and there was no hopes that he ever would be removed, except to his grave! All these misfortunes rendered him the more interesting to the lovely Araby, who attended him unremittingly, notwithstanding her uncle's bitter taunts. How I admired the angelic creature, as she kneeled beside his couch, administering the cordial to his parched lips with the tears in her eyes, smoothing his couch, or bathing his beating temples with vinegar! The heart of woman all over the world is alive to pity. As for Fin, he was as selfish as the Jew; for, though I lacked no attendance nor kindness that he could bestow, he would not attend to the prince, and seemed offended at Araby's attentions. I was frightened lest the lovely and amiable girl might fall a prey to that unaccountable creature's wiles, knowing his boundless command of money, and suspecting that her uncle kept her very bare; but, as she could speak a little broken French, I often held a friendly *tête-à-tête* with her, and trembled to hear her speak so well of Fin.

Naturally healthy and cheerful, I recovered fast, and had begun to sit up in bed, and take my food with a good deal of zest. But news arrived that the king of Sweden had gone away into the southern parts of the Russian empire, into provinces from which it was impossible he could ever return, and that a great army of the Czar's was approaching Smolensko for the reconquest of Poland. This was terrible news for me, and for many gallant Swedes who were lying wounded there, as well as at Holosin; and ere we could resolve what to do, or how to escape them, a party arrived to convey all the wounded Swedes, every one, to Moscow, there to be healed of their wounds, previous to their setting out for Siberia.

Fin came to me with the news that there was a Russian guard on the cathedral, and that the officer was searching the town for more prisoners; but the little fellow seemed rather elevated than depressed with the news. He was sick of Smolensko, and longed for a change; but, when I told him what sort of a place it was whither we were to be banished, his countenance fell, and he sat biting his fingers, and considering the matter with a grotesque and flippant seriousness. At length, cocking up his Polish cap, he said, "Well, then, I shan't go.

Depend on it, my dear master, since you tell me that there are neither money nor pretty women in that same Siberia, I for one shan't go near it. Nor shall you go either, unless you have a mind to it."

"I would dedicate my life to the man or woman," said I, "who would save me this day from going into exile. But I perceive no scheme by which it may be practicable. Peter, I know, is determined that not one officer or soldier of the Swedish army, who comes within the limits of his power, shall ever return to his home again."

"Whew!" cried Fin, snapping his fingers, "servile slaves, every officer in Peter's army!–men who, for a little money, would sell any thing in Muscovy save the life of their emperor. But I'll not even condescend to buy off this count. Remember, you are a servant of Peter's, one to whom matters of great trust are confided. But Charles, being master of the country, you durst not acknowledge it. See, do you remember aught of these?"

With that he took out the papers formerly mentioned, which he had picked up among the Russian slain, and which I remembered having seen and disregarded. Fin had got them deciphered, and they proved to be a passport from the Czar to General Count Fleming, ambassador to Augustus king of Poland, with some other sealed credentials. I thought there was something to be made of this; but the experiment was dangerous, as I could not conceive how the documents could have come there. I knew that Charles used every art to waylay and seize Count Fleming, and get possession of the correspondence; but I knew also that Fleming had escaped safe into Poland. The credentials were for General Count Fleming *and suite*, and it was probable that they had duplicates of these documents; and that some part of *the suite* had been chased back into Peter's army, and there fallen. I was so puzzled what to do, that my heart grew sick, and I felt that I was incapable of doing any thing. Fin waited for a while for orders; but I could not, durst not, come to any definitive resolution.

"Come, come," said he, "something must be done. We must seek out this Count Pollowowsky, and appear first before him; for if he have to find us out, we shall not escape so easily:" so away he went, and I saw no more of him all that day and the following night, nor the next day, till past noon, when I saw two noblemen, well attended, pass by on horseback, on their way to the cathedral. I waited till their return, expecting to see the whole of the Swedish wounded pass; but they came back as they went, and the most splendidly dressed one, whom I took to be the Count Pollowowsky, and who rode on the right hand, cast a look up to my window, and I perceived that it was Fin! I declare, at that moment, a suspicion struck on my heart that the creature was the devil. It was manifest that he had at once imposed on the Russian count, and passed himself off for a greater man than he; leaving me and my fears and scruples altogether out of the account.

The Swedes were all packed off that night towards Moscow in waggons, dung-carts, and sledges, without the least regard to their sufferings or deaths. It was a sight that oppressed my heart for many a day, and even till this present time my dreams are troubled by it. I still see some hundreds of brave men lying bound in pairs, writhing with pain, dragged off by their mortal enemies, never more to be heard of by their country or friends, and all to gratify the spleen of a fool–a born idiot! Oft has it caused me sinfully to say in my heart, "There can be no supreme and just ruler of the universe, else he would not suffer one madman thus recklessly to throw away an hundred thousand of his creatures,–a prey to death and bondage."

I could not, however, but feel grateful to the wayward and unaccountable being who had thus, by the most consummate duplicity, rescued me from a fate so dreadful, and I awaited his return with the most fearful anxiety. The poor Prince Iset was even more impatient than myself, expecting every minute a visit from his brother officer; but the latter left the town without deigning to call on him, and, I greatly suspect, without knowing he was there. His situation, doubtless, was most deplorable; for I had hitherto paid all the griping demands of old Zebulon, to prevent the prince's being laid on the street; and, as Fin's boundless wealth was both strangely situated, and under ticklish management, I feared it was not to be depended on.

Fin returned a grandee of the first rank, perfectly unknown to the prince, and every one of the Jew's family. He only deigned to tell me, in English, that I was now his subordinate officer, and that he was the most noble General Count Fleming, ambassador from the Emperor of Russia. I nodded assent, for I durst not converse freely, even in English, on so ticklish a point, before the prince and Araby, who had now heard a great deal of our language. When this elevated and proud diplomatist disowned all knowledge of the prince of the Baschkeirs, and let him know that the Count Pollowowsky did the same, Iset writhed in distress, and, I suppose, cursed the latter in bitterness of spirit. But I have no doubt that Fin concealed even the prince's name, lest the count should have come to our domicile, and learned more than he ought to have learned. Besides, Fin hated the prince, for what reason I could not guess, save that he had no feelings but those of selfishness and affection for me; an affection so strong and unalterable, that it hardly seemed natural. On the present occasion, he with a face of brass assumed the ambassador, and told the count that, for the preservation of these precious parchments, he had been obliged to assume the dress of a lowly Polish peasant, and pass as his own officer's servant. The count could not read a word; but he knew the seals, and believing all the great lies that Fin told him, he became obsequiousness itself, set Fin on his right hand, did him all honour, and would never part with him while he remained in Smolensko.

It was necessary now that we should depart, for winter was setting in, and we already ran the risk of being cooped up where we were in rather equivocal circumstances; but that which pained my heart the worst of all was leaving Prince Iset in such a deplorable state. He begged to go with me, saying he would follow me to any part of the world, for the whole earth was now alike to him, as he should never see his home again. There was a Chinese Jew in the town who knew a little of the prince's language, and explained some things to us; but we could not find out where his country lay, as, by his own description, more than half the world lay between him and it; but his father was the head khan of thirteen different tribes, which had each a subordinate khan of its own. He described this country as a perfect Eden, with great rivers and ships. What was to be done? he had no friends, no money; and mutual sufferings had rendered him so dear to me, that I felt strongly disposed to take him along with me, notwithstanding Fin's aversion to him, and the great trouble which I saw it would cost us, for he could still only lie on his back. So a bed was made for us in a covered waggon, and off we set, his excellency the ambassador riding in his chariot before us.

The description of this journey would take a whole volume, it was so disastrous; but the worst thing attending it was, that the ambassador, in spite of all our guides could say, would take his own roads, for a reason which I understood well. He had hidden treasures all the way; and the snow having fallen to a great depth, it was most difficult to find them. He searched for the coffer full of gold at the great morass, where the waggons were lost no less than a whole week, by which time the roads were quite impassable, and we lying all the while in a hovel. He gained the prize however at last, but told no one of it but me.

What a terrible country we had to traverse among snow and ice! At one time we stuck among the snow, and remained there all the night, and in the morning two of our horses were dead. At another time we were plunged into a river through the ice, and lost our waggon, but extricated the horses. We at length had to resort to sledges; and one having been constructed suitable for the two invalids, we made considerable progress; for his excellency having an order signed by Peter's own hand, pressed horses, carriages, and attendants whenever he chose into his service, and carried things with as high a hand as if he had been the grand vizier of the Turks.

All the attendants and guides that left Smolensko with us had long ago deserted, and returned homeward, excepting one boy, who continued close with us, and was most attentive to all our wants day and night. When we reached a town called Wilna, by which we were obliged to go, the ambassador paid the boy his wages, and ordered him to return home. I called him in to bid him farewell and give him a small present, and found him drowned in tears. On inquiring the cause, he could not tell me, but sobbed till his heart was like to burst. I said if he did not like to return home he was welcome to continue in my service, for that I esteemed him very highly for his attentions; on which the poor fellow kneeled, clasped my knees, and kissed my hand, and in a few minutes was as blithe as a lark.

From that time my heart was knit to the boy, and indeed he had been a favourite, and deservedly so, from the time of his engagement. The river of Wilna, on which we meant to have embarked for Koningsberg, being at that time shut up by the frost, we were obliged to continue our journey by land, anxious to get fairly out of the czar's reach, lest our sly escape should have been discovered; and as we were now approaching the country where the real General Count Fleming was well known, Fin dropped the ambassador, and again took his own name with a new title, General Finlay, by which appellation he continued to conduct all our movements.

From Wilna we journeyed by land, and on a dreadful road, towards a town called Kowna, that had been represented as only fifty miles distant; but which we did not reach till the evening of the fourth day, by which time we were quite overcome with fatigue, and ready to perish, our guides having fallen down through exhaustion by the way, owing to the great frost. The prince had very nigh perished; and poor William, for so we called the Russian boy, fainted, and was carried in quite lifeless. My whole efforts were exerted towards his recovery, and I soon succeeded in restoring animation; but he remained so faint and feeble, that I trembled for his life. At length he fell into a profound sleep, and, as I was unbuttoning his frozen fur frock to wrap him in warm blankets, I discovered, to my utter amazement, that poor William was a young maiden, and no other than the beautiful Araby the Jewess! My heart was quite overcome by various sensations, and my hand trembled so, that I could hardly conceal the youthful bosom from my own eyes and those of (as I wished to do) all the world beside.

At first I had no doubt that this diabolical act was one of Finlay's machinations, and my blood boiled with indignation at the thought. But when I considered that he had paid her her wages as a boy, and wished her to return to her native place before going quite out of the reach of it, I knew not what to think. I had heard him speak to her in a careless manner, as a servant lad about whom he was indifferent, ask anent her parents, and advise her to return home as the most prudent step she could take; so that if he really had gained her affections, and persuaded her to follow him in that guise, there was a duplicity in his whole behaviour that I could not believe him or any man capable of.

The truth is, I was in a fine quandary, for, after drawing every inference that I could from existing circumstances, I came to this conclusion, that a romantic passion had induced the girl to make that singular elopement; and I thought it most probable that the attachment was to myself. I had never been in love all my life, excepting that I felt a preference in my heart towards my beautiful preserver. I had never yet had time to fall in love, at least to any great depth; but felt a strong predilection to do so now. Here was a lovely and innocent virgin, of a race that had been the wonder of the world–one who had left every earthly relative for my sake–had cut off her beautiful raven locks–assumed the dress of a peasant-boy, and slept nightly at my feet in the waggon, often warming my feet in her bosom. In short, I thought of her with so much affection, that I often felt the tear smarting my eyes: this I called pity; but strong compassion is allied to love.

Day after day did my eyes follow the beautiful boy, out and in, early and late; and still, whatever vehicle we rode in, she attended us as our humble companion. She perceived at last, and that before we reached the coast, that I regarded her with more than ordinary attention; and I marked the very moment when suspicion first reached her heart that I knew her sex. It was beautiful. Her eyes met mine, and they spoke to each other, telling what language could not so impressively have revealed. The blush on her cheek came not suddenly; it began like the morning's dubious tint; and still, as suspicion imbued her heart, the cheek reddened and reddened, till all from the brow to the bosom was one ruddy glow, and then she hastened from my presence.

"She is mine," said I to myself; "wholly in my power! But may every misfortune be my lot, if I use that power to her disadvantage or ruin!" She came seldomer into my presence now; but being vexed at this, I spoke and looked to her as I was wont to do, or as nearly so as I could. But I saw that an explanation was necessary, for she was often exposed to the company of vulgar men in her present capacity, which I could not endure; and having now watched Finlay strictly, and thoroughly considered all his behaviour from first to last, I was convinced he was ignorant of her sex.

This was confirmed one day at Koningsberg as we were shipping our baggage. I was standing on the wharf giving some orders, when I heard a cry, and looking about, there was the great General Finlay beating my interesting maid cruelly with a cane. Without stopping to inquire the cause, I rushed to the spot, and with one blow of my crutch knocked him down. Some said I had killed the gentleman; and at that time I was so incensed, I cared not though I had. But the very next minute there was the beautiful Araby kneeling over him, weeping, and bathing his bloody face with cold water! "She is betrayed! she is betrayed! and his mistress after all!" thought I; "but I'll have his heart's blood for it, and then make her what reparation I can."

Boiling with rage and indignation, I went on board without regarding what became of Finlay or his degraded attendant. The prince inquired of me, in his broken English, what I ailed at the great little man, who surely had a right to beat his own servant boy. As I could make no answer, he went on, saying that he was a good and a kind gentleman, and we could not have lived without him; and so many kind things, while the tear often stood in his eye, that my heart relented, and I went to ask for him, for I knew if alive he would be on board, as he neither would nor durst separate from me. We were by that time half way to Lubeck, and I found him in his cabin, and Araby still in attendance. He had his head bound up, and still looked very ill; but as soon as he saw my face he begged my pardon, adding that he had forgot the boy was my servant, which he certainly was from the time that he had paid him off, and I had retained him.

I said, that with regard to his maltreating the boy as my servant, that was what I could easily forgive; but there was something under it of so vile and flagrant a nature, that I could never forgive it, and as soon as we reached Scotland it must part us for ever.

He then fell a crying outright, and said, though he had been guilty of many crimes, he had never been guilty of one towards me; and for the rest he was answerable himself. This answer confirmed me in his guilt with regard to the wretched maid in whom I had felt my heart so much interested, and I left them without any explanation.

Shortly after she came into the prince's cabin and mine, and told us that the general had discarded her as not belonging to him, and ordered her still to wait on us as usual, for he was better, and had another boy; and at the same time she looked so blithe and happy at the change, that I was again mightily puzzled, and knew not what to think. She remained with us, and slept in a small hammock off our cabin, and was so cheerful and attentive, that I began to love her better than ever. One night at Lubeck, being a little elevated with wine, and the prince having retired to his chamber, I began to question her about Smolensko, and if she did not wish again to retire home, proffering her at the same time the means of doing so directly by Petersburg. She answered unhesitatingly, that she had no such desire, and was still busy with some work when I inadvertently said something about her uncle Zebulon. Looking towards her, quite unconscious of having disclosed her great secret, such a statue of astonishment I never beheld. The work had fallen from her hands, and her face turned to crimson; but instantly it grew pale as death; the colour left her lips, and I, thinking she was fainting, took her in my arms, and set her on a sofa.

"Captain, what was it you said to me?" said she. "What or whom were you talking about?"

"Araby," said I, "could you ever conceive that I did not know you?"

The poor creature kneeled, and wept abundantly, and at once confessed that an unconquerable attachment had caused her to follow me; but that she had resolved never to have disclosed her sex as long as she lived. But I was transported with delight when she informed me that neither Finlay nor the prince knew or had ever manifested the least suspicion of her sex; and then in the height of my transport I dried her tears, kissed her lips, charged her to keep the secret inviolable till we reached Scotland, and then every thing should be according to her wishes. In this she readily acquiesced. I flew, and made friends again with Finlay, and every thing went right. I was deeply in love, and whenever Araby's eyes and mine met each other, they conversed in a language known only to ourselves.

No sooner had we reached Edinburgh than I equipped my darling in all the finery of the day; and when I took her into the great tavern, leaning on my arm, and introduced her to the prince and Finlay, I never saw such another scene of amazement and joy. The former, notwithstanding his crutches and wry neck, skipped about the floor, till I thought he had lost his senses; and then again and again he came and laid Araby's hand on his crown, and at the last prostrated himself in order to put her foot upon it; but this I would not permit. I had never seen her laugh so heartily before.

The city was at this time in great confusion; but time went on joyfully and happily with us, until I at last thought it time to unite myself with the maiden of my heart, who had left her country for my sake, and thus cast herself entirely on my honour. So, taking her hand one day, I asked her fervently when she was going to make me happy.

"You need not ask that," returned she; "for you know that every day and every hour I am ready and willing to make you happy, as far as honour and virtue will permit me, and farther I know you never will ask."

"Never, while I live, dearest Araby," said I; "but, in one word, when are you willing to become my wife?"

"Your wife, sir? What can you mean? Are you serious in such a question?"

"Quite serious, by all my hopes of earthly happiness!" said I. "And, moreover, was not this matter understood between us long ago?"

"Alas, never by me, sir!" said she; "but the very reverse of it."

"What!" said I; "did you not tell me at Lubeck that an unconquerable attachment had caused you to follow me from your native country?"

"Yes, I did, sir; but I never said that attachment was for you. If I did not make you to understand this, I thought I had done so; or, perhaps, I weened that every one saw into my heart as well as I did."

"Oh, very well, madam!" said I, in high dudgeon; "I see how it is! I am deceived, cheated, fooled by you and your paramour. And so you are Mr. Fin's mistress after all? I might have known as much when I saw you crying over his bloody coxcomb. But I'll bait him–I'll bang him for it, the deceitful wretch!"

"Alas, sir, how far you misread all my motives!" said she; "I had no feeling toward the gentleman, but pity for his ill usage; whereas you think that the heart of one of the lost sheep of Israel can entertain none but selfish passions. I like him not, for he is too cold hearted for me; but it is Prince Iset with whom my heart is bound up, and that so firmly, as to be incapable of removal, except with death!"

I was so transfixed with amazement, that I could not speak; but, as I lifted up my hands and eyes towards heaven, I prayed inwardly for blessings on that young and benevolent heart, and then, as if speaking in a dream, I exclaimed fervently, "He is mutilated, and maimed for life,–an outcast–a beggar–a helpless stranger in a foreign land!"

"Ay, there you are right," cried she; "these are the things that have endeared him to me! But as long as I am attached to him he cannot be very destitute. I will do every thing for him with so much delight; for his heart is ever as it should be. He is so grateful, so kind, so cheerful, and contented under every privation and every affliction; and then so utterly helpless, that, O! I could not suffer him to go away into a strange country by himself."

"You are a most extraordinary creature," said I; "a being of which I have no comprehension! Your affections, your delights, and even your very nature, appear to run counter to those of all other maidens of the race of Adam. But this romantic attachment, so disinterested, and so out of the common course of woman's love, shall never be thwarted by me. I am disappointed, it is true, in the attainment of the only heart I ever coveted; but, for all that, I am bound to admire it more than ever. I too love the prince with a brother's love, and it shall be my study to assist and protect you while I live; but come with me, we will now astonish him more than ever."

"O no! no!" cried she; "I cannot have it told him–no, not for the world would I discover to him the depth of my affection. I desire merely to live with him as his menial, as his servant-maiden, and be allowed to love and take care of him. I take on myself voluntary slavery, which you know every free woman has a right to do."

"No! no!" said I; "there is no such thing allowed in this country as slavery of any kind; and since you have appeared here as my equal in rank, it is only as his wife or mine that you can remain with us."

Araby cried, and was greatly distressed about the *éclaircissement*, and regretted that I had first found out her sex, and then the state of her affections, which I never should have done if she could have avoided it; but I persisted in introducing her to the prince as his betrothed, or, at least, as the maid he was bound in honour to wed, she having refused my hand and independence therewith, out of pure affection for him.

We went forthwith, and laid the whole case before the prince. But in place of being overjoyed, as he was at the first sight of her in Scotland, he was quite cast down, and in the deepest distress; and at last, after weeping abundantly, peremptorily refused to make her his wife, and thereby reduce her to a state of beggary. He next besought her to become my wife, and suffer him to live with her as a friend and humble dependant.

We were now in a sad dilemma, and, for my part, I knew not what to do, for I was terrified for Finlay, knowing that what he set himself about he would accomplish; and he was beginning to look very kind upon her. The prince *would not* marry her, and she *would not* marry me; and to live with us all three as a sister or relation would not do; so I boarded her with two old maiden ladies of high rank in the Lawn Market.

Before proceeding with my own history, I must digress a little to give the history of Prince Iset. The czar's army, after the battle of Smolenkso, having taken different routes, it was a good while before the prince was missed. But as soon as he was missed every search was made after him, and it came to be ascertained that he had been carried into Smolensko alive; but there all traces of him were lost. The powerful army that he commanded neither would nor could be led by any other general than their own prince, whose language and signals they understood; so that the czar was obliged to send an express for the old khan, Iset's father, to command the Baschkeirs, who came, but died on his march to Pultowa, through age, cold, and fatigue.

The search was then renewed for Iset with more ardor than ever, and by some means it was discovered that he had been removed from Smolensko by General Count Fleming. An express was sent to Dresden, and there it was found that the count had not been in the czar's dominions that year. But at Smolensko they found the Jew, who gave the marks of the prince, and then with ease they traced him to Leith.

One day, as I was sauntering down the Cannongate with Captain Drummond, with whom I had again met, one of the city criers was standing with his drum, braying away amid a crowd of giggling idlers. Drummond, who was deeply concerned in matters public and private at that time, drew me near to hear the proclamation; but when he heard what it was, he turned away, smiling, and saying to himself, "Oh! is that all?" I asked him what it was: he said it was only the Calmuck prince, whom they had been crying every day for this half year. I returned again to the spot, and heard the following extraordinary proclamation brayed out from the lungs of a genuine Campbell of Kilmun; for the Campbells had at that period every post high and low.

"Husha! And a more husha! Tis was to brought te believe tat tere was stolen or strayed from te creat man's of te Moss–cubhaid one creat prhince, all but te one leg and te neck,–feith his name is prince Iset Dog-at-brew; whisky cuach of tirteen peoples; whaever shall brought him to te pear of Leith, liffing or not liffing, shall pe gotting fifty toozand livers for te saiffety of him."

I heard at once, that though the Russians and the Highlander had not been able to comprehend each other properly, it was my beloved friend for whom the reward was offered; and without saying a word to Drummond, I posted off to the Lawn Market with the news to Araby, that she might discover her favourite to his countrymen, receive the reward offered, which amounted to £2,400, and then accompany him home to his regal dominions.

On reaching Miss Cumins I found that Araby was not there; and more, that she had been absent for three days; that I had sent for her express, and she had left the home in a chair for my lodgings on Sunday evening. This was the sharpest thrust of all; to have the dear affectionate creature ferreted from me in that clandestine manner, I could not bear. Suspecting Finlay at once, I hastened home, and in presence of the prince, charged him on his life to tell me where he had that amiable girl concealed, before I hewed him in pieces. He grew as pale as death, and sank on his knees, without being able to articulate a word; and jealousy, which is as cruel as the grave, prompted me to believe that this was nothing less than a fair avowal of his guilt; so, in the plenitude of my wrath I drew my sword, and had it not been for the interference of the prince, who came hopping between us, struck up my sword with his crutch, and offered to stand surety with his life for the innocence of his friend the general, I certainly had cleft the villain's head.

We now came to speaking and hearing, when Finlay protested his innocence in the most solemn manner, saying, that if I judged of him from former circumstances, I judged amiss; it being his opinion that whatever took place between a man and woman, if it was agreeable to both, and no other person concerned, then there was no injury done. But in this case, where he knew his only friend and protector to be so deeply interested, he would have laid down his life before attempting an abduction.

I was still but half convinced of his honesty, and told him to find her out, that I might hear the truth from her own lips, else I would hold him guilty to the day of my death; and he and I both instantly set out in search of her, without knowing well what to do first. My mind was at that time so wholly taken up with the loss of my beloved Araby, that I forgot even to mention to the prince his good fortune in the restoration to his father's throne.

I went again to the Misses Cumin, and told them I would make them answerable for the young foreigner I had left under their care with their lives and fortunes. I saw they were very much afraid, and, to intimidate them still farther, I had them apprehended and brought before the sheriff, who examined them very sharply; but they really seemed to know nothing. Finlay was more successful, for he had collected a whole posse of chairmen and caddies, and had them sworn and examined before the council, by which means he found out one of the men who had carried Araby from her lodgings. But then he had been released by a livery-servant at the Fountain well, and all that he knew was that the lady was carried down towards the palace.

I proffered him a high reward if he would find out any of the bearers, and he promised that he would. Finlay and I continued our search, having agreed that each of us was to whistle and sing alternately a Jewish melody, which we had learned from Araby. We did so, and about the fall of the evening a fellow came running after me in a street called Cannongate, and laying his hand on my shoulder, requested me to come and speak with a young lady, who had sent him expressly after me.

"Where is she?" said I.

"In a house down by here," said he: "for the L—'s sake, sir, follow me directly, for I fear she is in a very bad taking."

I still hesitated, for the man wanted the bonnet, and had a wild raised look; so I asked him who the lady was, and what she wanted with me.

"It is the lady you brought from High Germany, sir, your mistress, you know. By ——, sir, if you don't follow me directly, you will rue it all your life. I could not answer for the consequences, no, not for a minute," quoth the man; and so, turning, he ran down the street, and I after him. He led me into a narrow street on the right, where he rapped loudly at a door, and it was not till he had rapped six or seven times, that a voice within, in deep and angry tones, inquired what we were wanting. The man said this was the gentleman whom the young lady wanted to see; but the inmate of the house ordered him to go about his business for an ignorant and impertinent scoundrel; and with that we heard another door bolted inside. My conductor then swore most terribly, vowing the most ample revenge on some villanous aggressor; but the man was in such a fluster, it was impossible to understand him. He ran down the close, bareheaded as he was, and coming to a fine front or entrance door facing the south, he ran to that, calling me with curses to follow him; and without waiting to knock, tried to force the door, which he would soon have effected, had not a gentleman fired on him from a balcony above. The poor fellow fell, and tumbling down the steps, grovelled on the green, swearing without intermission.

I was standing in a sort of stupor, not knowing well either what to say or do, when the screams of Araby crying out my name struck my ears, at which both caution and discretion vanished. I flew to the door, and at the first effort bursting it open, I ran along a circular corridor, till coming to a grand stair, I there on the second step met the same gentleman who had shot my conductor, who, with his drawn sword, attacked me in the most furious and brutal style. Being in a foreign uniform, I was armed, but my sword in the scabbard; so I was obliged to fly with all my might, and before I got to the green before the door, I was wounded slightly in both shoulders. I was obliged to jump into the garden over a parapet of at least eight feet high, before I had time to draw my sword. My gentleman entered by the gate, running all the way. He was a beautiful and handsome man, with long curled hair over each shoulder. I called to him to restrain his rage, and grant me a word of the young foreign lady in that house; but he only advanced the quicker, saying he would teach such foreign puppies to burst into his house, and attacked me furiously with his weapon. I knew that no man in Scotland could be my superior in wielding the cut-and-thrust sword; so that now, getting leisure to draw, I stood his attack, and made play. He was agile and acute at the sword-exercise, and, I dare say, valued himself on his science; but in that he was a child to me. I tried three times to disarm him, but could not, and, at the third time, receiving a sharp wound in the thigh, I lost patience, and with a back stroke cut him across the breast, and killed him on the spot.

With my bloody sword in my hand, I ascended the steps from the garden, and was going straight to attack the house, when the wounded man on the green arrested my attention with a "Hem! hem!" I looked towards him: he was holding out his hand, which I took, and squeezed fervently in the perturbation of the moment. "Fly!" said he, "fly for your life! you are a brave fellow, and 'tis pity you should die. But you little know what you have done. Fly! the lady is safe *now*. I say, take the first street-door on the right, and bolt it behind you. You will find your way quite safe!"

I left him, and sheathing my sword in the close, walked quietly and deliberately out of the entry, looking carelessly around me. The first right-hand door in the street I found with the upper half open, like a barn-door; and entering, without any person that I could discern noticing me, or looking that way, I left the door open as it was, and watched a while from the interior. Instantly there was a rush of officers into the close. I could not help being alarmed, and, trying to work my way in the interior, I found it easily to a first and second story of curious antique appearance. The door of the first floor having an iron bolt as thick as my arm, I drew it, and was going to wait the issue, watching what I saw. But perceiving a barber's light dress, apron, and wig, I loosed off my sword, and put them on. This I had not well effected, ere I heard voices in the lower shop, calling out, "Barber! Barber! What the devil's become of Suds?"

As I heard the men speak in the English Northumberland tongue, I knew that they were strangers, and with my white apron, jacket, and yellow wig, I went down to them and began officiating as a barber, hoping to hear who the gentleman was whom I had slain, and if they had heard any thing of the lady. I prepared the suds and fell a-shaving; but the Northumbrian made a wry face, and cursed me. While still busy, with a trembling hand, a fourth Englishman came running in, crying, "Let us gwo bwoys! let us gwo." They would not consent, asking the reason of his haste, when he was obliged to tell them reluctantly before me that some of Mar's rebels were in town, who within these few minutes had broken into a house, and slain a near relation, and head general of king George's; and that the whole city was in arms, searching for them to cut them in pieces. "Whoy than, Lwoghd, we aghe gwone evehy swole of us!" cried the fellow I was shaving, starting up, all suds, and half-shaven as he was; and I never saw four fellows in greater agitation. They offered me a high reward if I would conceal them till midnight, which I accepted, and bolting the shop-door as I had at first been desired to do, I led the way up stairs, bolted the second door, and then up to a dark inscrutable third story, from which there led a long narrow passage, having a low black door at the farther end. On laying my ear to this, I heard indistinct sounds of wo, and was convinced it was the house in which my beloved Araby was secreted, and where her violator lay a corpse, killed by my hand. Feelings of indefinable perturbation seized me. I suspected that the occupier of the house we were in was the poor fellow who was shot, and that it must have been by that door he had obtained communication with Araby. As I was casting about in my mind if it was not possible to get her conveyed by that private door once more under my own protection, I was alarmed by a terrible noise at the street-door. The strangers had been seen to enter, and a company of the military were

*Captain Lochy in the Barber's Dress*

London Published by Cochrane & Co 1832.

breaking open the door. The men rushed from me to defend the second door, and in the mean time I easily shut the inner bolt of the private door, for which a convenience had lately been made by a small hole, in which there was an awl sticking. I found myself in a sort of confused concealed armoury, where I could easily have concealed myself in a coat of mail, and taking out the awl and bolting the door behind me, I attempted it. But aware that I could not live long, I thought it as good to venture forward and endeavour to escape while the great commotion was in the street; so finding the doors all on the latch, I passed on till I came to a sort of grand narrow gallery, in which a number of ladies were sitting all in tears; but Araby was not there. At the sight of me they all screamed and fled, taking me for the ghost of the barber who was shot, in whose daily dress I had appeared. I heard some expressions of dreadful terror; but all fled from my face, and I passed whom I pleased. Agitated as I was, in the middle of the saloon I sung aloud a stave of the plaintive Jewish melody; but there was no answer, no scream, but a solemn silence; and then I knew that Araby was either shut up from my hearing, or no more; and so escaping by the front door, without any obstacle, I went down through the garden and over the wall into a low road, which following, I came into the street called Cowgate, and soon reached my own lodgings. Neither Finlay nor the prince knew me, and assured me I might travel through all the world in that dress without being recognised by one individual. The yellow wig in particular so disguised me, that had it not been removed, they would not have been convinced of my identity.

This was a great comfort, and I immediately set out with Finlay to learn the fate of the Northumbrians; but we met the military coming up the High-street with them all prisoners, and saw them consigned to the prison called the Tolbooth; so we returned home, and, to our infinite joy and surprise, found Araby there before us. She had been sent back to the house of the Misses Cumin in a sedan-chair, almost on the instant after I had slain the gentleman; the ladies of the mansion appearing very anxious to get quit of her.

That was a night of joy with us, but one of great perplexity. We could make nothing of Araby's story, as the people she was with spoke in a different language, save when they spoke to her, and her English was imperfect. She said it was a great foreign prince that I had killed, and that she was to have gone abroad with him next day, to personate a queen or princess for a season, we could not make out which. But then she had told them of my name; the Misses Cumin also knew of our connexion, and it was apparent that my life was in momentary danger. There was no violence offered to her, except restraint, but, on the contrary, the greatest kindness; and they spoke to her of riches and grandeur. The story was inexplicable; but we hoped to hear all explained by the trial of the Northumbrians, who were to be examined in the council-chamber next day.

We knew not what to do first; it was necessary to disclose to the prince and Araby their good fortune, and have them consigned to the emperor's emissaries. It was also absolutely necessary that I should make my escape, else my fate was inevitable, as the disguise of the barber would ere that have been discovered; and in that garb only should I now be sought after and recognised. We sat together all night, maugre every danger, consulting together, and making reflections on the strange reverses of fortune, that seemed to attend us all individually, and myself in particular, whose life had been one tissue of danger and difficulty. When I told the prince that the great czar's messengers were awaiting him to take him home to his father's dominions, and that the thirteen nations would not draw a sword, but under his command, I never saw a human creature agitated by such a diversity of feelings. He wept bitterly, took my hand and squeezed, and kissed it, protesting that he would never part with me. Then he spoke again of his people and his kindred, lauded their love and fidelity, and wept again. Araby likewise shed some tears, but no one could guess whether of joy or grief. She was a singular girl, the Jewess, and different in all her feelings from any that I ever saw. When the prince said that he rejoiced that he now had it in his power to reward her by setting the crown of his father and mother on her head, she smiled, and said with the utmost decision, "No, no, prince, that is no station for me, nor one of which I will ever accept. I rejoice that you are going again into the bosom of your friends, where you will have no more need of me. If I saw that your life and comforts depended on my attention, I would have followed you to the end of the world; but as it is, I will remain where I am, and serve my masters here. All that I request of you is, sometimes to remember me."

It was in vain that he declared his life and happiness depended more on her than ever, and that he never would go home without her; she remained inflexible; saying, the queen, and princes, and great men, would soon thrust the poor daughter of Israel from among them, and that she had no heart or desire after greatness. But she wished him well and happy, and there was no fear of her. She could work well for her bread any where, and looked for nothing higher.

After all our entreaties proved of no avail, I mentioned Queen

Esther to her, and what a blessing she had been to her people by being raised to royalty; and hinted that there were doubtless great numbers of the scattered race of Israel in the prince's native dominions. Then a new light seemed to break upon her soul, and she turned her lovely dark eyes towards the prince for information. He assured her that one-fourth of all the people of his dominions were Jews, the richest and most industrious; and that they would rejoice in her exaltation, and keep jubilees, and bring gifts; and then I saw by her looks that her heart clung to the prosperity of her people. Her heart was made for conferring benefits, not for receiving them, and I felt that I was to lose her for ever.

I now equipped myself in the dress of a British captain, which I thought myself entitled to do, though so basely deprived of my rank by Marlborough, and ventured out to the council-chamber to hear the examinations of the Englishmen. It was a very curious one. There was a sufficiency of evidence to have hanged the fellows at once, had the council of Edinburgh not been divided, almost equally, between the houses of Brunswick and Stuart; and the latter seemed to be the strongest party over the greater part of Scotland. The magistrates durst not expose one another; and it was impossible to have any cause tried fairly and fully there. The name of the foreigner whom I had slain was even strictly concealed during the trial; but they could not prove his death by the hand of any of the Northumbrians; although they clothed one of them in my apparel, which they had found where I had concealed it, and made the ladies of the house make oath, they all denied that any one of them was the man. At last it was fairly concluded that the murderer had escaped in the disguise of the barber; and then the utmost vengeance was breathed against me. My bloody sword was produced in court, which brought the worthy magistrates into a fine puzzle. It was a fine cut-and-thrust blade, with the basket and handle of silver; a present to me from the king of Sweden; and sorry was I to part with it. But when they found *Carolus Rex* engraven on it, I never saw men look so dumbfoundered. They looked at one another; then they looked at the ceiling, as if in deep contemplation. Then the lord-provost put his hands in his breeches-pockets, and shook his head; the baillies put their hands in their pockets, primmed their mouths, winked, and shook their heads. They were all convinced that they had the Pretender within the city, and his sword in their hands; but farther they comprehended not. At length one of them spoke nearly as follows:–

"Aw doot, ma luord an' breethren, ye'll differ frae me; but it's maw hoomle opunion, that since we hae the true air o' the croon o' Scotland amang us, we shood let him slip awa' like a knotless thread, an' no bring oursels in guilty o' the blude royal, whilk wad be a stain on the auld town for evermair."

"Do ye no think, my lord," said another, "that our friend wha spak last should gang straught away to Perth, and try to assist Lord Mar wi' his counsels, and no bide here to distract ours ony langer, as we ken weel what cause he wishes to prevail?"

"Ooerder! Ooerder! Maw luord, aw cry to ooerder!" said the first speaker.

"No, sir, begging your pardon," continued the other, "I'm not out of order; and, as a friend and weelwisher to you, let me hint, that if it *was* the Pretender whose hand committed this slaughter, what a deadly misfortune to himself! Why, it is the most extraordinary manifestation of Divine vengeance on a cause, perhaps, that is to be found in history, and a certain signal that that cause is not to prosper."

Every one present acknowledged the singularity of the event. I know not what I would then have given to have known who this illustrious foreigner, whom I had blamelessly slain, was; but that was strictly concealed, even from a part of the council, who were not suffered to ask publicly.

The last speaker was at this time examining my sword, with closer minuteness than I liked. However, he noticed nothing new, till a gentleman, looking over his shoulder, pointed out the half obliterated figures to him. This kindled another flame, and put them all on another scent, not so agreeable to me. "My lord, there is something here we didna see. This is the king of Sweden's sword," cried he; "and this strange sacrilegious murder must have been committed by some trusted emissary of that dangerous man, who has lately espoused the cause of the Stuarts. And, my lord, since this is manifestly the case, it is absolutely necessary for our own honour and safety that we secure that foreign delinquent. He is perhaps the king of Sweden's first minister; at all events, some great accredited person. And I cannot help observing, that if the king of Sweden's agent have been led to commit this slaughter, it is a more extraordinary coincidence than the other."

In short, after a whole forenoon's wrangling among these wiseacres, the Northumbrians were dismissed, with orders to keep their mouths shut, and return straight home. Their dispatches were burnt before them, for they were written on a principle of concealment, through which the magistrates could not penetrate; and they did not wish their ignorance to be discovered. And finally, it was determined to offer a great reward for the apprehension of the king of Sweden's officer.

This was a ticklish announcement for me, for they had the clothes that I had worn, and my sword, in their possession; so that they could describe my appearance minutely; and they could have direct information from the Misses Cumin, and the people where I lodged beside. I was also known to Captain Drummond; but of him I was not afraid. Then there was a transaction in the bank, the only one then in Edinburgh, which was made out in my name by Finlay, who took the whole charge of my money concerns on himself; for knowing I had so good an agent, I made him master of my funds entirely. He had lodged a deposit in the bank at interest, in my name, that utterly astonished me; and as a great part of that was in foreign coinage, there I was not only sure to be detected, but to lose my all, as a foreign traitor to the cause of the king of England.

We left our lodgings that very afternoon, as if going out to take a walk. But I knew there would be an instant chase after me, and went straight to a furnishing tailor's, and exchanged my scarlet uniform for that of a Highland chief; and putting an auburn wig over my own dusky locks, I never valued myself on my appearance till then, in my life before, and I could have defied my nearest friend to know me. Still, that was not a dress for Edinburgh at that present time on one who could give no better account of himself; and I knew neither what to do, nor what I had done, which was the thing that distressed me worst of all.

In this extremity, I sent Finlay in search of Captain Drummond; but during his absence I heard myself called at the drum-head, and a thousand marks offered for my apprehension: while, worse than all, the very broker from whom I had the Highland dress was with the officers, to point out to them the man. It was on the shore at Leith I heard this; and being in a sort of dark coffee-room, I determined not to be taken; because, though conscious of no guilt, I saw my case looked bad; so I watched their motions. They repeated the proclamation. A servant at the tavern, or the tavern-keeper, went out bareheaded, and spoke to them, apparently in a jocular way: they regarded him with eager attention, and I saw him point to my window. I rushed out at the back-door into a stable-yard, where I came upon a beautiful girl, hanging some clothes on a cord. "I am pursued, my dear. Save me!" said I. She pointed to a door, and continued her song, without being in the least moved. I ran in; and behold! it was a small dark stable without any egress; and being fairly at bay, I flew to the darkest corner, with a cocked pistol in one hand and my drawn sword in the other. The whole party rushed after me in one moment; but the girl put them on a wrong scent: they took another door, and I heard them running past where I stood, like so many wild horses. She then called me out, and led me into a large cellar. "You need have no fear, sir," said she. "I am mistress here, and not for worlds would I betray one of the bold adherents of the Stuarts. Let these go, the dogs! They are fairly on a wrong scent. Take the use of every thing here. I must to my work again. They will be back."

I was so much affected by the spontaneous chivalry of this young and beautiful female, that I caught her in my arms, and kissed her cheek and lips, a freedom I had scarcely ever taken with a girl before; for mine had been a life of toil and danger, not of love. She gave me a playful slap, and ran out to her work in the yard. I saw her through the iron-stanchions of the cellar, as she began a clapping her muslins between her hands, and singing. She had scarcely begun when several of the party came back, and examined her over again. I now heard every word, and could not but admire her careless and indifferent air. To their queries, if such a man really passed through the yard, she answered, "To be sure there was. I had no occasion to lie about it. I saw a Highland gentleman pass through the yard. He went close by my side; but as he seemed in a hurry, I did not follow him with my eye. I thought he went out at that door. If he did not, he must be in the stable, he can be no where else."

They searched the stable, and came out convinced that I had eluded them in the back close. "Who is the gentleman? And what has he done?" said she.

"Who is he!" said the head-officer. "D–n him! he's the king o' Sweden, come over here to help the Pretender, and drive our true Protestant king frae the throne, as he has done half a dozen already. And to begin the work, he has killed with his own hand a great foreign prince or bishop, or something. Confound the knave! There's a thousand pounds set on his head, and they are doubling it every hour."

"I wish I had catched him by the kilt as he went by, and squealed out till ye came to me! I could easily have done it. But I hope you will get him still. Mind, you are to give me a hunder pounds of it for telling you the right door." The officer then ran off after the others, swearing great oaths to have the king of Sweden before he slept.

The delightful creature then came back to me, like to burst with laughter at the ridiculous idea that she had the great king of Sweden locked in her back cellar. She addressed me by the title of majesty, and treated me with various sorts of wine. A more intense jacobite never existed, and she told me there were a thousand of her name in the northern army who would die for king James every man of them, but they would place him on his throne once more. She was of the clan M'Kenzie. Yet, for all so completely as she had me in her power, and a high reward offered for me, she had the delicacy never once to ask who I was, or to hint that it was requisite she should know, which I admired exceedingly; but did not think it proper to tell her, though it was evidently my duty to have done so. I told her however that I expected Lord Drummond's brother to call on me every minute, in company with general Finlay, and described their appearance when they should come into the coffee-room, and ask for the Highland chieftain.

She appeared quite delighted with every thing she heard or saw; so I sat down on the end of a brandy cask, and took her on my knee; but at that moment, hearing the voices of strangers above stairs, she sprang off and left me: turning round however on the trap-stair, she made me a low and graceful courtesy, saying, in a whisper, "Good bye, your majesty, I will be back anon."

I felt the reproof, but could not help admiring the ease and animation of this captivating girl, and wished from my heart that Finlay and Captain Drummond might not come to part me from her. They had come already, and a fine pickle they were in. Drummond had been summoned before the council as a suspected person, and not choosing to risk a trial and find securities, he was obliged to abscond, and was proclaimed a rebel. Finlay had a still worse story. The officers, in their search for me, had laid hold of Prince Iset, and finding him a foreigner, had taken him prisoner. Finlay saw him stumping away with his tree leg, and his face on one shoulder, between two officers, in a fine dilemma, for the men could not understand one word he said. As we knew not what had become of Araby, every thing now with us had got into complete confusion; and, though ashamed to say it, I found that I was in love with our landlady, and unwilling to leave the house, urgent as matters were. I tried every expedient in order to remain, charging Finlay with the whole concern; for I had no fear of danger to him, he being more cunning than the serpent. He was willing to undertake any thing that I ever desired; but here both he and Captain Drummond expostulated on the great danger we two should brave if we remained. So much, they said, that no vigilance could save us for twenty-four hours more. I resisted flight strenuously, saying I knew not what was become of

Araby, whom it behoved me to see placed in safety. It was moreover absolutely requisite that I should see the prince liberated. These were weighty motives for remaining; but there was one stronger than them all, and that was a design I had formed on my charming landlady, whom I had deemed a virgin of such unmatched beauty and qualifications, that I determined to win her at all risks, even at that of marriage.

However, finding expostulation vain, the love of life prevailed, and I yielded, promising that if they would but suffer me to remain in that house concealed for another day and night, until I could hear of Araby and the prince, I would then fly and accompany Drummond to the earl of Mar's army. From this resolution I would not be broken, and there they were obliged to leave me.

I had nearly paid dearly for my temerity. The house was again searched for me at midnight, and all the premises, as if they had been searching for a rat; and had not my beloved landlady been endowed with an ingenuity superior to other women, I must have been taken. I escaped by such a measure as never was contrived, and occupied a position for some time, which I choose not to describe, and which would soon have proved as fatal to me as the executioner's axe.

The next night came, and with it came Finlay, in great perplexity about my life. He said it was ascertained that I was in that house, and I might expect a search every minute. I was more loth to go away than ever, but could find no more pretences for remaining: so flying up stairs to my charming girl, I in the most passionate way declared that I could not part with her, after the devotion she had shown to me; and that therefore I offered her my hand and heart. She laughed in my face, and told me she was a married woman! I stared in amazement, but was far from letting belief take hold of me. It was true! she had married a smuggler! one who had amassed immense riches by evading king George's new taxes, and who had at that time great stores purchased abroad, and imported free at almost no expense. I chided her for not telling me at the very first that she was a married woman. "Would I?" said she, in her sharp Highland tongue; "ha, bee my faith, and that would I not, though you had remained here these six months."–"Thou art another than a good one, Joanna," said I, "but not the less sweet and engaging;" and imprinting a warm kiss on her lips, I left her laughing at me, and entreating that I would come back and accompany her to Prince James's coronation.

The impression which this wild girl left on my heart was astonishing even to myself. I could not get her image removed from it; which incident, little to my credit, greatly softened the parting from Prince Iset and Araby, the care of whom I was obliged to trust wholly to Finlay. It was in vain that I tried to reason with myself, Joanna M'Kenzie was still uppermost in my thoughts, and till that period I did not deem myself so inconsistent a being. I wished to get the smuggler's wife from him by any means. The atrocity was not called into account, provided I could get the enchantress into my power. I wished the smuggler might drown himself in the sea, or fall a victim to the broken laws of his country, and get his head chopped off, so that by any means I might come into the possession of his wife. I am ashamed to tell this, but truth obliges me to do it; besides, this lawless attachment proved afterwards instrumental in modelling some of my actions.

On the first of October Captain Drummond and I made our escape at break of day across the Firth. The danger of my being seized was imminent, but he reached the pinnace in safety, and was waiting for me between Leith and Newhaven. I was so hotly pursued by one officer, that I was obliged to take to the tide, and the fellow following, seized me after I was waist deep. A hard struggle now ensued; but I saw Drummond rowing toward me, and took courage, though I found my opponent was the stronger man; and besides, there was another coming running up the head of the bank. He continued to drag me toward the land, and, in a desperate struggle, we came both down in the sea, and I uppermost, and there I held him till I drowned him; but he bit my left hand terribly under water.

Drummond reached me, and took me in just as the other officer was entering the water. We saw him reach his companion and carry him ashore, but whether dead or alive, we could not tell. There appeared to be a great disturbance on the Fife coast before us, with armies mustering on the shore, and we wist not well what to do; but return we durst not; and so holding on, to our joy and astonishment, we found the young Lord Sinclair with a body of horse acting as a rear-guard to a body of the Highland army that had performed a very gallant action that morning, in capturing a government ship laden with arms, off Burntisland; and joining this body, we journeyed with them to Perth, where we were introduced to the earl of Mar by Sinclair, as two of the king of Sweden's officers. He received us with a politeness which I never saw equalled in a general, except Marlborough, who, villain as he was, was certainly the most accomplished gentleman as well as commander of the age.

I could not help despising Mar from the beginning; for when he learned that I had served as a captain under Marlborough, as well as the king of Sweden, he deemed it incumbent on him to have a *tête-à-tête* with me about the tactics of these great commanders. He had plenty of cunning, and was shy of his own observations; but I easily saw through him, and that he knew no more about bringing the energies of an army into effect than a mere child. He was a pompous, bustling, polite, insignificant body; and though I intended to have raised a company at my own expense, as soon as I saw through our generalissimo I declined it. He however gave me a company at once of brave M'Raes, under Lord Seaforth. Captain Drummond took the principal command of his brother's regiment; and we two, being regarded as efficient officers, were very much employed in drilling.

Mar had the whole strength and puissance of Scotland north of the Forth, and why he should not at the very first have attacked Argyle and his handful of men, appeared to every brave man a perfect anomaly. It was evident to me, as well as to my colonel, Seaforth, that there was no hope of any gallant or decisive campaign under Mar. True, his army was a motley one. Such an army I never before had seen, excepting one division of the Muscovite army. But for all that they were men of strength and courage, and the Highlanders, at least, devoted to the cause; and it ought to have been his first measure to have rushed with them to battle as long as he had at least six men for every one under Argyle. Yet there we lay grumbling and assessing the country, and cutting the throat of our own cause.

It having been found out that I had plenty of money at command, (rather a scarce article in our army,) and having given my own company some largesses, I became a great favourite among Seaforth's soldiers. I said Mar's was a motley army; but when I first joined Seaforth, I could not keep my gravity at witnessing his muster. Sir John Falstaff's regiment were nothing to those of the great earl of Seaforth. Such a set of naked, shaggy, ragamuffins I had never beheld, rank and file before, the Lewis men in particular. Yet, on acquaintance, I found them orderly, civil, and rather well-bred; but they stole every thing they could lay hands on.

But the most original figures of the whole army were some of the squadrons of horse, of which the Strath-Bogie regiment was one, and perhaps the most whimsical of the whole. The riders were strong, powerful men, with broad bonnets on their heads, and rig-and-fur stocking-boots on their legs, reaching more than half way up the thighs. Their saddles were mostly made of sacking, stuffed with straw, or goat-skins, without stirrups. Their bridle reins were made of plaited hair, and acted by a gin on the nose, instead of bits in the mouth: so that to see those soldiers at drill was a treat, the like of which I have no hopes of ever seeing again. Their horses were constantly wheeling with them out of the ranks, and, as every soldier carried a strong whip, in place of spurs, he would then strike it violently on the cheek to make it wheel in again, which frequently set the animal on a rotatory motion, like a millstone: and there was then one expression which I frequently heard, "Dumm the bleed of ye! Far ye gaun, ye —?" But it is disgusting to dwell on this ill-managed business.

On the 23rd of November Finlay arrived at Perth. He had been several days with Borlam and his Mackintoshes, thinking to find me there with the regiment of the Drummonds. His approbation of Borlam's army was extravagant; and he said he was widely mistaken if the old fellow was not a hero, every inch of him.

The news that Finlay brought was of the most thrilling interest to me. Prince Iset was put safely into the hands of his friends, and Finlay, who never suffered gain to escape him, had pocketed the high reward. Araby, my beloved and amiable Araby, had clung to the prince in the end, finding herself otherwise totally deserted. I cannot tell how I felt on hearing this. I rejoiced in Araby's good fortune, but I felt a blank in my heart, and as if I had been a creature deserted,–an isolated and lonely being, who seemed thrown upon the world to be a football in it; a creature,–the sport of every misadventure that could fall to the lot of man.

All this time, from the day of my birth, I knew not who I was, or from whom descended; and this day, the 7th of February, 1731, when I write this, I am as ignorant of my parentage as I was the first day of my remembrance. I was merely Captain John Lochy, which was always pronounced Lockie, both abroad and at home: and that was all that I knew about myself, farther than that I had been the tennis-ball of fortune in a pre-eminent degree. It was in a mess of the officers at Perth, where the marquis of Huntly chanced to mention that I had a singular resemblance to the duke of Argyle, in which he was joined by every one present. Mar himself declared that, intimately acquainted as he was with Argyle, he could not, for several days, divest himself of the impression that I was that august person, come in disguise to reconnoitre his army and position. The only feeling that I had at the time was that of extreme awkwardness, not being able to explain who I was, or how related to his grace; and when pressed to tell in what way I was related to the family, for that I was nearly related to Argyle no one doubted, and not knowing what to say, I expressed myself in my confusion to the purport that, considering our relative situations, it was at present as good not to divulge my relationship to the duke. No more questions were then asked: the matter was perfectly understood.

Not many days thereafter Finlay came to me with a laughing face, and asked me if the report current in the army was true, that I was a natural son of the late duke of Argyle.

I answered Finlay ingenuously, that I believed I was, for that I knew I was the son of a nobleman, and was reared under the protection of the Campbells; but farther I knew not.

"The officers have your lineage cut and dry now, however," said he, "part of which I know to be not true. They say you are son to the late duke of Argyle, and half-brother to the present duke, and that your mother was the honorable Miss Helen Lockhart; and that you took her name, and she bought you a commission in the allied army."

I was thunderstruck at this news, believing it throughout. "Well then, sir," said I, "what part of this information do you know not to be true?"

"I know that your mother was not a Miss Lockhart," said he, "but a lady of the highest rank in England. And I farther know, or at least believe, that you are not a natural child, but that your parents were man and wife; for of this I am certain, that had you known who you were, to have asserted your own rights, you were heir both to extensive domains and titles; and on that account your life was sought in your youth, with an intensity which no human power could have circumvented. Now, ask me no farther, for farther I cannot tell you. It is but little more that I do know, and that most imperfectly; but if you knew even that little, it would soon cost you your life."

"Sir," said I, drawing out a loaded pistol, and cocking it, "tell me who is my mother, or I'll instantly shoot you through the head."

"I don't know, sir," said he, with a fierce and settled determination.

"Who is my father, then?"

"I don't know, sir; and if I did I would not tell you."

"I conjure you to tell me, at all events, every thing that you know of my parents."

"No, I won't, sir; I thought I had told you as much already."

"By the God that made me, sir, then I'll shoot you through the head this instant."

"You dare not, for your blood, sir; for your soul you dare not."

Every part of my flesh crept with impatience, with madness. I lifted up the pistol, and presented it at the head of the man who had again and again saved my life: he stood unmoved and indignant: my eye caught his face, and that moment I dashed the pistol out of my hand into a gutter, and holding out my hand, I begged his pardon. "I take your hand only on the condition that you never mention the subject to me again."–"It is a hard condition," returned I; "but as it is an injunction which I have no right to infringe, I accept of it." So there was no more about it. I was conscious that I could not live without Finlay, and he had from his boyhood the impression that he could not live without me. Thus was I left in a state of mind which I cannot describe. Hitherto I had thought very little about my parentage, regarding it as a secret that never was to be revealed by the parties concerned, and by any other means inexplicable. These late insinuations raised a burning desire within me to know what I have never learned to this day; but since I became acquainted with the duke of Argyle, I am persuaded that we are brothers.

However, to return to my narrative. I found that Finlay had brought money with him to raise a whole regiment for king James; from which I dissuaded him, telling him how poor an opinion I had of our commander-in-chief. "We seem to have more soldiers already than we can either pay or arm properly," said I; "and though sheer necessity obliged me to join this army, I account myself in honour bound to share its fortunes; but as a friend, I would advise you not to enter it, or if you do, enter it merely as a gentleman volunteer; for depend on it, John earl of Mar is not the man to keep this ardent and miscellaneous mass long together. If I had had the command, I should have been in possession of both Edinburgh and Glasgow a month ago."

Thus admonished, Finlay attached himself to the Kintail regiment as a volunteer, by the appellation of Captain Finlayson; John M'Kenzie of Assynt was our colonel, but I was, in fact, the commander of the regiment. Lord Seaforth had five regiments in the army, and five colonels under him, but he himself was head colonel, the sole leader of that division. He was a most powerful chief at that time; for, besides these five regiments, consisting of upwards of three thousand men, he had a great army in the north, under his brother Colonel Alexander M'Kenzie, keeping the Sutherlands in check. Our regiment, consisting of the M'Raes of Kintail, was by far the best regiment his lordship had. They were powerful, strong-bodied men, and perfectly subordinate; consequently I took great pains in perfecting them in the art of war, and I brought them to such a pitch of excellence, that I knew they would do credit to the division of the army in which they fought. As for the Lewis regiment, under Colin M'Kenzie, they were the drollest-looking kernes I ever beheld. The rest were so-so.

Nothing more happened worth noting during our stay at Perth, save that Mar had many foraging parties out, and parties lifting contributions at every town on the eastern coast. The redoubted Finlay contrived to get himself extensively employed in that capacity, whether always by Mar's authority or not, is rather doubtful. But true it is, that he contrived to amass a great deal of wealth during that short campaign. I never knew of this till it was all over, and, of course, out of time to check it: but I took it very ill, and reprimanded him for it in a way that he never forgot.

At length, word arriving at Perth that the Forth was frozen to such a degree, as to bear horses and carriages, Mar was obliged to move forward to fight the duke of Argyle. The frost had rendered Stirling no pass to defend, the whole of the river being bridged over from end to end; so the Highland army could pass over where they pleased. Thus his lordship, having no excuse left, was compelled, as I thought, with great reluctance, to set off, bag and baggage, to cross the Forth, and fall down upon the Lowlands; and, of course, to fight Argyle and his handful of rebels, as we called them, those base slaves to the elector of Hanover.

At a village, the name of which I have forgotten, we were joined by general Gordon and the flower of the clans, among whom there were some of the finest regiments I ever saw; for every one of the four clans M'Donald had a regiment made up of men, not only picked, but most of them gentlemen. There was a spirit in the looks of these men that clearly bespoke their capabilities, and they were, besides, in excellent training, which I could not comprehend. On expressing my astonishment at this circumstance, one of their chiefs said to me with exultation, "Sir, these men have been trained to battle from their cradles;" alluding to a regiment of his own, denominated the Moidart regiment: General Gordon was a gentleman who had seen much service. The clans confided in him and he in them, but with all the rest the case was otherwise.

Mar was a craven, there can be no doubt of it; would he else ever have come to guide the attack of the clans, while General Gordon, who was ten times better qualified to lead the attack than he, was with them, and by that means leaving all the rest of the army without a general? It was sheer cowardice: whenever he saw the ardor and spirit of the clans, he clung to them, not daring, for his life, to trust himself any where else; and thus left the main body and left wing to fight or run away, as they chose; the last of which they did, and could not be blamed for it, for they had no one to direct their general movements. I know the M'Donalds wanted none of his directions, and wished him at the devil when he came and placed himself at their head: so did I, with all my heart, for I was next to them, being on the right hand of Seaforth's line that day, and consequently next to the Skye men, who were on the left of the M'Donalds. I had the sole command of the Kintail regiment that day, for Assynt committed it to me, and rode with his chief.

Mar's own fear and folly ruined the success of the battle, and along with it the cause of his master, and many a brave man. The English regiments, horse and foot, did not stand the attack of the M'Donalds above ten minutes. It was the most furious simultaneous assault that I ever saw made by foot-soldiers, and reminded me very much of the king of Sweden's attacks with cavalry. Being determined that my M'Raes should not be the last, I hurried them on so quickly that I was before the left and centre of them all the time of the assault. The right of the M'Donalds was always foremost; and bloody work they made; but one of their bravest chiefs was slain, which irritating them still more, they hewed down all that came before them; for me, I took every man prisoner who asked quarter.

I relate only what came under my own eye, which was not much, leaving the general detail to historians. There was a fine-looking regiment of English dragoons, which were drawn up a little to the left of the right forward course, which it behoved the Kintail regiment to follow. I should have faced to the east and flanked this regiment: I saw and felt the necessity of it, but there were no orders to that effect: our general was a cipher; would he had been nothing worse! so I durst not quit my line, but held on straight forward, being obliged to run for a good space in order to keep up once more with the intrepid M'Donalds. It was however manifest, that, had that regiment been commanded by an officer of sense or experience, it might by a wheel either to flank or rear of us have cut my brave M'Raes all to pieces, and I expected nothing else. But, to my astonishment, that gallant regiment seeing itself cut off from its companions to the left, and perhaps not being able to see over the ridge what was going on in the right, took fright, and galloped off without striking a stroke, or any body striking one at it.

We had nearly the half of Argyle's army before us flying in confusion, the foot entirely at our mercy, the horse scouring away quite in advance, and we hard upon Stirling, without one thing to stop or stay us. We ought to have entered Stirling pell-mell with the fugitives, smashing them down as we went; and where would Argyle have been then, between two armies, either of them larger than his own? I insist on it, that we had the ruin, the total ruin of the duke's army entirely in our power; and I should have sought no more than the M'Donalds and the Kintail men to have effected it. But no; Mar took fright, even in the pursuit; called a halt, and ordered a retreat. There was a brave old captain in my regiment, called John Gun, who swore at our commander, and cursed him, till he foamed at the mouth; at this order, both Glengarry and Keppoch expostulated sharply with the general; but he had a tongue and a manner peculiarly conciliating. They were silenced at once.

But the worst was yet to come: he drew us up on the top of a little craggy hill, from whence we had complete command of the road. Argyle's retreat was cut off–fairly cut off. A single regiment of Highlanders would have broken his remnant, and scattered them like sheep, before they could have winded round the bottom of that little hill, even suppose they had had no weapons but the stones that lay among their feet. Argyle saw he was entrapped, and drew up, waiting an assault, for to proceed was out of his power. If we had but kept our situation, he must have fled to the mountains, for to have attacked us up the steep was impracticable: to have passed two or three men abreast below our feet was equally so; and certainly I never saw an army more entirely at the mercy of another.

Could any man have believed what followed? With all this, set plain before his craven eyes, Bobbing John ordered an instant retreat. When it was communicated to me, I laughed as loud as I could laugh, and even clapped my hands; and I saw the general turn a malicious look on me; but it had no effect; the order was given, and persisted in. I wonder to this day that some of the high-spirited Highland chiefs did not cut off his head.

There was an elderly gentleman, with a grey head, rode up to him at this time, and seemed expostulating most vehemently with him; but I was not so near as to hear the words. I expected when the old gentleman first rode up to him, that he would cut him down, for he had his drawn sword over his shoulder, and appeared resolute, and in a rage. I heard him mention the cause of the king and the nation, and I thought he asked the command of the clans but for one hour. I could not hear what Mar said; but the worthy old gentleman turned from him, and came away wiping his eyes.

I had done with Mar for ever. There was no standing such mean behaviour as this, after the commanders I had fought under: so, committing the retreat to Captain Gun, I rode straight to Lord Seaforth, and gave up my commission.

I found his lordship in even worse humour than myself. He said the main body of the army were left without either guide or direction, and knew not whether to advance or retreat. They lost sight of the right wing at the very first, and knew not how the battle was going there. On the other hand, they saw the left wing retreating; and as there were no troops ever came to attack the centre division, they had nobody to fight with. When I told him how the clans of the M'Donalds, and his own Kintail men, had the power of Argyle at their command, and that Mar refused to let them take the advantage, he bit his lips, and said, "I believe the fellow is a specious traitor, and has ruined the Highlands to aggrandise himself."

"No, my lord," said I, "I do not think so. He is a fool and a coward, and utterly incapable of executing the great charge committed to him. His pusillanimity yesterday surpassed aught I ever witnessed on a field of battle; and, you may depend on it, the cause is ruined, notwithstanding the preponderance of strength on your side; for, as every thing depends upon the commander-in-chief, so, in truth, success under such a general is out of the question."

"I wish to God every one of us could as easily get quit of the concern as you can!" said he: "and though I regret your dereliction, I cannot blame you."

I then took leave of his lordship and old Assynt, and never saw them afterwards; and being merely a soldier of fortune, though Drummond had inspired me with a little enthusiasm on the side of the Stuarts, my natural and original bias leant to the Protestant succession; and now that I fairly saw the incapacity of the jacobite general, I judged it utter madness to involve myself farther; and, in company with Finlay, I left Perth, resolved to offer my services to the Duke of Argyle. I know I shall be blamed for this volatility of purpose; I cannot help it. It is true; and it is farther true, that ever since I was made to believe that I was the duke's brother, I had an insatiable desire to be acquainted with him, to serve and to oblige him.

Thinking it requisite that two dashing captains, who had fought abroad, should at least have a servant between them, I hired a young ragged peasant at Alloa, the only one I could get. I could not help laughing at his appearance and address; and when I asked his name, he said it was Bobby Bunker! I took this for a nickname, it sounded so odd; and asked if it was his right name. "Aum shure aw dinna ken, mun, but aw never heard masel' ca'd aught else!"

I got him rigged out in a new suit, and bought a shaggy Highland pony for him to ride on; but such a simpleton as Bobby I never saw. The first day that I brought him in to wait at dinner, ere ever I wist, he drew in a chair, and sat down at table! "What do you mean, you scoundrel?" said I. "Think you I hired you to sit at table with me? Get up, and stand behind my chair till dinner be over."

"Ay," said he, with perfect good humour, his mouth choke full, and rose.

"Bobby, have you no more sense of manners than this?" said I.

"Oo, what did I ken, mun? Aw thought aw wood hae to get my meat, un' it was as good soon as syne," said Bobby.

"And, moreover," continued I, "when you speak to me, or any gentleman, especially a stranger, be sure always to denominate him SIR."

"'Sir!'" said he, with a lilt of disdain. "An' what the better will he be o' that?"

"If the duke of Argyle, for instance, ask you any question," said I, "will you just call him *mun?*"

"Aha billy! Catch me there!" said Bobby. "Nah! I wad ca' him naething ava!"

"What! you would not call him Sir?"

"Oo ay, if ye insistit on't. I dinna think it's any grit sin; but I never ca'd a man *Sir* a' my life."

When we came near Stirling, I ordered him to ride into the town, and find stalls for our horses, and be ready to take ours. But his pony had a will of its own. It had been accustomed to follow, not to lead; and not, if Bobby should have felled it, could he make it go past our horses. It ran forward full speed, till it had come parallel with the foremost; and then stopping short in one moment, uniformly threw Bobby forward over its head, among the snow and ice. "Aw comes aye aff at the mooth," said he, with perfect good humour; and mounted again.

When we arrived at Stirling, he alighted at a respectful distance; and a number of officers and gentlemen volunteers being present, he wanted to be very mannerly; so taking off his cap, he held it in the one hand, his horse's bridle in the other, and his stick in his teeth, across. In that guise he attempted to come to us. But no, his horse would only go backward; not a step would it lead. "Aw wonder what ails the beast, aw wonder!" said Bobby, with the staff in his mouth. If some other servant had not taken our horses, they had never been taken by our own. The greater part of servants are a great plague, and the more one has of them, his own cares are the greater. For me, I never saw one I could live with, except Finlay, whom I now acknowledged as my equal in every company, though he never assumed that consequence himself, but was constantly employed in looking after every thing that belonged to me, and putting all to rights. My interest was his, and he looked after the interest of none else beside.

I applied to the duke's equerry for an introduction to his grace. The equerry took me to Major Campbell, the duke's secretary, who asked our names. I gave him both, telling him plainly that we were two foreign officers, who had deserted from the Chevalier's standard, and were come to offer our services to his grace.

The major smiled, and said the general had more officers and gentlemen of his own clan than he had companies or posts of honour of any description for. He would, however, introduce us to him when he next saw him; for he was nowise difficult of access. We were introduced accordingly, and at the first sight and salutation my heart was knit to him. How different my feelings were with regard to him, to what they were with Mar! The latter was a specious, insidious character; the duke, a free, downright honest gentleman, qualities to which every look and every word bore testimony. I felt at once that I was in the presence of a hero, and of a man superior to the rest of his species. He repeated my name, Lochy, to himself several times, and looked at me with a suspicious interest. I was abashed, and dreaded something, I know not what. He asked if we had any warrantice to show that we were not spies from the Pretender's army. I said we had none, save that we brought honest hearts and good intentions, and were so disgusted with Mar's ignorance of every thing like military tactics, that we could not fight under him.

"Ha! Do you think so?" said he, rather as if displeased. "Pray, may I ask what school of military tactics you adhere to?"

I answered that I had served both under the duke of Marlborough and the king of Sweden; generals, whose measures were directly opposed to each other. I was going on to make some wise remarks on the military tactics of the two being carded together to make a complete system; but he interrupted me, by saying, that I certainly had a good right to find fault with the military tactics of the day in Scotland, which ranked very low; and he added, "But we are just obliged to do as things will do with us. In the mean time," continued he, "I must send you to prison."

"I trust, my lord duke, you will not do so," said I. "We have trusted ourselves to your honour, and mean to serve you truly. We came not to serve you for bounty or reward, but to fight under your banner, until we have proved ourselves worthy of your patronage."

"It is spoke like a gentleman, Sir, and I do not discredit your present intentions," said he. "But why did you not join the royal standard at first? It is this instability of purpose which I dislike, and of which I am always suspicious."

"We are mere soldiers of fortune," said I, "and neither know nor care much about the rival claims of the two competitors for the crown. But you know it is natural for a man to join the side that he is convinced will be ultimately successful, whatever may be the justice of his claim."

"True," said he. "What you have said is common sense. But you must have had some motive which regulated your choice of sides at first?"

"Why, my lord duke," said I, "the truth is, that I fell in with a gallant Scots officer, first in the Netherlands, and afterwards in the king of Sweden's army, who somewhat impressed on my mind the right and title of the family of Stuart to the throne of this realm. On coming home to Scotland I again met with him, and at his persuasion went with him, and joined what he called the royal army, in which I would have continued and fought you, and conquered you too, had I not felt convinced that I was fighting with a general under whom no man of spirit could fight. I can assure your grace, and you may take it as you please, that if I had had the command of the Highland army for two hours, on the afternoon of the 13th, I should have made my own terms with you."

"And you would perhaps have found your calculations incorrect," said he; "but that is over, I am thinking of something else. So you met with this jacobite officer on your return to Scotland?" I answered in the affirmative. "And you left Edinburgh together about the beginning of October?"

"I–I–am sure I do not remember exactly," said I, hesitating, and visibly in a quandary.

"Oh, but I remember well enough," said he, "and know more than you think I do. Do you remember any thing of a certain royal sword that was found, and what event it proved the instrument of effecting?"

I stood like a condemned criminal. Not a word had I to say for myself; but I looked at Finlay, and he gave me such a look! It said in plain English, What a fool you are! You have done for yourself now! The duke laughed at our dilemma, and having previously rung the bell, he ordered his guards to conduct these two gentlemen deserters to prison, and see that they were well guarded. We were accordingly consigned to the state-prison of the castle, apart from the prisoners taken in the battle.

I was greatly cast down, and vexed at my stupidity; but I never once thought of the duke knowing aught of the affray in the Cannongate, of which I was moreover conscious of being blameless. I felt assured, however, that I was at the disposal of a great and good man, who was incapable of any act of injustice. Finlay soon cheered up his spirits, saying he had plenty of money, and should purchase my freedom underhand that night, if I chose; but this I treated with derision.

I asked Finlay how he liked the duke. He answered, that there was only one thing he liked about him. He was, in fact, very like me, and he had not a doubt that we were brothers. For my part, hardly as I judged of his behaviour, my heart clung to him in a manner that I was ashamed to own; and I did not own it, but waited patiently to see what would be the end of this unlooked-for adventure. The duke was indeed a noble looking person, and had a dignity of manner to which neither I nor any man I ever saw could pretend. As to our personal resemblance, it was not apparent to me; but there must have been something in it, for every person said so, and I have since that period often been taken for him. What a yearning desire I now felt to know something of my parents, and the circumstances of my birth. The imminent and inexplicable dangers to which it had exposed me made me the more and more suspect there must have been something highly criminal connected with it. But for a long while, about that period, I would have braved any danger to have come at a glimpse of the truth.

Well, here in the castle we lay for several days, ignorant of what was to be our fate, the duke having been at Edinburgh on some business relating to the foreign auxiliaries, then on their way to join him. The morning after his return he sent for me into his office, where I found him with Major Campbell and Colonel Cadogan busily engaged. He had on a dressing-gown of crimson velvet, and his hair being long and elegantly dressed, I never saw a finer looking man. He received me with cool civility, and desired me to wait a few minutes in the anti-room. After waiting a long space, he at length came, and spoke to me with all the freedom of an old acquaintance, yet without any familiarity; from the nobleman and the high-born chief he never descended. After a number of inquiries, every one of which I answered candidly, he addressed me nearly as follows:–

"You have been telling me the truth, Captain Lockie; I know it. You have told me the truth all along, and I have therefore set you down in my mind as an honest man. But by this murder in Edinburgh you have subjected yourself to a criminal trial; and, as matters stand just now, it will go hard with you for your life. Tell me truly, are you really ignorant who the person was whom you slew there?"

"Totally ignorant, my lord duke, on the honour of a gentleman; and perfectly blameless. I slew the ruffian sheerly out of self-defence, for I tried thrice, at the risk of my life, to disarm him, but could not; and in one of those close scuffles I was wounded, so I was obliged to kill him." The duke turned away his face at this speech, unable to suppress laughter.

"But it is averred," said he, "that no man in Scotland could have mastered his sword with fair play."

"I could not master his sword, certainly," said I, "but I mastered himself with great ease, and could have done it with equal ease the first round. As the assailant, he ought to have called a parley, for he perceived well enough that he had met with his master."

"Indeed!" said the duke, "are you so much master of that noble science?"

"Give me a good cut-and-thrust blade in my hand, such as the king of Sweden's, which I lost, and, in a good cause, I'll meet any man in Europe, hand to hand, and foot to foot," said I.

"You take high ground, indeed!" said he; "but I hope there are many of my Campbells with whom you might still improve. You smile: speak out: I know you would say, 'They would in that case have stood the M'Donalds and M'Raes a little longer.' Well, we shall have a trial with foils to-morrow. In the mean time let us consider the proper destination for you. It is probably as well for the present to let you remain in ignorance of the enormity of your crime. But I am amused at the circumstances in which you stood. Had it come out in the Pretender's army what you had done, you would have been in a fine dilemma! Why, captain, you knocked one of the finest Popish plots on the head that ever was devised: one set on foot, too, by foreigners, in favour of the Pretender! It would, in all probability, have proved futile in the end, but you settled it at once. Now I know what the councils of Edinburgh are at present, and what they will be as long as the Chevalier has a party in Scotland. Apprehended you will be, and that instantly. Are you willing to take your trial, and run all risks, or will you go for me on a distant mission, and secure your safety till these troubles are settled one way or other?"

"I am quite subservient to your grace's pleasure," said I; "but my choice would be to remain and fight under your grace; for depend on it, the Chevalier will very soon have no party in Scotland. I shall run my risk of that event."

"Here is a letter from your chief, Seaforth, proffering terms of joining me. But he is a turbulent spirit; I'll none of him. This must be yourself he alludes to–'the distinguished foreign officer.' You have cast yourself on my honour, and it is my advice that you absent yourself for a space from Scotland. I have at this instant an express to send to my father-in-law, the Lord Mayor of London, as well as a packet for my lady, who is at present ill and in his house. These I will entrust to your care, with proper credentials and a passport. Your friend may remain with the army, or go with you, as he chooses."

I had nothing for it but to obey, and after receiving my credentials, and a general order for post-horses all the way, Finlay and I rode to Hamilton the first night; and changing horses at every post, the next night we crossed the border. We were dressed as dragoon officers of king George's, and proceeded without question, till we came to a place called Appleby, where we were obliged to enter into a fierce dispute with the master of the inn, a rude boorish fellow, who refused us fresh horses, on the pretence that he suspected us for two rebel officers, making our escape in that disguise. He would not so much as look at our passport or order, saying, "he cwold nwot reawd wony of them domm'd scrowls, and cared nwot a domm about them."

Our high words brought a mob about us, many of whom, without doubt, saw that we were government messengers; but no one interposed on our behalf; and the fellow being quite unreasonable, refusing either to give us horses for our order or money, we were obliged to go to the mayor, get a warrant, and press horses. This hubbub lost us a good part of that short day, and as we were pushing on under cloud of night, there were five or six men came on to the road at a right angle, and joined us. One of them addressed us in rather a genteel polished style, asking if we were the Scottish officers who left Appleby with some forged credentials.

"Forged credentials, sir!" said I; "what do you mean? I have my credentials from the lord-lieutenant of Scotland, of which I will satisfy any man, as soon as we reach a place where light is to be had."– "O you are perfectly well known," returned he. "You are discovered; so you must please to return with us, who have a warrant for that purpose. It was a bold expedient; but it is up; you are discovered."

"Sir, my errand is express; and of my identity, as the duke of Argyle's special messenger, I will satisfy any magistrate you please, who resides on the way before us; but return I will not for any man's pleasure."

"Well, then, sir, I am sorry we must take you by force."

"I'll shoot the first man through the head who dares to attempt it," said I, seeing two of them drawing up before me. I was that moment struck on the head with prodigious force; but kept my horse, and shot one of my assailants dead. The second blow brought me down; and I remember no more.

On coming to myself, I found I was in the house of a poor miner in a straggling hamlet, and grievously mangled. Finlay had escaped with very little injury, by counterfeiting death, and was waiting anxiously upon me. But never were two poor fellows in a more miserable plight, for we were robbed of every thing, clothes, watches, money, dispatches, and passports; and had only some plain clothes left to us, which seemed to have belonged to peasants. The people in whose house we were, being poor, rude, and uncivil, insisted on our going away. Alas! I could neither move nor be moved, for my whole body was bruised, my skull fractured, and my face beat to a jelly. I had shot one of the scoundrels, and they had murdered me, as they supposed, in the most brutal manner. Finlay was sadly put to his shift: he had lost, he said, a thousand pounds in Bank of Scotland notes and gold. I had gold on me to the amount of thirty-two pounds, and a gold watch, sword, and pistols. All were gone; and what were we to do? For my part, I could do nothing but lie wishing for death every night; for I was far worst in the night with delirium of the most terrible description. The people believed nothing that we told them, and insisted on taking me from house to house in a cart home to Scotland. Finlay at last found out a Dr. Campbell, originally from Ayrshire, who interested himself deeply in our affairs, and hearing a plain tale from Finlay, sent off a message to the duke of Argyle all the way to Stirling; and the same day caused our late landlord, with whom we quarrelled at Appleby, to be apprehended; Finlay assuring him that the fellow was of the party. I could say nothing, as I had neither seen him, nor recognised his voice, in the attack made on us. But Finlay, who had most emphatically groaned and sprawled to death, perceived every thing perfectly well; and, among other things, the direction in which they bore off their dead or wounded companion. A search was instituted, and the man was found in the house of a poor Catholic priest, who disclaimed all knowledge of his inmate's person or circumstances, declaring that he sheltered him for pity's sake alone as a dying person. He turned out to be a Mr. Abraham Taylor, brother to one Edward Taylor, who had made himself peculiarly obnoxious to government, by inflaming the country in favour of the Stuarts. He had joined the rebels with thirty men at Preston; but in the confusion he and his brother, the wounded man, and some more adherents, had escaped in the habits of countrymen. The matter was fairly brought home to the landlord, who had these men in hiding, he himself being known as a papist and a fierce jacobite: it brought him to the gallows very easily. In his dying declaration he asserted that the party wanted nothing but the passport to carry them to London, where they could secure their safety, and that the robbery and murder, (which he still believed in,) arose out of contingent circumstances to which he had never given assent.

He was hung, however; but of this we were not the better, our wealth and our precious trust were gone, and we found ourselves in much like an enemy's country, with the exception of Dr. Campbell, whose interest with the Lonsdale family was of great benefit to us. His messenger to Argyle returned in due course of time, bringing a letter to the earl of Lonsdale, and a short note to me, with a remittance; and, lest any person should suspect these adventures to be a fabrication, I shall here give the duke's note to me, in his own words:–

"SIR,

"Though I deplore the severe misfortune that hath happened to you and your friend, I, at the same time, must reprobate your imprudence in exposing your credentials to public view, knowing, as you ought to have done, the value of such at this moment. These should never have been shown but to an accredited magistrate. But what is done cannot be undone. Remain in England until you hear how the campaign in the north ends. We leave Stirling to-morrow. I transmit a small sum for present emergencies, and have written to my friend Lord Lonsdale in your behalf.

"ARGYLE.

"Stirling, Jan. 26, 1715–16."

We were instantly removed to the gardener's house at Lowther Castle, to comfortable lodgings; and every attention paid to my wounds, of all of which I soon recovered, save the one in my head, which continued to enfeeble and distress me very much; and I became so altered in my appearance, that my nearest friends could not have known me.

I did not feel at all comfortable here. I was like a dependant or hanger-on, and was not noticed by any of the family, save that the young ladies sometimes visited me. Among these I observed one very beautiful and very young lady, who always regarded me with great interest, and, on inquiring her name of the gardener's wife, I was told that she was a Miss Van, daughter to Lord Barnard; but, as I neither knew who Miss Van nor Lord Barnard were, I thought no more of the circumstance.

Finlay being obliged to go to Edinburgh for a supply of money, he asked an order from me on the bank. I asked what funds I had remaining in the bank: he answered, that we had a part there as yet; but it was lodged in such a way that he could not lift any more without my name along with his own. The fancy struck me at that moment that I would accompany him; and notwithstanding all the poor fellow's remonstrances, I persisted in my resolution. Will any person believe me, that it was the smuggler's wife at Leith who influenced me to this wild undertaking, while I was neither in a fit state to travel, nor had funds to enable me to travel as my situation required? Lord Lonsdale gave us a passport, and forwarded us on our journey as far as Carlisle in his chariot, and there we were left to our own resources. We hired horses to a place called Langholm, on the Scottish side; and on reaching that place, we found that neither my strength nor our funds were adequate to the journey. With great difficulty we reached Hawick on the evening of the third day, where I was left quite exhausted, while poor Finlay was obliged to proceed to Edinburgh on foot, for want of funds to hire a horse; the scoundrelly landlord of the Douglas Arms refusing to give him one, pretending that not one horse had been returned to him for the last six months. Our appearance was certainly much against us, and we were treated accordingly. I never received more niggardly and uncivil treatment than I did in that inn, not even among the outlandish Russians. His name was Ekron, a Philistine both by name and nature; and I should not have been much grieved to have seen him go the same way as my last landlord. But the trouble in my head made me exceedingly peevish and unhappy at this period.

When Finlay returned, in a splendid foreign uniform, and one for me also, as well as a fine horse, Mr. Ekron's countenance changed. He waited on us at table himself, and pretended to be a great wit, saying every droll and ridiculous thing that he could invent for our amusement; and seeing that he would not be affronted, but laughed at every thing, I was fain to be reconciled to the scrub, and pretend to be amused with him. We staid here for the space of seventeen days from our arrival, and at our inn fell in with some of the gentlemen-farmers on market-days, whom we found social, plain fellows, real stems of the old border warriors, and all firmly attached to the Protestant succession.

There were only three gentlemen of that neighbourhood who had joined the rebels, we were told; Scott of Walle, Scott of Whitsled, and Pringle of Hawthorn; and one of these estates being then in the market, I could have purchased it for a mere trifle. I liked the country; Finlay was exceedingly fond of it, as well as of the people; but that confounded smuggler's wife upset the only rational scheme I had perhaps ever formed. I had ordered Finlay to make some inquiries concerning her, on pretence that I lay under deep obligations to her. He brought me word that she was a widow, her husband having been killed on the English coast. All other motives vanished from my mind at once, but the attainment of that woman. I imagined I was a favourite, and resolved to be first in hand with her. I found her clothed in deep mourning, lovelier than ever, and as kind and affable as heart could wish. I could not ask her hand until a decent time had elapsed from the death of her husband; but I was invited back, visited her, conducted her to church, and to every place to which she proposed going; was given to understand that I was the favourite, and certainly no one could appreciate the favour more highly than I did; for, beside her great wealth, she was a most fascinating woman, and I loved her passionately. Every thing went swimmingly on, and I anticipated our approaching nuptials with a thrilling fondness which I could not express.

One day I went as usual to wait on her, and found her alone, with her countenance, as I thought, a little flushed. I thought I had taken her by surprise, and went forward to salute her. But such a rebuff as I got! one which I never can forget, should I live to the age of Methusaleh. "Stand off, and keep your distance, sir!" said she, fiercely. "Think you I would allow a traitor and a coward to approach my presence, far less my person?"

"Madam!" said I, with astonishment, "what do you mean? It is fortunate that you are a lady, else——."

"No, sir! It is unfortunate that I am a lady, else your life or mine should have paid for your falsehood and pusillanimity! So you deserted your true prince, to whom you swore allegiance, and went and joined with the ungrateful rebel Argyle against him?"

All was over with me at once! I saw it, and was utterly confounded.

The mistaken loyalty of the men of Scotland to their insignificant exiled prince is mixed with selfishness. That of the women is pure and disinterested, and as much above that of the men, as the ardour and generosity of their nature are above ours. I was dismissed with the utmost contempt, and debarred from ever looking her again in the face!

I felt myself now bereaved of every bond of affection; every thing that could tend to link me to my country or my race; and my heart began again to renovate the half-extinguished traces of affection for Araby, the Jewess, and my beloved Prince Iset, now a king and a queen somewhere in distant Asia, I little knew in what place. But in a few days I took up the resolution of going and spending the rest of my days in their service; and the day but one before writing this I mentioned it to Finlay, who I find is willing to go, at least as far as Poland, where the war is still raging, and where he hopes still to raise a considerable gleaning from a late harvest.

---

Here the journal of Captain Lochy breaks off abruptly, and nothing is known, with certainty, regarding his future adventures or fate. This would make it appear that he went abroad, and that his journals had never reached Britain. But I find, that in the year 1725-6, there was a law-suit between a Captain John Lochy and the laird of Borthwicksheils, regarding some superiority over the lands of Parkhill and Musely, which would make it appear that he had ultimately bought some lands about Borthwick, in Roxburghshire, for the surname was till then unknown; and there are sundry families of that name remaining in the district. But the most curious thing of this eventful memoir is, that, at this distance of time, I should have been able to discover what he never could do himself, namely, who were his parents. And though I cannot vouch for the authenticity of the intelligence conveyed in the following letters, there is a particularity about them, which undoubtedly entitles them to consideration. In the year 1827 the following advertisement appeared in two Scots papers:–

"INFORMATION WANTED.

"Whereas it has been reported to the advertiser, that the singular incidents, relating to the birth and parentage of a certain Captain John Lockie, or Lochy, are well known to two or three families in

Scotland; this is to give notice, that whoever will give such information to James Laidlaw, W. S. Edinburgh, or Mr. Alex. Reid, Trongate, Glasgow, shall be liberally rewarded."

In consequence of this advertisement, the two following letters were handed to the editor:–

"Aberdeen, Dec. 2nd, 1827.

"SIR,

"I presume to answer your advertisement, knowing, as I do, from my grandfather, who was one of the men that bore the child; and according to certain dates, the child was born on the 12th of August, 1691, and that privately, too, in the bed of a gentlewoman at Crieff. On the 14th, my grandfather and a nurse, and Hugh Campbell of Griskin, bore the child into the way of the hunters, and watched till he was taken. His father was the Hon. Colonel James Campbell of Argyle, and his mother Lady Mary Wharton, only daughter of Lord Wharton, a greaty beauty and a great fortune. Colonel Campbell and she made a runaway marriage from this town, and lived together for a few days and nights, I cannot certainly say how long. But it having been alleged that the lady got not fair play, a criminal action was laid against the colonel, who was obliged to fly the country. But Sir John Johnston of Caskiben, our provost, who assisted him in the wild prank, was catched and hanged. On the very week that Sir John was executed the marriage was dissolved by act of parliament. But behold! the young lady afterwards had a son; and the indignation of her great and powerful friends that the child of the ravisher should inherit that immense property was such, that the lady, out of terror for her offspring, was obliged to abscond into the highlands of Perthshire for six months.

"I have heard my father say that the marriage was law-abiding; and, if so, that boy was legal heir to the great estates of Boquhan and Burnbank, in Scotland, and two lordships in England; for neither of his parents had any other son. With regard to his persecutors, I know nothing. The colonel soon after returned home, and became a great man, and a member of parliament, and was married to Lady Margaret Leslie. These are the principal things that have come to my knowledge, and the certainty of them is not to be disputed. If any man were to dispute them, I would say he might as well dispute his own existence or mine. Do not I know, and cannot I prove, that the lady was taken from her mother's house in Broad-street, in fair daylight, wiled away to Grennan, and married to Colonel James

Campbell; that he narrowly escaped with his life; and that his friend, Sir John Johnston, was taken and executed for being art and part with him? Now, when it is considered that this boy, legitimate by the law of Scotland, and presumptive heir, not only to the earldom of Argyle, but to Lord Wharton's great estates, it is little wonder that there were some who eagerly desired to have him out of the way. I have heard it said that he was made a general and a count, and died abroad.

"I am, Sir,
"Your obedient servant,
"GEORGE M. MOIR."

Badly expressed as this letter is, it bears strong marks of authenticity, and has convinced me that our extraordinary adventurer, Captain John Lochy, was indeed the fruits of this runaway marriage. The other is to the same purport. It is dated Inverkielar, May 17th, 1827, and addressed to Mr. Laidlaw.

"SIR,

"You may acquaint your friend the advertiser that I am certain Captain Lockie was the son of Lady Mary Wharton. I do not remember any of the circumstances, but have often heard them related; for I had a grand-aunt present when the boy was born, and she used to cry, and tell how his mother loved him and wept over him. For when she saw that she had brought a fine boy into a world of enemies, and was obliged to throw him out destitute, her heart yearned over him, and her very soul clung to her child. She was but fifteen years old when she became his mother, and there was she obliged to give him up to be laid down in the wild, to be lifted and brought up as a foundling among his own kinsmen. He was born in the house of Mrs. Marrion Oliphant, in Crieff, and found in Glen-Lochy on the 12th of August, 1691. His mother never lost sight of him all his life, but kept constantly a confidential servant under her pay to keep guard over him. At first my grand-aunt was employed, and then others in succession; and I have heard it said that his was such a life of adventure and hair-breadth escapes as never was since the time that man was born in the world. I neither ask nor expect any reward for this intelligence, but only wish I had been able to have given it you more circumstantially; but I think I know those who can; and am, in the mean time,

"Sir, your humble servant,
"JAMES M'KINLAY."

From these simple documents the reader is left to judge for himself; they require no exposition of mine. But I only regret that our intrepid hero did not write out his autobiography to the last of his life; yet perhaps he did, as I know not what became of him.

# THE PONGOS:

## A LETTER FROM SOUTHERN AFRICA

---

MY DEAR FRIEND,

IN my last I related to you all the circumstances of our settlement here, and the prospect that we had of a peaceful and pleasant habitation. In truth, it is a fine country, and inhabited by a fine race of people; for the Kousies, as far as I have seen of them, are a simple and ingenuous race; and Captain Johnstone having insured the friendship and protection of their chief, we lived in the most perfect harmony with them, trafficking with them for oxen, for which we gave them iron and copper in exchange, the former being held in high estimation by them. But, alas! sir, such a fate has befallen to me since I wrote you last, as I am sure never fell to the lot of a human being. And I am now going to relate to you one of those stories which, were it to occur in a romance, would be reckoned quite out of nature, and beyond all bounds of probability; so true is it, that there are many things in heaven and earth that are not dreamed of in our philosophy.

You knew my Agnes from her childhood: you were at our wedding at Beattock, and cannot but remember what an amiable and lovely girl she then was. I thought so, and so did you, at least you said you never had as bonny a bride on your knee. But you will hardly believe that her beauty was then nothing in comparison with what it became afterwards; and when she was going about our new settlement with our little boy in her arms, I have often fancied that I never saw so lovely a human being.

Be that as it may, the chief Karoo came to me one day, with his interpreter, whom he caused to make a long palaver about his power, and dominion, and virtues, and his great desire to do much good. The language of this fellow being a mixture of Kaffre, High Dutch, and English, was peculiarly ludicrous, and most of all so when he concluded with expressing his lord's desire to have my wife to be his own, and to give me in exchange for her four oxen, the best that I could choose from his herd!

As he made the proposal in presence of my wife, she was so much tickled with the absurdity of the proposed barter, and the manner in which it was expressed, that she laughed immoderately. Karoo, thinking she was delighted with it, eyed her with a look that surpasses all description, and then caused his interpreter make another palaver to her concerning all the good things she was to enjoy, one of which was, that she was to ride upon an ox whose horns were tipped with gold. I thanked the great Karoo for his kind intentions, but declared my incapability to part with my wife, for that we were one flesh and blood, and nothing could separate us but death. He could comprehend no such tie as this. All men sold their wives and daughters as they listed, I was told–for that the women were the sole property of the men. He had bought many women from the Tambookies, that were virgins, and had never given above two cows for any of them; and because he desired to have my wife, he had offered me as much for her as would purchase four of the best wives in all the two countries, and that therefore I was bound to give her up to him. And when I told him, finally, that nothing on earth could induce me to part with her, he seemed offended, bit his thumb, knitted his brows, and studied long in silence, always casting glances at Agnes of great pathos and languishment, which were perfectly irresistible, and ultimately he struck his spear's head in the ground, and offered me ten cows and a bull for my wife, and a choice virgin to boot. When this proffer was likewise declined, he smiled in derision, telling me I was the son of foolishness, and that *he foretold I should repent it.* Three times he went over this, and then went away in high dudgeon. Will you, sir, believe, or will any person alive believe, that it was possible I could live to repent this?

My William was at this time about eleven months old, but was still at the breast, as I could never prevail on his lovely mother to wean him, and at the very time of which I am speaking, our little settlement was invaded one night by a tribe of those large baboons called ourang-outangs, pongos, or wild men of the woods, who did great mischief to our fruits, yams, and carrots. From that time we kept a great number of guns loaded, and set a watch; and at length the depredators were again discovered. We sallied out upon them in a body, not without alarm, for they are powerful and vindictive animals, and our guns were only loaded with common shot. They fled at the first sight of us, and that with such swiftness that we might as well have tried to catch deer; but we got one close fire at them, and doubtless wounded a number of them, as their course was traced with blood. We pursued them as far as the Keys river, which they swam, and we lost them.

Among all the depredators, there was none fell but one youngling, which I lifted in my arms, when it looked so pitifully, and cried so like a child, that my heart bled for it. A large monster, more than six feet high, perceiving that he had lost his cub, returned brandishing a huge club, and grinning at me. I wanted to restore the abominable brat, for I could not bear the thought of killing it, it was so like a human creature; but before I could do this several shots had been fired by my companions at the hideous monster, which caused him once more to take to his heels; but turning oft as he fled, he made threatening gestures at me. A Kousi servant that we had finished the cub, and I caused it to be buried.

The very morning but one after, Agnes and her black maid were milking our few cows upon the green; I was in the garden, and William was toddling about pulling flowers, when, all at once, the women were alarmed by the sight of a tremendous ourang-outang issuing from our house, which they had just left. They seem to have been struck dumb and senseless with amazement, for not one of them uttered a sound, until the monster, springing forward, in one moment snatched up the child and made off with him. Instead of coming to me, the women pursued the animal with the child, not knowing, I believe, what they were doing. The fearful shrieks which they uttered alarmed me, and I ran to the milking-green, thinking the cows had fallen on the women, as the cattle of that district are ticklish for pushing when any way hurt or irritated. Before I reached the green where the cows stood, the ourang-outang was fully half a mile gone, and only the poor feeble exhausted women running screaming after him. For a good while I could not conceive what was the matter, but having my spade in my hand, I followed spontaneously in the same direction. Before I overtook the women, I heard the agonised cries of my dear boy, my darling William, in the paws of that horrible monster. There is no sensation of which the human heart is capable that can at all be compared with the horror which at that dreadful moment seized on mine. My sinews lost their tension, and my whole frame became lax and powerless. I believe I ran faster than usual, but then I fell every minute, and as I passed Agnes she fell into a fit. Kela-kal, the black girl, with an astonishing presence of mind, had gone off at a tangent, without orders, or without being once missed, to warn the rest of the settlers, which she did with all expedition. I pursued on, breathless, and altogether unnerved with agony; but, alas! I rather lost than gained ground.

I think if I had been fairly started, that through desperation I could have overtaken the monster; but the hopelessness of success rendered me feeble. The truth is, that he did not make great speed, not nearly the speed these animals are wont to make, for he was greatly incumbered with the child. You perhaps do not understand the nature of these animals–neither do I: but they have this peculiarity, that when they are walking leisurely or running down-hill, they walk upright like a human being; but when hard pressed on level ground, or up-hill, they use their long arms as fore-legs, and then run with inconceivable swiftness. When flying with their own young, the greater part of them will run nearly twice as fast as an ordinary man, for the cubs cling to them with both feet and hands; but as my poor William shrunk from the monster's touch, he was obliged to embrace him closely with one paw, and run on three, and still in that manner he outran me. O may never earthly parent be engaged in such a heart-rending pursuit! Keeping still his distance before me, he reached the Keys river, and there the last gleam of hope closed on me, for I could not swim, while the ourang-outang, with much acuteness, threw the child across his shoulders, held him by the feet with one paw, and with the other three stemmed the river, though then in flood, with amazing rapidity. It was at this dreadful moment that my beloved babe cast his eyes on me as I ran across the plain towards him, and I saw him holding up his little hands in the midst of the foaming flood, and crying out, "Pa! pa! pa!" which he seemed to utter with a sort of desperate joy at seeing me approach.

Alas! that sight was the last, for in two minutes thereafter the monster vanished, with my dear child, in the jungles and woods beyond the river, and there my course was stayed; for to have thrown myself in, would only have been committing suicide, and leaving a destitute widow in a foreign land. I had therefore no other resource but to throw myself down, and pour out my soul in lamentation and prayer to God. From this state of hapless misery, I was quickly aroused by the sight of twelve of my countrymen coming full speed across the plain on my track. They were all armed and stripped for the pursuit, and four of them, some of whom you know, Adam Johnstone, Adam Haliday, Peter Carruthers, and Joseph Nicholson, being excellent swimmers, plunged at once into the river, and swam across, though not without both difficulty and danger, and without loss of time continued the pursuit.

The remainder of us, nine in number, were obliged to go half a day's journey up the river, to a place called Shekah, where the Tambookies dragged us over on a hurdle; and we there procured a Kousi, who had a hound, which he pretended could follow the track of an ourang-outang over the whole world. Urged on by a sort of forlorn and desperate hope, we kept at a running pace the whole afternoon; and at the fall of night came up with Peter Carruthers, who had lost the other three. A singular adventure had befallen himself. He and his companions had agreed to keep within call of each other; but as he advanced, he conceived he heard the voice of a child crying behind him to the right, on which he turned off in that direction, but heard no more of the wail. As he was searching, however, he perceived an ourang-outang steal from a thicket, which, nevertheless, it seemed loath to leave. When he pursued it, it fled slowly, as with intent to entice him in pursuit from the spot; but when he turned towards the thicket, it immediately followed. Peter was armed with a pistol and rapier; but his pistol and powder had been rendered useless by swimming the river, and he had nothing to depend on but his rapier. The creature at first was afraid of the pistol, and kept aloof; but seeing no fire issue from it, it came nigher and nigher, and seemed determined to have a scuffle with Carruthers for the possession of the thicket. At length it shook its head, grinning with disdain, and motioned him to fling the pistol away as of no use; it then went and brought two great clubs, of which it gave him the choice, to fight with it. There was something so bold, and at the same time so generous, in this, that Peter took one as if apparently accepting the challenge; but that moment he pulled out his gleaming rapier, and ran at the hideous brute, which frightened it so much, that it uttered two or three loud grunts like a hog, and scampered off; but soon turning, it threw the club at Peter with such a certain aim, that it had very nigh killed him.

He saw no more of the animal that night; but when we found Carruthers, he was still lingering about the spot, persuaded that my child was there, and that if in life, he would soon hear his cries. We watched the thicket all night, and at the very darkest hour, judge of my trepidation when I heard the cries of a child in the thicket, almost close by me, and could well distinguish that the cries proceeded from the mouth of my own dear William, from that sweet and comely mouth, which I had often kissed a hundred times in a day! We all rushed spontaneously into the thicket, and all towards the same point; but, strange to relate, we only ran against one another, and found nothing besides. I cried on my boy's name; but all was again silent, and we heard no more. He only uttered three cries, and then we all heard distinctly that his crying was stopped by something stuffed into his mouth. I still wonder how I retained my reason, for certainly no parent had ever such a trial to undergo. Before day we heard some movement in the thicket, and though heard by us all at the same time, each of us took it for one of our companions moving about; and it was not till long after the sun was up that we at length discovered a bed up among the thick branches of a tree, and not above twelve feet from the ground; but the occupants had escaped, and no doubt remained but that they were now far beyond our reach. This was the most grievous and heart-breaking miss of all; and I could not help giving vent to my grief in excessive weeping, while all my companions were deeply affected with my overpowering sorrow.

We then tried the dog, and by him we learned the way the fliers had taken; but that was all, for as the day grew warm, he lost all traces whatever. We searched over all the country for many days, but could find no traces of my dear boy, either dead or alive; and at length were obliged to return home weary and broken-hearted. To describe the state of my poor Agnes is impossible. It may be conceived, but can never be expressed. But I must haste on with my narrative, for I have yet a great deal to communicate.

About three months after this sad calamity, one evening, on returning home from my labour, my Agnes was missing, and neither her maid-servant, nor one of all the settlers, could give the least account of her. My suspicions fell instantly on the Kousi chief, Karoo, for I knew that he had been in our vicinity hunting, and remembered his threat. This was the most grievous stroke of all; and, in order to do all for the preservation of my dear wife that lay in my power, I and three of my companions set out and travelled night and day, till we came to the chief's head-quarters. I have not time to describe all the fooleries and difficulties we had to encounter: suffice it, that Karoo denied the deed; but still in such a manner that my suspicions were confirmed. I threatened him terribly with the vengeance of his friend Captain Johnstone, and the English army at the Cape, saying I would burn him and all his wives and his people with fire. He wept out of fear and vexation, and offered me the choice of his wives, or any two of them, showing me a great number of them, many of whom he recommended for their great beauty and fatness; and I believe he would have given me any number if I would have gone away satisfied. But the language of the interpreter being in a great measure unintelligible, we all deemed that he said repeatedly that Karoo would not give the lady up.

What was I now to do? We had not force in our own small settlement to compel Karoo to restore her; and I was therefore obliged to buy a trained ox, on which I rode all the way to the next British settlement, for there are no horses in that country. There I found Captain Johnstone, with three companies of the 72d, watching the inroads of the savage Boshesmen. He was greatly irritated at Karoo, and despatched Lieutenant M'Kenzie, and fifty men along with me, to chastise the aggressor. When the chief saw the Highlanders, he was terrified out of his wits; but, nevertheless, not knowing what else to do, he prepared for resistance, after once more proffering me the choice of his wives.

Just when we were on the eve of commencing a war, which must have been ruinous to our settlement, a black servant of Adam Johnstone's came to me, and said that I ought not to fight and kill his good chief, for that he had not the white woman. I was astonished, and asked the Kaffre what he meant, when he told me that he himself saw my wife carried across the river by a band of pongos, (ourang-outangs,) but he had always kept it a secret, for fear of giving me distress, as they were too far gone for pursuit when he beheld them. He said they had her bound, and were carrying her gently on their arms; but she was either dead or in a swoon, for she was not crying, and her long hair was hanging down.

I had kept up under every calamity till then; but this news fairly upset my reason. I fell a blaspheming, and accused the Almighty of injustice for laying such fearful judgments on me. May he in mercy forgive me, for I knew not what I said! but had I not been deprived of reason I could not have outlived such a catastrophe as this, and whenever it recurs to my remembrance, it will make my blood run chill till the day of my death. A whole year passed over my head like one confused dream; another came, and during the greater part of it my mind was very unsettled; but at length I began to indulge in long fits of weeping, till by degrees I awakened to a full sense of all my misery, and often exclaimed that there was no sorrow like my sorrow. I lingered on about the settlement, not having power to leave the spot where I had once been so happy with those I loved, and all my companions joined in the cultivation of my fields and garden, in hopes that I would become resigned to the will of the Lord, and the judgments of his providence.

About the beginning of last year a strange piece of intelligence reached our settlement. It was said that two maids of Kamboo had been out on the mountains of Norroweldt gathering fruits, where they had seen a pongo taller than any Kousi, and that this pongo had a beautiful white boy with him, for whom he was gathering the choicest fruits, and the boy was gambolling and playing around him, and leaping on his shoulders.

This was a piece of intelligence so extraordinary, and so much out of the common course of events, that every one of the settlers agreed that it could not be a forgery, and that it behoved us immediately to look after it. We applied to Karoo for assistance, who had a great number of slaves from that country, much attached to him, who knew the language of the place whither we were going, and all the passes of the country. He complied readily with our request, giving us an able and intelligent guide, with as many of his people as we chose. We raised in all fifty Malays and Kousis; nine British soldiers, and every one of the settlers that could bear arms, went with us; so that we had in all nearly a hundred men, the blacks being armed with pikes, and all the rest with swords, guns, and pistols. We journeyed for a whole week, travelling much by night and resting in the shade by day, and at last we came to the secluded district of which we were in search, and in which we found a temporary village, or camp, of one of these independent inland tribes. They were in great alarm at our approach, and were apparently preparing for a vigorous resistance; but on our guide, who was one of their own tribe, going up to them, and explaining our views, they received us joyfully, and proffered their assistance.

From this people we got the heart-stirring intelligence that a whole colony of pongos had taken possession of that country, and would soon be masters of it all; for that the Great Spirit had sent them a queen from the country beyond the sun, to teach them to speak, and work, and go to war; and that she had the entire power over them, and would not suffer them to hurt any person who did not offer offence to them; that they knew all she said to them, and answered her, and lived in houses, and kindled fires like other people, and likewise fought rank and file: that they had taken one of the maidens of their own tribe to wait upon the queen's child; but because the girl wept, the queen caused them to set her at liberty.

I was now rent between hope and terror–hope that this was my own wife and child, and terror that they would be torn in pieces by the savage monsters, rather than given up. Of this last, the Lockos (the name of this wandering tribe) assured us we needed not to entertain any apprehensions, for that they would, every one of them, die, rather than wrong a hair of their queen's head. But that it behoved us instantly to surround them; for if they once came to understand that we were in pursuit, they would make their escape, and then the whole world would not turn or detain them.

Accordingly, that very night, being joined by the Lockos, we surrounded the colony by an extensive circle, and continued to close as we advanced. By the break of day we had them closely surrounded. The monsters flew to arms at the word of command, nothing daunted, forming a circle round their camp and queen, the strongest of the males being placed outermost, and the females inmost; but all armed alike, and all having the same demure and melancholy faces. The circle being so close that I could not see inside, I went with the nine red-coats to the top of a cliff, that, in some degree, overlooked the encampment, in order that, if my Agnes really was there, she might understand who was near her. Still I could not discover what was within; but I called her name aloud several times, and in about five minutes after that the whole circle of tremendous brutal warriors flung away their arms and retired backward, leaving an open space for me to approach their queen.

In the most dreadful trepidation I entered between the hideous files, being well guarded by soldiers on either hand, and followed by the rest of the settlers; and there I indeed beheld my wife, my beloved Agnes, standing ready to receive me, with little William in her right hand, and a beautiful chubby daughter in her left, about two years old, and the very image of her mother. Conceive, if you can, sir, such a meeting! Were there ever a husband and wife met in such circumstances before? Never since the creation of the world! The two children looked healthy and beautiful, with their fur aprons; but it struck me at first that my beloved was much altered: it was only, however, caused by her internal commotion, by feelings which overpowered her grateful heart, against which nature could not bear up; for on my first embrace she fainted in my arms, which kept us all in suspension and confusion for a long space. The children fled from us, crying for their mother, and took shelter with their friends the pongos, who seemed in great amazement, and part of them began to withdraw, as if to hide themselves.

As soon as Agnes was somewhat restored, I proposed that we should withdraw from the camp of her savage colony; but she refused, and told me, that it behoved her to part with her protectors on good terms, and that she must depart without any appearance of compulsion, which they might resent; and we actually rested ourselves during the heat of the day in the shades erected by those savage inhabitants of the forest. My wife went to her hoard of provisions, and distributed to every one of the pongos his share of fruit, succulent herbs, and roots, which they ate with great composure. It was a curious scene, something like what I had seen in a menagerie; and there was my little William, serving out food to the young ourang-outangs, cuffing them, and ordering them, in the broad Annandale dialect, to do this, that, and the other thing; and they were not only obedient, but seemed flattered by his notice and correction. We were then presented with delicious fruits; but I had no heart to partake, being impatient to have my family away from the midst of this brutal society; for as long as we were there, I could not conceive them safe or fairly in my own power.

Agnes then stood up, and made a speech to her subjects, accompanying her expressions with violent motions and contortions, to make them understand her meaning. They understood it perfectly; for when they heard that she and her children were to leave them, they set up such a jabbering of lamentation as British ears never heard. Many of them came cowering and fawning before her, and she laid her hand on their heads; many, too, of the young ones came running, and lifting the children's hands, they put them on their own heads. We then formed a close circle round Agnes and the children, to the exclusion of the pongos, that still followed behind, howling and lamenting; and that night we lodged in the camp of the Lockos, placing a triple guard round my family, of which there stood great need. We durst not travel by night; but we contrived two covered hurdles, in which we carried Agnes and the children; and for three days a considerable body of the tallest and strongest of the ourang-outangs attended our steps, and some of them came to us fearlessly every day, as she said, to see if she was well, and if we were not hurting her.

We reached our own settlement one day sooner than we took in marching westward; but there I durst not remain for a night, but getting into a vessel, I sailed straight for the Cape, having first made over all my goods and chattels to my countrymen, who are to send me down value here in corn and fruit; and here I am, living with my Agnes and our two children, at a little wigwam about five miles from Cape Town.

My Agnes's part of the story is the most extraordinary of all. But here I must needs be concise, giving only a short and general outline of her adventures; for among dumb animals, whose signals and grimaces were so liable to misinterpretation, much must have been left to her own conjecture. The creatures' motives for stealing and detaining her appeared to have been as follows:–

These animals remain always in distinct tribes, and are perfectly subordinate to a chief or ruler, and his secondary chiefs. In their expedition to rob our gardens, they had brought their sovereign's sole heir along with them, as they never leave any of the royal family behind them, for fear of a surprisal. It was this royal cub which we killed, and the queen his mother, having been distractedly inconsolable for the loss of her darling, the old monarch had set out by night to try, if possible, to recover it; and on not finding it, he seized on my boy in its place, carried him home in safety to his queen, and gave her him to nurse! She did so. Yes, she positively did nurse him at her breast for three months, and never child throve better than he did. By that time he was beginning to walk, and aim at speech, by imitating every voice he heard, whether of beast or bird; and it had struck the monsters as a great loss, that they had no means of teaching their young sovereign to speak, at which art he seemed so apt. This led to the scheme of stealing his own mother to be his instructor, which they effected in the most masterly style, binding and gagging her in her own house, and carrying her from a populous hamlet in the fair forenoon, without having been discovered. Their expertness, and the rapidity of their motions, Agnes described as inconceivable by those who had never witnessed them. They showed every sort of tenderness and kindness by the way, proffering her plenty of fruit and water; but she gave herself totally up to despair, till, behold! she was introduced to her own little William, plump, thriving, and as merry as a cricket, gambolling away among his brutal compeers, for many of whom he had conceived a great affection;–but then they far outgrew him, while others as fast overtook him in size.

Agnes immediately took her boy under her tuition, and was soon given to understand that her will was to be the sole law of the community; and all the while that they detained her, they never refused her in aught save to take her home again. Our little daughter she had named Beatrice, after her maternal grandmother. She was born six months and six days after Agnes's abstraction. She spoke highly of the pongos, of their docility, generosity, warmth of affection to their mates and young ones, and of their irresistible strength. She conceived that, however, to have been a tribe greatly superior to all others of the race, for she never could regard them in any other light than as dumb human creatures. I confess that I had the same sort of feeling while in their settlement, for many of the young females in particular were much comelier than negro savages which I have often seen; and they laughed, smiled, and cried very much like human creatures. At my wife's injunctions, or from her example, they all wore aprons: and the females had let the hair of their heads grow long. It was glossy black, and neither curled nor woolly; and, on the whole, I cannot help having a lingering affection for the creatures. They would make the most docile, powerful, and affectionate of all slaves; but they come very soon to their growth, and are but short-lived, in that way approximating to the rest of the brute creation. They live entirely on fruits, roots, and vegetables, and taste no animal food whatever.

I asked Agnes much of the civility of their manner to her, and she always described it as respectful and uniform. For a while she never thought herself quite safe when near the queen; but the dislike of the latter to her arose entirely out of her boundless affection for the boy. No mother could possibly be fonder of her own offspring than this affectionate creature was of William, and she was jealous of his mother for taking him from her, and causing him instantly to be weaned. But then the chief never once left the two queens by themselves; they had always a guard day and night.

I have no objection to the publication of these adventures in Britain, though I know they will not obtain credit; but I should not like that the incidents reached the Sidney Gazette, as I intend emigrating to that country as soon as I receive value for the stock I left at the settlement, for I have a feeling that my family is scarcely safe as long as I am on any part of the coast of Africa. And for the sake of my rising family, I have an aversion to its being known that they were bred among creatures that must still be conceived to be of the brute creation. Do not write till you hear from me again; and believe me ever, your old affectionate friend,

WM. MITCHELL

Vander Creek, near Cape Town,
Oct. 1, 1826.

# MARION'S JOCK

THERE wad aiblins nane o' you ken Marion. She lived i' the Dod-Shiel, and had a callant to the lang piper, him that Squire Ridley's man beat at the Peel-hill meeting. Weel, you see, he was a gilliegaupy of a callant, gayan like the dad o' him; for Marion said he wad hae eaten a horse ahint the saddle; and as her shieling wasna unco weel stored o' meat, she had ill getting him mainteened; till at the lang and the last it just came to this pass, that whenever Jock was i' the house, it was a constant battle atween Marion and him. Jock fought to be at meat, and Marion to keep him frae it, and mony hard clouts and claws there passed. They wad hae foughten about a haggis, or a new kirning o' butter, for a hale hour, and the battle generally endit in Jock's getting a good share o' ilka thing. When he had fairly gained the possession, by whatever means, he feasted with the greatest satisfaction, licking his large ruddy lips, and looking all about him with eyes of the utmost benevolence. Marion railed all the while that the poor lad was enjoying himself, without any mercy and restraint, and there wasna a vile name under the sun that had ony signification of a glutton in it, that she didna ca' him by. Jock took the bite wi' the buffet;–he heard a' the ill names, and munched away. Oh, how his heart did rejoice o'er a fat lunch o' beef, a good haggis, or even a cog o' milk brose! Poor fellow! such things were his joy and delight. So he snapped them up, and in two or three hours after he was as ready for another battle as ever.

This was a terrible life to lead. Times grew aye the langer the waur; and Marion was obliged to hire poor Jock to Goodman Niddery, to herd his kye and his pet sheep. Jock had nae thoughts at a' o' ganging to sic a job at first; but Marion tauld him ilka day o' the fat beef, the huge kebbucks, and the parridge sae thick that a horn spoon wadna delve into them, till he grew impatient for the term-day. That day came at length, and Marion went away hame wi' her son to introduce him. The road was gayan lang, and Jock's crappin began to craw. He speered a hunder times about the meat at Goodman Niddery's house, and every answer that Marion gae was better than the last, till Jock believed he was gaun hame to a continual feast. It was a delightful thought, for the craving appetite within him was come to a great height. They reached the place, and went into the kitchen. Jock's een were instantly on the look-out; but they didna need to range far. Above the fire there hung two sides of bacon, more than three inches deep of fat, besides many other meaner objects: the hind legs of bullocks, sheep, and deer, were also there; but these were withered, black, and sapless in appearance. Jock thought the very substance was dried out o' them. But the bacon! How it made Jock smack his lips! It was so juicy, that even the brown skin on the outside of it was all standing thick o' eebright beaming drops like morning dew. Jock was established at Goodman Niddery's: he would not have flitted again and left these two sides of bacon hanging there for an estate. Marion perceived well where the sum of his desires was fixed, and trembled for fear of an instant attack. Well might she; for Jock had a large dirk or sheathed knife (a very useful weapon) that he wore, and that he took twice out of its place, looked at its edge, and then at the enormous bacon ham, which was more than three inches deep of solid fat, with the rich drops of juice standing upon the skin. Jock drew his knife on his sandal, then on the edge of a wooden table that stood beside him, examined the weapon's edge again, and again fixed his green eyes on the bacon. "What do the people mean," thought he to himself, "that they do not instantly slice down a portion of that glorious meat, and fry it on the coals? Would they but give me orders to do it–would they even give me the least hint, how slashingly I would obey!"

None of them had the good sense to give Jock ony sic orders. He was two or three times on the very point of helping himself, and at last got up on his feet, it was believed, for the sole purpose of making an attack on the bacon ham, when, behold, in came Goodman Niddery!

"There's your master, sirrah!" whispered Marion; "haste ye and whup aff your bonnet."

Jock looked at him. There was something very severe and forbidding in his countenance; so Jock's courage failed him, and he even took aff his bonnet, and sat down with that in his one hand and the drawn knife in the other. Marion's heart was greatly relieved, and she now ventured on a little conversation.

"I hae brought you hame my lad, Goodman, and I hope he'll be a good servant to you."

"I coudna say, Marion: gin he be as gude as you ca'd him, he'll do. I think he looks like ane that winna be behind at his bicker."

"Ay, weel I wat, Goodman, and that's true; and I wadna wish it were otherwise. Slaw at the meat, slaw at the wark, ye ken."

"That is a good hint o' my mother's!" thinks Jock to himsel:

"What though I should show the auld niggard a sample? The folk o' this house surely hae nae common sense."

The dinner was now, however, set down on the kitchen-table. The goodman sat at the head, the servants in a row on each side, and Jock and his mother at the foot. The goodwife stood behind her servants, and gave all their portions. The dinner that day consisted of broad bannocks, as hard as horn, a pail of thin sour milk, called whig, and a portion of a large kebbuck positively as dry as wood. Jock was exceedingly dissatisfied, and could not but admire the utter stupidity of the people, and their total want of all proper distinction. He thought it wonderful that rational creatures should not know what was good for them. He munched, and munched, and gnawed at the hard bread and cheese, till his jaws were sore; but he never once looked at the food before him; but leaning his cheek on his hand to rest his wearied grinders somewhat at every bite he took, and every splash of the sour shilpy milk that he lapped in, he lifted his eyes to the fat bacon ham with the juice standing on it in clear bells.

Marion wished herself fairly out of the house, for she perceived there would be an outbreak; and to prepare the good people for whatever might happen, she said before going away,–"Now, goodwife, my callant's banes are green, and he's a fast growing twig: I want to ken if he will get plenty o' meat here."

"I winna answer for that, Marion;–he shall fare as the lave fare; but he's may-be no very easily served. There are some misleared servants wha think they never get enough."

"Tell me this thing, then, goodwife; will he see enough?"

"Ay; I shall answer for that part o't."

"Then I shall answer for the rest, goodwife."

Jock had by this time given up contending with the timber cheese, and the blue sour milk, and, taking a lug of a bannock in his hand, the size of a shoe sole, he went away and sat down at the fireside, where he had a full view of the bacon ham, three inches thick of fat, with the dew standing on its brown skin.

The withered bread swallowed rather the better of this delicious sight; so Jock chewed and looked, and looked and chewed, till his mother entered into the security mentioned. "That is a capital hint," thought Jock; "I shall verify my good mother's cautionry, for I can stand this nae langer." He sprang up on a seat, sliced off a large flitch of bacon, and had it on the coals before one had time to pronounce a word; and then turning his back to it, and his face to the company, he stood with his drawn dirk, quite determined to defend his prey.

The goodwife spoke first up. "Gudeness have a care o' us! see to the menseless tike!" cried she. "I declare the creature has na the breeding o' a whalp!"

Jock was well used to such kind of epithets; so he bore this and some more with the utmost suavity, still, however, keeping his ground.

Goodman Niddery grinned, and his hands shook with anger, as if struck with a palsy; but for some reason or other he did not interfere. The servants were like to burst with laughter; and Jock kept the goodwife at bay with his drawn knife, till his slice was roasted; and then, laying it flat on his dry piece of bread, he walked out to the field to enjoy it more at leisure. Marion went away home; and the goodman and goodwife both determined to be revenged on Jock, and to make him pay dear for his audacity.

Jock gave several long looks after Marion as she vanished on Kettlemoor but he had left no kind of meat in her shieling when he came away, else it was likely he would have followed his mother home again. He was still smacking his lips after his rich repast, and he had seen too much good stuff about the house of his new master to leave it at once; so he was even fain to bid Marion good bye in his heart, wipe the filial tear from his eye, poor man, and try to reconcile himself to his new situation.

"Do you carry aye that lang gully knife about wi' you, master cow-herd, or how do they ca' ye?" said his master, when they next met after the adventure of the bacon.

"I hae aye carried it yet," said Jock, with great innocence; "and a gay gude whittle it is."

"Ye maun gie that up," said Niddery; "we dinna suffer chaps like you to carry sic weapons about our house."

Jock fixed his green eyes on his master's face. He could hardly believe him to be serious; still there was something in his look he did not like; so he put his knife deeper into his pocket, drew one step back, and, putting his under row of teeth in front of those above, waited the issue of such an unreasonable demand.

"Come, come; give it up I say. Give it to me; I'll dispose of it for you."

"I'll see you at the bottom o' the place my mother speaks about whiles," thought Jock to himself, "afore I gie my gully either to you or ony that belangs to you." He still kept his former position, however, and the same kind of look at his master's face, only his een grew rather greener.

"Won't you give it up, you stubborn thief? Then I will take it, and give you a good drubbing into the bargain."

When Jock heard this, he pulled out his knife. "That is a good lad to do as you are bidden," said his master. But Jock, instead of delivering up his knife, drew it from the sheath, which he returned to his pocket. "Now I sal only say this," said he; "the first man that tries to take my ain knife frae me–he may do it–but he shall get the length o't in his monyplies first." So saying, he drew back his hand with a sudden jerk.

Goodman Niddery gave such a start that he actually leaped off the ground, and holding up both his hands, exclaimed, "What a savage we have got here! what a Satan!" And without speaking another word, he ran away to the house, and left Jock standing with his drawn knife in his hand.

The goodman's stomach burned with revenge against Jock; so that night he sent him supperless to bed, out of requital for the affair of the fat bacon; and next day the poor boy was set down to a very scanty breakfast, which was not fair. His eye turning invariably to one delicious object, the goodman perceived well what was passing in his heart; and, on some pretence, first sent away all the servants, and then the goodwife. He next rose up himself, with his staff in his hand, and, going slowly away into the little parlour, said, as he went through the kitchen, "What can be become o' a' the folk?" and with that entered the dark door that opened in a corner. He made as though he had shut the door; but he turned about within it and peeped back.

The moment that he vanished was the watchword for Jock: he sprang from his seat at the bottom of the table, and, mounting a form, began to whang away at the bacon ham. Some invidious bone, or hard object of some sort, coming unfortunately in contact with the edge of his knife, his progress was greatly obstructed; and though he cut and sawed with all his might, before he succeeded in separating a piece of about two pounds' weight from the main body, his master had rushed on him from his concealment, and, by one blow of his staff, laid him flat on the floor. The stroke was a sore one, for it was given with extreme good-will, and deprived Jock of sensibility for the time being. He and his form both came down with a great rumble, but the knife remained buried in the fat bacon ham; and the inveterate goodman was not satisfied with felling the poor lad, but kicked him, and laid on him with his stick after he was down. The goodwife at length came running, and put a stop to this cruelty; and fearing the boy was murdered, and that they would be hanged for it, she got assistance, and soon brought Jock again to himself.

Jock had been accustomed to fight for his meat, and, in some measure laid his account with it; so that, on the whole, he took his broken head as little to heart as could have been expected, certainly less than any other boy of the same age would have done. It was only a little more rough than he had been prepared to look for; but had he succeeded in his enterprise, he would not have been ill-content. The goodwife and her maids had laid him on a kitchen bed and bathed his temples; and on recovering from stupefaction, the first thing he did was to examine his pockets to see if he had his gully. Alack! there was nothing but the empty sheath. Then he *did* lose the field, and fell a blubbering and crying. The goodwife thought he was ill, and tried to soothe him by giving him some meat. He took the meat of course, but his heart was inconsolable; till, just when busy with his morsel, his eye chanced to travel to the old place, as if by instinct, and there he beheld the haft of his valued knife, sticking in the bacon ham, its blade being buried deep in sappy treasures. He sprang over the bed, and traversing the floor with staggering steps, mounted a form, and stretched forth his hand to possess himself again of his gully.

"Aih! Gudeness have a care o' us!" cried the goodwife: "saw ever ony body the like o' that? The creature's bacon mad! Goodman! Goodman, come here!"

Jock, however, extricated his knife and fled, though he could scarcely well walk. Some of the maids averred that he at the same time slid a corner of the ham into his pocket; but it is probable they belied him, for Jock had been munching in the bed but the moment before.

He then went out to his cows, weak as he was. He had six cows, some mischievous calves, and ten sheep to herd; and he determined to take good care of these, as also, now that he had got his knife again, not to want his share of the good things about the house, of which he saw there was abundance. However, several days came and went, and Jock was so closely watched by his master and mistress all the time he was in the house, that he could get nothing but his own scanty portion. What was more, Jock was obliged every day to drive his charge far a-field, and remain with them from morn till evening. He got a few porridge in the morning, and a hard bannock and a bottle of sour milk to carry along with him for his dinner. This miserable meal was often despatched before eleven o'clock, so that poor Jock had to spend the rest of the day in fasting, and contriving grand methods of obtaining some good meat in future.

There was one thing very teasing: he had a small shieling, which some former herd had built, and plenty of sticks to burn for the gathering or cutting. He had thus a fire every day, without any thing to roast on it. Jock sat over it often in the most profound contemplation, thinking how delightfully a slice of bacon would fry on it; how he would lay the slice on his hard bannock, and how the juice would ooze out of it! Never was there a man who had richer prospects than Jock had: still his happiness lay only in perspective. But experience teaches man wisdom, and wisdom points out to him many expedients.

Among Jock's pet sheep there was one fat ewe-lamb, the flower of the flock, which the goodwife and the goodman both loved and valued above all the rest. She was as beautiful and playful as innocence itself, and, withal, as fat as she could lie in her skin. There was one rueful day, and a hungry one, that Jock had sat long over his little fire of sticks, pondering on the joys of fat flesh. He went out to turn his mischievous calves, whose nebs were never out of an ill deed, and at that time they had strayed into the middle of a corn field. As bad luck would have it, by the way he perceived this dawted ewe-lamb lying asleep in the sun; and, out of mere frolic, as any other boy would have done, he flew on above her and tried if he could hold her down. After hard struggling he mastered her, took her between his feet, stroked her snowy fleece and soft downy cheek, and ever, as he patted her, repeated these words, "O but ye be a bonny beast!"

The lamb, however, was not much at her ease; she struggled a little now and then; but finding that it availed not, she gave it over; and seeing her comrades feeding near her, she uttered some piteous bleats. They could afford her no assistance; but they answered her in the same tremulous key. After patting her a good while, Jock began to handle her breast and ribs, and found that she was, in good earnest, as fat as pork. This was a ticklish experiment for the innocent lamb. Jock was seized with certain inward longings, and yearnings that would not be repressed. He hesitated long, long, and sometimes his pity awoke; but there was another natural feeling that proved the stronger of the two; so Jock at length took out his long knife and unsheathed it. Next he opened the fleece on the lamb's throat till its bonny white skin was laid bare, and not a hair of wool to intervene between it and the point of his knife. He was again seized with deep remorse, as he contemplated the lamb's harmless and helpless look; so he wept aloud, and tried to put his knife again into its sheath; but he could not.

To make a long tale short, Jock took away the lamb's life, and that not in the most gentle or experienced way. She made no resistance, and only uttered one bleat. "Poor beast!" said Jock; "I dare say ye like this very ill, but I canna help it. Ye are suffering for a' your bits o' ill done deeds now."

The day of full fruition and happiness for Jock was now arrived. Before evening he had roasted and eaten the kidneys, and almost the whole of the draught or pluck. His heart rejoiced within him, for never was there more delicious food. But the worst of it was, that the devils of calves were going all the while in the middle of a cornfield, which his master saw from the house, and sent one running all the way to turn them. The man had also orders to "waken the dirty blackguard callant if he was sleeping, and gie him his licks."

Jock was otherwise employed; but, as luck would have it, the man did not come into his hut, nor discover his heinous crime; for Jock met him among the corn, and took a drubbing with all proper decorum.

But dangers and suspicions encompassed poor Jock now on every side. He sat down to supper at the bottom of the board with the rest of the servants, but he could not eat a single morsel. His eyes were not fixed on the bacon ham as usual, and moreover, they had quite lost that sharp green gleam for which they were so remarkable. These were circumstances not to be overlooked by the sharp eyes of his master and mistress.

"What's the matter wi' the bit dirty callant the night?" said the latter. "What ails you, sirrah, that you hae nae ta'en your supper? Are you weel eneugh?"

Jock wasna ill, he said; but he could not enter into particulars about the matter any farther. The goodman said, he feared the blade had been stealing, for he did not kythe like ane that had been fasting a' day; but after the goodwife and he had examined the hams, kebbucks, beef-barrel, meal-girnel, and every place about the house, they could discern nothing a-missing, and gave up farther search; but not suspicion.

Jock trembled lest the fat lamb might be missed in the morning when he drove out his flock; but it was never remarked that the lamb was a-wanting. He took very little breakfast, but drove his kine and sheep, and the devils of calves, away to the far field, and hasted to his wee housie. He borrowed a coal every day from a poor woman, who lived in a cot at the road-side, to kindle his fire, and that day she noticed, what none else had done, that his coat was all sparked over with blood, and asked him of the reason. Jock was rather startled by the query, and gave her a very suspicious look, but no other answer.

"I fear ye hae been battling wi' some o' your neighbours?" said she.

This was a great relief for Jock's heart. "Ay, just that," said he, and went away with his coal.

What a day of feasting Jock had! He sliced and roasted, and roasted and ate till he could hardly walk. Once when the calves were going into a mischief, which they were never out of, he tried to run, but he could not run a foot; so he was obliged to lie down and roll himself on the ground, take a sleep, and then proceed to work again.

There was nutrition in the very steams that issued from Jock's hut; the winds that blew over it carried health and savoury delight over a great extent of country. A poor hungry boy that herded a few lean cows on an adjoining farm, chancing to come into the track of this delicious breeze, became at once like a statue. He durst not move a step for fear of losing the delicious scent; and there he stood with his one foot before the other, his chin on his right shoulder, his eyes shut, and his mouth open, his nose being pointed straight to Jock's wee housie. The breeze still grew richer, till at last it led him as straight as if there had been a hook in his nose to Jock's shieling; so he popped in, and found Jock at the sublime employment of cooking and eating. The boy gaped and stared at the mangled body of the lamb, and at the rich repast that was going on; but he was a very ignorant and stupid boy, and could not comprehend any thing; so Jock fed him with a good fat piece well roasted, and let him go again to his lean cows.

Jock looked very plump and thriving-like that night; his appearance was quite sleek, somewhat resembling that of a young voluptuary; and, to lull suspicion, he tried to take some supper; but not one bite or sup was he able to swallow. The goodwife, having by that time satisfied herself that nothing was stolen, became concerned about Jock, and wanted him to swallow some physic, which he peremptorily refused to do.

"How can the puir thing tak ony meat?" said she. "He's a' swalled i' the belly. Indeed I rather suspect that he's swalled o'er the hale body."

The next morning, as Jock took out his drove, the goodman was standing at the road-side to look at them. Jock's heart grew cold, as well it might, when the goodman called out to him, "Callant, what hae you made o' the gude lamb?"

"Is she no there?" said Jock, after a long pause, for he was so much astounded that he could not speak at the first.

"Is she no there!" cried the goodman again in great wrath, imitating Jock's voice. "If ye binna blind, ye may see that. But I can tell you, my man, gin ye hae letten ought happen to that lamb, ye had better never hae been born."

"What can be comed o' the beast?" said Jock. "I had better look the house, she's may be stayed in by herself."

Jock didna wait for an order, but, glad to be a little farther off from his master, he ran back and looked in the fold and sheep-house, and every nettle bush around them, as he had been looking for a lost knife.

"I can see naething o' her," said he, as he came slounging back, hanging his head, and keeping aloof from the goodman, who still carried his long pike-staff in his hand.

"But I'll mak you see her, and find her baith, hang-dog!" said he; "or deil be in my fingers an I dinna twist your neck about. Are you sure you had her yestreen?"

O yes! Jock was sure he had her yestreen. The women were examined if they had observed her as they milked the cows: they could not tell. None of them had seen her; but they could not say she was not there. All was in commotion about the steading, for the loss of the dawted pet-lamb, which was a favourite with every one of the family.

Jock drove his cattle and nine sheep to the field–roasted a good collop or two of his concealed treasure, and snapped them up, but found that they did not relish so well as formerly; for now that his strong appetite for fat flesh was somewhat allayed, yea, even fed to loathing, he wished the lamb alive again: he began, moreover, to be in great bodily fear; and to provide against the probability of any discovery being made, he lifted the mangled remains of his prey, and conveyed them into an adjoining wood, where he covered them carefully up with withered leaves, and laid thorns above them. "Now," said Jock, as he left the thicket, "let them find that out wha can."

The goodman went to all the herds around, inquiring after his lamb; but could hear no intelligence of her till he came to the cottage of poor Bessie, the old woman that had furnished Jock with a coal every day. When he put the question to her, the rock and the lint fell out of Bessie's hand, and she sat a while quite motionless.

"What war ye saying, goodman? War ye saying ye had lost your bonnie pet-lamb?"

"Even sae, Bessie."

"Then, goodman, I fear you will never see her living again. What kind o' callant is that ye hae gotten? He's rather a suspicious-looking chap. I tentit his claes a' spairged wi' blude the tither day, and baith this and some days bygane he has brought in his dinner to me, saying that he dought nae eat it."

Goodman Niddery could make no answer to this, but sat for a while grumphing and groaning, as some late events passed over his mind; particularly how Jock's belly was swollen, and how he could not take any supper. But yet the idea that the boy had killed his favourite, and eaten her, was hardly admissible: the deed was so atrocious he could not conceive any human being capable of it, strong as circumstances were against his carnivorous herd. He went away with hurried and impatient steps to Jock's wee house, his old colley dog trotting before him, and his long pike-staff in his hand. Jock eyed him at a distance, and kept out of his path, pretending to be engaged in turning the calves to a right pasture, and running and threshing them with a long goad; for though they were not in any mischief then, he knew that they would soon be in some.

The goodman no sooner set his nose within Jock's shieling than he was convinced some horrid deed had been done. It smelled like a cook's larder; and, moreover, his old dog, who had a very good scent, was scraping among the ashes, and picking up fragments of something which he seemed very much to enjoy. Jock did not know what to do when he saw how matters stood, yet he still had hopes that nothing would appear to criminate him. The worst thing that he saw was the stupid hungered boy on the adjoining farm coming wading through the corn. He had left his dirty lean kine picking up the very roots of the grass, and had come snouking away in hopes of getting another fat bit for his impoverished stomach. But when he saw Goodman Niddery come out of the cot with impassioned strides, he turned and ran through the strong corn with his whole might, always jumping up as he proceeded.

The goodman called angrily on his old dog to come after him, but he would not come, for he was working with his nose and forefeet among Jock's perfumed ashes with great industry; so the goodman turned back into the house, and hit him over the back with his long pike-staff, which made him glad to give over, and come out about his business; and away the two went to reconnoitre further.

As soon as the old dog was fairly a-field again he took up the very track by which Jock had carried the carcass that morning, and went as straight as a line to the hidden treasure in the thicket. The goodman took off the thorns, and removed the leaves, and there found all that remained of his favourite and beautiful pet-lamb. Her throat was all cut and mangled, her mouth open, and her tongue hanging out, and about one half of her whole body a-wanting. The goodman shed tears of grief, and wept and growled with rage over the mangled form, and forthwith resolved (which was hardly commendable) to seize Jock, and bring him to that very spot and cut his throat.

Jock might have escaped with perfect safety, had he had the sense or foresight to have run off as soon as he saw his master enter the wood; but there seems to be an infatuation that directs the actions of some men. Jock did not fly, but went about and about, turning his kine one while, his nine sheep another, and always between hands winning a pelt at one of the ill-conditioned calves, till his incensed master returned from the fatal discovery, and came up to him. There was one excuse for him; he was not sure if the carcass had been found, for he could not see for the wood whether or not his master went to the very place, and he never thought of the sagacity of the dog.

When Goodman Niddery first left the wood he was half running, and his knees were plaiting under him with the anticipation of horrid revenge. Jock did not much like his gait; so he kept always the herd of cows, and the sheep too, betwixt himself and this half-running master of his. But the goodman was too cunning for poor Jock; he changed his step into a very slow careless walk, and went into the middle of the herd of cows, pretending to be whistling a tune, although it was in fact no tune, but merely a concatenation of tremulous notes on C sharp, without the least fall of harmony. He turned about this cow and the other cow, watching Jock all the while with the tail of his eye, and trilling his hateful whistle. Jock still kept a due distance. At length the goodman called to him, "Callant, come hither, like a man, and help me to wear this cow against the ditch. I want to get haud o' her."

Jock hesitated. He did not like to come within stroke of his master's long stick, neither did he know on what pretence absolutely to refuse his bidding; so he stood still, and it was impossible to know by his looks whether he was going to comply or run off altogether. His master dreaded the latter, and called to him in a still kinder manner, until Jock at last unfortunately yielded. The two wore the cow, and wore the cow, up against the ditch, until the one was close upon her one side, and the other upon her other. "Chproo! hawkie! chproo, my bonnie cow!" cried the goodman, spreading out his arms, with his pike-staff clenched fast in his right hand; then springing by the cow in a moment, he flew upon Jock, crying out, with the voice of a demon, "D–n you, rascal! but I'll do for you now!"

Jock wheeled about to make his escape, and would have beaten his master hollow, had he been fairly started, or timeously apprised of his dreadful danger; but ere he had run four or five steps the pike-staff came over the links of his neck with such a blow, that it laid him flat on his face in a mire. The goodman then seized him by the cuff of the neck with the one hand, and by the hair of his head with the other, and said, with a triumphant and malicious laugh, "Now, get up, and come away wi' me, my braw lad, and I'll let you see sic a sight as you never saw. I'll let you see a wally-dy sight! Get up, like a good cannie lad!"

As he said this, he pulled Jock by the hair, and kicked him with his foot, until he obliged him to rise, and in that guise he led him away to the wood. He had a hold of his rough weather-beaten hair with the one hand, and with the other he heaved the cudgel over him; and as they went, the following was some of the discourse that passed between them.

"Come away, now, my fine lad. Are nae ye a braw, honest, good callant? Do nae ye think ye deserve something that's unco good frae me? Eh? Ay, ye surely deserve something better nor ordinar'; and ye shall hae it too."–(Then a kick on the posteriors, or a lounder with the staff.)–"Come your ways, like a sonsy, brave callant, and I'll let you see a bonny thing and a braw thing in yon brake o' the wood, ye ken."

Jock cried so piteously that, if his master had not had a heart of stone, he would have relented, and not continued in his fatal purpose; but he only grew the longer the more furious.

"O let me gang! let me gang! let me gang!" cried Jock. "Let me gang! let me gang! for it wasna me. I dinna ken naething about it at a'!"

"Ye dinna ken naething about what, my puir man?"

"About yon bit sheep i' the wood, ye ken."

"You rascal! you rogue! you villain! you have confessed that you kend about it, when I wasna speiring ony sic question at you. You hound! you dog! you savage wolf that you are! Mother of God! but I will do for you! You whelp! you dog! you scoundrel! come along here." (Another hard blow.) "Tell me now, my precious lad, an ye war gaun to be killed, as ye ken something about killing, whether would you choose to have your throat cut, or to have your feet tied and be skinned alive?"

"O dinna kill me! dinna kill me!" cried poor Jock. "My dear master, dinna kill me, for I canna brook it. Oh, oh! an ye kill me I'll tell my mother, that will I; and what will Marion say t'ye, when she has nane but me? Oh, master, dinna kill me, and I'll never do the like o't again!"

"Nay, I shall take warrant for that: you shall never do the like o't again!"

In this melancholy and heart-breaking manner he dragged him on all the way by the rough towsy head, kicking him one while, and beating him another, till he brought him to the very spot where the mangled remains of the pet-lamb were lying. It was a blasting sight for poor Jock, especially as it doubled his master's rage and stern revenge, and these were, in all conscience, high enough wrought before. He twined the hapless culprit round by the hair, and knocked him with his fist, for he had dropped the staff to enable him to force Jock to the place of sacrifice; and he swore by many an awful oath, that if it should cost him his life, he would do to Jock as he had done to that innocent lamb.

With that he threw him on the ground, and got above him with his knees; and Jock having by that time lost all hope of moving his ruthless master by tears or prayers, began a-struggling with the force which desperation sometimes gives, and fought with such success that it was with difficulty his master could manage him.

It was very much like a battle between an inveterate terrier and a bull-dog; but, in spite of all that Jock could do, the goodman got out his knife. It was not, however, one like Jock's, for it had a folding blade, and was very hard to open, and the effecting of this was no easy task, for he could not get both his hands to it. In this last desperate struggle, Jock got hold of his master's cheek with his left hand, and his nails being very long, he held it so strait that he was like to tear it off. His master capered up with his head, holding it back the full length of Jock's arm; yet still being unable to extricate his cheek from Jock's hold, he raised up his knife in his right hand, in order to open it with his teeth, and, in the first place, to cut off Jock's hand, and his head afterwards. He was holding down Jock with his right knee and his left hand; and while in the awkward capering attitude of opening his knife, his face was turned nearly straight up, and his eyes had quite lost sight of his victim. Jock held up his master's cheek, and squeezed it still the more, which considerably impeded his progress in getting the knife open; and, at that important moment, Jock whipped out his own knife, his old dangerous friend, and struck it into the goodman's belly to the haft. The moment he received the wound he sprang up as if he had been going to fly into the air, uttered a loud roar, and fell back above the dead pet-lamb.

Lord, how Jock ran! He was all bespattered with blood, some of it his own, and some of it his master's; wanted the bonnet, and had the bloody knife in his hand; and was, without all doubt, a wild frightsome-looking boy. As he sped through the wood, he heard the groans and howls of his master in the agonies of death behind him. Every one of them added to Jock's swiftness, till it actually became beyond the speed of mortal man. If it be true that love lends a pair of wings, fear, mortal fear, lends two pair. There is nought in life I regret so much as that I did not see Jock in this flight; it must have been such an extraordinary one. There was poor Jock flying with the speed of a fox from all the world, and yet still flying into the world. He had no home, no kindred to whom he durst now retreat, no hold of any thing in nature, save of his own life and his good whittle; and he was alike unwilling to part with either of these. The last time he was seen was by two women on Kirtle-common. He appeared sore bespent, but was still running on with all his might.

The goodman was found before the evening, but only lived to tell how he had come by his end. All his friends and servants were raised, and sent in pursuit of Jock. How he eluded them no man knows; but from that day Marion's Jock has never been more seen or heard of in this land.

END OF VOL. I.

# Appendix:
## MS Fragment of 'The Adventures of Captain John Lochy'

Of Hogg's manuscript material for *Altrive Tales* the only survivor appears to be a hitherto-unidentified fragment of 'The Adventures of Captain John Lochy' in the National Library of Scotland, MS 8887, fol. 38. This is the upper portion of a single unwatermarked leaf of Hogg's manuscript for the tale, paginated 5 by him on the recto and 6 on the verso. It bears a compositor's mark 'B 17' on the recto, at the point in the printed text of the first edition where gathering B begins on page 17, showing that it was used as printer's copy for that edition. The text of this fragment, transcribed below, is equivalent to passages on pp. 86–88 (recto) and 89–90 (verso) of the present text. There are some gaps at the end of each section of text where Hogg's words are not precisely aligned with the cut in the manuscript: gaps are indicated thus: [TEAR].

[*start of page 5*]

told me a part and that small part was all that ever I knew of them. I remember yet every word she said

"Your parentage you never must know for with the knowledge all your prospects and happiness in this world become extinct and most probably the day that you came to the knowledge of it would prove your last and the last of others. One gallant knight has suffered death on your account already and were the secret of your birth divulged heaven knows what would be the consequence. Enquire no more concerning it but be assured of this that the best blood of the kingdom flows in your veins"

"This is strange and most oppressive!" said I "It is not to be borne of course then I am an illegitimate child?"

"No" replied she "Your father and mother were married solemnly married. But the houses of both your parents have inadvertantly and without intending it rendered you illegitimate, and by an act of parliament, obtained by power in an unhallowed rage, ere ever you saw the light made you an outcast and a vagabond in the earth; and though only one individual out of the two families knows of your existence you see how you have been persecuted and will be to the death. Therefore for the sake of all that is dear to you and to me never enquire more about your parents In three days I will present you with a Cornet's commission in Wharton's dragoons. Lord Wharton himself the Colonel's father hath procured it for you; look to him as your patron, and win your way to rank and honour in the service of your country"

Obedience and respect being my bounden duty to such a sweet and benevolent being as this I promised that I never would disgrace the good sword which her kindness had put in my hand and that I would never enquire farther about my parents. I only begged to have her own address and she should be to me father and mother sister and brother as well as the earthly object of my idolatry. She declined giving me it saying it could be of no avail to me as she was only commissioned to put me in a fair way to honour and fame and might never have it in her power to assist me farther or haply to see me again. With this answer I was obliged to be content though my heart yearned for more of her dear society

The day following the hostel boy said to me "Captain your horse is come" on which I went to the stable and found a jet black steed of great beauty and fully caparisoned Of all the gifts I ever recieved I valued this the most. I had a passion for beautiful horses and cannot tell how delighted I was when I mounted that fine animal that caprioled and cantered away so beautifully. I felt as light as the wind and perfectly dizzy with rapture. I will be excused for this when it is considered that I was but the other day lying chained in a dungeon ready to be hanged with only one dark step before me into eternity and now here was I bounding away upon a gallant steed and men taking off their hats to me and calling me Captain!

My commission soon arrived signed and sealed with a letter of instructions but by whom either these or the horse was brought I was kept in profound ignorance, and not having any money by me to bear my expenses on the road I knew not what to do or whom to apply. My time was limited and I began to dread that all would go wrong together, when on the morning of the very last day I had to remain I heard a sweet and beloved voice below enquiring for the young captain. I knew it to be the voice of my lovely protecting angel and hoped that all would yet go well. Heavens how was I astounded when on running to the head of the stair to welcome her I percieved only poor old Mora in the entrance! I recieved such a shock of dissapointment that for a good while I could not speak, which was very bad in me for there was no one living to whom I was more indebted than to poor Mora I at length half articulated "Oh poor dear Mora is it you"

"Yes it is I captain just come to see you [TEAR] with a fawning accent for the people of the house heard us "For you must [TEAR]

"Yes Mora I must give you something [TEAR] had thrown me into a quandary [TEAR]

[*start of page 6*]

remorse in the most dashing stile imaginable without any delinquency being attached to the deed. I practised early and late to attain proficiency and at length challenged my then master a country man of my own one Corporal Renwick whose prowess I pretended to hold cheap but he disarmed and wounded me making at the same time a remark which cut me to the heart. From that time forward I studied the science harder than ever one while under the celebrated Donald Bawn and another under Van Malloch a Saxon until quite concious of superiority I watched a fit opportunity until one evening I found Renwick somewhat inebriated and making terrible vapouring among his pupils on which I challenged him again, and after a very few passes slew him on the spot

Grieveously did I repent of this! A fencing master's life was not accounted much of, but yet my brother officers accounted this unfair and cried shame shame! I had not a word to say, for my heart told me it was a murder. It was malice prepence. I had prepared myself for it, and taken him at a disadvantage when too elevated by drinking and I found that I had done a deed which would hang like a milstone about my neck as long as I lived

This happened after we had left the Netherlands and were on our march to the upper Rhyne I had been introduced to Prince Eugene and had seen the prince of Baden both great heros, but the latter I never liked, nor could any of the English officers bear him, but Eugene was the darling of all ranks. The first time I saw the French face to face was at a strong military station in Bavaria on the second day of June. I had a curious disagreeable sensation that day. The French nation had always been liked in Scotland as its ancient friends and the English hated and here was I joined with our inveterate enemies against our old friends. Nevertheless I was eager for the fight and resolved to distinguish myself at all hazards We attacted the enemy at a dreadful disadvantage for the hill was strongly fortified and their lines of circumvallation appeared to me almost interminable. The Dutch Infantry commenced the attack on the left and the English shortly after, but they were so hotly handled that in fifteen minutes the Dutch lines were first staid then driven into confusion and beat back Our regiment was ordered to their support and went up the slope at a canter cheering on the Dutch who rather looked gruff and dispirited but the Bavarian infantry that were opposed to us we rode over like a field of thistles and restored that part of the field for the present but we came upon the lines at a half angle which confounded us exposing us to the fire of the lines behind. A great number fell. I saw them dropping in whole files and among the rest our brave young Colonel fell under his horse. I was at his side in a minute and extricated him mounted him on my own horse and that moment sprang on behind him for I had no idea of being left in that confusion without a horse and mine was the best on the field. "Lockie I am crushed a little" said he "Take you the rein and let us lead on. We [TEAR] by this time [TEAR]

# Note on the Text

The publication history of *Altrive Tales* as a whole is given in the Introduction to the present edition. The volume was prepared by Hogg during his London visit of January to March 1832 as the first of a series of his collected prose fiction, designed to secure its permanent preservation. For this Hogg revised his earlier published work to appear in conjunction with tales that were either newly-written or that he had failed to publish earlier in periodicals or within his separate volume publications. Each component part of the volume, therefore, also has an individual history and identity.

The present edition seeks to preserve the integrity of the collection created by Hogg in 1832, and therefore each component part is reprinted from the first edition of *Altrive Tales*. It also seeks to provide summaries of the individual history of those parts: this Note on the Text attempts to give these and account for each item's inclusion in the first volume of the projected series of 'Altrive Tales'.

Knowledge of Hogg's revisions can be essential to a nuanced reading of a late version of one of his works. In his 'Memoir of the Author's Life' Hogg creates a multi-layered effect, revisions often acting as accretions to, or reflections upon, segments of earlier versions, rather than simple replacements for them. The present edition attempts to provide an outline of the relationship between all surviving versions of individual items by means of the following notes, which are supplemented by further information in the explanatory Notes.

In listing emendations the page and line numbers are given for each item, followed by the emended reading. After a single square bracket the original reading of the copy-text is given, together with the reason for the emendation (within parentheses) where this may be helpful to the reader.

## Dedication

There is apparently no surviving manuscript version of Hogg's verse dedication 'To the Right Honourable Lady Anne Scott, of Buccleugh'. It was initially published as the preface to his first conventional collection of prose fiction—see *The Brownie of Bodsbeck; and Other Tales*, 2 vols (Edinburgh, 1818), I, i–xii. It was therefore natural that it should appear at the start of a series intended to summarise and preserve the best work of his long career as a fiction-writer.

*The Brownie of Bodsbeck; and Other Tales* was planned and produced at a time when Hogg had newly settled at Altrive in Yarrow, a small farm granted to him rent-free by Charles, 4th Duke of Buccleuch. Although the poem's dating from Altrive is 1 April 1818, shortly before the May publication of the work, Hogg's intention to include a dedication of *The Brownie* to his patron's eldest daughter is clear from the earliest surviving references to the publication. Hogg's letter asking his patron's permission to include such a dedication has not apparently survived, but the Duke's reply, dated 20 December 1816 (NLS MS 2245, fols 25–26), states, 'Lady Ann will be proud of the honour you intend her provided there is nothing profane or irreligious in the Tales'. This, it should be noted, precedes Hogg's letter to the Edinburgh publisher William Blackwood of 4 January 1817 offering him the work: 'My "Cottage Winter Nights" is ready for the the [*sic*] press if you are for them tell me' (NLS MS 4002, fols 153–54). Having recently settled in Yarrow Hogg seems at this period to have felt close to his patron emotionally as well as geographically, as well as to his literary mentor Walter Scott at nearby Abbotsford. Writing from Abbotsford, for example, he instructed Blackwood in a letter of 5 January 1818 to send any proof sheets of the work 'under cover to the Duke of Buccleuch' (NLS MS 4003, fols 84–85). This sense of neighbourhood is reflected in the poem itself, which refers to Hogg's relationship with Lady Anne's mother (the late Harriet, Duchess of Buccleuch) and also recalls a recent visit to Bowhill, during which the tranquillity of the ducal family circle inside the mansion contrasted with the tempestuous storm taking place outside.

The poem was quickly recognised as one of Hogg's most successful pieces by the Tory coterie centred on *Blackwood's Edinburgh Magazine*. In the issue of the magazine for October 1818 (Volume 4, pp. 74–76) the editor apologises for his delay in reviewing *The Brownie* (a work, after all, published by the Blackwood firm and written by one of the magazine's chief supporters):

> We have as yet, by accidental circumstances, been prevented from laying before our readers any account of the Prose Tales lately published by Mr Hogg. In the mean time, we have great pleasure in extracting the following very beautiful Poetical Dedication to a Young Lady of the Noble Family whose enlightened patronage has been so liberally extended to the Ettrick Shepherd. (p. 74)

The poem is then reprinted in full. Further showcasing of the poem from *The Brownie* occurred the following year in another Blackwood publication. In Lockhart's anonymously-published *Peter's Letters to His Kinsfolk*, 3 vols (Edinburgh, 1819), the narrator Dr Morris describes Wordsworth as 'a solemn, wrapped-up contemplative genius' (II, 312), a voice of distant nature, 'what the Ettrick Shepherd finely calls' (quoting from the poem, clearly from memory) 'Great Nature's hum,/ Voice of the desert, never dumb' (see lines 69–70).

In the four-volume *The Poetical Works of James Hogg* (Edinburgh, 1822) 'Verses Addressed to the Right Honourable Lady Anne Scott of Buccleuch' is placed at the end of the second volume (pp. 325–39). It thus concludes a series of poems written during Hogg's Edinburgh years, reflecting the ending of that period of his career with the building of a house and his settlement at Altrive. Most of the changes between the 1818 and 1822 versions consist of adjustments to spelling and punctuation, likely to be the result of the use of a different house-style by the printers. The most significant differences are the deletion of two lines (equivalent to ll. 165–66 of the present text) of Hogg's description of his disembodied voyaging after death, and the re-ordering of 'As minstrel must, and lady ought,' to read 'As lady must and minstrel ought'. The change from 'little wist' in the final paragraph to 'never wist' seems likely to be authorial, but a shift from 'wild dark streamlet raves' to 'wild dark streamlet waves' perhaps represents an error introduced in the course of the printing. The 1822 version of the poem retains the end-dating of the poem from Altrive on 1 April 1818.

The version in *Poetical Works* of 1822, however, appears to be a textual dead-end, since it looks as though Hogg worked from a copy of the 1818 text in revising the poem for its appearance in *Altrive Tales*. Many of the changes made for 1822 are negated, so that 'waves' is once more 'raves', and 'never wist' reverts to 'little wist'. Line 108 reads 'As minstrel must and lady ought;' and the two lines deleted in 1822 reappear in *Altrive Tales*.

*Altrive Tales*, however, does not merely reprint the 1818 text. Obvious errors are corrected again just as they were in 1822 (for example, l. 7 has 'rural hind' not 'rural kind'), but in addition Hogg smooths the flow of his verse and makes a number of minor adjustments. At l. 29, for instance, 'Even babes catch the beloved theme' is ellided to 'Even babes will catch the 'loved theme', while 'the scene' has become 'these scenes' at l. 218. Most strikingly, Hogg introduces a new four-line passage (ll. 171–74) into the description of his disembodied voyaging after death. The deletion of the end-date was perhaps motivated by a wish to make the poem relate more directly to the 1832 volume, even though the circumstances recounted are more relevant to the earlier date–see explanatory Notes.

Only one change has been made to the present reprinting from *Altrive Tales*, as follows:

l. 174 night, ] night.

## Memoir of the Author's Life

Hogg seems to have written a form of his literary autobiography as early as 1803, when he was living with his parents and managing for their support the small farm of Ettrickhouse in his native district. Hogg described the 'original sketch' of his 'Memoir' as 'written more than a twelvemonth ago at Ettrickhouse' in a letter to Scott of 18 January 1805 (NLS MS 3875, fol. 39), and as 'written in a large folio amongst others which I mean to publish'. It was probably intended to form the basis of a biographical account of Hogg to appear under Scott's name in a projected volume of Hogg's songs. In a letter to Scott of 24 December [1803] (NLS MS 3874, fols 248–49) Hogg consults him 'if we might front the songs with a letter to you giving an impartial account of my manner of life and education, and which if you pleased to transcribe putting He for I'. At just this time Hogg had been enjoying an increase of reputation gained through the appearance of his songs and other poetry in the *Edinburgh Magazine* and *Scots Magazine*, and the projected volume would capitalise on this.

The volume of songs did not materialise, but it is possible that Hogg published his 'Memoir' for the first time in association with his work for the *Scots Magazine* all the same. There is a two-part article, signed 'Z.' and entitled 'Farther Particulars of the Life of James Hogg, the Ettrick Shepherd' in *Scots Magazine*, 67 (July and November 1805), 501–03 and 820–23. This, dated from 'Banks of Ettrick', refers to Hogg in the third person but gives many highly specific details of his early life. Edith Batho, in her study *The Ettrick Shepherd* (Cambridge, 1927), convincingly remarks, 'These articles follow the phrasing of the 1807 Memoir so closely that it is safe to conclude that they were written either by Hogg or by one of his intimate friends under his supervision' (p. 224). If 'Z.' is Hogg himself then this would explain his assertion at the opening of the 'Memoir' in *Altrive Tales* (p. 11) that the work is then being published 'for the fourth time, at different periods of my life'.

The manuscript of Hogg's 'original sketch' does not appear to have survived, though it is clear from *Altrive Tales* that he kept a journal for many years as the basis for subsequent versions of the 'Memoir'. The relationship of journal to published work is stated explicitly at the conclusion of the 1821 'Memoir', in a passage carried over into *Altrive Tales* as follows:

> In this short Memoir, which is composed of extracts from a larger detail, I have confined myself to such anecdotes only as relate to my progress as a writer, and these I intend to continue from year to year as long as I live. There is much that I have written which cannot as yet appear; for the literary men of Scotland, my contemporaries, may change their characters, so as to forfeit the estimate at which I have set them, and my social companions may alter their habits. (p. 52)

Among the subjects Hogg refers to in the 'Memoir' as subjects in his journal excluded from the 'Memoir' itself are his experiences as a farmer in Dumfriesshire from 1807–09 (p. 23), character sketches of his fellow members of the Forum debating society (pp. 27–28), his visit to the Lake District in 1814 (p. 33), and the proceedings of the Right and Wrong Club (p. 47). He draws a distinction between 'this short Sketch of my Literary Life' and 'the extended memoir' (p. 36), excluding his farming and domestic life, and various social experiences unrelated to literature. Hogg seems to have kept his manuscript journal up to date until shortly after the publication of the 1821 'Memoir' in the third edition of *The Mountain Bard* (see p. 53). Unfortunately, the journal does not appear to have survived. It may well have been among the manuscripts entrusted to John Wilson after Hogg's death to enable him to write a biography, and never returned by him to Hogg's widow when the intention was abandoned (see Garden, p. 330). There is apparently no surviving manuscript material for any version of Hogg's 'Memoir'.

The earliest surviving version that can be unequivocally ascribed to Hogg is the one printed at the start of *The Mountain Bard* (Edinburgh, 1807), pp. i–xxiii, which concluded with his frustrated attempt to move to Harris as the tenant-farmer of Seilibost in the summer of 1804. *The Mountain Bard* itself, with its collection of ballads and songs, was the crowning point of Hogg's literary career to date. Another notable achievement was the publication of a handsomely produced and illustrated subscription edition of his best-known long poem, *The Queen's Wake* in 1819. Hogg was clearly tempted to attach an updated version of the 'Memoir' to this significant volume, for he asked the publisher, William Blackwood, in a letter of 12 October 1818 (NLS MS 4003, fols 99–100) 'How do you think it would do to give a short abstract of my literary life in the subscription edition [...]?' In the event, however, an updated version of the 'Memoir' did not appear until the third edition of *The Mountain Bard* itself in 1821 (pp. ix–lxxvii).

A full account of the differences between the 1807 'Memoir' and the 1821 'Memoir' will be given in the forthcoming S/SC Edition volume of *The Mountain Bard*, edited by Suzanne Gilbert. A brief outline of them, however, facilitates understanding of the later version of *Altrive Tales*. (Page references in this paragraph are to the 1821 edition of *The Mountain Bard* published by Oliver and Boyd in Edinburgh.) Most obviously, Hogg brought the 'Memoir' up to date, continuing his narrative with a substantial account of his years as a literary man in Edinburgh up to the publication of his most recent volumes, *Winter Evening Tales* (1820) and the second series of *Jacobite Relics* (1821). The 1821 'Memoir' is indeed more than double the length of the 1807 'Memoir'. Hogg's retention of the prefatory remarks by Scott, and the letter-opening of his own narrative, complete with the dating of November 1806 from Mitchelslacks, further emphasises the difference as one of a naive coupling of a later block of text to the end of a pre-existing one. Hogg's strategy is rather more complex, however, and appears to be designed to increase the space between himself as author and himself as subject. Some of the alterations to the earlier text, it is true, relate merely to matters of fact. A reference to Hogg's parents being 'living, and in good health', for example, has clearly been deleted because both of them were dead by the end of 1820. Overall, however, the writing is made smoother between 1807 and 1821–'hired to a farmer' becomes 'hired by a farmer' (p. xi), for example. Hogg also adds passages where the self as author mocks the self as subject: when the youthful Hogg first reads poetry, for example, and fails to recognise a triplet, the 1821 'Memoir' adds 'I thought the author had been straitened for rhymes, and had just made a part of it do as well as he could without them' (p. xvi). Other newly-introduced phrases are scornful of Hogg's early poems–instances of this are 'in all respects miserably bad' (p. xviii); a piece is full of faults 'like all the rest' (p. xix); and 'Indeed, all of them were sad stuff, although I judged them to be exceedingly good' (p. xxv).

The 'Memoir' in *Altrive Tales* (pp. i–xciii) was the last version published in Hogg's lifetime, and was followed by a distinct section of 'Reminiscences of Former Days' that follows the journal-based 'Memoir' with what Hogg termed 'reminiscences at random'. The

'Memoir' itself apparently ends at the same point as the 1821 'Memoir', but in fact has been substantially revised. Hogg inserts sections of new material that sometimes reflect upon portions of the earlier text and sometimes replace them, making it clear to the attentive reader that different portions of the narrative have been written at different times. The overall effect is curious, as reading comes then to resemble the work of archaeological excavation, an uncovering of layers of pre-existing yet co-existing text. A sensitive and innovative reading of this kind is the distinctive feature of Douglas Mack's edition of *Memoir of the Author's Life* and *Familiar Anecdotes of Sir Walter Scott* (Edinburgh and London: Scottish Academic Press, 1972). It would have been logical for Hogg to revise the whole 'Memoir' to suit the time of publication in 1832, but his strategy instead mimics the processes of memory itself, with an awareness of the coexistence in the mind of different times. (Intriguingly, this foreshadows Freud's model of the unconscious.) The opening of the 'Memoir', for example, at first appears to introduce a straight reprinting of the previous text: Scott's original prefatory remarks are retained and the first section of the 'Memoir' still takes the form of a letter to him, dated from Mitchelslacks in November 1806. Several pages later, however, the narrative is interrupted by a passage that is clearly marked as a later addition, Hogg following his account of his first encounter with the poetry of Burns in 1797 by a paragraph beginning 'I remember in the year 1812' (p. 18). (Both passages occur only in the 1832 text.) Since Hogg could not have been recollecting an event of 1812 in a narrative composed in 1806 the reader is alerted to the coexistence of the four years 1797, 1806, 1812, and 1832 at this point in the narrative, and that it mimics and reflects the mental process of recollection in its writer. Hogg's awareness of mental processes in the 1832 'Memoir' renders it a more Romantic text than any of its predecessors, and this fact is emphasised by the many additional passages relating to his early life. Details of Hogg's early literary productions given in the 1821 'Memoir' disappear, and new material tracing the development of an original and primitive genius is added. These new passages belong in an established literary tradition of which one influential example is James Beattie's *The Minstrel* (1771–74), also a precursor of Wordsworth's *The Prelude: or, Growth of a Poet's Mind* (1805). Hogg runs races against himself on the hills as a child (p. 13), falls in love with a country maiden (pp. 13–14), writes songs for the admiration of the lasses (p. 17), and then achieves a moment of epiphany as to his true vocation on first hearing of Burns (pp. 17–18). Hogg's situation in 1832 also impinges upon his earlier narrative in a clearly-marked fashion. After describing the publication and reception of his *Scottish Pastorals* in 1800 and 1801, for example, Hogg expresses his annoyance that instead of the work having been long ago 'consigned to eternal oblivion' (p. 21) it was quoted from liberally by a London critic in April 1830. A passage about the publication and reception of *Queen Hynde*, published at the end of 1824, is also added to the 1821 'Memoir' (pp. 42–43). Once the reader has been alerted to the effect of the reflecting author of 1832 modifying the earlier narrative, several of the new passages can be seen to represent Hogg's concerns and situation at that time. Hogg's relations with William Blackwood, for instance, were a preoccupation during his London visit: having quarrelled with Blackwood before his departure from Edinburgh he found that in the metropolis everyone identified him with the literary group of the 'Noctes Ambrosianae' and of *Blackwood's Edinburgh Magazine.* These mixed feelings probably motivated the expansion of the section dealing with his introduction to Blackwood after Goldie's bankruptcy in 1814 to include new material stressing the part played by Samuel Aitken in rescuing the copies of the third edition of *The Queen's Wake* (p. 32), and another defending his claim to have originated 'Translation from an Ancient Chaldee Manuscript' in the magazine (pp. 44–45). Hogg's claim to importance in a wider literary circle is also pointed by a new section concerning his relations with Byron (pp. 39–40). Hogg states specifically 'I write this in London' (p. 45).

Hogg probably intended to include his 'Memoir of the Author's Life' in *Altrive Tales* from the inception of the project, for *The Athenaeum* of 7 January 1832 mentions it in the course of announcing Hogg's arrival in London:

> It seems, that the Ettrick Shepherd, obeying the call of these times for cheap reprints of works of genius, has arrived in London and made arrangements with Cochrane & Co. for the reproduction of his prose works in monthly volumes. They are to be called 'The Altrive Tales,' and a memoir of the Poet's Life is to accompany them. (p. 19)

Despite this early announcement, however, it seems clear that Hogg produced copy for the 'Memoir' in *Altrive Tales* in London rather than in Edinburgh, by marking up a copy of *The Mountain Bard* of 1821 obtained during his visit. A letter of January 1832 to the publisher of *Altrive Tales*, James Cochrane (NLS MS 14836, fol. 40) requests him to send Hogg 'The Mountain Bard 3$^{d}$ Edition published by Whitaker' (Whittakers being the London partner of the Edinburgh publishing firm of Oliver and Boyd who produced the 1821 edition). The punctuation of the 1832 'Memoir' also seems consistent with its having been typeset from a copy of the 'Memoir' from *The Mountain Bard* of 1821. Larger additions and more substantial changes presumably accompanied the copy on separate manuscript sheets.

The appearance of the 'Memoir' in *Altrive Tales* was clearly meant to promote the work as the production of an original genius labouring under difficulties, and formed part of Hogg's self-promotion and literary celebrity during his London visit. It is also very much a work of the Reform period, appealing to a new populist mood in British culture.

The following changes have been made to the text of the 'Memoir' in *Altrive Tales* in reprinting it in the present edition:

p. 17, l. 42–p. 18, l. 1 Tam o' Shanter ] Tam O' Shanter
p. 22, l. 28 gay queer chiel, ] gay, queer chiel [as in 1821 'Memoir']
p. 38, ll. 26–27 alas for my unfortunate Pilgrims! ] alas! for my unfortunate Pilgrim!
p. 41, l. 2 Bridge ] bridge [as in 1821 'Memoir']
p. 41, l. 29 suggestion ] suggestions [ as in 1821 'Memoir']
p. 42, l. 28 who gave ] whog ave
p. 45, ll. 37–38 "The Brownie of Bodsbeck, and other Tales," ] "The Brownie of Bodsbeck," and other Tales

## Reminiscences of Former Days

'Reminiscences of Former Days' divides into two main parts. The first (pp. 53–60) claims to be a continuation of the 'Memoir', carrying the narrative of Hogg's literary life past 1821 when an earlier version was published in the third edition of *The Mountain Bard*. Hogg refers to it as 'this Memoir' twice (pp. 55, 60), but is nevertheless careful to distinguish it from the preceding text by use of a new heading and by beginning a new page in the first edition. On a superficial level it appears to continue the roughly chronological sequence of the 'Memoir', extending the account of Hogg's literary life and principal works from 1821 up to 1832. Hogg's opening sentence, however, notes that this narrative is rather different from the preceding one in not being based on his journal: 'I must now proceed with my reminiscences at random, as from the time the last journal was finished and published I ceased keeping any notes' (p.

53). And in fact the narrative begins with the history of Hogg's settlement in Yarrow in 1815 rather than with the events of the early 1820s. This part of 'Reminiscences of Former Days' is substantially an attempt to explain Hogg's motivation in publishing the series of 'Altrive Tales' itself. A brief summary of the narrative sequence is revealing. Hogg gives an account of his settlement at Altrive and marriage; of his leasing of the Mount Benger farm and the unsuccessful attempts to meet the expenses of renting and stocking it by his writings, leading to his ruin at the end of the lease in 1830; of his domestic happiness and his major works produced in financial desperation; of Blackwood's grudging dealings with him over a bill for the profits of *Queen Hynde*, as contrasted with the generosity of Robert Cadell of the Constable firm; of his resort to periodical contributions for an income in the 1820s and Blackwood's reluctance to publish collections of his work; and of his unsuccessful attempts to get his collected prose fiction published in Edinburgh and his successful attempt in London. It seems probable that this section of 'Reminiscences of Former Days' was written towards the end of January or beginning of February 1832, Hogg writing to Blackwood on 5 February (NLS MS 4033, fols 123–24) as follows:

> Smarting as I still am under your total disregard of my circumstances and most simple request you need not wonder that I have been most bitterly severe on you in the memoir of my life which I have brought forward to the present hour at which I write. [...] I will send you a proof though without the promise of altering any of it

Blackwood's response in his reply of 13 February (NLS MS 30312, pp. 331–32) was to state that he declined to answer Hogg's 'late absurd letters' on any other footing but that of a man of business. Presumably, therefore, he did not receive a proof of this part of 'Reminiscences of Former Days', and was not able to influence the eventual text of it. No manuscript material or proofs for it have survived. The final paragraph concludes with a statement of Hogg's intentions for his 'Altrive Tales' series, 'to give the grave and gay tales, the romantic and the superstitious, alternately, as far as is consistent with the size of each volume' (p. 60).

The second part consists of 'a few reminiscences relating to eminent men' (p. 60). This may perhaps be seen as the fulfillment of an intention expressed in a passage at the end of the 1821 'Memoir' carried forward into *Altrive Tales*. 'I have written out, at great length, my opinion of all the characters of these literary gentlemen, with traits of their behaviour towards each other, principally from reports on which I could depend, and what I myself knew of their plans and parties; but this would fill a volume as large as the present work' (p. 32). References within this section of the 'Reminiscences', however, suggest that Hogg was writing in London from memory, at least in part, rather than reproducing a manuscript created before 1821. Hogg says, for instance, that he first met Galt in 1804 and has known him for twenty-eight years (p. 72), concluding his sketch by anticipating his return to Altrive when he will reminiscence about his literary acquaintances in London (p. 73). Again, in his reminiscence of Lockhart, Hogg reflects that the 'generality of mankind have always used me ill till I came to London' (p. 74). Reminiscences by the literary lion of the London season of his famous contemporaries would naturally attract attention to the first volume in the projected series of 'Altrive Tales', and extracts could easily be reprinted as attractive column-fillers by the newspapers (see Introduction, pp. liv–lv). Hogg would be well aware of the advantages of such publicity.

While no manuscript material or proofs have apparently survived for this portion of the 'Reminiscences' either, two sections of the reminiscences of eminent literary men had appeared in the *Edinburgh Literary Journal* previous to Hogg's London visit under the same general title employed in *Altrive Tales*, 'Reminiscences of Former Days'. The section on 'Sir Walter Scott' had previously been published in the issue for 27 June 1829 (pp. 51–52), and the section on 'Allan Cunningham' had previously been published in the issue for 16 May 1829 (pp. 374–75). These sections therefore demand separate consideration textually. Hogg wrote to his Edinburgh friend John Aitken on 17 January 1832 (Fales Library & Special Collections, New York University: Fales MSS 89: 20):

> Please send me here with your first parcel the No. of the literary Journal which contains the account of my first meeting with Sir Walter Scott and that which contains my first meeting with Allan Cunningham as I want them immediately and know not where to find them here.

Hogg's letter appears to have been addressed wrongly by the person who franked it for him, and took longer than usual to reach its recipient, but Aitken eventually replied on 28 January (Bodleian Library, Oxford, MS Montagu d. 11, fols 20–21):

> I now inclose you slips of the two articles you want–not having any opportunity of sending the whole Numbers by a

> parcel, and no Stampt copies being left. These I presume will serve your purpose equally well, and I can send them free by a friends frank.

Comparison of these two articles in the *Edinburgh Literary Journal* with the relevant sections of 'Reminiscences of Former Days' in *Altrive Tales* suggests that Hogg made his revisions on the slips that Aitken sent him and passed them to Cochrane's printers. The punctuation largely coincides and a passage of indirect speech is mistakenly given speech marks in both–see the emendation below for p. 61, ll. 21–22. Most revisions are relatively minor in the section on 'Sir Walter Scott', smoothing the style, correcting the grammar, and rectifying the odd printer's error such as 'away' for 'awry' in 'his grave face [...] went gradually awry' (p. 61). The most significant change is the introduction of a long new section detailing a night-time fishing expedition on Tweed during which Scott demonstrated his phenomenal memory in being able to repeat Hogg's ballad of 'Gilmanscleuch' (pp. 63–64), and adjustments to the surrounding text necessitated by its inclusion. The section on 'Allan Cunningham' in *Altrive Tales* is even closer to the original *Edinburgh Literary Journal* article.

The second part of 'Reminiscences of Former Days' seems from Hogg's correspondence to have been shaped by the author's closeness, both in geographical and emotional terms, to John Gibson Lockhart during his London visit. For most of this time Hogg was staying at 11 Waterloo Place, near to The Athenaeum on Pall Mall, of which club Lockhart was a member. As the editor of the *Quarterly Review* Lockhart also frequented the premises of the owner and publisher, John Murray, in nearby Albemarle Street. Hogg dined with Lockhart, in his own home and elsewhere, and there are surviving notes exchanged between them. One of these, unfortunately undated, shows that Hogg was passing proofs of *Altrive Tales* to Lockhart for his suggestions, and that he had originally intended to include in his 'Reminiscences' a section about the Edinburgh critic Francis Jeffrey:

> As I cannot possibly get out to day I send you the proofs altered in a way which I hope will pass[.] Jeffery I have cancelled altogether and though you have made me leave out the only parts I set a value upon yet in the counsel of a true friend there is safety. Supply the number of stanzas in Gilmanscleuch and the boy will wait if you like and bring back the proofs [...] Look at p 107 there is something wrong in it (NLS MS 924, No. 80)

An exchange in late February is worth detailing at length, since it suggests that Lockhart provided Hogg with an outline of the section about himself for the work. In another undated note Hogg asked for Lockhart's assistance with this as follows:

> I think it a pity that I should close my reminiscences without something about you who has been so long my immoveable friend. But the truth is that I have altogether forgot where or how we first met and wish very much that you would help me out with some queer thing. [...] Write me. (NLS MS 924, No. 85)

Lockhart's response, dated 25 February, is an obliging one and, as it provides the bones of several details fleshed out by Hogg in his recollections of Lockhart as well as demonstrating the intimacy between the two writers at this time, it is worth quoting at length here:

> It is no wonder you have no recollection of our first meeting for in those days I was little more than a boy (it was long before Blackwood had ever been seen or even *by me* heard of)–I well remember however that I first saw you in the links. I was walking w old Sym & he introduced us: but what was I? an idle youth, fresh from college, dancing after the misses, & drawing caricatures I had never read your poems & thought there was little poetry worth reading under 2000 years standing. A year or two after you will begin to recollect meeting me w Hamilton, Wilson, & that set–& I daresay you can recall one or two jolly doings when I lived in Maitland Street. I remember the first time you visited me there you expressed great horror to somebody at my extravagance in having *four* black men to wait on a party of six or seven *whites* but found out that this was the result of keeping only *one* black man, whose friends of that complexion clustered round him whenever they smelt a fleshpot. If Elizabeth Wilson were here she could tell us more of those days than either you or I–& has I daresay some of my graceless caricatures of your noble person still in her possession. Let me see what you write in proof & I will put in some devilry. (Pierpont Morgan Library, New York: PML 52349, fol. 158)

Lockhart's response opens up the possibility that the reminiscence of Lockhart is to some extent a collaborative effort between himself and Hogg, and that he may have revised other sections of these reminiscences of eminent men in proof.

The following emendations have been made to the *Altrive Tales* text of 'Reminiscences of Former Days' in the present edition:

p. 57, l. 23 I hae gotten ] I hae gottin
p. 61, l. 3 indeed, ] in [*eol*] deed, [as in *Edinburgh Literary Journal*]
p. 61, l. 8 they're ] they 're [as in *Edinburgh Literary Journal*]
p. 61, ll. 21–22 I said [...] ballads. ] "I said [...] ballads."
p. 67, l. 1 said James; "for ] said James; for
p. 77, l. 41 Still, there ] Still there

## The Adventures of Captain John Lochy

'The Adventures of Captain John Lochy' was published for the first time in *Altrive Tales* (pp. 1–142). It was never reprinted, neither in Hogg's lifetime nor in the posthumous six-volume collection of *Tales and Sketches by the Ettrick Shepherd* published by Blackie and Son of Glasgow between 1836 and 1837. Hogg's correspondence with William Blackwood indicates that the story originated in a proffered contribution for *Blackwood's Edinburgh Magazine*, and the correspondence between Hogg and Blackwood reveals a surprising amount of information about its genesis.

Hogg may have shown Blackwood an early version of the tale in the summer of 1830, during Hogg's June visit to Edinburgh or perhaps when the two men met with Lockhart at Chiefswood to discuss plans for a collected edition of Hogg's prose fiction (see Introduction, pp. xvii–xviii). Hogg's tale is first mentioned in his letter to Blackwood of 13 August (NLS MS 4027, fols 190–91) as then in the publisher's hand in an incomplete state: 'I am not sure about Captain Lochy. Some of your remarks have been crawing in my croppin I wish you would return it with these remarks in writing and I will alter and finish it'. Blackwood's reply of 26 August (Alexander Turnbull Library, Wellington: MS Papers 42, Folder 9) sheds light on the nature of his objections, and indicates that the tale was of a length to be divided between two or more issues of the magazine:

> The story as you say in your last will be greatly improved if you leave out the introductory & concluding Highland gibberish, in the way we talked of. I therefore return it to you for this purpose, and I could also wish you to conclude the story in whatever way you intended, as I always wish to see a story complete, as then I can judge best how it should be divided, and whether or not it requires any filling up or omissions.

From the postscript it is clear that Blackwood's son Robert was unable to locate the manuscript to accompany this letter, but it was eventually sent with Blackwood's letter of 25 September (NLS MS 30312, pp. 81–82).

Hogg's subsequent letters to the Edinburgh publisher indicate that his revisions to the tale were substantial ones. Promising to alter and finish the story on 30 September (NLS MS 4027, fols 194–95) Hogg confessed 'I have mislaid the second part and cannot find it if I should die', while by 8 October his original design has been completely superceded:

> Capt Lockie has run away with me altogether and grown far too long. It is grown very like an original document and as such I intend to pass it. (NLS MS 4027, fols 196–97)

Even though the increased length of the revised tale may have made it less suitable for the pages of *Blackwood's Edinburgh Magazine* Hogg still sent it to William Blackwood, for he requested in a letter probably written on 10 September 1831 that if it were published Blackwood should 'give no hint about the Ettrick Shepherd but merely insert "The Adventures of Capt John Lochy" + "Written by himself"' (NLS MS 4719, fol. 181). Hogg's manuscript was still in Blackwood's hands at the time of Hogg's quarrel with him early in December that year, for Hogg mentions it by name in his letter of 6 December 1831 (NLS MS 4029, fols 268–69) as among the manuscripts to be returned to him at once. Blackwood subsequently sent Hogg's unused manuscripts and an outstanding payment for his magazine contributions under cover to a lawyer, a Writer to the Signet, in Selkirk, from whence they were forwarded by Margaret Hogg to her husband in London.

Hogg clearly had 'The Adventures of Captain John Lochy' to hand not long after his arrival in London, and he must have welcomed the opportunity to publish it in *Altrive Tales* after Blackwood's repeated rejection of it.

Only a small fragment of Hogg's manuscript of the story as it apears in *Altrive Tales* survives, in the National Library of Scotland (MS 8887, fol. 38). This is the upper portion of a single leaf, without a watermark but paginated by Hogg 5 on the recto and 6 on the verso. It bears a compositor's mark 'B 17' on the recto, at the point in the first edition where gathering B begins on p. 17, showing that it was used as printer's copy for that edition. As the only surviving printer's copy for *Altrive Tales* this fragment is of particular interest in assessing the process by which James Cochrane's chosen printers, A. J. Valpy of Fleet Street, turned Hogg's copy into print, and a transcription is given in the Appendix to the present edition (pp. 187–90).

From a comparison of this manuscript fragment and the equivalent portions of text in the published volume of 1832 it seems likely that the process of turning manuscript into first edition was much the same as the one that took place with respect to a subsequent work Cochrane published for Hogg, *Tales of the Wars of Montrose* (1835). In the case of Hogg's later work the whole of Hogg's copy used by the printers has fortunately survived and forms the basis of the relevant S/SC volume–see 'Note on the Text', in *Tales of the Wars of Montrose*, ed. by Gillian Hughes (S/SC, 1996), pp. 236–57. One obvious difference in the production process for the two works is that Hogg himself does not seem to have received proofs for *Tales of the Wars of Montrose*, whereas when *Altrive Tales* was being printed he clearly did so. Indeed, during his visit to London Hogg was living for the most part in his publisher's house in daily contact with him. Some of the differences between the manuscript and the first edition, therefore, could be the result of authorial proof correction and revision. It also seems unwise to implement tentative conclusions based on a comparison between such a small fragment of 'The Adventures of Captain John Lochy' with the equivalent passage in the first edition. Such a comparison, however, is suggestive.

The majority of the differences between the text of the manuscript fragment and the equivalent passage in the 1832 printed text are the result of the routine work of the printers in preparing Hogg's work for its public appearance. His idiosyncratic spelling of words like 'recieved', 'dissapointment', and 'the Rhyne' are corrected, and some slightly old-fashioned orthography such as 'stile' is modernised. A great many commas and other punctuation marks are added, to complete Hogg's rather spare system of punctuation in the manuscript. Where Hogg, near the end of the fragment, has spelled the hero's name as 'Lockie' this has been standardised to the more usual 'Lochy', and the Dutch-sounding name of 'Van Malloch' has been changed to the more Germanic 'Von Malloch' as its bearer is described as coming from Saxony. Hogg's use of initial capitals in words such as 'Colonel', 'Cornet's', and 'heaven' has also been standardised in accordance with general contemporary usage. Such changes, almost certainly the work of intermediaries such as compositors, are the legitimate completion of the author's work. Other changes might be viewed as less satisfactory, in that they appear to distort rather than complete that work. On several occasions the printed text interferes with Hogg's original sentence breaks, adding new ones or ignoring those present in the manuscript. For instance, where Hogg's original read that the regiment had 'restored that part of the field for the present but we came upon' (p. 189 in the Appendix transcription of the manuscript) the printed text has 'restored that part of the field for the present. We came next upon' (p. 90 in the present text). Hogg's language is also altered on occasion, so that his style appears to be more formal and less colloquial, less oral and more written–a dubious shift in a narrative composed of the supposed recollections of a soldier. A good example of this is in Lochy's account of his disappointment when he realises that his female visitor at the inn is only old Mora. Hogg's manuscript reads 'for a good while I could not speak, which was very bad in me' (see p. 188) and the printed text 'for a while I could not speak; which was very bad of me' (see p. 88). Such changes are perhaps more likely to be the work of the pressmen than of Hogg himself.

The possibility of using Hogg's manuscript fragment as the copy-text for the equivalent small section of 'The Adventures of Captain John Lochy' in the present volume has been rejected. Not only would a reversion to the manuscript have risked undoing changes made by Hogg himself and revisions that met with his approval, but it would also have destroyed the evenness of the tale by producing a patchwork effect at this point. A transcription of the manuscript fragment has, however, been supplied in the Appendix (pp. 187–90) to the present volume. The following conservative changes have been made in the present text to 'The Adventures of Captain John Lochy' as printed in *Altrive Tales*:

p. 80, l. 25 me, with sweetmeats, when ] me, with sweetmeats when

p. 92, l. 38 cut-and-thrust ] cut and thrust [as at p. 125, l. 23]

p. 125, ll. 32–33 "Hem! hem!" ] "hem! hem!"

p. 130, l. 42 After all our entreaties proved of no avail, I mentioned ] After all, our entreaties proved of no avail. I mentioned

p. 131, l. 42 but it's ] but its

p. 144, l. 27 Bobbing John ] bobbing John [a well-known personal epithet]

p. 148, l. 32 affirmative. "And ] affirmative." And

## The Pongos

'The Pongos' (pp. 143–63 in the original edition of *Altrive Tales*) had first been published as 'A Singular Letter from Southern Africa.

Communicated by Mr Hogg, the Ettrick Shepherd', in *Blackwood's Edinburgh Magazine*, 26 (November 1829), 809–16. Although no details are known about its composition it seems likely that it was written specifically for the magazine, as it appears to pick up on accounts of Africa given in the pages of *Blackwood's* itself. In particular, an early article 'Bowdich's Mission to Ashantee', *Blackwood's Edinburgh Magazine*, 5 (June 1819), 302–10, provides a description of great apes which accords with Hogg's fictional presentation of orang-outangs in this tale as Wild Men, or primitives, and continues an earlier debate maintained by writers such as Lord Monboddo (1714–99) and the French naturalist Buffon (1707–88) about whether they were animals or primitive men. They have 'the cry, visage, and action' of very old men, and they imitate the natives in carrying heavy burdens through the forest, though without understanding the purpose of the action. They are reported to build houses in imitation of men, though preferring to sleep outside or on the roofs of them. They are so attached to their offspring that they will carry their dead bodies about until the remains decay quite away (p. 309). Hogg certainly kept back-issues of *Blackwood's*, for his letter to the proprietors of 18 February 1835 (NLS MS 4040, fols 287–88) makes it clear that he had them bound into sets, and it seems likely that he sometimes used those volumes as a quarry for ideas for poems and stories intended for the magazine. Hogg also knew several settlers and travellers returned from Africa in the course of his career, from his early Selkirk acquaintance Mungo Park (1771–1806) to Thomas Pringle (1789–1834), one of the editors of the first issues of *Blackwood's Edinburgh Magazine* and a contributor to Hogg's own *The Poetic Mirror* (1816). Hogg's probable sources of information about orang-outangs are explored in more detail in the explanatory Notes to the present volume.

'The Pongos' is an almost verbatim reprint of 'A Singular Letter from Southern Africa' and must have been typeset from a copy of the earlier tale in *Blackwood's Edinburgh Magazine*. Cochrane's printers, A. J. Valpy, tended to replace some commas with semi-colons and to prefer 'queen' to 'Queen' but there are very few differences in punctuation between the two printings. There are a few minor changes in wording and word-order, the effect of which is to make the narrative a little smoother and more conventional–for instance, 'rent in pieces' becomes 'torn in pieces' (p. 167), perhaps because the word 'rent' has already been used near the start of the same sentence. Either the printer or Hogg himself might have been responsible for this kind of minor alteration.

Hogg was amused that readers thought his tale was a genuine letter from a South African colonist (see Introduction, p. lviii), and such manifest tribute to his imaginative gifts might well have induced him to include this particular tale in the first volume of his 'Altrive Tales' series. It was subsequently reprinted from *Altrive Tales* in the Edinburgh weekly paper *The Schoolmaster* of 16 February 1833, pp. 106–09.

In the present edition 'The Pongos' is reprinted from *Altrive Tales* without change.

## Marion's Jock

'Marion's Jock' (pp. 164–90 in the original edition of *Altrive Tales*) had originally appeared as 'The Laird of Peatstacknowe's Tale', part of the tale-telling contest held at Aikwood Tower among the members of the Warden's embassy to Sir Michael Scott in Hogg's three-volume novel *The Three Perils of Man*, published in London by Longmans in 1822 (II, 188–224).

Although modern critical opinion places this Border Romance among the best of Hogg's work, he had clearly become dissatisfied with it himself by the time that *Altrive Tales* was being produced. In a letter to William Blackwood of 26 May 1830 (NLS MS 4036, fols 102–03) discussing plans for his collected prose fiction, Hogg told him, 'The Perils of Man which contains some of the best parts and the worst of all my prose works I would divide into seven distinct tales [...]'. Hogg's account of the work in the 'Reminiscences of Former Days' in *Altrive Tales* is in accordance with this letter and may provide a clue as to how the dismemberment was meant to be implemented:

> Lord preserve us! what a medley I made of it! [...] I dashed on, and mixed up with what might have been made one of the best historical tales our country ever produced, such a mass of diablerie as retarded the main story, and rendered the whole perfectly ludicrous. (p. 55)

At this time, then, Hogg clearly valued the main plot about the siege of Roxburgh highly and dismissed the magical sub-plot concerning the devil and the wizard of Aikwood as 'perfectly ludicrous'. In the posthumous *Tales and Sketches by the Ettrick Shepherd* (1836–37), published in six volumes by the Glasgow firm of Blackie and Son, the main plot appears on its own as 'The Siege of Roxburgh' (VI, 67–274). It has long been known that Hogg himself was involved to some extent in the preparation of copy for this edition before his death in November 1835, and it seems quite likely that he engineered the separate appearance of the main plot from his Border Romance there. In Hogg's plan for the contents of the first seven volumes of his projected series of 'Altrive Tales', dated 19 March 1832 (Beinecke Rare Book and Manuscript Library, Yale University: GEN MSS 61, Box 1, Folder 17), 'The Seige [*sic*] of Roxburgh' is set down for the third volume. Another part of *The Three Perils of Man*, from 'The Poet's Tale' (III, 41–81), was turned into verse and published within Hogg's lifetime as 'The Three Sisters' in *Fraser's Magazine*, 11 (June 1835), 666–79. It seems likely that Hogg dismembered *The Three Perils of Man* at about this time, so that the component parts could appear in various volumes of his 'Altrive Tales' series. Presumably 'The Siege of Roxburgh' and the five tales related during the contest at Aikwood would comprise six of the 'seven distinct tales' mentioned in his letter to Blackwood. The probable content of the seventh tale is much more difficult to determine.

No manuscript for 'Marion's Jock' appears to have survived, but Hogg's manuscript for *The Three Perils of Man* forms part of the Fales manuscript collection of the Fales Library & Special Collections, New York University. A comparison of 'The Laird of Peatstacknowe's Tale' in the manuscript and in the first edition of *The Three Perils of Man* with 'Marion's Jock' reveals, however, that Hogg was almost certainly working from a copy of the printed novel rather than the manuscript when he prepared his tale for *Altrive Tales*. In most cases, where the manuscript and first edition differ 'Marion's Jock' follows the reading of the first edition. A suitable example occurs at the point where Jock, having been felled by the goodman in attempting to cut a piece from the bacon ham, lunges towards the ham again as soon as he recovers his senses. The manuscript reads as follows:

> He sprang over the bed, and with staggering steps traversing the floor, he mounted the form and stretched his hand to the bacon ham (p. [2]77)

The first edition reading is identical with that of *Altrive Tales* (p. 177):

> He sprang over the bed, and traversing the floor with staggering steps, mounted a form, and stretched forth his hand to possess himself again of his gully. (II, 201)

Both wording and punctuation are so close generally between 'Marion's Jock' and 'The Laird of Peatstacknowe's Tale' in the published novel of 1822 as to imply that the one was set from a copy of the other. Most of the few differences between the two texts are consonant with changes made elsewhere in *Altrive Tales*, and continue the work of correcting grammar, regularising the use of upper- and lower-case initial letters and hyphenation and the like. Typical examples are the change to correct grammar, from Jock 'would have beat his master' (II, 218) to Jock 'would have beaten his master' (p. 184), and the change to avoid close repetition of a word, from 'Among Jock's fat sheep there was one fat ewe lamb' (II, 203) to 'Among Jock's pet sheep there was one fat ewe-lamb' (p. 178).

There are two major differences only between the 1822 and 1832 versions of the story, one of which was probably authorial and one of which can safely be attributed to misapprehension on the part of a London compositor unfamiliar with Scots expressions and social customs. The first is the deletion of a bracketed phrase alluding to the threatened starvation of the imprisoned group in Aikwood tower, '(I wish we had sic things here, even though we had to fight for them!)' (II, 188). This allusion to the wider context of *The Three Perils of Man* is clearly inappropriate to the new context of *Altrive Tales*, of course. The second major difference is that the words 'goodman' and 'goodwife', the male and female heads of a Scottish peasant household, appear as 'good man' and 'good wife' throughout 'Marion's Jock', except when these are given initial upper-case letters and serve as titles (as in 'Goodman Niddery'). This is clearly the result of compositorial misunderstanding, though it is somewhat surprising that Hogg himself did not spot the repeated error at the proof stage. It is silently corrected throughout in the present edition's reprinting of 'Marion's Jock' from the first edition of *Altrive Tales*. One further printing error has also been corrected, as follows:

p. 183, l. 21 plaiting under ] plaiting un- [*eol*] under

# Hyphenation List

Various words are hyphenated at the ends of lines in the present edition. The list below indicates those cases in which such hyphens should be retained in making quotations. As elsewhere, in calculating line numbers, titles and running headlines have been ignored.

p. 25, l. 29 leanest-looking
p. 53, l. 5 last-mentioned
p. 54, l. 15 Mount-Benger
p. 63, l. 8 shoe-lachets
p. 68, l. 18 arm-in-arm
p. 82, l. 8 night-gown
p. 85, l. 23 a-puling
p. 99, l. 37 dumb-foundered
p. 101, l. 15 pocket-money
p. 129, l. 32 sedan-chair
p. 131, l. 30 cut-and-thrust
p. 138, l. 3 *tête-à-tête*
p. 139, l. 11 ill-managed
p. 139, l. 33 tennis-ball
p. 158, l. 29 Glen-Lochy
p. 168, l. 39 orang-outangs
p. 172, l. 29 term-day
p. 179, l. 10 corn-field
p. 182, l. 35 fore-feet
p. 183, l. 23 half-running

# Notes

In the Notes that follow, page references include a letter enclosed in brackets: (a) indicates that the passage found is in the first quarter of the page, while (b) refers to the second quarter, (c) to the third quarter, and (d) to the fourth quarter. Where it seems useful to discuss the meaning of particular phrases, this is done in the Notes: single words are dealt with in the Glossary. Quotations from the Bible are from the King James version, the translation most familiar to Hogg and his contemporaries; in the case of the Psalms, however, reference is sometimes given to the metrical *Psalms of David* approved by the Church of Scotland, where this seems apposite. For references to plays by Shakespeare, the edition used has been *The Complete Works: Compact Edition*, ed. by Stanley Wells and Gary Taylor (Oxford: Clarendon Press, 1988). For references to other volumes of the Stirling/South Carolina Edition the editor's name is given after the title, with the abbreviation 'S/SC' and date of first publication following in parentheses. References to Sir Walter Scott's fiction are to the Edinburgh Edition of the Waverley Novels (EEWN). The National Library of Scotland is abbreviated as NLS. The Notes are greatly indebted to the following standard works: *Dictionary of National Biography*, *Oxford English Dictionary*, and *Concise Scots Dictionary*. The Notes on Hogg's 'Memoir of the Author's Life' are particularly indebted to the ground-breaking work of Douglas Mack in his edition of the work, listed among the following works used in the notes and referred to by these abbreviations:

**1807 Memoir**: 'Memoir of the Life of James Hogg', in James Hogg, *The Mountain Bard; consisting of Ballads and Songs, founded on Facts and Legendary Tales* (Edinburgh, 1807), pp. i–xxiii

**1821 Memoir**: 'Memoir of the Life of James Hogg', in James Hogg, *The Mountain Bard; consisting of Legendary Ballads and Tales*, third edition (Edinburgh, 1821), pp. ix–lxxvii

**Corson:** James C. Corson, *Notes and Index to Sir Herbert Grierson's Edition of the Letters of Sir Walter Scott* (Oxford: Clarendon Press, 1979)

**Garden:** Mary Gray Garden, *Memorials of James Hogg, the Ettrick Shepherd* (Paisley, undated)

**Harris:** Stuart Harris, *The Place Names of Edinburgh: Their Origins and History* (Edinburgh: Gordon Wright Publishing, 1996)

**Mack:** James Hogg, *Memoir of the Author's Life* and *Familiar Anecdotes of Sir Walter Scott*, ed. by Douglas S. Mack (Edinburgh and London: Scottish Academic Press, 1972)

**Parr:** Norah Parr, *James Hogg at Home: Being the Domestic Life and Letters of the*

*Ettrick Shepherd* (Dollar: Douglas S. Mack, 1980)

**Rogers:** Charles Rogers, *The Modern Scottish Minstrel*, 6 vols (Edinburgh, 1855–57)

**Rubenstein:** James Hogg, *Anecdotes of Scott*, ed. by Jill Rubenstein (S/SC, 1999)

**Z.:** 'Z.', 'Farther Particulars of the Life of James Hogg, the Ettrick Shepherd', *Scots Magazine*, 67 (July and November 1805), 501–03 and 820–23.

**Illustrations**

**Frontispiece** Hogg's portrait was drawn during his London visit by Charles Fox specifically for engraving as the frontispiece to the first edition of *Altrive Tales*, according to *The Athenaeum* of 11 February 1832:

> A very clever drawing of the Ettrick Shepherd has just been completed by Mr. Fox, well known for his fine engraving of the head of Burnet: it bears the true stamp and impress of the poet, and will form a characteristic frontispiece to the forthcoming edition of his works. (p. 97)

Charles Fox (1794–1849) worked at the studio of the engraver John Burnet in London. Like Burnet, Fox engraved plates from a number of paintings by the Scottish artist David Wilkie, including 'Village Politicians'. He also engraved some illustrations by Wilkie for the *magnum opus* edition of Scott's Waverley Novels, and was employed on plates for various Annuals. His own painting, mostly in watercolour, consisted largely of portraits of his friends, and it seems likely that he was among the artists with whom Hogg associated during his London visit in 1832. This portrait may be the one now in the National Portrait Gallery, London (NPG 426)—see Richard Walker, *Regency Portraits*, 2 vols (London: National Portrait Gallery, 1985), I, 254. The similarity in Hogg's pose and dress is indeed striking, but Walker dates the portrait to 1830 rather than 1832, and notes that it was acquired in 1876 as a portrait by Stephen Poyntz Denning. It may indeed be a similar portrait by Denning. The engraving of the Fox portrait for *Altrive Tales* was the work of William Campden Edwards (1777–1855), an engraver whose early work was on illustrations to editions of the Bible and Bunyan's *The Pilgrim's Progress* published at Bungay in Suffolk. During his London career he specialised in and excelled at portrait engraving.

**128 Captain Lochy in the Barber's Dress** this engraving was made by George Cruikshank (1792–1878) as an illustration to 'The Adventures of Captain John Lochy', presumably during Hogg's London visit from January to March 1832. Cruikshank, after his earlier satirical engravings, enjoyed great popularity as a book illustrator. Advertisements for James Cochrane's series, 'Roscoe's Novelist's Library', on which the projected 'Altrive Tales' series was partly modelled, specify that the first volume included 'Illustrations by GEORGE CRUIKSHANK, who is engaged to illustrate the WHOLE SERIES of THE NOVELIST'S LIBRARY', and it was natural for Cochrane to employ the same artist for his other fiction series, 'Altrive Tales'. It is clear from Hogg's correspondence that he was frequently in company with Cruikshank in London, whom he later described as 'stately and solemn'—see *A Series of Lay Sermons on Good Principles and Good Breeding*, ed. by Gillian Hughes with Douglas S. Mack (S/SC, 1997), p. 33. A paragraph in the *Edinburgh Weekly Chronicle* of 24 December 1831 (p. 414) implies that Cruikshank had been engaged to illustrate *Altrive Tales* before Hogg's arrival in London: 'During the Ettrick Shepherd's stay in London he is to superintend the publication of some volumes of Tales proposed to be brought out, with humorous cuts by

Cruikshanks'. Cruikshank is best known today for his illustrations to the early works of Charles Dickens.

**Dedication**

Lady Anne Elizabeth Montagu Scott was the eldest daughter of Charles, 4th Duke of Buccleuch: she was born in 1796 and died unmarried in 1844. A version of this verse dedication had appeared in Hogg's *The Brownie of Bodsbeck; and Other Tales*, 2 vols (Edinburgh, 1818), I, i–xii, where it was favourably noticed (and indeed reprinted) in *Blackwood's Edinburgh Magazine*, 4 (October 1818), 74–76. It then appeared in *The Poetical Works of James Hogg*, 4 vols (Edinburgh, 1822), II, 325–39. For further details of the poem's textual history see Note on the Text, pp. 191–94.

l. 10 **themes of many a winter night** a generic description for many of Hogg's tales, which sought to replicate in print the kind of stories told around the fire during the long winter evenings in the cottages and farmhouses of his childhood. In 1820 he had published a collection called *Winter Evening Tales*, a counterpart to the 1818 collection in which this dedication originally appeared–see Ian Duncan's Introduction to his edition of *Winter Evening Tales* (S/SC, 2002), pp. xv–xviii.

l. 38 **once an angel trod** Lady Anne Scott's mother, Harriet, Duchess of Buccleuch, had been a warm friend and patron of Hogg until her early death in 1814. She had sent Hogg a hundred guineas in return for his dedication of *The Forest Minstrel* to her in 1810, and the grant of the farm of Altrive Lake rent-free to Hogg for his life, was made by her widower in compliance with her wish that he should do something to benefit the poet.

l. 77 **Our creeds may differ** Hogg was a member of the established Church of Scotland, which was presbyterian, whereas the Buccleuch family were episcopalians.

l. 96 **Thy fathers bled** perhaps an allusion to Lady Anne's descent from James Scott, Duke of Monmouth and 1st Duke of Buccleuch (1649–85), who was a natural son of Charles II and was executed after leading an unsuccessful rebellion against the Catholic James II and VII.

l. 124 **Lover or sister** Lady Anne Scott had five younger sisters: Charlotte (1799–1828), Isabella (1800–1829), Katherine (1803–1814), Margaret (1811–1846), and Harriet (1814–1870). However, by 1832 when *Altrive Tales* was published only the two youngest were still alive, while by the conventions of the day Lady Anne would be considered a middle-aged spinster: the situation envisaged would appear to be more appropriate to 1818 when the poem was first published than to 1832.

ll. 165–66 **That curls [...] springs of day** these lines were cut for the 1822 printing, but restored for *Altrive Tales*.

ll. 171–74 **By azure blue [...] of the night** a new passage for *Altrive Tales*.

l. 186 **short the time since it befel** these lines occur in the earlier version of the poem, published in 1818.

l. 199 **love and peace within** Hogg is presumably recalling a visit paid before 1818 to the Buccleuch mansion at Bowhill, near Selkirk.

l. 201 **thy woodland harp** the harp was a fashionable ladies' instrument during the Regency years as well as the traditional symbol of a bard or minstrel.

l. 213 **flowers that spring where others grew** Lady Anne is seen as the natural successor of her mother, Harriet, Duchess of Buccleuch, who was Hogg's patron.

l. 227 **Caledonian name** after these closing words earlier versions of the poem had been end-dated, from Altrive, on 1 April 1818.

**Memoir of the Author's Life**

**11(a–c) I LIKE to write [...] Memoir in 1806** a new passage in *Altrive Tales*.

**11(a) an Edinburgh editor** no specific printed source has been identified for this comment, which may of course have been a verbal remark. William Blackwood, besides being Hogg's chief Edinburgh publisher, also acted as editor of his own *Blackwood's Edinburgh Magazine*, and may be the person referred to here.

**11(b) the fourth time** Hogg's autobiography was only published three times under his own name in his lifetime: besides its appearance in *Altrive Tales* it had prefaced *The Mountain Bard* of 1807, and *The Mountain Bard* of 1821. Mack (p. 3) suggests that Hogg may be including in his count the two different issues of *The Mountain Bard* of 1807 which were set from the same type. It is possible, however, that Hogg is including in his count an anonymous article entitled 'Farther Particulars of the Life of James Hogg, the Ettrick Shepherd', which appeared under the initial 'Z' in the *Scots Magazine*, 67 (July and November 1805), 501–03, 820–23. For further details, see Note on the Text, pp. 194–99.

**11(b) plain truth, and nothing but the truth** a reference to the oath taken in a court of law, a promise to tell 'the truth, the whole truth, and nothing but the truth'. Hogg indicates slyly that he does not necessarily tell the whole truth.

**11(b) The following note** the version of Hogg's 'Memoir' which appeared in the 1807 *Mountain Bard* takes the form of a letter of November 1806 addressed to a friend, and is prefaced by that friend's apology for 'committing it to the public'. The friend is named as Sir Walter Scott only in *Altrive Tales*.

**12(a) Mitchell-Slack, Nov. 1806** the original date given to the 1807 Memoir. While in service as shepherd to Mr Harkness at Mitchelslacks farm in Closeburn parish, Dumfriesshire, from Whitsunday 1805 to Whitsunday 1807 Hogg prepared much of the material for *The Mountain Bard* (1807), in which that version of the 'Memoir' was published.

**12(b) As if [...] secret sins of men** see John Home, *Douglas*, ed. by Gerald D. Parker (Edinburgh: Oliver & Boyd, 1972), p. 44 (Act 3, lines 75–76).

**12(b) four sons** Hogg's parents, Robert Hogg and Margaret Laidlaw, were married in Ettrick on 27 May 1765 (Ettrick OPR), where the baptisms of their four sons are also recorded–William (12 July 1767), James (9 December 1770), David (10 January 1773), and Robert (25 February 1776). The gravestone of Hogg's parents in Ettrick churchyard also records the burial of 'three of their sons': no names are given and presumably these are children who died in early infancy.

**12(b) Robert Hogg** Robert Hogg was born in 1729, and he died on 22 October 1820–see *Dumfries and Galloway Courier* of 31 October 1820.

**12(b) Margaret Laidlaw** Margaret Laidlaw was born in 1730 and seems to have died in the summer of 1813, although her death is not recorded in the Ettrick or Yarrow parish registers. In Hogg's letter to Harriet, Duchess of Buccleuch of 7 March 1813 (NLS MS 3884, fols 96–97) he mentions both parents as living: his letter to General Dirom of 3 September 1813 mentions his mother's death as recent–see Coutts & Co, London: Dirom Papers 124 (Box 602). This letter is cited by permission of the Directors of Coutts & Co.

**12(b) and was born on the 25th of January, 1772** a phrase added in *Altrive Tales*. The date is clearly influenced by Hogg's wish to be viewed as the successor to Robert Burns, who was born on 25 January 1759. Hogg's baptism on 9 December 1770 (Ettrick OPR) probably means that he was in fact born towards the end of November 1770.

**12(b) a considerable sum of money, for those days** a phrase added in *Altrive Tales*, replacing 'some substance' in previous versions of the 'Memoir'.

**12(c) became bankrupt** this would probably have been in 1776 or 1777.

**12(d) his untimely death** according to his grave-stone in St Mary's churchyard,

Yarrow, Walter Bryden of Crosslee was killed on 16 March 1799 when a tree fell on him at Newark–see James Hogg, *Scottish Pastorals*, ed. by Elaine Petrie (Stirling: Stirling UP, 1988), p. 50. Hogg's 'A Dialogue in a Country Church-Yard', included in that collection, was written as an elegy for Bryden. His son, George (1786–1837) was subsequently farmer of Crosslee, and is mentioned on p. 63 as the host of Hogg and Scott. At the conclusion of this sentence the 1821 Memoir continued with a reference to this poem in *Scottish Pastorals*, one of a number of passages dealing with Hogg's early work eliminated from *Altrive Tales*.

**12(d) the Shorter Catechism** a catechism is a series of questions and answers designed as instruction in the fundamental doctrines of Christianity. As Garside explains, the presbyterian Church of Scotland subscribed to the Larger and Shorter Catechisms of the Westminster Assembly of 1647–48–see *The Private Memoirs and Confessions of a Justified Sinner*, ed. by P. D. Garside (S/SC, 2001), p. 227.

**12(d)–13(a) my wages for the half year [...] found them all** a new passage in *Altrive Tales*, as Mack (p. 5) notes. Hogg had previously presented a similar picture of his solitary childish athletics in his poem 'The Minstrel Boy', in *Friendship's Offering* (London, 1829), pp. 209–13.

**13(a) a lad named Ker** this youth has not been identified, but according to Z. (p. 501) William Ker was Hogg's teacher for four months.

**13(c) old John Beattie** John Beattie (*c.* 1736–1826), whose daughter Mary married Hogg's elder brother William on 28 December 1798 (Yarrow OPR). His gravestone in Ettrick churchyard records that he and his father together had been schoolmasters in the parish for 101 years.

**13(c)–14(a) It will scarcely be believed [...] what to do** a new passage in *Altrive Tales*, as Mack (p. 6) notes. It is very much in keeping with his persona of the Shepherd in the 'Noctes Ambrosianae', whose fondness for women is the subject of frequent comment there. They are described as forming his 'besetting imagery' as a poet, for instance, in No. XXXV in *Blackwood's Edinburgh Magazine*, 23 (January 1828), 112–36 (p. 127). The devotion of a boy to an older girl who is out of his reach is a recurrent theme in Hogg's fiction. Barnaby of 'The Wool-Gatherer', for example, shows similar devotion to the country maiden Jane, who at the tale's conclusion is married to his master–see *The Brownie of Bodsbeck; and Other Tales*, 2 vols (Edinburgh, 1818), II, 89–228.

**14(b) Solomon avers** see Proverbs 22. 1. The book of Proverbs is supposed to have been written by Solomon.

**14(b) while with one shepherd** Z. gives his name as Grieve (p. 502).

**14(c) our version of the Psalms of David** as Mack records (p. 7) Hogg's affection for the metrical Psalms of the Church of Scotland is apparent in his 'A Letter from Yarrow. The Scottish Psalmody Defended', in *Edinburgh Literary Journal*, 13 March 1830, pp. 162–63.

**14(d) an old violin** Z. makes the point that, as Hogg's practice on his violin was necessarily done at night in the byres and outhouses where he slept and where he had no means of procuring a light, 'he was much more obliged to the ear than the eye for any advances he made' (p. 501).

**14(d) and my associate quadrupeds [...] utter indignation** a new passage in *Altrive Tales*, as Mack (p. 7) notes.

**15(a) Mr. Scott of Singlee** Singlee is a farm on Ettrick Water. In giving details of his subsequent employment at Elibank Hogg implies that his previous term of service at various farms was usually one year, so he was probably employed at Singlee from Martinmass (11 November) 1785 to Martinmass 1786, when his next employment at Elibank began. Martinmass is one of the Scottish Quarter Days used to fix the term of farm servants' contracts. Hogg's master was probably William Scott, brother to Henry Scott, the tenant of Wester Deloraine and father to the girl commemorated in Hogg's song 'The Bonny Lass of Deloraine'–see Richard D. Jackson, 'The Pirate and the Bonny Lass of Deloraine', *The Scott Newsletter*, No. 40 (Summer 2002), pp. 9–21. William Scott seems to have been the tenant of this farm for many years. The birth of his eldest son, Robert Scott, is recorded in the Yarrow OPR for 22 June 1772, and he was still there in August 1800, when two of his adolescent daughters along with a visiting Miss Anderson and Miss Ayres were accidentally drowned in Ettrick Water–see *Edinburgh Evening Courant* for 23 August 1800. His wife was Margaret Potts.

**15(a) a short distance from the house** as Mack notes (pp. 7, 8) this phrase replaces 'on some necessary business' in the 1821 Memoir, paralleling the replacement towards the end of the paragraph of 'with disordered garments' by 'speechless with affright'. Hogg was presumably aware that references to bodily functions might be termed indelicate.

**15(c) lately been considerably annoyed himself** Hogg was fifteen years old while serving at Singlee, and was clearly only just mastering the old violin he had purchased the previous year. Z. recounts that Mr Scott himself coming home late one night and deciding to stable his own horse had overheard Hogg's playing, and 'upon opening the stable door, he was saluted with a voice so unharmonious, that he run into the house with the greatest precipitation, crying that he believed the devil was in the stable; and was with considerable difficulty convinced of his mistake by some of his family better acquainted with our musician's inclination and abilities than he was' (p. 502). The 1821 Memoir has 'stunned' rather than 'annoyed' here.

**15(c) Elibank upon Tweed** near Clovenfords and only a few miles from Scott's pre-Abbotsford home at Ashiestiel. Hogg described it as 'the most quiet and sequestered place in Scotland'–see *A Series of Lay Sermons on Good Principles and Good Breeding*, ed. by Gillian Hughes with Douglas S. Mack (S/SC, 1997), p. 74. Hogg's master has not been identified.

**15(c) three half-years** Hogg must have moved to Elibank at Martinmass (11 November) 1786, since his next employment at Willenslee began at Whitsunday 1788.

**15(c) Willenslee** a hill farm in Innerliethen parish in Tweeddale. Hogg's master was presumably an elderly man, since he is mentioned as the father of the farmer of Elibank. The William Laidlaw of Willenslee who married Miss Sarah Anderson of Traquair on 9 December 1806 is presumably a younger man, possibly one of his sons–see Innerleithen OPR. Hogg's bed was in a stable that stood in front of the Willenslee burn–see *A Series of Lay Sermons on Good Principles and Good Breeding*, ed. by Gillian Hughes with Douglas S. Mack (S/SC, 1997), p. 74.

**15(c) two years** Hogg must have moved to Willenslee on Whitsunday 1788, since his next contract began at Whitsunday 1790. Whitsunday (15 May) is another of the Scottish Quarter Days, used to fix the term of farm-servants' contracts. Z. agrees that it was at Willenslee that Hogg was first 'entrusted with the charge of a hirsel' (or flock) of sheep (p. 502), rather than being employed as a general agricultural labourer.

**15(d) "The Life and Adventures of Sir William Wallace,"** the poem by Blind Harry, which Hogg probably read in the paraphrase by William Hamilton of Gilbertfield. It was widely read in eighteenth-century Scotland, and known to Burns–see Mack, p. 8.

**15(d) "The Gentle Shepherd;"** a pastoral comedy of 1725, written by the Scottish poet Allan Ramsay (1686–1758).

**16(a) Bailey's Dictionary** Nathan Bailey's dictionary dates from 1721, but was frequently reprinted in the eighteenth century. This particular anecdote may have been a standing joke, since 'Bailey's Dictionary' recurs as a toast at a wedding in 'The Shepherd's Calendar'–see *Winter Evening Tales*, ed. by Ian Duncan (S/SC,

2002), p. 402 and note on p. 581.

**16(b) "Bishop Burnet's Theory of the Conflagration of the Earth."** Mack thinks that this is probably Thomas Burnet's *The Sacred Theory of the Earth* (1684), although this Burnet (1635?–1715) was a Yorkshire divine and Master of Charterhouse and not a bishop. He supposes (p. 9) that Hogg confused him with Bishop Gilbert Burnet (1643–1715).

**16(b) the grand millennium** a thousand years during which Christ will return to earth and live with the saints, before taking them to heaven. The idea derives from Revelation 20. 2–7.

**16(b) new heavens and a new earth** see Revelation 21. 1 ('And I saw a new heaven and a new earth').

**16(c) balm of Gilead** a popular patent medicine, frequently advertised in the newspapers, produced by a 'Dr Solomon' of Gilead House near Newcastle. An advertisement in the *Edinburgh Evening Courant* of 18 January 1813 gives a long list of Scottish sellers of the medicine at eleven shillings a bottle: it was described as good for a surprising variety of complaints including 'inward wastings, loss of appetite, indigestion, depression of spirits [...] and consumptive habits'. As it was also efficacious as a pick-me-up the morning after 'a nocturnal debauch of wine' it seems likely that alcohol featured largely in its composition.

**16(c) a letter to my elder brother** Z.'s similar account is that 'being obliged to write a letter to his elder brother William, he had so far forgot the way, that he actually was under the necessity of printing some of the letters as he saw them in the beginning of the Catechism' (p. 502).

**16(c) Whitsunday 1790** this date enables Hogg's two preceding periods of employment to be fixed.

**16(c) Mr. Laidlaw of Black House** James Laidlaw was the father of Hogg's life-long friend William Laidlaw (1780–1845), who later became Steward of Abbotsford. Surviving family papers in James Laidlaw's hand record payments to 'my servant' James Hogg for lambs for the start of 1792, 18 December 1793, and 27 December 1794–see NLS Acc. 9084/8. The farm is a hill-farm on the Douglas Burn in Yarrow.

**16(d) having taken a wife** William Hogg had married Mary Beattie in Yarrow on 28 December 1798, and on 4 May 1800 their daughter Margaret was baptised (Ettrick OPR)–their expanding family was perhaps one reason for the move.

**16(d) another residence** William Hogg seems to have moved to another house in Ettrick in the first instance, since the baptisms of his next two children, Robert (14 June 1802) and William (1 April 1804) are recorded in the Ettrick OPR. The baptism of his third son, James, on 20 June 1807, however, is recorded for Tweedsmuir, Peebles. In later life William lived at Stobohope near Peebles.

**16(d) lease expiring at Whitsunday 1803** Hogg and his parents seem to have removed from Ettrick House to Craig Douglas, since Hogg dates a letter to Scott of 16 January 1805 (NLS MS 3875, fols 35–36) from there during a period of unemployment. His coded self-description as 'J. H. Craig, of Douglas, Esq.' on the title-page of his drama *The Hunting of Badlewe* (1814) implies that Hogg's father remained there until Whitsunday 1815, when he moved to Altrive Lake. Craig Douglas is a farm in Yarrow parish, lying between the heights of Blackhouse and the river. It seems to have been tenanted by Hogg's old master, James Laidlaw of Blackhouse. An advertisement for the farm as to let in the *Edinburgh Evening Courant* of 27 February 1817 refers to it as 'belonging to the right honourable the Earl of Traquaire, and lately possessed by the deceased Mr James Laidlaw, containing about 1500 acres of pasture, and about 20 acres of arable haugh land'.

**16(d)–17(a) spring of the year 1796** earlier versions of the 'Memoir' state that Hogg began to write verse in 1793. His first published poem, 'The Mistakes of a Night', appeared anonymously in the *Scots Magazine*, 56 (October 1794), 624. It is identified as Hogg's work by Z. (p. 503).

**17(a) For several years [...] "Jamie the poeter."** a new sentence in *Altrive Tales*, replacing a longer and more detailed account of Hogg's early compositions in previous versions of the 'Memoir', as Mack (p. 10) notes.

**17 (a–b) I had no more difficulty [...] at a sitting** a new sentence in *Altrive Tales*, as Mack (p. 10) notes.

**17(b) the Italian alphabet** Hogg probably means that he copied printed letters: Italian or Roman type is used in printing.

**17(c) never write two copies of the same thing** as Mack indicates (p. 11), this passage was written for the 1807 Memoir and probably only represents Hogg's early practice. Among Hogg's papers in the Alexander Turnbull Library, New Zealand, for example, are a number of draft manuscript versions of both poetry and prose from the 1820s and 1830s–see P. D. Garside, 'An annotated checklist of Hogg's literary manuscripts in the Alexander Turnbull Library, Wellington, New Zealand', *The Bibliotheck*, 20 (1995), 5–23.

**17(d) the above practice** Mack points out (p. 11) that as this passage is included in the 1807 Memoir it does not necessarily represent Hogg's practice in 1832.

**17(d) alteration of any part of it** the 1821 Memoir continues, 'for instance, how is the Scottish public likely to receive an improved edition of the Psalms of David, faulty as they are?' (p. xx). This argument was less forceful, following William Tennant's proposal in 1830 to produce just such an improved version of the Scottish metrical psalms–see Hogg's 'A Letter from Yarrow. The Scottish Psalmody Defended', *Edinburgh Literary Journal*, 13 March 1830, pp. 162–63.

**17(d)–18(c) The first time I ever heard of Burns [...] he may do."** a new passage in *Altrive Tales*, as Mack (p. 12) notes. Hogg's first encounter with Burns is the moment he becomes aware of his vocation as a poet, and bears a striking resemblance to a first-person conversion narrative. Hogg's familiarity with this tradition is shown, for example, in Robert Wringhim's reaction to being assured of his election ('I wept for joy to be thus assured of my freedom from all sin')–see *The Private Memoirs and Confessions of a Justified Sinner*, ed. by P. D. Garside (S/SC, 2001), p. 80. Another account of this incident was given by Hogg in his final years in his letter to an unknown correspondent of 21 April 1834 (Manuscripts Division of the Department of Rare Books and Special Collections, Princeton University Libraries: RTCO1, Box 9): 'I was petrified with delight and never suffered him to quit me until I had it all by heart [...]'. (Published with permission of the Princeton University Library.) Hogg also refers to the 'supreme youthful delight' with which he heard the poem in his edition of the works of Burns–see note to 17(d).

**17(d) a half daft man, named John Scott** see also *The Works of Robert Burns*, ed. by James Hogg and William Motherwell, 5 vols (Glasgow, 1834–36), I, 203. There Hogg also dates the episode to summer 1797, describing Scott as 'a great original, but accounted "rather harum-scarum ways"': 'He had taken a fancy to me, and thought nothing of coming five or six miles out to the wild hills to visit, and well did I like to see him coming, he had so many songs and stories of all sorts'.

**18(a) 21st of August** Robert Burns actually died on 21 July 1796.

**18(b) I could not write** an allusion probably referring to Hogg's difficulties in composition rather than the mechanical operation with the pen–see Mack, p. 12.

**18(b) Rev. James Nicol** James Nicol (1769–1819) was minister of Traquair, and the author of *Poems, chiefly in the Scottish Dialect* (1805). Hogg gives a portrait of him as a poet in 'Mr Shuffleton's Scottish Muses' in *The Spy*, No. 5 (29 September 1810), pp. 33–39 (pp. 36–37). For further information about Nicol, see Simon Curtis, 'James Nicol, Minister of Traquair and Poet', *Studies in Hogg and his World*, 7 (1996), 80–86.

**18(c) Mr. John Grieve** John Grieve (1781–1836) was the son of Walter Grieve, who had been minister of the Reformed Presbyterian church in Dunfermline before retiring to Cacrabank in Ettrick, where he died in 1822. Walter Grieve's wife, Jane Ballantyne, was the maternal aunt of Hogg's friend William Laidlaw. She had previously been married to Thomas Bryden, and had a son, Walter Bryden, born on 4 January 1762 and christened in Ettrick on 10 June (Ettrick OPR). John Grieve had been brought up largely in Ettrick, and had been in business in Greenock and Alloa before entering into copartnership with Chalmers Izett, a hat-manufacturer of the North Bridge in Edinburgh–see Rogers, III, 43–45. He was a generous patron to Hogg during the latter's early years in Edinburgh (see p. 27 and notes).

**18(c) Mr. William Laidlaw** Hogg's life-long friendship with William Laidlaw (1780–1845) was formed during his ten-years' service at Blackhouse in Yarrow to Laidlaw's father, James.

**19(a) to appeal to you** that is to Walter Scott, the unnamed friend to whom the letter that comprises the 1807 Memoir was addressed. Laidlaw was in correspondence with Scott in 1801 about ballads for *Minstrelsy of the Scottish Border*–see Hogg's letter to Laidlaw of 20 July 1801 (University of London Library, [S. L.] V. 14).

**19(b) the year 1798** 1796 in previous versions of the 'Memoir'.

**19(b) Alexander Laidlaw** Hogg's life-long friend Alexander Laidlaw, of Bowerhope farm in Yarrow. He is mentioned in William John Napier's *A Treatise on Practical Store-farming* (Edinburgh, 1822) as keeping weather records (pp. 29–44), as building sheep-stells for his master (pp. 123–32), and as a scientific experimenter and friend of the African explorer Mungo Park (pp. 274–75). He is also quoted as an authority in the account of Ettrick parish in the 1845 *Statistical Account of Scotland.* He helped to nurse Hogg in his last illness, and wrote to a friend after Hogg's death that 'Mr. Hogg and I were in our youthful days almost inseparable companions'–see Garden, pp. 326–28.

**19(d) "Reflections on a view of the Nocturnal Heavens."** the contest is dated to 1796 in Hogg's 1821 Memoir, as well as by Z. (p. 820), who gives the following extract from the poem:

'Tis solemn silence all, and not a breath,
In this sequestered solitude, I hear;
Save where the bird of night his mournful scream
Sends from the ruins of yon lofty dome.
Great Source of all perfection, how I'm lost
In wonder and amazement, when I view
That ample space, spread by thy potent arm;
Where worlds unnumbered float at thy controul.

**19(d) a paraphrase of the 117th Psalm** an extract from Hogg's paraphrase (or rather elaboration of the ideas in this two-verse shortest psalm of all) is also given by Z. (p. 821), as follows:

Ye straggling sons of Greenland's rigid wilds,
Y' inhabitants of Asia's distant isles,
With all between, make this your final aim,
Your great Creator's goodness to proclaim.
* * * * * *

The highest seraph that in glory sings,
In heavenly strains; on earth the mighty kings,
The poor, the rich, the wicked, and the just,
The meanest reptile crawling in the dust,
All share his bounty, all his goodness prove,
And all proclaim him God of truth and love.

**19(d)–20(a) a violent inward complaint** as Mack notes (p. 14), in the 1807 Memoir Hogg refers to it as 'a violent pain in my bowels' (p. xvii).

**20(a) in a friend's house** Z. dates this final attack to November 1798, and explains that Hogg was 'from home, assisting a neighbouring farmer to smear his sheep' (p. 821).

**20(b)–21(a) My first published song [...] subsequent transactions** a new passage in *Altrive Tales*, replacing information about Hogg's early poetry, as Mack (p. 15) notes. The inclusion of the new material was perhaps motivated by the successful publication of *Songs by the Ettrick Shepherd* in 1831, in which 'Donald MacDonald' (see below) appears as the first song (pp. 1–5).

**20(b) "Donald M'Donald,"** there is a copy of Hogg's 'Donald M'Donald' printed by John Hamilton and with an 1801 watermark in Stirling University Library. It was subsequently reprinted in Hogg's *The Mountain Bard* of 1807 (pp. 179–82) and in *The Forest Minstrel* of 1810 (pp. 190–93), as well as in *Songs by the Ettrick Shepherd* of 1831 (pp. 1–5).

**20(b) Crown Tavern, Edinburgh** Marie W. Stuart, in her account of the Edinburgh taverns of Fergusson's day, mentions a Crown Tavern in Kennedy's Close run by James Austen–see *Old Edinburgh Taverns* (London: Robert Hale, 1952), p. 51.

**20(b) one of them** probably Andrew Mercer. According to 'R. G.', the author of an article entitled 'The Ettrick Shepherd's First Song' in the *Edinburgh Literary Journal* of 8 May 1830 (pp. 275–76), Hogg showed the song to Mercer, 'then editor of the *North British Magazine*', who invited him to dine at a chop-house in Fleshmarket Close. On hearing Hogg then perform it, Mercer said, ' [...] to put it into the Magazine would not bring it into the hands of the great bulk of the people, whose song it must, and *shall* be. I'll tell you what I'll do,–I'll get Mr — to sing it at the meeting of the Grand Lodge of Scotland, which takes place next week'.

**20(b) Mr. John Hamilton** the Stirling University Library copy of this song gives the publisher's address as 24 North Bridge Street. Rogers (I, 117) describes him as the composer of several airs, a music-seller and instrumental teacher, adding the detail that he married one of his music pupils against the wishes of her family. He died aged fifty-two on 23 September 1814.

**20(c) masonic meeting** the Freemasons was a secret society flourishing in England and Scotland from the eighteenth century onwards. The meeting Hogg refers to is possibly the one described as a meeting of the Grand Lodge of Scotland by 'R. G.' in 'The Ettrick Shepherd's First Song', in *Edinburgh Literary Journal*, 8 May 1830, pp. 275–76, although he says that the chairman of the meeting was George, 9th Earl of Dalhousie (1770–1838) rather than the Earl of Moira: both men were distinguished soldiers. W. M. Parker suggests that this meeting took place on 30 November 1804, and that it was on this occasion that Hogg first became acquainted with Thomas Oliver as the singer of his 'Donald M'Donald'–see 'The House of Oliver & Boyd. A Record from 1778 to 1948' (undated and unpublished typescript, Edinburgh Room, Central Library, Edinburgh), p. 24.

**20(c) the Earl of Moira** the British general Francis Rawdon Hastings (1754–1826) succeeded to the title of Earl of Moira in 1793, and in 1803 he was appointed Commander-in-Chief of Scotland. He was made Marquess of Hastings in 1816, and acted as Governor-General of India between 1813 and 1822.

**20(c) Mr. Oliver** Thomas Oliver had begun printing 'on an extremely modest scale in his mother's house in North Richmond Street, Edinburgh in 1778. There, it is believed, he used the hearth as an "imposing" stone'–see W. M. Parker, 'The House of Oliver & Boyd. A Record from 1778–1948' (undated and unpublished typescript, Edinburgh Room, Central Library, Edinburgh), p. 1. After several years of producing small books, mostly of poetry, under the imprint of T. or Thomas Oliver or Oliver & Co. from a variety of addresses, he found a partner in

1807 or 1808 in the bookbinder George Boyd (pp. 1–2).

**20(c) house of Oliver and Boyd** this publishing firm, founded in 1807 or 1808, produced Hogg's *Winter Evening Tales* of 1820, and *The Mountain Bard* of 1821, by which time they had acquired premises in Tweeddale Court–see W. M. Parker, 'The House of Oliver & Boyd. A Record from 1778 to 1948' (undated and unpublished typescript, Edinburgh Room, Central Library, Edinburgh), p. 37.

**20(c) It was loudly applauded** according to 'R. G.' 'It is a feeble expression to say that it was received with rapturous applause. The walls of the Grand Lodge literally shook with the acclamations. The Earl of Dalhousie was in the chair, and eagerly asked who was the author. He was told that it was a shepherd lad in Ettrick. His Lordship then said, that were the song published, he was sure it would go off well, and that he himself would take fifty copies. The song was accordingly published, and never was triumph greater, or popularity more complete'–see 'The Ettrick Shepherd's First Song', *Edinburgh Literary Journal*, 8 May 1830, pp. 275–76 (p. 276).

**20(d) General M'Donald** perhaps the Major-General Donald M'Donald who, according to the army list for 1805 (p. 378) was Lieutenant-Governor of Fort William.

**20(d) comical anecdotes** see *Songs by the Ettrick Shepherd* (Edinburgh, 1831), pp. 4–5. Of the two anecdotes given there the first was contributed by Hogg and the second by his nephew Robert Hogg, working from his recollections of his uncle's oral reminiscences–see Robert Hogg's undated letter to William Blackwood in NLS MS 4719, fols 202–03.

**21(a) publishing a pamphlet** the publishing history of this 1801 production is given in *Scottish Pastorals*, ed. by Elaine Petrie (Stirling: Stirling UP, 1988), pp. ix–xii. The work was printed by John Taylor, whose business was located opposite the sheep pens in the Grassmarket in Edinburgh. Z. places his account of the publication (pp. 821–22) immediately after Hogg's decision to give up his spare-time occupation as a sheep-dealer partly because he was temperamentally unsuited to it and partly because of his 'natural propensity to literary pursuits'.

**21(c) "unhousell'd, unanointed, unaneled, with all their imperfections on their heads."** from the account of his murder given to Hamlet by the ghost of his father in Shakespeare's *Hamlet*, I. 5. 77–79.

**21(c) some periodical publications** 'Will an' Keatie' appeared in the *Scots Magazine*, 63 (January 1801), 52–54, where it was described as 'no unfavourable specimen' of Hogg's publication. No other reprinting is known.

**21(c–d) The truth was [...] mortification** a new passage in *Altrive Tales*.

**21(d) a London critic** see 'Literary Characters.–By Pierce Pungent. No. I. James Hogg', *Fraser's Magazine*, 1 (April 1830), 291–300 (pp. 295–96). There are quotations from 'Willie an' Keatie: A Pastoral' and 'A Dialogue in a Country Church-Yard'.

**21(d)–22(a) On the appearance [...] composition** substantially rewritten in *Altrive Tales*, eliminating material about *The Mountain Bard* (1807), 'Sandy Tod', and Hogg's Highland journeys, as Mack (p. 16) notes.

**21(d) "The Minstrelsy of the Scottish Border,"** Scott published the first two volumes of his ballad collection in early spring 1802, and a second edition with a third volume with ballad imitations by himself and friends in the following year. His researches for this collection led to his making the acquaintance of Hogg in 1802.

**22(a) Poetical Trifles** details of Hogg's earliest compositions given in 1807 were replaced by other material in *Altrive Tales*. An account of these will be given in the forthcoming S/SC volume of *The Mountain Bard* of 1807/1821, edited by Suzanne Gilbert.

**22(a) my return from the Highlands in June last** the 1807 Memoir is dated from Mitchelslacks farm in November 1806, but Hogg refers here to events in the summers of 1803 and 1804. He signed a five-year lease to subset the farm of Seilibost on Harris from William Macleod of Luskintyre on 13 July 1803 (NLS Ch. 413), and was to enter on the farm at Whitsunday 1804 paying his first year's rent of £150 at Martinmass. According to Z., 'At Whitsunday 1804, James, with other two acquaintances went away again to Harris, to take possession of the farm; which they at length reached, after a long and dangerous voyage. But though the proprietor had shown considerable anxiety to see James, through an unlucky coincidence of misfortunes and disasters, this meeting was prevented, which no doubt led to consequences of the last import to him. Returning home again, he purchased a good many sheep, with which, when he was finally setting out for Harris, about the middle of July, he received notice that the tacksman's right to the subject was called in question, and a plea entered at the Court of Session accordingly' (p. 822). Hogg then decided not to go with his stock to Harris, and in his subsequent letter to Scott of 23 October 1806 (NLS MS 865, fols 74–75) Hogg names a sum of £150 lost on the venture, representing the first year's rent.

**22(b) "Farewell to Ettrick,"** first published as 'Jamie's Farewell to Ettrick' in the *Scots Magazine*, 66 (May 1804), 377, and reprinted in *The Mountain Bard* of 1807, pp. 164–69, in which the 1807 Memoir appeared.

**22(b) the remainder of the summer** Hogg's whereabouts during this brief sojourn in England during the summer of 1804 are unknown, but he was possibly in the Lake District. In giving his reminiscences of Southey (p. 66) Hogg says of their meeting in 1814 that he 'had previously resided a month at Keswick'. In the note to his song 'Caledonia' in *Songs by the Ettrick Shepherd* (Edinburgh, 1831) Hogg mentions an intended tour of Wales at about this time, which ended at Lancaster at the time of the assizes, after which he 'set off for Scotland by the Lakes of Westmoreland and Cumberland' (p. 26). Z. in his account of this 1804 summer simply refers to 'the North of England' (p. 822). The 1807 Memoir ends at this point, as Mack notes (p. 17).

**22(c) Mr. Harkness of Mitchell-Slack, in Nithsdale** Mitchelslacks farm is in Closeburn parish, Dumfriesshire. Hogg served as a shepherd there for two years, from Whitsunday 1805. His master, James Harkness, came from a family renowned for their earlier support of the Covenanters.

**22(c) here that I published "The Mountain Bard,"** this was advertised at five shillings, or ten shillings and sixpence 'fine', among the list of 'New Works Published in Edinburgh' in the *Scots Magazine*, 69 (February 1807), 112.

**22(c) I went to Edinburgh** Hogg almost certainly made two visits to Edinburgh in the winter of 1805–06 to promote the publication of *The Mountain Bard*. Scott, whom Hogg says accompanied him to see the Edinburgh publisher Archibald Constable (1774–1827), was in London from the end of January until early March 1806—see Edgar Johnson, *Sir Walter Scott: The Great Unknown*, 2 vols (London: Hamish Hamilton, 1970), I, 250–53. While Hogg's letter to Constable of 11 March 1806 (NLS MS 7200, fols 199–200), accepting his offer for the first edition of *The Mountain Bard*, is dated from Edinburgh it is clear from his letter to Scott of 17 March, dated from Mitchelslacks (NLS MS 3875, fols 150–51), that he had not seen Scott since Scott's return from London. Therefore Hogg must have seen Scott before Scott's departure from Edinburgh. It is unlikely, though, that Hogg would have been able to leave his master's sheep for weeks at a time.

**22(d) half-guinea copies** the printer's account for *The Mountain Bard* of 1807 has survived as a loose paper in a copy of the work itself in the Craig-Brown Book Collection at the Scottish Borders Archive and Local History Centre, Selkirk. A thousand copies were printed in the 12mo size, and there was also a charge for 'Enlarging to 8vo', for which seventeen reams of paper ('hot press'd') was used.

These copies set from the same type in the larger format, advertised as 'fine' at ten shillings and sixpence (or half a guinea), were presumably the subscribers' copies Hogg refers to here.

**22(d) "Hogg on Sheep;"** this is *The Shepherd's Guide: being a Practical Treatise on the Diseases of Sheep, Their Causes, and the Best Means of Preventing Them [...]*, published by Constable in 1807 and sold at 7s. 6d. It was listed among the 'New Works Published in Edinburgh' in *Scots Magazine*, 69 (June 1807), 440.

**23(a) one pasture farm** Corfardin on the Water of Scaur in Tynron parish in Dumfriesshire. It was advertised in the *Dumfries Weekly Journal* of 9 September 1806 as to let on an 18-year lease from Whitsunday 1807, and as consisting of around 300 acres altogether, with 'an excellent steading of new houses built upon the farm'. Hogg mentions the farm in his letter to Scott of 12 December 1806 (NLS MS 3875, fols 250–51) as 'a pretty convenient thing with an elegant set of houses but for want of a residence I took it dear [...]'.

**23(b) another extensive farm** Locherben, in Closeburn parish, which Hogg farmed in partnership with his friend Adam Bryden of Aberlosk–see Hogg's letter to [Bryden] of 4 December [1806], in NLS Acc. 10190. It was advertised as to let from Whitsunday 1807 in the *Dumfries Weekly Journal* of 21 October 1806 and described as 'very extensive' though no acreage is given. Hogg's letter to Scott of 10 January 1807 (NLS MS 3876, fols 6–7) reveals that the agent for the lease was the brother of Scott's neighbour, Robert Laidlaw of Peel.

**23(b) for three years** Hogg had insufficient capital to stock the farms properly, and though his lease of Locherben was for seven years the venture was effectively over when he wrote to Scott on 28 July 1809 (NLS MS 3878, fols 97–98). Hogg mentions that his books have been 'rouped off', presumably to pay arrears of rent and other debts incurred during his tenancy, and laments that he had never 'been able to attain to any thing better than labouring for [...] daily bread'.

**23(b) a larger MS. work** Hogg clearly kept a journal or book of notes about his life until approximately 1821–see Note on the Text, pp. 194–95.

**23(c) never asked any settlement** by failing to agree a composition with his creditors at this stage Hogg left it open to them to claim his future earnings in payment of outstanding debts, and this is what seems to have happened after his success with *The Queen's Wake* in 1813. In his letter to Scott of 3 April 1813 (NLS MS 3884, fols 122–23) he wrote, 'The little old debts and claims which one would have judged quite forgot are pouring in upon me without any limit or mitigation'. See also note to 31(d).

**23(c) returning again to Ettrick Forest** Hogg must have returned to his native district from Dumfriesshire shortly after his letter to Scott of 28 July 1809 (NLS MS 3878, fols 97–98) was written.

**24(b) correspondents** the table of contents of *The Forest Minstrel* of 1810 names Hogg himself and Thomas Mounsey Cunningham, but also gives the initials 'A', 'B', 'C', and 'D' for other anonymous contributors. Contributor A is clearly Hogg's old friend William Laidlaw, as one of the songs so marked is his 'Lucy's Flittin''. Rogers (III, 44) states that 'C' is John Grieve. A marked copy of *The Forest Minstrel* owned by Peter Garside names 'Jas Gray Esqr–High School' as 'B' and 'Mr Jn. Ballantyne Booksr' as 'D' on Hogg's authority.

**24(b) the ingenious Mr. T. M. Cunningham** Thomas Mounsey Cunningham (1776–1834) was the second of ten Cunningham children, and brother to the poet Allan Cunningham. He had been apprenticed to a mill-wright but left Scotland in 1797 for various employments in England: from 1812 onwards he was employed by Rennie the engineer. Between November 1804 and January 1810 he contributed verses to the *Scots Magazine* above the signature 'T. M. C.', and these presumably attracted the attention of Hogg who was also a contributor. Hogg's poetical epistle

'To Mr T. M. C. London' appeared in the *Scots Magazine*, 67 (August 1805), 621–22 and was followed by Cunningham's reply, 'Answer to the Ettrick Shepherd', in volume 68 (March 1806), 206–08. Hogg included Cunningham's contributions to the *Scots Magazine* in *The Forest Minstrel* of 1810, with his permission according to Rogers (II, 225).

**24(c) Walker and Greig** this firm, of Foulis Close (1806–09) and then Parliament Stairs (1810–30) in Edinburgh, had printed Hogg's *The Forest Minstrel* of 1810 for Constable.

**24(d) Mr. Ballantyne** John Ballantyne (1774–1821), the younger brother of James Ballantyne, the printer of Scott's works, and the contributor of 'Mr Pitt's Anniversary Song' (pp. 202–03) to *The Forest Minstrel*. In 1808 Scott had set him up as a publisher in Edinburgh. The Edinburgh Postal Directory for 1810–11 (p. 17) gives the address of John Ballantyne and Company, booksellers, as 48 South Hanover Street.

**24(d) David Brown** the Edinburgh postal directory for 1810–11 (p. 30) lists the booksellers' firm of Brown and Crombie, with an address of 53 South Bridge Street. The directory of 1811–12 (p. 32) gives the name of the firm at the same address simply as David Brown.

**24(d) James Robertson** Robertson, of 16 Nicolson Street, published the first thirteen weekly issues of *The Spy*. The Edinburgh postal directory of 1810–11 gives his private address as 3 Hill Place.

**25(a) the imprint** see *The Spy*, ed. by Gillian Hughes (S/SC, 2000), pp. 11, 31. There was clearly some confusion about who was to receive the money paid for copies of the weekly paper by its subscribers. A note at the conclusion of No. 1 of *The Spy* reads:

> THE SPY will continue to be published, and delivered to Subscribers in *Edinburgh* and *Leith* every Saturday, Price FOUR PENCE if called for.–A copy of this Number is sent to such literary Gentlemen as are known to the Proprietors; and to those who chuse to retain it when asked for, the succeeding Numbers will be sent till further orders.

No mention was made at this stage of how the subscribers' money was to be collected, and this clearly led to confusion, with some people paying for it at the printing-office and some paying the boy who delivered it. A uniform system was needed to enable proper accounts to be kept, and No. 3 ends with the following note:

> ⁂ *The editor of the* Spy *desires it as a favour of his subscribers, that for preventing confusion, they will desist from paying any money to those employed to deliver it, until the expiry of one quarter, when their receipts will be sent; and likewise, that they will not send to the office for the paper, as it will in future be delivered every Saturday at their houses, without any additional expense.*

**25(b) subscribers** Hogg's letter to Scott of 8 September [1810] (in NLS MS 3879, fol. 184), written on the day the second number of *The Spy* was published, states: 'I had not one Subscriber in Edin. save yourself when the first No. was published and I see I have this day upwards of 100 esq's exclusive of others [...] I am this incoming week to make out a regular list of them [...]'.

**25(b) third or fourth number** the second part of Hogg's 'Life of a Berwick-shire Farmer'–see *The Spy*, ed. by Gillian Hughes (S/SC, 2000), pp. 32–43. No. 4, published on 22 September 1810, relates the seduction of the narrator by his artful housekeeper, after which she grows 'nearly double her natural thickness about the waist' (p. 33).

**25(c) the Cowgate** one of the two main thoroughfares in Edinburgh, leading from the Grassmarket to the Pleasance in Edinburgh's medieval Old Town, and a busy commercial street. It gradually declined in importance in the nineteenth century, being shadowed by the heights first of the South Bridge built in 1788 and later by George IV Bridge built in 1829–32.

**25(c) My youthful habits** in an unpublished 'Letter to Timothy Tickler' (Alexander Turnbull Library, Wellington, New Zealand: MS Papers 42, Folder 9) Hogg states of his consumption of spirits that 'as long as I remained at my pastoral employment, I could not calculate on more than a bottle in the year at an average'.

**25(d) Messrs. Aikman** Andrew and James Aikman's *Edinburgh Star* newspaper was produced from their office at 227 High Street in Edinburgh. They printed issues 14 to 52 of *The Spy*. Andrew Aikman's somewhat bitter account of these dealings with Hogg, dated 2 May 1832, is given in James Browne's anonymous pamphlet, *The 'Life' of the Ettrick Shepherd Anatomized; in a Series of Strictures on the Autobiography of James Hogg* (Edinburgh, 1832), pp. 16–18. Aikman claimed that Hogg's subscription list was misrepresentative: some of the booksellers whose names were given were only agents who had the work on sale or return so that copies were returned unsold, and it included the names of subscribers who had withdrawn after the appearance of the fourth issue. He also accuses Hogg of receiving money from the sale of the paper, despite agreeing that all such sums should be collected by the Aikman firm who would subsequently render an account and pay Hogg his share of the profits.

**26(b–c) "They have [...] editor of 'The Spy.'"** see 'The Spy's Farewell to his Readers', in *The Spy*, ed. by Gillian Hughes (S/SC, 2000), pp. 515–16. There are a number of minor differences between the original passage and the quotation here, and in the original Hogg wrote 'could neither write nor read with accuracy when twenty', and also included the phrase 'should run away from his master' between 'knowledge' and 'leave his native mountains'–see Mack, p. 21.

**26(c) Mr. and Mrs. Gray** James Gray (1770–1830), then senior master at the Edinburgh High School and living at 4 Buccleuch Place. He had made Hogg's acquaintance in 1808. On 25 October 1808 he married as his second wife Mary Peacock (1767–1829), who had been an Edinburgh acquaintance of Hogg's before her marriage–for further information on the Grays and the other contributors to Hogg's paper named in this paragraph, see *The Spy*, ed. by Gillian Hughes (S/SC, 2000), pp. 557–71.

**26(d) Robert Sym** (1752–1845) was a Writer to the Signet, living at 20 George Square. See pp. 76–78 for Hogg's personal reminiscences of him, and the note to 76(c) for further information.

**26(d) Professor T. Gillespie [...] an occasional lift** a new sentence in *Altrive Tales*. Thomas Gillespie (1777–1844), born at Closeburn, Dumfriesshire, contributed to *Blackwood's Edinburgh Magazine* and other periodicals. He was appointed assistant and successor to the Professor of Humanity at St Andrews University in 1828, although not succeeding to the Chair until 1836.

**26(d) Rev. Wm. Gillespie** William Gillespie (1776–1825) succeeded his father as minister of Kells in Galloway in 1806. He was the author of *The Progress of Refinement* (1805) and *Consolation, with Other Poems* (1815).

**26(d) J. Black of the Morning Chronicle** John Black (1783–1855) had been employed as a clerk in Edinburgh, before removing to London in 1810, where he was employed first as a reporter and translator of foreign correspondence by the *Morning Chronicle*, and from around 1817 as editor. He had been a friend and protégé of James Gray.

**26(d) like the sibyl's papers** that is, were mostly lost or destroyed, only a small part surviving, like the Sybilline Books of ancient Rome. The Cumaean sibyl offered to sell King Tarquin nine books of oracular utterances, and when he refused her offer she burnt three of them and offered the remaining six at the same price. Again being refused, she burnt three more, and then Tarquin out of curiosity bought the remaining three at the original price.

**26(d) if indeed there is one** a new phrase in *Altrive Tales*, as Mack (p. 22) notes.

**27(a) Mr. John Grieve** see note to 18(c). By 1810 the hatters' firm, on the North Bridge, was known as Grieve and Scott's. Grieve was a contributor to *The Forest Minstrel*, and to various periodicals, according to Rogers, III, 44. Hogg dedicated *Mador of the Moor* (1816) to Grieve, and portrayed him as the bard who sings 'Mary Scott' in *The Queen's Wake* (1813). He retired from business through ill-health in 1817. In his retirement Grieve lived with his sister at Newington, near Edinburgh.

**27(b) Mr. Scott** Grieve's partner, Henry Scott, was 'a native of Ettrick', according to Rogers, III, 43. Richard Jackson suggests that he may have been a member of the Scott family of Wester Deloraine, a farm in the vicinity of the Grieve cottage at Cacrabank in 'The Pirate and the Bonny Lass of Deloraine', *The Scott Newsletter*, No. 40 (Summer 2002), pp. 9–21. Richard Jackson's more recent research has shown that he was Henry Scott of Deloraine's nephew, the son of Hogg's old master, William Scott of Singlee.

**27(c) the Forum** for further information see Gillian Hughes, 'James Hogg and the Forum', *Studies in Hogg and his World*, 1 (1990), 57–70. George Goldie disputed Hogg's account in his vituperative *A Letter to a Friend* (Edinburgh, 1821)–see Mack, pp. 88–89. Goldie states that Hogg was paid a £20 salary one year, and part of the second year's salary before the Society broke up. He also makes the offensive insinuation that Hogg was so mistrusted by his fellow office-bearers that they would not allow him to disburse charitable funds alone.

**27(c) though far from being a young man** a new phrase in *Altrive Tales*.

**27(d) the larger work** Hogg's journal–see Note on the Text, pp. 194–95.

**28(b) a musical farce** this does not appear to have survived. Possibly, like Hogg's journal of these years, it formed part of the papers given by Hogg's widow after his death to John Wilson and then lost. Hogg subsequently (see p. 33) suggests that it was written in the same year as *The Hunting of Badlewe*, that is, 1813.

**28(c) another musical drama of three acts** possibly an early version of 'The Bush Aboon Traquair; or, The Rural Philosophers. A Pastoral Drama, With Songs', which is in three acts–see *Tales and Sketches by the Ettrick Shepherd*, 6 vols (Glasgow, 1836–37), II, 275–338. This is clearly modelled in some respects on Allan Ramsay's *The Gentle Shepherd*. Hogg subsequently (see p. 33) suggests that it was written in the same year as *The Hunting of Badlewe*, that is, 1813.

**28(c) Mr. Siddons** Henry Siddons (1774–1815) was the son of the famous actress Sarah Siddons, and manager of the Edinburgh theatre from 1809 until his death.

**28(c) some pieces in "The Spy"** two of Hogg's longer poems in his weekly paper were reprinted in *The Queen's Wake* of 1813, 'King Edward's Dream' from No. 20, and 'Macgregor.–A Highland Tale' from No. 40–see *The Spy*, ed. by Gillian Hughes (S/SC, 2000), pp. 209–12 and 402–05.

**28(d) lived at Deanhaugh** Deanhaugh in Stockbridge was developed as a suburb of Edinburgh at about this time, 1812. R. P. Gillies in his *Memoirs of a Literary Veteran*, 3 vols (London, 1851), II, 121, relates that Hogg 'tenanted a room at a suburban residence near Stockbridge. It was a weather-beaten, rather ghostly, solitary looking domicile, like an old farm-house in the country'.

**29(a) to Buccleugh Place** James and Mary Gray lived in a flat at 4 Buccleuch Place on the south side of Edinburgh. The boarders were probably country boys attending the Edinburgh High School, where Gray taught.

**29(a) a young lady** possibly Hogg's future wife, Margaret Phillips, who was Gray's sister-in-law, and visited Gray and his wife on a number of occasions at about this time.

**29(d) George Goldie** in *A Letter to a Friend* (Edinburgh, 1821), p. 12, Goldie disputed the claim made here by Hogg that they became acquainted at the Forum, saying 'I never was a member of the Forum, nor had I ever any connection with it as a collective body [...]'. However, Goldie ran a circulating library at 34 Prince's Street, where he sold sixpenny tickets of admission to the debates of the Forum–see the *Edinburgh Evening Courant* of 23 November 1811. Goldie also stated that Hogg waited on him because 'Mr Constable had refused to publish for him', an assertion contradicted by Hogg's letter to Constable of 24 September 1812, offering him the work (NLS MS 7200, fol. 202). In this letter he says, 'Geo. Goldie requests a share of it that shall be as you please'. Goldie gives his age at this time as twenty-three (p. 5).

**29(d) he had differed with Mr. Scott** Scott was in financial difficulties in the autumn of 1812: the Ballantyne printing firm was insufficiently capitalised and Scott had moved into Abbotsford. Constable wished to take a share of his new poem, *Rokeby*, but his offer was refused by Scott–see Edgar Johnson, *Sir Walter Scott: The Great Unknown*, 2 vols (London: Hamish Hamilton, 1970), I, 402–03.

**30(a) in the spring of 1813** the title-page of the first edition of *The Queen's Wake* gives George Goldie's business address as 34 Princes Street. The work was published in conjunction with the Longmans firm in London, and printed by Andrew Balfour. Hogg's poem was advertised as 'This day is published [...]' in the *Edinburgh Evening Courant* of 1 February 1813, but in his letter to Robert M'Turk of [28 January 1813] (NLS MS 3218, fol. 37) Hogg says that 'the Queen's Wake is to be published on Saturday', that is 30 January.

**30(b) Mr. William Dunlop** William Dunlop (1777–1839) was a wine and spirit merchant, and brother-in-law to John Usher of Toftfield. There is a rhyming epistle to Hogg which may be by him, signed 'Your William' and dated from the Canongate on 2 March 1829 (NLS MS 2245, fols 140–41) about the treatment proper to a cask of beer which has been sent to Mount Benger with Ebenezer Hogg, the Yarrow carrier. Hogg's letter of 26 February 1825 (cited with the permission of The Poetry/Rare Books Collection, University Libraries, University at Buffalo, The State University of New York), about an order of whisky, is addressed to him in the Grassmarket. Goldie mentions him in *A Letter to a Friend* (p. 6) as 'one of the chief magistrates' of Edinburgh, and a 'Bailie Dunlop' is recorded as having voted for the election of John Wilson to the Chair of Moral Philosophy of Edinburgh University on 17 July 1820–see *Edinburgh Weekly Journal*, 26 July 1820, p. 237. As Mack notes (p. 26), in the 1821 Memoir Dunlop is reported as using the word 'b–h' (presumably 'bitch') rather than 'deevil'.

**30(d) save the Eclectic** the poem was reviewed in the *Eclectic Review*, 9 (June 1813), 647–53. The reviewer found that Hogg's work when imitating the ballads 'may for a while be simple and natural' but criticised its 'finery and verbiage' elsewhere: comparing Hogg's own poetry to that of the Rizzio of the work (criticised by the Scots for its artificiality) the reviewer commented sarcastically that 'we wish that the greater part of Mr. Hogg's bards had been deterred by this *disdain* from following in the taste of Rizzio' (pp. 650–51).

**30(d) Mr. Jeffery** Francis Jeffrey (1773–1850), the editor of the *Edinburgh Review*, and a lawyer who became Lord Advocate in 1830. Jeffrey's review is in the *Edinburgh Review*, 24 (November 1814), 157–74, and is followed by his review of William Tennant's *Anster Fair* (pp. 174–82). As Mack has previously noted (p. 27), this second review contains the phrase 'Mr Tennant is a kind of prodigy as well as Mr Hogg–and his book would be entitled to notice as a curiosity, even if its pretensions were much smaller than they are on the score of its literary merit' (pp. 174–75).

**31(a) any literary connexion** Hogg fears that his support for the Tory *Blackwood's Edinburgh Magazine* may have prevented the Whig Francis Jeffrey from reviewing his works in the *Edinburgh Review*.

**31(b) sold two editions of it** the second edition of 1813 seems to have been made up of remaining copies of the first edition with a new sheet, and with a poem by Bernard Barton added. It was advertised as 'This day is published' in the *Edinburgh Evening Courant* of 14 June 1813. Barton's enthusiastic response to *The Queen's Wake*, 'To James Hogg, The Ettrick Shepherd, Author of the Queen's Wake. By a Gentleman of Suffolk', had appeared in the *Edinburgh Evening Courant* of 29 April 1813.

**31(b) a general failure** in writing of 1813 Edgar Johnson says that 'Clarke of St. Andrew Street, Walker of Hunter Square, and numbers of smaller houses had all gone under, leaving masses of dishonored bills'–see *Sir Walter Scott: The Great Unknown*, 2 vols (London: Hamish Hamilton, 1970), I, 412.

**31(b) A third edition** a third edition of *The Queen's Wake* was advertised as 'This day is published' in the *Edinburgh Evening Courant* of 14 July 1814. In *A Letter to a Friend* (Edinburgh, 1821) Goldie declared that 'even a second edition was not called for; but Mr Hogg represented it as "*the third*" to Mr Constable, which, together with other statements equally untrue, respecting my declining again putting it to the press, he succeeded in persuading Mr Constable to engage in the publication; but Mr Hogg's falsehood being subsequently seen through by Mr Constable, that gentleman declined proceeding any farther in the business [...]' (p. 7).

**31(d) in Goldie's name** the third edition of *The Queen's Wake* of 1814 was printed by James Ballantyne for Goldie. The London firm of Henry Colburn is also named on the title-page.

**31(d) he stopped payment** Goldie's failure appears to have occurred at the beginning of September 1814, less than two months after the publication of the third edition of *The Queen's Wake*. Hogg says in a letter to Byron dated 13 September 1814 that Goldie 'broke last week' (Bodleian Library, University of Oxford, MS Dep. Lovelace Byron 155, fols 51–52). In *A Letter to a Friend* (Edinburgh, 1821), pp. 7–8, Goldie stated, 'As to the edition not being lodged in my premises a week before I stopped, it is unfortunate for Mr Hogg, that, by a comparison of dates, he will find this week to have been several months!'

**31(d) to sell, or give away, more than one half of the copies** Goldie seems to have been particularly angry at what he saw as a charge of clandestinely disposing of property on the eve of bankruptcy, a criminal act according to law. In *A Letter to a Friend* (Edinburgh, 1821) he declared that to this 'I can only say, that my affairs were carefully examined by Mr Francis Bridges, Mr Blackwood, and Mr Samuel Aiken [...] in the certificate, or discharge, which was afterwards granted by my creditors, on the recommendation of these gentlemen, the very contrary is stated; and what is perhaps more extraordinary, Mr Hogg's signature is appended to that document, and now in my possession!' (p. 8).

**31(d) some old farming debts** having failed to secure a settlement with his creditors when he gave up farming in Dumfriesshire in 1809, Hogg was now obliged to pay debts outstanding from then out of his recent literary profits. Walter Cunningham of Catslackburn, for instance, began to agitate in 1814 for repayment of a debt dating back to Hogg's farming days in Locherben in 1808, and this became the subject of a legal action in May 1821 when Hogg's tenancy of the large farm of Mount Benger would also have suggested that he was in good financial standing–see John Chisholm, *Walter Scott as Judge: His Decisions in the Sheriff Court of Selkirkshire* (Edinburgh, 1918), pp. 100, and Appendix, pp. 204–14.

**31(d)–32(a) Mr. Blackwood [...] one of the trustees** the Edinburgh bookseller William Blackwood (1776–1834). In his letter to William Blackwood of 28 October 1814 (in NLS MS 4001, fols 207–08) Hogg states that the third edition of *The Queen's Wake* consisted of 1030 copies published as a joint venture between himself and Goldie, and requests that half the copies be made available to him.

**32(a) the two Messrs. Bridges** one of the trustees of Goldie's bankruptcy was called Francis Bridges–see Goldie's *A Letter to a Friend* (Edinburgh, 1821), p. 8. The Edinburgh postal directory for 1814–15 (p. 32) gives his address as Hill Place. The other Mr Bridges was perhaps Hogg's friend, David Bridges (1776–1840) of the clothiers' firm of David Bridges and Son–see note to 34(a).

**32(a–b) I applied to [...] kindness of the trustees** a new passage in *Altrive Tales*, as Mack (p. 28) notes.

**32(a) Mr. Samuel Aitken** the Edinburgh Postal Directory for 1814–15 (p. 6) lists him as a bookseller of 6 Parliament Square. Goldie mentions in *A Letter to a Friend* (1821) that his affairs were examined by 'Mr Francis Bridges, Mr Blackwood, and Mr Samuel Aiken' (p. 8).

**32(b) paid me more than double** Mrs Oliphant in *Annals of a Publishing House: William Blackwood and his Sons*, 2 vols (Edinburgh and London, 1897), I, 36 says there is a balance sheet in the Blackwood archive giving an account of the transaction over *The Queen's Wake* between Hogg and Goldie, and that it shows Hogg received £245 for it from Blackwood and Murray. This has not been traced, and there seems to be no record of such a payment in the Murray Archive. Goldie in *A Letter to a Friend* (Edinburgh, 1821) stated that Hogg gained 'something more than L. 70 over and above what he would have received had I been able to meet all my engagements to him in the regular way!' (p. 8). The fourth edition of *The Queen's Wake*, published by Murray and Blackwood, was advertised as 'just published' in the *Edinburgh Evening Courant* of 15 December 1814.

**32(c) Reverend Dr. Morehead** probably Robert Morehead (1777–1842), a Scottish episcopal clergyman and minor poet. An advertisement for a volume of his sermons in the *Edinburgh Evening Courant* of 6 January 1810 describes him as 'Of Baliol College, Oxford, junior Minister of the Episcopal Chapel, Cowgate, Edinburgh', while the Edinburgh postal directory for 1811–12 (p. 181) gives his address as 21 Hill Street. Corson (p. 566) says he was the third son of William Morehead of Herbertshire, and married Margaret Wilson on 27 November 1804, the daughter of Charles Wilson, Professor of Church History at St Andrews University.

**32(c) name of Lowes** these ladies have not been identified, though they may possibly have been relations of the Thomas William Lowes of Ridley Hall, who died in Edinburgh on 18 September 1812.

**32(d) Mr. Wilson's "Isle of Palms,"** the poet and miscellaneous writer John Wilson (1785–1854), the 'Christopher North' of *Blackwood's Edinburgh Magazine*, and from 1820 Professor of Moral Philosophy at Edinburgh University. His *Isle of Palms and Other Poems* was published on 20 February 1812–see Elsie Swann, *Christopher North (John Wilson)* (Edinburgh: Oliver and Boyd, 1934), p. 46. There is a presentation copy of the poem, 'To the Ettrick Shepherd from his friend the Author', in the James Hogg Collection, Special Collections, University of Otago Library, Dunedin, New Zealand.

**32(d) a Scottish Review** this may allude to *The Scotish* [*sic*] *Review*, a quarterly periodical printed by D. Schaw and Son of the Lawnmarket, Edinburgh. A new series was advertised in the *Edinburgh Evening Courant* of 9 July 1814.

**32(d) for the space of six months** suggesting that Hogg's acquaintance with Wilson began in the autumn of 1812: probably, though, it was formed after the publication of *The Queen's Wake*, early in 1813.

**33(a) hair like eagles' feathers [...] birds' claws** in Daniel 4. 33 Nebuchadnezzar was 'driven from men, and did eat grass as oxen, and his body was wet with the dew from heaven, till his hairs were grown like eagles' *feathers*, and his nails like birds' *claws*'. This description clearly rankled with Wilson himself, for in a savage review of *The Three Perils of Woman* in *Blackwood's Edinburgh Magazine*, 14 (October 1823), 427–37, two years later, he commented sarcastically that Hogg in his 'Memoir' 'describes his friends by "hair like feathers," and "nails like eagle-claws," and so forth, which is all very proper and pretty portraiture' (p. 428).

**33(a) the Road of Gabriel** Hogg's letter to Margaret Phillips of 26 October 1814 (Stirling University Library, MS 25, Box 4, Item 5) gives his address as 'No. 2 Gabriel's Road'. However, Hogg only moved from his previous lodgings at Deanhaugh after his success with *The Queen's Wake*: his letter to Constable of 20 May 1813 (NLS MS 7200, fols 203–04), for example, is still dated from Deanhaugh. If Wilson called upon Hogg for the first time at 2 Gabriel's Road, as Hogg suggests, this could not have been as early as the autumn of 1812.

**33(a) at four** as Mack notes (p. 29), in 1821 the words were followed by 'and if not, he might stay at home'.

**33(b) at his seat in Westmoreland** Wilson built a large house at Elleray near Windermere in 1808, which was demolished in the 1860s although the original cottage he lived in while the mansion was being built survives and is known as Christopher North's Cottage–see Grevel Lindop, *A Literary Guide to the Lake District* (London: Chatto & Windus, 1994), pp. 40–41. Hogg's stay was made during a visit to the Lakes in September 1814, also referred to in his reminiscences of Southey and Wordsworth (pp. 65–69). Hogg's letter to Byron of 13 September 1814 (Bodleian Library, University of Oxford, MS Dep. Lovelace Byron 155, fols 51–52) is dated from Elleray.

**33(d) "The Hunting of Badlewe;"** Hogg's drama was composed in 1813, and Hogg persuaded George Goldie to print a few copies for private circulation among his literary advisors: in his letter to William Laidlaw of 22 July 1813, for instance, Hogg says, 'Only half a dozen copies are printed merely to prevent *holographs* being known [...] To friends such as you they are intended as *proof-sheets*; for the hunting of Badlewe shall not be given to the world without some certainty of poetical superiority' (Beinecke Rare Book and Manuscript Library, Yale University: GEN MSS 61, Box 1, Folder 39). It was published anonymously (as 'By J. H. Craig, of Douglas, Esq.') by Goldie in a larger impression the following year, price five shillings, and advertised as 'This day was published' in the *Edinburgh Evening Courant* of 31 March 1814.

**33(d) not favourably received** in his letter to William Roscoe of 28 July 1814 (Liverpool Record Office, Liverpool Libraries and Information Services: 920 Ros 2049) Hogg says of it, 'It is reviewed in both our minor reviews in the one with a good deal of asperity [...]', before discussing the one in 'the Scottish published yesterday'. An advertisement in the *Edinburgh Evening Courant* of 9 July 1814 for No. II of *The Scotish Review* notes that this included a review of *The Hunting of Badlewe*, presumably the one summarised in Hogg's letter, though unfortunately no copy of this particular issue appears to have survived.

**33(d) the *fifth edition*** this was a one-guinea subscription edition printed by Oliver & Boyd for Blackwood, with Murray's name also appearing on the title-page, and published in 1819. The plates include a frontispiece portrait of Mary Queen of Scots, 'Sketched by Sir John Medina from a Picture in the Royal Cabinet at Versailles', a double-page plate between pp. 76 and 77, illustrating the witches' visit to Lapland in 'The Witch of Fife' which is the work of Charles Kirkpatrick Sharpe, and a drawing of Queen Mary's harp between pp. 328 and 329 'Drawn and Engraved by Daniel Somerville 1807', this latter reprinted from the frontispiece to John Gunn, *An Historical Enquiry Respecting the Performance on the Harp in the Highlands of Scotland [...]* (Edinburgh, 1807).

**33(d) Charles Sharpe** Charles Kirkpatrick Sharpe (1781–1841), editor, author and amateur artist. His illustration of 'The Witch of Fife' was made at Hogg's request and he also seems to have acted as Hogg's agent in his dealings with the engraver Lizars about the production of the two new plates for the subscription edition of

*The Queen's Wake*–see Hogg's letter to Sharpe of 24 November 1818 (inserted in Case Y 185 ·H6745, James Hogg, *The Queen's Wake* (Edinburgh: Blackwood, 1819), The Newberry Library, Chicago).

**33(d) Mr. Walter Scott** the original prospectus for a subscription edition of *The Queen's Wake*, dated 24 May 1817, is in Scott's hand (NLS MS 30921). In his letter to Lord Montagu of 8 June [1817] Scott says, 'This is a scheme which I did not devise for I fear it will end in disappointment but for which I have done and will do all I possibly can'–see *The Letters of Sir Walter Scott*, ed. by H. J. C. Grierson and others, 12 vols (London, 1932–37), IV, 460–61.

**34(a) Mr. David Bridges, junior** of the Edinburgh clothiers' firm of David Bridges and Son. James Nasmyth, the son of the painter Alexander Nasmyth, recalls him as a connoisseur of painting in his *Autobiography*, ed. by Samuel Smiles (London, 1883), p. 36. He was secretary of Edinburgh's Dilettanti Club, of which Hogg was also a member. Robert Chambers paints a lively picture of the scene in his shop 'at the south-east corner of Bank Street, and entering from the Lawnmarket' and describes Bridges's appearance in his *Walks in Edinburgh* (Edinburgh, 1825), pp. 71–78.

**34(a) dedication** the dedication (which is not dated) in the first edition of *The Queen's Wake* reads 'To Her Royal Highness Princess Charlotte of Wales, A Shepherd among the Mountains of Scotland, dedicates this Poem'.

**34(a) the Princess Charlotte** Princess Charlotte Augusta (1796–1817) was the only daughter of the then Prince Regent and therefore heir presumptive to the throne, although estranged from her father after his quarrel with her mother. In December 1813 she became engaged to William, Prince of Orange, but the match was broken off and in May 1816 she married Leopold, Prince of Saxe-Coburg. She died in childbirth in November 1817.

**34(b) Dr. Fisher, bishop of Salisbury** John Fisher (1748–1825) had been tutor to Prince Edward, later the father of Queen Victoria, from 1780–1785, and became bishop of Exeter in 1803. George III made him the superintendent of Princess Charlotte's education in 1805. He was translated from the bishopric of Exeter to that of Salisbury in 1807.

**34(b) let the original date remain** the original dedication of *The Queen's Wake* was undated, though in the fifth edition it is dated 'ELTRIVE, *May* 1811'. This is something of a puzzle, as Hogg relates that *The Queen's Wake* was composed after *The Spy* had been discontinued at the end of August 1811–also he was not granted the farm of Altrive by the Duke of Buccleuch until January 1815.

**34(b) Kinnaird House in Athol** about six miles from Dunkeld, overlooking the Tay. Mack (p. 31) points out that during 1823–24 it was tenanted 'by the Bullers, whose tutor, Thomas Carlyle (1795–1881), here wrote most of his *Life of Schiller* and the first part of his translation of *Wilhelm Meister*'. Chalmers Izett appears to have sold the 820-acre estate in 1820, when the house was described as 'built within these few years' and as containing 'three public rooms [...] and seven Bedrooms, besides Kitchen, Servants' Rooms, Water Closets, &c.'–see *Edinburgh Weekly Journal*, 10 May 1820, p. 152.

**34(b) the seat of Chalmers Izett** Izett had formerly been a partner in the hatters' firm now run by Grieve and Scott in Edinburgh.

**34(b) whose lady** Eliza Izett was one of Hogg's closest friends during this period of his life, and retained a long-term interest in his fortunes. Hogg's earliest surviving letter to her is dated 23 July 1808 (NLS MS 3278, fol. 62), and when his quarrel with Blackwood was made up in 1834 Hogg remarked in an undated letter to Wilson that besides his wife's relief 'Mrs Izet too will rejoice beyond measure' (NLS MS 4039, fols 35–36). Elizabeth Stewart was baptised at Dowally, Perthshire on 13 June 1774 and married Chalmers Izett, hatmaker, there in or around April

1792. (I thank Janette Currie and Richard Jackson for this information from Dowally OPR.) Before her removal to Kinnaird Mrs Izett had been a neighbour and intimate friend of the novelist Mary Brunton, both women living in St John Street, Canongate, while from about 1830 onwards the Izetts had clearly returned to Edinburgh and (on the evidence of postal directories) were living in Blacket Place, near John Grieve in Newington.

**34(c) the summer of 1814** it appears probable that the composition of *Mador of the Moor* was begun during Hogg's visit of 1813 rather than 1814. In a letter to Alexander Bald of 14 November 1813 (NLS Accession 9953) Hogg wrote, 'Since my return from the Highlands I have been very busy with a new poem which already extends to 1100 lines and no appearance of any close. It is in the stanza of Spencer [*sic*] and much of it descriptive of Highland scenery and manners'. Again in a letter to Byron of 3 June 1814 (Beinecke Rare Book and Manuscript Library, Yale University: GEN MSS 61, Box 1, Folder 5) he wrote 'I have finished another poem in the Spenserian stanza six months ago but I am terrified for publishing too much and [...] I have prevailed upon myself to let it lie over for some time'. The 'Literary Intelligence' of the *Scots Magazine*, 76 (April 1814), 296 states: 'Mr Hogg will likewise shortly publish a new poem entitled Morice [*sic*] of the Moor. It is a Highland tale, and descriptive of the manners, superstitions, and scenery, of that romantic country. From all that we have learned of this poem, we are led to expect that the public will derive from it the same gratification which they have so amply received from the Queen's Wake'.

**35(b) "Mador of the Moor"** Hogg's *Mador of the Moor; a Poem* was published by William Blackwood in 1816. It was advertised as 'This day is published' in the *Edinburgh Evening Courant* of 22 April 1816, and included in the list of new works published in Edinburgh in the *Scots Magazine*, 78 (April 1816), 292.

**35(b) left out [...] one whole book** the poem as published consists of five cantos, so the omitted section may have been as much as a sixth of the whole poem.

**35(b) "Ode to Superstition"** Hogg's 'Superstition' was first published in *The Pilgrims of the Sun; a Poem* (Edinburgh and London, 1815), pp. 129–48.

**35(c) "Midsummer Night Dreams,"** a title given, presumably, in allusion to Shakespeare's comedy, *A Midsummer Night's Dream*. The title-page of the second volume of Hogg's *Poetical Works*, 4 vols (Edinburgh, 1822) shows that at this time Hogg envisaged an extended collection under the same title.

**35(c) a friendly advice** the 1821 Memoir employs the more self-critical phrase 'chance adulation' (p. l).

**35(c) "Connel of Dee,"** see 'Country Dreams and Apparitions. No. II. Connel of Dee', in *Winter Evening Tales*, ed. by Ian Duncan (S/SC, 2002), pp. 410–25. It was first published in the first edition of 1820.

**35(c) "The Pilgrims of the Sun."** *The Pilgrims of the Sun; a Poem* was advertised 'This day is published' in the *Edinburgh Evening Courant* of 15 December 1814, though the published work bears an 1815 title-page. It is also listed, price 7s. 6d. under 'New Works Published in Edinburgh' in *Scots Magazine*, 76 (December 1814), 932. Publication in London, however, appears to have been delayed until early in 1815.

**35(c) Mr. James Park of Greenock** James Park (1778?–1817) was the son of the keeper of the White Hart tavern in Greenock, and an early friend of the novelist John Galt. He contributed to various periodicals, including Hogg's *The Spy* of 1810–1811. In his reminiscences of Galt (pp. 72–73) Hogg claimed that his acquaintance with Park began in the summer of 1804, but Hans de Groot has demonstrated that the acquaintance must date back to 1803 at least–see 'When did Hogg meet John Galt?', *Studies in Hogg and his World*, 8 (1997), 75–76.

**35(d) also that of publishing Mador** Park's visit, and Hogg's change of heart, must have taken place before the end of July 1814. Hogg had offered Constable *Mador of* *the Moor* ('a poem of 2200 lines or thereabout') in a letter of 1 February 1814 (NLS MS 7200, fols 207–08), but on 25 July [1814] offered him *The Pilgrims of the Sun*, commenting 'I spoke to you some months ago about publishing a poem price 12/ about which I believe we were mostly agreed but on mature calculation I am resolved first to publish one not half so long [...]' (NLS MS 7200, fols 209–10).

**36(a) "half-naked, for a warld's wonder,"** this quotation has not been identified, although the expression 'a world's wonder' was clearly in common use. Scott's Edgar Ravenswood, taking farewell of Lucy Ashton after her breach of faith with him, for example, says, 'I have nothing farther to say, except to pray to God that you may not become a world's wonder for this act of wilful and deliberate perjury'–see *The Bride of Lammermoor*, ed. by J. H. Alexander, EEWN 7a (Edinburgh: Edinburgh UP, 1995), p. 253.

**36(c) Hang him** as Mack indicates (p. 33) the 1821 Memoir has 'D–n him' (p. liii).

**37(b) your friend Mr. Paterson's** as Mack notes (p. 34), *The Legend of Iona, with Other Poems*, by Walter Paterson, was published by Constable in 1814. It was advertised as 'this day is published' in the *Edinburgh Evening Courant* of 24 February 1814.

**37(b) Mr. Miller** the Edinburgh bookseller Robert Miller, of the firm of Manners and Miller of 208 High Street.

**37(b) *Discipline*** a novel by Mary Brunton, published by Manners and Miller in 1814. As it was advertised in the *Edinburgh Evening Courant* of 12 December 1814 as to be published 'tomorrow', Hogg must be mistaken in recalling that Constable had mentioned Miller's sales of it. This conversation took place in the summer of 1814, since in his letter to Byron of 14 August (John Murray Archive, Box A 31 5) Hogg says 'Constable and Manners and Miller have bought the first edition of the poem I was mentioning to you'.

**37(c) eighty-six pounds** £80, according to the 1821 Memoir (p. liv)–see Mack, p. 35.

**37(d) I left Edinburgh** Hogg was planning to visit Wilson at Elleray near Windermere in the Lake District. In his letter to Byron of 14 October 1814 (John Murray Archive, Box A 31 5) he mentions his recent return to Edinburgh 'after an absence of 9 weeks'.

**38(a) wrote Mr. Miller a note** as Mack indicates (p. 35) Hogg's letter to Byron of 14 October 1814 (John Murray Archive, Box A 31 5) makes his role in the affair much less passive: 'I told you I had sold an edition of a new poem to Constable and Miller–on my return to town after an absence of 9 weeks, by which time it was to have been published, I found it in the same state in which I left it, and the m. s. taken out of the press and passing thro' all the notable *blues*. I went to the shop in a tremendous rage, threatened Miller with a prosecution, and took the M. S. out of his hands–So that if Murray and I do not agree I am in a fine scrape'.

**38(b) Mr. Blackwood introduced me to Mr. John Murray** William Blackwood had been the agent for Murray's publications in Edinburgh since August 1810 (I, 256). While Blackwood may have brought about a personal introduction of Hogg to Murray, it is clear that Murray's attention had been drawn to Hogg's poem beforehand by Byron. Hogg had written to Murray on 17 August 1814 (NLS MS 20437, fols 40–41) regretting that his poem had just been placed with Constable and Manners and Miller.

**38(b) Albany Street** in the Broughton district of Edinburgh.

**38(c) would not allow his name to go to the work** there are two different states of the title-page for *The Pilgrims of the Sun*. The imprint of the Edinburgh copies reads 'London:\ Printed for John Murray, 50, Albemarle Street:\ And William Blackwood, South Bridge Street,\ Edinburgh.\ [rule]\ 1815.' and that of the London copies 'Edinburgh:\ Printed for William Blackwood, South Bridge\ Sreet;\ And Sold by J. Murray, London.\ [rule]\ 1815.'. This reflects a last-minute withdrawal by John Murray from his role as the principal publisher of the work. Full details of the publication history of the work will be given in the forthcoming S/SC volume of *Midsummer Night Dreams*.

**39(a) the Eclectic** see *Eclectic Review*, new series, 3 (March 1815), 280–91.

**39(a) reprinted in two different towns in America** *The Pilgrims of the Sun; a Poem* was reprinted in Philadelphia by Moses Thomas in 1815, and again the following year–see Stephanie Anderson-Currie, *Preliminary Census of Early Hogg Editions in North American Libraries*, South Carolina Working Papers in Scottish Bibliography 3 (Columbia, South Carolina: Department of English, University of South Carolina, 1993), p. 7. There is no evidence, however, that it was reprinted in two different American towns or cities.

**39(b) a poem from every living author in Britain** Hogg's plan was for a half-yearly publication, priced at five shillings, partly containing original poetry and partly reviews of poetry. R. P. Gillies and John Wilson were to be his co-editors, and it was to be entitled the 'Edinburgh Poetical Repository'. The projected publication seems to have been modelled on the *Poetical Register*, to which Hogg had sent contributions the previous year with his letter to Robert Anderson of 3 May [1813] (NLS MS 22.4.11, fol. 23). This journal contained a section of critical notices of volumes of poetry published in the year to which each issue related, and another of short original poems. Interestingly R. A. Davenport, the projector of the *Poetical Register*, wrote to Byron on 16 February 1815 (John Murray Archive: Miscellaneous Letters to Byron) about rumours that his periodical was regarded unkindly in Edinburgh and that Hogg had started 'a rival publication' to which Byron himself was named as a contributor.

**39(b) Southey** the poet Robert Southey (1744–1843) had contributed to Hogg's periodical paper *The Spy*, and Hogg seems to have made his personal acquaintance at Keswick in the summer of 1814 (see pp. 65–66). Hogg solicited a poem from Southey for his poetical repository in his letter of 4 June 1814 (NLS MS 2245, fols 4–5).

**39(b) Wilson** John Wilson's contribution was presumably requested in person.

**39(b) Wordsworth** Wordsworth's letter to R. P. Gillies of 12 November 1814 reveals that he had already given Hogg 'Yarrow Visited' for the proposed poetical repository–see R. P. Gillies, *Memoirs of a Literary Veteran*, 3 vols (London, 1851), II, 148.

**39(b) Lloyd** the poet, novelist, and translator of Alfieri, Charles Lloyd (1775–1839), who had been settled at Low Brathay house near Ambleside since 1800. He was a friend of Coleridge and of Southey.

**39(b) Morehead** for information about Robert Morehead see note to 32(c).

**39(b) Pringle** Thomas Pringle (1789–1834), who from 1811 was employed as a copyist at Register House in Edinburgh and devoted his spare time to literature. He was subsequently one of the original editors of *Blackwood's Edinburgh Magazine*, and then editor of Constable's rival *Edinburgh Magazine*. In 1819 he published *Autumnal Excursions, and other Poems*, but finding he could not make a living by literature returned to his old job at Register House. He emigrated to South Africa with a group of his own and his wife's relations in February 1820, but returned to Britain in July 1826 and settled in London, where he was appointed secretary to the Anti-Slavery Society.

**39(b) Paterson** for information about Walter Paterson see note to 37(b).

**39(c) Lord Byron** the poet George Gordon Noel Byron, 6th Baron Byron (1788–1824). Hogg and Byron never met, but Hogg initiated a correspondence when he applied to Byron for a contribution to the poetical repository in his letter of 3 June 1814 (Beinecke Rare Book and Manuscript Library, Yale University: GEN MSS 61, Box 1, Folder 5). From a subsequent letter of 30 July [1814] (John Murray Archive, Box A 31 5) it is clear that Byron had promised to send him *Lara*, which was published with Samuel Rogers's *Jacqueline* in 1814.

**39(c) Rogers** Samuel Rogers (1763–1855), was a banker and also a poet, the author of *The Pleasures of Memory* (1792).

**39(c)–40(b) In one of Lord Byron's [...] my publication** a new passage in *Altrive Tales*, as Mack (p. 38) notes, giving an account of Hogg's relations with Byron.

**39(c) one of Lord Byron's letters** no letter of 1814 with the expression 'he would appear in my work in his best breeks' appears to have survived.

**39(c) Lord Byron's letters to me** of the six letters Hogg mentions here only two appear to have survived–see *Byron's Letters and Journals*, ed. by Leslie A. Marchand, 12 vols (London: John Murray, 1973–82), IV, 84–86 and V, 37–38. Marchand (V, 13) also gives an extract from a third letter to Hogg of 1816 on the evidence of a record in Henry Crabb Robinson's diary of 1 December 1816.

**40(a) I had been quizzing him** Byron was married on 2 January 1815 to Anna Isabella Milbanke (1792–1860), the daughter of Sir Ralph Milbanke (later Noel). Hogg's letter to him making this pun, of 14 October 1814 (John Murray Archive, Box A 31 5), makes a number of sexual innuendos and implies there was a mercenary aspect to the marriage.

**40(a) shortly after the birth of his daughter Ada** Byron's daughter Augusta Ada was born on 10 December 1815. Byron's letter to Hogg of 1 March 1816 says 'My family about three months ago was increased by a little girl–who is reckoned a fine child–I believe–though I feel loth to trust to my own partialities.–She is now in the country'–see *Byron's Letters and Journals*, ed. by Leslie A. Marchand, 12 vols (London: John Murray, 1973–82), V, 37.

**40(a) the news that soon followed** by early February 1816 Byron and his wife were discussing their separation, and by the end of April Byron had left the country. Byron's 'Fare Thee Well', and a letter from Sir Ralph Noel of 18 April to the editor of the *Morning Chronicle* about the breakdown of the Byron marriage, were printed in the *Edinburgh Evening Courant* of 9 May 1816. When Byron went abroad his correspondence with Hogg appears to have been discontinued, and he died at Missolonghi in Greece in April 1824.

**40(b) his poems as they were printed** a bound volume of Byron's poems in the James Hogg Collection, Special Collections, University of Otago Library, Dunedin, New Zealand contains *Hebrew Melodies* (1815), *The Siege of Corinth* and *Parisina* (1816), *The Prisoner of Chillon, and Other Poems* (1816), *The Lament of Tasso* (1817), and *Manfred, A Dramatic Poem* (1817). A note by Hogg's daughter, Mrs Garden, records that the volume once bore an autograph inscription by Lord Byron, since stolen. Part of the fly-leaf has been cut away.

**40(c) sent him a very abusive letter** this does not appear to have survived, though Hogg relates in his letter to Byron of 14 October 1814 (John Murray Archive, Box A 31 5) that he has quarrelled with Scott. According to this letter Scott had agreed to contribute to the second number of the poetical repository, and their quarrel was about Scott's criticisms of a drama by Hogg. Mack is almost certainly correct, however, in suggesting that Hogg had strong reasons for concealing from Byron that Scott had refused to help with the poetical repository, since 'Byron would be unlikely to contribute if Scott had refused, and a contribution from either Scott or Byron was essential if the project were to succeed' (p. 91).

**40(d) "The Poetic Mirror, or Living Bards of Britain."** was published by John Ballantyne and Longmans in October 1816. It was advertised for 1 October in the *Edinburgh Evening Courant* of 5 September, and as 'Today is published' in the paper for 12 October, price 7s. 6d. It was included among the 'New Works Published in Edinburgh' in *Scots Magazine*, 78 (October 1816), 773.

**40(d) my imitations of Wordsworth and Lord Byron** the Wordsworth imitations in the volume were 'The Stranger' (pp. 131–53), 'The Flying Tailor' (pp. 155–70), and 'James Rigg' (pp. 171–87). The first poem in the book, 'The Guerilla' (pp. 3–

26), was an imitation of Byron.

**40(d) Mr. Ballantyne** possibly John Ballantyne (1774–1821), the publisher of the work, though this may have been his elder brother James Ballantyne (1772–1833), who was noted as a particularly fine reader. A second, anonymous, account of this performance was written by Hogg and has partly survived in NLS MS 2245, fols 301–02.

**41(a) the Bridge** that is, the North Bridge joining Edinburgh's New Town and Old Town.

**41(a) except a very small proportion** recollecting his visit to Wilson at Elleray in the autumn of 1814 in his *Songs by the Ettrick Shepherd* (1831) Hogg says, 'I likewise wrote "The Stranger" and "Isabelle" there, both to be found in the Poetic Mirror' (p. 118).

**41(a) Epistle to R— S—** for further information on Thomas Pringle see note to 39(b). Mack remarks (p. 39) that the poem gained Pringle Scott's friendship and there is an undated note from Scott to Hogg praising the poem in the Beinecke Rare Book and Manuscript Library, Yale University (GEN MSS 266, Box 1, Folder 17). After Pringle's name in the 1821 Memoir Hogg had written 'who has now left this country (a circumstance ever to be regretted)' (pp. lix–lx).

**41(a) another small secret** two possible explanations may exist of this secret. Firstly, the imitation of John Wilson's poetry in 'The Morning Star' consists largely of rearranged lines of his own work, as Antony Hasler has pointed out: 'most of "The Morning Star" is by Wilson, with a few minor but devastating readjustments by Hogg'—see 'Ingenious Lies: *The Poetic Mirror* in Context', *Papers Given at the Second James Hogg Society Conference (Edinburgh 1985)*, ed. by Gillian Hughes (Aberdeen: ASLS and the James Hogg Society, 1988), pp. 79–96 (p. 83). The review of Hogg's *Altrive Tales* in *Fraser's Magazine*, 5 (May 1832), 482–89 (p. 489), however, goes further than this in saying, 'Apropos, Hogg is absurd when he says that there is a secret connected with his *Poetic Mirror* which he is not at liberty to unfold; it is merely that Wilson wrote the parody of himself, as Croker very well guessed in his review of that book in the *Quarterly*'.

**41(b) another of seven hundred and fifty copies** a second edition of *The Poetic Mirror* was published in December 1816, though with an 1817 title-page. It was advertised as 'This day is published' priced 7s. 6d. in the *Edinburgh Evening Courant* of 16 December, and included among the 'New Works published in Edinburgh' in the *Scots Magazine*, 78 (December 1816), 934. Hogg's letter to George Boyd of 8 March 1820 (NLS Acc. 5000/188) states that each of the two editions of *The Poetic Mirror* consisted of 750 copies. Perhaps because Hogg was known to be the author by the time the second edition was published, sales were surprisingly slow. Hogg's letter to the publisher George Boyd of 5 May 1821 (NLS Acc. 5000/188) refers to unsold copies which he wished him to put out as a third edition.

**41(b) "The Gude Greye Katte,"** Hogg later thought of republishing this self-parody among his other ballads in *A Queer Book* (1832)—see his letter to Blackwood of 9 March 1831 (NLS MS 4029, fols 249–50).

**41(b) two volumes of Tragedies** Hogg's *Dramatic Tales* was published in two volumes by John Ballantyne in 1817, price 14s. It was advertised as 'This day is published' in the *Edinburgh Evening Courant* of 24 May 1817.

**41(c) "Sir Anthony Moore"** was published in *Dramatic Tales*, I, 135–274. The plot of Hogg's play seems to owe something to Shakespeare's *Romeo and Juliet*.

**41(d) "All-Hallow Eve"** was published in *Dramatic Tales*, I, 1–134. For Robert Morehead see note to 32(c).

**42(a) "The Profligate Princes"** was published in *Dramatic Tales*, II, 1–187.

**42(b) "The Haunted Glen"** was published in *Dramatic Tales*, II, 189–271.

**42(b) an epic poem on a regular plan** Hogg's *Queen Hynde* was published in December 1824, and advertised as 'This day is published' in the *Edinburgh Weekly Journal* for 8 December 1824.

**42(c)–43(b) Several years subsequent [...] no interest in it** a new passage in *Altrive Tales*, as Mack (p. 41) notes. The preceding phrase 'I determined to write no more poetry' replaced 'I have never written another line of poetry' in the 1821 Memoir (p. lxii).

**42(c) "Queen Hynde,"** for the history of this poem, published at the end of 1824, see *Queen Hynde*, ed. by Suzanne Gilbert and Douglas S. Mack (S/SC, 1998), pp. xiv–xvi, xlvii–lix.

**42(c–d) Blackwood [...] claimed the half** Longmans' letter to Blackwood of 28 October 1824, offering Blackwood a quarter-share of the edition, is quoted in *Queen Hynde*, ed. by Suzanne Gilbert and Douglas S. Mack (S/SC, 1998), pp. 221–22.

**42(d) the Highlandman's character** in his 'Anecdotes of Highlanders' in the *Edinburgh Literary Journal*, 24 October 1829, pp. 293–95 Hogg relates that the anecdote was told to him by Rev. James M'Queen of Skye about 'a man of the name of M'Pherson, from the Braes of Lochaber' who wanted one of his children baptised (p. 293).

**42(d) Jerdan** William Jerdan (1782–1869) was editor and part-proprietor of the weekly London literary paper, *The Literary Gazette*, and in 1821 assisted in establishing the Royal Society of Literature. *The Literary Gazette* was often the first periodical to issue a review of a newly-published book, and reviewed *Queen Hynde* on 25 December 1824, pp. 817–19.

**42(d) Mr. Wordsworth's plan** perhaps a reference to Wordsworth's two-volume *Poems*, published by Longmans in 1815. Reacting to his critics in the Preface (I, vii–xlii) he looked forward to the justification of posterity from 'a recollection of the insults which the Ignorant, the Incapable, and the Presumptuous have heaped upon' his writings (p. xxxi). An 'Essay, Supplementary to the Preface' (I, 341–75) attempts to prove that most of the major poets of the past have been undervalued by their contemporaries, and that by analogy with painting 'the qualities which dazzle at first sight, and kindle the admiration of the multitude, are essentially different from those by which permanent influence is secured' (I, 373).

**42(d)–43(a) a public dinner** *Queen Hynde* was advertised in the *Edinburgh Evening Courant* as 'This day is published' on 18 December 1824. The same issue records a dinner of the Scottish Border Club at Barry's Hotel, Prince's Street, on the previous day, with 'Dr Aitken in the chair, supported by the Ettrick Shepherd'. Although the toasts are not specified it seems probable that one to the success of Hogg's new work might well have been included.

**43(b) Mr. Thomas Pringle** see note to 39(b).

**43(c) Mr. Gray** see note to 26(c) for further information on Gray. He seems to have been involved with another periodical at this time, for Hogg's letter to Pringle of 21 August 1818 (cited with permission of the Department of Special Collections, Kenneth Spencer Research Library, University of Kansas: MS P146:1) mentions among other annoyances 'the stopping of Gray's review'.

**43(d) inclosed it in another** this letter does not appear to have survived.

**43(d) Cleghorn** James Cleghorn (1778–1838) had been a farmer, but moved to Edinburgh in 1811 and edited the *Farmer's Journal*. He was the founder of the Scottish Provident Assurance Company, and a well-thought-of actuary. His address is given as 'Rose bank' in the Edinburgh postal directory for 1814–15 (p. 53).

**44(a) a letter from Mr. Blackwood** the magazine was first published in April 1817, so that the fourth month would be July of that year. Blackwood's letter does not appear to have survived, but Hogg's letter to him of 12 August 1817 (NLS MS 4002, fols 155–56) reveals that he had recently been in Edinburgh and contains a refusal to come in to town again. By that time Blackwood had clearly resolved on parting company with Pringle and Cleghorn and making a fresh start with the magazine, for Hogg says: 'I regret much that you have told me so little of your plan; if the name is to change who is to be Editor &c.'.

**44(b) enlisted under the banners of Mr. Constable** a new series of the *Scots Magazine* under the title of the *Edinburgh Magazine and Literary Miscellany* 'for August 1817' was advertised as to be published on 1 September, price 2s., in the *Edinburgh Evening Courant* of 28 August 1817. A subsequent advertisement in the same newspaper for 27 September states, 'The Editors of the Edinburgh Monthly Magazine, a work of which the discontinuance has just been announced, beg leave to intimate, that they have now undertaken to act as Editors of the Edinburgh Magazine and Literary Miscellany. They are happy in being enabled to state, that they have received the most satisfactory assurances of support, not only from the extensive circle of literary friends, with whose assistance they planned and so successfully carried on their former publication, but also from a number of other distinguished individuals, who have engaged to contribute their effective aid to this new series of the earliest and most esteemed Repository of Scottish Literature'.

**44(b) letters from both parties** these have not apparently survived.

**44(c) the "Chaldee Manuscript,"** Hogg's original manuscript (in NLS MS 4807, fols 2–4) seems to have accompanied his letter to Blackwood of 25 September 1817 (fol. 1). The published version is 'Translation from an Ancient Chaldee Manuscript', *Blackwood's Edinburgh Magazine*, 2 (October 1817), 89–96. The additions are generally attributed to Lockhart and Wilson.

**44(d)–45(a) Certain of my [...] responsibility there** a new passage in *Altrive Tales*, as Mack notes (p. 44).

**44(d) sneer at my assumption** there are a number of passages mocking Hogg's claim to be the author of the Chaldee Manuscript in the 'Noctes Ambrosianae' series of *Blackwood's Edinburgh Magazine*–in the very first number, for example, Odoherty declares 'I'll claim it myself. I'll challenge Hogg if he disputes the point' (*Blackwood's Edinburgh Magazine*, 11 (March 1822), 369–71 [mispaged] (p. 374)).

**44(d)–45(a) the original proof slips** a set of four proof slips of 'Translation from an Ancient Chaldee Manuscript' marked with Hogg's corrections and additions survives in the British Library (C.60.k.4), but since the printed text appears to be the result of changes made by Blackwood's Edinburgh contributors they do not show which parts of the article are attributable to Hogg himself. They appear to be the proofs referred to in Hogg's letter to Blackwood of 19 October 1817 (NLS MS 4807, fols 34–35). Hogg marked his corrections on these for his own satisfaction while realising that it was too late for him to influence the published text. Hogg says of its faults, 'I have remedied that in proof in a great measure but alas it is out of time!'.

**45(a) three of Mr. Blackwood's letters relating to the article** these have not apparently survived.

**45(b) confessed the matter to Mr. George Thomson** in his letter to Thomson of 29 November [1817] (British Library Add. MS 35,264, fols 320–21) Hogg is clearly responding to Thomson's comments on the 'Chaldee Manuscript' when he writes, 'I have laughed immoderately at one part of yours You should take very good care my dear George how you mention such anonymous things in a Magazine and to whom. You could not possibly have been more unfortunate in your remarks'.

**45(c) a long continuation** fragments of this continuation, describing the artists of Edinburgh, survive in the de Beer Collection, Special Collections, University of Otago Library, Dunedin, New Zealand: MS 16.

**45(c) "My little finger [...] father's loins."** see 1 Kings 12. 10.

**45(d) a large pamphlet** Hogg underestimates his own fear of the possible consequences of being recognised as author of the 'Chaldee Manuscript', displayed, for example, in his letter to William Laidlaw of 28 October [1817]—see R. B. Adam, *Works, Letters, and Manuscripts of James Hogg, "The Ettrick Shepherd"* (Buffalo, 1930), p. 7.

**45(d) "The Brownie of Bodsbeck, and other Tales,"** *The Brownie of Bodsbeck; and Other Tales* was published in two volumes by William Blackwood and advertised as 'This day is published' in the *Edinburgh Weekly Journal* of 20 May 1818, price 14s.

**45(d) "Old Mortality,"** Scott's tale about the Covenanters, part of the first series of his *Tales of My Landlord*, advertised as 'This day are published' in the *Edinburgh Evening Courant* of 2 December 1816. Douglas Mack reviews the evidence on the date of composition of Hogg's tale and concludes that it is consistent with Hogg's claim here—see *The Brownie of Bodsbeck*, ed. by Douglas S. Mack (Edinburgh: Scottish Academic Press, 1976), pp. xii–xv.

**46(b) "The Bridal of Polmood"** this was published as the lead story in the second volume of Hogg's *Winter Evening Tales* of 1820—see *Winter Evening Tales*, ed. by Ian Duncan (S/SC, 2002), pp. 259–357.

**46(c) "The Wool-Gatherer,"** was published in *The Brownie of Bodsbeck; and Other Tales*, 2 vols (Edinburgh, 1818), II, 89–228. Hogg seems to have sent this tale to Blackwood with his letter of 13 January 1818 (NLS MS 4003, fol. 86).

**46(c) their minions** during the later 1820s Blackwood frequently sent Hogg's contributions to *Blackwood's Edinburgh Magazine* to David Macbeth Moir, who acted as a publisher's reader for the journal.

**46(d) an intruder in the paths of literature** Hogg expresses the same idea elsewhere, for example in the closing number of *The Spy*—see *The Spy*, ed. by Gillian Hughes (S/SC, 2000), p. 518.

**47(a) the proceedings of a club** another account of the Right and Wrong Club, which seems to have been formed towards the end of 1814, was given by R. P. Gillies in 'Some Recollections of James Hogg', *Fraser's Magazine*, 20 (October 1839), 414–30 (pp. 424–25).

**47(b) Oman's Hotel** Gillies states that this was in the vicinity of Hogg's lodging in Gabriel's Road—see 'Some Recollections of James Hogg', pp. 424–25. The hotelier Charles Oman appears to have changed his premises fairly frequently. In 1805 his tavern was at 29 West Register Street, and in 1810 he opened another in Princes Street, but in 1815 he changed to 22 St Andrew Street—see Marie W. Stuart, *Old Edinburgh Taverns* (London: Robert Hale, 1952), pp. 82–83 and the Edinburgh postal directory for 1811–12, p. 192. Either West Register Street or St Andrew Street would be close to Hogg's lodgings.

**47(d) between two and three in the morning** Gillies in 'Some Recollections of James Hogg' (p. 425) remembers calling on Hogg during his illness 'at three o'clock of a December morning'.

**48(a) John Ballantyne** in a letter to Hogg postmarked 8 January 1815 (NLS 2245, fols 11–12) Ballantyne says, 'The Right Wrong & Right went off ill without you yesterday: The Company, as the invitation was mine, a newly adopted member (or rather a stranger to the Club) & generally acceded to, was smaller than was polite, & I got drunk in pure vengeance'.

**48(a) Dr. Saunders** the Edinburgh postal directory for 1814–15 lists a Dr James Saunders, with an address at 26 Elder Street. Hogg may have become acquainted with Dr Saunders through the Forum, since an advertisement for the debating club in the *Edinburgh Star* of 21 June 1811 mentions a sum of £7 given to 'Private objects of charity under the sanction of Dr. Sanders [*sic*]'. Blackwood's letter to Murray of 21 January 1815 reports Hogg's first outing that day after his illness (John Murray Archive, Blackwood Correspondence, Box 2), while by the time Hogg wrote to Laidlaw on 29 January 1815 (Garden, pp. 81–82) he seems to have recovered sufficiently to have been out curling.

**48(d) wrote an apology to Sir Walter** Hogg's letter to Byron of 14 October 1814 (John Murray Archive, Box A 31 5) helps to date Hogg's quarrel with Scott, since he mentions it in this letter. His letter of apology to Scott is probably the one of 28 February [1815] (NLS MS 3886, fols 84–85).

**49(b) Mr. Wilson [...] "The Field of Waterloo,"** 'The Field of Waterloo' was written in the autumn of 1815, and is mentioned in Hogg's letter to Scott of 16 November [1815] (NLS MS 3886, fols 229–30). Hogg's letter to Wilson of 2 January [1816] calls Wilson 'an officious impudent scoundrel' and 'an ideot and a driveller' (Pierpont Morgan Library, New York: Gordon Ray Collection, GNR MA 4500 H). The first known printing of the poem seems to have been in Hogg's *Poetical Works*, 4 vols (Edinburgh, 1822), II, 281–323, though there may have been a previous pamphlet publication.

**49(c) amused himself [...] at my expense** an allusion to the 'Noctes Ambrosianae' of *Blackwood's Edinburgh Magazine*.

**49(c) one instance** perhaps an allusion to an application for a pension for Hogg made to the Royal Society of Literature. In his letter to Blackwood of 6 April 1830 (NLS MS 4027, fols 181–82) Hogg wrote, 'Every churchman voted against me on the ground of my dissipation as described in the *Noctes* and neither denied by myself nor any friend publicly'. No such vote is recorded, however, in the minutes of meetings of the RSL.

**49(d)–50(a) Of this work it is proper to mention [...] poetical epistle** a new passage in *Altrive Tales*, as Mack (p. 49) notes.

**49(d) the Highland Society of London** a letter from Colonel David Stewart of Garth (1772–1829) of 11 October 1817 (NLS MS 2245, fols 28–29) proposed that George Thomson should compile a collection of Jacobite Songs on behalf of the Highland Society of London, and offered a fee of a hundred pounds or more plus 'assistance in the first instance in making the necessary research, and afterwards in promoting the sale of the work'. Thomson clearly passed the commission on to his friend Hogg. Stewart is the author of *Sketches of the Character, Manners and Present State of the Highlanders of Scotland* (2 vols, Edinburgh, 1822). He assisted Scott in organising the reception of George IV in Scotland in August 1822–see *DNB*, and John Prebble, *The King's Jaunt* (London: Collins, 1988).

**49(d) the Duke of Sussex** Augustus Frederick, Duke of Sussex (1773–1843) was the sixth son of George III.

**50(a) whose language I did not understand** Hogg may not have comprehended spoken Gaelic well, but a number of his works suggest that he certainly had a smattering of Gaelic words and phrases–see, for example, 'Julia M,Kenzie' in *Tales of the Wars of Montrose*, ed. by Gillian Hughes (S/SC, 1996), 138–53. In this passage, as in *Jacobite Relics* itself, Hogg treats Jacobite song as an almost exclusively Gaelic affair, glossing over the predominance of episcopalians and Scots speakers in the tradition–see *The Jacobite Relics of Scotland. [First Series]*, ed. by Murray G. H. Pittock (S/SC, 2002), p. xiii.

**50(a) a poetical epistle** see 'To the Most Noble and Honourable President and Members of the Highland Society of London', *The Jacobite Relics of Scotland. [First Series]*, ed. by Murray G. H. Pittock (S/SC, 2002), pp. v–vi.

**50(a) the first volume in 1819** the first series of *Jacobite Relics* was advertised as 'This day are published' in the *Edinburgh Weekly Journal* of 15 December 1819.

**50(a) second volume until the following year** the two-year gap indicated by the title-page of the second volume is deceptive, for in fact it was advertised as 'This day is published' in the *Edinburgh Weekly Journal* of 21 February 1821, not much more than a year after the appearance of the first volume, as Hogg indicates here.

**50(a–b) The jealousy [...] never do."** a new passage in *Altrive Tales*, as Mack (p. 49) notes. Elsewhere Hogg emphasises that he learned Jacobite songs from the Scots speakers that he socialised with in Edinburgh: 'When I was engaged in collecting the Jacobite relics, my pleasure as well as interest led me very much among the old Jacobite families of Angus and Mearns settled in Edinburgh, for all the Episcopalians of those districts were wonderfully attached to the house of Stuart. In these gentlemen's houses we had numerous supper parties, into which none were invited save sterling Jacobites'–see *The Works of Robert Burns*, ed. by James Hogg and William Motherwell, 5 vols (Glasgow, 1834–36), V, 24.

**50(b) "The Winter Evening Tales,"** the two volumes were advertised as 'This day are published' in the *Edinburgh Weekly Journal* of 26 April 1820, price 14s.

**50(b) written in early life** Hogg may have collected the stories in *Winter Evening Tales* during his years as a shepherd, but he rewrote and revised them extensively before publication in 1820, as Ian Duncan indicates–see *Winter Evening Tales*, ed. by Ian Duncan (S/SC, 2002), p. xiii.

**50(c) indelicacies hinted at by some reviewers** the introduction of the prostitute Clifford Mackay in 'The Renowned Adventures of Basil Lee', *Winter Evening Tales*, 2 vols (Edinburgh, 1820), I, 1–99 seems to have been particularly objected to. The *British Critic* mentions 'characters, whom it is a shame even to talk about, and such as never can be, and never ought to be represented, without exciting nausea and disgust' (new series, 13 (June 1820), 622–31 (p. 622)). The reviewer of *The Scotsman*, 29 April 1820, pp. 143–44 thought that Hogg should read his tales over to his recently-acquired wife and 'strike out every paragraph which, either as to thought or expression, offends her delicacy' (p. 143).

**51(b) Sacred Melodies** presumably *A Selection of German Hebrew Melodies* published in London by C. Christmas. Although Hogg subsequently mentions being applied to for verses 'in 1815', the work appears not to have been published until early in 1818. In his letter to William Blackwood of 5 January 1818 (NLS MS 4003, fols 84–85) Hogg refers to it as 'a London work but not yet published', while by the time he wrote to the composer W. E. Heather on 1 April 1818 (Boston Public Library/Rare Books Department, Mss. Acc. 70: Courtesy of the Trustees), the work must have been published, as Hogg complains of not having received any copies of it.

**51(b–d) To these may now be added [...] man's life** a new passage in *Altrive Tales*, as Mack (p. 51) notes, replacing a paragraph which mentions some of these works in the context of an explanatory passage about the previous context of the 1821 edition of *The Mountain Bard*.

**51(d) a celebrated composer of music** the music for *A Selection of German Hebrew Melodies* (London: C. Christmas, [*c.* 1818]) was composed by W. E. Heather.

**52(a) never paid a farthing** Hogg mentions having eleven copies to sell in his letter to Blackwood of 26 December 1818 (NLS MS 4003, fols 103–04), with the implication that this is all he has for a promised payment of £30. An advertisement for *A Border Garland* in the *Edinburgh Weekly Journal* of 28 April 1819 also advertises this other song-collection at sixteen shillings. The 1821 Memoir (p. lxxvi) continued with a mention of Hogg's design, abandoned by 1832, for a series of song publications under the 'Border Garland' title.

**52(b) allowance for the failing** the 1821 Memoir ends at this point, as Mack (p. 52) notes, with Hogg's 'Reminiscences of Former Days' being entirely new for *Altrive Tales*.

## Reminiscences of Former Days

**53(a) ceased keeping any notes** Hogg's missing journal seems to have been discontinued when Oliver and Boyd published the third edition of *The Mountain Bard*, containing the 1821 Memoir.

**53(b) a letter from the late Duke Charles of Buccleugh** Charles William Henry Scott, 4th Duke of Buccleuch (1772–1819) succeeded to the title in January 1812. This letter survives in NLS MS 2245, fol. 13, and is dated 26 January 1815.

**53(b) by the hands of his chamberlain** according to Hogg's letter to William Laidlaw of 29 January 1815, Major Charles Riddell of Muselee (1755–1849) waited on him the previous day in Edinburgh and gave him the letter–see Garden, pp. 81–82.

**53(b) quite unsolicited** Hogg did not solicit the Duke at the time when the farm was granted, but he had applied to the Duchess for it previously in a letter of 7 March 1813 (in NLS MS 3884, fols 96–97).

**53(d) his beloved partner's death** Harriet, the wife of Charles, 4th Duke of Buccleuch (1773–1814) was the daughter of the 1st Viscount Sidney, and died on 24 August 1814–see Corson, p. 390. She was greatly lamented by both Scott and Hogg as well as her husband. Hogg's poem *The Pilgrims of the Sun* (1814) closes with a lament for her by the Yarrow people she has cherished and by Hogg himself, who declares that when he began the poem he did not realise 'That sad and low the strain should close,/ 'Mid real instead of fancied woes!' (p. 127). He also wrote a poem on hearing of her death which was presented to her widower and published in the Edinburgh newspapers–see Gillian Hughes, 'Hogg's Poetic Responses to the Unexpected Death of his Patron', in *Studies in Hogg and his World*, 12 (2001), 80–89.

**54(a) an untimely grave** Charles Scott, 4th Duke of Buccleuch died on 20 April 1819. He had been born in 1772.

**54(a) lovely in their lives [...] divided** from David's lament for Saul and Jonathan in 2 Samuel 1. 23.

**54(a) built a handsome cottage** Garden (pp. 85–86) records that when Hogg took posession of Altrive in 1815 the old house there was barely weatherproof, and that the inhabitants hung plaids around the door as a screen from the cold. The house Hogg built in 1818 was basically a four-room stone-built structure, with an arrangement that all the smoke from the fires should come out of the kitchen chimney so as not to advertise Hogg's presence at home and encourage idle calls from visitors.

**54(a) married in 1820** Hogg signed the marriage-contract in Dumfries on 27 April 1820, and was married on the following morning at his bride's home of Mouswald Place, a few miles to the east of Dumfries (Parr, pp. 6–7).

**54(a) debts due [...] to the amount of a thousand pounds** Hogg took a nine-year lease of Mount Benger farm from the Buccleuch estate, beginning at Whitsunday (15 May) 1821. John Murray was joint publisher of *The Brownie of Bodsbeck* and an edition of *The Queen's Wake* with William Blackwood, who also published the two volumes of *Jacobite Relics*; Oliver and Boyd published the 1821 edition of *The Mountain Bard* and two editions of *Winter Evening Tales*; and Longmans were to publish the forthcoming *The Three Perils of Man*. It is not known what sums Hogg had been promised for all these publications: but John Murray's ledger for his joint publications (p. 231) states that the author's share of the sixth edition of *The Queen's Wake* was to be £100 (John Murray Archive); on 27 August 1821 Blackwood proposed to give Hogg £80 from himself and Murray as payment for the edition of 1500 copies of *The Brownie of Bodsbeck* (NLS MS 30301, p. 201); a letter from Blackwood to Hogg of 7 December 1819 (NLS MS 2245, fols 34–35) suggests that Hogg was to be paid £150 for the first series of *Jacobite Relics*; a letter from Blackwood to Hogg of 3 August 1820 (NLS MS 2245, fols 42–43) offers £150 for the second series of *Jacobite Relics*; and on 2 August 1819 Oliver and Boyd promised £100 for the first edition of *Winter Evening Tales* (NLS Acc. 5000\188).

**54(b) the Right Honourable Lord Montague** Henry James Scott-Montagu (1776–1845) was the third son of the third Duke of Buccleuch. He was guardian to his nephew, the fifth Duke of Buccleuch, during his minority. Walter Francis Montagu Douglas Scott had been born in 1806, and succeeded as Duke of Buccleuch on the death of his father in April 1819–see Corson, pp. 564, 390.

**54(c) I had not half enough of money** Hogg is silent here, presumably out of consideration for his wife's feelings, as to one reason why he could not afford to stock the Mount Benger farm adequately. His father-in-law, Peter Phillips, had offered to advance Margaret Hogg's inheritance of £1,000 to help with the stock, but had suffered severe financial losses himself in the spring of 1821 and was unable to perform this promise (see Parr, pp. 18, 34–35).

**54(c) seven hundred and fifty pounds** Hogg seems to be thinking of his earnings from book-length publications, and not including his contributions to magazines which would presumably account for the 'smaller sums paid in cash' mentioned here. Hogg states below (p. 55) that he was paid £150 each for *The Three Perils of Man* and *The Three Perils of Woman*. Longmans' payment for *The Three Perils of Man* (1822) cannot be confirmed, but from their letter of 5 May 1823 (University of Reading Library: Longman Archives part 1, Item 101, Letter-book 1820–1825, fol. 357) they do seem to have paid £150 for *The Three Perils of Woman* (1823). The *Confessions of a Justified Sinner* (1824), published on the half-profits plan, appears to have produced little or nothing for Hogg according to Blackwood's letter to him of 23 September 1826 (NLS MS 30309, pp. 385–87), which also reveals that Hogg was to have been paid £150 for *Queen Hynde* (1824). Constable seems to have paid £200 for Hogg's four-volume *Poetical Works* of 1822–see Cadell's letter to Hogg of 16 February 1822 (NLS MS 791, p. 497).

**54(d) without a sixpence in the world** in his letter to Blackwood of 6 April 1830 (NLS MS 4027, fols 181–82), written towards the end of his lease, Hogg stated, 'Times are very bad with me. The cheapness of the live stock will leave me at Whit Sunday without a farthing exclusive of an annual loss I will loss [*sic*] £600= between the buying and the selling'.

**55(b) "George Cochrane,"** see 'The Love Adventures of Mr George Cochrane', in *Winter Evening Tales*, ed. by Ian Duncan (S/SC, 2002), pp. 166–228. Had the series of *Altrive Tales* been continued it would have been reprinted in a subsequent volume. Hogg's claim here that the tale embodied some of his own youthful love adventures is supported by a review of *Winter Evening Tales* in *Blackwood's Edinburgh Magazine*, 7 (May 1820), 148–54 (p. 148), in which the reviewer remarks, 'Not a few of the stories we have of old heard him tell in nearly the same words, with this difference, that instead of the Basil Lees, George Cochranes, Adam Bells, &c. who now figure as their heroes, the adventures were then commonly narrated as having befallen no less a person than the Ettrick Shepherd himself'.

**55(c) rendered the whole perfectly ludicrous** Hogg's expressed view here suggests that it may have been he who removed the supernatural sub-plot from *The Three Perils of Man* to create 'The Siege of Roxburgh' and 'Marion's Jock'–see Note on the Text, pp. 209–10.

**55(c) Allan Cunningham** for further information about Allan Cunningham (1784–1842), see notes to pp. 69–71 below. His three-volume novel, *Sir Michael Scott: A Romance* was published in London by Henry Colburn in 1828. Cunningham's novel opens at Flodden, where the wizard Sir Michael Scott appears and takes James IV of Scotland on a long journey to an abbey, fairyland, Westminster, the land of chivalry, and the gates of heaven. Visions of the Pope and of the future of Scotland are also vouchsafed to the dead king. A modern reader might well agree that Cunningham 'made matters rather worse'.

**55(d) published anonymously** the poor sale of *Confessions of a Justified Sinner* is unlikely to have been due to the fact that it was published anonymously, as it was very generally attributed to Hogg by reviewers as soon as it was published–see

Gillian Hughes, 'The Critical Reception of *The Confessions of a Justified Sinner*', *Newsletter of the James Hogg Society*, 1 (1982), 11–14.

**56(a) "The Lives of Eminent Men;"** this proposed work was to include a number of tales which were later rewritten for *Tales of the Wars of Montrose*–see *Tales of the Wars of Montrose*, ed. by Gillian Hughes (S/SC, 1996), pp. xi–xiii. No letter with the remark quoted appears to have survived, and it is possible that Hogg's negotiations with Longmans for the work were verbal ones. Owen Rees of the Longmans firm was in Edinburgh in September 1825, and Hogg wrote to Blackwood on 1 September expressing his anxiety to meet with him: 'But should I miss Mr Rees tell him that I am going to publish two small works about Martinmass about 7/6 each "The Shepherd's Callander" and "Some passages in the lives of eminent men" and he must send the paper for both on the instant" (NLS MS 4014, fols 289–90).

**56(b) wrangling between Mr. Blackwood and me** Blackwood's account of this transaction is given in his letter to Hogg of 23 September 1826 (NLS MS 30309, pp. 385–87). According to this Blackwood paid Hogg £150 as the entire author's profits for *Queen Hynde* on the understanding that the £100 Hogg had previously received from Longmans would be covered by author's profits from *The Private Memoirs and Confessions of a Justified Sinner.* The London firm, however, included this £100 payment in the account they sent Blackwood subsequently of the expenses of *Queen Hynde.* The bill was to repay Blackwood this debt, since Hogg could not make a cash settlement.

**57(a) Mr. Robert Cadell** Robert Cadell (1788–1849) became Constable's junior partner in 1811, and later made a fortune as the publisher of Scott's and other works.

**57(a) our club** possibly the Dilettanti Society, of which both Hogg and Cadell were members. For details see note to 74(b).

**57(a) a perfect Nabal** Nabal's story is told in I Samuel 25. David and his followers had been careful not to waste the wealthy Nabal's flocks and other goods, but he then denied them food when they asked for it.

**57(a) not the smallest objection** the Constable Letter Book for 1820–1822 (in NLS MS 791, pp. 488–89, 497) confirms Hogg's statement here. Cadell undertook the edition partly at Scott's persuasion and initially offered Hogg £150, but seemed ready enough to accede to Hogg's request for £200, adding 'perhaps we may give you a bill due in 1823'.

**57(b) Mr. Fyffe, his cashier** Corson (p. 463) gives his name as Archibald Fife.

**57(d) what soon after followed** this appears to be a reference to the failure of the publishing firm of Constable & Co. in January 1826, and the part played by Cadell in helping to revive Scott's profitability as an author.

**57(d)–58(a) Sir Walter Scott [...] a hundred pounds** Scott's letter to Ballantyne of [18 October 1822] says, 'I fancy you must renew poor Hoggs bill for him. I suppose I shall have to pay it at last–but will not if I can help it having given him enough'–see *The Letters of Sir Walter Scott*, ed. by H. J. C. Grierson and others, 12 vols (London, 1932–37), VII, 268–69.

**58(b) my best songs** *Songs by the Ettrick Shepherd*, a gift-book style volume, containing 113 songs, was meant to be published at the end of 1830. The *Edinburgh Literary Journal* of 11 December 1830 (p. 365) mentions it as 'to be published on Christmas day', but the issue for 25 December itself speaks of Hogg as 'at present in town, in excellent health and spirits, superintending the publication of his songs' (p. 407): this with the 1831 date on the title-page suggests that the volume was not actually published until very early in the following year. There is a review of it in the *Edinburgh Literary Journal* of 8 January 1831, pp. 23–25.

**58(b) exceedingly well received** Blackwood reported to Hogg in his letter of 26 February 1831 (in NLS MS 30312, pp. 154–56), 'Your Songs are liked by every body, and the sale is going on well' (p. 155).

**58(b) a good sum already** Blackwood's letter to Hogg of 12 March 1831 (NLS MS 30312, pp. 160–61) reveals that he paid Hogg £120 for this edition.

**58(b) the year before last** as Garside shows, production of the volume that was to be published by Blackwood in late April or early May 1832 as *A Queer Book* seems to have been started in March 1831 and completed early in the summer of that year—see *A Queer Book*, ed. by P. D. Garside (S/SC, 1995), p. xxi. Hogg wrote this at the beginning of 1832 during his London visit, and is exaggerating somewhat when he says that the book was printed 'the year before last'.

**58(b) that great bugbear, Reform** in his letter to Hogg of 25 June 1831 (in NLS MS 30312, pp. 200–01) Blackwood explained how the agitation over parliamentary reform was ruining the trade of himself and other publishers: 'Our trade never was in such a state as it is in just now. This cursed Reform agitation has completely put a stop to the sale of Books in London and every where else. It would be ruin therefore to attempt to publish your Ballads till business gets into a more healthy state. I was never so out of spirits in my life, for we have no orders almost at all, and Longman & C° and every publisher is in the same state. Maga is the only thing that keeps us alive' (p. 201).

**58(d) "Oh [...] insufferable beast!"** Blackwood's insolent comments on one particular author, James Hogg, were the subject of a remonstrance in Hogg's letter to him of 2 March 1832 (NLS MS 4033, fols 125–26). Hogg accused him of 'saying before my own wife with your accustomed delicacy "O its delightful to see what a rage he's in when I send him back a cartfu' Manuscripts! It's quite grand!"' (fol. 125r). Hogg's attitude to his wife was particularly protective.

**58(d) now otherwise occupied** probably referring to John Gibson Lockhart, who in 1825 moved to London to become editor of the *Quarterly Review*. Lockhart did, as Hogg suggests, continue to write occasionally for *Blackwood's Edinburgh Magazine* after this date—see, for example, his memorial piece 'Death of Mr Blackwood', *Blackwood's Edinburgh Magazine*, 36 (October 1834), 571–72.

**58(d) worth his weight in gold** John Wilson was certainly as mercurial and undependable as Hogg suggests here, but in fact he continued to be the mainstay of *Blackwood's* until after Hogg's death.

**58(d) Ebony** a black wood, a pun on the Edinburgh publisher's name used in the 'Chaldee Manuscript'.

**59(a) much pain to my family and relations** a reference to the characterisation of the Shepherd in the 'Noctes Ambrosianae'. The evidence suggests that Hogg's wife, Margaret, was particularly resentful of ill treatment of her husband in *Blackwood's Edinburgh Magazine*: in his letter to Blackwood of 4 September 1821 (NLS MS 4007, fols 38–39), for instance, Hogg says 'there are other feelings now beside my own that I am bound to respect, and on these the blows that you inflict wound deeper and smart with more poignancy, nor can any palliatives that I can use heal them. I warned you of this when I saw you, and you who are yourself a husband ought to have known it without such a hint'.

**59(a) a solemn written promise** this probably refers to Blackwood's letter to Hogg of 2 and 5 December 1820 (NLS MS 30,002, fols 16–17), in which he stated 'All I can now say is this, that whatever be the consequence, there shall nothing appear in the Magazine of or concerning you, but what you yourself shall previously see'. This is only a promise to give Hogg a previous inspection of such material, and there may have been another to obtain his previous consent to publication. Blackwood's letter of 23 August 1821 (NLS MS 30301, pp. 197–201), (written after Wilson's attack on the 1821 Memoir had been published in *Blackwood's Edinburgh Magazine*) remarks, 'You will tell me however that I ought not to have done this without your consent according to what I wrote you when we had our former disagreeable correspondence' (p. 199). Hogg's letter to Scott of 3 October 1821 (University of London Library, [S.L.]. V. 14) also uses the word consent and gives an earlier date for 'a written promise dated 19 months back most solemnly given "that my name should never be mentioned in his mag. without my own consent"'.

**59(b) a Masque or Drama** Hogg's *The Royal Jubilee* of 1822 was written to commemorate George IV's visit to Scotland in August of that year, and published on 14 August (see the *Edinburgh Advertiser* of 13 August 1822, p. 103). Peel's letter, dated 'Melville Castle, Edinburgh, Thursday morning, six o'clock' was addressed to Scott and not to Hogg himself–see the James Hogg Collection, Special Collections, University of Otago Library, New Zealand (MS Item 1).

**59(a) In the spring of 1829** although a new urgency entered Hogg's correspondence with Blackwood on the subject of a collected edition of his prose fiction after the expiry of his lease of the Mount Benger farm, he seems to have been discussing a collected edition of his tales with his Edinburgh publisher as early as January 1825 at least–see Introduction, pp. xii–xvii.

**59(c) He and I waited on Mr. Lockhart subsequently** in his letter to Blackwood of 26 May 1830 (NLS MS 4036, fols 102–03) Hogg said, 'as my good taste has been watched with a jealous eye by the literati I would have the work published under the sanction of Lockhart'. His subsequent letter of 21 June 1830 (NLS MS 4027, fols 188–89) says, 'I reccollect [*sic*] my tryste at Mr Lockhart's on the 3[d] of July'. Lockhart and his family were staying at Chiefswood on the Abbotsford estate on a visit to Scott and their other Scottish friends.

**59(d) whither I had proposed going** the expiry of Hogg's lease at Mount Benger at Whitsunday 1830 left him penniless but also meant that his time was less occupied with farming, and he seems then to have had a hankering after London. In his letter to Blackwood of 28 April 1830 (in NLS MS 4027, fols 185–86) he asks, 'Do you not think that in London I could be well employed in some literary capacity'.

**59(d)–60(a) I carried it at once to London** Hogg travelled to London immediately after his rupture with Blackwood in December 1831, arriving on 31 December.

**60(a) more than one friend** besides Lockhart, Hogg seems to have counted on the assistance of Allan Cunningham and Thomas Pringle in preparing his *Altrive Tales* for the press.

**60(b) a partial conclusion** Hogg died on 21 November 1835, and his Memoir was never updated again.

***Sir Walter Scott***

**60(b) One fine day** 'Reminiscences of Former Days' includes sections on Scott and on Cunningham previously published by Hogg as articles under that title in the *Edinburgh Literary Journal* of 1829. 'Reminiscences of Former Days. My First Interview with Sir Walter Scott' appeared in the issue for 27 June 1829, pp. 51–52 (referred to below as *ELJ*)–see Note on the Text, pp. 201–02.

**60(b) the summer of 1801** this must have been 1802, as Hogg goes on to mention that he had seen the first two volumes of *Minstrelsy of the Scottish Border*, published in February of that year. Hogg's first meeting with Scott is difficult to date more precisely. Hogg's memory is more likely to be correct about the season than the precise year, and there is evidence that Scott planned to be in Ettrick Forest in July. This appears to be the time favoured by Rubenstein (p. 109). Hogg's correspondence with Scott, however, is ambiguous on the point: his letter to Scott of 30 June [1802] (NLS MS 3874, fols 114–15) describes his correspondent as 'a person I had seen and conversed with', suggesting an earlier meeting, while that of 10 September [1802] (NLS MS 877, fols 243–44) reveals a greater ease and intimacy and may imply that the meeting took place just before this letter was written in early autumn. As with the date of Hogg's birth, the date of this crucial first meeting with Scott may never be precisely identified.

**60 (b) Ettrick House** the small farm Hogg tenanted as a home to his parents between 1800 and 1803–see p. 16.

**60(b) Wat Shiel** has not been identified. As Garside indicates, in his exploration of possibilities for the William Shiel who excavates the corpse of a Yarrow suicide, Shiel is a common name in the district–see *The Private Memoirs and Confessions of a Justified Sinner*, ed. by P. D. Garside (S/SC, 2001), pp. 249–50.

**60(c) Ramseycleuch** this farm was tenanted by Walter and George Bryden, cousins of William Laidlaw–see Edgar Johnson, *Sir Walter Scott: The Great Unknown*, 2 vols (London: Hamish Hamilton, 1970), I, 191.

**60(c) the Shirra** Scott had been appointed Sheriff-Depute of Selkirkshire on 16 December 1799 with a salary of £300 per annum–see Edgar Johnson, *Sir Walter Scott: The Great Unknown*, 2 vols (London: Hamish Hamilton, 1970), I, 170.

**60(c) a number of old ballads** *ELJ* has 'a number of old things' (p. 51).

**60(d) the ballad of Old Maitlan'** published in the third volume of Scott's *Minstrelsy of the Scottish Border* (Edinburgh, 1803), pp. 1–41. Rubenstein (pp. 109–10) notes that Hogg had sent Scott a copy of the ballad through Laidlaw in the spring of 1802, and that Scott quoted an extract from Hogg's letter to him of 30 June 1802 in his introduction to it in *Minstrelsy* (pp. 9–10). She also notes Hogg's other account of this encounter between his mother and Scott in his 'Lines to Sir Walter Scott, Bart.', *The Poetical Works of James Hogg*, 4 vols (Edinburgh, 1822), IV, 131–40.

**60(d) from the singing of another Laidlaw** Hogg seems originally to have transmitted his copies of ballads to Scott through William Laidlaw, subsequently opening a direct correspondence with Scott by his letter of 30 June [1802] (NLS MS 3874, fols 114–15), which mentions recovering another portion of 'Auld Maitland'. The Laidlaw mentioned as a singer here is probably Hogg's maternal uncle, William Laidlaw (1735–1829).

**61 (a) Andrew Moor** Andrew Moore was the servant of the Rev. Thomas Boston, minister of Ettrick from 1707 to 1732. Hogg mentions Moore in his notes to *The Mountain Bard* (Edinburgh, 1807) as follows: 'Andrew Moore, who died at Ettrick about 26 years ago, at a great age [...]. This singular old man could repeat by heart every old ballad which is now published in the "Minstrelsy of the Border," except three, with three times as many; and from him, *Auld Maitland*, with many ancient songs and tales, still popular in that country, are derived' (p. 69).

**61(a) Baby Mettlin** a familiar form of Isabella Maitland.

**61(a) the first laird o' Tushilaw** a Mr Anderson was the first laird of Tushielaw from 1688 to 1721 or 1724 (Rubenstein, p. 110).

**61(a) George Warton** has not been identified.

**61(a) James Steward** has not been identified.

**61(b) Mr. Scott's liveryman** has not been identified.

**62(a) near the beginning of the Black Dwarf** alluding to the first chapter of Scott's anonymous tale, published in 1816 as part of the first series of *Tales of My Landlord*. In Scott's tale Jedidiah Cleishbothom really does misunderstand the terms of the dispute in question–see *The Black Dwarf*, ed. by P. D. Garside, EEWN 4a (Edinburgh: Edinburgh UP, 1993), pp. 12–13. During this period the old black-faced sheep traditionally stocked in the Borders were gradually being replaced by the less hardy, but finer-woolled Cheviot sheep.

**62(a) The next day** Hogg commemorated this expedition in verse in his 'Lines to Sir Walter Scott, Bart.', in *Poetical Works of James Hogg*, 4 vols (Edinburgh, 1822), IV, 131–40.

**62(a) Buccleuch or Mount-Comyn** Rubenstein (pp. 110–11) gives a description of the site of the church from the account of Selkirkshire given by the Royal Commission on the Ancient Monuments of Scotland, and comments on Buccleuch as the place from which the Dukes of Buccleuch, heads of the Scott clan, derive their title. As she indicates, an early Scott clan chief, Sir Walter Scott of Rankleburn (renamed by Hogg at Scott's insistence Sir Ringan Redhough of Mount Comyn), is an important figure in Hogg's novel *The Three Perils of Man* (1822).

**62(a) old Satchells** as Rubenstein notes (p. 111), Walter Scott of Satchells (1616?–94?) was the author of a rhyming history of the Scott clan entitled *A True History of Several Honourable Families of the Right Honourable Name of Scot, in the Shires of Roxburgh and Selkirk, and Others Adjacent: Gathered out of Ancient Chronicles, Histories, and Traditions of our Fathers* (1688; reprinted Edinburgh, 1776). The actual passage (presumably quoted by Hogg from memory here) is 'If Heather-tops had been Meal of the best,/ Then Buckcleugh-mill had gotten a noble grist' (p. 43).

**62(d) an ancient consecrated helmet** Rubenstein (p. 111) points to a possible allusion to the helmet of Mambrino in Cervantes's *Don Quixote*, I, 21. There is also a resemblance to the passage in Scott's own novel *The Antiquary*, where Edie Ochiltree ruins Jonathan Oldbuck's identification of the Praetorium of the Kaim of Kinprunes by calling, 'I mind the bigging o't'–see *The Antiquary*, ed. by David Hewitt, EEWN 3 (Edinburgh: Edinburgh UP, 1995), p. 30.

**62(d) a terribly high-spirited horse** possibly Brown Adam, on which Scott had executed a series of showy leaps in Selkirk while being instituted as Sheriff of Selkirkshire–see Edgar Johnson, *Sir Walter Scott: The Great Unknown*, 2 vols (London: Hamish Hamilton, 1970), I, 173.

**63(a) our shoe-lachets** Rubenstein (p. 111) notes that in *Rob Roy* Scott mentions the eponymous outlaw's unusually long arms as verging upon deformity, enabling him to 'tie the garters of his hose without stooping' and giving him a resemblance to 'the old Picts' who were also noted for their length of arm. *ELJ* (p. 52) simply uses the word 'shoes' here.

**63(b) Mr. Brydon of Crosslee** George Bryden of Crosslee (1786–1837) was the son of the Hogg family's early friend and patron, Walter Bryden–see note to 12(d).

**63(b)–64(b) His memory, or, perhaps [...] next day was no worse** a new passage for *Altrive Tales* that is not in the previous version of the Scott section of Hogg's reminiscences published in *ELJ*, as Mack (p. 65) notes.

**63(b) a pleasant instance of it recorded lately** the occasion of Scott's recalling 'The Pleasures of Hope' from memory has not been identified; but see Rubenstein (pp. 113–14) for a possible origin.

**63(c) Skene of Rubislaw** Scott's friend James Skene of Rubislaw (1775–1864) had antiquarian and artistic interests and shared his love of the Scottish countryside.

**63(c) Elibank March** Scott's country home until the spring of 1812 was at Ashiestiel, near Clovenfords, in the neighbourhood of Elibank.

**63(c) Rob Fletcher** Rubenstein (p. 114) suggests that this may be James Fletcher, gamekeeper to the Duke of Buccleuch.

**63(c–d) "Gilmanscleuch." [...] never been either printed or penned** the incident therefore dates from before the first appearance of 'Gilmanscleuch' in *The Mountain Bard* (Edinburgh, 1807), pp. 35–49. The poem, which relates to the history of the Scott clan, appears to have been a favourite with Scott.

**63(d) "The Abbot of Aberbrothock,"** as Rubenstein notes (p. 114) Southey's 'The Inchcape Rock' (the title of his poem about the Abbot of Aberbrothock) was published in his *Metrical Tales and Other Poems* in 1805. Scott and Southey visited each other that year.

**64(a) old Laidlaw of the Peel** Robert Laidlaw (known as 'Laird Nippy') was tenant of Peel, a farm adjacent to Ashiestiel, and sublet the sheep farm portion of Ashiestiel from Scott (Rubenstein, p. 114).

**64(a) the more mischief, the better sport** a proverb associated with Lord Lovat, who is supposed to have used these words at his execution for treason after the failure of the Jacobite Rising of 1745, on hearing that a gallery filled with spectators had collapsed and that many deaths had resulted.

**64(a) "An' gin the boat [...] to row;"** identified by Rubenstein (pp. 114–15) as from the song 'The Weary Pund o' Tow', cited from Robert Chambers, *The Songs of Scotland Prior to Burns* (Edinburgh, 1862), pp. 203–05.

**64(b) leaving Altrive Lake** Hogg did not take possession of the small farm of Altrive Lake until Whitsunday 1815–see Peter Garside, 'Hogg, Eltrive, and *Confessions*', *Studies in Hogg and his World*, 11 (2000), 5–24 (p. 8). Rubenstein (p. 115) dates the expedition to the summer of 1817.

**64(b) my dear friend William Laidlaw** *ELJ* (p. 52) reads 'the same Mr. Laidlaw', the revision being necessitated by the introduction of the preceding anecdote with its mention of 'old Laidlaw of the Peel'.

**64(b) Sir Adam Fergusson** Scott's friend Sir Adam Ferguson (1770–1855) was the son of the philosopher, Adam Ferguson, and Scott's tenant at Huntlyburn on the Abbotsford estate.

**64(b) The Grey Mare's Tail** a spectacular waterfall between St Mary's Loch in Selkirkshire and the town of Moffat, fed by a burn from Loch Skene in the hills above it.

**64(b) Clavers** the persecutor of the Covenanters, John Graham, Earl of Claverhouse and Viscount Dundee (1649?–1689). Even his horse was supposed to be demonic: Hogg relates that 'the marks of that infernal courser's feet are shewn to this day on a steep, nearly perpendicular, below the Bubbly Craig, along which he is said to have ridden at full speed, in order to keep sight of a party of the flying Covenanters'–see *The Brownie of Bodsbeck*, ed. by Douglas S. Mack (Edinburgh and London: Scottish Academic Press, 1976), p. 75.

**64(b–c) to Moffat [...] some of his family** the party were probably on their way to the Buccleuch mansion of Drumlanrig, near Thornhill, Dumfriesshire.

**64(c) his subsequent works** Hogg presumably had in mind an earlier description of the scene in the Introduction to Canto Second of *Marmion*, as Rubenstein indicates (p. 115).

**64(d) if I outlive him** this intimation of Hogg's *Familiar Anecdotes of Sir Walter Scott* (New York, 1834) was first given in the original of this section, 'Reminiscences of Former Days. My First Interview with Sir Walter Scott', *Edinburgh Literary Journal*, 27 June 1829, pp. 51–52 (p. 52). On Scott's death *The Athenaeum* noted (29 September 1832, p. 635), 'THE papers are filled with anecdotes, narratives, and memoirs of Sir Walter Scott: [...]. We shall have many biographies of him; Hogg threatens one [...]', going on to quote this passage from *Altrive Tales*.

**64(d) five months and ten days younger** Scott had been born on 15 August 1771, and Hogg (having been baptised on 9 December 1770) was certainly the older of the two. However, he gives his date of birth as 25 January 1772 in the 'Memoir' (see p. 12 above), from which he calculates the difference in their ages here.

**65(a) inspired me with a determination immediately** in the 'Memoir' (see p. 21) Hogg states that dissatisfaction with the ballad imitations of the third volume of *Minstrelsy of the Scottish Border* was the immediate spur to his own composition of ballad imitations, rather than Scott's earlier enthusiasm for the traditional ballads themselves. But in both passages Scott's influence inspires Hogg's creativity.

**65(a) dedicated "The Mountain Bard"** *ELJ* (p. 52) reads 'Of course I dedicated The Mountain Bard to him'. The dedication reads 'To Walter Scott, Esq. Sheriff of Ettrick Forest, and Minstrel of the Scottish Border, the following Tales are respectfully inscribed by his friend and humble servant, the Author.'

**65(a–b) Bless'd be [...] o'er my cradle sung** a quotation from Hogg's tribute to

'Walter the Abbot' in the conclusion to his best-known narrative poem–see *The Queen's Wake: A Legendary Poem*, fifth edition (Edinburgh and London, 1819), pp. 336–37.

***Southey***

**65(b) My first interview with Mr. Southey** Hogg appears to have met the poet Robert Southey (1774–1843) during his visit to the Lakes in September 1814. He was on a visit to Wilson at Elleray, and had been accompanied by Wordsworth and his wife for part of the journey–see p. 67. The two poets had, however, previously corresponded and Southey had sent Hogg the poem 'To Mary'–see *The Spy*, ed. by Gillian Hughes (S/SC, 2000), pp. 220–21 and note on p. 600. Hogg's trip to the Lakes seems to have been partly motivated by his desire to elicit contributions to his projected 'Poetical Repository' (see pp. 39–41).

**65(b) Queen's Head inn** the inn, in the vicinity of the market-place, in Keswick, was extensively refurbished in the Victorian period and is now known as the Queen's Hotel. It was presumably one of the town's principal inns, since John Hatfield, the imposter who married the 'Maid of Buttermere' established himself there in 1802, posing as an aristocrat and Member of Parliament–see Grevel Lindop, *A Literary Guide to the Lake District* (London: Chatto & Windus, 1994), p. 168.

**65(c) Greta Hall** Mack (p. 67) says, 'Southey moved to Greta Hall, Keswick, in 1803 and made it his home for the rest of his life. In 1795 he had married Edith Fricker, whose sister became the wife of Coleridge. Greta Hall consisted of two houses under one roof, and Coleridge and his family moved into one of these houses in 1800. By 1809 Coleridge had practically left his family, and they became Southey's dependants'.

**65(d) little that is worth drinking** an allusion to Scotch whisky, which is still a powerful icon of national identity. Hogg himself was famous for brewing whisky punch, and it is a sign of the foreignness of Keswick that the spirit in the punch there is rum instead.

**65(d) his nephew, young Coleridge** Samuel Taylor Coleridge had two surviving sons in 1814, Hartley (born in 1796), and Derwent (born in 1800). It seems probable that the literary Hartley is intended here.

**66(a) a poem and ballad of his own** Southey's letter to Hogg of 1 December 1814 (in NLS MS 2245, fols 7–8) refers to 'the Ballad of the Devil & the Bishop which Hartley transcribed for you', and which Hogg was to use in his 'projected publication' before it was reprinted in Southey's 'miscellaneous poems collected into three volumes'. The poem is probably 'A True Ballad of St Antidius, the Pope, and the Devil', in *The Minor Poems of Robert Southey*, 3 vols (London, 1815), III, 171–80. It is end-dated '1802'.

**66(a) previously resided a month at Keswick** this may have been in the summer of 1804, ten years previously, after the failure of Hogg's plan to move to Harris–see note to 22(b).

**66(a–b) but of three** in his letter to Byron of 13 September 1814, written from Elleray (University of Oxford, Bodleian Library, MS Dep. Lovelace Byron 155, fols 51–52) Hogg mentions Southey's own family, adding 'Colridge's family likewise reside with him as well as another widow lady who was left without a shilling'.

***Wordsworth***

**66(c–d) the summer that the "Excursion" was first published** Wordsworth's poem was published in July 1814, during his visit to Scotland with his wife Mary and her sister Sara Hutchinson. The party left Rydal Mount on 18 July and reached Edinburgh on 25 August, after making a tour of the Highlands–see Mary Moorman, *William Wordsworth A Biography: The Later Years 1803–1850* (Oxford: Clarendon Press, 1965), pp. 258–59.

**66(c) Mr. James Wilson** the naturalist James Wilson (1795–1856) was the youngest brother of Hogg's friend John Wilson of *Blackwood's Edinburgh Magazine*, and known as 'the Entomologist'.

**66(d) his mother's house** the Wilsons' widowed mother, Margaret, lived at 53 Queen Street–see Elsie Swann, *Christopher North (John Wilson)* (Edinburgh, 1934), p. 56.

**66(d) the celebrated horse-dealer** the other well-known Mr Wordsworth had been operating at the head of Leith Walk as a horse-dealer since at least 1801, as an advertisement in the *Edinburgh Evening Courant* of 2 February 1801 reveals. This mentions that 'his Sale for the SUMMER SEASON, from this date, is to be every Wednesday, and to begin at One o'clock'.

**67(b) I had not then seen his ponderous "Excursion."** the first edition of Wordsworth's poem was an expensive purchase at two guineas. In a letter to Byron of 17 August 1814 Hogg commented that he had only seen it 'on the counter', but when he wrote to Byron again from Elleray on 13 September he reported having read the poem there with Wilson (University of Oxford, Bodleian Library, MS Dep. Lovelace Byron 155, fols 49–50 and 51–52 respectively).

**67(b) Old Dr. Robert Anderson** Dr. Robert Anderson (1750–1830) was a literary man rather than a practising physician. He had been editor of the *Edinburgh Magazine* and was a great encourager of young poets. He had earlier contributed to Hogg's paper *The Spy*–for further information see *The Spy*, ed. by Gillian Hughes (S/SC, 2000), p. 558. Wordsworth had been greatly influenced by Anderson's *A Complete Edition of the Poets of Great Britain*, 13 vols (1792–95). Wordsworth later recalled, 'We had lodged the night before at Traquhair, where Hogg had joined us and also Dr. Anderson, the Editor of the British Poets, who was on a visit to the Manse. Dr A. walked with us till we came into view of the Vale of Yarrow and, being advanced in life, he then turned back'–quoted from Simon Curtis, 'James Nicol, Minister of Traquair and Poet', *Studies in Hogg and his World*, 7 (1996), 80–86 (p. 80).

**67(c) my father's cot** Robert Hogg was probably still living in a cottage on the Laidlaw farm of Craig Douglas in Yarrow (see note to 16(d)), since Hogg did not acquire Altrive until the following Whitsunday. This Yarrow excursion took place on 1 September, according to Sara Hutchinson's letter to her sister-in-law of 2 September [1814]–see *The Letters of Sara Hutchinson from 1800 to 1835*, ed. by Kathleen Coburn (London: Routledge & Kegan Paul, 1954), p. 79. Sara Hutchinson's journal notes record 'had refreshment at Hogg's Fathers' Cottage he being a Shepherd in Yarrow–An old man upwards of 80–a fine old Creature' (The Wordsworth Trust, DCMS 77).

**67(c) visited St. Mary's Lake** this visit is referred to by Wordsworth in his 'Extempore Effusion upon the death of James Hogg'. Hogg also accompanied the Wordsworth party to Newark Tower.

**67(c) "Yarrow Visited"** a poem inspired by Wordsworth's visit to Yarrow with Hogg, and the only poem from this Scottish tour to be published in his *Poems*, 2 vols (London, 1815), II, 20–23. It is dated 'September, 1814' and is immediately preceded by 'Yarrow Unvisited' of 1803 (II, 16–19). It was originally (and appropriately) intended as Wordsworth's contribution to Hogg's projected 'Poetical Repository'–see R. P. Gillies, *Memoirs of a Literary Veteran*, 3 vols (London, 1851), II, 148. Hogg says (see p. 39) that Wordsworth afterwards reclaimed his contribution, presumably for publication in his own collection of 1815.

**67(c) "Yarrow Unvisited;"** a poem relating to Wordsworth's 1803 visit to Scotland, first published in his *Poems, in Two Volumes*, 2 vols (London, 1807), II, 31–35.

**67(d) Wordsworth had business** after parting with Hogg the Wordsworth party visited Abbotsford, where they breakfasted with Scott's wife and his daughter

Sophia, although Scott himself was absent. They then lunched with the Earl of Buchan at Dryburgh–see Mary Moorman, *William Wordsworth A Biography: The Later Years 1803–1850* (Oxford: Clarendon Press, 1965), p. 260. Sara Hutchinson's letter to her sister-in-law of 2 September [1814], referred to above, is dated from Kelso and the party intended to be at Hawick on the following day and then to proceed to Burnfoot in Eskdale to collect the Wordsworths' son John, who had been left there with the Misses Malcomson during the Scottish tour.

**67(d) Ryedale Mount** Wordsworth had moved to Rydal Mount early in 1813 and lived there for the remainder of his life.

**67(d) a day and a night before him** that is, on 8 September since the Wordsworth party arrived home to Rydal Mount on 9 September–see Juliet Barker, *Wordsworth: A Life* (London: Viking, 2000), p. 462.

**67(d) his sister** Dorothy Wordsworth (1771–1855) was her brother's constant friend and companion, both before and after his marriage in 1802.

**67(d) the children** Dorothy (born 1804) and William (born 1810). John (born 1803) accompanied his parents home (see note to 67(d)), and Catharine and Thomas had both died in 1812.

**68(a) caricaturing his style in the "Poetic Mirror."** for references to Hogg's Wordsworth imitations in *The Poetic Mirror* see note to 40(d).

**68(a) brought forward in the "Noctes Ambrosianæ,"** in No. XVII, which appeared in *Blackwood's Edinburgh Magazine*, 16 (November 1824), 585–601 (p. 592).

**68(a) one night, when I was there** Sunday, 11 September, from the following report from Whitehaven of a 'Celestial Phenomena', printed in the *Edinburgh Evening Courant* of 15 September 1814:

> WHITEHAVEN, September 13.–A most beautiful streamer was observed here on Sunday night, having much the appearance of a rainbow. Its direction was nearly from east to west; the air perfectly calm, and the sky studded with innumerable stars, which seemed to acquire a milder lustre from the pale steady light of the stranger, which made its appearance about a quarter before eight, and continued nearly three quarters of an hour, when it gently faded away, and was seen no more.

Wordsworth's angry reaction to Hogg's account was expressed in a letter to Edward Quillinan of [14 April 1832], in which he casts doubt upon Hogg's memory of an event that took place eighteen years previously. Wordsworth relates that Hogg and Wilson 'were on their way either to or from Grasmere when they saw the arch and very obligingly came up to tell us of it, thinking, w[h] was the fact, that we might not be aware of the phenomenon'. He seems to have been affronted that Hogg reported him as having uttered the supposedly vulgar word 'fellow', while admitting 'I might on that occasion have been tempted to use a contemptuous expression, for H. had disgusted me not by his vulgarity, w[h] he c[d] not help, but by his self-conceit in delivering confident opinions upon classical literature and other points about w[h] he c[d] know nothing'–see *The Letters of William and Dorothy Wordsworth: Volume V Part II, 1829–1834*, second edition, ed. by Ernest de Selincourt, revised by Alan G. Hill (Oxford: Clarendon Press, 1979), pp. 517–18.

**68(b) Lloyd** see note to 39(b).

**68(b) De Quincey** Thomas De Quincey (1785–1859), the author of *Confessions of an English Opium Eater* (1822), was living at the cottage of Townend in the Lake District in 1814.

### *Allan Cunningham*

**69(b) some three-and-twenty years ago** this passage of the 'Memoir' was first published as 'Reminiscences of Former Days. My First Interview with Allan Cunningham', in *Edinburgh Literary Journal*, 16 May 1829, pp. 374–75, and as Mack

(p. 71) notes was reprinted in *Altrive Tales* with a few minor alterations in the wording–see Note on the Text, pp. 201–02. This first printing is dated '*Mount-Benger, May* 6, 1829' so that the phrase 'some three-and-twenty years ago' probably refers to the autumn of 1806.

**69(b) my master's ewes** Hogg was employed as a shepherd by Mr. Harkness of Mitchellslacks near Thornhill in Dumfriesshire for two years from Whitsunday 1805 until Whitsunday 1807, when he became tenant of two farms, Corfardin and Locherben, leased with the profits of *The Mountain Bard* and *The Shepherd's Guide*.

**69(b) by their way of walking** a shepherd would be able to walk along the slope of a steep hill at speed: an old joke has it that for this reason a shepherd can be recognised by the fact that he has one leg longer than the other.

**69(b) my old dog Hector** Hector was commemorated in 'A Shepherd's Address to his auld Dog Hector', *Scots Magazine*, 67 (December 1805), 943–44, reprinted as 'The Author's Address to his auld dog Hector' in *The Mountain Bard* of 1807 (pp. 183–89). He also features largely in 'Dogs' in *The Shepherd's Calendar*, ed. by Douglas S. Mack (S/SC, 1995), pp. 57–67. Hogg's letter to Eliza Izett of 11 December 1808 (Beinecke Rare Book and Manuscript Library, Yale University, GEN MSS 61, Box 1, Folder 13) reveals that he was fatally injured by a horse towards the end of 1808.

**69(c) seemingly approaching to forty** James Cunningham, the eldest of the Cunningham brothers, had been born in 1765–see Rev. David Hogg, *Life of Allan Cunningham* (Dumfries and London, 1875), p. 7. Hogg therefore slightly underestimates his age.

**69(c) youth of about eighteen** Allan Cunningham had been born on 7 December 1784, making him rather older than Hogg's estimate here. At the age of eleven he had been apprenticed as a stonemason to his brother James in Dalswinton in Dumfriesshire, but had begun reading and writing poetry–see Rev. David Hogg, *Life of Allan Cunningham* (Dumfries and London, 1875), pp. 17–18.

**69(d) an accusation regarding some of the lasses** it was during his Dumfriesshire years that Hogg fathered at least two illegitimate daughters: his daughter Catherine was probably conceived around Hallowe'en 1806 while he was serving at Mitchelslacks–see Gillian Hughes, 'James Hogg and the "Bastard Brood"', *Studies in Hogg and his World*, 11 (2000), 56–68.

**69(d) the Duke of Queensberry** William Douglas became 4th Duke of Queensberry in 1778 and died in 1810, when this title passed to the Duke of Buccleuch.

**70(b) Thomas Mouncey** for information about Thomas Mounsey Cunningham (1776–1834) see note to 24(b). It seems probable that he and Hogg never actually met.

**70(b) put his poetical vein under lock and key** Thomas Cunningham's output as a poet was spasmodic. On leaving for England in 1797 he was advised by his father's employer, Mr Patrick Miller of Dalswinton, to renounce poetry, and his contributions to the *Scots Magazine* in 1806 were preceded and followed by a nine-year silence. After contributing a series of papers entitled 'Literary Legacy' to the *Edinburgh Magazine* from 1817 he relapsed into silence again, periodically destroying many of his manuscripts–see Rogers, II, 223–26.

**70(d) the Cunninghams [...] at Dalswinton** the father of the Cunninghams had been land-steward to Mr Patrick Miller of Dalswinton in Dumfriesshire, and James Cunningham was established as a stone-mason and builder there.

**71(a) some imitations of Ossian by him** Cunningham had contributed some poems under the signature of 'Hidallan', the name of one of Ossian's heroes, to a London periodical called *Literary Recreations*, edited by Eugenius Roche, in 1807, telling Roche 'it was the writer's first attempt to have his verses put in print, so as to obtain the high title of an author'–see Rev. David Hogg, *Life of Allan Cunningham* (Dumfries and London, 1875), pp. 41–42.

**71(a) Cromek's "Nithsdale and Galloway Relics"** the engraver Robert Hartley Cromek (1770–1812) made Allan Cunningham's acquaintance while touring Scotland to collect old songs in 1809. Cunningham provided him with his own work, thinly disguised as old songs, which were then published in the *Remains of Nithsdale and Galloway Song* of 1810–see Rev. David Hogg, *Life of Allan Cunningham*, (Dumfries and London, 1875), p. 79. Cunningham was introduced to his subsequent employer, Chantrey, by Cromek.

**71(b) Mr. Morrison** the surveyor John Morrison (1782–1853). His visits to Hogg in Dumfriesshire are recorded in his 'Random Reminiscences of Sir Walter Scott, of the Ettrick Shepherd, of Sir Henry Raeburn, &c., &c.–No. 1', *Tait's Edinburgh Magazine*, 10 (September 1843), 569–78 (pp. 573–74).

**71(b) "Mermaid of Galloway,"** published in *Remains of Nithsdale and Galloway Song*, ed. by R. H. Cromek (London, 1810), pp. 229–48.

**71(b) Gray** Hogg's friend and future brother-in-law, James Gray of the Edinburgh High School–see note to 26(c).

**71(b) Grieve** Hogg's early friend John Grieve–see note to 18(c).

**71(c) to Mr. Jeffrey** that is, presumably, for insertion in the *Edinburgh Review*, of which Jeffrey was editor. Hogg's review and Jeffrey's note do not appear to have survived.

*Galt*

**72(a) most original and most careless writer** the Scottish novelist John Galt (1779–1839), author of *Annals of the Parish* (1821), *The Entail* (1823), *Ringan Gilhaize* (1823), and other works.

**72(a) the summer of 1804** Hans de Groot has shown that this meeting could not have taken place in 1804, as Galt had then left Greenock for London–see 'When did Hogg meet John Galt?', *Studies in Hogg and his World*, 8 (1997), 75–76. De Groot suggests that Hogg probably met Galt for the first time in the summer of 1803, during his return journey from the Outer Hebrides, and that in this reminiscence, written many years subsequently, he unconsciously telescoped two visits to Greenock together.

**73(a) James Park, Esq., junior** see note to 35(c).

**73(a) until I get back** this section of the 'Memoir' was composed during Hogg's visit to London in the first three months of 1832–see Note on the Text, pp. 199–204.

*Lockhart*

**73(b) Lockhart** John Gibson Lockhart (1794–1854), Scott's son-in-law and editor of the *Quarterly Review*, had, like Hogg, been one of the mainstays of the early *Blackwood's Edinburgh Magazine*.

**73(b) I scarcely recollect any thing** for his reminiscences of J. G. Lockhart Hogg seems to have elaborated on information supplied by Lockhart himself in a letter of 25 February 1832–for details given in this and the following notes, see Note on the Text, pp. 202–03.

**73(b) He was [...] everyone who came in contact with him** in his letter of 25 February 1832 Lockhart had written '[...] what was I? an idle youth, fresh from college, dancing after the misses, & drawing caricatures', referring subsequently to 'my graceless caricatures of your noble person' (Pierpont Morgan Library, New York: PML 52349, fol. 158).

**73(b) Oxford puppy** after studying as a teenager at Glasgow university Lockhart won a Snell exhibition to Balliol College where he went in 1809, and took a first-class degree in classics in 1813. He describes himself in his letter of 25 February 1832 as having read none of Hogg's poems and thinking 'there was little poetry worth reading under 2000 years standing' (Pierpont Morgan Library, New York: PML 52349, fol. 158).

**73(c–d) Even his household economy [...] invited his friends also** Lockhart's letter of 25 February 1832 reads 'I daresay you can recall one or two jolly doings when I lived at Maitland Street. I remember the first time you visited me there you expressed great horror to somebody at my extravagance in having *four* black men to wait on a party of six or seven *whites* but found out that this was the result of keeping only *one* black man, whose friends of that complexion clustered round him whenever they smelt a fleshpot' (Pierpont Morgan Library, New York: PML 52349, fol. 158).

**73(d) Sym** see Hogg's reminiscences of him on pp. 76–78, and in particular the note to 76(c).

**73(d)–74(a) supporting Blackwood** Blackwood had begun a magazine in April 1817 with Pringle and Cleghorn as editors, but they quarrelled and the editors soon attached themselves to the rival publisher, Archibald Constable. Hogg, Wilson, and Lockhart adhered to Blackwood and supported the revitalised *Blackwood's Edinburgh Magazine*.

**74(a) his brother, Captain Lockhart** Lockhart was the eldest son of the family, and had four surviving brothers: Laurence (1795–1876); Robert (1805–1859); Richard Dickson (1807–1826); and Archibald Inglis (1810–79). Laurence became a clergyman, and Robert a merchant in Glasgow, but both Richard and Archibald were in the army. Richard was recruited as an ensign in the 63rd Bengal Regiment, but was drowned in the Bay of Bengal in Calcutta in December 1826. Archibald became an ensign in the 92nd Highland Regiment and rose to become a Lieutenant-General. It is not clear whether 'Captain Lockhart' is Richard or Archibald. I thank Mr Richard Jackson for this information about the Lockhart family.

**74(a) Peter Robertson** Patrick Robertson (1794–1855), known as Peter, was a friend of John Wilson's, a successful advocate who was also known for his social and convivial abilities. Scott called him 'Peter o' the Paunch' because of his figure, and Lockhart gives a description of him at the 1819 Burns dinner in *Peter's Letters to his Kinsfolk*, 3 vols (Edinburgh, 1819), I, 142–43.

**74(a) Sheriff Cay** John Cay (1790–1865), was Sheriff of Linlithgow from 1822 onwards, and a friend of Lockhart's. The present editor's copy of the subscription edition of *The Queen's Wake* (1819) contains Hogg's signed receipt for a guinea for copy No. 55, from 'John Cay, Esq. Advocate'.

**74(a) James Wilson** see note to 66(c).

**74(b) Dr. Scott** James Scott, a Glasgow dentist and the 'Odontist' of *Blackwood's Edinburgh Magazine*–see also pp. 75–76. In the *Edinburgh Evening Courant* of 27 May 1813 Scott notified his patients that he had 'sometime ago, been induced, by the increase of his friends at Edinburgh, to extend his practice there for their convenience'. He had just moved from 24 St James's Square to 10 South St Andrew's Street, both addresses in the fashionable New Town of Edinburgh. Scott, whose practice was clearly a busy one, requested that patients should make appointments to see him, to avoid disappointment. Mrs Gordon reproduces a caricature of him by Lockhart, and also mentions his Glasgow address as 7 Miller Street–see *'Christopher North': A Memoir of John Wilson*, 2 vols (Edinburgh, 1862), I, 272.

**74(b) James and John Ballantyne** James Ballantyne (1772–1833) was Scott's old friend and the printer of his works, and John (1774–1821) his younger brother. The mention of John Ballantyne in this connection indicates that Hogg is alluding to the earlier days of his association with Lockhart, for Ballantyne died in June 1821.

**74(b) Sam Anderson** occasionally referred to in the 'Noctes Ambrosianae' of

*Blackwood's Edinburgh Magazine*. Mackenzie has the following note to No. XVI for August 1824: 'Mr. Samuel Anderson, then a wine-merchant in Edinburgh, afterwards, by favor of Lord Brougham, Registrar of the Court of Chancery in London'–see *Noctes Ambrosianae*, ed. by R. Shelton Mackenzie, 5 vols (New York, 1854), I, 476. He features, as 'The Registrar', as a character in 'Noctes Ambrosianae. No. LXV' for May 1834, and is also referred to on p. 77 in Hogg's reminiscences concerning Robert Sym.

**74(b) poor Baxter** has not been identified.

**74(b) the Dilletanti Society** James Nasmyth gives an account of the involvement of his father, the artist Alexander Nasmyth, with the Dilletanti Society in his *Autobiography*, ed. by Samuel Smiles (London, 1883), pp. 35–36: 'Its meetings were held every fortnight, on Thursday evenings, in a commodious tavern in the High Street. The members were chiefly artists, or men known for their love of art. [...] The drinks were restricted to Edinburgh ale and whisky toddy'.

**74(c) Bridges** David Bridges (1776–1840), of the firm of David Bridges and Son–see notes to 32(a) and 34(a). He was the Secretary of the Dilletanti Society.

**74(d) O'Dogherty's principle** Morgan O'Doherty is one of the interlocutors of the 'Noctes Ambrosianae'. In No. I, in *Blackwood's Edinburgh Magazine*, 11 (March 1822), 369–71 [mispaged] (p. 372) he declares, 'I follow one great rule,–never to own any thing that is my own, nor deny any thing that is not my own'.

**74(d) in future, I would sign my name or designation** remarkably few of Hogg's periodical contributions between his arrival in Edinburgh in 1810 and the beginning of *Blackwood's Edinburgh Magazine* in 1817 have been identified. The passage suggests that many of these were anonymous.

**74(d) they signed my name** several spurious articles were assigned to Hogg in *Blackwood's Edinburgh Magazine*. Within the period Hogg mentions his name had been attached to 'Song to a Salmon' and 'L'Envoy; an Excellent New Song in Honour of Dr Scott', 5 (August and September 1819), 610 and 640, 'Letter from the Ettrick Shepherd', 6 (January 1820), 390–93, and 'Sonnet, by the Ettrick Shepherd', 6 (January 1820), 464. In his letter to Margaret Phillips of 14 February 1820 (Stirling University Library, MS 25, Box 4, Item 12) Hogg says, 'They have likewise attached my name to several of their grovelling productions, but not a line in that work has been wrote by me for the last nine months'.

**74(d) those too often applying to my best friends** Norah Parr (p. 40) gives two examples of such embarrassing sayings of the magazine's Shepherd, about Rev. James Russell of Yarrow and Sir Walter Scott respectively. Hogg comments on the one about Russell in his letter to Blackwood of 29 October [1819] (NLS MS 4004, fols 154–55).

**75(a) some humorous poetry** Lockhart seems to have been chiefly responsible for the rhyming Notices to Correspondents in early issues of *Blackwood's*, for example, as well as for 'The Mad Banker of Amsterdam' published in instalments between July 1818 and March 1819–see Alan Lang Strout, *A Bibliography of Articles in Blackwood's Magazine Volumes I through XVII 1817–1825* (Lubbock, Texas: Texas Technological College, 1959), pp. 29, 158–60. Hogg praises the rhyming Notices of the magazine in his letter to William Blackwood of 15 July 1818 (NLS MS 4003, fols 95–96).

**75(a) married on the same day with myself** Hogg married Margaret Phillips on 28 April 1820, and Lockhart married Sophia Scott on 29 April the same year, as Mack (p. 77) indicates.

**75(c) "The Odontist's" songs** James Scott was perhaps less complaisant about Lockhart's assumption of his personality than Hogg suggests here. He wrote to Blackwood on 22 August 1822 and to Galt on 25 August 1822 protesting about 'these objectionable articles where I am alluded to'–see Mrs Oliphant, *Annals of a*

*Publishing House: William Blackwood and his Sons*, 2 vols (Edinburgh and London, 1897), I, 212–13.

**75(d) Captain Tom Hamilton** Thomas Hamilton (1789–1842) was a soldier, and had served in the Peninsular War before retiring to Edinburgh on half-pay in 1818. He lived at Chiefswood on the Abbotsford estate during several summers, was among the writers to *Blackwood's Edinburgh Magazine*, and in 1827 published the novel *The Youth and Manhood of Cyril Thornton*.

**75(d) the original O'Dogherty** the character of Morgan O'Doherty in the 'Noctes Ambrosianae' soon became associated with the Irishman William Maginn (1793–1842).

**75(d) "The Lament for Captain Patton,"** 'Captain Paton's Lament. By James Scott, Esq.' was published in *Blackwood's Edinburgh Magazine*, 5 (September 1819), 735–36, and is generally attributed to Lockhart.

**75(d) a trip to Liverpool** no specific occasion has been identified.

**76(a) Dean Swift** Jonathan Swift (1667–1745), the poet, satirist, and author of *Gulliver's Travels*, had been made Dean of St Patrick's, Dublin, in 1713.

**76(b) his works [...] with his portrait at the beginning** a self-mocking allusion perhaps to the projected series of 'Altrive Tales'.

**76(c) the bibliopole's** John Ballantyne was in business from 1813 as an auctioneer of books and fine art with premises in South Hanover Street.

*Sym*

**76(c) Timothy Tickler** one of the interlocutors of the 'Noctes Ambrosianae', modelled on John Wilson's maternal uncle, Robert Sym. Sym, the second son of a Glasgow merchant, had been born in Glasgow on 29 February 1752, but moved to Edinburgh when he was fifteen years old to be apprenticed to his uncle of the same name, a Writer to the Signet. He was admitted as a W. S. himself in 1775 (making him the oldest member of the body in Edinburgh by the time of his death in 1845), and was reasonably successful in his profession for some years. Although he claimed that he had never cost his father a shilling or received the slightest assistance from him since leaving home, he did inherit a share of his father's large fortune at his death, and then withdrew from business to pursue his literary interests. He contributed anonymously to various periodicals. His sister Margaret was the mother of Hogg's friend John Wilson. He was a member of the Royal Edinburgh Volunteers, and an intimate friend of Lord Melville, Baron Dundas and other leaders of the Tory party in Edinburgh. He was six feet four inches tall with a slender figure, and generally considered an exceptionally handsome man. John Kay's portrait of him, dated 1787, shows him fashionably dressed, going for his daily constitutional walk in the Meadows. At one time he lived in the buildings known as 'The Society' in Brown Square, but for the last forty years of his life at 20, George Square. He never married, though for many years he was noted for his gallantry towards and popularity with women. Apart from the Wilsons he had another nephew, John Sym, who was one of the ministers of Old Greyfriar's Church in Edinburgh–for further information and a reproduction of Kay's portrait of Sym, see John Kay, *A Series of Original Portraits and Caricature Etchings*, 2 vols (Edinburgh, 1877), II, 455–57 (portrait facing p. 455).

**76(d) Mr. Robert Wilson** John Wilson's mother had been Margaret Sym before her marriage and her son Robert Sym Wilson (1792–1868) was named after her brother. He became Secretary to the Royal Bank–see Kay, II, 457.

**76(d) "The Spy,"** see pp. 24–26 and notes.

**76(d) first on the list of subscribers** in a letter to Walter Scott written on the publication of the second number on 8 September [1810] (NLS MS 3879, fol. 184) Hogg mentions that he intends to draw up a list of subscribers for *The Spy* during the following week, and that he now has upwards of a hundred names for it. He adds, 'I had not one Subscriber in Edin. save yourself when the first No. was published'.

**77(a) some written advices anonymously [...] some very clever papers** Sym's contributions probably consisted of 'Edmund Hoyle's Defence of Card-Playing' (No. 23), 'The Twa Craws' (No. 23), 'T. M.'s Letter to the Spy in Answer to the Observer' (No. 27), and 'On Monumental Honours' (No. 43)–see *The Spy*, ed. by Gillian Hughes (S/SC, 2000), pp. 570–71.

**77(b) Mr. Aikman** see note to 25(d).

**77(c) Samuel Anderson** see note to 74(b).

**77(d) North** Christopher North was the fictitious editor of *Blackwood's Edinburgh Magazine* and chief character in the 'Noctes Ambrosianae', an alter ego for Sym's nephew, John Wilson.

**78(c) I outlive him** Robert Sym in fact outlived Hogg by almost a decade, dying on 28 April 1845 at the age of ninety-three–see the announcement of his death in the *Gentleman's Magazine*, new series, 24 (July 1845), 100.

## The Adventures of Captain John Lochy

**79(b) the third William came to the throne** William of Orange became King of England in 1688 and King of Scotland in 1689: the ambiguity about Lochy's year of birth is compounded at the end of the story by letters giving the year as 1691. This uncertainty about the date perhaps reflects that of Hogg's own birth. It is also similar to the uncertainty over the births of George Colwan and Robert Wringhim, either side of the 1688 Revolution–see *The Private Memoirs and Confessions of a Justified Sinner*, ed. by P. D. Garside (S/SC, 2001), p. 200. Like Robert Wringhim, Lochy's parentage is uncertain, while the date given here is the first of a series of half-formulated Jacobite references in the tale.

**79(d) the chief of M'Nab** the homeland of the Macnab clan is in the Breadalbane district of Perthshire. Hogg refers to Francis, 12th Laird in No. 40 of *The Spy*, ed. by Gillian Hughes (S/SC, 2000), p. 397. Hogg's poem 'Jocke Taittis Expeditioune till Hell' depicts 'the doughtye chieftaine of M,Nab/ [...] playing at hydde-and-seike' in the infernal regions–see *A Queer Book*, ed. by P. D. Garside (S/SC, 1995), p. 141. The chieftain referred to here is probably Robert Macnab, 10th Laird of Macnab, who married Anne Campbell, a sister of the Earl of Breadalbane.

**80(a) Earl of Breadalbane** John Campbell, 1st Earl of Breadalbane (1635–1716) was a kinsman of the Earl of Argyll, and had been entrusted by the government with the task of ensuring the Highland chiefs were quiet on the accession of William III. He is notorious as the instigator of the massacre of Glencoe of 13 February 1692. At the onset of the Jacobite Rising of 1715 the government had ordered him, among other suspected Scottish noblemen, to appear at Edinburgh and give security for his good behaviour. He failed to come, and joined the Earl of Mar at Perth on 20 September. His support for James Stuart was no better than lukewarm in 1715, however, and after Sheriffmuir the Breadalbane Highlanders went home and the Earl was allowed his discharge by the government. The third Highland chief is not named.

**80(b) the wilds of Glenorchy** a river valley in Argyllshire.

**82(b) Loch Dochart** Loch Dochart is to the north of Beinn Suidhe in Lorn, Argyllshire.

**82(d) Sir James Innes** has not been identified, though Hogg clearly flags him later as a whig and an adherent to the Protestant succession–see p. 89.

**83(c) a buck in April** the male deer would presumably be at his leanest at the end of the winter before the spring growth of grass and other plants, and there may also be a reference to the seasonal shedding of his horns. The Scottish red-deer stag sheds his horns from mid-March through April each year, and almost immediately they are replaced by the velvet-covered buds that will grow into the new horns. The new horns are generally fully grown by July, in preparation for the autumn rut, or mating season.

**83(c) the sweat of his brow** an allusion to God's punishment of Adam for his transgression in Genesis 3. 19: 'In the sweat of thy face shalt thou eat bread, till thou return unto the ground'.

**84(c) the judge, Lord Erskine** he is later described (p. 85) as 'one of the Marr family', and is perhaps James Erskine, Lord Grange (1679–1754), brother to the Jacobite leader the 11th Earl of Mar (1675–1732).

**85(b) on the 29th of May** oak-apple day, celebrated as the day of the Restoration of the earlier Stuart King Charles II, the day of his accession also being his birthday.

**85(c) the queen** Queen Anne, who came to the throne in 1702, after the death of William III. William's wife, Mary II, the previous queen, had died at the end of 1694, when Lochy would still have been a young child.

**85(d) the M'Kenzie's arms** a false clue as to Lochy's parentage, since his mother is later revealed to be Mary Wharton. The armorial bearings of the Mackenzies were a stag's head and horns. The Mackenzies of Seaforth were a Jacobite family: William, 5th Earl of Seaforth (1675–1732) was engaged in the 1715 Rising.

**86(a) my mother** although Lochy argues that the lady is too young to be his unknown mother, she is later announced as 'Mademoiselle de Whartoong' (p. 97), and at the end of the tale it is stated that his mother was only fifteen years old when he was born (p. 158).

**87(a) an act of parliament** necessary to end a legal marriage at this time.

**87(b) Wharton's dragoons** regiments were normally called by the name of their Colonels prior to the modern system of numbering.

**87(b) Lord Wharton himself, the colonel's father** Thomas, 1st Marquis of Wharton (1648–1715) was an important Whig politician and had been a privy councillor of William III. He succeeded to his father's title of Baron Wharton in 1696. He was the author of the song 'Lillibulero', and known as a rake. His first wife, Anne (the poet) died in 1685, and the marriage was childless. He was married again in 1692, to Lucy, the daughter of Viscount Lisburne, and the couple's only son Phillip (1698–1731) later became 2nd Marquis and 1st Duke of Wharton. At the time of the Flanders campaign Phillip was in his infancy and could not have been colonel of a regiment.

**87(d) calling me captain!** a piece of flattery, the rank of lieutenant standing between that of a cornet and a captain in a cavalry regiment. The cornet was the fifth commissioned officer, responsible for carrying the colours.

**88(d) Lieutenant Drummond** since Hogg later describes Drummond as about the same age as Lochy (p. 89) and brother to Lord Drummond (p. 135), he must be referring to a younger son of the Earl of Perth. One potential candidate is Edward Drummond (1690–1760), son to the Earl of Perth by his third wife, Mary, the widow of Urquhart of Meldrum. Edward 'went early to France, but was in Scotland during the rising of 1715, and left this country the following year. He became Gentleman-in-waiting at the Court of St Germains, was a general of cavalry in the French service, and received the royal and military order of St Louis'–see *The Scots Peerage*, ed. by Sir James Balfour Paul, 9 vols (Edinburgh, 1904–19), VII, 56. On the other hand he is described in a contemporary peerage as a much more contemplative character, who 'spent almost all his life in France in literary retirement, and devoted to religious duties'–see Sir Robert Douglas, *The Peerage of Scotland*, revised by John Philip Wood, 2 vols (Edinburgh, 1813), II, 364. Rev. Robert Patten lists a 'Master *John Drummond* Brother to the Lord *Drummond*' with his brother as among the suspected men summoned to appear at Edinburgh at the time of the outbreak of the 1715 Jacobite Rising—see *The History of the Late Rebellion. With Original Papers, and Characters of the Principal Noblemen and Gentlemen Concern'd in it* (London, 1717), p. 168. David Groves has drawn attention to a resemblance between the Drummond of this tale and the Thomas Drummond wrongfully accused of murdering George Colwan in Hogg's *The Private Memoirs and Confessions of a Justified Sinner*—see 'The *Confessions* and *The Adventures of Captain John Lochy*', in *Newsletter of the James Hogg Society*, 6 (1987), 11–13. Peter Garside correctly identifies the Drummond of *Confessions* as the second son of the Duke of Melfort by his second marriage, and points out that a 'Captain Thomas Drummond' was listed as having been taken prisoner at Sherrifmuir—see *The Private Memoirs and Confessions of a Justified Sinner*, ed. by P. D. Garside (S/SC, 2001), p. 226. It appears probable, therefore, that Hogg is not referring to the same historical personage in each tale, but to two cousins.

**88(d) Blackheath** a south-eastern district of London.

**88(d) an armament for Flanders** Lochy is about to be drawn into the War of the Spanish Succession (1701–14). Charles II of Spain was childless, and there had been two contenders to succeed him, Louis XIV of France and Leopold I, Emperor of Austria. Neither England nor Holland were willing to see Spain united to either France or Austria, and because of this Louis XIV claimed the throne for his second grandson, Philip of Anjou, while Leopold claimed it for his second son, Archduke Charles. When Charles died in November 1700 Philip of Anjou was proclaimed Philip of Spain in accordance with his will. The French occupied fortresses in the Spanish Netherlands, which were still claimed by Austria, and a Grand Alliance was formed to oppose the French by England, Holland, Austria, Prussia and most of the other German states. England declared war on France on 15 May 1702.

**88(d) Marlborough** John Churchill (1650–1722) had been created Duke of Marlborough in December 1702 for his services against the French, previously being Earl of Marlborough. Lochy joins Marlborough's army at the start of the Blenheim campaign of 1704.

**89(b) his brother** Lieutenant-General Charles Churchill (1656–1714) landed in Holland with his brother, the Duke of Marlborough, on 21 April 1704.

**89(b) the earl of Orkney** Lord George Hamilton, Earl of Orkney, (1666–1737) was a general who served at the battle of Blenheim in 1704. He was grandson to the Marquis of Douglas.

**89(d) the celebrated Donald Bawn** perhaps a reference to Donald M'Bane, a celebrated swordsman who was in General Mackay's army at the Battle of Killiecrankie in 1689. According to Robert Chambers, an account of his life was subsequently published as a pamphlet—see *History of the Rebellions in Scotland, under the Viscount of Dundee, and the Earl of Mar, in 1689 and 1715* (Edinburgh, 1829), p. 318.

**90(a) our march to the Upper Rhine** in May 1704, without informing the Dutch of his intentions, Marlborough marched towards the Rhine valley, leaving about sixty thousand men behind to protect Holland.

**90(a) Prince Eugene** Prince Eugen of Savoy (1663–1736) had joined the Austrian army in 1683, and served against the Turks, relieving the siege of Vienna and going on to achieve victories at Mohacs and Zenta. In the War of the Spanish Succession he co-operated with Marlborough at the battle of Blenheim in 1704, carried out a successful campaign in North Italy, and took part in the victories of Oudenarde and Malplaquet. He became governor of the Austrian Netherlands in 1724.

**90(a) prince of Baden** Louis William, Margrave of Baden, commanded a force on the Upper Rhine. Marlborough met with him and Prince Eugen of Savoy for a planning conference at Mondelsheim which lasted from 10 to 13 June 1704.

**90(b) the second day of June** Lochy describes the Battle of the Schellenberg, an audacious surprise attack by Marlborough on the fortified Schellenberg Hill over looking Donauworth. In fact this battle took place in the evening of 2 July 1704.

**90(b) its ancient friends** as Scotland's traditional enemy had been England, an 'auld alliance' existed between Scotland and England's traditional enemy of France. This alliance, however, had been considerably weakened by the Scottish Reformation, since Scottish protestants were naturally inclined to look for support to protestant England.

**90(c) A great number fell** the heavy casualties were a subject of reproach to Marlborough subsequently. Of his English troops 1,500 were killed or wounded, including many high-ranking officers. The Dutch blamed Marlborough for their heavy casualties, and the medal struck to mark the occasion included a relief of the Margrave of Baden but not of Marlborough himself–see Christopher Hibbert, *The Marlboroughs: John and Sarah Churchill 1650–1744* (London: Viking, 2001), p. 140.

**91(a) a hideous view of the pomp and circumstance of war** an ironic allusion to Othello's invocation of the 'Pride, pomp, and circumstance of glorious war!' in *Othello*, III. 3. 359.

**91(b) General Gower [...] mortally wounded** the Dutch lieutenant-general, Van Goor.

**91(c) The gallant Prince Eugene** in fact Eugen and Marlborough joined forces only on 12 August, after Schellenberg–see *The Encyclopedia of Military History from 3500 B. C. to the Present*, ed. by R. Ernest and Trevor N. Dupuy, second edition (London: Jane's, 1986), p. 620.

**91(c) the next day we took the town of Donawert** Donauworth gave the Allied forces a bridgehead on the Danube, and large amounts of provisions and other stores fell into their hands since the enemy had fled the town in haste when the fortress on Schellenberg Hill was taken.

**91(d) offence taken at the Elector** Maximilian II, Elector of Bavaria (1622–1726) was an ally of the French. Marlborough hoped by laying waste western Bavaria to occupy the Elector's army in defending his own territory, as well as denying supplies to the enemy. The burning of crops and villages was generally regarded with distaste by Marlborough's allies.

**92(d) Colonel Scrivener** has not been identified.

**93(b) the great battle of Blenheim** fought on 13 August 1704, near the village of Blindheim, or Blenheim, in Bavaria, a success made possible by skilled co-ordination and co-operation between Marlborough and Prince Eugen. French prestige was severely weakened, and the Elector of Bavaria's country was subsequently annexed by Austria.

**93(c) General Wilkes** has not been identified.

**94(a) Saint Christopher** Saint Christopher was a highly appropriate saint for a soldier to call on in battle. He was not only the patron saint of travellers but was also invoked against sudden death–see David Hugh Farmer, *The Oxford Dictionary of Saints* (Oxford: Clarendon Press, 1978), pp. 78–79.

**94(a) killed, drowned, or taken** Hibbert quotes a letter from Marlborough to the English envoy at the Hague of 28 August 1704, in which he says 'We have intercepted severall Letters going to Paris by which the Enemy own their loss to exceed fforty [*sic*] Thousand men killd, taken prisoners and by the great Desertion in their fflight [*sic*] towards the Black Forest'–see *The Marlboroughs: John and Sarah Churchhill 1650–1744* (London: Viking, 2001), p. 154. As the Danube was behind the French lines, the panic-stricken French force would head for the river in their flight.

**94(c) Austrian general's sword** Lochy's possession of valuable property belonging to a fallen commander of his own side was presumably interpreted as evidence that he was well behind the line of fighting.

**95(b) the king of Sweden** an alliance against Charles XII of Sweden (1682–1718), then just sixteen years old, had been formed in 1698–99 by Peter the Great of Russia, Augustus II of Poland, and Frederick IV of Denmark. Peter the Great of Russia (1626–1725) became czar jointly with his half-brother Ivan in 1682. He modernised Russia and, being especially interested in ship-building, created the Russian fleet. Hogg alludes to his visit to England in 1698 in Robert Wringhim's delusion that the demonic Gil-Martin is Peter the Great of Russia–see *The Private Memoirs and Confessions of a Justified Sinner*, ed. by P. D. Garside (S/SC, 2001), pp. 89 and 233. Charles subsequently invaded Zealand in August 1700 threatening Copenhagen, and in November advanced on Narva, scattering the Russian forces attempting to block his approach. At the battle of Narva on 20 November 1700, fought for two hours during a snow-storm, Charles virtually annhilated a Russian army nearly five times the size of his own. He then, unwisely, turned his attention away from the Russian army and invaded Poland. In May 1703 Peter the Great occupied and fortified the mouth of the River Neva, gaining an outlet on the Baltic, and founded St Petersburg. Meanwhile civil war was raging in Poland, as Charles had placed Stanislas Leszczynski on the Polish throne. On 9 August 1704, only a few days before Blenheim, Peter the Great had retaken Narva and massacred all the Swedish inhabitants. For information about literary portrayals of Charles XII of Sweden see the note to 114(b).

**97(a) in a fine puzzle** Marlborough returned to England after Blenheim on 14 December 1704 and left again the following April, but far from being in difficulties he was at the height of his power, rewarded as the nation's triumphant general and saviour. His political difficulties at home did not begin until 1706.

**97(d) de Whartoong** the similarity of this name to 'Wharton' implies that the mysterious lady may be Lochy's mother, or a family connection.

**98(b) Madam Vilshoven** the lady, presumably Prince Eugen's mistress, has not been identified.

**98(b–c) a mysterious understanding** subsequently explained by James M'Kinlay's statement (p. 158), 'His mother never lost sight of him all his life, but kept constantly a confidential servant under her pay to keep guard over him'.

**98(d) such a one as the Highlands of Scotland only can produce** a similar view of the Highland character is expressed by Hogg in his story 'Julia M'Kenzie': 'It is or rather was a trait in the character of this patriarchal race and rather a mean subservient one that they only saw heard felt and acted in conformity with their chiefs and superiors [...]'–see *Tales of the Wars of Montrose*, ed. by Gillian Hughes (S/SC, 1996), p. 144.

**98(d) Saxony [...] the army of the king of Sweden** Augustus II of Poland, the king whom Charles XII of Sweden had deposed, was also Elector of Saxony. Charles entered Saxony in the early autumn of 1706. The Treaty of Altranstadt of 24 September of that year allowed Charles's army to stay in Saxony over the winter to rest, await recruits and replace worn clothing and equipment–see Ragnhild Hatton, 'Charles XII and the Great Northern War', in *The New Cambridge Modern History: Volume VI. The Rise of Great Britain and Russia 1688–1715/25*, ed. by J. S. Bromley (Cambridge: Cambridge UP, 1970), pp. 648–80 (pp. 662–63).

**99(a) Gustavus** Gustavus Adolphus (1594–1632), who was king of Sweden from 1611 onwards. His Protestant force invaded Germany in 1630 and defeated the Count of Tilly (1559–1632), the commander of the Catholic Imperial forces in the Thirty Year's war, at Breitenfeld near Leipzig on 17 September 1631. Gustavus then defeated another Imperial leader, von Wallenstein (1583–1634) in battle at Lützen on 16 November 1632, where he was killed. Walter Scott's fictional mercenary soldier Dugald Dalgetty constantly refers to him and has named his horse after him—see *A Legend of the Wars of Montrose*, ed. by J. H. Alexander, EEWN 7b (Edinburgh: Edinburgh UP, 1995).

**99(d) charge and trouble** Lochy's ignorance of the world is shown in his failure to recognise that Fin's supposed wife is in fact his whore.

**100(a) Leipsic** the chief town of Saxony, seized by the Swedish army in the autumn of 1706 without any real opposition being made.

**100(a) a diplomatic capacity on behalf of the exiled Stuarts** Charles XII of Sweden is praised in Jacobite songs such as 'Here's to the King', his bravery and folly later linking him to Charles Edward Stuart—see James Hogg, *The Jacobite Relics of Scotland [First Series]*, ed. by Murray G. H. Pittock (S/SC, 2002), pp. 110–11, 283, 457–58. In *Jacobite Relics* Hogg correctly dates the connection between Charles XII and the Jacobites to a period after the succession of the Elector of Hanover to the British throne (p. 271). Denmark annexed the Swedish possessions of Bremen and Verden in 1712 and sold them to Hanover in May 1715. Presumably Hogg brings this forward for the sake of creating a narrative link between the Northern Wars and Lochy's later involvement in the 1715 Jacobite Rising in Scotland.

**100(a) Czar Peter was farther humbled** Charles XII of Sweden had humbled Peter the Great at the battle of Narva of 20 November 1700 (see note to 95(b)), but the town had recently been recaptured by the Russians on 9 August 1704.

**100(a) Marshall Rennyson** Hogg's footnote reference to 'Marshall General Renschild' indicates that the Swedish marshall Karl Gustav Rehnskiold is the person signified here. He had been partly responsible for the king's youthful military training, and his brilliant battle-plan had made an important contribution to the Swedish victory at Narva in 1700.

**100(c) 16th of April** Lochy's introduction to Charles XII in April 1707 coincides with the Duke of Marlborough's visit to the Swedish king at his headquarters at the Castle of Altranstadt near Leipzig. Louis XIV was thought to be trying to enlist Charles on his side in the War of the Spanish Succession, but Marlborough had the impression that the Swedish king had an aversion to France. Voltaire's account of the meeting was that Charles's eyes 'always kindled at the name' of Peter when Marlborough mentioned it and that Marlborough noticed 'a map of Russia lying on the table'—see Christopher Hibbert, *The Marlboroughs: John and Sarah Churchhill 1650–1744* (London: Viking, 2001), p. 200. Hogg's account of Charles's obsession with revenge on Peter the Great at this time may well have been taken from a translation of Voltaire's *Histoire de Charles XII*—see the following note.

**100(d) covered them with his upper lip** in Book VIII of his *Histoire de Charles XII* Voltaire remarks on the unpleasant appearance of the king's mouth in a generally favourable description: 'Charles XII was tall and nobly shaped; he had a fine forehead, large blue eyes full of sweetness, and a handsome nose: but the lower part of his face was disagreeable, and often disfigured, by a frequent laugh which hardly opened his lips; he had little beard or hair; he spoke little, and it was habitual to him to answer only with that laugh' (pp. 260–61). In Hogg's day Charles XII's unsuccessful invasion of Russia led to obvious comparisons with Napoleon, and several English translations of Voltaire's history were printed in 1815—citations in this and the following notes are from one of these, *The Life of Charles XII. King of Sweden, including Memoirs of Several of the Crowned Heads of Europe, particularly of Peter the Great, Emperor of Russia. Translated from the French of M. de Voltaire* (Newry: Alexander Wilkinson, 1815). The Editor's Preface notes that 'the attentive reader will perceive some strong points of resemblance between the fate of the French emperor and that of the Swedish king. The strength and resources of a nation wasted in the prosecution of mad and criminal enterprises, are apparent in both instances. In short, the history of Charles and that of Napoleon, equally admonish the rulers of the earth to "fling away ambition," and to study, above all things, to promote the peace and prosperity of their subjects' (p. iv).

**101(a) his blue surtout** Voltaire comments that although before his accession to the throne Charles had been fond of gaiety and dress, he was 'ever after clad like a common soldier'–see *The Life of Charles XII*, p. 30.

**101(b) route towards Lithuania** the route chosen by Charles XII to Moscow was a northern one from Poland and Lithuania by Vilna, Minsk, and Smolensk. The purpose of Charles XII's stay in Saxony was to prepare for his Russian campaign. Recruits had arrived from Sweden and German volunteers formed into dragoon regiments.

**101(c) the Russians fled before us** Ragnhild Hatton comments: 'The campaign began with impressive success. By keeping the Russians guessing as to his route and choosing the Masurian marshes and woods, never before traversed by a large army, Charles was able to avoid battle and yet force the Russians out of Poland'–see 'Charles XII and the Great Northern War', in *The New Cambridge Modern History: Volume VI. The Rise of Great Britain and Russia 1688–1715/25*, ed. by J. S. Bromley (Cambridge: Cambridge UP, 1970), pp. 648–80 (p. 664). As Charles prepared for an invasion of Russia, Peter concentrated his forces at Grodno and Minsk.

**101(d) He was tried, found guilty** Voltaire comments on the strict discipline maintained by Charles in the Swedish army: 'There was not a soldier who dared to refuse payment for whatever he bought, much less go a marauding, or even stir out of the camp. He would not so much as allow his troops, after a victory, the privilege of stripping the dead, till they had his permission [...]'–see *The Life of Charles XII*, p. 35.

**102(b) Grodno** after waiting until the rivers were frozen Charles crossed the Vistula into Russia with an army of 45,000, and took Grodno on 26 January 1708. The town, just across the border with Poland, in Belorussia, had effectively been abandoned by Peter the Great, who had decided to conserve his army for a decisive battle and rob the Swedes of subsistence by destroying crops and farms as he retreated.

**102(c) Dr. Rymmer** has not been identified.

**104(c) Prince of Wirtemburg** Maximilian of Wurttemberg had been entrusted to the care of Charles XII at the age of thirteen, and was regarded affectionately by him. Hogg's reference to him as Charles's nephew (p. 107) agrees with Voltaire's statement that he was related to Charles–see *The Life of Charles XII*, p. 132.

**105(a) Minsk** an important city on the way to Smolensk.

**105(b) General Levenhaupt** General Adam Loewenhaupt with a small relief army was stationed in Livonia at this time. Subsequently he was ordered to bring his forces with a large waggon train of supplies to join Charles XII in the Ukraine in July 1708. Loewenhaupt, however, only reached Charles on 21 October 1708 with 6,000 survivors of an army originally numbering 11,000. He had made slow progress along roads rendered difficult by an unusually wet summer, and had been forced to burn his supply train when his army had been defeated by a larger Russian force at the battle of Lyesna on 9 and 10 October, just east of the Dnieper.

**105(c) forbidden him taking any gratuities from gentlemen** Hogg is perhaps mocking the rigid proprieties of this historical period. In Richardson's *The History of Sir Charles Grandison* (1753–54), for example, Harriet Byron's cousin, on offering to reward the eponymous Sir Charles's servant for bringing news of her escape from her abductor, is told 'that he was under an obligation to the most generous of masters to decline all gifts'–see *Sir Charles Grandison*, ed. by Jocelyn Harris (Oxford: Oxford UP, 1986), p. 130.

**105(c) General Horn's division** Ragnhild Hatton mentions Arvid Horn with Rehnskiold as a Swedish officer involved in the military training of the young Charles XII and under whom he had fought at the victory of Narva in November 1700–see *The New Cambridge Modern History: Volume VI. The Rise of Great Britain and Russia 1688–1715/25*, ed. by J. S. Bromley (Cambridge: Cambridge UP, 1970), pp. 648–80 (pp. 654–55).

**105(c) a great battle was expected at the crossing of the river Berezine** Charles crossed the River Berezina at Borisov on 29 June 1708. The first large-scale attempt by the Russians to stop the Swedish army gaining command of the road to Smolensk occurred at Holowczyn on the river Vabitch on 14 July. In this battle the Russians were scattered by the forces of Charles XII.

**105(d) General Ross** has not been identified.

**107(a) Prince Gallitzin** this Russian General has not been identified.

**107(b) On the 7th of August** after the encounter at Holowczyn Charles XII proceeded to the Dnieper at Mogilev, which he reached on 8 July.

**109(b) mentioned [...] by Lord Keith** James Keith (1696–1758), brother of George Keith, 10th Earl Marischal (1693?–1778). He was clearly too young to have taken part in military action in 1708, but Hogg may imply that he was a source of information about the Russian service before as well as during his own career. As a young man he took part in the Jacobite Rising of 1715 along with his brother and both were attainted for high treason. Keith escaped abroad and became an officer in the Spanish army, entering the Russian service as a major-general in 1728, and becoming Governor of the Ukraine in 1740. In 1747 he left the Russian service and entered that of Frederick the Great of Prussia as a field-marshal. He was killed at the battle of Hochkirche, and buried in Berlin. Frederick erected a statue of him in Berlin, and presented a replica of it (which Hogg may have seen) to the town of Peterhead–see *The Scots Peerage*, ed. by Sir James Balfour Paul, 9 vols (Edinburgh, 1904–19), VI, 61–62. *A Fragment of a Memoir of Field-Marshal James Keith. Written by Himself 1714–1734* was published in Edinburgh by the Spalding Club in 1843, but mostly relates to events subsequent to the 1715 Rising.

**109(c–d) last week of September [...] pursued a retreating foe for exactly a twelvemonth** according to Voltaire in Book IV of his history, on 22 September 1708 Charles attacked a body of ten thousand Russian horse and six thousand Calmuck Tartars near Smolensk with only six regiments of horse and four thousand foot soldiers. The Russian forces made their way to the king's person, killing two aid-de-camps: 'The king's horse was slain under him; and as one of his equerries was giving him another, both the equerry and horse were struck dead upon the spot. Charles fought on foot, encircled by some of his officers, who immediately flew to relieve him, by surrounding him'–see *The Life of Charles XII*, p. 120.

**110(b) some old heroes** notably John Graham of Claverhouse, Viscount Dundee (1649?–1689), killed at the battle of Killiecrankie, supposedly with a silver button because the devil had granted him immunity from lead bullets. Claverhouse is an important character in Hogg's novel *The Brownie of Bodsbeck* (1818).

**111(a) What a vain fuming creature is man!** Hogg's reflections on the futility of war here resemble those in his 'Sermon IV. Soldiers' in *A Series of Lay Sermons on Good Principles and Good Breeding*, ed. by Gillian Hughes with Douglas S. Mack (S/SC, 1997), pp. 40–47. His portrait of Charles XII of Sweden as a power-hungry half-wit was presumably strengthened by living through the Napoleonic era, and agrees with his criticism in *Lay Sermons* of the way in which 'if a statesman, to gratify his pride, his ambition, or aspiration at fame or dominion, forms a plan, in the execution of which a million of innocent unoffending people shall by the sword be hurried into eternity, we applaud his valour and the daring greatness of his spirit' (pp. 40–41). See also note to 114(b).

**111(b) an Asiatic prince [...] Baschkeirs** Bashkir is on the eastern side of the Russian empire, near the Ural mountains. During the final years of the Napoleonic conflict the presence of Asiatic troops from the Russian army in western Europe excited public comment. The *Edinburgh Evening Courant* of 6 November 1813, for instance, remarks that 'Baschkir Cossacks are the only troops now seen in Europe who continue to use the bow as a military weapon'. Hogg would probably have been familiar with Bashkir weapons and clothing through his friendship with the painter William Allan (1782–1850), who had travelled widely in Russia. Lockhart describes his studio as covered with Turkish, Circassian, Georgian, Armenian and Tartar military accoutrements and weapons and the artist himself is described and engraved wearing 'a dark Circassian vest, the breast of which was loaded with innumerable quilted lurking-places, originally, no doubt, intended for weapons of warfare, but now occupied with the harmless shafts of hair-pencils'—see *Peter's Letters to his Kinsfolk*, 3 vols (Edinburgh, 1819), II, 234–35 (portrait between these pages). A public exhibition of Allan's paintings 'including Three lately purchased by the Grand Duke NICHOLAS of RUSSIA, together with a Collection of the COSTUME and ARMOUR of different nations in the Eastern Part of Europe, and Borders of Asia' was held at 32 Princes Street during January and February 1817—see *Edinburgh Evening Courant*, 4 January 1817.

**111(c) as rich as Crœsus** Crœsus, the last king of Lydia (560–546 BC) and patron of Aesop and the poet Solon, was famous for his power and wealth.

**112(a) Araby, the niece of old Zebulon** the noble Araby clearly owes something to the Rebecca of Scott's *Ivanhoe* (1820), but also perhaps to William Allan's painting of the youthful bride in his *A Jewish Family in Poland making merry before a Wedding*. In describing this picture Lockhart comments that 'the Polish Jews are a very different kind of people from our ones. They form a population of several hundred thousands, and occupy whole towns, villages, and tracts of territory by themselves.[...] The character of these Polish Jews, with their quiet and laborious lives, with their firm attachment to the principles of honesty, with their benevolence and their hospitality, and, above all, with their fervid and melancholy love for their old Faith [...] cannot surely be denied to be a highly poetical one'—see *Peter's Letters to his Kinsfolk*, 3 vols (Edinburgh, 1819), II, 245–46.

**112(a) a complete Nabal** Zebulon is a stereotypically grasping Jew clearly descended from Marlowe's *Jew of Malta* or the Shylock of *The Merchant of Venice*. For the story of Nabal, see 1 Samuel 25, briefly summarised in the note to 57(a).

**112(c) the southern parts of the Russian empire** after Dobry the Swedish army began to suffer severely from shortage of provisions and fodder, and, as a result, Charles XII abandoned the northern route to Moscow via Smolensk, turning south on 25 September 1708 to adopt an alternative route across Severia and the Ukraine by Kiev and Kaluga. In the Ukraine he was hoping to join forces with the Cossack chief Mazeppa. Hogg would almost certainly have known of Byron's popular poem *Mazeppa* (1819), which was founded on the account of this part of the campaign in Voltaire's *Histoire de Charles XII*. The winter of 1708–09 was perhaps the coldest winter ever known in Europe, and the Swedish army suffered terrible losses from the cold in addition to being harrassed by the Russians. By the spring Charles XII had barely 20,000 men fit for fighting; and, after a crushing defeat at the battle of Poltava on 28 June 1709, he retreated to Turkey, remaining there until November 1714.

**112(c) the reconquest of Poland** after the defeat of Charles XII at Poltava, Peter the Great marched westwards to occupy Poland between August and December 1709. Augustus II was then reinstated as king.

**112(d) Siberia** this north-eastern Russian province with its harsh Arctic climate has long been used as a place of internal exile for prisoners of the Russian state. Voltaire dates the establishment of a Swedish community in Siberia to the period following the defeat at Poltava in 1709—see *The Life of Charles XII*, pp. 138–39.

**113(b) General Count Fleming, ambassador to Augustus king of Poland** the Saxon field-marshal, Count Jakob Heinrich von Flemming.

**114(b) one madman** Hogg draws on a literary tradition which regarded Charles XII of Sweden as a monomaniac intent on personal glory at the expense of the well-being of his country and his subjects. To Samuel Johnson, for instance, he exemplifies the false pride of the warrior in a famous portrait concluding, 'He left the Name, at which the World grew pale,/ To point a Moral, or adorn a Tale'—see 'The Vanity of Human Wishes', in *The Poems of Samuel Johnson*, ed. by David Nichol Smith and Edward L. McAdam, second edition (Oxford: Clarendon Press, 1974), pp. 110–33 (lines 191–222). Hogg's shepherd Watie draws a parallel between loss of European liberties under Charles and under France, comparing the deference shown to Charles 'when th' impetuous Prince o' Sweden/ Thro' Saxony in blude came waedin'' with his friendless state after Pultova, when enemies 'On him turn'd a' their arms anon,/ 'Til a' his richest lands were won'—see 'Dusty, or, Watie an' Geordie's Review of Politics; An Eclogue', in *Scottish Pastorals*, ed. by Elaine Petrie (Stirling: Stirling UP, 1988), pp. 3–12 (lines 111–28).

**115(b) winter was setting in** presumably the winter of 1709–10, although Hogg is necessarily imprecise about dates here since by the time Lochy returns to Scotland the year is clearly 1715.

**116(a) Wilna** Vilna, or Vilnius. Lochy and his companions retrace the route of the Swedish army back through Lithuania to the Baltic port of Königsberg on the border of Poland, from which they take ship for the port of Leith in Scotland, pausing at the North German Hanseatic port of Lübeck on the way.

**116(c) Kowna** or Kaunas, between Vilna and Königsberg.

**117(b) a romantic passion** Araby's guardianship of her lover in the disguise of an attendant boy is similar to that of Marsali's attendance on her lover in 'The Adventures of Colonel Peter Aston'—see *Tales of the Wars of Montrose*, ed. by Gillian Hughes (S/SC, 1996), pp. 99–137, particularly p. 122 onwards.

**120(a) in great confusion** because of the Jacobite Rising of 1715. The accession of the Elector of Hanover to the British throne as George I following the death of Queen Anne on 1 August 1714 was greatly resented. His predecessor had been the daughter of James VII, whereas there were more than fifty members of European royal houses whose claim to the throne was better than that of the Elector of Hanover but who were passed over because they were Catholics—see *The Jacobite Relics of Scotland [First Series]*, ed. by Murray G. H. Pittock (S/SC, 2002), p. 455.

**121(c) slavery** many miners and salters in Scotland were serfs, if not quite slaves, until 1799. Despite this, however, Scottish liberty and Russian tyranny were contrasted in essays such as James Gray's 'Duty of Servants and Masters'—see *The Spy*, ed. by Gillian Hughes (S/SC, 2000), pp. 213–20 (pp. 214–15).

**122(a) the Lawn Market** the upper part of the High Street of Edinburgh, above the Parliament Square and Tolbooth prison.

**122(b) on his march to Pultowa** to join Peter of Russia at the battle of Poltava on 28 June 1709.

**122(d) Calmuck prince [...] every day for this half year** another way by which Hogg indicates the passage of time. From Lochy's narrative it seems as if his party, including Prince Iset, have only just arrived in Scotland, but if the Russians have traced them to Scotland from inquiries made after their departure from Smolensk and been advertising in Edinburgh for six months a longer period must have elapsed than would otherwise appear.

**122(d) a genuine Campbell** the chief of the Campbells was John Campbell, 2nd

Duke of Argyll (1678–1743), the most powerful of the Highland chiefs and a staunch supporter of the Hanoverian King George I, who had appointed him commander-in-chief of the royal forces in Scotland. The Campbells would therefore benefit from the patronage of their chief at this time.

**122(d) te Moss–cubhaid** possibly meant as a Gaelic pronounciation of Muscovite. Alternatively, *cubaid* is Gaelic for 'pulpit', which would mean that the Highlander had misunderstood the Russians to say that Iset had been 'stolen from the great manse of the Moss'. I thank Tom McKean for this latter suggestion.

**123(a) whisky cuach** a *cuach* is the more familiar Scots *quaich*, a shallow dish used for drinking whisky, normally with two small flat handles. Perhaps the Highlanders have heard the word 'khan', meaning an Asiatic lord or prince, and have selected this expression as including the nearest-sounding familiar Gaelic word.

**123(b) Miss Cumins** have not been identified.

**124(a) chairmen and caddies** chairmen would carry the sedan chairs hired by the ladies of Edinburgh to transport them on their visits, while the caddies were an unofficial corps of errand-boys in the city. Edward Topham gives a favourable picture of their exceptional information and efficiency in his *Letters from Edinburgh in 1774 and 1775*, facsimile of 1776 edition (Edinburgh: James Thin, 1971), pp. 86–87.

**124(a) the Fountain well** this well was part of the city's water-supply, completed in 1681 and situated off the High Street of Edinburgh—see Harris, p. 278.

**124(b) whistle and sing [...] a Jewish melody** a common Romance convention. Richard I of England was supposedly recognised in captivity by his faithful minstrel Blondel hearing him reply to his singing of a favourite air.

**124(b) Cannongate** a continuation of the High Street, from the Netherbow Port down towards Holyrood Palace. Many of Scotland's most important families had town-houses in the Canongate.

**125(c) cut-and-thrust sword** the type of sword has not been identified, but is presumably a weapon between the light, sharp rapier and the heavy broadsword.

**126(b) some of Mar's rebels** after lingering in London for almost a year after the arrival of George I, John, Earl of Mar (1675–1732) left London secretly for Scotland on 2 August 1715, arriving at Braemar on 20 August, where he held a hunting-party on 27 August as a cover for a meeting of leading Jacobites. The leaders of the party met again at Aboyne on 3 September, and the standard of James VIII and III was raised at Braemar on 6 September 1715. At this point the narrative must have reached the final days of September, since Lochy and Drummond leave Edinburgh on 1 October (p. 137).

**126(c) slain** accounts of the person slain differ substantially: here he is 'a near relation, and head general of king George's', but subsequently 'a great foreign prince' (p. 129), acting in the Stuart interest.

**129(b) Cowgate** see note to 25(c).

**129(c) the Tolbooth** the old prison of Edinburgh, situated to the north of St Giles Cathedral on the High Street. It was demolished in 1817 once the new jail on Calton Hill had been built, and was commemorated in Scott's novel *The Heart of Midlothian* in 1818.

**130(d)–131(a) Queen Esther** the chief wife of King Ahasuerus of Persia, whose story is told in the biblical Book of Esther. The king's preference for her over his other women enabled her to shield Jews from the destruction threatened to them by their enemies, especially Haman.

**131(c) Northumbrians** the government had received early information that Roman Catholics and discontented Protestants in Northumberland, Cumberland and Durham would rise, and warrants for the arrest of leading men in the north-east were issued on 21/22 September, though most of those named were warned in time to evade arrest–see Leo Gooch, *The Desperate Faction? The Jacobites of North-East England 1688–1745* (Hull: Hull UP, 1995), p. 41. Hogg's Northumbrians were perhaps in Scotland to ask for reinforcements from the Earl of Mar.

**131(d)** ***Carolus Rex* [...] the Pretender** in 1715 'the Young Pretender' Charles Stuart (1720–1788) was as yet unborn: his father, 'the Old Pretender' (1688–1766) and son of James II and VII, was named James. The assumption might be that James Stuart was carrying a family weapon once belonging to his uncle, the former Charles II.

**131(d) the lord-provost** the chief magistrate of the royal burgh of Edinburgh. Until 4 October 1715 this was Sir George Warrender, who was then succeeded by Lord Provost Campbell.

**132(a) to Perth [...] to assist Lord Mar** Perth had been taken for the Jacobites on 14 September, and by the end of the month the Earl of Mar had an army of between four and five thousand men there–see Alistair and Henrietta Tayler, *1715: The Story of the Rising* (London and Edinburgh, 1936), pp. 49, 53.

**132(b) Divine vengeance on a cause** the belief that the Stuarts' failure to regain the crowns of England and Scotland was due to the effectiveness of the prayers made against them by the Covenanters whom they had persecuted is to be found in other works by Hogg, notably *The Brownie of Bodsbeck* (1818) and *The Three Perils of Woman* (1823).

**132(c) lately espoused the cause of the Stuarts** Charles XII of Sweden had reached the Swedish-controlled German port of Stralsund in November 1814. He supported the Jacobites as a means of annoying George I, who as Elector of Hanover had purchased the Swedish possessions of Bremen and Verden from Denmark in May 1715–see also note to 100(a).

**133(a) the bank, the only one then in Edinburgh** when the Bank of Scotland was founded in 1695 it was granted a twenty-one year monopoly. The rival Royal Bank of Scotland was not founded until 1727.

**133(c) called at the drum-head** this may indicate that Edinburgh was under martial law because of the Jacobite threat. Hugo Arnot provides details of other defensive measures taken in 1715 by the Edinburgh town council: 'The council of Edinburgh provided for the security of the town, and the support of government, by ordering the city walls and gates to be repaired and the sluice upon the north-loch to be dammed up, and trenches to be made; the town-guard to be augmented; the trained bands to be armed; 400 men to be raised and maintained at the city's expence; and armed vessels to be fitted out, to assist the King's ships, in preventing the rebel army from crossing the Forth'–see *The History of Edinburgh*, fifth edition (Edinburgh: West Port Books, 1998), p. 107. The original publication was in 1779.

**133(c–d) the shore at Leith** Leith is the sea-port of Edinburgh, and at this time was a separate burgh.

**134(c) half a dozen already** Charles XII of Sweden had dispossessed Augustus II of Saxony, crowning another king of Poland in his place–see note to 95(b). The reference to 'half a dozen' is perhaps a rhetorical exaggeration.

**135(b) Lord Drummond's brother** probably Edward Drummond or his brother John–see note to 88(d). James, Lord Drummond himself (1673–1720), the eldest son of the Earl of Perth, had distinguished himself in the early stages of the Rising of 1715 by a daring attempt to take Edinburgh Castle on 8 September–Hogg gives an account of this in *The Jacobite Relics of Scotland. Second Series* (Edinburgh, 1821), pp. 230–32.

**136(d) king George's new taxes** although the 1707 Union with England opened the way for the expansion of Scottish trade, particularly with America, the imposition of English taxes was greatly resented in Scotland. James Keith records that on raising the Standard at Braemar the Earl of Mar 'sent orders to all the touns to pay the taxes and duties only on the old Scots footing'–see *A Fragment of a Memoir of Field-Marshal James Keith. Written by Himself 1714–1734* (Edinburgh, 1843), pp. 11–12. Rev. Robert Patten, who accompanied the Borders Jacobites, notes that when the Earl of Mar's manifesto was read at Kelso on 24 October the people shouted, 'NO *Union!* NO *Malt,* NO *Salt*-TAX!'–see *The History of the Late Rebellion. With Original Papers, and Characters of the Principal Noblemen and Gentlemen Concern'd in it* (London, 1717), p. 49.

**137(d) the young Lord Sinclair** John Sinclair (1688–1750), Master of Sinclair and son of Harry, 8th Lord Sinclair. His waspish account of the 1715 Rising from the Jacobite perspective was published as *Memoirs of the Insurrection in Scotland in 1715* in Edinburgh for the Bannantyne Club in 1858.

**137(d) a very gallant action** the Master of Sinclair had been informed by a friend of his father's at Perth that the master of a ship carrying arms and ammunition from Edinburgh Castle to the Whig Earl of Sunderland in the north had put in at Burntisland on the forth of Firth to visit his wife. Travelling to Burntisland by night Sinclair's party passed within ten miles of Stirling Castle, posted sentries around the town at Burntisland to prevent any alarm spreading, and set out in boats to capture the ship on 2 October 1715. According to Sinclair's own account: 'At last, those boats brought in the ship by maine force, against the contrarie wind; and those aboard of ours, being seamen, did their dutie very well. I stood in the water to the middle of the leg, and, with my oun hands, receaved all the armes from the ship's side, and found, to my great grief, but three hundred, wanting one [...] We seized the armes of a big ship which lay in the harbour, which were about tuentie-five firelocks, and with them a barrell of pouder; and, at sametime, the armes of the Toun Guarde, about thirtie'–see John, Master of Sinclair, *Memoirs of the Insurrection in Scotland in 1715* (Edinburgh, 1858), p. 100.

**138(a) pompous, bustling, polite, insignificant body** in his notes to *The Jacobite Relics of Scotland. Second Series* (Edinburgh, 1821), Hogg again expresses the common view that 'Mar acted like a fool, and without either energy or spirit, in not making a dash into the Lowlands before Argyle got his forces concentrated [...] but he knew nothing of the Highland character, which rises to the sublimity of vigour with action, but fades and dies away with inactivity. [...] Mar had no such feeling, certainly, else he would not have lain idle about Perth till the middle of winter [...]' (p. 233).

**138(b) brave M'Raes** a minor Ross-shire clan, subordinate to the Mackenzies of Seaforth, whose badge is the fir-club moss. When the Earl of Seaforth's lands were forfeited after the 1715 Rising the clan was so loyal to him that the government found it impossible to collect his rents–see William Anderson, *The Scottish Nation*, 3 vols (Edinburgh and London, 1865), III, 69–70.

**138(b) Lord Seaforth** William Mackenzie, 5th Earl of Seaforth (d. 1740) joined the Earl of Mar at Perth in November 1715 with between three and four thousand men, and fought on the Jacobite side at the battle of Sheriffmuir. After the battle he returned to the north to protect his own estates, which were then threatened from Inverness–see Alistair and Henrietta Tayler, *1715: The Story of the Rising* (London and Edinburgh, 1936), pp. 94–95, 102.

**138(d) Sir John Falstaff's regiment** Falstaff's comical recruiting for the royal army to suppress the rebellion of Archbishop Scroope, Mowbray, and Hastings is depicted in Shakespeare's *2 Henry IV*, III. 2. Falstaff's force consists of those men who are not able to bribe him to let them off serving in the army.

**138(d) the Strath-Bogie regiment** the Earl of Huntly's horsemen were also objects of ridicule to the Master of Sinclair, who described them as '[...] a troop of fourtie or fiftie great lubbertlie fellous, in bonnets, without boots, or any such thing, and scarce bridles, mounted on longe-tailed little horses, less then the men, who were by much the greatest animalls of the tuo, without pistells, with great rustie musquets, tyed on their backs with rope; and those he called light horse. I must oun, the grotesque figure those made moved everie bodie's laughter [...]'–see *Memoirs of the Insurrection in Scotland in 1715* (Edinburgh, 1858), p. 160.

**139(a) saddles [...] bridle reins** cheap country substitutes for more costly leather horse-tack. For an account of an uncontrolled ride on a horse with straw sunks and a hair halter see Hogg's 'Seeking the Houdy' in *The Forget Me Not* (London, 1830), pp. 399–413.

**139(b) On the 23rd of November** Hogg's dating seems odd here, for Finlay clearly arrives at Perth before the battle of Sheriffmuir on 13 November: perhaps 23 October is the intended date.

**139(b) Borlam and his Mackintoshes** the clan Mackintosh was one of the first to declare for the Jacobite cause and took Inverness on 14 September 1715. Brigadier William Mackintosh of Borlum (1662–1743) with about seven hundred of the clan later joined the Earl of Mar at Perth, and he was dispatched to the south with a force of two thousand men to liase with Jacobites in the Borders and the north of England. He crossed the Firth of Forth on 12 October, but was then invited by Edinburgh Jacobites to try to take the city and marched westward to occupy Leith before retreating to Haddington. It was 22 October before Mackintosh and the Northumbrian Jacobites joined forces at Kelso–see Leo Gooch, *The Desperate Faction? The Jacobites of North-East England 1688–1745* (Hull: Hull UP, 1995), pp. 49, 76.

**139(c) thrown upon the world to be a football in it** Douglas Gifford has commented on Hogg's similar expression with reference to his own situation in literary Edinburgh–see *James Hogg* (Edinburgh: The Ramsay Head Press, 1976), p. 196. Hogg referred to his dislike of being treated as 'a tennis ball between contending parties' in his letter to Blackwood of 20 November 1820 (NLS MS 4005, fols 169–70).

**139(c) 7th of February, 1731** the date appears to have no significance in itself.

**139(d) marquis of Huntly** Alexander Gordon, Marquis of Huntly (1678?–1728) was the eldest son of the Duke of Gordon. On the outbreak of the 1715 Jacobite Rising he proclaimed James Stuart king at Gordon Castle and then joined the Earl of Mar at Perth on 6 October. He returned to Gordon Castle, however, after the battle of Sheriffmuir, and after the Rising was eventually pardoned by the government.

**139(d) duke of Argyle** John Campbell, 2nd Duke of Argyll (1678–1743) had held a major command under the Duke of Marlborough at Oudenarde in the Netherlands, and was a field-marshal in the British army. He was an able politician and had been Commissioner to the Scots Parliament in 1705. He was one of the prime movers in passing the Act of Union. He supported the accession of George I, and was appointed commander-in-chief of all the government forces in Scotland.

**140(b) the honorable Miss Helen Lockhart** Miss Lockhart was presumably selected as the putative mother of Captain Lochy because his surname could be interpreted as an abbreviation of hers. However Lochy himself says that his name was given to him from that of the river on the banks of which he was found as an infant (p. 80).

**141(d) John M'Kenzie of Assynt** Hogg probably refers to John Mackenzie of Assynt in Sutherland, second son to Kenneth, 3rd Earl of Seaforth. He had taken his degree at King's College, Aberdeen in 1684, and been M. P. for Fortrose from 1702 until his death on 26 June 1705–see Duncan Warrand, *Some Mackenzie Pedigrees* (Inverness: Robert Carruthers & Sons, 1965), p. 28. Even though John Mackenzie died ten years previous to the events related here Hogg's subsequent reference to 'old Assynt' (p. 145) and his use of the Christian name John render it unlikely that he means John Mackenzie's son, Kenneth.

**141(d) Colonel Alexander M'Kenzie** as Hogg states, Colonel Alexander Mackenzie was brother to the 5th Earl of Seaforth. He was entered at the Scots College at Douai in September 1685, afterwards renouncing his Catholicism and accepting a commission in the British Army. He was married to Elizabeth Paterson, daughter to the Bishop of Ross–see *The Scots Peerage*, ed. by Sir James Balfour Paul, 9 vols (Edinburgh, 1904–1919), VII, 510.

**142(a) the Lewis regiment** by 1718 Mackenzies formed the greater part of the tacksmen (chief tenants subletting land to lesser tenants) in Lewis, even though Macleod remains the commonest surname there–see *Collins Encyclopaedia of Scotland*, ed. by John Keay and Julia Keay (London: Harper Collins, 1994), pp. 659–60.

**142(c) general Gordon** Alexander Gordon (1669–1751) was the eldest son of Lord Auchintoul, and a professional soldier. After joining the French army he was present at the siege of Namur in 1690. He joined the Russian service in 1695. In November 1700 he was wounded and taken prisoner at Narva, and was kept a captive in Sweden for seven years before being exchanged for another prisoner. Peter the Great appointed him first a brigadier and then a major-general. He resigned his commision on his father's death and returned to Scotland to take possession of the family estates. After the raising of the Jacobite standard at Braemar he enlisted men in the western Highlands, failed to take Fort William, and rejoined Mar in Perth on 10 November with about four thousand men. After Sheriffmuir he led the retreating Jacobite army northwards, and eventually escaped to France. He was attainted as Thomas rather than Alexander Gordon, and in 1720 had his estates restored on pleading that the attainder was therefore invalid. Although too old to fight in the 1745 Rising he acted as a valued adviser to the Jacobite forces. He was the author of a life of Peter the Great, and of a heroic poem entitled 'The Prussiad'–see Alistair and Henrietta Tayler, *1715: The Story of the Rising* (London and Edinburgh, 1936), pp. 231–35.

**142(c) four clans M'Donald** the various branches of the Clan Donald operated as independent clans under their respective chiefs. Hogg lists the Macdonald chiefs on the Jacobite side as 'Sir Donald of Sky, the captain of Clan-Ranald, Glengarry, Keppoch, and Glenco'–see *The Jacobite Relics of Scotland. Second Series* (Edinburgh, 1821), p. 232. In fact the two brothers of Sir Donald Macdonald, 4th Baronet of Sleat, commanded the Skye Macdonalds at Sheriffmuir–see William Anderson, *The Scottish Nation*, 3 vols (Edinburgh and London, 1865), II, 715.

**142(d) the Moidart regiment** Moidart was the seat of the Clanranald chieftains. The 14th Clanranald chief led his clan at the battle of Killiecrankie in 1689 at the age of sixteen, and was killed at Sheriffmuir. According to Chambers he was 'famed in the Highlands to this day for maintaining the character of a chief with almost princely state, and for an almost Ossianic degree of heroism. He was led off the field, uttering expressions of encouragement to his men, and wishing success to the glorious cause they were engaged in'–see *History of the Rebellions in Scotland, under the Viscount of Dundee, and the Earl of Mar, in 1689 and 1715* (Edinburgh, 1829), p. 260.

**143(b) Mar's own fear and folly [...] the battle** Hogg gives a similarly unfavourable account of Mar's behaviour at the battle of Sheriffmuir (fought on a moor near Dunblane in Perthshire on 13 November 1715) in *The Jacobite Relics of Scotland. Second Series* (Edinburgh, 1821), pp. 238–40. He says, for instance, that Mar 'stood behind a clump of trees that flanked the clans to the right till he saw the onset given; and when he saw the clans bear down their opponents, and break their ranks, he made his appearance, but had better staid where he was' (p. 239).

**143(b) one of their bravest chiefs was slain** Allan Macdonald, 14th Chief of Clanranald–see note to 142(d).

**143(c) the general detail** while the right of the Jacobite army obtained a complete victory over the opposing left wing, the left wing after three hours' fighting was driven by the government forces downhill to the river Allan.

**143(d) not being able to see over the ridge** Alistair and Henrietta Tayler argue that 'such is the lie of the land that neither army had a complete view of the other'–see *1715: The Story of the Rising* (London and Edinburgh, 1936), p. 98.

**144(a) hard upon Stirling** 'The right centre of the Jacobite army, under the personal command of Mar, [...] drove the enemy with great slaughter almost to Stirling. The Jacobite cavalry never drew rein till they reached Causewayhead, and were under the impression that they had won the battle, the configuration of the ground preventing their knowing what was happening on their own left'–see Alistair and Henrietta Tayler, *1715: The Story of the Rising* (London and Edinburgh, 1936), p. 99. Mar's return to Sheriffmuir was in fact prompted by news of the disaster that had befallen his own left wing.

**144(a) Glengarry** Alasdair MacDonnell of Glengarry (d. 1724) had led his clan at Killiecrankie, and was one of the first Highland chiefs to rally to the Earl of Mar in the 1715 Rising. His clansmen occupied a position on the right wing of the Jacobite army at the battle of Sheriffmuir.

**144(a) Keppoch** Coll Macdonald of Keppoch had succeeded as Chief at the age of eighteen, and was known as one of the boldest and most warlike of the Keppoch chieftains. At the battle of Killiecrankie he had fought at the head of his clan on the Jacobite side, and he distinguished himself on the right wing of the Jacobite army at Sheriffmuir. He was one of the last to lay down arms after the failure of the 1715 Rising, and died around 1728–29. He was married to Barbara, the daughter of Sir Donald MacDonald, 10th Baron Sleat–see Donald J. Macdonald, *Clan Donald* (Loanhead, Midlothian: Macdonald Publishers, 1978), pp. 381–87.

**144(b) a little craggy hill** named by Hogg as Kippendavy hill in *The Jacobite Relics of Scotland. Second Series* (Edinburgh, 1821), p. 240. After returning to Sheriffmuir Mar remained inactive all afternoon, hesitating to attack the small remnant of Argyll's army remaining there and even allowing the government troops returning from the pursuit of his own left wing to pass by the foot of the hill and return to Dunblane–see Alistair and Henrietta Tayler, *1715: The Story of the Rising* (London and Edinburgh, 1936) p. 100.

**144(c) Bobbing John** a nickname for the Earl of Mar, originating in his reputation for changing sides. Before heading the 1715 Rising, he had been a prime mover in the 1707 Act of Union.

**149(d) the foreign auxiliaries** six thousand Dutch troops were sent to help to crush the Jacobite Rising.

**149(d) Colonel Cadogan** William Cadogan (1675–1726), who is supposed to have fought as a boy cornet at the Battle of the Boyne. He enjoyed a distinguished military career as a trusted colleague of the Duke of Marlborough in the Wars of the Spanish Succession, and was for a while minister plenipotentiary to the Estates General of Holland. After the battle of Sheriffmuir the government appointed him colleague and adviser to the Duke of Argyll, and he sent confidential reports to London that Argyll was being too lenient with his fellow Scots among the Jacobites. He was later created Earl Cadogan for his diplomatic and military services to the government.

**151(b) my father-in-law, the Lord Mayor of London** the Duke of Argyll's first wife, Mary Brown, the daughter of John Brown, was the niece of Sir Charles Duncome, Lord Mayor of London.

**151(c) Appleby** in Westmorland, south-east of Penrith. Rev. Robert Patten in 1717 describes it as 'an ancient Corporation, and the Head Town of the County of *Westmorland*: The Assizes are held here. It was formerly a famous *Roman* Station'–see *The History of the Late Rebellion. With Original Papers, and Characters of the Principal Noblemen and Gentlemen Concern'd in it* (London, 1717), p. 86. The Jacobite force in the north of England, led by Mackintosh of Borlum, entered Penrith on 3 November, and passed through Appleby and Kendal before reaching Lancaster on 7 November. They surrendered to the government forces at Preston in Lancashire on 14 November 1715—see Leo Gooch, *The Desperate Faction? The Jacobites of North-East England 1688–1745* (Hull: Hull UP, 1995), pp. 79–83. Lochy is travelling through a Jacobite area and among people who are anxious to escape from the retaliation to be inflicted on supporters of the losing side after Preston.

**153(a) Mr. Abraham Taylor, brother to one Edward Taylor** neither has been identified.

**153(a) at Preston** the Jacobites from northern England and the Scottish Borders surrendered to the government forces at Preston, Lancashire, on 14 November 1715.

**153(c) the earl of Lonsdale** Henry Lowther succeeded as third Viscount Lonsdale in 1713, on the death of his elder brother Richard, 2nd Viscount Lonsdale, and died unmarried in 1751.

**153(d) Jan 26, 1715–16** the Gregorian reform of the calendar was adopted by England and Scotland in 1752, when the beginning of the year was also altered from 25 March to 1 January. The date that is now reckoned to be 26 January 1716 would therefore have been reckoned by contemporaries as 26 January 1715. Double-dating was sometimes used, since Britain adopted the Gregorian system long after many other countries on the Continent.

**153(d) Lowther Castle** the seat of the Earl of Lonsdale, to the south of Penrith in Westmorland.

**154(a) the young ladies** although the implication is that the young ladies of the family were Lord Lonsdale's daughters, Henry, 3rd Viscount Lonsdale was unmarried.

**154(a) Miss Van, daughter to Lord Barnard** a daughter of Christopher Vane, Baron Barnard of Barnard's Castle in county Durham. He was born on 21 May 1653, created a baron in 1698, and had married the sister of the Duke of Newcastle in 1676—see *Complete Peerage of England, Scotland, and Ireland, &c*, ed. by G. E. C[ockayne], 9 vols (London, 1887–98), I, 425.

**154(c) Douglas Arms** the inn is presumably named for an ancient and dominant family of local landowners in the south-west of Scotland. Sir William Douglas was a supporter of Wallace and died in prison in London in 1298. An Earl of Douglas features in Hogg's Border Romance, *The Three Perils of Man* (1822).

**154(d) Ekron, a Philistine** the name of a district of Philistine, mentioned in various places of the Old Testament, notably Zechariah 9. 5, 7.

**155(a) Scott of Walle** Woll is in Ettrick Forest, south of Selkirk. Walter Scott of Woll married in 1694 and died in 1744—see Keith S. M. Scott, *Scott, 1118–1923: Being a Collection of "Scott" Pedigrees* (London, 1923), p. 161.

**155(a) Scott of Whitsled** is one of the oldest branches of the Scott clan, based at Whitslade Tower near Ale Water on the borders of Selkirkshire and Roxburghshire. John Scott, the eighteenth and last of Whitslaid, sold the family estates—see Keith S. M. Scott, p. 112. According to T. Craig-Brown, 'In 1714 his lands were disjoined on petition of himself, Sir Patrick Scott of Ancrum, Thomas Scott of Todrig, and William Scott in Milsington. This was followed by a sale of the paternal acres in 1722'—see *The History of Selkirkshire or Chronicles of Ettrick Forest*, 2 vols (Edinburgh, 1886), I, 444–45. Disjoin is a Scots legal term, meaning to separate or disconnect one part from another.

**155(a) Pringle of Hawthorn** has not been identified.

**155(d) the age of Methusaleh** see Genesis 5. 27: 'And all the days of Methuselah were nine hundred sixty and nine years: and he died.'

**156(a) That of the women is pure and disinterested** Hogg expresses similar views about the disinterested and zealous loyalty of female Jacobites compared to that of males through his characterisation of Lady Balmillo in his novel *The Three Perils of Woman* of 1823–see *The Three Perils of Woman*, ed. by David Groves, Antony Hasler and Douglas S. Mack (S/SC, 1995), pp. 313–17, 325–31. In *The Jacobite Relics of Scotland. Second Series* (Edinburgh, 1821) he quotes a contemporary source: 'Ray, the volunteer, in his journal, says, "I found always the ladies most violent–they would listen to no manner of reason."' (p. 290).

**156(c) Borthwicksheils** about 6 miles west of Hawick in Roberton parish, near Alemoor Loch. In 1834 the landowners of the parish included 'George Pott, Esq. of Borthwickshiels'–see *The New Statistical Account of Scotland*, 15 vols (Edinburgh and London, 1845), III, 90.

**156(c) Parkhill and Musely** Muselee Burn and Hill are ten or so miles SW of Hawick, and there are many names including the word 'Park' in that neighbourhood. I thank Jean Moffat for this information. The Chamberlain of Hogg's landlord and patron, the Duke of Buccleuch was Major Charles Riddell of Muselee–see Corson, p. 609.

**157(a) James Laidlaw, W. S. Edinburgh** a Writer to the Signet named James Laidlaw appears in the Edinburgh postal directory for 1827–28, which lists his office address as 28 India Street and his home as 13 Hope Street (p. 101). In the subsequent directory for 1828–29 his home address has changed to 10 Manor Place (p. 213). However, Laidlaw is a common Border name and Hogg may not have had a specific person in mind here.

**157(a) Mr. Alex. Reid, Trongate, Glasgow** the Glasgow Post-Office directory for 1828–29 does not list an Alexander Reid with a Trongate address, but the booksellers William Reid and Son are listed there (p. 213). Hogg may not have a specific person in mind here, but is simply giving a plausible Glasgow name.

**157(b) Hon. Colonel James Campbell of Argyle** James Campbell of Burnbank and Boquhan was a younger son of Archibald, 9th Earl of Argyll and therefore a brother to Archibald, 1st Duke of Argyll (*c.* 1658–1703). John Lochy is supposedly the first cousin of the Duke of Argyll who led the government forces at Sheriffmuir. James Campbell served as a soldier, rising to the rank of Colonel, and was M. P. for Renfrew from 1699–1702, and for the Ayr burghs from 1708–10. He married Margaret Leslie, third daughter of David Leslie, Lord Newark, the victor of the Battle of Philliphaugh–see *The Scots Peerage*, ed. by Sir James Balfour Paul, 9 vols (Edinburgh, 1904–19), I, 367–68.

**157(b) Lady Mary Wharton, only daughter of Lord Wharton** Mary Wharton was the daughter of Sir George Wharton, and therefore a family connection of Lord Wharton but not his own daughter–see *The Scots Peerage*, ed. by Sir James Balfour Paul, 9 vols (Edinburgh, 1904–19), I, 367.

**157(b) a runaway marriage** details of this celebrated case are given in 'Papers Relative to the Abduction of Miss Wharton, by the Hon. James Campbell of Burnbank, and the Execution of Sir John Johnston, Bart. for his Concern Therein', in *The Argyle Papers*, ed. by James Maidment (Edinburgh, 1834), pp. 43–57. James Campbell and his friend Sir John Johnston called at Queen Street in London on 10 November 1690, and took Mary Wharton away with them from her aunt's house. She was married privately to Campbell, and spent two nights with him before being taken away on a warrant. Campbell and Johnston were both accused of forcible abduction, though claiming the lady had gone with them and been married voluntarily. Campbell escaped into Scotland but Johnston was arrested, found guilty, and executed at Tyburn on 23 December. The marriage was subsequently annulled by Act of Parliament, but there is no surviving record of any child born to Mary Wharton as a result of this episode.

**157(c) Sir John Johnston of Caskiben, our provost** Sir John Johnston, 3rd Baronet of Caskiben, was an army officer who had served in Flanders and been a captain at the battle of the Boyne. He never married, and is not the same person as the John Johnston who was forced on the city of Aberdeen as Provost in 1697 by the outgoing incumbent, his father-in-law, Robert Cruikshank of Banchory. A protest was made to the Privy Council about the Aberdeen election, the Council declaring that no one should hold the office of Provost for more than two years at a time—see Alexander Keith, *A Thousand Years of Aberdeen* (Aberdeen: Aberdeen UP, 1972), pp. 562, 265. In transferring the Wharton abduction from London to Aberdeen, Hogg has blended the identities of two men of the same name.

**158(a) the earldom of Argyle [...] Lord Wharton's great estates** Hogg overstates the claims of a child born to James Campbell and Mary Wharton. Even if Mary Wharton had been Lord Wharton's daughter, he had a male heir in his son Phillip—see note to 87(b). On the Campbell side Lochy was supposedly the cousin of John, 2nd Duke of Argyll, and even if acknowledged as legitimate he would not have taken precedence of the Duke's brother, Archibald (1682–1761), to succeed to the title and family estates.

**158(b) Inverkielar** Inverkeilor is in Angus, between Montrose and Arbroath.

**158(c) but fifteen years old** Mary, daughter of Sir George Wharton, and the inheritor of an estate of £1,500 per annum, was thirteen at the time of her abduction—see *The Scots Peerage*, ed. by Sir James Balfour Paul, 9 vols (Edinburgh, 1904–19), I, 367.

**158(c) Crieff** a town in Perthshire, famous for its October cattle market, and associated with the Drummond family of the Earls of Perth, whose home of Drummond Castle lies nearby.

## The Pongos

**title** pongos are sometimes identified with gorillas or chimpanzees, as well as with orang-outangs, which are not native to Africa but to Borneo and Sumatra. The meaning of orang-outang in Malaysian is 'wild man', close to Hogg's notion of pongo in this tale. There was a great deal of speculation in the eighteenth century about the nature of the larger apes, Lord Monboddo, for instance, giving it as his opinion that they were 'a barbarous nation, which has not yet learned the use of speech' and that they were humans 'in one of the first stages of society, and in the progress towards a more civilized state'—see *Of the Origin and Progress of Language*, second edition, 6 vols (Edinburgh, 1774–92), I, 270, 361. Hogg discusses Monboddo's theory as 'a most ingenious one' and as 'excellent' in 'A Letter About Men and Women', *Blackwood's Edinburgh Magazine*, 26 (August 1829), 245–50 (pp. 245–46). Other possible sources of information for Hogg are a translation of the French naturalist, Buffon, as *Natural History, General and Particular, by the Count de Buffon, Translated into English [...] by William Smellie*, second edition, 9 vols (London, 1785), VIII, 77–105 (hereafter referred to as Buffon). These apes had also been mentioned in 'Bowdich's Mission to Ashantee', in *Blackwood's Edinburgh Magazine*, 5 (June 1819), 302–10 (p. 309). Hogg was a frequent contributor to the magazine, and regularly received successive numbers from its publisher, William Blackwood. Hogg's friend Thomas Pringle (1789–1834) may have been a source of detailed information both about pongos and South Africa in general. The topography and colonists of 'The Pongos' seem to relate specifically to the Cape settlement of Albany and Somerset East in the early 1820s by about four thousand British subjects. Pringle was the leader of a Borders party which settled at Glen Lynden near Somerset East, and one of the founding editors of the short-lived *South African Journal*—see the prefatory remarks by A. M. Lewin Robinson in *South African Journal, Nos I and II (January–April 1824)*, 2 vols, South African Library Reprint

Series 4 (Cape Town: South African Library, 1974). On Pringle's return to Britain in 1826 he published several accounts of his time in the colony. His 'Anecdotes of South-African Baboons' was published in the *Juvenile Keepsake* (London, 1830), pp. 209–12. Hogg himself was invited to contribute to this Annual–see an undated letter to him from the editor, Thomas Roscoe (NLS MS 2245, fols 321–22). A subsequent letter from Roscoe dated 'March. 15' acknowledges 'three little pieces from your hand [i. e. Hogg's] for the purpose of inserting in the "Juvenile Keepsake"' (NLS MS 2245, fol. 323), but it seems likely that as these did not appear in this Annual they were held over by Roscoe, for they appeared in his later Annual, *The Remembrance* of 1831. Pringle's *African Sketches* (London, 1834) provides much information about the colony and the geography and peoples of this specific part of Africa. Although Pringle's publications appeared after the first publication of Hogg's tale in *Blackwood's Edinburgh Magazine* in 1829 (see Note on the Text, pp. 207–08) it is probable that as a friend Pringle may have previously informed Hogg about his experiences. His letter to Hogg of 22 May 1828 (NLS MS 2245, fols 118–19), for example, refers to previous letters written since his return from South Africa.

**160(b) Kousies** the address 'To Correspondents' prefacing the second (and as it turned out final) number of Pringle's *South African Journal* states, 'We mean by-and-bye to overhaul the Caffers and Koosas–the Tambookies and Mambookies [...]'–see *South African Journal, Nos I and II (January–April 1824)*, 2 vols, South African Library Reprint Series 4 (Cape Town: South African Library, 1974), II, [n. p.].

**160(c) many things in heaven and earth** an allusion to Hamlet's rebuke to Horatio for his scepticism in *Hamlet*, I. 5. 168–69.

**160(c) Beattock** a town in Annandale in Dumfriesshire, south of Moffat. Pringle's *African Sketches* (London, 1834) reveals the strongly Scottish identity of the 1820s settlement of the Somerset East and Albany districts. A map facing page 117 (reproduced on p. 280, from the copy in the Bodleian Library, University of Oxford: RHO: 620. 12r. 77) shows a concentration of Borders place-names around Glen-Lynden. Pringle's discussion on 7 June 1820 with the acting governor at the Cape, Sir Rufane Donkin, also reveals a tendency to the replication of Scotland in South Africa:

> The upper part of the valley formed by the Bavian's River had been surveyed for the reception of my party; while the unoccupied territory to the eastward was destined for five hundred Highlanders, who were expected out [...] and for a smaller party from the west of Scotland, who were understood to be also on their voyage out. A district town, to be called New Edinburgh, he added, was intended to be founded in a convenient situation, where a resident magistrate and a clergyman of the Scottish church would be placed for the civil and religious benefit of the settlers. The Highlanders, moreover, were to be formed into a body of local militia, for the defence of that part of the frontier. [...] It was now for me, he said, to decide whether I would accede on behalf of my party to that plan, or avail myself of the option allowed by the original scheme of the home government, to select a location among the English emigrants in some other part of the disposable territory nearer the coast' (pp. 138–39).

After consultation with the heads of families of his party, Pringle informed the governor that they preferred to settle near their own countrymen.

**160(d) the chief Karoo** is named after a topographical feature, an arid high plain or scrubby desert. The 'Great Karoo' desert is in central South Africa.

**160(d) Kaffre** clearly an African language is indicated. Mungo Park defines *Kafir* as 'A Pagan native; an unbeliever'–see the prefatory Glossary of African words in his

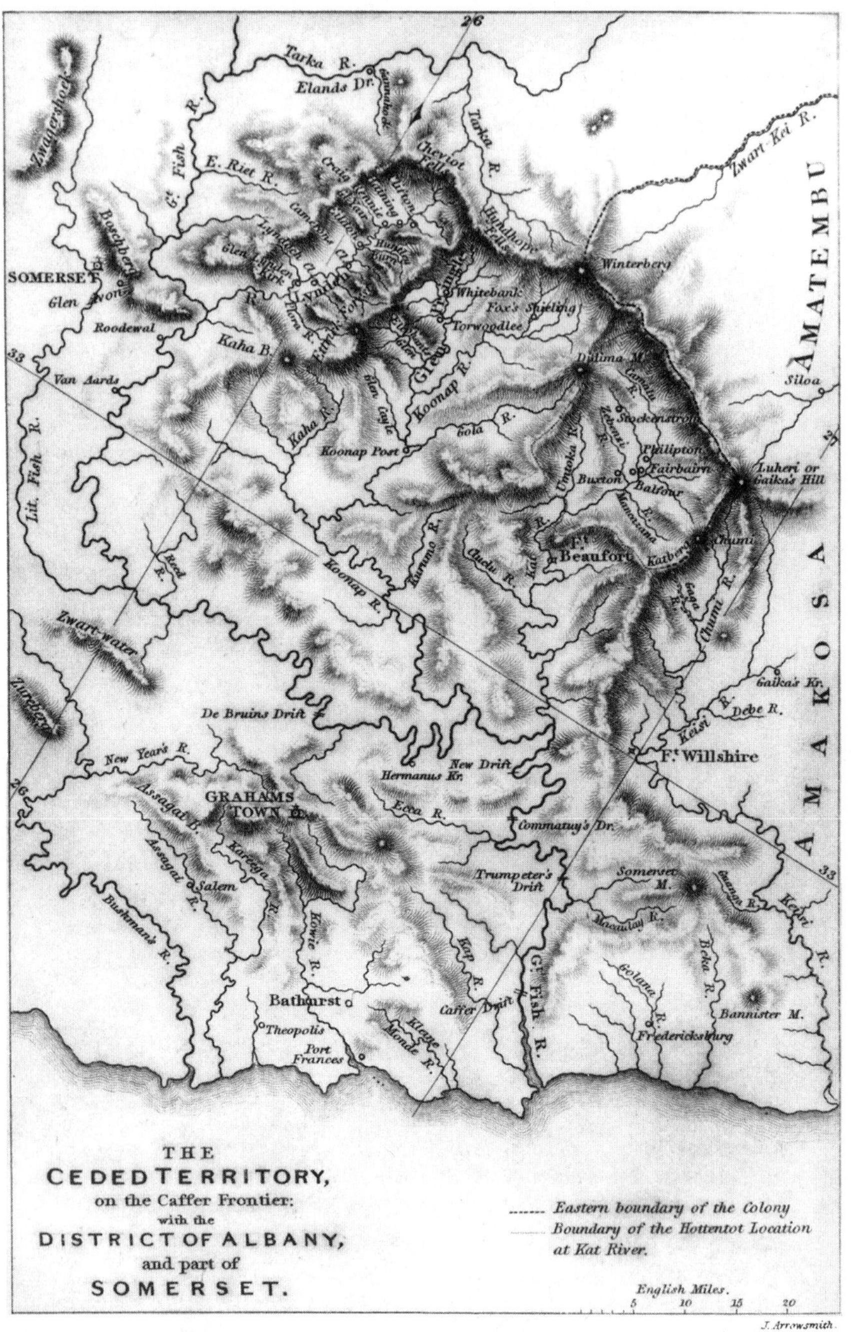


London, E. MOXON, Dover Str.t 1834.

*Travels in the Interior Districts of Africa [...] in the Years 1795, 1796, and 1797*, second edition (London, 1799). Pringle explains, however, that the term 'though sometimes still applied in a more extensive sense, is generally used in the Cape Colony, to denote the three contiguous tribes of Amakosa, Amatembu, and Amaponda'. He adds, 'The Caffers are a tall, athletic, and handsome race of men, with features often approaching to the European or Asiatic model; and, excepting their woolly hair, exhibiting few of the peculiarities of the negro race [...] Their principal wealth and means of subsistence consist in their numerous herds of cattle'–see *African Sketches* (London, 1834), p. 413.

**160(d) High Dutch** German, especially the language of South Germany.

**160(d) in exchange for her** Mungo Park comments on polygamy and the purchase of wives in Africa as follows: 'The value of two slaves is a common price, unless the girl is thought very handsome; in which case, the parents will raise their demand very considerably'–see *Travels in the Interior Districts of Africa [...] in the Years 1795, 1796, and 1797*, second edition (London, 1799), p. 266.

**161(a) one flesh and blood** an allusion to Christian marriage, ultimately deriving from a detail in the story of Adam and Eve in Genesis 2. 23–24. An article on the 'Mission from Cape Coast Castle to Ashantee' in *Blackwood's Edinburgh Magazine*, 5 (May 1819), 175–83, pictures a similar clash of values about marriage: 'When the English women were represented not only to possess the advantage of enjoying the sole affections of a husband, but the more amicable privilege of choosing that husband, the effect was truly comic. "The women sidled up to wipe the dust from our shoes; [...] the husbands, suppressing their dislike in a laugh, would put their hands before our mouths, declaring they did not want to hear that palaver any more, abruptly change the subject to war, and order the women to the harem"' (p. 180).

**161(a) Tambookies** evidently the name of an actual South African tribe. Thomas Pringle's *Some Account of the Present State of the English Settlers in Albany, South Africa* (London and Edinburgh, 1824) includes a prospectus for the *South African Journal*, advertising 'A Series of Articles on the Native Tribes of South Africa' to appear in its pages, including 'No. VI. The Tambookies' (p. 125). In *African Sketches* (London, 1834), he refers to 'Tambuquas, *i.e. Amatembu*' (p. 414), the people living nearest to the Scottish settlement around Glen-Lynden, beyond the eastern boundary of the colonised area–see map on p. 280.

**161(c) great mischief to our fruits** Pringle reported that the South African baboon 'appears to be in reality a very harmless and inoffensive creature; making allowance for a thievish propensity, which he has in common with roguish schoolboys, to rob gardens, orchards, &c., when he can contrive to get at them'–see 'Anecdotes of South African Baboons', *Juvenile Keepsake* (London, 1830), pp. 209–12 (p. 210).

**161(d) Keys river** perhaps the Zwart Kei River, marked within the homelands of the Amatembu tribe–see map on p. 280.

**162(b) the monster [...] snatched up the child** Pringle relates a similar episode with similar motivation. 'There is, indeed, one story told at the Cape, and said to be quite authentic, of a party of these cynocephali carrying off an infant from a farm house in the vicinity of Cape-town, and only resigning it after having been hunted for a whole day, by a numerous party of men and dogs, over the tremendous precipices of the Wynberg mountains. The child, however, when recovered, was found perfectly uninjured; and perhaps this extraordinary abduction (the only instance of the sort I ever heard of in the colony), may have been prompted rather by the erratic affection of some mother bereaved of her own offspring, than by any more ferocious or mischievous propensity'. He emphasises the fondness of these animals for their young: 'I have frequently witnessed affecting instances of this attachment, when the inhabitants pursued them from their orchards to the mountains; the females in such emergencies returning to search for the young ones they had lost through the very midst of their mortal enemies'—see Thomas Pringle, 'Anecdotes of South-African Baboons', *Juvenile Keepsake* (London, 1830), pp. 209–12 (pp. 210–11).

**163(a) the cubs cling to them** 'The young Pongo hangeth on his mother's belly, with his hands fast clasped about her' (Buffon, p. 83).

**163(d) Adam Johnstone [...] Joseph Nicholson** several of these surnames are associated with Annandale in Dumfriesshire. A Johnston was once Steward of Annandale, and Haliday is also the name of an Annandale clan. The surname Carruthers is derived from a parish of the same name in Dumfriesshire, while Hogg's mother-in-law was a Carruthers and Hogg's Dumfriesshire wife had several Carruthers cousins. The government plan for the colonisation of South Africa required emigrants to form parties containing at least ten adult males, so it was natural for settlements to consist of friends and relations from the same neighbourhood. The Border names of these settlers also appear to reflect the composition of the Glen-Lynden colony associated with Thomas Pringle—see note to 160(c).

**163(d) Shekah** has not been identified.

**164(b) two great clubs** Lord Monboddo describes the pongos as being 'armed with sticks, with which they attack even elephants, and drive them out of their woods'—see *Of the Origin and Progress of Language*, second edition, 6 vols (Edinburgh, 1774–92), I, 273.

**164(b) so bold [...] so generous** this is one of the episodes in which Hogg portrays the pongos as more civilised than the colonists. Absurdly the pongo abides by the European convention of duelling, whereas the Scots settler breaks it by accepting a challenge to fight using clubs and then surprising his challenger by using another weapon.

**164(c) grunts like a hog** perhaps a reference to Hogg himself, who was sometimes treated as a sort of missing link between animal and man by the Edinburgh literati. Interestingly, John Wilson in his review of Hogg's 1821 Memoir had gone on from calling Hogg a stout country lout to ask rhetorically, 'What would he himself have thought, if a large surly brown bear, or a huge baboon, had burst open his door when he was at breakfast, and helped himself to a chair and a mouthful of parritch?'—see *Blackwood's Edinburgh Magazine*, 10 (August 1821), 43–52 (p. 45).

**165(d) the 72d** a Highland regiment originally raised by Lord Seaforth in 1778 and known after 1823 as The Duke of Albanys Own Highlanders. They wore a version of the Royal Stuart tartan known as Prince Charles Edward. The regiment did indeed serve at the Cape at one time—see *Collins Encyclopaedia of Scotland*, ed. by John Keay and Julia Keay (London: Harper Collins, 1994), p. 859. Pringle relates an experience of his father's at Glen-Lynden which indicats that Karoo's fears of the regiment were probably well founded. Old Mr Pringle had granted a party of five native warriors shelter and food at Glen-Lynden for the night when a 'disbanded serjeant of the 72nd regiment, who then occupied a farm on the location belonging to Mr. Sydeserff, came to the place in great haste with his gun. He informed my father that he had heard of the arrival of the strangers; and having been engaged in many commandoes, and consequently well acquainted with the "nature" of the Caffers, (who, he said, "were just the same as wolves, and very *treacherous*") [...] he coolly proposed, as the best plan to prevent all this mischief, to surround the hut with their servants, while the Caffers were busy with their supper, *and shoot them all dead on the spot!* Happily not so "experienced" as his martial countryman, my father rejected this proposal with horror and indignation!' (*African Sketches* (London, 1834), p. 457).

**166(a) savage Boshesmen** from the Dutch name boschjesman, a tribe of native Africans. Pringle has much to say of the government-ordered 'legalised butcheries of the Bushman race'. The tribesmen were desperate people and also demonised by the settlers who had dispossessed them of their homelands. He describes the 'regular mode' of expeditions to repress their aggressions. 'The kraal was surprised, the males consigned to indiscriminate slaughter, and such of the women and children as survived the massacre were carried into captivity' (*African Sketches* (London, 1834), pp. 371–72).

**166(b) my wife carried across the river by a band of pongos** Buffon describes abductions of women and young girls, but with a sexual motivation that is carefully replaced by parental concern in Hogg's tale: 'Dampier, Froger, and other travellers, assure us, that the orang-outangs carry off girls of eight or ten years of age to the tops of trees, and that it is extremely difficult to rescue them. To these testimonies we may add that of M. de la Brosse, who assures us, in his voyage to Angola in the year 1738, that the orang-outangs [...] "endeavour to surprise the Negresses, whom they detain for the purpose of enjoying them, and entertain them plentifully. I knew a Negress at Loango who remained three years with these animals"' (pp. 84–85).

**166(c) no sorrow like my sorrow** an allusion to Lamentations 1. 12.

**166(d) Norroweldt** has not been identified, but the term 'veldt' is a South African word of Dutch origin for unenclosed country or pasture land. Pringle's *African Sketches* (London, 1834) reveals that during the 1820s Dutch place-names were gradually being replaced by Scottish ones in the district. He refers, for example, to 'The *Baviaans-River*, or River of Baboons, (now the Lynden)' (p. 148), and to ' a subsidiary rivulet, called *Bosch-Fontein*–now the Plora' (p. 149).

**167(c) lived in houses, and kindled fires** points discussed by Hogg's probable sources in determining the humanity or otherwise of the pongos. Monboddo gives among his evidence in favour of the pongos' humanity that they 'make huts, to defend themselves against the sun and rain; and, when one of them dies, the rest cover the body with a heap of branches and foliage'–see *Of the Origin and Progress of Language*, second edition, 6 vols (Edinburgh, 1774–92), I, 274. Buffon, in retailing evidence as to their animal nature adds their failure to make fire to their lack of speech: 'They cannot speak, and have no understanding more than a beast. The people of the country, when they travel in the woods, make fires where they sleep in the night; and in the morning, when they are gone, the Pongos will come and sit about the fire, till it goeth out; for they have no understanding to lay the wood together' (p. 82).

**167(c) fought rank and file** like the proffered duel earlier, an adoption of European fighting conventions. Rank refers to soldiers in line abreast or side by side, and file to men standing one behind another–i.e. the pongos supposedly adopt the square fighting formations of European troops.

**167(d) the Lockos** have not been identified as a specific tribe. There is an interesting verbal echo of the name of the eponymous hero of 'The Adventures of Captain John Lochy'.

**168(a) demure and melancholy faces** Buffon retails the following description of the pongo: 'His air was melancholy, his gait grave, his movements measured, his dispositions gentle, and very different from those of other apes' (p. 86).

**168(d) cuffing them, and ordering them** William's unquestioned supremacy over creatures larger and stronger than himself presumably derives from the 'dominion over [...] every living thing that moveth upon the earth' given to man by God in Genesis 1. 28.

**170(a) aim at speech** speech was a crucial part of the eighteenth-century definition of man, and the pongos' lack of language was frequently mentioned in accounts of them. Buffon quotes Froger to the effect that the 'most part of the Negroes imagine them to be a foreign nation come to inhabit their country, and that they do not speak for fear of being compelled to work' (p. 94), but presumably this is intended as evidence of the simple-mindedness of black Africans. Monboddo argued that the fact that the pongo could not speak did not indicate that he was not human, but only that he was in the first or most primitive stage of civilisation: 'The objection, therefore, when thoroughly examined, comes to this, that the Orang Outang has not yet learned the several arts that we practise; and among others which he has not acquired, is that of Language'–see *Of the Origin and Progress of Language*, second edition, 6 vols (Edinburgh, 1774–92), I, 347.

**170(c) six months and six days after Agnes's abstraction** making it clear to the reader that Beatrice was conceived in the colonists' settlement, and avoiding the suggestion in some of Hogg's sources that the pongos abducted women as sexual partners–see also note to 166(b).

**170(d) dumb human creatures [...] much comelier than negro savages** Monboddo, who also classifies orang-outangs as dumb human creatures, argues similarly: 'And, indeed, it appears to me, that they are not so much inferior to the Americans in civility and cultivation, as some nations of America were to us, when we first discovered that country'–see *Of the Origin and Progress of Language*, second edition, 6 vols (Edinburgh, 1774–92), I, 347–48.

**170(d) the most docile [...] of all slaves** the reference to slavery in connection with the British imperial agenda was probably intended to make the reader uncomfortable, as opposition to slavery was a mark of liberal feeling at the time of composition. Hogg's friend and possible informant Thomas Pringle, for example, was Secretary to the Anti-Slavery Society from 1827 until the British abolition shortly before his death in 1834. By contrast, a Scot of an older generation could argue that the pongos' habit of carrying off children to make slaves of them proved them to be humans living in society, who 'must have made some progress in the arts of civil life; for we hear of no nations altogether barbarous who use slaves'–see Monboddo, *Of the Origin and Progress of Language*, second edition, 6 vols (Edinburgh, 1774–92), I, 344–45.

**171(b) Sidney Gazette** the *Sydney Gazette and New South Wales Advertiser* was a weekly newspaper published by G. Howe of Sydney in Australia between 1803 and 1842.

**Marion's Jock**

**172(a) the Peel-hill meeting** has not been identified, though there is a Peel Fell among the Cheviots, bordering Roxburghshire and Northumberland.

**172(c) took the bite wi' the buffet** to accept blows when accompanied by food, to bear with ill-treatment if it comes with certain advantages–see 'A Collection of Scots Proverbs' in *The Works of Allan Ramsay: Vol. V*, ed. by Alexander M. Kinghorn and Alexander Law (Edinburgh and London: Scottish Text Society, 1972), pp. 63–129 (p. 109). Walter Scott refers to this as a 'Scottish phrase'–see *The Bride of Lammermoor*, ed. by J. H. Alexander, EEWN 7a (Edinburgh: Edinburgh UP, 1995), p. 166 and note.

**172(c) aye the langer the waur** see 'The longer the worse' in *The Oxford Dictionary of English Proverbs*, third edition, rev. by F. P. Wilson (Oxford: Clarendon Press, 1970), p. 481.

**173(d) Slaw at the meat, slaw at the wark** proverbial–see 'A Collection of Scots Proverbs' in *The Works of Allan Ramsay: Vol. V*, ed. by Alexander M. Kinghorn and Alexander Law (Edinburgh and London: Scottish Text Society, 1972), pp. 63–129 (p. 107).

**174(a) The goodwife [...] gave all their portions** Hogg describes the farmhouse community of his childhood and youth in similar terms in his essay 'On the

Changes in the Habits, Amusements, and Condition of the Scottish Peasantry', *Quarterly Journal of Agriculture*, 3 (February 1831–September 1832), 256–63 (p. 258): 'Formerly every master sat at the head of his kitchen table, and shared the meal with his servants. The mistress, if there was one, did not sit down at all, but stood at the dresser behind, and assigned each his portion, or otherwise overlooked the board, and saw that every one got justice'.

**174(c) banes are green** Jock's bones are immature, i. e. he is still growing.

**175(b) Kettlemoor** has not been identified, but Hogg probably envisages a setting in Eskdalemuir. Tam Craik in *The Three Perils of Man*, where the tale originally appeared, says that the night after the homicide he slept at the head of a water called Lanshaw Burn–see *The Three Perils of Man*, 3 vols (London, 1822), II, 280–81. Jean Moffat suggests that this is a phonetic spelling of 'Langshaw Burn' in Eskdalemuir.

**175(d) the place my mother speaks about whiles** presumably hell.

**177(a) a kitchen bed** probably a box-bed in an alcove or closet off the kitchen. Norah Parr (p. 10) gives a plan of Hogg's own cottage at Altrive which includes such a kitchen bed as well as a bed closet leading off the parlour.

**177(a) lose the field** lose the battle or contest, in this case Jock's assumed stoicism gives way to tears.

**178(a) experience teaches man wisdom** a proverbial commonplace. See 'Experience is the mother of wisdom' in *The Oxford Dictionary of English Proverbs*, third edition, rev. by F. P. Wilson (Oxford: Clarendon Press, 1970), p. 235, and 'Experience teaches Fools' in 'A Collection of Scots Proverbs' in *The Works of Allan Ramsay: Vol. V*, ed. by Alexander M. Kinghorn and Alexander Law (Edinburgh and London: Scottish Text Society, 1972), pp. 63–129 (p. 76). John Ray has 'Experience may teach a fool', in *A Compleat Collection of English Proverbs*, third edition (London, 1737), p. 285.

**178(d) the lamb's harmless and helpless look** here the pet lamb suggests the sacrificial lamb, a notion reinforced by Jock's subsequent assertion that it is killed for its sins.

**180(b) poor hungry boy** this herd-boy (and Jock himself) probably reflect Hogg's own experience during his childhood farm service. In the 'Memoir' (p. 14) he recalls, 'From some of my masters I received very hard usage; in particular, while with one shepherd, I was often nearly exhausted with hunger and fatigue'.

**184(a) seized him by the cuff of the neck** in its original context as 'The Laird of Peatstacknowe's Tale' this probably implied demon-like power. As the transformed warriors leave Aikwood subsequently, they see Satan holding out Tam Craik (a name subsequently assumed by Jock) 'by the nape of the neck' so that he is 'spurning the air over an unfathomed void'–see *The Three Perils of Man*, 3 vols (London, 1822), III, 154. In similar fashion Robert Wringhim recalls as a gesture of his degradation that Gil-Martin 'pushed me by the neck before him'–see *The Private Memoirs and Confessions of a Justified Sinner*, ed. by P. D. Garside (S/SC, 2001), p. 161.

**184(d) throat cut [...] feet tied and be skinned alive?** the Goodman's equation of murder with butchery confuses the human and animal, also a feature of 'The Pongos'.

**186(a) love lends a pair of wings** Cupid traditionally is depicted as a winged boy. Hogg's application of the saying to fear relates to the proverb 'Fear gives wings'–see *The Oxford Dictionary of English Proverbs*, third edition, rev. by F. P. Wilson (Oxford: Clarendon Press, 1970), pp. 249–50.

**186(b) no hold of any thing in nature** another indication of hellishness, shared both by the wizard Master Michael Scott in *The Three Perils of Man* and Gil-Martin in *Confessions*.

**186(b) Kirtle-common** has not been identified.

# Glossary

This Glossary sets out to provide a convenient guide to Scots, English, and other words in *Altrive Tales* which may be unfamiliar to some readers. It is greatly indebted to the *Oxford English Dictionary*, to the *Scottish National Dictionary*, and to the *Concise Scots Dictionary*, ed. by Mairi Robinson (Aberdeen: Aberdeen University Press, 1985), to which the reader requiring more information is advised to refer. The Glossary concentrates on single words, and guidance on phrases and idioms of more than one word will normally be found in the explanatory Notes.

*ahint:* behind, at the back of
*aiblins:* perhaps
*an:* if
*anathemas:* sentences of excommunication; curses, imprecations
*a-puling:* whining, complaining
*a'thegither:* altogether
*auld:* old
*aurora borealis:* the northern lights, a luminous atmospheric phenomenon at the North Pole
*ava:* at all
*awl:* a shoemaker's sharp pointed tool, used for making holes in leather
*ay:* always, ever, continually
*aye:* yes, just so

*baith:* both
*banes:* bones
*bang:* thrash, beat
*bannocks:* round flat cakes of oat-, barley-, or pease-meal
*basket:* a wickerwork shield for the hilt of a sword
*battling:* fighting
*bells:* bubbles
*bibliopole:* a dealer in books, a bookseller
*bicker:* beaker, wooden drinking-cup or bowl
*billy:* brother, friend, comrade
*blate:* timid, diffident, modest
*bletherin':* talking foolishly or loquaciously
*boardly:* burly
*bonnie, bonny:* pretty, beautiful
*bothy:* a rough hut, accommodation for workmen
*boud:* behoved
*braw:* fine, handsome, splendid
*breeks:* trousers, breeches
*brose:* a dish of oatmeal or peasemeal made with boiling milk or water
*buck:* a male deer
*budget:* a bundle, bag, or wallet, usually made of leather
*buisting:* marking sheep by branding or painting
*bygangin:* in passing, passing by

*ca':* call, summon
*caddies:* messengers or errand-boys
*callant:* a lad, a youth
*cambric:* fine white linen, originally made at Cambray in Flanders
*cannie:* cautious, prudent, astute; lucky
*caparisoned:* decked or harnessed
*caprioled:* leaped high in the air without advancing
*capuchin:* a Franciscan friar, so called because of his capuche or hood
*carded:* made to lie parallel, from the

process of carding fibres preparatory to spinning
*certes:* assuredly
*chapeau:* a covering for the head
*chiel:* man, fellow
*cipher:* someone who fills a place but is of no importance
*claws:* strokes, scratches
*clouts:* heavy blows with the hand
*cog:* a wooden container with staves, a bowl
*coits:* quoits, a game where the players try to throw rings over pins stuck in the ground; also used to mean the game of curling
*collop:* a slice of meat
*cornet:* the fifth commissioned officer in a troop of cavalry, who carried the colours
*cot:* cottage
*counterscarp:* the outer wall or slope of a ditch which in fortifications supports the covered way
*crappin:* the crop or stomach

*dawted:* caressed, made much of
*deil:* devil
*deil a:* not a, never a
*dens:* narrow valleys, especially ones with trees
*dinna:* do not, does not
*dirk:* a short dagger
*divan:* an oriental council of state
*dought:* to have been able (to do)
*dragoons:* originally mounted infantrymen armed with a type of carbine called a dragoon; now the name of certain cavalry regiments
*draught:* the entrails of an animal
*drum-head:* a court-martial held around an upturned drum, for summary trial of offences during military operations

*eebright:* bright to the eye
*een:* eyes
*eldron:* old

*fold:* a pen or enclosure for sheep

*gang:* go
*gar:* to cause or make someone do something
*gash:* pale, grim, dismal, ghastly
*gay:* very, great
*gayan:* very
*gie:* give
*gilliegaupy:* a stupid person, a gaping fool
*gin:* if, whether
*gin:* a bolt or bar
*goodman:* male head of a household
*goodwife:* female head of a household
*gowan:* daisy
*gude:* good
*gully:* a large knife

*haggis:* a savoury pudding made from sheep's offal and oatmeal
*hale:* whole
*haud:* hold
*hawkie:* a pet name for a cow; a cow with a white face
*High Dutch:* language pertaining to the South Germans
*hurdles:* portable rectangular frames of bars interwoven with withes of hazel, willow, &c.

*ilka:* each, every
*iron-stanchions:* upright iron bars, often stays or supports in a window

*jogged:* trudged

*kebbuck:* a cheese
*kelpie:* a water demon
*ken:* know
*kernes:* Irish or Scottish Highland foot-soldiers
*khan:* a princely title, specifically one relating to the descendants of Genghis Khan who were supreme rulers over the Turkish, Mongol, and Tartar tribes
*kine:* cows
*kirk:* church
*kirning:* the quantity produced by one complete act of churning
*kye:* cows

*kythe:* show, display, or reveal oneself

*lair:* a mire or muddy place
*langsyne:* long ago, long since
*lave:* the rest
*league:* a measurement of distance, varying from country to country, but generally of about 3 miles
*leeing:* lying, telling lies
*linn:* a deep, narrow gorge
*lint:* flax in the process of manufacture for spinning
*lord-provost:* courtesy title of the chief magistrate and head of the town-council of Edinburgh
*lounder:* deal heavy blows upon
*lout:* a bumpkin, a clown, an awkward fellow
*lucubrations:* literary works showing signs of careful elaboration or study
*lug:* a flap or projection; an ear
*lunch:* a lump or large slice of food

*manes:* the shade of a dead person, regarded with reverence
*mark:* sum of money amounting to two-thirds of a pound, either in Scots or English
*masonic:* relating to the secret fraternity of freemasons
*maugre:* notwithstanding, in spite of
*meal-girnel:* a storage chest for meal
*meat:* food in general
*menseless:* unmannerly, behaving objectionably
*mess:* a division of a regiment, the members of which take their meals together
*mill:* female pudend
*mire:* a boggy place, wet or swampy ground
*misleared:* greedy, ill-bred, rude, unmannerly
*missive:* a letter in which a transaction is agreed upon, which may be legally binding
*moiety:* a half payment, an installment of a total payment
*monish:* an imitation of the Yiddish pronunciation of 'money'
*monyplies:* the third stomach of a ruminant; guts
*muckle:* much in quantity or degree, a great deal of
*mutchkin:* a quarter-pint Scots, or three-quarters of an Imperial pint

*neb:* nose

*park:* an enclosed piece of land
*Pechs:* Picts, ancient inhabitants of Scotland
*pelt:* a hard blow or buffet
*pike-staff:* a long walking-stick with a spike on the bottom
*pinnace:* a small, light ship
*plaid:* a long rectangle of twilled woollen cloth worn as an outer garment
*ploy:* a venture or undertaking; a piece of fun, a trick or joke
*pluck:* the heart, liver, and lungs of an animal, used as food
*pongos:* large anthropoid apes, variously identified with chimpanzees, gorillas, and orang-outangs
*pontoon:* a flat-bottomed boat used as a ferry-boat
*pouch:* pocket containing money, one's own purse or finances
*puir:* poor
*puissance:* power or influence

*queer:* amusing, entertaining
*quiz:* a hoax, a piece of banter or ridicule
*quizzing:* making fun of or mocking someone

*rig-and-fur:* ribbed
*rock:* distaff

*saddle-laps:* flaps hanging from a horse's saddle
*saloon:* a large room or hall suitable for entertainments or exhibitions
*Sassenach:* a non-Gaelic Lowlander, English or Scots
*scrip:* a small wallet or satchel

*scrub:* a mean, avaricious person, a hard bargainer
*second-sight:* the ability to see future or distant things as though present
*sedan-chair:* a closed vehicle for one person, carried on poles by one person in front and one behind
*shaw:* a thicket, a small copse or grove
*shieling:* a small house or hovel; a shepherd's hut
*shilly-shally:* vacillating, irresolute
*shilpy:* thin, insipid, no longer fresh
*Shirra:* Sheriff, the chief officer responsible for the peace and order of a county
*shottle:* a small compartment at the top of a trunk
*siller:* silver coin; money in general
*slack:* remiss, backward
*slounging:* walking in an idle, slouching, lethargic way
*smeddum:* spirit, energy, drive
*snouking:* hunting, nosing, scenting out
*sonsy:* friendly, hearty, jolly
*spairged:* sprinkled, bespattered
*sparked:* spattered with mud or liquid
*specie:* pieces of precious metal minted, coins
*speer, speered:* asked, made enquiries, questioned
*speir:* to ask, to make questions, to enquire
*squadron:* a body of cavalry, usually composed of between one and two hundred men
*steading:* the buildings on a farm, sometimes including the farm-house itself
*swalled:* swollen

*Tartar:* a native of the region of central Asia to the east of the Caspian Sea
*tentit:* observed, took notice of
*term-day:* one of the four Scottish quarter-days on which contracts of farm employment began and ended
*ticket:* a notice posted in a public place
*tickler:* an irritant; a puzzler or teaser
*tike:* a dog or cur; a rough or boorish person
*timber:* wooden, made of wood
*tither:* the other, the second of two
*Tontine:* built by a fund, the subscribers to which all enjoy a life-time annuity which increases as their number diminishes, until the last survivor enjoys the whole income

*umber'd:* of a reddish brown colour
*unco:* remarkable, extraordinary; great

*vizier:* the chief minister or administrator of the Sultan

*wally-dy:* alas! an exclamation of sorrow
*warrantice:* a warrant, a document of guarantee
*wat:* know, knew
*waur:* worse
*wear:* to conduct animals into an enclosure
*wee:* little, tiny; small
*ween'd:* surmised, guessed, imagined
*whalp, whelp:* puppy
*whiles:* sometimes, at times, occasionally
*whisky cuach:* a drinking cup with two flat handles, *quaich* in Scots
*whittle:* a knife
*wight:* a human being, a person
*woo:* wool

*yestreen:* yesterday, sometimes yesterday evening

# Index

['Memoir of the Author's Life' and 'Reminiscences of Former Days']